I wanted to shout my objection to the sky, to reject the very idea that I could be thinking about Wake and the mad god as if they were real, as if I believed they actually existed. And yet I couldn't deny what my own eyes had seen, the words I had heard. I couldn't pretend away the power I felt—the fire I still felt coursing through every single vein in my body, no matter how hard I tried to will it away.

"Who are they?" I asked Nika, with one last desperate attempt to find clarity. "The Scion, and the Zealot? *Who are they?*"

She shook her head.

"Nika," I said. "What am I?"

CONTINUE THE JOURNEY WITH TARIK AND HAYLI
IN

# THE HOLLOW KING

## (COMING SOON)

OTHER BOOKS BY J. LEIGH BRALICK

**THE LOST ROAD CHRONICLES**

*Down a Lost Road* (Lost Road Chronicles #1)
*Subverter* (Lost Road Chronicles #2)
*Prism* (Lost Road Chronicles #3)
*Down a Lost Road: Special Extended Edition*
*The Lost Road Chronicles: The Complete Series*

**CHAOS LIES BENEATH THE NIGHT**

*Episode 1: Gifts*
*Episode 2: Omens*

**SHORT STORIES**

*Of Smoke and Wind* (Fantasy)
*The Silence Between* (Sci-Fi)

# A SEA LIKE GLASS

### BOOK THREE IN THE MADNESS METHOD

## J. LEIGH BRALICK

VORONA BOOKS

2023 Vorona Books Edition

Originally published in the United States by SisterMuses in 2018.


Published by Vorona Books, the publishing division of Vorona, LLC, Texas. 580 Decker Dr, Suite 105, Irving, TX 75062


ISBN: 9781941108222 (Paperback) | ISBN: 9781941108215 (Hardcover) | ISBN: 9781941108239 (eBook)

Cover and book design by Jennifer Lee

Vorona Books

*For Hannah, Eoin, Veronica and Clare*

*In loving memory of Patrick Tinning*

"*Yet I am not mad — and very surely do I not dream.*"

Edgar Allan Poe, "*The Black Cat.*"

# Part One:
# Threnody

# Chapter 1 · Tarik

"NOT MANY AS WOULD MAKE THE CROSSING TO ISTIA, THIS TIME OF THE winter," said the man at my elbow, as I leaned over the schooner *Hastol*'s rail and stared out at the wild and desolate sea. "One wonders what drives you."

He spoke Cavnish, which surprised me, and I turned from the wind to study him. I didn't recognize him, but all the fishermen still looked so much the same to me—all bundled in furs and oilskins, cheeks ruddy and unshaven, lips cracked from the cold and the wind— and none of them had taken the time to introduce themselves to me. We were three days into our voyage already, but besides the Istian schooner's captain, Agnir, I'd only exchanged words with the cook, a wiry, wide-eyed man named Sevnar who claimed he could make soup from saltwater.

"Name's Mattac," the sailor said, holding out his hand.

It was bound thick with wool and patchwork leather, so only the chafed and pitch-stained tips of his fingers showed. I untucked one of my poorly-gloved hands and took it, shaking it as firmly as my numb fingers could manage.

"Taumir," I said, giving him the Istian version of the name *Shade* that I'd chosen so long ago, when I first went to the streets in Brinmark.

Mattac slanted me a long glance. "Istian name. Istian by the looks of you, too, I'd wager. So how is it you speak Cavnish?" When I didn't answer he went on, half under his breath, conspiratorial, "I've heard you talking to Agnir. Half the time you're speaking Cavnish, but I can't understand why, if you're both Istian."

"You're Cavnish," I evaded. "Sailing on an Istian schooner. What does that make you?"

"*Was* Cavnish. Don't belong anywhere now, or to anyone, except *her.*" He leaned his arms on the cracked wood of the rail and nodded toward the silver-grey waves, and I smiled. When I didn't speak, he said, "I notice you didn't answer me. Where do you belong, Taumir? Istia? Or Cavnal?"

"Both, maybe," I said. I looked away. "Or maybe neither. I belong to a sea as well. A sea like glass…"

A sharp pain lanced through my head and I bowed over my hands, pressing my forehead against the cracked leather of my gloves. Mattac clasped my shoulder, and I thought I heard him saying my name, but it sounded far away…lost in the toss of waves, the rustle of ropes and heavy sails. The ship pitched in a sudden gust of wind and I caught the rail for support, shaking my head to ward away Mattac, and to drive back the pain.

"You need to sit down?" Mattac asked, his face close to mine so I could hear him above the wind. "You look a bit grey. You apt to be sick?"

"I don't get seasick," I said, pushing him back. "I just need a moment."

I left him standing there, staring after me in surprise, and made my way to the prow of the ship. I'd never sailed in a vessel like *Hastol* before. She was a sleek schooner, two-masted, with long, elegant lines and a hull crafted of the famous north Cavnish darkwood—Istia having no timber of her own for their shipwrights to use. The snap and flutter of the tawny sails was a sound I'd already come to love, almost as much as the creak of the beams and the soft rush of the waves against her hull.

Agnir had told me that the voyage would last ten days if the weather held, and so far it had. We'd come three days from the Cavnish coast under blue skies and a good stiff breeze, colder than anything I'd ever felt, but I'd seen Agnir watching the skies and frowning at his charts and knew it was better not to trust the winds.

I stood at the prow long enough to let the cold break over me and drive back the pain, then picked my way over the ropes and nets and the little fishing dories to the captain's cabin. It had taken me almost a full two days of sailing to get my sea legs, but I still hadn't figured out how to navigate the clutter of the deck without tripping over something. It amazed me how the sailors could move about so nimbly, even the old sea devils who were as weathered as *Hastol* herself.

Agnir spotted me coming and left his cabin to meet me—it was too cramped inside to talk comfortably. Despite the cold he had the sleeves of his wool jumper pushed back, revealing a pair of blue forked-lightning tattoos tracing his forearms, and he wore neither hat nor scarf, as if the biting wind couldn't touch him. He couldn't have been more than fifty. His hair was dark, speckled with silver, and his eyes were deep and keen, framed by creases that spiderwebbed his coarse and reddened skin. An honest face, I thought, Istian through and through.

"Godarson," he said, and gave me a smart nod.

I stifled a grimace. When we'd first set sail I had asked him not to call me by any title, and although he'd readily agreed, he still called me *Godarson* every bloody time we spoke.

"*Skeyfyr*," I said, using his Istian title.

"Voyaging well?"

"Well enough," I said. I nodded toward a few of the sailors manning the sheets. "Do they know who I am yet, Agnir?"

"To them?" He eyed me curiously. "Or to Cavnal?"

"What do you mean, to Cavnal?"

"Come now," he said with a knowing smile. "*Veka* knows your manners are too good to be Istian, and Godar Eyid never claimed any Istian for his son. I know you were raised in Cavnal…in the aristocracy too, I'd wager, given your demeanor and way of speech. And with the stories we've been hearing of late, well. Didn't take too much thinking to figure you out." I must have still looked alarmed because he gave a low laugh and clapped a hand on my arm. "Don't worry. Not my secret to tell."

I knew enough of Istian custom not to ask if he meant it. Above all else, Istians valued honesty and loyalty. It was enshrined in their laws—I'd heard that if an Istian falsely accused another person of lying, it was considered a crime so terrible that the insulted man had the right, by law, to kill his accuser. So if Agnir had sworn himself to silence, I knew that silence would follow him to the grave.

"Did Ambassador Eskir say—" I started.

3

Agnir shook his head. "He said nothing but that he'd found Eyid's son, and all that had happened in the Cavnish Court during his stay."

"Well, then, what was your first clue?" I asked. "If I'm doing something wrong, tell me. If I'm not...*Istian* enough. You know I can't afford to make mistakes."

He laughed. "This is why we believe in honesty," he said. "When you're honest there's no need to worry that your secrets will find the ears of the wrong people. Want to know what you're doing wrong? Well, for one thing, you don't swear like an Istian."

"I swear," I protested, an inexplicable blush warming my cheeks.

"Oh, sure," Agnir said. "You use the proper sort of swear words that every well-bred Cavner gentleman would use. That's not what I mean."

I'd heard the sailors tossing around strings of words I'd assumed were profanity, but apart from the standard obscenities, most of the literal translations made no sense—I still couldn't figure out what was meant to be insulting and what was meant simply as peculiar metaphor.

"I'm sure I picked up a few words on the street," I muttered.

"Hah! Like what?"

"What do you mean, *like what*? I'm not going to just say them if I have no reason to."

He chuckled and patted my back, a strangely familiar gesture that only a few months ago I never would have tolerated—from anyone. "See what I mean? If you're Istian, you're the damn most soft-spoken Istian I've ever met."

"I am *not* soft-spoken—"

I was interrupted by an uproar of wild laughter and raucous shouts from somewhere behind me on the deck, and Agnir raised an eyebrow meaningfully at me. I lifted my hands in a gesture of defeat.

"I didn't say it was something to be ashamed of," Agnir said, quietly. "In a nation full of people who talk too loud and say too much, saying little and hearing much can be a far greater power."

Somehow his words made me think of Trabin, who, of all the men in the Cavnish government, had been a master of keeping his thoughts. I'd learned early on that the only way to get his true opinion about anything was to provoke him to irrational anger—I had never appreciated the strength of his will in governing his thoughts in the ordinary course of his days. It was Kor who had helped me understand how Trabin let his own silence draw out the truth of other people's thoughts.

It should have saved him, in the end. Or I should have.

I turned abruptly to look back the way we had come, shielding my eyes against the low-hanging sun. This far north, in the dead of winter, the days were unnaturally short, and they only got shorter the farther northeast we sailed. Only a few hours earlier we'd eaten a light midday supper, and yet the sun was already beginning to set. It cast a few ragged clouds gathering from the north ablaze, and turned the sea to a flickering dance of fire.

"Will the weather hold?" I asked.

Agnir followed my gaze toward the clouds and shrugged. "Not likely. We've had good luck so far, but don't trust it to last."

I gestured at his forearms. "Was it luck, Agnir?"

"Ah," he said. "Luck, and a bit of magic. But not even I can hold back the storms a full voyage. The crossing this time of year is always bad."

"Could I help you?" I asked. "I've got a Wind's powers, though not a Mist's. I don't know how useful I could be."

He laughed. "No offense, Godarson, but you'd do more harm than good if you don't understand the sea and her moods. It's not just about making the wind blow or not. It's a wisdom takes years to gain. And only a fool would pit his pride against the sea's."

We stood side by side in companionable silence, as Agnir watched his men working on the deck, and I thought about the fickle sea and the changeable winds.

Presently I said, "Are many Istian sailors weather-workers?"

"Some," he said. "Most vessels like to have one on board, and will pay a higher wage to those as have an aptitude for weather magic. Even if they're not powerful, they can make a difference between life and death for a ship on these waters. But magic won't make a man a sailor." He was quiet a moment, then he smiled and said, "My son, Iskari. He knows the sea like a mistress. Born with both hands in the water, that one. He has no magic of his own but he's the damned finest sailor I've ever known. Put him behind the wheel and he makes me look like a *skatrdrakkeyn* cabin boy, I'm not ashamed to say."

"Does he sail with you often?"

"Been on the water all his life, but he started sailing the sea with me when he was twelve, after he left the *Karavasthir*. But lately..." He waved a hand. "I've asked much of him, these past few years, sending him in my stead to the moot. But it's not the best arrangement for either of us, and I'm sure he must resent me for it."

He drifted over to the ship's weathered rail, leaning out to watch the waves. Since he hadn't dismissed me, I followed.

"*Karavasthir?*" I asked. "What is that?"

"Ah, it's a school," he said, and nothing else.

"And the moot?"

He thought for a moment. "Closest thing I reckon you Cavners have to it is your *katzpotivyek*."

"The Lower Chamber? The nobility?"

Agnir's mouth twitched—apparently he wasn't entirely satisfied by the comparison. "I imagine our *sodthari* have more power in their own right than your katzpotoi. Your nobles mostly just exercise the authority of the Court of Ministries, am I right?"

"It's a little subtler than that. They exercise the authority of the King, codified by the Court."

He shrugged and ran his fingers over the rough wood. "At any rate, the *sodthari* meet every season to discuss issues concerning all of Istia. When there is a Godar, the moot is called the *Godartheng*, and he presides. When there is no acting Godar, it's an *eyltheng*. Someone may serve as acting Godar in times of emergency, but the primary business of the *eyltheng* is deciding who will take the *aydrding*."

"That's the crown?"

"Nothing so spectacular as the Cavnish crown, I wager. But the stones look like fire, hence the name."

I leaned onto the rail beside him, shoulders hunched against the wind. "And since Eyid's death? What is the state of things in Istia?"

"Not good," he said. "Man named Rigvar has taken the chair—unofficially, of course, as we've not had an *eyltheng* since Eyid's death. But he doesn't seem too keen on letting go of the power, either. He had the notion he might challenge your father for the title, before Eyid died." He eyed me sidelong. "You have to understand, Istia has had no knowledge of your existence for, what, eighteen years?"

I glanced away, and didn't correct him—*eighteen* sounded too young already for this madness. I didn't really feel the need to inform him that he had misjudged me by a year.

"Rigvar has no claim to the title, though," Agnir added. "Just temerity. Too young yet to be wise, but old enough to be dangerous."

"And me?" I asked, low. "Aren't I too young, then?"

"Ah. There's young, and there's young." He gave me an appraising glance. "You've been raised to rule. It's not just in your blood, it's woven in every thread of your life. People will see that. They'll respect it." He waved a hand, turning back to the sea. "Well, and don't let Istian pride fool you. We claim we want to do everything ourselves but deep down we need our Godar, just as Cavnal needs its King."

"When I sent word to you asking for passage on *Hastol*," I began, and paused. He nodded for me to go on. "How did you know my claim was true? That I was actually Eyid's son?"

"Well, there was the letter from Eskir, so I knew there *was* a son. And it wasn't common knowledge, so I didn't see how anyone would be claiming that title if they didn't already know it was possible. Then I just waited to see you for myself, to settle my opinion. And I was right. You're the spitting image of Godar Eyid."

I smiled, faintly, and bowed my head. Would he have believed me, then, if I'd shown up in Ridgemark looking like Tarik? I wondered what would he do now, if he knew I was Masked—if it would make him doubt me, or doubt my claim.

I had no proof of my identity except my face, and that was nothing but a lie.

# Chapter 2 • Hayli

*I* AM INVISIBLE.

From the crown of the lofty pine tree that overlooks the smelter fence, I *watch as a motorbike chuffs down the river road toward the gate. Even though I know it isn't Tarik riding the bike, my wings flutter in agitation, and a part of me dares to hope—maybe he will have decided not to leave. Maybe he will have decided he wanted me with him after all.*

*Hayli's mind is a chaos of regret and grief behind my own.*

*It's all my fault, Piper,* she whispers.

*I can't help smiling. Piper is the name she gave me not two days ago, when she finally got tired of not having anything to call me. I'm not sure I understand why she chose that name for me, but I like it, and it amuses me to hear her say it.*

Tarik would have let me go with him, *she goes on,* if I hadn't been so afraid. If I hadn't abandoned him when he needed me most, when he'd just lost everything else he'd ever loved.

*I have nothing to tell her to comfort her. For my part, my greatest regret in all of it is that I wasn't even there when he left. I didn't even see him go.*

*That is my burden now, and my punishment is seeing the face of the rider come clear, and realizing it is only Derrin.*

*A cold wind lances through the tree branches and I hunch closer to my perch, drawing one foot up into the warmth of my downy feathers as I observe the scene below. Derrin brings the motorbike to a stop outside the gate, even though I know the guards would have let him through straight away. He has stopped so he can talk to them, there at the fence line, away from the smelter where there are no secrets.*

"Well," *Derrin says, hooking his arms over the bike's handlebars. He wears his black cap slouched low over his eyes, so I cannot see his face.*

"Did he go through with it?" *asks one of the guards—Anuk. He is bundled up against the fierce cold, his red hair hidden under a wool cap, but I would know his tall, muscular frame anywhere.*

"He did."

"I guess he must have, since you've brought back his bike."

*Coins, who has been standing guard with Anuk, lets out all his breath and slumps back against the gate post.*

"What do we do now?" *he asks.*

*Derrin shrugs.* "We wait. And pray he comes back before war breaks out."

"I'm worried about him," *Coins says after a restless pause.* "We shouldn't have let him go alone. He didn't give any of us the chance to go with him. But Derrin, you..."

"Respected his wishes," *Derrin interrupts.* "He wanted to go alone. Maybe it's something he needed to do alone. Who am I to oppose him?"

"His friend," *Anuk says, fire in his voice.*

*Derrin shakes his head, then tilts it back, just enough that I can see the sadness in every shadow of his face.* "I have no right to call myself his friend."

*I shift my weight, unhappy. Maybe Shade wouldn't have let me go with him after all. Maybe he left when he did so that I would never be able to follow him. Like Coins and Anuk.*

"Any sign of..." *Derrin starts, the words trailing off on a hope.*

*Anuk and Coins say nothing, and I cannot see the looks on their faces. But Derrin nods.*

"Would you give me a minute?"

*The two of them slip through the gate and wander away across the factory yard, leaving Derrin on the bike by the fence. He doesn't move for endless minutes, and I watch him, wary, suddenly uncertain.*

"Hayli," *he says. He doesn't look up.*

*I freeze, everything inside me tight and ready to flee. My wings flutter, and a part of me wants nothing more than to fly away, far away, and never come back. Cast myself to the ocean sky and fly until I can't go on.*

"I know you're here," *he goes on.* "Please. Please come down. Talk to me. You don't have to hide any more."

*But I do, Hayli shouts at him in my mind. I never had a place among you, and now I never will. Can't you see that?*

9

*And her words are my own, and I want to convince myself of their truth so badly, but somehow I cannot.*

*I shift on my perch. If anyone can understand what Hayli is feeling, it's Derrin. And if Derrin was the last person Shade allowed to see him before he left for Istia...then maybe we have a reason for hoping.*

*Finally Derrin glances up, and it's like he knows exactly where to find me. He says, "I have a message from Shade."*

*I cock my head, staring down at him, then I dive from the branch.*

I LANDED JUST INSIDE THE SMELTER gate, Shifting into a crouch near a soddy drift of half-melted snow. My fingers felt a bit buzzy inside, which got me realizing how long it'd been since I'd used these hands. Seen with these eyes. It took a good tick for my vision to make sense of the dull-colored world about me, a blurred confusion of forgotten details.

Derrin swung off the motorbike and came through the gate, slowly, hands open at his sides like he thought I was still bird and might fly away on him.

"Hayli," he said, choking on the name.

I stood up—too fast, making the world spin—and threw my arms around his neck.

"We've been so worried about you," he murmured. "Two weeks! Where have you been?"

I blinked, surprising myself with the heat of tears on my cheeks. "Mostly right here," I said. "I div'n gan far. Stars, I wanted to. I wanted to gan away and never see anybody again. Stay a crow forever. But..."

He didn't say anything, but a minute and he let me go, brushing the tears off my face with his thumbs.

"What did Shade..."

"He begged you to come back. Asked me to tell you that he needs you. And even though there's nothing to forgive, he wants you to know you're forgiven."

I covered my face with my hands. "Why? How can he forgive me so easy? After all I did..."

Derrin took my hands and tugged them down so he could look me long and hard in the eye. "Hayli, listen to me. He said he needs you, but I say he needs you even more than he realizes. Especially now that..."

His voice skitted out on him, but he held my gaze.

 10

"Zagger," I whispered, the name a shard of grief in my heart. I squeezed my eyes shut. "I miss him, Derrin. I div'n know him for long, but I miss him so much."

"He was a good man," Derrin said. "I wish I might have known him better. And...we could really use him here now."

I studied Derrin through a frown, because suddenly I got to wondering what my life would be like if I lost him. I'd known him less than ten years, and he'd always just been part of life at the Hole, someone I respected more than anybody else. But that was nothing to what Zagger had been to Tarik. I'd thought I understood what Tarik had lost, but I realized all at once that I didn't understand at all, and my heart ached at the thought of his loss, and his grief.

"Well," Derrin said finally, straightening up and returning to the motorbike. "Are you coming in? It's freezing out here."

"I can't. There's more folks here than ever, what since the King's funeral..."

"So? You'll be just one more face in a crowd. Most of the people won't recognize you."

"Not even after what happened..."

*In the plaza, when I shot Tarik? When Zagger sacrificed his life to save mine?*

"You had your back to the people," he said. "Trust me. Only the folks who knew you before will recognize you. And Tarik was pretty adamant that nobody hold you liable for what happened."

"He was?"

Derrin nodded, rubbing a hand over the motorbike's steam gauges. "He gave the pointy end of the boot to three people who were saying they wouldn't welcome you back."

"Anybody I know?"

He hesitated, then shook his head.

"What about Jig? Jig's a'right with me coming back?"

"I think he fears—or respects—Tarik more than he dislikes you. And I'm not sure he dislikes you, anyway."

That surprised me, and I couldn't think of aught to say. Me and Jig had always danced around the idea of being friends, and what with all that had happened, I'd been dead sure he would be among those who wanted me gone—and Red right along with him, because I thought Red liked me even less than Jig.

11

Derrin squeezed my arm briefly, then swung onto the bike and took it into the factory yard. I followed on foot with my arms wrapped tight about me, the bird in me still wanting every instant to take to the sky and fly away. The feeling got ten times worse when I tailed Derrin into the smelter and found myself face to face with Coins and Anuk.

Coins didn't say aught at all but reached out and grabbed me, pulling me into the tightest possible hug. I realized all at once that I hadn't seen him with Hayli's eyes since I'd watched Shiver carrying his broken body to safety, after he'd destroyed the transmitting station to save us all, and almost got killed in the moments after. Maybe that was why my breath burned so bad in my throat. Maybe that's why everything inside me felt like drowning.

And then there were other arms around me, other hands on my arms—Anuk and Jig. Pika and Luce and Shiver sending a shuddery jolt all through me at their touch. Bobs and Zip with their arms wrapped tight about my waist. When the world blurred too bad for me to see, I buried my head against Anuk's chest, my arms around as many shoulders as I could reach.

I'd been so sure they would hate me. I'd thought they would turn me out, turn their backs on me, turn their hearts against me. Somehow I'd never let myself remember that they were my family, this wonderful, strange, frustrating, beloved collection of people, and that now, finally, I was home.

I was home, but Tarik was not.

The unexpected thought cut through my heart like glass. Standing there surrounded by people who cared about me, who forgave me despite everything, who loved me and made me a part of their lives... all I could think was that somewhere out on the wild, empty sea, Tarik was alone.

I only hoped he would remember that we cared about him, that we needed him, that we loved him. That I loved him. Somehow I wasn't sure what would happen to him if he ever forgot.

After the fuss had died down and everybody mostly left me to myself, Coins and Anuk took me back to Nan's corner of the smelter to fetch me some food. The smell of soup reminded me how dead skapped I was, and I tried to block out Piper's memories of everything she'd eaten over the last few weeks, because just the thought was enough to

12

drive the hunger straight away again.

I took my steaming bread bowl to a fire someone had built between two of the potlines, and sat on the narrow cement lip of the reduction pots as the lads took their seats across from me. They let me eat in peace, but I couldn't tell if it was because they didn't know what to say, or if they were just waiting for me to talk first.

When I'd finished off the last of the bread I hooked my arms over my knees and leaned close to the fire, letting the pungent smoke sting my eyes. "So, what happens now?"

Anuk bent his head, but Coins made a funny kind of face—uncertain, skeptical—and looked away, tugging one hand through his unruly mop of curly dark hair.

"What?" I asked. "Did something happen I dan' na about?"

"No," Coins said. "We've just been asking ourselves the same thing since Tarik lammed off, right? Got no noodle. Feels like we're just holding our breath, waiting for the blow to fall."

"Well, it's not like nobody's got any ideas," Anuk said, cross. "It's just the ideas they've come up with are all bloody awful, so."

"Lemme guess," I said. "Jig wants to take down the Court of Ministries?"

"Jig and Scorch, yeah. That about sums it up. They think the Ministers betrayed Tarik too bad for us to let them stay standing."

"They can't do that. They'd be idiots to try."

"Well..." Coins started, and I laughed.

"I know, they *are* idiots. But they'd be bigger idiots than usual to try this."

"I don't know," Anuk said, softly. "They almost had *me* convinced."

I stared at him in alarm. "But Anuk...if we topple the Ministries, who'd hold the reins? *Jig?* Stars, we'd be in such a ruck. Better or worse, the Ministers all we've got. We can't look weak right now. The whole world's watching us."

"But if we leave them in charge, they'll sign that treaty with Meritac and Cromis, and send us straight into war against Istia and Tulay. *And* sentence you mages to who knows what kind of fate." He rubbed a hand over his face. "Not saying I want to see Jig in charge—hell, I can't imagine a worse nightmare—but either way, we're gonna be in a ruck."

"Can they do that?" I asked. "Sign that treaty? Thought that was the King's job."

13

"Yeah, well, we don't bloody have a King right now, do we?"

Coins sighed and leaned his head back against the smelter pot with his arms tight across his chest. Somehow I knew what he was thinking, because it was the same thing I was.

*Why did Tarik have to leave us now? Now, when we need him the most?*

Finally Anuk got to his feet, dropping a hand on my shoulder as he did. "Get some sleep. You look rotten."

I stuck my tongue out at him but didn't protest. Getting wearily to my feet, I scanned the potlines for some halfway decent place I could bed down for the night. I'd got used to Luce's little corner of the smelter, with its scattered piles of fabric and blankets and half-mended clothes making a cozy kind of nest, but I always felt a bit like I was a nuisance to her. So in the end I gave up trying to find a place for Hayli, and let Piper roost in her favorite tree, where we both felt so much more at home.

# Chapter 3 · Tarik

AGNIR LEFT ME STANDING BY THE SHIP'S RAIL. HE STRODE ACROSS THE deck like a maelstrom, shouting orders at his crew, but for some time after he'd gone I stayed where I was, watching the turbulent waves roil against the ship's hull, considering Agnir's words. From the few times I'd spoken with him, and from his insistence on calling me *Godarson* despite my protests, I knew Agnir believed I was going to Istia to claim the *aydrding* for myself. And maybe that was what I was supposed to do...but I had no clarity.

All I knew was that the last thing Trabin had asked of me was to go to Istia, to lead them. I wished he'd had the chance to tell me what he meant by that. A part of me desperately wanted to believe I could lead them from the ranks, and let someone else wear the fire crown—I would gladly give up any right I had to it. Hell, as far as I knew, this man Rigvar might be a better Godar for Istia than I could ever be.

I sighed and leaned my head on my arms, breathing in the smell of salt and fish and pine tar. The hatch behind me suddenly slammed open and I, startling, turned to see Sevnar's blond head poking above deck. He was staring straight at me like he'd known I would be there, and when I met his gaze he jerked his chin at me and scuttled back down the ladder. I followed him after a moment, down into the cramped galley that stank perpetually of fish and oil.

"Did you need me?" I asked, in Istian.

He grunted and pushed a bucket crammed full of dead fish into my arms. "Make yourself useful. No idle hands on this boat."

When I just stood there staring at him, the bucket held awkwardly between us, he rolled his eyes and took it back from me, slamming it down on the rough slab that served as both cooking counter and dining table in the galley. He pulled out one of the cold fish and waved it at me, then slapped it on the slab and hacked its head and tail off with two swift strokes of a cleaver. I watched, torn between fascination and disgust, as he pulled the skeleton out in one flourish and peeled off its thick skin.

"Understand?" he said, tossing the cleaned fish into a deep pot. He slid the cleaver across the slab to me and waved at the bucket. "Well, get to work. These men need to eat."

I glared at him but didn't complain—when I'd bartered passage with Agnir I'd known that I would be expected to pull my weight, regardless of who Agnir believed I was. As Sevnar said, on a boat this size, out in the deep, there was no room for idle passengers. Already I'd learned more than I ever cared to know about scrubbing deck planks, and gathering and mending fishing nets.

With a sigh I tugged off Zagger's leather coat, pushing down a sudden spike of grief as I left it on a stool by the ladder with my gloves and hat. It was warm enough in the galley, anyway, out of the frigid wind with Sevnar's coal furnace blazing like an inferno. Sevnar didn't speak while we worked—me cleaning the fish, him preparing what he called *stew*, which looked to me more like a mashed mess of potatoes and vegetables—but I didn't mind the silence. I even found I didn't mind the gory work. It was mindless, methodical, with a strange sort of rhythm that somehow quieted the noisy chaos of my thoughts. Even the glassy, staring eyes of the fish didn't bother me overly much.

As I tossed the last fish into the pot and dropped the empty bucket onto the floor, Sevnar glanced at my work and sniffed. "Not bad. You only mutilated half of them. Better than my first try."

"Must be I had a better teacher than you did," I said, giving him my most charming smile.

He just scowled and lugged the pot of fish over to the furnace, but I thought I heard him mutter, "Cavnish," under his breath.

I folded my arms and leaned back against the slab. "What was that supposed to mean?"

"What?"

"You heard me. What did you mean by calling me Cavnish?"

 16

"What do you think?" he asked, wiping his hands off on his apron front as he turned to face me. "You don't talk like an Istian. There's more to you than you let show. I just can't figure what."

"Keep it that way," I growled.

His mouth twitched in a smile. "*Now* you sound Istian." He worked silently for a time, cooking the fish into the stew while I sat on the stool and watched, then he waved a hand over his shoulder and said, "Call in the men."

That at least I knew how to do. There was an iron bell just outside the hatch, so I climbed the ladder and braved the frigid wind long enough to tug the cord and send the bell clanging a few times. There was an instant clamor of activity on the deck above, someone bellowing orders, then four of the sailors piled down the ladder into the galley.

"Eat fast, lads," one of the men said as he grabbed a bowlful of stew from Sevnar. "*Skeyfyr's* orders."

"We're eating early. Are we at the passage already?" an older sailor asked, pulling a wool cap off his shockingly bald head.

"Not quite, by my reckoning," the first said. "Must be something on the wind."

"What passage do you mean?" I asked.

The two men exchanged a quick glance. I wondered if they were more surprised by the question, or the fact that I had asked it; if the sailors had kept their silence around me up until now, I'd returned silence in kind.

"Gull's Folly," he said at last. His eyes narrowed slightly and he added, "Which, of course, you must have passed through on your way to Cavnal in the first place."

I hesitated. The Prince in me wanted to feel indignant at their blatant hostility, to demand to be treated with the respect I deserved. But Shade seemed to understand the Istian temperament a bit better, though I wasn't quite sure how. Maybe it was in my blood after all. So I just shrugged and took the bowl Sevnar offered me, and leaned back against the edge of the ladder.

"It's your job to pay attention to those things," I said. "Not mine."

The first man held my gaze evenly for a moment, then went back to eating his stew. The hatch above me opened, pouring a gust of icy wind into the galley as Agnir made his way down the ladder. I moved aside until he got the hatch closed again.

"You're not a sailor, lad," the second man said to me, "nor a fisherman. So what are you?"

Agnir paused at the bottom of the ladder, glancing from me to the older man.

"My business is my concern," I said.

Sevnar gave Agnir a bowl and the skipper slid onto the bench at the slab table. Apparently he was the only one who ever sat down to eat, since I'd never seen any of the other sailors join him there for meals; they seemed to prefer leaning against the walls instead.

"Are we at Gull's Folly, *skeyfyr*?" one of the other sailors asked.

"We should hit it late tonight, early tomorrow, barring other obstacles. But the seas are getting rough," Agnir said. "When you're finished get back to your posts. Send the others down."

They stacked their dishes and went without a word, leaving just Sevnar and me with the captain. I took my seat on the stool again while Sevnar busied himself over the furnace, raking out ash and piling in fresh coal.

"The men giving you problems?" Agnir asked me.

"No," I said.

Sevnar shot me a quick glance over his shoulder but didn't offer any comment. I wondered if he thought I was lying.

I shrugged and added, "I'm a stranger. I'm not one of them. They treat me as well as I expect."

"Still, let me know if they take it too far. I won't stand for it."

"I will."

The four remaining sailors blustered their way into the galley. Mattac clapped my shoulder as he passed, flashing me a broad smile, but the others did their best to ignore me. I didn't mind being ignored; it was far preferable to being challenged.

"Feeling better?" Mattac asked me, speaking Istian as perfectly as any of the other sailors.

"Seasick?" one of the other men asked with a smirk. "Just wait."

"It was just a headache."

"Ah well. There's a bucket in your berth if you get sick during the night. We're like to have some rollers."

"Storm waves," Mattac said, guessing my unspoken question. "They can make the boat pitch and roll quite a bit, but she's a sturdy vessel. Old but sturdy, like our *skeyfyr*, aye?"

"Aye!" the others shouted, and Agnir laughed as he got up.

The ship pitched abruptly, but I was the only one who reached to grab something for support. None of the other sailors seemed worried, but Mattac grinned when he saw me hanging onto the railing.

"*Hastol* will take care of us," he said. "Nothing to worry about, right, *skeyfyr*?"

"For now," Agnir said, and disappeared back topside.

"You look a bit white," Sevnar said. "Don't worry. Agnir knows this ship through and through. She won't let him down. More blood than paint in her timbers."

I frowned, and almost made the mistake of asking what he meant—asking if Istians really believed the ancient folklore about mages' blood. Somehow I rather doubted Sevnar would answer me even if I found a safe way to ask the question, so I kept my doubts to myself, but I wondered.

The rest of the men ate quickly and silently—from what I'd seen so far, there were no leisurely meals on board a ship, even when the weather was fair. Mattac finished first and headed for the ladder, but paused at my shoulder before going up to the deck.

"Get some sleep, Taumir. We'll wake you if we need you."

"For what?" I asked, baffled.

"Ballast," one of the other sailors muttered, jostling me as he reached for the ladder.

Sevnar chuckled but Mattac said, "Don't mind them. They treat every passenger like this."

"That makes me feel so much better," I said.

He grinned and disappeared through the hatch with the other sailors. As Sevnar busied himself cleaning the bowls, apparently intent on ignoring me, I decided I didn't want to risk him saddling me with scullery duty. So I grabbed Zagger's coat and my wraps and headed to my berth behind the ladder instead. It had room for only one small table nailed to the floor and two narrow beds set in the outer wall, both meant for passengers, but since I was the only one on board, I had the whole berth to myself. Not that it mattered; I was too tired from the wind and the chaos of the day to enjoy the extra space—or the solitude.

I extinguished the lantern on the wall and threw myself onto the lower of the two beds, pulling up the heavy wool blankets and clutching

19

my hands under my arms while my body shivered stubbornly in the cold. The ship keeled and tilted, timbers groaning, as the waves crashed and raged against the porthole. Then, slowly, I felt the wind die down, and the waves settle, and the ship pick up speed.

I closed my eyes.

*It is snowing.*

*I stand once again on the dais in Avnaya Square, facing a turbulent crowd. But I don't see the crowd. I don't feel the snow, or taste the fear and anger on the wind. All I know is that Hayli is walking up the steps toward me with her gaze riveted on mine. She holds something in her hands. When she lifts them up, I see that it is a small crow, watching me keenly from one bright eye. But then the crow flies away and instead Hayli is holding a revolver, and I know what will happen next.*

*I don't want to see it, but I cannot stop it.*

*The gun fires. I feel nothing, but I watch, paralyzed, helpless, as Zagger grabs her amidst a rain of bullets and they both fall...and fall...lost in the sea and the endless dark.*

*"Zagger!"*

# Chapter 4 · Tarik

T HE SOUND OF MY VOICE CALLING FOR ZAGGER SHOOK ME FROM MY DREAM, just as the boat pitched wildly to the side. I could hear the shriek of the wind, the crack of a splitting beam, shouting from up deck-side. My hand flashed out, grabbing at the rail of the bed for support. And for all I swore otherwise, my stomach lurched until I was sure I'd be sick.

Someone was hammering on the door of my berth. "Get the hell up on deck! All *thrigun stodadrakkeyn* hands, damn it!"

I rolled off the bed, still sleep-dazed and fighting back the haunting ache of grief, and stumbled out into the narrow passage. Whoever had called me had already disappeared, so I made my way toward the ladder, bracing my hands on the passage walls to keep from falling as the ship rocked and heaved. I pushed open the hatch and was met by a spray of sea foam mingled with a swirl of snow and rain, tasting of tears, or blood. Coughing and numb, I climbed onto the deck and nearly lost my footing on the slick wood.

"Taumir!" someone called.

I turned to see Agnir waving at me from the quarter deck. Whatever else he said was lost on the wind, but he was pointing emphatically at something behind me. I squinted through the gusting rain. The other sailors were fighting to secure the rigging and sheet the storm sails as the ship reared to crest a massive wave, while the helmsman wrestled the wheel to keep the ship from keeling. But one of the mainsail sheets was snapping loose, the wind tossing the heavy hemp like a bit of spider silk.

I ran without thinking and grabbed the rope. I had no idea what to do with it, so I just hung onto it with all my strength, the coarse rope shearing through the thin leather of my gloves until my hands were chafed and bloody.

Agnir had stopped shouting at me. He stood with his arms outstretched, head bowed, a rain-drenched statue with snow fringing his beard and hair. I closed my eyes and tried to focus, tried to find the trace of the wind trailing through the night. Somehow I could sense Agnir's magic—fingers smoothing the warp and weft of the wind like a master weaver. And in my mind I stood back and watched, mesmerized by the deft skill of his power.

One of the deckhands tugging the rope from my bloody grip brought me back to the ship and the squall.

"Let go, damn it!" he shouted in my ear.

I made sure the sailor had the rope firmly in hand before releasing it and stumbling back. The wind was dying down, slowly. Little by little the waves receded and calmed, then the clouds pulled back to reveal the stars and the boat settled to rock gently on the water.

I took a deep breath of bitter sea air and pressed my hands against the soothing chill of the wet rail, shuddering with the pain, and the trailing remnants of fear. One of the deckhands retched over the side of the ship. Two sat against the mainmast, heads buried in their arms. After a moment I realized that Agnir was standing beside me, watching the still-roiling bank of clouds to the east.

"I don't understand," he said, voice low. "I already soothed the winds once. They have no *drakkeyn* will of their own. If I tell them to go one way, they go. They don't fight back. They don't return angrier than before. What happened?"

"Was it a different storm?"

He shook his head, too distracted for a moment to answer. Then he glanced down at me and said, "They are all connected. The winds that bring a storm here leave warmth and sun in their wake, and flow into other storms in other lands. They weave into each other like the currents of the sea. If I drive the storm away here, it touches all the currents of air and water. Hell, what I do probably sends a deluge on some other unsuspecting land, but regardless…they don't *come back*."

"If what you do can change the weather elsewhere," I said, "is it possible that another mage changed our weather here?"

He pursed his lips. "It's possible, in principle, but...that isn't what I felt here," he said, very quietly. "I don't know how to explain this, but the storm was...it was *irrational.*"

I bit my tongue on asking how any storm could be considered *rational.*

But Agnir seemed to sense my thought, because he added, "Most storms, you can see the pattern of them, even when they've been touched by magic. It is all by perfect and flawless design. You can trace the logic of them from beginning to end, from the front that moves here to the swell of cold air there, and the way they intertwine." He gestured across the sky as he spoke, as if he were seeing a tapestry that was invisible to me. "It *makes sense.* But this storm... If I didn't know better I would say the storm was..." I gestured him to finish, a little knot twisting in my stomach. "Rage," he said. "And grief."

I jolted, and jerked my gaze away from his. Shame and horror flashed through me—because like a lightning bolt I understood exactly what had happened. It was only recently that I'd learned how dangerous my emotions could be, how they could somehow control the winds if I didn't control *them.* I'd seen it happen before, more often than I cared to admit. I'd gotten fairly adept at harnessing my anger, my fear...when I was awake. But when I was asleep?

Could I tell Agnir that the storm was my fault? Could I tell him that I'd had a nightmare that nearly destroyed his ship?

Agnir left me when I offered no comment, weaving through the sailors' huddled forms to the ship's helm, where the exhausted helmsman stood draped over the wheel like a bit of damp rag. And I, I stayed on the deck even when the wind shifted colder and turned the spray on the wood planks to frost. If my nightmares put the ship in danger, then I vowed I wouldn't sleep again until we reached Istia.

As the night shifted toward morning, we came to the stretch of treacherous sea called Gull's Folly, passing through it with what the other sailors called good sailing. After the night squall, I was willing to admit the passage wasn't as bad as it could have been, but I would never have considered it *good sailing.* The ship heaved, constantly, once nosing forward so steeply that I was sure we would topple stern over bow. Even with Agnir's unceasing efforts, the winds were too strong, the current too turbulent, for him to control entirely.

Still, we passed through the worst of the Folly in just under nine agonizing hours, with only two of the deckhands getting sick from the rolling of the ship. By the time the half-shrouded sun had begun to dip toward the horizon, we had reached calmer seas and Agnir had stepped down from his post.

I watched him disappear into his cabin and shut the door behind him, unsurprised. I'd found it exhausting just watching him. Using my own magic never wearied me, at least not beyond bearing—or maybe I never noticed it because of the way it fractured my thoughts instead. I sighed and leaned back against the ship's bulwark, fighting to keep my eyes open. They stung from the salt spray and the wind, and all I wanted was to close them…to just sleep…

"Well, you survived Gull's Folly," Mattac said, loudly, leaning over the rail beside me. "Didn't even retch your guts out. You should get some sleep."

"I'm fine," I said.

"You look terrible. Take the rest you can get, when you can get it. That's what you learn on the sea." When I didn't answer, he said, "The tattoo on your face. Can I ask what it means?"

"It's my mage sign."

He gave a low whistle. "So you're a mage, too? Knew the *skeyfyr* was, of course, but none of the other crew are. Why the mask symbol?"

"Because that's what I am," I said, but when he just regarded me blankly I added, "I can change my appearance. Put on another face, even another body, for what it's worth. So, I'm a Mask."

He turned from the rail to face me and folded his arms. There was no hostility in his manner, just a sudden uncertainty, and I found I couldn't meet his gaze.

"The face I'm looking at right now—is that your real face?"

And even though I'd always felt like Shade's face was a lie, I hesitated. *Was* it real? I wasn't sure what *real* would even mean. Who was I, when I wore Shade's face—myself, or someone else? Was this face just an outward expression of something deep inside me? Maybe…maybe if my soul had a face, this was it.

The thought made me shudder, because suddenly I remembered the first time I had looked into Shade's eyes, in my armoire mirror in Brigun Palace, and saw a darkness there that Tarik's eyes never held.

"I don't know," I said, keenly aware of Mattac's expectant silence. "But this face is a part of me."

He grunted in response. "Taumir, what's troubling you?"

"What do you mean?"

"I don't know that I've ever seen anyone who looked so sad."

I lifted my brows in surprise. I thought I had learned at least that much from Trabin—that behind the mask of Shade's face I could hide all the turmoil I felt inside. Apparently I was wrong.

"My...father," I faltered. "He passed away a few weeks ago."

"*Oh*. Taumir, I'm sorry to hear that," he said. "Truly."

*You probably mourned him and didn't even realize it*, I thought.

But I didn't tell him that Trabin's death was not what weighed most heavily on my heart. His death was a constant ache, numb and hidden in the corners of my heart, but it didn't burn the way Zagger's death did. And I realized with some surprise that I missed the smelter. I missed the cold and drafty space, the crowds of people, the smell of Nan's soup, the endless rush of noise and activity. I missed the routine of watches and meetings and taking rounds, the comfortable confines of my room and office that felt more *mine* than any room in Brigun Palace ever had. I even missed the constant vigilant presence of Jig and Scorch at my back. Coins and his insufferable high spirits.

Hayli.

And, though I'd always tried to convince myself that I hated being put in charge, forced to take up responsibility for the people who had gathered around me...I even missed that. More than anything I worried about them. Were they safe—the skitters and the mages and the *krizanyi* who'd lost what little work they had in the uprising? Would they plot foolishness in my absence? Would the Ministers who had betrayed Trabin try to bring order to the chaos they'd left behind? I wished I knew; I had no way to know.

"You're alone," Mattac said suddenly. There was no question in the words, but the gentle sympathy of them jolted me.

Gritting my teeth, I just lifted my chin and faced the endless sea, dark and turbulent under the quiet stars.

"I always was," I said.

# Chapter 5 · Hayli

"*Hayli!*"

*The sound of shouting startles a flock of sparrows roosting in the tree beside mine, and it takes every bit of my self-command to stay still, and not to fly away with them. Down in the smelter yard I see Coins and Anuk—they look terrified, but Derrin, coming out behind them, wears a look of tolerant frustration.*

*It is morning, late morning from the height of the sun, and I realize with something that Hayli would probably call guilt that the lads must have been looking for me for some time, because they have given up looking at the ground, and are all staring up at the trees.*

*I give in, and fly down to join them, but just as I prepare to Shift and let Hayli come out, a handful of folks I don't know straggle out of the smelter. They are likely going to find work in the city, but they frighten me, and in the back of my mind Hayli is even more anxious than me.*

Don't let them see me, *she whispers.* I'm not…I'm not ready for them to know I'm back yet.

You'll have to show yourself eventually, I *tell her, cross, and flit away from the lads before any of them can reach out to me. I perch up on a rung of the fire escape ladder.*

*Coins is the first to see me. Perhaps he heard me fly past him, but he ducks around now and frowns up at the ladder.*

*"Hayli, come on!" he calls. "What are you doing?"*

*"Hayli!" I shout back, taunting.*

*Hayli grumbles at me, but I laugh at Coins's wide eyes.*

"What's she doing?" Anuk asks, coming beside Coins.

I peck at the shiniest spot on the ladder rung I can find, and eye them sideways. Coins climbs a few steps up, but I flit out of his reach.

"Why did you Shift again?" he asks, softly now. "You worried about those folks?"

I don't know how to say what I want to say in Hayli's words, so I duck my head, pretending to examine my toes. Coins smiles sadly and stretches his hand up toward me. I watch him cautiously, fearing to be trapped, then make a show of trust and hop onto his fingers. Carefully, gently, he climbs back down to the ground.

"We won't let anybody do anything to you, right?" he says. Anuk and Derrin watch us, looking like they are afraid to so much as breathe. "You're safe here."

Not safe, Hayli mutters in my thoughts. Not as Hayli. I only feel safe when I'm you.

This pleases me, though I know it is not good for Hayli to feel that way. Still, I understand her caution, and deep inside I know I am a little jealous of my time. I don't want to retreat again. I've lived gloriously for two weeks, and the thought of giving way to Hayli makes me strangely sad.

Fly away, Hayli says. I'll go back tonight, when it's quiet. I just don't want to be here when it's day, when there's so many folks about.

"Night!" I shout, because I can say that word, then I launch myself from Coins's hand before he can catch me, and glide up to a high perch on a thin branch that even Coins could never reach.

"Damn it!" Anuk shouts, but Derrin holds up a hand.

"Give her time," he says. "If she says she'll be back tonight, she'll be back tonight."

Coins claps Anuk on the shoulder and heads for the smelter gate. Anuk trails him after a minute, and then Derrin, all alone, vanishes into the air. I think he understands more than anyone my need to be apart.

PIPER FINALLY MADE ME SHIFT BACK as the sun was beginning to sink over the trees. I crept into the smelter while everybody was back in the back claiming skappers from Miss Nan, and hovered near the potline closest to the door, wanting to hide, wanting to be found. Just as I'd made up my mind to have a go at the food line, I caught a goggle of a slim figure slipping in through the half-barricaded smelter door. I frowned.

I'd recognize Doc's long white hair anywhere, but I'd never seen him wearing a coat before, as if he didn't get cold the way the rest of us did. But it was definitely Doc, and he was definitely wearing a long black trencher that fell to his ankles, with a black courier bag slung over one shoulder. And if I didn't know any better, I almost thought he was sneaking in like a skitter who'd been out past curfew.

"Doc!" I called. He jumped a bit and spun to face me, looking, if possible, paler than ever, and when I folded my arms and glared up at him, he wouldn't look at me at all. "Where you been? I—or the crow, rather—saw you leave after...after Zagger. We've not seen you about since. Where'd you gan?"

He edged past me toward his infirmary, tossing his black bag down by one of the old wooden crates and picking up a stray bandage. For much too long he fiddled with the linen, his gaze fixed on something across the smelter. His lips moved like he meant to say something, but he never said a word.

"Doc?"

"I had to investigate something," he said, turning abruptly away.

"Did you find what you were looking for?"

A glance, flitting toward me, then away. "No. But what I didn't find confirmed what I...suspected."

It took me a tick too long to reckon that. "Is that good?"

"Enough," he said, throwing a hand out. "No more questions."

"But—"

"Go!"

I flinched back, my heart aching in the strangest way. I knew it was so much more than just Doc being snappish at me—it was Doc, and Zagger, and Tarik gone, and a bullet I could never put back, and the terrors of my own mind, lurking in the darkness like a trap set to cage me again.

I turned away and leaned against the wall, my arms wrapped tight about my waist, my face catching the wind that gusted through the splintered boards over the door. A minute and something brushed my shoulder, naught but a snowflake touch, and when I glanced back I found Doc behind me, one hand hovering ghostly between us.

"I'm sorry," he murmured. "You did nothing to deserve that."

I nodded, not trusting myself to answer, and left him standing there with his hand tracing an apology to the shadows. But I'd barely rounded the corner of the nearest potline when I heard Rivano's voice hailing Doc, and instinctively I ducked behind the reduction pots where they wouldn't see me.

I was always too curious for my own good.

From my spot I could peek through a gap between the pots and get a good goggle at the infirmary, where the two men now stood face to face. Tension laced the air.

"You've been gone for two weeks," Rivano said. "May I ask where?"

Doc straightened up, letting the bandage he'd been fussing with drop unheeded to the ground. Somehow he didn't seem the least bit fitsy now, not like when he'd talked to me. If I'd been Rivano, I might have been a bit intimidated to face that fire in his eyes.

"No," Doc said. "It's really none of your concern."

"What my mages do is always my concern," Rivano said.

Doc gave him a frigid smile. "That's where you're mistaken, then." He leaned close to Rivano and said, almost too soft for me to hear, "I am not, and never have been, one of your mages."

I stifled a noise of surprise, but Rivano just measured Doc evenly. As they stood there face to face, unmoving and silent in those deep shadows, with the barest light from a nearby torch touching their faces, I got a strange feeling like I was looking on a painting from ages ago. Doc had always been a mystery to me, but lately I felt like even Rivano was some kind of cryptic text I didn't have the cipher for. I couldn't make sense of them at all.

Finally Rivano said, "You were looking for him, weren't you?"

Doc laughed. I didn't think I had ever heard him truly laugh before. It reminded me of the crow's laughter, harsh and airy, and a bit otherworldly.

"Of course I was looking for him. I know you can't stand the thought of him out there, free on the wing, any more than I can."

"Did you find him?"

"Why? What would you do if I did?" Doc moved to pass him, but stopped at Rivano's shoulder and said, "I know what you would do with him. I know what you would do with both of them. You are no better than Kippler." He hesitated, then added, "They are both safer far away from here."

Rivano spun and grabbed Doc's arm, forcing Doc to face him again. He leveled a finger at his throat. "You think you would have done any differently, if you had been there in my place when it happened? Would you have interfered? I had no idea then that he would turn out to be such a threat. What in Wake's name would have made *you* think he would?"

Doc held Rivano's gaze, his glass green eyes cold as sea ice, then he shook Rivano's hand off his arm and gave him a bitter smile. "Wake?" he asked. "You dare invoke Wake's name? I thought you Istians couldn't abide a lie."

Without another word he strode away, disappearing noiselessly into the shadows. Rivano watched him go, the surprise on his face hardening into some other expression I couldn't quite decipher. Anger, perhaps. Or fear.

He didn't linger there long, though, and soon as he had faded away into some other corner of the smelter, I said, "Shiver."

Because I knew, I just *knew* that Shiver was somewhere nearby, and that he'd heard every word of the conversation too. Sure enough, a tick later he melted out of the smelter pot beside me. I half expected him to be wearing some kind of smug grin, but the lines of his face were oddly serious.

"What was that all about?" I said. "You heard it too, yeah?"

He folded his arms and leaned back against the pot, which made me suddenly wonder if he actually had to try *not* to pass through the things he touched. In the torchlight the strange tattoos on his hands seemed to twist and curl, and against the warm copper of his skin, his green eyes were strangely bright.

"Yeah, and dan' that strike you as odd?" he asked. "No secrets in the Clan. No secrets here in the smelter. Everybody knows it's true. *Doc* knows it's true. So...dan' it seem peculiar that he'd have a gab with Rivano right here in plain sight, where anybody might get a clam on it?"

"Not sure," I said. "I think he *wanted* me to hear it. He knew I hadn't cleared out yet. I'd barely walked away when Rivano came along." I shrugged. "Doc dan' ever say what he dan' want. If he said it, he had a reason for it. But, I just can't figure *why*."

"Who were they even talking about?"

I glanced around the quiet smelter, patches of inky darkness cut by halos of firelight and shadowed whispers, and said, "No secrets."

He nodded, and without a word we both headed out into the smelter yard. It was near night now, the overcast sky hanging low overhead in dark rusty waves, and behind us the wind had turned the factory yard into a great big snow globe with the drifty white flakes swirling about till we couldn't even see the other buildings. Not that there was aught to see behind us anyway. All the folks who were still at the smelter had gathered inside the main building for what little warmth it offered.

I hunched my shoulders and tucked one foot up behind the other calf, because the ground was so cold I thought my feet might freeze clean off if they both were standing on it. Shiver just laughed at me.

"What's funny?" I asked, cross.

"You look like a great dafty bird is all," he said, mimicking my pose, making me laugh.

"Can't help myself. Been her for too long. Can't remember all of how to be Hayli."

Serious again, he reached out to touch my arm. "Dan' lose yourself inside her, savv?"

"What, Shiver, you worrying about me?" I asked, and tried not to feel alarmed by the thought that it might be possible...that if I stayed the crow too long, maybe I'd forgot I'd ever been Hayli.

*Not likely,* Piper whispered. *You're too stubborn. You'd never let me hear the end of you.*

Shiver shrugged. "I worry about everybody these days, seems like. We're all falling apart here. Ship without a rudder."

And I did shudder then, because his words made me think of Tarik adrift on the wild sea, and the weird certainty I had that he was in some kind of danger that none of us could ever understand.

"So, who d'you ken Doc was pecking about for, out in the city?" Shiver asked, interrupting my musings.

"Wish I knew," I admitted. The wind nipped the words from my mouth soon as I said them, chasing them away like ghost-tails in the dark. "I know he can't have been looking for Tarik."

"Then Kor, maybes?"

"Why would Doc be looking for Kor?" I heaved a great sigh, poking at a snow drift with the toe of my boot. "Stars, I hate secrets."

"Me too," said a voice behind us, and we both spun about to see Coins lounging against the wall, arms and ankles crossed. He grinned and added, "That's why I make it my business to know everyone's."

"Sneak-thief," I muttered.

31

He shoved away from the wall and came to join us out in the dark and the snow. He wore an old leather coat with almost as many patches as pockets, and had a wool watchcap tugged firmly down over his tangle of dark curls. Bundled up like that, he had to be the warmest person in our little group, but he never stopped moving.

"Everything jake?" he asked, bouncing on his toes. "What're you lot doing out here? Hayli threatening to fly off again?"

That last he asked Shiver, but I scowled and muttered, "No."

Coins chuckled and threw an arm about my shoulders. "Luce was looking for you earlier. I tried to tell her you'd gone bird again but that didn't make her feel better."

"Hey," Shiver said suddenly, smacking Coins's arm. "Who's that?"

I jumped and we both turned to see a dark bundle of a human being trundling through the gate. Since the sentry guards had let him past without a ruckus, he had to be someone friendly, but for the life of me I couldn't figure who. Then, as he came into the little puddle of light that dripped out through the smelter doorway, I realized it was Tam.

My stomach turned queasy and I glanced away from him. Beside me I felt Coins tense. I didn't think either of us could look at Tam, with the patch over his ruined eye, and not think of Vim. The grenade. The Chernayi guard whose throat I'd cut.

I wiped my hand on my pant leg, again, again, but the blood never came off. It was burned into my skin forever.

"Tam," Coins said, forcing a cheerful voice. "Did you come all this way just to see me?"

"Oy, shut it," Tam said, but he grinned fair enough and clapped him on the arm. "Where's Tarik? Need a gab with him."

"Tarik!" I exclaimed, not sure what had got me more shocked—that Tam claimed he needed to see Tarik, or that, somehow, he had connected Tarik to us.

Tam gave me a surly glare. "Dan' be daft. I can put two bobs together. I know who he is. So, you ganna let me jabber with him or what?"

When I hesitated, Coins gave me a little encouraging nod.

"You can talk to me till he gets back," I said.

"I can wait, 'specially if you let me sit by the warm nobby for a bitty tick."

Shiver and I exchanged a glance, then Coins shook his head and said, "It'll be a long wait. He's gone."

When Tam just frowned at him, uncomprehending, Shiver added, "He went to Istia. You knew that, right?"

"But—" Tam started, and pointed toward the smelter gate. "Not possible, mate. I just saw him out city way, not two hours past. Meant to gab with him then, but he div'n seem too keen on company. But I got news I think all you lot need to hear, so."

I stared at Tam like he'd grown another head, or like he might up and bite me like a rabby dog.

Coins drew a ragged breath and said, "You can't possibly have seen Tarik."

"You calling me a fib, Coins?"

Coins knotted his hands, but he backed down when I stepped between them with a hand on his chest. Behind him I spotted Derrin standing in the smelter doorway. I knew he'd heard enough to realize what Tam was claiming, but he didn't make any comment, or any move to join our group. I watched him sidelong to see if I could read aught in his expression. Was it possible Tam was being truthsome? Could Tarik have decided to stay? And…if he did, did Derrin know?

"Where'd you see him?" I asked Tam, trying to sound like I was actually willing to believe him.

"Was up near the Avnaya. Well. On a rooftop overlooking the Avnaya."

"Avnaya?" I echoed, scowling.

Coins cleared his throat gently. "Avnaya Square. That's the name of the plaza."

I blushed. At least he didn't do aught else to make me feel foolish at my ignorance—I felt foolish enough all on my own. Tam didn't know what the other lads knew about me, that I didn't have a ken what any of the streets were called, or the special buildings. To most of the Hole rats, the plaza was always just *the plaza*, as if that was its name, spelled in proper decorated capitals, as 𝕿𝖍𝖊 𝕻𝖑𝖆𝖟𝖆 or some such. Stars, the palace probably had a name of its own too—I was sure I'd heard Tarik call it something or other before—but I had no ken what it was. It just never mattered.

"You said he was on a roof?" I asked, to change the subject. Even I had to admit that sounded an awful lot like Tarik, what with his manic tendency to climb on roofs and all.

When Tam nodded, Shiver asked him, "Did he say aught to you?"

33

"Said he was trying to make sense of something. Sounded a bit Jixy to me so I figured I'd steer clear till he'd got his nog on straight." He frowned at me, then Coins. "You really thought he went to Istia?"

"He did," Derrin said, finally leaving the shadows to join us. "I watched him set sail myself."

Tam gave him a grudging nod of greeting. "Then how's it possible—"

"Oh stars," I gasped, snatching Coins's arm. "Oh, no."

"Hayli?" Shiver said.

I almost didn't hear him. Realization and fear showered through me like ice, then confusion, and all I saw, over and over again, was the dais in the plaza, and the mage who looked like Tarik. The mage Dr. Kippler had sent me to kill, making me believe he was the enemy. Could it be...? Nobody had seen the impostor mage at all since that terrible day, and me, I'd almost forgotten about him.

"Tam," I said. "Did he...did he look like Tarik? Or like Shade?"

"Tarik," Tam said, after a tick. "Why?"

"Because Tarik's not looked like himself since the whole incident on the dais. He Masked to Shade and hasn't changed back since." I shot a glance at Coins and Derrin. "Has he?"

They both shook their heads.

"But I saw him," Tam said. "Plain as rain I saw him, not further than you from me. Who could it've been if not him?"

"Did he know who you are?" Derrin asked, voice low.

Tam got very pale all at once. "Well, that was the oddness of it. I div'n reckon he did. Just stared at me like he div'n quite see me. I couldn't figure why. But..." Coins prompted him to go on, and he swore as he rubbed a hand over his face, letting his fingers linger over the edges of his eyepatch. "D'you think I bodged up? I called him *Shade*."

He didn't say aught else to explain himself. He didn't need to. If he'd called that other mage *Shade*...then he, whoever *he* was, would know Tarik's secret. He'd know that Shade—the mage everyone was calling the Zealot—and Prince Tarik were really one and the same person. Even though Tarik had shouted the truth to the whole city from the dais, most folks, far as I knew, never quite believed it unless they'd known it already.

Derrin cussed something fierce and stalked away, leaving me, Shiver and Coins with a distraught Tam.

"Maybe he div'n draw the dots," Shiver said, but Tam looked sore to slug him for saying it.

I drifted a step away from them, too. My thoughts were churning and turning like mad, and I had the nagging sense I was stumbling over something obvious. I just couldn't see it.

Finally I turned back to face the lads. "Dan' worry about it tonight, a'right? We dan' even know if that mage is dangerous." I gripped Tam's arm lightly. "We'll figure it out. But dan' gan looking for him. That ain't Shade, and whatever he is, I dan' want him knowing more about us than he already does. Got it?"

He nodded.

"But you said you had news for us?"

Tam hesitated, and Coins said a bit sharply, "Shade ain't here. If there's something we need to know, you'd better just spit tips and tell us, right?"

Tam regarded us a long while, head canted to the side like he wasn't quite sure what to make of us. Then, mouth twitching in a grimace, he said, "Look, it's bad, a'right? It's bad in the city. You think things've smoothed? They've not. Not a jot. It ain't just Ministers truppin' the fuss o'er what's the game now, but all those folks as got their lives bodged up by the muckery. All them as div'n flock here to Shade's banner. Them as div'n feel too keen on the way he and the King spun a knot up there on the dais like that. The anarchists and what. Div'n you wonder what came of them?"

Coins and I exchanged a glance. "I wondered," I said. "They're still around? I never heard tell of them causing trouble so I figured they'd had enough, since the King died."

"Figured dan' fix," Tam said. "Just because they're laying low dan' mean they've thrown in the pot."

"What do you know?" Coins asked, stern enough that even Shiver regarded him in surprise.

Tam took half a step back, raising his hands. "Dan' get tetchy on me, Coins," he said. "I div'n have to come and I dan' have to tell you pittance."

"C'mon, Tam," I said.

"Y' know the Bricks dan' exist no more," he said. "But remember the Cleavers?"

Coins swore under his breath. My face must have mirrored Shiver's blank confusion, because Tam looked from me to him and flicked us both a crude gesture.

"Really? You got no ken at all? Where's your nog been hid all these years? Up—"

"I dan' mix with the street gangs," Shiver snapped before Tam could finish, with a bit more arrogance than he probably needed. "Never have."

"*Oh*," Tam said. "Right. Sorry, *Mage*. Div'n mean to trash your high and mighty."

"Leave it be," I said.

Tam glared a minute longer at Shiver, then turned back to Coins with a shrug, ignoring me altogether because he probably reckoned I was too ignorant to talk to.

"Well, they've all grown up a bit since what in the Avnaya. Not just bangers no more. Like I said, these are folks as wanted to see Shade turn full-out revolutionary, *down with the Crown* and all, and never liked him being so cautious-like, always playing both sides."

"Yeah," Coins said. "Can't please everyone, right? So?"

"So," Tam said, and let that word hang in the air much too long. "So take it you ain't noticed your mate Red's slipped the roost?"

That got all of our attention. Coins and I looked at each other, then at the smelter like we expected to see Red walking out that minute with an armful of his cursed political pamphlets.

"Aw hell," Coins said. "Where is the idiot?"

"Where d'you think?"

"Cleavers?"

"Yeah, and not just. Told 'em where you lot are hiding out, none less. I heard some of their boys talking. Mages, most, who dan' stand for being second-rate citizens no more. They've a mind to come out, jaw with Shade, work out an understanding. Think they've a mind to win him to their side. Topple what's left of the old regime, put up a new. *That's* what I wanted to tell him about. Give him a head's up. You got company coming."

"If they find out Shade ain't here?" I asked Coins, digging my fingertips into my palms. "If they already div'n like how Shade was angling with the King and all, then if they think he's gone...if they think he's abandoned them..."

"Reckon they either want you signing the ticket and boarding the

 36

train, or getting the hell off their tracks," Tam said. "Reckon they're willing to use force if need be. They're fed up, and got nobody to stop them. They know if you lot dan' join up, you'll be standing in their way, and I dan' think they're keen to let you. Just ain't their style."

Coins took a step closer to him. "How exactly did you learn what Red did? How d'you ken what he told them?"

Tam said nothing.

"They got a stoolie in the ranks?"

Finally Tam gave him a nasty glare and threw one hand between them like an insult. "Maybes I heard 'em myself, Coins. Not exactly had any place to gan what since the King bowed out and the country went to pot." He shrugged. "They offered me a place. I took it. Dan' see as I like 'em over much, an' like 'em less and less every day. Mad as cats, that lot. Then this. This was the last egg. Figured it was time to haul out what I knew, see what Shade had a mind to do with it."

"Thanks," I said, and everybody looked at me in surprise. "What? He div'n have to come and warn us. Too much to say thanks?"

Coins just waved in dismissal, but Tam gave me a sharp nod and turned away.

"Stay with us, Tam."

He glanced at me over his shoulder. "Why?"

"You dan' like that lot. Maybe you'll like us better."

He hesitated, his one eye scanning the broken smelter, Red's burned-out office, the piles of snow and patches of ice.

"Dan' like this place already," he said. "But I s'pose I got naught left to lose." He turned his head. "I got naught at all."

"You've come to the right place then," Coins said. "We've all got nothing but each other here, right?"

I nodded in agreement, but Coins's words left me strangely sad. A minute and I wandered away from them, taking deep breaths of the frigid night air to clear my head. The snow was coming down thicker than ever, tickling my cheeks and clinging to my hair, chilling every inch of me until I wanted to turn bird just to enjoy the cozy warmth of downy feathers. But all the snow and all the cold couldn't bring sense to my thoughts.

I couldn't stop thinking about how Tam claimed he'd seen Tarik up in Brinmark. Part of me had hoped that the mysterious impostor mage had just…gone…when the chaos in the plaza had ended, like maybe he was some kind of an illusion and not really a man at all. But if he was still alive, and still here in Brinmark, loose on the streets, then Wake only knew what havoc he meant to rain down on us all.

I startled when someone laid a hand on my arm, and turned to find Tam frowning anxiously at me.

"What's bothering?"

"You really dan' get it, do you? You lot…you're all in such danger. Why dan' you listen to me?"

"We are listening," I protested. "I'll think of something, dan' worry. We'll keep these folks safe."

He flung his hands in the air. "That's just what I mean. You dan' have *time* to figure something out."

"Why not? You said the Cleavers had a mind to come see us, but I mean to clear us out before they can. We'll find some place safe to gan and…" My voice trailed off, feebly.

"No bloody time," he said then, punctuating each word. "Yeah, they've got a mind to come jaw with you lot. But they're on their way *right now.*"

## Chapter 6 ∞ Hayli

*I* GRABBED TAM'S ARM, SO TIGHT HE JERKED BACK IN SURPRISE. "THEY'RE coming *now?* Why div'n you say that in the first place?"

"Thought it was plain as rain," he muttered.

I released him and turned back toward the others, my thoughts whirling and twirling like mad leaves in a gale. Coins was watching me like a hawk, but Shiver had a thoughtful, wary look about him like he already guessed what Tam had told me.

"So what're you ganna do about it?" Tam asked, following me. "How d'you figure you can protect these folks?"

"They're coming to talk? Or to fight?"

"Stars, I dan' na. Cleared out before I heard that bit. Figured either way Tarik oughta know."

I glowered at him and shrugged up my shoulders, fighting the sudden urge to sprout wings and fly to the top of my favorite tree, where I could see the world so much more clearly.

*They're like rabid dogs,* Piper said, harsh, disdainful. *If they find out Shade's not here, it'll be like dogs drawn to the smell of a wounded beast. They'll come after you all. Put you down so you can't cause them mischief.*

*I know,* I thought back at her. *But what can I do?*

*Draw them away from the nest. It's the only thing you can do right now.*

"Where are they?"

"Holed up in the south streets," he said. "Not two bobs from the Hole. But like as not on their way here already."

"Shiver," I said, heading straight for him. "Come with me."

"Where d'you plan on going?" Coins asked.

"We're ganna gan and meet these folks," I said, "and we're not ganna do it here. If things hit the rails we're the two most like to get away safe, 'specially since I dan' na where Derrin's lammed off to again. I'm not ganna risk anyone else. We'll hear what they've got to say, and see what to do from there."

"And if things do hit the rails?" Tam asked.

I fired the engine on Tarik's motorbike. "Dole out the guns and double the guard on the gate and the roof," I said, as the steam built pressure, "and hope to Wake you dan' need to use them." I swung my leg over the motorbike, then jerked my head at Shiver. "C'mon."

He got on behind me, holding me almost too tight as the motorbike swerved and skidded on the loose gravel.

"You sure you can drive this thing?" he hissed in my ear.

"Course I can," I said, and spurred the bike through the gate.

The motorbike picked up speed on the river road, trailing clouds of steam like ghostly ribbons in the darkness. The cold wind bit my cheeks and brought tears stinging to my eyes, and even the leather of Tarik's riding jacket couldn't keep the chill from my bones. We'd almost reached the outskirts of the city when I spotted movement off the road in a broad field, a few flickers of torchlight glinting off the blanket of snow. I braked the motorbike so fast it skidded and almost bucked us off into the hedges.

Shiver tensed behind me, and I knew he was seeing what I'd already seen. There had to be fifty people there off the road, trying to trace a shortcut through the open fields to the smelter. In the patchy torchlight, I realized that probably half the folks were carrying weapons. I let my breath hiss out.

"Dan' look like they're in a chatty kind of mood," I said.

"We should get back," Shiver said. "Warn the others."

"Not yet." I climbed off the motorbike and took a few steps away from it, then shouted, strong as I could, "Hoy, on the road!"

The group came to a stop, and ten torches all flashed in my direction. I flung a hand over my eyes, but too late—I'd already lost what little night vision I had.

"Hayli?" someone called.

I waited, hands in knots, as a familiar figure ambled toward me, with two goons at his back carrying rifles that looked much too big for them. A third followed with a torch, but at least he had the sense to keep the beam trained on the ground, and not on my face.

"Hullo, Red," I said curtly, as they joined me. "Wondered where you'd lammed off to."

"Someplace warm, since I got burned out of my last space."

I bit my lip on bickering with him. We could argue for hours, Red and me, and it would never do anybody a jot of good.

"What's the fuss tonight?" I asked. "You lot look like you'd a mind to head down my way. Planning to join us again, or is there something I should know about?"

"What put you on the road tonight, at this time?" Red countered. I could see suspicion in his eyes, an ugly, twisted kind of thing. "Not a civilized time to be out."

"No, it ain't, is it?" I said. "I had business in the city. Saw what looked to be trouble heading toward my home, so you wonder that I stopped?"

He shrugged and stepped onto the road. Two of the others stayed back, but one of them came forward with Red—an older man, maybe in his late thirties, who had a mean look about him and a mage sign I guessed was a Knack's on his temple. I swallowed, trying to remember everything Pika had ever taught me about guarding my thoughts from nosy Knacks. For all I'd practiced with her, I'd never been very good at it. I just hoped I was good enough.

Red stopped too close to me. "So? Talk. Where you headed?"

"My business is my business," I said, and nodded toward the little mob. "But your business looks like my business, so maybes you're the one as should be talking."

"Who is this girl, Red?" the older man asked. "Why are we wasting time with her?"

"I'm not talking to you," I snapped. "I asked *him* a question."

"Don't get your feathers ruffled, Hayli," Red said, the words laced with mockery. "This is Klissen. He's in charge of the Grey Mist."

"The Grey Mist? Is that s'posed to sound intimidating?"

Klissen's mouth twisted and he took a half step toward me. "Funny thing," he said, "little girl like you, having such airs, thinking yourself so important."

Red cleared his throat softly. "She's important," he said, half under his breath. "She's Shade's girl."

My cheeks flushed hot at his words, but somehow I found I didn't mind the title. I'd snapped at Shiver once for calling me *Kantian's girl*, but that was entirely different.

Klissen's brows shot up. One was singed off in a bad way, webbed with scars, but the other was unnecessarily thick, and it stuck out from his forehead like a protest. I couldn't get a sense of the color of his eyes, but they were cold, and hard, and made me feel far too young.

"Really," he said.

He folded his hands behind his back and took another step toward me. Behind me I could sense Shiver drawing himself up, and I suppressed a smile.

"We've a mind to speak to Shade," Klissen said. "Will you take us to him? Maybe we'll get a friendlier reception if you lead us in."

"Not likely. If you think I'm ganna lead an enemy right through my own gates, you dan' na me a bit."

"Enemy!" Klissen echoed. "You've got us figured all wrong."

"Well," I said, waving a hand toward the field. "What else was I s'posed to think, seeing a mob of folks hedgehogged with guns sneaking off toward me home in the fox hours of the night? I mean, obviously that's how I'd send out a delegation if I meant to jaw with someone peaceful-like."

"*Delegation*," Klissen said. "Listen to you with the proper words. Then I'll tell you what. You run home, tell your boy Shade that we're on our way to talk We'll even give you a five-minute head start."

"Shade ain't a boy," I snapped. "And that dan' suit me. You keep coming like this, and I'll tell our guards to open fire soon as they see you. I'll tell you what. You lot turn about, gan off home, and come back in two weeks, just the two of you and your two lackeys, and then we'll listen to what you have to say."

I didn't much like the smile Klissen wore now. "Red, you never told me Shade kept company with master tacticians like this," he said. Then, turning back to me, "Makes me almost wish you were one of mine. Suppose Shade would lend you to me for a while?"

"No," I said, crosser than I meant, and crosser than ever when it just made him laugh.

"All right, girl, we'll—"

"Name's Hayli, not *girl*," I interrupted.

He pursed his lips, then finished, "We'll play it your way. We have time. But two weeks is an eternity these days. Anything might happen in that amount of time. No chance he'd see us sooner?"

"Shade's a very busy person," I said, "or why d'you suppose he sent me an' him out to run his errands?" I jerked my thumb at Shiver. For half a tick I hesitated, then gambled and said, "Not like I'd *choose* to go spy on the Cleavers in the middle of the night if I div'n have to."

Klissen's eyes sparked, but he kept his face neutral. "The Cleavers? What does Shade want with that lot?"

"He heard a rumor they were plotting something big. Some kind of alliance with the Chernayi, way I heard it." I cocked my head. "Heard aught like that on the street?"

Klissen and Red exchanged a glance, but Red looked a bit more nervous than I thought he had any right to. Maybe I'd struck a nerve without meaning to. I'd just tried to say the most unlikely thing I could think of, but...he almost looked guilty.

*Always scheming, that one,* Piper whispered. *He's weaving himself into a web he can't get out of.*

I got a sudden scratching feeling at the corners of my mind, and panic flared up inside me.

*Piper, he's trying to read me,* I told her, frantic. *What do I do? I can't blank my thoughts like Tarik can.*

I felt her smile. *Let go of your mind,* she said, *and let me do the thinking.*

I grinned, mentally, because I knew the way Piper's thoughts worked, and it was nothing like the way mine did.

"Shiver," I said, very softly, "you should go."

I barely sensed him retreating, step by step, into the shadows, and I thanked all the stars that he hadn't picked this moment to argue with me. I waited until he'd gone, then I turned my attention back to Klissen, and smiled, and let down the wall in my mind.

*The man stares at Hayli, confusion in his eyes. I carry my thoughts to the skies and set them free, in the clouds and the currents of the wind and the rhythm of color in tree branches, the vastness of forever and the smallness of a carrion rat seen from hundreds of feet aloft, fur and claws and twisted tail, dull in the brightness of gleaming light, a roost and a cacophony of voices and the taste of fear under the watchful eye of a hawk...*

*"What are you?" Klissen asks. He steps away from Hayli. "I don't...I can't..." He turns to the boy with the red face and suspicious eyes. "You didn't*

43

*say she was a mage. What…what kind of power…"*

*All at once the fingers of his mind withdraw, and Hayli is released, and I return her mind to her control.*

"BEEN A CROW FOR A WHILE now," I said, catching in a quick breath. "Can't keep my thoughts quite sorted yet." I looked him full in the eyes. "Not in proper order yet for folks to go snooping about in."

Klissen actually blushed bright red at that, which surprised me a fair bit. "You're a Moth," he said. The man with the torch startled, but Klissen just studied me a long time, not saying aught at all. Then he asked, "Why did you send your friend away?"

"Div'n need him here, and you dan' respect people's thoughts."

"Why," Klissen said, smoothly, "is there something on your mind I shouldn't know about?"

"Not a thing," I said. "Just dan' care much for folks who muck about in other folks' heads without their ken, is all." I took a step back toward the motorbike. "I'll see you in two weeks. Better know what you mean to tell him, because Shade dan' have much patience for nonsense these days."

"Wait," Red said. "Where…where are you going?"

"Told you," I said. "Trying to hunt down where the Cleavers roost."

"You don't know where they are?"

"Got no grobbing clue," I lied. "Got a ken?"

"Nah," Red said, too quick.

Klissen said, too glib, "Think I heard they were holed up in a building that got burned out in the uprising. East of the Avnaya."

"Much thanks," I said, and flashed them both a grin. "Shiver's gone back already. He'll have told my people about you lot being out here, and what I told you. So they best not see you prowling about tonight. You'd never know what you walked into."

They nodded, and I fired the engine on the motorbike, letting it chuff and build pressure before kicking up the stand. As I turned the bike toward the city, Klissen turned to one of the other men.

I didn't hear what he said, but Piper's sharp ears did: *"Follow her."*

# Chapter 7 • Hayli

I WOVE THE MOTORBIKE THROUGH THE STREETS OF BRINMARK, ALL TOO AWARE of Klissen's man following behind me, too fast to be human. Or, too fast to be possible without magic. My heart was pattering like mad. I could get clear of the man easy enough if I Shifted, but that would mean abandoning the motorbike someplace and risking it being stolen off. I wasn't much willing to do that, but the deeper I trailed into the city, the less likely it seemed that I'd have any kind of choice.

I made a show of going the direction Klissen had pointed me, toward Avnaya Square and the streets beyond where we'd searched for the transmitting tower, where Tam had lost his eye, where I'd betrayed Tarik to Dr. Kippler, where Coins had almost died. The streets were still a mess from the fighting—windows shot out, walls scorched from incendiaries and rogue fires, rubble piled in the streets. There was no light. It brought a sick ache to my heart to be there again, and the farther I went, the less reason I gave myself to continue my charade.

But if Klissen's man saw me give up my search before finding anything, he would report back to him and Red that I'd been lying. And that would put everyone in danger all over again.

So I kept moving, and presently I came to a tall building just east of the plaza, which looked like a fire had raged through every one of its stories. The walls around the windows were charred black, and there wasn't a single pane of glass left unbroken in the whole building. Even weeks after the fighting had ended, it still stank of ash and smoke. I cut the motorbike's engine at the end of the street, walking it into the mouth of an alleyway as if I were still set on sneaking inside. With Zagger's revolver clutched tight in my hand, I crept up to the building's broken door and poked my head into the shadows.

I heard the growl before I saw the gleam of eyes, and I jerked away, stumbling back over the rubble-strewn street until I hit the wall of the building behind me. A minute and a dog appeared in the doorway, all mottled fur and gleaming teeth and eyes. I couldn't quite tell if it was a dog or a wolf—either way, it didn't look friendly.

And yet I could feel the pulse of energy lingering all around it, and felt a sudden sharp certainty that the dog was actually Klissen's man.

In all my life, I'd never met another Shifter. For the longest time I'd thought I was the only Moth in all of Brinmark. Some bitty part of me wanted to talk to him, to ask him if he and his dog had the same kind of kinship me and Piper had, but the look in the dog's eyes was all feral, all wild. There was nothing human about it.

Another guttural growl drifted across the street toward me.

"Wait," I said, holding out my hand. "I know you're a mage. You're a Shifter like me. Please, *please* dan' hurt me!"

The dog stopped midway across the street, shoulders lowered in a warning crouch.

"Look, I could get away from you any time I want. But I wanna talk. Can we talk?"

The dog crept forward one more step, then, in a flurry of shadow and wind, Klissen's man appeared in front of me. He wasn't a big man, and his hair was almost as mottled as the dog's, but his face would have been pleasant enough if not for the dark suspicion in his eyes.

"So," he said, sidling forward. The way he moved still reminded me of a dog, lithe and rangy. "A fellow Shifter."

"Never met another Moth before," I said, brave as I could.

"Klissen doesn't want me to hurt you," the man said. "But this is a dangerous part of town."

At least he was halfway honest. I gave him a wild kind of smile and took a step closer to him. "You have no idea."

He just laughed. "Cute, kid. Not impressive."

He stopped laughing when I leveled Zagger's revolver at him. "Why'd you follow me?"

"Why are you looking for the Cleavers?"

"Told you that already. But they ain't here, are they?"

 46

"How do you know? They may be."

"'Cause Red may be an absolute leadhead and Klissen dan' seem much brighter, but still, dan' think they'd go gabbing off the location of their safe house to the likes of me."

"You know?" he asked. "Then why would you come all the way here? Pretend to be looking for them?"

"Maybes I just wanted to lure you out here, all alone, away from your friends," I said. "Worked, div'n it?"

"You are cracked, girl," the man said, but he watched me warily now, like I was some kind of snake in the grass—like he thought I might actually use Zagger's gun on him. "You're half my size, half my age, and you think you can take me on?"

"Got no desire to take you on. Just wanted to talk. Shifter to Shifter." When he opened his mouth I held up my hand and said, "I ain't magic-deaf, y'know. I felt you following me the whole time."

"All right," he said. "You want to talk? I'll talk to you."

"Talk honest."

He dipped his head in agreement.

"Your folks div'n really want to talk to Shade, did they?"

"Well," he said. "We meant to surprise him, put his back to the wall so he would have no choice but listen to us. We meant to convince him to join us, if he wasn't too bull-headed and belligerent to reason with. Otherwise, I suppose they meant to just get him out of the way."

"What for?"

He waffled, so I fired the gun near his feet. That made him jump back, breathing hard. "Stars, girl," he said. "You're insane."

"You think *I'm* dangerous?" I asked. "You might think twice before trying to cross Shade, or reckoning you could do aught to put him at a disadvantage." I waved the gun at him, just carelessly enough to make him nervous. Doing it made *me* nervous, too. "Answer my question."

The mage shifted his weight, scanning the narrow street around us. If I didn't know better, I might've thought he was gauging his odds of escaping me if he bolted. Funny, I was wondering the same thing.

"Look," he said, finally. "It wasn't my idea. I like Shade well enough but I liked the stability of the monarchy better, even if we got a rough end of the deal now and then. This is all madness. It's never going to work. But they won't listen to me."

I studied him curiously. His support of the monarchy might've surprised me, except he spoke fair and proper like a high street gentleman, which made me wonder if he was one. Or had been.

"Can't make heads or horns of what you're saying," I said. "Who wants to do what, why?"

"Red, and Klissen," he said, as if it was obvious. "They mean to topple what's left of the old regime, start fresh with all power in the hands of the mages. Turn the tables on the establishment—if we were kept out of power before on account of being born mages, now they want to keep everyone else out on account of them *not* being born mages."

"And...Shade?"

"They'd a mind to ask if he would take the reins."

"Red did?" I asked, astonished, because I was fair certain Red hated Shade as much as it was possible for one person to hate another.

"It was his idea. And if Shade doesn't agree, I guess they figure he'll be standing in their way."

"Do they really think they can stop him?"

"Maybe he can stop those Chernayi weapons, but I don't think he can stop a plain old bullet."

I laughed out loud. "They've got no idea."

"He's too dangerous," he whispered with a violent shudder. Then his gaze flashed to my face and he held up his hands. "I'm sorry. I know you care about him. But surely you see..."

"The only folks who should worry about him being dangerous are the folks who've a mind to hurt the people and the things he cares about. Including Cavnal."

"They say he's Istian."

"He's a lot of things."

"They say that too."

We stood in uneasy silence, me trying to make sense of what the mage had said, the mage still looking about as if hoping to find someone to rescue him. I heard a clatter of rocks some distance away—at the end of the street, maybe, or within the burned out building. It put all my senses on alert, but nothing followed except the wind whistling through the broken windows and the distant wail of a fire siren.

"If Red wants to set up Shade as some kind of Mage King, why's he dealing with the Chernayi?" I asked. "And what's in all this for Red anyway? He ain't a mage."

I didn't know for sure that he was dealing with the Chernayi, I was just playing a hunch because Red had acted so nervous about it before. The mage shook his head violently.

"I don't know anything about that, I swear. What you said earlier—that's the first I've heard about it. Makes no sense. I mean, as you said, *Red* isn't a mage, but now all his allies are, unless..."

"Unless he's not being completely forth with you," I said.

He scrubbed a hand over his jaw. "It wouldn't surprise me. Still, it doesn't quite fit with his plans for Shade."

I took a step closer to him, holstering the revolver in a show of good faith. "Listen. You obviously aren't too keen on what Klissen and Red are up to. You dan' trust Red, and I dan' blame you for that. Shade dan' want aught to do with overthrowing the monarchy *or* the Ministries. He never did. But he won't give up on the mages either."

He considered that, studying me under his heavy eyebrows. "Maybe I'm standing on the wrong side of the street then," he said.

"Maybe you could stay there," I said, "and tell me what you see."

He nodded slowly. "Stupid thing, telling a dog to chase a crow," he said. He held out a hand. "Name's Creech."

I hesitated, then took it, but my gaze never left his other hand. It didn't even twitch, and Creech just shook my hand warmly and dropped it again, welly fair and proper, like a gentleman.

"You realize I can't trust you just like that," I said, quiet.

"I know how it works."

"I'll come back here in a week, in the evening. You can tell me if you've learned aught useful."

He nodded and turned away, and the next minute I saw the black and tan dog trotting placidly away down the street, leaving me standing there alone in the dark.

WHEN I GOT BACK TO THE smelter, I let out a breath of relief when I saw no plumes of fire and smoke staining the sky, no signs of any kind of mischief. Instead I found Shiver out in the yard, still talking to Tam. Coins and Derrin were nowhere to be seen.

"Hayli, thank the stars!" Shiver said, soon as he saw me. "You jake? What happened? Did he read you?"

Tam shot him an alarmed look, but I waved a hand at them both. "The crow took care of it," I said, fighting a grin. "You should've seen his face. I'm surprised she div'n show him a whole lot of crow memories of eating dead rats."

*You wouldn't have been able to handle it either,* Piper said, smug.

Shiver laughed, but Tam said, "You were gone a bloody long time. What's the what?"

"Had to trick a way clear of them," I said. "Klissen's man followed me into the city, but we had a nice chat." I shook Tam's arm. "C'mon, mate, why dan' you come in and get warm?"

"That bodged up stack of bricks?" he said. "Dan' look warm to me."

"Warmer than out here."

He shrugged, and finally gave in. We found a corner of the smelter where someone had left a fire burning, and Shiver did the kindness of bringing Tam a cup of hot tea, which, that time of night, was all Miss Nan's makeshift kitchen had to offer. We sat around the fire, and little by little the rest of Tarik's crew drifted over to join us, first Coins, then the rest. When Jig sat down across from Tam they exchanged a glare so fierce that I was dead sure they'd start throwing fists for no reason at all, but then Jig shrugged and Tam looked away, and that was that.

"You two got a history I need to know about?" I asked.

"Exchanged words a few times," Tam said.

Jig grinned at him, feral. "Yeah, what you threw at me sure div'n count as punches, like."

Tam tensed, looking apt to jump over the fire at him, but Coins flung an arm around his shoulders with a cheerful grin. "Don't let him rib you, Tam," he said. "He's just sore you've got a bigger vocabulary than him, right?"

"I dan' even know what that means," Tam said.

"Me either," Jig said. "But wha'ever it is, I'm sure mine's bigger."

Coins just laughed, and I caught Griff stifling a smirk. I scowled, part because I had no ken what Coins was talking about either, and part because I was sure Jig and Tam hadn't seen the end of their quarrel yet. But Shade had won Jig over, too, and they hadn't started out friendly, so maybe there was hope for Tam and Jig yet.

Come to think of it, Shade had made a lot of folks friends who hadn't been before. I glanced at Anuk and Coins, sitting side by side, jostling each other good-naturedly. Before Shade had come along, they'd been indifferent to each other at best, but now, close as brothers. Shiver and Scorch—those two weren't quite friendly yet, but at least content to sit in each other's company without spitting insults. Shade had made us all a family. A big, messy, quarrelsome family, sure…but family all the same.

"So Tam," I said, hooking my arms over my knees. "Now we've got some time, anything else you can tell us about the Cleavers?"

"Cleavers!" Jig spat. "Stars, not that lot. Bloody awful scumbags."

Tam ignored him. "It's as I said. They've got in thick with the mages who want your kind to take the upper in society. They've got a common enemy, anyway, in the Ministers."

"Klissen called the folks heading our way the Grey Mist," I said. "You ever heard aught of that?"

"Aye, that's the faction of mages holding hands with the Cleavers. Klissen and Red, they're the what, unified front? Mage and non-mage, working together for the good of society, *tok dalzhu*. Red ain't in charge of the Cleavers, but they trail him more an' more every day, and that dan' set with me neither."

"They planning anything yet, or just talking big?" Anuk asked.

I held my tongue to see what Tam would say.

"Chits and chats, mostly," Tam said. "Still trying to sort what they dan' agree on. The mages have a mind to treat with Tarik, make him see sense as *they* see it, put him on the throne and make mages respectable again. Cleavers dan' want nobody at all on the throne, nor in the Ministries. Want the common folk in charge. Which, they can't even agree on their own name, so how they figure to agree on laws is trups to me. But your mate Red, he's got big plans he wants everyone to know about. Plans that're too big for his head, way I see it, but Red's got their ear and I dan', so."

That all seemed to confirm what Creech had said, so, I thought maybe I could trust the other Shifter after all.

"Shade should've taken Red down when he had the chance," Anuk muttered.

"Shade should've done a lot of things when he had the chance," Tam said. "But wishing dan' change dung to diamonds, though, now do it?"

Everybody got a thorny kind of annoyance about them at his words, and he lifted his hands.

"Dan' mean I dan' respect Shade. Div'n have to come, did I? But he left us a royal mess, no laugh intended."

"He did what he thought was right," I said. "He did what he

51

thought would help the most."

"Am I disagreeing with you? Dan' change the facts though, love."

"But what can the Cleavers possibly do?" Griff asked. "I've heard of them—long story. But they're just a street gang, right?"

Jig snorted and Anuk folded his arms, muttering, "*Katzo.*"

If the *katzpotivyek* called mages *Jixies* as an insult, south-streeters liked to call the high street folks *katzoi.* They usually got a mite skundered at being called little piggies, but Griff just laughed.

Anuk went on, "Street gangs already caused a mighty mess in this city, Farro. Not something I'm particularly proud of, but don't be too quick to dismiss them. And the Cleavers have got numbers we never had, so. Adults, too. Not just a bunch of kids like us."

I looked instinctively for Zagger, to grin at him for being called one of the kids, only to remember he wasn't there. My breath escaped in a sigh and I hunched my shoulders up.

"And mages," Scorch said. I almost hadn't noticed him, lingering in the shadows at the corner of the potline. "Militant mages," he added, "who won't sit quiet by a fight."

Shiver glared at him. "Dan' tell me, you've got a mind to join up? Wave their little banner, tear down the Court?"

"Don't insult me, Shiver," Scorch hissed, sidling closer to the fire. "Their ambitions are petty."

I frowned. Tarik had said the same thing, once, about Red. *He sees one problem and one solution,* he'd said, *but he doesn't really want change.* Had Tarik talked to Scorch about that? Was it change that Scorch wanted? And if so...what kind of change?

"Thought Rivano had most of Brinmark's strongest mages tight in his corner," I said, looking at Scorch thoughtfully.

"I don't hear Rivano preaching against the evils of the Grey Mist, do you?"

"What do you mean by that?" Shiver asked.

Scorch held his gaze briefly, a grim smile on his lips. "Don't tell me you haven't noticed," he said. "Rivano has plans that he's not talking about to anyone. It wouldn't surprise me if he wasn't working in the background to build up this Grey Mist. Use them for his own purposes, just like he's been using that damn Cromner book. And no one would be the wiser until it was too late."

# Chapter 8 · Tarik

*I* SPENT THE ENTIRE NIGHT PACING BACK AND FORTH ALONG THE DECK, desperate to stay awake, until even the sailors who kept watch throughout the night gave up trying to tell me to go to sleep. As the sun broke free of the horizon, Mattac emerged from below-decks and took one long look at me, but he didn't have time to do more than shake his head before one of the sailors called him to help with the fishing dories. I left the rail a few moments later, offering my poor help to the fishermen as they cast the little boats into the gold-glimmering expanse of the sea and laid out the nets.

A part of me wanted to go down into one of the dories with them, but the sea was too unpredictable; only the most experienced of the fishermen took that job. So I stayed on deck with Mattac, and helped to haul in the morning catch. By the time the morning had shifted to afternoon—the daylight already fading—and the work had ended, I was stumbling from exhaustion. Mattac kept saying something in my ear, but I couldn't focus long enough to comprehend it.

Finally he grabbed me by both shoulders and turned me to face him. "You're a dead man walking!" he shouted.

The wind had picked up; that was why he was shouting. I hadn't even noticed.

I pushed him away, shuddering at his words, and didn't answer.

"*Skeyfyr's* orders, mate. You're to stay below-decks for the rest of the day." I glanced back at him, surprised, but he just came closer and yelled, "Go to sleep!"

*I can't…don't make me sleep.*

But I knew if I didn't sleep they would make me work…and if my fatigue put the crew at risk, I would never forgive myself. Maybe, if I only took a short nap, I could avoid the nightmares.

"Fine. But wake me up in an hour, will you?"

"Why in *Veka's* name should I? You need the rest. And food. You haven't eaten anything since last night, have you?"

"Please," I said. "Don't ask. Don't…don't make me explain. Just do it, won't you?"

He shook his head and waved a hand at me. "All right. An hour."

I slipped through the hatch and claimed some leftover food from the sailor's lunch, but the bread and salted fish turned strangely dry in my mouth, and I couldn't bring myself to eat more than a few bites. Finally I gave up and stumbled into my berth, but for a few long moments I just sat on the edge of the low bed, head in my hands.

*Don't let me dream. I don't want to dream any more…*

But my head was already nodding, so I rolled onto the thin mattress and pulled the pillow over my head.

I'M STANDING AT THE EDGE AGAIN, *but this time, not the dais, in the snow. I stand at the edge of the sea, staring out over endless dark water, so smooth it catches the light of the stars and scatters it back to the sky. A wind—hot or cold, I can't tell—howls around me, but its raging breath doesn't touch the surface of the sea. I can feel its fingers on my neck, and my mouth opens to scream…but I make no sound.*

*"Tarik," a voice says, and when I look again I see Zagger standing in front of me.*

*He is holding a crow, cradling it close to his chest, and both his hands are made of flesh. But they are bleeding, or the crow is bleeding, because in the monochrome of my night vision, the red of blood trickling through his fingers is the only color I can see.*

*"Where are you?" I whisper. I want to step closer to him, but I'm at the very edge, the brink of the abyss, and I know no one will catch me if I fall. "Come onto the wall, won't you? What are you doing out there?"*

*I try to reach for him, but he is right in front of me and a million miles away, and my hand moves like it's trapped in water. He looks down at the crow, and I realize all at once that the crow is dead, its parted beak gently touching the edge of his finger, a hollow where its eye was meant to be. Grief lances through me. I can't breathe.*

*And already Zagger is fading, as if he is part of the night, and part of the wind, and nothing but the darkness between the stars.*

*"Zagger! Zagger...don't leave me. Don't you see I need you?"*

*"They say you shouldn't fear death," Zagger says. He is looking at the crow, but then he lifts his gaze to mine, and his eyes are white and empty. "They're wrong."*

*And the sea opens beneath him, swallowing him into shadow.*

*"Zagger!" I scream.*

*And the wall heaves and cracks under my feet, and I am falling into the darkness with him...falling endlessly...*

I SLAMMED INTO THE FLOOR, LANDING on my stomach. For a moment I lay shaken, my breath coming in ragged, broken gasps through the fire of grief in my heart. Almost too late I saw the wooden pail in the corner of the cabin tip and roll straight for me, and I swung out an arm to knock it away. It spun across the tiny space and rolled again as the ship lurched beneath me.

I could almost hear the beams and boards of the ship's hull screaming.

In a wild panic I dragged myself to my feet, stumbling through the narrow corridor and up the ladder to the deck, but halfway through the hatch I froze. My mind couldn't process the chaos. The ship's mainmast was split in half, the base barely standing, the other hanging like a broken twig over the side of the ship, a skeletal hand dragging through the foaming waves. Black clouds scarred with lightning churned overhead like roiling water. The gale tore the sails like bits of gauze. One of the sailors was overboard, clinging desperately to a splintered timber as the sea heaved beneath him. The other men couldn't spare the time or the hands to save him.

Agnir stood behind the helmsman, arms outstretched to the sky, but the sky wasn't listening.

"Taumir!" he shouted when he saw me.

I caught a mouthful of ocean water as a massive wave crashed over the deck. Blind, choking and sputtering, I somehow managed to gain my feet. But I couldn't go any further.

I couldn't erase that image of Zagger, blood on his hands, eyes white with death. I couldn't forget his words.

"You've got to help me!"

The voice came from beside me now, and I glanced up to find Agnir leaning over me, face pallid with fear and desperation. I was on my knees. I didn't remember falling.

"I can't..." I said. "You said it, I'd do more harm—"

"Not now! There's no more harm can be done!" He straightened up, staring into the sky, saying over and over again, "*Veka...Veka...*"

"What should I do?" I asked.

"Help me. Soothe the winds. Whatever you know how."

He closed his eyes and opened his arms at his sides, and I turned my focus inward to find his magic like I'd done before. But the ship pitched again and a flash of lightning just off the starboard bow stood my hair straight on end. The immediate crash of thunder set my ears ringing, deafened. I lost the thread of Agnir's magic but reached for the sky with my own power, trying to find the electrical currents in the clouds. If I could draw them down to me, like I'd done once in Esobor, then maybe I could send them away, too...

*"They say you shouldn't fear death..."*

"Taumir—damn it, I can't control it! Help me!"

"I can't," I gasped, grinding my teeth and focusing with all my strength. Threads of power slid endlessly through my fingers. "I'm trying. I can't..."

*"They were wrong."*

My head pounded. I knew it wasn't just from the crack of thunder too close to my head. The world swam before my eyes, starlight in water, blood in the moon.

*"Couldn't you have saved me?"*

I was on my knees. Drinking sea water. The ship was dying all around me and I couldn't move to save her.

The timbers groaned and the ship keeled, and somewhere I heard the crack and whine of breaking wood.

"Taumir, look out!"

## Chapter 9 • Tarik

*T*HE SEA WAS SWALLOWING ME.

One minute I clawed free of the waves, gasping for breath, the next I was hurtling through the black, the currents tearing me apart. Broke the surface, breathed water instead of air, plunged back into the depths, lower, lower. I couldn't tell the night from the sea. Couldn't force my arms to claw the waves. Couldn't kick, couldn't swim. Too numb to move. I was sinking, or rising, tumbling or climbing. Dizzy, bewildered, lungs caving in.

The sea spat me out. I tried to catch a breath but again the waves crashed over me, filling my nose, filling my mouth. Bitter salt abraded my throat, burned my lungs. Something brushed my leg but I couldn't see what. Couldn't see anything except foam and swirling black, the heaving sea, waves like mountains looming above me, on the verge of falling. Then something grabbed the collar of my coat, dragging me back, dragging me free…

Too numb to feel.

My ears rang and I couldn't hear anything else, but I found myself sprawled on my stomach across slick wood, wood that shook and lurched under the tearing waves. Someone's boot was planted next to my face.

Slowly the ringing in my ears narrowed to a shrill, constant whine, then faded away.

"*Veka…*" someone said.

I closed my eyes, coughing feebly with the first broken gulps of air. Blood pulsed at the edges of my blurry vision. Somehow I knew I should be doing something about the storm, but my thoughts scattered too wildly.

*Breathe...focus...*

I turned my gaze inward again, found the chaos of the storm at the heart of the night. Agnir's magic was there, working desperately, weakly, but it was like watching a man trying to stop a raindrop in a downpour.

*But at least he's alive...and at least he's still fighting. Unlike you.*

*No.*

I slammed a mental hand down with that word, striking the surface of the water.

And a calm fell, and the waves, and the sea grew still.

"What the devil?"

That was Agnir, and he was standing directly over me. I blinked against the saltwater once, then again, and realized it was his boot so close to my face. I rolled limply onto my back and found him staring at the night-dark sea, hands listless at his sides. From what I could tell we were in one of the fishing dories, battered from the storm but still watertight. Mattac lay over one of the rear benches, unconscious or dead. One of the other sailors— the one who'd said I would only be useful for ballast—sat hunched over his knees beside him.

What would he think of me now, if he knew the truth?

I glanced up again and found Agnir watching me, an unreadable expression haunting his eyes. Terror, grief, awe, relief...an odd jumble of emotions that made no sense put together, but which somehow felt strangely right. He bent and helped me to a sitting position, and as I coughed up water he crouched down in front of me.

"Taumir," he said. His voice was hoarse from screaming. "Thank *Veka*...I thought you were lost to the sea."

"I am," I said. The words fell from my lips like saltwater, and I pressed my head into my hands.

He gripped my shoulder fiercely. "We're alive, do you understand? We're alive. And...I don't know how. Another minute and this boat would've gone the way of..." His voice broke, and I looked up to see him staring out at the settling waves, dotted with driftwood and bits of canvas. "My ship," he whispered, the words honed with a keening sadness that I wasn't sure I would ever understand.

I turned away so I wouldn't see him weep. The other sailor was watching me now, so steadily that I wanted to turn away from him too, but I forced myself to hold his gaze.

"Why did the sea spare *you?*" he asked. "Of all the souls on that boat?"

Mattac groaned and his head lolled back. In the thin moonlight I could just glimpse the gleam of a livid cut across his forehead. The other sailor bent to blot away the blood, and Agnir sat down wearily on the bench behind me.

"You should be grateful she did," he said.

"Why?"

"Because he just saved your life. Didn't you, Taumir."

*Saved your life, after destroying all the others.*

And for some reason—I didn't know why—my heart flinched with grief at the thought of Sevnar, surly, cross, impossible...and now, lost to the waves forever. *God forgive me.*

I was too weary to argue, so I only nodded.

"Saved us?" the sailor asked, scoffing. "If he's powerful enough to stop that storm, who do you think started it, *skeyfyr?*"

"He was asleep!" Agnir shouted.

"You know that for certain, do you?"

I pressed the backs of my numb fingers to my mouth and looked away. For too long the little boat bobbed on the choppy water, in silence, the emptiness of the sea around us nothing compared to the emptiness between us. Finally Agnir moved, drawing a pair of long, slim oars from their brackets along the inner wall of the dory. The other sailor followed his example, taking his position at the stern bench and shoving his set of oars a bit too violently through their thole pins.

"Mattac is going to die," he said over his shoulder as he set his oars to the water.

I tried to stand but my legs were still numb, too weak from battling the sea to support me. But I managed to pull myself over Agnir's bench, and edged across the wet planks to Mattac's side. He still hadn't gained consciousness. Blood mixed with seawater pooled in the tangled fringes of his beard, and his round cheeks, always red from the wind and cold, were almost as pale as the foam on the sea.

"What're you about?" the other sailor asked me. "We've got

59

no stock on this *skatr thrigundrakkeyn* boat. No medicine, bandages, nothing. *Thu gyr drakkeyn vinga drakkur.* Do you hear? We hold out till we reach shore."

"And when will that be?" I asked, shooting him a dangerous look.

He exchanged a glance with Agnir and didn't answer. As they plied the oars in silence, I focused my attention back on Mattac.

*It isn't much. Just a little more magic. If you didn't fight it so much, do you really think it would damage you so badly?*

*Don't fight the sea.*

*You are the sea.*

I shook my head, trying to banish the nonsense whispered in the back of my mind, and placed my hands on Mattac's temples.

*Should I let you have him back?*

I tore my hands away, shaking all over. That voice...I knew that voice. It was the voice constantly in my thoughts, the voice that sang blood to the moon, the voice in every darkest moment of my life. But...I had never heard it like that before. Before it had always come with my own words, my own thoughts, the voice of my fragmenting mind. But this...this was different.

Like it belonged to someone else.

"Taumir?" Agnir asked, shaking me from my bewilderment. "Is he dead?"

"No." I gritted the word through my teeth. "Because I won't let him die."

I took Mattac's head in my hands again and closed my eyes, feeling out with my magic for some slip of life I could take hold of. Finally I found it, a tangled, fraying thread fast unraveling. And I did what I had seen Agnir do with the winds, smoothing the fibers, untangling the knots, ordering its warp and weft like a master weaver.

I tried to ignore how every movement of my magic unraveled something inside my own mind just a little more.

All at once Mattac gasped and lurched forward, and I caught his shoulders to steady him. The other sailor almost dropped one of his oars.

"Oh, stars," Mattac said, his gaze fixing blearily on my face. "I thought...I thought I'd died."

"Not quite," I said.

This time I managed to actually stand up, and I climbed carefully

 60

over Agnir's bench to sit on the one behind him, facing away from the others so they wouldn't see my pain.

AGNIR AND THE OTHER SAILOR ROWED for almost an hour, then handed off the oars to Mattac and me so they could rest a while in the belly of the boat. I let Mattac lead, since he had a better sense for the direction we were supposed to be heading, and lost myself in the rhythm of the sweeping oars.

"There are four of us on this boat," the other sailor said, when it felt like we'd been rowing for an eternity.

"Aye," Agnir said.

He was lying on the floorboards in the middle of the dory, arms wrapped tight around him against the cold night wind. The other man was nestled in the narrow stern, past Mattac, so I couldn't see his face at all. But Mattac twisted slightly to catch my gaze, and shook his head as if that might mean something to me.

"We've got no water, no *skatrdrakkeyn* food," the other sailor said, leaning against the edge of the boat to see us both. "We can't all survive. If we could have rigged a *drakkeyn* sail we might have made better headway, but how are supposed to row all the way to Istia?"

I was starting to get a sense for what the ubiquitous word *drakkur* meant. I had to appreciate the loving way the Istian sailors lingered over it, giving each syllable a particular emphasis. It seemed that Istians said everything fast except their profanity.

"There was no canvas fit for a sail, Vaskar," Agnir said.

And that was all. He made no effort to argue the sailor's other points, which made me more nervous than anything he might have said. *Istian honesty.*

"How far out are we?" I asked.

"Five days, if we still had *Hastol*." Agnir lowered his arm and studied me thoughtfully. "Fewer, maybe, if we can get the sea on our side."

I turned away, staring at the foam glittering in starlight where my oar cut through the waves.

"Taumir," Agnir said, just when all my focus had been swallowed by the sea. "Can you help me?"

Mattac darted a glance at me over his shoulder. Vaskar said nothing, and I wouldn't look at him, but I felt the hostility of his stare like a candle too close to the skin.

"I don't know," I said.

Agnir joined me on my bench, sitting away from the others so he faced the boat's prow. "You healed Mattac," he said, voice almost soft enough to be lost in the splash of the sea on the dory's hull.

"Yes."

"And you can control the Wind."

I nodded.

"Yet your mage sign is a mask."

"Are you asking how many Gifts I have?" I asked.

He let out a quick breath that might have been a laugh. "*Gifts,*" he said. "I forgot how you people like to categorize magic that way."

"*You people?*" I echoed.

He shrugged. "Cavners. By upbringing if not by blood."

"What do you mean about categorizing magic?"

"You talk about Gifts as if that is the sum total of magic. As if magic could ever be so neatly defined. I was only marveling at the spectrum of powers you apparently have proficiency in."

I gritted my teeth and focused on matching my oar strokes with Mattac's. My mother had made an enigmatic comment to the same effect, I recalled. The thought plunged me into a memory of the Kalethelia ball, of standing on the balcony of Brigun Palace, in the snow and the wind, when I'd broken Samyr's heart and my mother had told me of my father Eyid's descent into madness.

"*You should know that being a mage is so much more than just having a Gift,*" she'd said. "*A Gift is an expression of magic, but not the fullness of it…*"

"What you call Gifts are like so many currents in the sea," Agnir said, startling me from my thoughts. "They aren't the sea."

*I am the sea…*

I struck my oar too hard against the water, spraying icy foam over me and sending the boat skittering sideways.

"Careful," Mattac said.

"I can't help you," I said to Agnir. "I'm not sure what would happen if I tried."

I must have said it too loud, because Vaskar started from his seat in the stern. The boat shuddered and dipped, and Agnir was off the bench and halfway to Vaskar before I could blink.

"Sit down, Vaskar."

"That *vingathur thrigundrakkim* as much as admitted he sank

*Hastol!*" Vaskar shouted.

I gave him a feral smile. "If I'd meant to sink the ship, do you think I would've chosen to save *you?*"

Vaskar lurched over Mattac's bench. Agnir planted a hand on his chest, positioning himself between us in the narrow hull. "I'm not telling you again. Sit down."

"What, Agnir?" Vaskar asked, pushing forward and forcing Agnir a step back. "You prefer this foreigner to Lekke? Avnan? Iskathur? Don't you care that they've been claimed by the sea, robbed of the sun before their time?"

"Of course I care," Agnir said. "But you have no idea who that man is."

"What is he? The scion of the mad god? I don't care."

"You're a blasphemer, Vaskar. Maybe it was your impiety that brought *Hastol* down."

"Can we focus on getting to Istia?" Mattac asked. "I can't steer with you two rocking the damn boat."

"Shut it, Cavner," Vaskar said. "You never belonged on the ship anyway, no more than this *vingaskatr* foreigner."

Mattac shoved himself off the bench, setting the boat rocking dangerously. "Do you want to say that to my face?"

I dipped the oars again, again, watching a strip of the sea turn to silver flame like a river of moonlight.

*Won't you stop them? They're fighting on account of you.*

I shook my head. It wasn't my concern what they did. I had only one concern, and that was to reach Istia. It didn't matter to me if I made the shore alone or in the company of three.

Did it?

*You can't really believe that.*

"Both of you, sit down, now!" Agnir shouted.

I glanced up to see the captain grab the two men by the front of their wool jumpers, driving them apart. Mattac sat down obediently, picking up his abandoned oars and slamming them rather too violently into the waves, but Vaskar refused to relent. He broke Agnir's grip on his shirt, his arm swinging so fast I couldn't make sense of what I was seeing until Agnir staggered back, blood pouring from his nose. Then Vaskar had him by both shoulders, holding him precariously over the edge of the dory.

"You were the one who took him on board in the first place," he growled. "Maybe it's you we should be blaming, *skeyfyr*. Weren't you supposed to be able to harness the seas? Those men trusted you with their lives!"

"Take your hands off me! You're a fool if you imagine you can navigate the coastal rocks without me," Agnir said.

As he spoke, he shifted his weight, carefully. I was just expecting him to kick Vaskar off when Vaskar moved, hooking his leg around Agnir's ankle and jerking it back. Agnir crashed against the boat's hull with a cry of pain, tipping the vessel precariously as half his weight dangled over the dark churning waters. A gust of wind crashed over us under the cloud-blackened sky, and Vaskar's head snapped up, his eyes on mine, wide with alarm.

I didn't even realize I had stood up. I watched myself as if from somewhere outside of myself, gripping the oar like a weapon, swinging, striking. I never felt the impact of wood on bone.

I felt nothing at all.

Vaskar crumpled, landing over Agnir. Both of them tumbled over the edge of the boat, nearly capsizing it as they went. Mattac shouted; I sprang forward, reaching blindly into the moonlight water, grabbing the collar of an oilskin coat. Mattac helped me haul Agnir into the boat, then scrambled back to the edge beside me. I was staring into the depths of the sea. I could still see Vaskar's pale face blurred by the deep, still see his eyes staring up at me, the blood threading from his head like a wisp of red smoke on the wind.

I didn't reach to grab him.

# Chapter 10 ~ Tarik

Hours dragged by. I had never been so bitterly cold in my life. The damp sea air kept our clothes from drying, but none of us were willing to risk exposure to the frigid wind by taking them off. As the temperature dropped to a glacial chill, I could feel my sleeves and pant legs starting to freeze, but my hair had long since frozen in a tangled mess, stiff and cold against my forehead and neck.

The three of us sat huddled close together in the belly of the boat, shivering like mongrel dogs, letting the waves jostle the dory with a rhythm and a force that was never quite gentle enough to lure us into sleep.

I'd never longed for death so keenly.

"We're going to die," Mattac said, as if he'd read my thoughts.

I gritted my teeth, biting back tears of frustration, grief…regret. Fear. My head pounded with a splintering ache, and that was the first moment I realized that something must have struck me when *Hastol* was sinking, because my scalp just above my left ear was torn and swollen. Bleeding. That ear still rang, a sharp, whining hum that turned my stomach sick.

"Move," I said, nudging Mattac away.

As he and Agnir shifted around, watching me uncertainly, I edged back until I sat against the bulwark, then cupped my hands in front of me. I closed my eyes and focused. Drew a deep breath. Heard Mattac gasp in surprise.

"Taumir," Agnir whispered. "Are you all right?"

I opened my eyes, just enough to see the little blossom of fire curling above my palms. The flame behaved itself, burning contentedly in the space I gave it and shedding the most wonderful warmth I'd ever felt. So why was Agnir staring at me in such pale alarm?

"I'm fine," I said. My lips felt numb.

"You're bleeding. Stop, whatever you're doing. *Stop.*"

I closed my eyes wearily. My face felt warm, from the fire, I guessed, until I saw something dark drip down onto my sleeves, my hands. Agnir reached out and grabbed my wrist, wrenching it so hard that I cried out in pain and pulled back. The fire winked out, leaving us cold and dark once again.

I coughed, tasting blood in my mouth and the back of my throat. Choked and spat, and stared at the red flecks spattered over my hands.

"God," Mattac said.

He caught me when my spine gave way without warning, and I searched the sky and wondered what it meant to ride the stars.

A BLARING SHIP'S WHISTLE STARTLED ME awake. It must have only been moments since I collapsed, because the blood on my face was still wet, cold but not frozen. But sure enough, the stars were blotted out on the starboard side of the boat, and a smell not of salt or rain drifted over us, as a steamship bore down on the dory.

It was little bigger than *Hastol* and had no sails, just a cloud of grey fog curling over a single funnel and a Cavnish flag snapping from a midship pole. In the dark I couldn't see its colors, but I would have recognized its stylized sun and diamond ordinary anywhere. The horn blared again, and suddenly, fearing the skipper would miss us in the darkness and catch us in the ship's wake, I lurched to my feet, stretching one hand straight above my head and calling the brightest spark of flame I could manage.

The boat slowed as it approached, and finally settled to a drifting stop as it drew up alongside us. Men shouted above us as a rope ladder cascaded over the hull, and I let my arm drop, staggering and dizzy with relief. Mattac had his arm around my shoulders but I barely felt it. Agnir climbed up the ladder first, then Mattac, but I only managed to twine my arms through the ropes before my strength gave out. Vaguely I felt the ladder swinging, pulling me up, then Agnir and Mattac were grabbing my elbows and hauling me onto the deck.

"Who are you?" one of the steamship's sailors demanded, standing over the three of us as we sprawled at his feet, wet, half-frozen, exhausted. "Do you speak Cavnish?"

"Yes," Agnir said. His Cavnish *was* good, if a bit overly formal and weighted with a heavy Istian accent. "We're fishermen. There was a storm. I...I lost my ship."

I let my head roll back so I could get a look at the Cavnish sailor. He wore a plain wool cap and heavy fisherman's coat, and with his sparse blond beard he looked fairly young, but the way the other sailors lingered behind him I guessed he was their skipper. At Agnir's words his expression changed from scowling suspicion to pity. He reached down and hauled Agnir to his feet.

"Captain," he said, and tipped the ridge of his hand to the middle of his forehead in a curious salute I'd never seen before. "My condolences."

Agnir returned the salute, then glanced over his shoulder at Mattac, standing close behind him, and the man's other sailors, who were busy lashing our dory to the side of their ship.

"We're half-frozen, Captain. Please, we beg a few hours by your fire. We'll work for a meal. And then just let us be on our way to Istia."

"Fishing vessel?" the Cavnish captain asked, and Agnir nodded. "Not military?"

"No."

The man glanced down at me. "And what's wrong with that one?"

"Our ship was entirely destroyed," Agnir said rigidly. "He was injured in the wreck."

"You said there was a storm but we've had naught but smooth seas. How long ago were you wrecked?"

I closed my eyes, fighting back a surge of anger, as my fingers drifted over the sticky blood under my nose and lips.

*Are you truly going to doubt our story because I'm still bleeding?*

"I'm sorry," the Cavner said then, waving a hand as if to will the question out of existence. "We saw a light on the water and came to investigate. It looked like a fire but it was too small, gone too fast."

"That was my doing," I said. "I'm a Flint. I was trying to save their lives. We were freezing to death. We are *still* freezing to death."

The man drew up in alarm, snapping his fingers at two of his sailors. He muttered something to one of them, and before I could blink they had circled behind me and hauled me onto my knees, twisting a bit of rope around my wrists.

"Honestly!" Agnir exclaimed.

"Who are you?" the Cavner asked, staring hard at me. "You look pure-blooded Istian but you speak Cavnish without a lick of accent."

"Does it matter who I am?" I gritted. "Let them get warm, and you can do whatever you want with me."

"You're here by my hospitality. You're in no position to make demands."

I staggered to my feet, dragging the two sailors with me as I brought my face inches from his and gave him a cold smile. "If you value your life and the lives of your crew, don't make the mistake of thinking you can mute my power by tying my hands."

Was it bravado? I didn't know.

"Are you threatening me, Mage? Because we can and will throw you back to the deep."

"Taumir…" Mattac said.

I glanced at him, his eyes red-rimmed, beard rimed with ice and salty seawater, body racked with shivers. Agnir, beside him, barely managing to stand upright.

If I didn't do something, this Cavnish captain would send us back into our dory, and we would be left to float helplessly adrift and await the hand of Death. If I pushed the threat too far, he would throw us overboard without the courtesy of returning us to our boat. I could defeat him easily enough, I thought, but what good would that serve in the end? But I didn't know what else to do. I had no authority here, no influence, unless…

"How long have you been at sea?" I asked the Cavner.

"Ten days…?" he said, baffled.

"You were in Cavnal before that?"

"Of course, yes."

I took a breath and swallowed back my doubt. I said, "And you don't recognize me?"

He grabbed a lantern from one of his sailors and swung it in my face so he could peer at me more closely. Then all at once he swore and stumbled a step back, pale and wide-eyed.

"Get *them* inside," he said. "Leave this one to me."

# Chapter 11 ∞ Hayli

AFTER THE MIDNIGHT CHASE THROUGH BRINMARK AND HOURS OF conversation with Tarik's crew after, I slept almost the whole of the next day away and didn't wake up till most everybody else had eaten dinner. Now, while the rest of the folks had gone to bed, I was wide awake, my thoughts a restless kind of chaos. I stood in the doorway of the smelter with Anuk beside me, both of us quiet and watching. It had to be late, near the middle of the night, and only the amber glow of a few low fires and a handful of magic-fueled torches broke the darkness.

I'd told Tam we would find someplace safe for everybody to go before the Cleavers could smoke us out, but the more I thought about it, the more muddled I felt. If only Shade were here, he would know exactly what to do to keep everybody happy and safe. I didn't have much of a mind for planning and strategy, and I couldn't think of anybody who did, except...

"Anuk!" I said, grabbing his arm so suddenly that he jumped in surprise. "What happened to Lieutenant Bridnow? Did he come back?"

"He did. Got pardoned by Minister Farro after the King's funeral. Could've gone anywhere once they set him free, even back to the Army, way I heard it, but he came back to stay with us here instead, so."

I nodded, relieved. Bridnow had training and experience none of the rest of us had, no matter how we puffed ourselves up and imagined we could change the world all on our own.

"A'right, that's good," I said. "Bring him to me."

He gave me a funny kind of look but sauntered off into the smelter, which made me realize that I'd gone telling him what to do, as if I could. I wasn't in charge—what made me think I could order him about like that? And not just tell *him* what to do, but tell him to wake up *Lieutenant Bridnow*, in the middle of the night, just because I'd a mind to talk to him.

I fretted, wondering if I ought to chase him down before he got to Bridnow, but faster than I thought was possible I saw them coming toward me, with Jig and Scorch trailing them, and Coins and Griff a few paces behind. A moment later Derrin stepped out of the shadows, and I'd a feeling Shiver was likely in the walls somewhere too. Tam was the only one missing, but he'd been keeping mostly to himself, and never seemed too keen to fit in with the crew.

A minute and the whole group of us stood in the doorway, awkward and silent. The lads looked cross, like as not because Anuk had woken them up—and I wanted to shake Anuk for doing it, too, because all I'd wanted was Bridnow.

"It's freezing. Let's talk somewhere else," I said, when they all kept watching me, and none of them spoke.

By habit I turned left inside the smelter, tracking down the long corridor to Shade's office. Even when we all crowded inside, the room felt strangely empty without him there, darker and colder than it should have been. Scorch stooped without a word and started a fire in the stove, then stirred his fingers toward the oil lanterns. The light brightened and steadied, showing us all our haggard and anxious faces.

"So, what's gannin' on?" Jig asked, watching me hawkishly through his shaggy black hair as I pulled myself onto the edge of Shade's desk.

"I actually just wanted to talk to the lieutenant," I said, peevish. "Div'n mean to wake all you lot up, too. But since you're all here, you might as well stay and give us your thoughts." I hesitated, hands clasped between my knees, and looked straight at Bridnow. "We can't keep living here, not like this. We need to move everybody out. And if the Cleavers mean us harm, we need to do it soon."

Of all of them, only Bridnow didn't seem shocked.

"What?" I said, when they said nothing. "Look at this place. It ain't fit for decent folks now, with everyone in everybody's business, and nowhere proper to eat and sleep. And what happens if we get attacked again? We'd never survive."

"Aw, hell," Coins said. "And I was just starting to enjoy sleeping on concrete."

"It ain't your call, is it?" Jig asked me. "Maybe we should wait on Shade getting back before we gan moving about. We dan' na what he even wants us to do, like. Maybe he'd rather we all just went home. Back to the Hole. Or wha'ever. Forget this whole mad business. It dan' concern us no more, what with the King corpsed and all."

"Dan' be a grobbing idiot," I said, then added softly, "And dan' talk about the King like that."

Jig shifted and no one else spoke, but I read a silent *thank you* in Bridnow's eyes.

"Anyway," I said, "Shade wouldn't want us just giving up and throwing in the kips, not after all..."

*Not after all we did. Not after all we lost.*

"Who put you in charge?"

"Shade's not here," Bridnow said, voice low. "Hayli is in charge."

I stared at him, as stunned speechless as the others. "Wha—" I faltered. "I am?"

"She is?" Jig asked at almost the same moment. "Why?"

"Because," the lieutenant said, "that's what Shade instructed me before he left."

"Yeah, but *why?*"

I was asking myself the same thing. Tarik had left me in charge of his crew? And not just his crew, but the whole motley group of mages and *krizanyi* who'd left all and everything to follow him? Why not Derrin, or Bridnow himself? Either of them would've been so much better for the job than me.

Bridnow measured me quietly. I couldn't tell if he was doubting the smarts of Shade's choice too, or if he just was trying to figure out if I deserved it. But under that hard gaze I felt much too young.

"Because he trusts her more than anyone," he said finally, answering Jig without taking his eyes off my face.

I glanced at Derrin, uncertain, but to my relief he didn't look sore about it. Maybe a bit sad, but I knew that had naught to do with me and everything to do with himself, even though he'd never done worse to Tarik than I'd done. In fact, *I* had done worse. I'd come that much closer to actually assassinating him, firing the bullet at his heart that ought to have killed him. I wasn't sure what made Tarik trust me in spite of all that, but I swore I'd do whatever I could to make sure I earned it.

"Fine, wha'ever," Jig said. "I dan' care. What's your plan, Hayli?"

"That's *why* I wanted to talk to the lieutenant. We're hundreds of people here. If it were just us, we could squirrel out in ten minutes tops and den up in any place we like. But we've all manner of folks with us now. Some old, some young. Some mages, some not. Some healthy, but a lot ain't. We *can't* just empty out on an hour's notice. We likely wouldn't even last a day."

"We've posted extra guards at the gates," Coins said. "And on the roof. We'll know if something's coming."

"Not good enough, Coins. We can't be here if something comes."

"You really want to take all these folks with us, wherever we go?" Anuk asked.

I chewed the inside of my cheek. It would be so much easier if it was just us, not having so many mouths to worry over feeding, not having to wonder if everybody hanging about was actually loyal. We could stay on the move, we could hole up in an abandoned house somewhere, and weather out the days until Shade came back. But somehow I knew that was never what Shade had in mind.

"These folks've got naught at all," I said quietly. "They've been burned out of their homes, lost their *stavos* and their work crews. They're hungry and desperate. And they came here because they trusted Shade to take care of them. Shade ain't here right now, so that means it's our job to do it. We're not ganna turn anybody away. So, Lieutenant." I turned to face Bridnow. "If we were a regiment deployed someplace far away from home, how would you gan about getting shelter for everybody?"

Bridnow's mouth quirked in a smile. "Well, you could either take over a site that already has enough space to house everyone, or you'd have to build a temporary bivouac. If you're planning to stay a while, you'd probably build a permanent post."

I ground my teeth, my stomach pitching into knots. Trouble was, I *did* know of a place that had plenty of room for all of us, safe and secure, warm and dry and tricked out with decent enough furniture. I just didn't know if I could ever force myself to go there. I could barely bring myself to think its name.

"What about Borokhev?" Derrin asked softly.

And that was exactly what I didn't want to hear. Every pair of eyes turned straightaway to me, waiting to see if I would melt down. And I wanted to. Everything inside me wilted just at the thought, and I wanted to throw something at Derrin for even saying it.

*It's not about you, Hayli,* I told myself, firm as I could. Or maybe that was Piper's harsh, airy voice I heard, scolding me deep in my mind. *What do these folks need? Remember what you just told the lads. Tarik left the folks in your charge. Are you going to let them suffer and freeze because you're too scared?*

I wanted to say *yes.* Part of me thought I'd happily let everyone stay in the smelter if it meant I never had to set eyes on Borokhev again. Too late I realized I had my arms clamped tight around my waist, that I was bending over, that my head pounded like a thunderstorm and my breathing was coming too shallow, too fast.

"Oh, God," I whispered, which wasn't what I meant to say at all.

*Pull yourself together. How can you be in charge of anything if you can't control your fears?*

*Borokhev.*

*I can't I can't I can't*

Coins said, his voice low and a little rough, "Would you give her a minute?"

"No," I said, willing myself to be calm. My shoulders shook and I dug my fingernails into my arms, fiercer, tighter, hoping the pain would drive away the fear.

"We'll go to Borokhev," I wanted to say.

I opened my mouth to say it, but those weren't the words that came out. Nothing came out but broken breath. An inhuman whimper that couldn't possibly belong to me. I dragged my gaze away from the door, the door I wanted to run through and never look back, and turned to Derrin.

I nodded.

All at once the room spun into motion—how long had time felt suspended, like a breath held too long? Everyone was talking, shuffling papers on Tarik's desk, and I sat alone like an island in the middle of the tempest, and tried to hold myself together.

I didn't notice Coins until I felt his hand gentle on my shoulder.

He sat against the edge of the desk beside me, worry in every line of his face.

"Hey, you jake?"

I hesitated, then shook my head, wishing desperately, stupidly, for Tarik to come walking through the door. He was the only one in the world who could take the terror out of my heart.

He was the only one *still alive* who could, I realized in a rush of grief, as I remembered how Zagger had comforted me when I'd seen Miss Farrady…

*Miss Farrady.*

The name pierced the fog in my thoughts like a shaft of lightning. *Oh stars, how's it I forgot about her?*

"Coins," I whispered. He waited, quiet and expectant, while I stared dumbly at the wall, trying to cage in my fluttering thoughts. Finally I jumped off the desk and dragged him out into the corridor. "What happened to Miss…to Miss Farrady?"

He let out all his breath in one exasperated puff. "Wish I knew, right? Honest. Either she had help, or she's got quickfinger skills that would put mine to shame."

"What d'you mean?"

"When we got back, after…after everything…she was gone. Door open, cuffs laid on the table neat as could be, holding down the kindest *thank-you* note you could ask for. She flew the stew."

"Flew the stew?" I echoed, but something had Coins bothered because he didn't even smile. "So we got no ken where she lammed off to?"

"No. I'm sorry. Wish we'd kept better guard on her. I don't like the thought that she's free on the wing again. That woman's a bloody lunatic."

I wanted to scream—in anger, in fear, I didn't even know—but I kept it trapped inside, holding it in with my arm tied like a chain about me. Drove my knuckles against my teeth. Bit down until I bled.

Coins swore and snatched my hand away from my mouth. "Stars, girl," he murmured, and caught me in a tight embrace. "It's all right. You're safe. We'll never let her hurt you, you know that, right?"

"She should die," I said into the rough wool of his jumper. The violence of my own voice startled me.

A minute and he didn't say aught at all, then he sighed and released me. "I know," he said. "But Shade let her live for some reason. Maybe he never got to do what he planned, I don't know. Maybe I could track her down and bring her back for him."

"Just dan' tell me, if you do. I dan' ever want to see her again."

"And you're sure you're all right, moving everyone to...the prison town?"

I was walking away from him before I realized I'd moved, but he caught up to me as I stepped out into the snow-swirl darkness. Everything inside me was so numb I didn't even feel the wind, but Coins beside me was bouncing on his toes to stay warm, hands tucked tight under his arms.

"I dan' na," I said finally. I tipped my head back, blinking against snowflakes, then dragged in one deep breath and grabbed him by the arms. "Dan' let them cage me again! I dan' wanna be caged up. Not ever."

I knew he wanted to ask what I meant, but he couldn't possibly understand. We all used that saying—*free on the wing*—but not a single person here had a ken what it really meant.

I took a step back, fingers stirring the wind and feeling its currents, longing to fly.

"I dan' wanna die," I whispered.

"Die?" he echoed. "Cage you? Hayli..."

"Haven't you ever noticed?" I threw my arms wide to the night and turned my face to the wind. "Wild birds dan' die."

## Chapter 12 – Tarik

THE SAILORS USHERED MATTAC AND AGNIR AWAY, THOUGH BOTH OF THEM kept glancing anxiously over their shoulders all the way to the ship's hold. I stood as straight and still as I could until they disappeared down the ladder, then I let out my breath and staggered to one knee.

"Shade, isn't it?" the captain asked, dropping his voice. "I don't believe it. What are you doing out *here*, halfway to Istia?"

"Please," I muttered. "I can't feel anything."

He straightened up, and the curiosity had left his eyes. All I read in them now was hatred.

"Brought low, are you?" Without warning he backhanded me across the face. I sprawled on the wet wood of the deck, unable to catch myself with the rope binding my hands behind my back, and fresh blood rushed from my nose and mouth. "Never thought you'd be at the mercy of a mere fisherman, did you? What did you do to the King, traitor?"

"I didn't do anything to him—"

"*Shut* up," he hissed, driving his boot into my stomach, just below my ribs.

I coughed and curled in on myself, the deck wobbling weirdly beneath me.

"Maybe you got some of the common folk flocking to your banner, *Zealot*, but we're not all turncoats. Some of us loved the King. Some of us were actually *loyal*."

"I loved him," I said. "More than you know. You know nothing about me."

He dragged me off the deck, but only so he could slam his fist into my face again. My vision showered sparks and I sagged in his grip. Then I closed my eyes and focused, directing all my strength, all my energy inward. A moment later I smelled the char of burning rope, and a comforting heat seeped over my wrists. I pulled outward against the bonds, testing, waiting until the precise moment the heat from my skin burned through the fibers.

The ropes snapped all at once and I threw my hands forward, planting them both against the captain's chest. And I Pushed. He flew across the deck, his back slamming against the metal-clad bulwark on the other side of the ship. I stumbled to my feet and staggered after him, rage burning through every vein in my body.

He shrank back, hands held defensively before his face. "Oh God," he gasped. "Don't kill me."

"I asked for nothing but a boon for those two men," I hissed, dropping to one knee beside him. My hand, sticky and red from my blood, clamped on his jaw. "I don't care what you think of me. Take care of them, and I'll leave you in peace. Give them any trouble, and I will sink your ship and everyone on it."

"Mad," he whispered. "It's true…"

I released his jaw. "What's true?"

"They said you were mad. The scion of the mad god. I thought they were fools for believing it."

"They are," I said. "The mad god has no claims on me."

I got to my feet, leaving him crouching against the bulwark, but not two steps away I heard his voice, or a voice, drifting after me, whispering, "Doesn't he?"

I hesitated, then shook my head and forced the thought away. Taking the ladder down into the hold of the ship, I found Agnir and Mattac laughing with the other fisherman over mugs of ale or grog. One of the Cavnish sailors glanced up at me when I appeared in the galley, eyes widening when he saw my face.

"The hell happened to you?"

"We came to an understanding," I said.

His gaze shifted past me, as if expecting to see his captain coming down the ladder on my heels. "Where's the Chief?"

I jerked my head toward the hatch. "On deck." When his face turned a ghastly shade of pale, I added, darkly, "Alive."

I pointed at his cup and beckoned, and he stood without a word and poured me my own mug. Mattac got up to give me his spot by the furnace, an oddly deferential gesture he probably didn't even realize he had made. I slipped onto the edge of the bench and leaned gratefully toward the fire. One of the sailors handed me a damp rag, which I took with a nod of thanks. Once I'd cleaned the blood from my face and hands, I tossed the cloth into the fire and watched it smoke and burn.

"Why'd, ah…why'd you burn that?" the sailor asked.

They were all staring at me, and the sensation was agitating. I focused on the cup of grog—it was hot, and strong, and the burn of it in my throat was so much pleasanter than saltwater and blood.

"I'm not leaving my blood here," I said.

For a moment no one said anything at all.

"You're joking, right?" Mattac asked then, staring at me like I'd said something absurd. "What would anybody do with your blood?"

Agnir shuffled his feet. "It's superstition," he said. "Fisherman's lore. I don't know that anyone actually does it any more."

"Does what?" the Cavnish sailor asked, frowning.

"Stars," one of the others said. "I told the Chief not to dabble in that nonsense."

"What nonsense?" the first sailor cried, thoroughly vexed. "Am I the only one here with no bloody idea what any of you are talking about?"

I ignored him, keeping my gaze on Agnir, fear and frustration and anger like a blaze inside my veins. "Was it true what Sevnar told me, that there was more blood than paint in *Hastol*'s timbers? Not that it worked, apparently."

Agnir rubbed a hand over the back of his neck. "My father believed the lore. He's the one who built *Hastol*, when I was a boy. And that's what he always said. More blood than paint."

The first sailor flung his hands up and slumped onto the bench.

"There's lore that working a mage's blood into a ship's timbers will give it special protections," the second sailor said, quietly. "Whatever the mage's particular ability. The blood of a Flint," and he nodded in my direction, "would protect a ship from being destroyed by fire."

"And a weather-worker's?" I asked. "Would it save a ship from being smashed by a tempest?"

"It's supposed to," Agnir said, regarding his forearms with their lightning tattoos. "And it always has. Until now. I suppose there are some powers stronger than blood."

"Just depends on whose blood, I suppose," I said, straightening a little and draining the mug. "It's not just fisher lore, either. Every culture has it in one form or another, but fishermen all share the same lore, regardless of what country they hail from. I suppose the sea claims stronger allegiance than any flag."

"You're thinking about Arnthor?" Mattac asked quietly.

I nodded. Everyone knew the story how, when the Cromners executed him at the end of the Scourge, the archmage Arnthor was left without so much as a drop of blood in his body. But every drop he had spilled was collected and taken to the Towers of the King. For a century they'd rubbed a drop of that blood into the skin over the heart of every Cromner born into the royal family. They'd despised Arnthor, and murdered him, and yet they didn't see the irony of using his blood like a talisman of protection. It was meant to keep them safe.

Maybe Arnthor's blood was never meant to stop bullets, because seven dead royals drew a heavy burden of proof.

I sighed and ran a hand over my forehead. Cromis had been the first country to turn away from the ancient piety of its people, but somehow they'd never managed to let go of that custom. They were the first to issue edicts permitting people to be executed for the crime of being born with magic in their veins, but they never stopped anointing their royal infants with a mage's blood. Sometimes, I thought, the world made altogether too little sense.

"You actually rubbed your blood into your ship's wood?" the Cavnish sailor asked Agnir as I shook myself out of my thoughts.

"Every sheet and timber, and every sail." Agnir rubbed his fingers over his forearms, and I noticed for the first time that every stroke of the blue-forked lightning tattoo was inked beside a scar. "I've been tied to that ship since I was five years old. And now she's gone."

The two sailors moved away after a while, going about their duties in the galley and leaving the three of us to dry ourselves out by the fire. Agnir was quiet—grieving the loss of his ship, I wagered—but I endured Mattac's curious attention until finally I turned to him, throwing my hand at him in a mildly obscene gesture.

"Spit it out, Mattac."

"With all your gifts, what…what do you suppose would happen if they used your blood on their ship?"

I met his gaze, surprised to realize I was grinning. "Honestly, if they tried it, I think it might just sink the damn thing."

Mattac stared at me; Agnir swore under his breath.

"Didn't you wonder what happened to *Hastol*?" I asked. My voice had pitched up; it sounded strange, raspy, almost manic—not the least bit like me. "I bled on your ship, Agnir. My blood was in the ropes and the rails. It's my fault. Vaskar was right. First I called down the storm and then my blood rotted the ship out from under you."

I put my head in my hands, shoulders shaking. Agnir reached over and clasped my upper arm. I flinched, expecting pain, feeling only reassurance.

"You need to rest, Taumir. And let someone see to that wound on your head."

"You think I'm delirious?" I whispered. "Don't you realize…it's madness."

"Raving lunacy," a voice behind us stated. I twitched my head, just enough to see the Cavnish captain standing at the bottom of the hatch, watching me in pale fear. He held a heavy rucksack in one hand and an armful of grey wool in the other. "Food and water. Blankets. Now get the hell off my ship."

I caught Agnir's eye and nodded toward the hatch. "Let me talk to Mattac a moment."

Agnir followed the Cavnish captain wordlessly, leaving Mattac and me huddled around the coal hearth.

"You should stay," I told him. "Let them take you back to Cavnal, find a new ship to hire out on. Agnir and I have to go to Istia, but it's not going to be a safe journey. You're better off here with these men than with me."

"Who are you, really?" Mattac asked. "The captain seemed to recognize you. Should I?"

I straightened slightly, considering the prudence of telling him the truth, then said, "It doesn't matter. I'm no one you need to concern yourself about."

He snorted. "I doubt that very much."

 80

He got to his feet as I did and trailed me up onto the deck of the ship, where Agnir and the Cavnish captain waited in tense silence. When we joined them, I expected Mattac to volunteer his services to the Cavner, but he stood uncertainly, weight shifting from one leg to another, watching me. I sighed.

"Let Mattac stay on board with you," I said to the captain. "When you make port in Cavnal again he's free to sail where he will. Just give him safe passage home."

"Is he a spy? One of yours?"

"I met the man less than a week ago. Draw your own conclusions."

He grimaced and spat to the side, then eyed Mattac skeptically. "What do you have to say on the matter?"

"If you'll take me, I'd be glad to go home," Mattac said, with an odd wistfulness in his voice. Perhaps the sea's claim on his heart was not as strong as he'd believed.

"Very well," the captain said. "You two?"

He glanced at Agnir and me and jerked his head toward the side of the ship without further comment, then swung away. Mattac embraced Agnir briefly and shook his hand, then turned to me.

"I'd wish you good fortune," he said, "but I've a feeling a man like you makes his own. Be safe, Taumir. If you ever need a place to stay, my family in Greydowns would welcome you. I'll see to it they know."

I clasped his forearm. "Thank you."

The other sailors had lowered the ladder for us again, bidding Agnir a polite farewell and watching me with suspicious scowls and folded arms until I was safely off their ship. Mattac leaned over the rail as the ship's engine built up steam, and we rowed the dory clear of her wake. I closed my eyes briefly, because suddenly I remembered how the Cavnish captain had struck me, and how I'd spat blood on the deck of the ship.

*Maybe it's all nonsense. Maybe it means nothing at all.*

"What are you, that your blood could sink a ship?" Agnir asked quietly as we rowed.

I tossed my head back to stare at the sky, the dark so deep. "I'm nothing," I said. "Just a shade."

# Chapter 13 ~ Hayli

"YOU REALLY NEED TO STOP STAYING UP ALL NIGHT," SOMEONE COMMENTED, AS I perched on the bottom wing of the downed aeroplane two nights later, when it was far too late to be civilized.

I leaned onto my elbow so I could look up at Shiver, who was laying on his stomach on the aeroplane's upper wing with his arms folded along its edge. He grinned when he caught my eye, and I scrambled up from my wing and onto his so I could sit beside him. It was colder up on the top wing, with no shelter from the sleet and wind and snow that swirled around us, but Shiver didn't seem to care two bobs about the weather.

"Can't sleep," I said.

"Psh," he said. "You been sleeping like a dog all day."

I made a face. "Well, maybe I like it better at night. Fewer folks to bother me."

"You really think everybody's that sore to have you back?" he asked in surprise. "Is that why you've been hanging about at night like a bitty owl instead of a crow?"

I shrugged. "True though, isn't it?"

"Maybe they dan' na what to think," he said. "Maybes it's time you set their minds at ease. *Talk* to them. Someone's ganna have to tell them we're moving out, anyway."

I grumbled in response and dropped down to the ground. "I know," I said. "I'll do it, just...let me do it in my own time."

He huffed and faded into the wing of the aeroplane, leaving me standing all by myself.Fighting a faint shudder at his peculiar leave-taking, I wandered out to check on the lads at the sentry post beyond the gate where, to my surprise, I found Bridnow standing on watch. He didn't seem surprised to see *me*, just nodded once in greeting, and turned back to face the road. He was on post with a younger man I didn't know, who goggled at me much too long before getting his mind back on his duty.

"D'you two need aught?" I asked. "Thought we'd doubled the guard on the posts."

"We've got two up on the road, keeping an eye at the turning. Lev and Quickly are in the hut."

He pointed at a small tent just off the side of the road, which glowed a bit from the can fire burning inside. I could see the two men's silhouettes as they hunched over a low table playing at a game, but I didn't hear a sound from inside besides the rattle and clatter of dice. That didn't surprise me over much—Quickly hardly ever said a word unless he had to.

"Good," I said. "Have the two up the road got flares or whistles?"

Bridnow nodded, but the younger guard suddenly smacked his arm and pointed at the road. We both turned to look, and saw the dancing splashes of light from a pair of torches, drifting to and fro over the gravel. When the two guards came into view of the sentry post fire, I narrowed my eyes, realizing it wasn't two, but three. And the third man was, inauspiciously, wearing the uniform of an Army officer.

"Krigs?" Bridnow said suddenly, starting forward.

"Oh, thank God," the officer said. "I was afraid you wouldn't be here, and these two would go on insisting I wasn't a friendly and nick me away for a hostage."

He jerked his arms roughly, and I realized the two guards had been marching him toward the post with their hands locked on his elbows. Bridnow stepped around the barricade and caught his friend in an embrace, which finally made the guards release him.

"It's good to see you," Krigs said. "After everything, I didn't know—"

Bridnow nodded, clapping a hand on his shoulder as he led him over to the fire. "It's late for a visit."

"Had to wait until now, when a friend was standing sentry at the garrison gate. We're not allowed off post otherwise."

"Not at all?"

"Not at all, unless under orders."

He rubbed his hands over the fire, and I watched him, curious. I remembered Bridnow telling us about his friend Krigs, the mage grenadier, and how he'd decided to stay in the Army and pass intelligence to us as often as he could. He was maybe a little older than Bridnow, with a thick black mustachio cutting a severe line across his round face, but his eyes were kind and warm, and I liked the look of him.

"Well?" Bridnow asked. "What news could be bad enough that you would come out in the middle of the night in this dastardly weather to tell us?"

Krigs studied me briefly as I tried to hide in the shadows, then he glanced back at Bridnow and said, "Word has it the King's assassin is here at this smelter."

"What?" Bridnow and I said at the same time.

I added, "That's bodgy. Nobody here laid hand or power on the King. We dan' even know that he *was* assassinated."

*It certainly wasn't me, if that's what you're thinking,* I wanted to add, but the words wouldn't come out.

"I know," Krigs said. "The inquest never turned up anything useful about how he died. But it doesn't have to be true, does it? That's the report. At any rate, the Army claims the assassin is here, and some of the highest ranking officers in the Ministry are intending to request permission to send a squadron out. They're going to recommend a kill-or-catch order."

Bridnow swore.

"What is that?" I asked.

"Open orders to kill or capture anyone they find in a certain location," Bridnow said quietly. Then, to Krigs, "Is Farro going to approve it?"

"I don't know. They were going to bring the intelligence to him in the morning. If he gives the order, it'll happen fast."

"Fast," Bridnow echoed, snorting.

"*Actually* fast," Krigs said, laughter in his eyes as he and Bridnow shared some private joke. Then he sobered and added, "Three companies have all been given a stand-by order, to be ready to march out as soon as they're given the nod."

"What?" Bridnow exclaimed. Obviously, by the horror in his eyes, this went against some sort of military policy I had no notion about. "Who gave that order? They can't even authorize a stand-by without Farro's approval."

"I know," Krigs said. "It's unheard of. As far as I'm aware, it was Lieutenant Commander Vickery."

"Vickery," Bridnow gritted.

"Bastard, I know," Krigs said. He gave me an apologetic nod. "Don't mind us, miss."

"Dan' mind me," I said. "Ain't aught I've not heard before."

He got a rather pitying look about him at that, which made me feel half prickly with indignation and wounded pride, and half ashamed of myself and the way I'd grown up wild, so far from the pretty manners and sensitivities of the Court.

"We're planning to clear out of the smelter," Bridnow told Krigs. "You'll understand if I don't tell you where we're removing to."

"Don't want to know," Krigs said, holding up a hand. "Just have a care. I don't know how soon they will act, but the sooner you can move out, the better. It's what I was coming to recommend, but you've already thought of it."

"We had reasons to," Bridnow said.

Krigs nodded and tugged a pocket watch from his inner coat pocket. "I should get back. Didn't trust a messenger with this news, and honestly, I needed an excuse to get off post or I'd've gone barking mad. But my friend will be changing shift in a few hours, so," he clapped Bridnow's shoulder, "best be off so I can get back in without a court martial on my head."

"Thank you," I said.

He nodded to me, and Bridnow shook his hand. "You're sure you won't join us?"

"How would you have heard about this if I'd joined you?" Krigs asked, and, waving a hand in farewell, disappeared down the dark street.

Bridnow watched him go, then said, "What a colossal mess." He laid a hand on my shoulder. "Try to get some sleep, if you can."

"My clock's all wrong. Can't seem to sleep at night these days."

His mouth twitched in a smile and he nodded, and I gave him and the other guard both a wave of farewell and headed back toward the smelter. I found Derrin by the gate, leaning against the post with his arms crossed and a dark scowl on his face. It cleared a bit when he saw me, and he straightened up as I joined him.

"What're you doing out and about?" I asked him, leaning against the wall beside him.

"Can't sleep," he said. "Too much on my mind, I guess."

"Anything you wanna talk over?" I asked.

He waffled a bit, then said, "Guess I'm just worried about that impostor mage. I don't understand him, and that makes me nervous."

"D' you suppose he's got a bad streak?"

"I don't know," he said. "I think I remember him from the Science Ministry."

"You do? Was he...was he a prisoner like us?"

He looked a bit uncomfortable, shifting his weight from one foot to the other. "I honestly don't know," he murmured. "My own memories... they're so confused. Was *I* a prisoner of Kippler's? I don't even know that. How much of it was my own choice? You know how it was. And it could be no different for *him*. Maybe he was Kippler's hostage. Or maybe he was cooperating with him. Plotting with him. One of the masterminds of the scheme that unfolded in the Avnaya. Stars, I wish I knew."

"D'you suppose he'd make a move for Tarik's crown?" I asked. "He did a fair job impersonating him once."

"There's no telling what he could do," Derrin said. "This is a nightmare."

I chewed the inside of my cheek, my mind whirling over possibilities and improbabilities, then let out all my breath in a weary sigh. "Drat," I said. "I gotta warn the Ministers."

"What? Warn them, why?"

"They need to know. They need to know he's still out there."

"Fine," he muttered. "Say you're right, and he does mean to kick up a fuss, and the Ministers do deserve to know. Why do *you* have to do it? What about Bridnow?"

I shook my head. "Reckon I've got a better chance than him. He was just a lieutenant. There's no way he'd be able to get in to see the Ministers."

"*Just* a lieutenant?" he echoed with a faint laugh. "*Just* an officer in the King's Army? And you're what, sixteen, seventeen? Street rat who knows more about picking locks than the customs and courtesies of the

Court? You think you could do more with them than Bridnow?"

"I can be persuasive."

"What about Farro?"

I clacked my teeth shut. Of course, Griff would be a much better choice than me, seeing as he actually *belonged* inside the Oval Wall... except sending him would mean making him face his father again. I had no notion if he'd be willing to do that, even for us. Even for Tarik.

"I'll ask him," I said. "But maybes...maybes I should go with him. I need to talk to the Ministers anyway—Farro especially."

"Why?"

I waved back toward the guard post where I'd left Bridnow, and didn't explain, and when I headed through the gate he didn't follow. He would go and ask Bridnow what the situation was, which was for the best. Bridnow could explain it all so much better than I could anyway, and maybe between the two of them they could scheme up some kind of plan to save us all.

## Chapter 14 ⚜ Hayli

I LEFT DERRIN AND HEADED INTO THE SMELTER, TORN BETWEEN TRYING TO find a spot to bed down for the night like a civilized person and tracking down Griff, who like as not was already asleep. But to my surprise I found him near Doc's infirmary, sitting up on top of one of the reduction pots along with Coins, Kite and Gem. Coins waved a greeting when he saw me, and Kite, who was sitting closer to Coins than I'd ever seen her, actually gave me a friendly kind of smile.

"Hey, Li!" Griff called cheerfully.

I startled, and stared at him, but all I could see was Vim's face—Vim, who had said that almost every day for three years until I'd half wished to strangle him for it. Vim, who had died in a clumsy accident, and would never say it again. I never would've believed it, but I almost missed it, and though we'd never got along, somehow I even missed *him*.

Griff must've seen something in my face because he sobered and dropped down to the ground beside me. "Sorry, did I say something I oughtn't've?"

"It's nothing," I said.

"You don't expect me to believe that, do you?" he asked. When I didn't say aught else he threw an arm around my shoulders. "Something we can do for you?"

"Need to talk to you," I said. Gem looked a bit sore at that so I made an effort to grin up at her. "I'll bring him right back, dan' worry."

She blushed and Griff threaded his fingers through his hair, and

Coins shot me a quirk smile that was all shared mischief. I laughed and pulled Griff after me, back toward Shade's office where we could talk in private. But when I opened the door, I found Scorch sitting inside—not in Shade's chair, which nobody had sat in since he left, but on the edge of the desk, staring down at Shade's maps of the city. He glanced up at us in surprise, one brow lifted in such a way that my face grew foolishly hot.

"Scram, Scorch. I gotta talk to Griff," I said, refusing to let him needle me. "What're you doing in here, anyhow? It's grobbing late to be up."

"It is, isn't it?" he said, just a bit maliciously. When I just crossed my arms and scowled at him, he shrugged. "I've been going over Shade's maps. I like the ones he drew."

He held one out to me and I took it, my mouth tugging into a faint smile. Shade always belittled his ability to draw accurate maps, but I agreed with Scorch—I liked his best. There was a firmness to every pencil stroke, bold and decisive but almost whimsical at the same time, so that even when the details weren't quite right, they seemed to show a deeper sort of truth than the official maps with their perfect measurements and scales. Like how he'd drawn the courthouse bigger than it should've been, taking up most of the space he'd allotted for Avnaya Square. Given everything that had happened there, the larger-than-life size of it seemed right.

I held the map as if it could keep me close to Shade, and even when Scorch stalked out of the room I kept hanging onto it. Griff rifled through the other papers on the desk while I looked on, torn between disapproval and curiosity. It felt like we were invading Shade's privacy by poking through his things, but, he'd left them strewn about his office when he left. He could've tidied the place up if he didn't want us seeing them.

"So what's this all about?" Griff asked finally, dropping a sheaf of newspaper clippings onto the desk. "Why are you owling about tonight?"

"Got a mission, and I need your help," I said. "I need to gan and talk to the Ministers."

"Stars," he said, brows lifting in surprise. "I'm sorry. Why? Because of this business with the Cleavers?

"Them—and Scorch, and Jig, and all the other grobbing anarchists who've a mind to see the Court fall." I studied the map a minute, tracing the shape of the plaza. "But they've got another problem, too. You know that mage who was there on the dais with Tarik, wearing Tarik's face, claiming to be the Prince?"

Griff's gaze snapped to mine, but he just nodded once and said nothing at all.

"Well, Tam says he's back. Or still around."

Griff sat down on the edge of the desk, whistling softly. "So...do we know what he has planned?"

"No..." I said, the word wisping away in uncertainty. "Dan' na if he's got aught at all *planned*. But just think, if he still looks like Tarik, how would anyone know if this bloke is the real Prince or not?"

"Surely they could question him and learn the truth?" Griff said, frowning. "He can't lie that well, can he?"

"Maybes," I said. "Got a strange sense he'd do a better job of it than we might think. Unless we could convince someone to test him with one of those EMS weapons..." My voice trailed off, as I worked out the likelihood that I could persuade the Ministers to fire one of those Chernayi guns at the man who looked like their Crown Prince. Then I pushed the idea aside and said, "Griff, what if he tries to claim Tarik's crown? What would the Ministers do? And if the Cleavers put us in a ruck by attacking the Court, will there be anybody left strong enough to stop him?"

Griff frowned at me like he didn't quite understand what I was saying. I didn't blame him—I barely knew myself. It felt all wrong. Backwards. Twisted and warped like a carnival mirror.

"So..." Griff said. "Let me get this straight. You want my help...to prop up the Court of Ministries? The seditious Ministers who hurt you so badly, who imprisoned the King, and tried to drive this nation into a civil war? You want to help *them*?"

*The seditious Ministers...like your father?* I wanted to ask.

"Let me rephrase," he added. "*You* want to help them?"

"What," I said, "you think I shouldn't bother about it?"

"It's not that I think you shouldn't, it's just surprising that you do. That anyone here does, really."

I laughed under my breath. "I'm surprised myself. Never did care two bobs about what they did up northside, not until Shade came along. Now, seems like I can't think about aught else." With a sigh I dropped the map onto the desk and sat down beside it, leaning my head in my hands. "They've got to be better than nothing. I just think Tarik would rather see the Court in power than a bunch of anarchists who dream big and dan' na aught at all about how the world works. He'd certainly rather see them in power than some mage who stole his face."

Griff leaned back on the desk beside me. A few long minutes and he didn't speak, and I only knew he was thinking hard about what I'd said by the flickering of his gaze over nothing at all.

"If it's a choice between my father, that impostor mage, and Red—or Scorch, or any other bunch of bloody anarchists—you're damn right I'd rather see my father in charge. He's not a bad man. I know what he did, but...I think he meant to do the right thing."

"Like us," I muttered. "Wake knows if we're ganna shift off as terribly wrong as he did. Times like these, how do you know if what you're doing is the right thing?"

"I wish I knew," he said quietly. "I really do." He heaved a great sigh and slapped his hands on his thighs. "All right. We'll warn my father and the Ministers about the little anarchists in the city, and the impostor mage, and hope that the lot of them together can be as strong a leader for this country as Trabin was."

He said those last words bitterly, eyes shining in the low light. Puzzled, I reached out and touched his arm.

"Did you think Trabin was a good king?"

He turned to me, now unabashedly distraught. He had one fist pressed against his heart, like a fealty gesture, and I didn't think he even realized it. "What kind of question is that? He was our King." When I didn't say aught, he sighed and said, "He wasn't perfect, and of course he made mistakes, but he was our father. That's something I think *my* father and his allies forgot about somewhere along the way. Cavnal's always had a king. Having a king reminds us...it reminds us that we're all brethren."

That reminded me of what Shiver had told me the very first time I'd met him, that we were both mages and that made us brethren. At the time, I'd thought it was absurd, but since then I'd seen enough to know what happened when those ties of brotherhood failed. Half the buildings in south Brinmark still bore the scars. They were the broken heart of the city.

I'd never considered that it was the King who held Cavnal together—not so much by forcing it into unity, but because he was the sign of trust among his people that everyone counted on without even realizing it.

Now he was gone.

Tarik, who might've taken his place, was gone.

And that was what made the impostor mage so dangerous. Cavnal needed her King, and apparently there was only one bloke around who could fill the role. Wake save us.

"So, what're we ganna tell them?" I asked.

"I'm not sure." He thrummed his thumbs on his legs. "Tarik was always the one with the head for politics. He insisted he didn't like it, but he watched everything. Drank it in. He would know what to say to get them to listen. Me, I just feel like a dog running home with my tail tucked. Nothing for it, though, I suppose. I'll check in with Luce and see if she's got anything proper for me to wear. I can't go looking like this."

I glanced at him sidelong. Coins had given him a pair of trousers and a worn jumper after Kor had snatched him from the nick, and though they were fine enough for the smelter, he'd surely be laughed out of the Palace if he showed up there wearing them. My own clothes weren't much better, with my breeches torn from a bullet hole and my boots all covered in mud.

So in the end we both went to see Luce, early the next morning as the smelter was just starting to wake up. She was in her usual corner, already busy mending a wee skitter's jumper that had got a big raggedy hole in the elbow, while the boy sat beside her chunnering on about Wake knew what. As we joined her she tucked a few last stitches through the sleeve and piled the jumper into the skitter's waiting arms.

"Thankth, Luthe!" he lisped through gappy teeth, and bolted off into the shadows.

"Well? What can I do for you?" Luce asked, leaning against the wall and tipping her head back to see us better.

Her sleek dark hair was hanging loose, framing her pale face and setting off the dark circles that made her eyes a brighter blue than ever. She looked dead tired, but then, we all looked tired these days.

"We need some clothes," Griff said, and I waved a hand at him to make him shut up.

"Y' a'right, Luce? D'you need a rest? You look grobbing horrid."

"Do I? Oh, Hayli, you're so sweet," she said, mocking a glare at me.

"Div'n you get any sleep last night?"

She just looked at me, then nodded and brushed her fingers over her eyes, which made me doubt she was being truthsome. Griff, oblivious as always, started listing off the things he needed, so I slipped away while she was busy with him and grabbed a cup of tea from Nan's corner. By the time I got back, Griff was describing the precise kind of shoes he would need. And Luce was just staring at him, mouth quirked in a skeptical smile.

"That's quite the laundry list," she said when he finished. "Don't know if I can oblige you quite so particularly. But I can scrounge up some decent stitches."

I sat down beside her and held the cup out. "Here. You look like you could use this."

"Thank you," she murmured, with so much warmth that my cheeks burned. "Nobody... Thank you." She took a small sip and smiled at me. "And you? What is your list of requests?"

"Not a thing," I said. "Just need to brush the muck off my trompers, and I should be good to gan."

"In *that*," she said flatly. "Say, I've got a dress you could wear. Looks decent enough for high society, but it won't turn you into a *katzpotim*." I nodded, and Luce shooed Griff away. "Go on, now. I'll have your things ready tomorrow. Will it be soon enough?"

I'd hoped we might get to warn Minister Farro about what the Army was planning before it happened, but amazing as Luce was, she couldn't work miracles. It wasn't like Griff or I could just pop effortlessly into high society.

"It'll be fine," I said. "We'll do our best."

As Griff wandered away, I curled up in the nest of fabric and folded my arms under my head like a pillow.

"Did *you* sleep at all last night?" she asked me.

"Eh," I said.

She glanced at me under a raised eyebrow. "Coins says you're in charge now. You could probably sleep in Shade's old room if you wanted, on a proper bed and everything."

I goggled at her, eyes wide, blushing fierce at the thought. She laughed and got to her feet, cupping her hands around the mug of tea and holding it close to her face so the steam could soothe her eyes.

"What were you ganna say earlier," I asked, "when I gave you the tea?"

She just gave me the saddest kind of smile and shook her head. "It was a kind thing to do. It just surprised me."

She took a few sips of the tea, then set the mug up on a bit of broken machinery and started sifting through her collection of garments. I watched, strangely melancholy, as she pulled out a pair of black trousers and a black waistcoat, faded a bit to grey around the edges—they were Shade's old clothes, the ones he'd been wearing when he first came to us, so long ago. They weren't fine by any stretch, but combined with a rather nice long-coat she tugged from the pile, they'd do well enough to make Griff presentable.

She left the clothes in a neat stack and climbed onto her own little pile of fabrics where she slept, and tugged out a dress in midnight blue silk and velvet. When she held it up against her, smoothing a hand over the lace-trimmed bodice, the lantern light caught and glimmered on bits of silver thread embroidered into the sweeping skirt. I reckoned it was the finest dress I'd ever seen.

"Where'd you get that?" I whispered, reaching out to touch the fine fabric. "It's beautiful."

Luce's eyes shadowed. "It was mine," she said. "My mother made it for me, when I was sixteen. She was a seamstress, like me, but my father was a watchmaker. He had a customer who always came to look at his wares. A young man. I guess he'd been studying abroad a few years, in Meritac, but he'd come back to see what he could salvage of... his family's fortune. My parents thought he was the finest young man in Brinmark. And I...I did too. He was handsome, wealthy, brilliant, but kind to a fault, always attentive to me, like I wasn't just a shopkeeper's daughter but a proper lady deserving of his notice. So one day my mum dressed me up in this gown and sent me into my father's workshop. I suppose she thought we'd make a smart pair."

Her voice trailed off, and her eyes grew dark and sad.

"Luce?" I whispered. "What happened?"

She caught in a sharp breath. "It's the past. I don't like to think about the past. I haven't thought about him in... Well, it doesn't matter."

Much as I wanted to hear how the story ended, I got her reluctance to talk. I respected it. Most of the kids in the Hole, and now the smelter, never talked about what came before, and what they'd left behind—all that was nobody's business. Our lives began when we joined the crew, and that was all anybody cared about.

For much too long she was much too quiet, and when I glanced up at her again there were tears on her cheeks that she tried—and failed—to wipe away before I saw. I scrambled to my feet and laid a hand on her arm.

"What's wrong?"

She pressed her lips together and shook her head, then whispered, "How do you all bear it?"

"Bear what?"

"All this. Living like this. Uprooting again and again. Never having a home. Living on the fringes of society like outcasts. I can't...I miss..." She covered her mouth, staring at the scar-pocked ceiling as if the sight of it could drive away her grief. "I miss my life," she whispered. "I'm not strong like you. I don't want to have to be strong like you."

I lowered my hand slowly, struggling to find something—anything—to say to her. It had never even occurred to me that Luce had only just been thrown into our life, and rather traumatically at that. She hadn't grown up in the Hole. She'd had a proper life, a proper family...even an honest job at a shop. I couldn't imagine how hard it had been for her, to be suddenly surrounded by strangers, and stripped of everything she'd ever known. She'd buried herself in her work, and nobody around her—even me—had cared enough to see how she was struggling. Except, strangely enough, Scorch. Scorch, who I thought had a burnt-out cinder in place of a heart, and the nastiest mean streak imaginable, had always seemed to care about Luce.

"I'm so sorry," I whispered.

And that was all I could say. She wrapped her arms around me unexpectedly, murmuring a *thank you* that I could barely make out through her tears. A minute and she let me go, rubbing a hand over her cheeks and offering me a wavering smile.

"Let's have a look at this," she said, shaking out the dress. "I doubt it'll fit you as it is, but it shouldn't be too much work to fix it up for you."

She helped me step into it, putting it on me inside-out so she could take in the side seams a bit, and when I told her I meant to wear my breeches underneath she just laughed. Eventually she persuaded me to leave them behind, but at least I won on the matter of wearing my boots instead of the pair of too-large fancy court slippers she offered me.

"I've never imagined wearing such a fine thing," I whispered, toying with the hand-tatted lace at the hems of the sleeves. "It's even pretty inside-out."

She laughed again and shrugged, almost shyly, and kept her attention on her needle. "It's proper enough. I'm just happy to see it get worn again." She worked a few moments in silence, then asked, "Are you nervous?"

I twisted a little to try to catch her eye. "Can't you tell?"

"I've been good," she protested, pouting her lower lip. "Mostly."

"I'm terrified," I admitted with a shaky laugh. "Luce…can you read Tarik at all? Do you know how he is?"

There was a strange pause, then she said, almost resentful, "I've never been able to read him." She tipped her head to meet my gaze and smiled faintly. "Sorry, Hayli. I've got nothing."

I sighed, then winced as Luce pinched in the dress a little tighter. "I think it was good the way it was," I gasped.

"Could you breathe normally?" she asked sourly, and I nodded. "Then it wasn't good enough."

I blew out all my breath in annoyance at that, and was rewarded with Luce taking the opportunity to pull it even snugger.

# Chapter 15 ∞ Tarik

WE TOOK TURNS ROWING ALL THROUGH THE NIGHT. IT WAS THE ONLY WAY TO keep the sea from carrying us farther adrift, since we had neither sails nor anchor to help us hold our course. By morning Agnir had gotten enough rest to use a little weather magic, drawing up a strong current to ease the burden of rowing. I would have helped by calling down a southerly wind, but without sails it would have made little difference. Instead I focused on the oars. At least I knew how to handle those from my years of crew, back when I had lived another life, in another world.

Agnir filled the time telling me stories from Istia's history and lore. I'd heard the Cavnish versions of most of them long ago, but there was a raw and sharp cleanness to the original tales that gave them a life all of their own. He turned to other topics after, and I marveled at the pride in his voice when he told me more than I'd ever wanted to hear about Iskari, his twenty-year-old son who so loved the sea, and Nika, the daughter a little over a year younger, who loved nothing at all. My heart burned, thinking of Trabin, wondering if he had ever looked on me with that sort of pride. It was too late to hope.

Near midday on the second day, we had both been rowing so long that neither of us had the energy for magic or the strength for oars. I heard a low thump behind me, and as the boat lost speed, I realized I was the only one still rowing. With a glance over my shoulder I saw that Agnir had shipped his oars, and had slumped down to lay in the belly of the boat, one hand flung over his face to ward away the cold, sharp sunlight.

"Take your rest, Godarson," he said, as he heard my oar strokes falter. "We'll be dead of exhaustion if we keep going like this, and that'll never serve to get us where we're going."

"The current…?"

"It's in our favor right now. Let the sea carry us a while."

I shipped the oars gratefully and turned around on my bench to face Agnir, but he was already asleep. The dory rocked, swayed by the low swells of the quiet sea. Overhead the sky was cloudless, but a blue so pale it almost looked white, and the sun was a bare glittering silver disk low on the horizon. The water reflected the pallid sky, so that the whole world was so cold and bright I could hardly bear to face it.

But I was terrified of falling asleep. I'd caught snatches of sleep over the last day and a half, but never for long, never long enough to dream. With Agnir asleep, I had no notion if I'd be able to wake myself in time to keep the nightmares from coming.

I leaned my arms along the top of the dory's bulwark and rested my chin on them, staring out over the endless expanse of sea. My mind was strangely calm; it occurred to me once that Agnir and I might never make the coast of Istia, but I dismissed the idea as soon as I became aware of it. There, adrift in the empty nothingness, I felt nothing at all—no fear, no worry, none of the paralyzing uncertainty that had plagued me the last two weeks.

If I felt anything at all, it was a pale sort of horror at my own indifference.

Presently I turned my gaze from the horizon that hung an eternity away from me, and lowered it to plumb the depths of the sea below me, a churning grey-green swarm of foam and water, the thin sunlight glinting every now and then off the silvery body of some lithe fish.

Then I saw the face.

It was Vaskar, I realized too late, pale, staring open-eyed straight up through the water, straight at me. Blood still curled and drifted from the wound in his head, and he stretched one hand toward me, reaching for help, perhaps, or pointing at me in silent accusation. My heart shuddered, and I gripped the edge of the boat, willing myself to look away. I could not.

*It's not real,* I told myself. *He's not there. He can't be there…*

Vaskar's lips lifted in a smile that was colder than the sea itself.

And then I realized it wasn't Vaskar at all, but Andon Vrey, with a hole in his head where one eye was meant to be. A choking breath escaped me, and I reached out toward the water, my fingers spasming on the empty air.

"You're not here," I whispered.

He said, "Neither are you."

He closed his one eye, and when he opened it again both his eyes were whole, but a slow white fire sparked at the heart of his irises, and spread, and spread, until his eyes were bright as lightning, staring and burning into my soul.

And still his hand stretched toward me, and somehow he reached me, and he grabbed my shoulder to pull me with him into the deep. I cried out and pulled back, my body wracked with tremors, and snatched my knife from its sheath behind my back.

"Taumir, wait! Wait, it's me!" Vrey shouted, and his face filled my vision, but it wasn't Vrey, and there was no brightness in his eyes, and I couldn't make sense of who was shaking me.

All that made sense was the frail sunlight on the edge of my knife, held like a warning in front of me.

"*Veka*, what's wrong? It's me, Agnir."

There was no sunlight on the blade's edge; it was the gleam of blood I saw.

*Did you kill him too?* whispered the voice in the back of my thoughts.

I let out all my breath in a strangled noise that somehow sounded like a sob, and tightened my fingers on the hilt. The hand never let go of my shoulder, but I couldn't blink away Vrey's face, leering over me. I squeezed my eyelids shut and those brilliant lightning-bright eyes seared into the darkness of my mind with a pain like fire.

I scrabbled backwards, and fell from the bench, and that was the first moment I realized that Agnir was leaning over me, that he had one hand gripping my shoulder, and one hand clasping my right wrist, muscling the point of my knife away from his throat.

"Agnir," I gasped.

My fingers slackened on the knife, and it fell to the bottom of the boat, and it was silver and clean and unstained.

"It's all right," Agnir said, releasing my wrist, holding his hand up in front of me as if I were a skittish child. "Taumir, look at me. You're all right."

The dizzy confusion faded to the edges of my mind, but slowly, too slowly. I lifted a shaking hand to my eyes and found my face wet with salt spray, or tears. Agnir reached down and gripped my elbow, helping me to sit upright, and claim my seat on the bench again. I kicked the knife as I stood; it clattered dully against the wall of the dory.

"Did I…did I hurt you?" I murmured.

I was still trembling as I sat on the bench, and Agnir wrapped one of the Cavnish captain's wool blankets around my shoulders as if it were the cold that shook me.

"No," he said. "Scared me a fair bit, that's certain, but no, you were waving that knife a bit too blindly to do any harm."

My cheeks warmed in a flush of shame, and I, not daring to look at the water again, bent my gaze to my hands instead. They were raw and red, chafed from wind and saltwater, and on my knuckles the aching skin had split and begun to bleed.

Agnir reached past me and retrieved my knife, handing it back to me without the slightest hesitation. When he'd settled in the belly of the boat again, he tipped his head back to look at me.

"What was it?" he asked softly.

"What do you mean?" I asked, pretending it was possible to misunderstand him.

"You were looking at the water and you were dead pale, shaking like a loose sheet. Looked at me like I wasn't even there. What…what were you seeing that had you so terrified? Were you asleep?"

"Not asleep, no," I said. "I wish I had been."

"Why?"

"Because what I saw would make sense in sleep, in dreams, in… in nightmares. It doesn't make sense, seeing it with my waking eyes." I shuddered again and pulled the blanket a little closer. Agnir waited patiently, saying nothing. He wasn't even looking at me now, but I could sense his expectation. I couldn't explain to him about the blazing eyes that I could still see like an afterimage seared against my eyelids, and I didn't want to explain to him about Andon Vrey, so instead I said simply, "I saw Vaskar. In the water."

"Ah," he said. He studied his hands briefly. "Vaskar was responsible for his own fate. It doesn't matter if you're on a schooner or a dory— mutiny is mutiny."

"I could have saved him."

He regarded me in surprise. "Would you have?"

 100

"I didn't," I said flatly, as if that answered the question.

And somewhere in the back of my mind I could hear Rivano's smooth voice, trying to give me counsel in one of the bleakest hours of my life: *"If someone dies at your hands, perhaps they were meant to die at your hands. Perhaps their lives were yours to take. Perhaps it was your right."*

*I don't believe that,* I told the voice, snatching at certainty as desperately as I had the first time I'd heard him say it. *I will never believe that.*

"I wouldn't have saved him either," Agnir said, interrupting my thoughts, "if that makes you feel better."

"He was one of your sailors."

"He stopped being that the moment he turned on me," he said, with an indifference that startled me. Then he reached out and clasped my knee. "You're not a murderer."

I flinched, seeing Andon's face in my mind again, and the ribbon of blood blossoming from the hole in his head. But I didn't say a word of it to Agnir. I pulled out the oars and set them to the water, and Agnir, sighing, followed my lead.

"The sea is going to drive me mad," I muttered.

# Chapter 16 ❖ Hayli

WHILE LUCE WAS BUSY FIXING UP THE CLOTHES FOR ME AND GRIFF, I SPENT all day with Bridnow and the lads, talking over our plans for getting the folks to Borokhev.

We decided that we'd get everyone moving the next morning.

Bridnow decided that I would be the one to tell them.

I didn't want to do it but pride or shame kept my protests locked away inside, and then Bridnow looked so pleased that I'd accepted that I couldn't bring myself to complain.

The next morning, when it was still too early and the sun hadn't even properly risen yet, I sent the lads to gather the folks together in the Chamber. As I waited for them to trickle in, I stepped up on the lip of the reduction pots where Shade had spoken to his people so many times before, and tried to calm my nerves. Little by little the people wandered in and gathered around me, regarding me with either open interest or wary suspicion. My heart was a knot of anxious hope and fear—this was the moment I'd been dreading, avoiding, for so long.

What would they think when I broke the news that we'd have to leave the smelter? Would they blame me for the necessity? They should, I thought. In so many ways, it was my doing, but I would do all in my power to make it right, even if it was the last good thing I ever did in my life.

When I reckoned most everyone had arrived, I straightened up and held up a hand to get their attention—not that it mattered, because they were already watching me.

"A'right," I said, but it came out hoarse, and much too quiet, so I cleared my throat and tried again. "Listen up, folks. While Shade's away, we're not safe staying here. We've got to move everybody out, and we've got to do it fair and quick-like."

My words hit the crowd like a wall, and I faltered. I'd meant the statement to have some authority behind it, maybe some conviction that would stir everybody to action, but they all just stared at me. I swallowed and looked for help among Shade's crew, but they were all watching the crowd too.

"Where we ganna gan?" someone finally called. "You're sending us home? Some of us haven't got a home to gan back to!"

"Not home," I said. "I know this place *is* home to most of you now, and we're not leaving behind anybody who needs a place to stay. We're gannin' to the old prison town, Borokhev, up by the quarry. It's abandoned now." I said that part all in a rush, brave as could be, but soon as the words were out, my voice choked, and my throat closed, and the room started fading to grey around the edges, cold and grey and empty and hateful. Finally I found Bridnow's face in the crowd and forced my hands to relax at my sides. "We'll be..." *Breathe.* "We'll be safe there."

"Borokhev," someone said. "Know the place. But how d'you mean for us to get there? That's no small jaunt."

That, at least, made me grin. "Once you've got your bits and bobs together, head up to the Web. There'll be a train waiting on you."

That had been Scorch and Jig's idea, and though it had sounded much too daring to me at the time, I kind of liked the brashness of it all now. They and a handful of other lads had gone up the night before to scout out the Web, waiting on their chance to hijack a northbound freight train and hold it in the yard for us to use. It was canny mad. I just hoped there were no coppers in the rail yard, or the lads might all end up in the nick and we'd never even know till it was too late.

But the folks in the crowd seemed satisfied by the answer, if not by the necessity.

Someone called out, "What're we supposed to do at Borokhev? Hide? How long do we mean to wait to get on with our lives?"

"Till we know how we stand in the city, mages and *krizanyi* alike. Griff and I are ganna find that out this morning. Soon as I know aught, you will too, but I'm not for lying and telling you something that ain't true or certain."

I caught sight of Bridnow in the back of the crowd, and he nodded in approval when he met my eye, which made me all manner of proud at myself—probably prouder than I had any right to be.

A few folks started murmuring, and I held up a hand to quiet them. "You've never been forced to stay here, and you won't be forced to gan to Borokhev either. If you want to leave, that's your right. Just be safe, and remember the safety of the folks you're leaving behind."

After I'd released them, folks wandered back to their spaces to start gathering up their few belongings. I stepped down from the cement step, feeling a bit shaky and more than a bit queasy. Not one of them had accused me. No one had complained, no one had questioned me. None of them had told me to stand down. I wasn't sure quite how I felt about that—I knew I should've been relieved, but I kept waiting for the hammer stroke to fall in some other way, when I least expected it. I felt oddly troubled, too, and it wasn't until I overheard some men talking about the prison town that I understood why.

Had I been right to tell the whole crowd of people where we meant to go? Maybe I should have told everyone who didn't want to move to leave first, and then told the folks who stayed that we were going to Borokhev. I worried until my stomach was in knots, and then I forced myself to put the fear aside. If it happened, we would deal with it.

*Face the situation in front of you,* Zagger had told me once, *not the situation you fear.*

Piper had a different way of saying the same thing, as always: *You can't eat the rat that's still running.*

And the situation was more than enough for us to deal with. Coins and Shiver had commandeered a coach first thing in the morning, even before I'd woke up, and headed out with Jig and Anuk to make sure the Borokhev facility was really and truly empty. Midmorning they came back to the smelter, and told me they'd delivered the all-clear to the lads hanging about the railyard, who had actually done the impossible and nabbed a clagger for us to use. I was out in the smelter yard, perched up on the lower wing of the aeroplane, when Coins and Shiver got back, but even the news of the lads' success wasn't enough to calm the twisty, uncomfortable knot in my stomach.

I knew part of it was because of the thought of going to the Palace, but part was the thought that soon we wouldn't be living at the smelter any more. I'd grown used to the way the wind moaned in the high rafters, the way Scorch and the other Flints had set the main room alight with magic-fueled torches, the way the potlines divided the endless space into manageable bits but still kept everyone together. I liked the way the sun slanted through the broken windows early in the morning, whenever there was sunlight to be had. I loved the Chamber and the Training Room and Luce's nest, and the way the smells of Nan's cooking filled every last corner of the building.

Besides, it was in those trees just beyond the fence line that we'd buried Bugs and Zagger, and Link and Kitty and the others we'd lost, in a clearing some of the lads had marked out with a crude woven fence and cairns made of river stones. When we left the smelter, who would go to visit them? Would anyone remember to clear the leaves in the autumn, and the snow in the winter? Would anyone even remember where the little graveyard was?

I sighed and drew up my knees, looping my arms tight about them. In the time I'd spent as the crow after Zagger's death, I'd been able to push the pain away. For all her mad brilliance, Piper just didn't feel things like I did—she watched Tarik and the lads bury Zagger with something like grief and something like regret, more because of Tarik's anguish than her own memory of him. It wasn't till I'd stopped by the grave with my own eyes and my own heart that I truly grieved.

My heart ached with a sick sort of pang, and I slid off the plane before I could get too lost in my own pain. Back in the smelter, I found Luce already helping Griff with his clothes, straightening a black silk cravat around his neck and settling a fine felt hat on his head. He looked a proper gentleman in Shade's old waistcoat and trousers, with the scruff shaved clean off his jaw and the dirt and engine grease scrubbed from his cheeks.

Seeing him so cleaned up got me brushing a hand self-consciously over my own face and hair, wondering what sort of state I was in. If I was a mess, though, I trusted Luce would see me straight before she let me go to the palace.

"You look fine now," she said, dusting imaginary lint from the brim of his hat. "Scram and let me take care of Hayli."

He tipped his hat to me with a suave little bow and sauntered off, which got me and Luce exchanging skeptical grins.

"He's much too comfortable in all that frippery," I said.

She snorted as she shook out the blue dress. "Your turn. Let's get you ready for your social debut."

I swallowed and nodded. She helped me into the dress, murmuring in satisfaction as she fastened up the back and saw that it fit perfectly, then made me kneel down so she could attack my hair with a comb. My hair was a bit manky, and it wasn't cut in any kind of order, just chopped to a manageable length with a pair of rusted kitchen shears Coins had dug up somewhere. My cheeks burned with embarrassment to have Luce trying to put it into something like a stylish fashion, but she didn't make any snide comments about it while she worked.

She just said, "Your hair is too short. I don't know what to do with it."

I scowled. "Then leave it down."

"How old are you?"

I shrugged. "Sixteen, I think? Maybe seventeen? Got no grobbing clue, honest."

"Let's just say you're seventeen, then. Sixteen and you'd have no place talking to the Ministers. At least if we say you're seventeen you're technically an adult. But that means the hair needs to be up."

She frowned and walked around me in a slow circle. Just when I wondered what she was thinking of doing to me, she snapped her fingers and started twisting my hair above my ears, then tugged it all up onto the crown of my head. She wrapped it tight with something until it stayed put—it was like a magic I couldn't understand. Then she fished around in her pile of belongings and pulled out a small felt hat decorated with a tiny rosette and a bit of black netting, which she pinned on top of my head at a dashing angle.

I gingerly touched the twists of my hair, afraid they'd fall out if I so much as twitched my head, but they seemed secure. Then, swallowing hard, I let my fingers drift to the back of my neck, and the clockwork tattoo that Luce had to have seen.

"The collar of the dress covers it," she said softly. "No one will see it."

I shivered and nodded, and let my hand fall back to my lap, while Luce fetched a cloth and a bit of water to wash my face and hands.

"There," she said, dabbing relentlessly at a spot on my cheek. "I think you're almost presentable now. See for yourself."

She pulled a small hand mirror from her carpet bag and held it up for me. I'd never looked in a proper mirror before, and for much too long I stared at the girl staring back at me. Her hair twisted softly around her face, and even though the face was a bit thin and pale, it was...almost pretty. I peeked a little closer. I had brown eyes? It wasn't a particularly interesting color, I decided, just dark and darker, but I guessed they suited well enough. They were rimmed with heavy circles, like as not from my habit of owling about all hours of the night, but there was no helping that.

I blushed and glanced away, suddenly ashamed of staring so intently at my own reflection.

"That's what I look like?" I muttered, focusing fierce attention on a handful of skitters marching out of the smelter with rolls of blankets strapped to their backs, like wee little soldiers.

Luce laughed. "You look like your mother."

"*What?*"

I spun around, heart wrenching in my chest, but Luce just dropped her gaze and fiddled with the mirror.

"Griff told me who you are. My mother used to sew Lady Lorin's gowns. She was always so kind to me." She glanced up at me, the saddest smile tugging at her mouth. "Her daughter was always into mischief though."

Blood rushed hot to my cheeks, worse because I had no memory of when I was such a wee skitter. I'd been a mischief? Somehow the notion didn't surprise me much, but I hated to wonder what I'd done that Luce would remember me for it.

"You...*knew* me?" I finally stammered. And then, as that old uncertainty crept into my heart, that feeling that I was forgetting someone who'd once meant the world to me, I asked, "Did...did you know the rest of my family?"

She turned abruptly. "You'd better go find Griff. It's getting late."

GRIFF WAS WAITING FOR ME OUT in the smelter yard, talking to some of the other lads about the aeroplane, and when all of them turned about and goggled at me, it took every last ounce of my will not to turn bird and fly far, far away.

"Well, Lady Lorin," Griff said, sweeping his hat off his head and offering me a courtly bow. "You sure cleaned up."

I scowled at him, but I had my hands full of the long skirts to keep them from trailing in the snow, otherwise I'd've punched him in the arm. He just laughed.

"You'd better not call me *Lorin*. That name's got a history to it."

"What should we call you then?"

Anuk shuffled his feet, a quirk smile on his mouth that I couldn't read at all. "How about Oramay?"

"Why? That dan' sound Cavnish," Shiver said.

"It's not. It's Meritian." Anuk bit his lip and glanced away as if he were about to burst out laughing, which got me sore because I didn't get the humor in it at all. He sobered a bit and said, "It means *disinherited*, I'm told."

"Oh," I said, and shrugged. "That should do a'right then."

A rattle of wheels on the river road interrupted us, and Griff settled his hat back on his head, looking pleased.

"Ah," he said. "Our ride, right on time."

A minute and Coins arrived, driving a fine, long-legged bay horse from the seat of a smart black cab, which didn't look at all like the run-down coach he and Shiver had taken to Borokhev. And Coins was wearing an elegant livery too, like a proper high streets chauffeur. For the life of me I couldn't imagine where he'd gotten it. I decided I likely didn't want to know.

He drew the cab to a stop close to us and jumped down from the seat, giving a low whistle when he saw me.

"Is that my little Hayli?" he asked, holding me at arm's length. "Good, at least you'll give that oaf some respectability."

He flashed a dazzling grin at Griff, who threw him an obscene gesture.

"Coins," I said, "where'd you get the cab?"

He opened the door with a deep bow and dramatic flourish. "Why, my dear, haven't you heard? I'm the best damn thief in Brinmark."

Griff shoved Coins's head aside as he climbed into the cab, then Coins handed me up after him. My hands were shaking, but at least the black lace gloves I wore kept Coins from noticing how sweaty my palms were. I was keenly aware how odd I'd look showing up at the palace in the winter cold without a coat or a muff for my hands, wearing just a dress and thin gloves that belonged to warmer weather and brighter days. But at least I looked halfway proper. Soon as I opened my mouth, though, I knew I'd give away what a pretender I was, and not the finest dress in Cavnal could hide the truth of me then.

"Good luck, Lady Oramay!" Anuk called.

Coins halted in the middle of shutting the cab door, gawping first at Anuk, then at me. "*Oramay!*" he exclaimed. "Did Anuk tell you... Do you know..."

"Means *disinherited*, right?" I said, bewildered.

Anuk turned away, fingers pressed against the bridge of his nose and shoulders shaking, but Coins laughed out loud as he clapped the door shut.

"Oh, absolutely," he said.

"Coins! What else does it mean?"

He just grinned and shook his head. "Not a thing," he said. "Not a thing at all."

I scowled and settled against the hard leather seat as he disappeared back to the driver's bench. A minute later the cab rolled out, jostling over bumps and pits in the road, and I put the whole business out of mind to focus on what was coming. I shivered—it was glacially cold inside the cab, and apparently Coins hadn't thought to steal a rug for us too. Griff studied me sidelong a minute, and then, without even asking, he shrugged out of his long coat and draped it over my shoulders.

I nodded my thanks, since my teeth were chattering too hard for words. The wool coat wasn't terribly heavy, and I felt a bit guilty that now Griff was sitting there in just a shirt and waistcoat, which had to be ten times colder than the velvet sleeves and layered bodice of my own dress. But he didn't seem fazed by the cold.

"I've got to get the aeroplane to Borokhev," he mused after a bit, when the outlying buildings of Brinmark started rising up around us. "Can't leave that beauty behind to go to waste."

"How're the repairs coming? Can it fly yet?"

"Oh, sure she can *fly*. Not quite sure about landing, but she'll get airborne at least."

I stifled a laugh, and for a while we rode in silence, watching the cab wind through the city streets. All too soon I spied the sprawl of the Oval Wall, and then Coins was slowing the cab to take us through the southern gate.

"Business?" the gate guard asked.

"Lady Oramay and escort on official business," Coins said.

"Escort?" I whispered to Griff. "Why div'n he say your name?"

"No telling what rumors he's heard about me. Safer for him not to know who I am," Griff said, tipping his hat forward just a bit so it shadowed his face.

"Are you worried?"

He hesitated, tracing a line of frost on the window. "Worried about what my father will say. What if he tells me to come home?"

"You wouldn't have to, would you?"

"In a month I could say no," he said, laughing quietly. "Right now I'm still in my minority. Stars, that's embarrassing."

The cab rattled up to the palace steps, and my heart rattled right along with it. The only time I'd ever got this close to the palace was when Kor had offered to get me inside. This time it was actually happening— and I wasn't there to hide and spy, but to stand in front of the Ministers and try to tell them what to do.

*I'm grobbing crazy,* I thought. *We are both grobbing crazy.*

As Coins drew the cab to a halt, a footman came down to open the door for us. I could feel Griff tensing beside me, but he kept his head bent as if that could hide him forever. The footman helped me down, then stood back so Griff could climb out on his own. He watched us both with sharp curiosity, but he never said a word as he led us up the long flight of steps and into the front hall.

I handed Griff his coat as we stepped inside, and then, in the middle of the grand entry, I stopped and gawped. The ceiling soared so high above my head I felt like I was back in the smelter, only here there was no concrete and steel, but shining panels of mahogany wood framed by carved marble, and glittering gold leaf bordering intricate tapestries. So much ornament might've looked gaudy anywhere else, but everything in the palace was elegant in a restrained and understated kind of way. Like Tarik, I realized, with a little hitch of my heart.

It struck me suddenly that this wasn't just the palace of the King— this was Tarik's home. He'd walked through these hallways, stood in this entryway, seen these paintings and columns every day of every year of his life until he came to us in South Brinmark. I couldn't even imagine what it would be like to grow up in a place like this, taking its way of life as a matter of course.

And yet he'd given it all up. For us.

A small man in formal livery approached us as one of the other servants offered to take Griff's hat. Griff's shoulders sank, but since he couldn't very well keep wearing his hat indoors, he swept it off his head and handed it with a sigh to the waiting servant. The small man drew up short at the sight of him, eyes wide with shock.

"Dear *God*," he said. I didn't know much about how servants were supposed to behave, but I'd a good notion that was *not* a proper thing for him to say. "Mr. Farro?"

"Morning, Pont," Griff said, giving the man a lopsided grin.

Pont's gaze drifted over me, disinterested, then he jerked his head at the other servants. They all scuttled back like little beetles, disappearing into the alcoves and shadows of the walls. Pont took hold of Griff's elbow and steered him farther into the palace, I suppose just to be doubly sure the other servants were out of earshot. We stood now almost at the entrance of a grand ballroom, and through the open doors I could see the marble railings of the curved double staircase swathed in black and auburn silk—still wearing mourning colors for Cavnal's fallen King.

"What are you doing here, Mr. Farro?" Pont asked Griff, his voice an urgent whisper. "Where have you been? We were told you'd been taken hostage by the Zealot."

"Nothing that exciting, I'm afraid. I'm here to see my father."

"He's in session with the Court," Pont said.

"Perfect," Griff said. "What I have to say concerns all the Ministers."

Pont looked a bit flustered at that, but he just looked at me and said, "And this young lady?"

"Lady Oramay is with me," Griff said, putting a stern edge to his voice that I'd never heard before.

"As you say," Pont murmured. "Please, follow me."

I did my best to keep my shoulders straight and my head up as I trailed Griff and Pont, trying to keep the south-street attitude from my stride. It was harder than I'd expected to walk with the easy elegance of the high-street ladies. My legs didn't seem to want to take the proper small steps, and my hips didn't seem built to sway, but I just hoped the folds of the skirt would hide what my talents couldn't. A minute and I realized I had my hands clamped in tight balls against my stomach, and I forced them to relax, to hang at my sides like this was something I did every day.

We passed a massive pair of carved and gilded doors, which I desperately wanted to peek through, and headed down a long paneled hallway lined with offices and scattered with stuffy looking officials and scurrying secretaries, all wearing black mourning epaulets on their shoulders. Toward the end of the hall we came to another set of double doors, but these were not nearly as ornate as the first pair. From beyond them I could just make out a sharp volley of raised voices, but the wood muffled them too much for me to make out any words.

I didn't have time to wonder, anyway. Pont nodded to two guards standing on either side of the doorway, who managed to keep their faces perfectly still as they looked down at us. I wondered what they thought of us, if they thought anything at all. Did they think we had no business there, demanding admittance into the Ministers' meeting? One of them hammered the butt of his rifle against the wood, then, without so much as a word to us, they each took a door and swung them open to let us in.

The argument inside the room cut off all at once, as eleven men in grey robes and dark wigs stopped shouting to stare down the long empty room at us. One of them—Minister Farro, I remembered— dropped the book he was holding on the long mahogany table. It hit with a deep thud that echoed oddly in the open space.

"Griff," he gasped.

He strode across the room, his steps too loud in the sudden quiet, almost doubling the low clack of the mantle clock's second hand. In the harlequin shadows I couldn't read the look on his face at all. It might have been relief. Maybe it was anger, or grief. Or maybe he didn't know himself what he felt. Griff stood straight and still beside me, his hands in loose fists at his sides, but I could hear the shallow sharpness of his breathing as he fought for calm.

Then he let out one shattered breath and said, "Father."

The Minister caught him in a tight embrace, holding fast to him like he imagined Griff might drift away if he let him go. "Griff," he murmured, so soft I almost didn't hear him. "Where is the Prince?"

# Chapter 17 • Tarik

On the third day rowing on the endless sea, Agnir and I ran out of the food the Cavnish captain had given us. By nightfall we'd finished the last of the water. On the fourth day we saw the coast of Istia rising like a scar from the ocean, dark and rugged and foreboding. Under the lowering storm sky, surrounded by steel-grey sea and facing the coastline with its black cliffs and black sands, I wondered suddenly if I'd lost my ability to see color. The world was wrought in monochrome, like a photograph or a charcoal sketch.

Even Agnir couldn't leash the wind that railed against us then, or tame the waves that crashed over the sides of the little dory as we drew closer to the shore. Less than a mile off the coast the boat capsized in a rogue wave, and as I tried to claw free of the surf long enough to breathe, I believed I was going to die in sight of my destination.

Agnir grabbed hold of me before the current could claim me, and before I could pull away from him, he was wrestling Zagger's coat off my shoulders.

"No," I tried to say, and swallowed saltwater instead. I thrashed against him. "Leave it...stop..."

But he didn't stop, and before I could make him, he had dragged the coat off of me. I fought him for it, but my arms would hardly move, and I watched, sick with rage and grief, as the coat slipped from his hands into the churning sea.

"It would have drowned you," Agnir said.

I was barely treading water now. The waves swelled around me, and

I fell beneath them once, again. One of the oars from the dory drifted by but I couldn't move quickly enough to grab it. Agnir was a stronger swimmer in the ocean current than me; he dragged my arm across his shoulders and struck out toward the shore, pulling me with him.

Halfway there I took over, looping my arm around him and fighting the waves with desperate strokes. Just when I was sure my legs were too numb to move anymore…when I began to wish the waves would swallow me then and there and be done with it all…my feet scraped the rocky sea floor.

Agnir pulled away from me, rested enough now to swim on his own. I kicked against the sand and swam a little farther until the water was shallow enough to hit my waist. Then I walked, fighting the treacherous undercurrent, then I crawled. Finally I sprawled face-first on the beach with the waves washing over me in heaving swells. I couldn't even feel the sharp black gravel that bit into my cheek.

It took me longer than it should have to realize that Agnir was beside me, on hands and knees, shaking my shoulder.

"Come on," he said, his head close to mine so I could hear him over the roar of the surf and the wailing wind. "Get up. You've got to get up."

I wasn't even cold any more. With cold brine cocooning me, drifting past my lips and tugging the coarse sand away from my hands, I didn't shiver. I didn't feel a thing.

"Taumir, damn it, get up!"

Agnir hooked one hand under my armpit and dragged me off the beach, staggering under my weight as he brought me upright. I managed to push myself the rest of the way to my feet.

"This way," he said, pointing inland. "I'll have you warm soon, I promise. Just stay with me now."

I dashed saltwater from my eyes and tried to see what he was seeing, but the whole beach was blanketed in a dank fog. Only a few outcroppings of jagged black rock pierced the cloud, showing vague outlines of sea cliffs and wind-carved monoliths.

Agnir turned, beckoning me, the rasp of his heavy boots in the shale lost in the crash of the waves. I hunched my shoulders against the biting wind that cut straight through the sodden linen of my shirt, and forced my legs into motion. They shook treacherously, weak and numb from swimming, and my fingers and toes ached with a bone-deep pain. I had to keep moving. If I stopped, I wasn't sure I'd have the strength to move again.

Agnir's long strides carried him quickly away from me, too quickly. I tried once to call after him but the wind stole the words from my lips and swallowed my voice. Step by step. I bent my head and just kept plowing forward, hoping Agnir would eventually turn back and see how far behind I'd fallen.

"Just on over the ridge," his voice said suddenly, startling me. He'd stopped to wait for me, and I hadn't even noticed. "Not much further. Let me give a hand."

He reached out to support me, but I waved him away and stumbled on toward the ragged stone. Everything in this place felt cold and desolate, even the yellow-green moss and the little tufts of sea grass clawing between the rocks. I'd faced the winter elements more in the last few months than I'd ever wanted to, but I'd never been to a place where even the sun felt cold—colder even that it had seemed on the wild winter sea. It hung low on the horizon among a shredded whirl of clouds, shedding only a pale, watery light, biting and merciless, over the scarred and broken earth. The whole landscape that spread before me seemed to have forgotten the meaning of color.

My feet slid on the icy moss as I scrambled up the ridge, my breath freezing in the woolen fibers of my wet scarf. Just a little further.

"There now, as I said," remarked Agnir, stopping beside me, barely out of breath.

He hardly looked cold, either, though he had relinquished his own leather fisherman's coat to the sea as well. He planted one heavy boot on the top of the ridge and pointed down to a tiny hut half-buried under a mound of stone and sod, crouched between the edges of the black coastline and a vast expanse of uneven turf.

"Good God," I said, forcing the words past my numb lips. "Who'd ever want to live there?"

Agnir shot me a glance, a faint smile flashing behind the frost-rimmed strands of his beard. "Why, I do. You didn't think I was steering us to no purpose, did you?"

"Mad," I said, but I followed him down the other side of the ridge.

At least the stony hillock gave some shelter from the sea wind. But I couldn't tear my eyes from the barren sweep of land before us, stretching back and back until it disappeared into the snowy slopes of the wildest and most terrible mountains I'd ever seen. There was absolutely nothing else in sight. Nothing to give any root to the little hut. No roads. No other buildings. Nothing but the cold earth and the cold sun, ice behind and ice ahead. And, I realized with a faint sinking feeling, nothing to serve as fuel for a fire. There were no trees or shrubs anywhere. The hut had no chimney, no curl of welcoming smoke to lead us home. Agnir had promised me warmth, but somehow I imagined he didn't know the meaning of the word.

By the time we reached the hut, I didn't care what it was like inside, as long as it was out of the howling wind. Agnir shoved open the door with some effort and waved me after him. In the wood of the door I recognized the warp and pitch-sealing of boat timbers, like it had been salvaged from some wreck not unlike the one we'd just survived. I wondered how much else Agnir had scraped from death to make a life here at the edge of nowhere.

I stepped through the door and stopped short as a gust of warm air washed over me. Agnir was already peeling off his soaked and torn shirt, humming under his breath as he moved through the tiny space. I took one more step in and closed the door behind me, staring all around as I unwound the stiff-frozen scarf from my neck. The hut had only one small window cut in its stone and daub walls, sealed from the cold with a thick pelt, and little by way of furnishings—two stout chairs fashioned from drift wood, a black stone slab for a table, a narrow cot beneath the loft at the far end of the hut and two thin mattresses above. In the middle of the room was a circular stone pit that looked a bit like a water well. At first I thought might be for a fire, but it was empty and bare.

"It's so warm," I said. "But the fire is out."

"So it is," Agnir said, smiling.

I narrowed my eyes. "What am I missing?"

Agnir lit a few oil lamps around the room to combat the shadows, then waved me toward the back of the hut. He heaved up the lid of a sea chest tucked under the loft and sifted through its contents until he found a linen shirt and a jumper woven of heavy grey and black wool. He handed them to me, then kept searching until he came up with a pair of woolen trousers, and an even thicker pair of wool socks to go with them.

"Here," he said. "Not the finest clothes, but they'll serve. Keep you from catching your death, at any rate."

He tugged a coarse red and grey blanket down from one of the beds in the loft and dropped it on the floor at my feet.

"Get yourself warm and dry, Godarson."

I stripped out of my sodden garments, shivering even in the warm air of the hut, and pulled on the clothes Agnir had given me. The wool was softer than I'd expected, and all the garments fit rather large, though Agnir himself was a little smaller than me. I guessed that they belonged to his son, Iskari. Any other time I might have bristled at the thought of wearing someone else's clothes, but I was too damned cold right then to care.

Agnir pulled on dry clothes of his own and went to drag one of the polished driftwood chairs closer to the stone pit, and then, when I was dressed, beckoned me over to sit. The air was even warmer near the pit—somehow. I peered down into the hole, down and down into the darkness, but Agnir laid a hand on my shoulder and pulled me gently back.

"Not a wise idea. We don't often get fires for warmth here, Godarson. The earth gives us all the heat we need."

"I don't understand."

He pushed me into the chair and tugged on a long string that hung down into the pit, smiling in satisfaction as he tested its weight.

"Nika's been in, thank *Veka*," he said, winding the string around his hand as he pulled it up. After a moment he drew out a small bundle wrapped in mesh cloth and left it to rest on the stone rim of the pit. "I imagine you're as hungry as I am. Care for a bit of soup?"

"Yes, thank you," I said, still scowling at the bundle. "What is that?"

"Bread," he said simply, as if it were obvious.

"You cook your bread in a hole in the ground?"

Agnir shook his head with a patient smile, like I was a daft child. "We use the steam, Taumir. There are pockets of hot water under the earth's surface. At certain places, the steam breaks through. You'll see more of that as you travel through Istia. Out here away from the cities and villages we try to build our houses over the vents when we can. They keep us warm, cook our food, and never die out. It's how we survive. It's the only way to survive here."

I gave a rueful laugh. "In Cavnal they imagine that they were the ones who first harnessed the power of steam, but it seems you've understood it longer than anyone." I paused, studying the pit thoughtfully. "What about in the summer? Doesn't it get too hot?"

He laid a heavy iron cauldron over the mouth of the vent, chuckling under his breath. "Summer? Ah, but summer's not much milder than winter here. Believe me. On a summer night you'd be glad to have the steam. On the rare occasion it gets warm enough, we lid the vent with stone. It keeps most of the heat trapped."

I pulled up my knees, bracing my stockinged feet against the lip of wood at the edge of my chair. I doubted I looked much like the Godarson at the moment, but I couldn't bring myself to care. I barely noticed when Agnir stopped beside me, a clay cup in his hands.

"Water, Godarson?"

I eyed the cup suspiciously, remembering my encounter with the South Brinmark water that had almost been the death of me.

He laughed, seeing my expression. "No need to fear the water sickness here. The earth here is made of the blood of volcanoes, turned to stone, and it keeps the water clean. No foreigner has ever gotten sick from it. Drink, Godarson. You haven't had enough to drink since you survived drowning."

I took the cup and swallowed down its contents—it was glacially cold, and perhaps the best thing I had ever tasted in my life. When I sat a few moments trying to drain the last few drops from the cup, Agnir laughed and refilled it for me without a word. He filled the cup three times before I was finally satisfied, then turned back to his stew preparations.

I tried to watch, but my thoughts were straying, and the room was shifting in blurry, watery lines around me. Finally I gave up and leaned my forehead on my knees, and closed my eyes. I didn't even care if I dreamed—I couldn't imagine wind and storms doing any damage to the earthbound hut.

"Ah," Agnir said some time later, startling me out of a faint doze. I glanced up to find him watching the door, as though he'd heard something outside through the whistling wind. "That'll be my *vaemi*."

I almost asked what he meant, but caught myself in time. *Vaemi* were children—or more than that, one's blood children. I remembered that much from my schooling.

Instead I asked, "How can you tell?"

He just waved a hand toward the door as he tended the cauldron,

 118

stirring around a lamb shank and a cluster of tiny potatoes. A moment later the door slammed open behind me. I jumped and turned as a young man strode into the hut, wind-blown and coated with ice, wearing no coat but a width of fur draped over his shoulders, pinned with a heavy copper clasp. I doubted he was much older than me, but he came in like a conqueror of old, with a sparse beard and his thick hair bound in knotted cords in a way Minister Batar would have called *p-p-positively* barbaric. He strode past me without even a glance and tossed a heavy-bladed knife on the table.

"You're back. I wondered, but I didn't see *Hastol*," he said to Agnir, leaning against the black stone slab and folding his arms—in spite of the cold, they were bare. "Nika is seeing to the horses. She said don't wait."

"Iskari," Agnir said. "Show some courtesy."

*So*, I thought with a little sinking feeling, *that is Iskari*.

# Chapter 18 ⚜ Hayli

OF ALL THE THINGS MINISTER FARRO MIGHT'VE ASKED GRIFF, THE CROWN Prince's whereabouts was the last thing I expected. Griff seemed just as surprised as me.

He tipped his head like he hadn't quite heard, and said, "Tarik?"

Minister Farro pursed his lips, eyes shifting to the side like he meant to glance behind him, at the long table where the other Ministers were gathered, watching us hawkishly.

"I know the truth, son," he said. "I know that Tarik and Shade—Tarik and the Zealot—are the same person. And I know for bloody certain that *he* is the one who got shot on that dais and taken away by that tattooed mage, not the other one who disappeared out from under everybody's noses. Is he...he isn't..."

"He's alive," Griff said. "He isn't here."

Minister Farro bent his head briefly, lips moving silently. I bit my lip when his gaze lifted and drifted toward me, disinterested at first, then shifting to alarm and a dark blaze of anger. "What...the *hell*... do you mean by bringing *her* here?" he hissed. "Is she not the one who—"

"Father," Griff said, gripping the Minister's elbows. "Please, just listen. She's all right. I'll explain everything to you, but not right now. We need to talk to the Ministers."

Minister Farro's eyebrow struggled to a low slope of doubt. "All of them, what the devil for? Stars, if you can stop the in-fighting and bickering, I'll nominate you to take over Bell the Younger's Ministry."

"Oh, hell no," Griff said, which made his father chuckle quietly.

"Listen," he said. "Since Bell died, we've been at an impasse. Five against five, loyalists versus the sedition. Of course, there's no sedition now that…"

His voice cut off abruptly and he turned his head, pressing his fingertips against his eyes. After a short tick, while Griff and I stood in awkward silence, he took a deep breath and scrubbed his hand over his face.

"Who's the holdout?" Griff asked. "You said five against five, but there are eleven of you left."

Minister Farro held his gaze a long moment, then turned away again.

"You?" Griff's hands knotted at his sides. "I don't understand. How is it even a question? How can you still even consider siding with those traitors? After all they did, I thought for sure you—"

"I know," Minister Farro interrupted. "Believe me, I know. But I'm not sure I agree with everything Batar and that damn scientist Baisell stand for, either." He waved a hand. "Well, maybe you can bring some light to our darkness. Come on."

He turned and strode back toward the table with his ground-devouring stride, leaving Griff and I standing in sudden uncertainty near the doors. I ground my teeth, because I'd meant to ask Minister Farro about the Army—to find out if the Army had brought him that intelligence report yesterday, and beg him not to authorize a strike against the smelter—but the chance had passed me by. Praying I'd get another one, I gave Griff's hand a little squeeze and followed his father toward the long table.

"Mr. Farro," one of the Ministers said. "So glad to see you safe and sound."

"I'm sure you were very concerned, Minister Blake," Griff said with frigid politeness.

I couldn't stop staring at Minister Von, standing beside Minister Blake with his hands resting on the table. But I didn't see him. I saw his son Risiya, and the look on his face when he had left me with a shattered knee to be burned alive in his house. They both had the same cruel, hard look in their eyes.

"What is this about?" one of the other Ministers asked, a stuffy, portly bloke with almost as many nose hairs as whiskers. "What business do these children have interrupting our session? No offense to your son, Farro." I lifted my chin and glared at him, watching the little spots of red blossoming on his puffy cheeks. "Beg pardon, my lady. I see…ahh…you…"

"You're all in danger," I said, cutting off his stammering. Gem had tried to teach me once how to talk with a proper high-street accent, and though I was dead sure I didn't have it down straight, I did my best. "We came to warn you."

"*Warn* us?" the portly Minister sputtered. "What sort of danger… nonsense…could you *possibly* know about that we don't? We have eyes and ears throughout the city, I assure you, and if there was any danger to our persons, we would *certainly* know about it without having to be told by…"

He waved a hand in our direction, obviously failing to find a word that captured his contempt without insulting us outright.

"Your eyes and ears in the city aren't very observant," I said, "or maybe they've got a bit of…selective blindness and deafness."

"*Katzpotim*, are you insinuating—"

"There are anarchist cells in the city who want to overthrow the Court of Ministries," Griff interrupted, hands knotted in frustration. "You know full well there are. After all, they're the ones you blamed for the first assassination attempt on King Trabin. Do you think they just gave up after Avnaya Square? If anything they're bolder than ever, because now the biggest obstacle is gone, and all that's left is the Court. And let's be honest, Ministers—you aren't exactly exuding an image of strength and power right now."

"How *dare* you—" the Minister blustered.

Before he could go on, I cut in, "And it's not just the anarchists you need to be worrying about. There's also the—"

I never got to finish. The double doors slammed open behind us, and we all turned to stare as Prince Tarik strode into the room, ablaze like lightning. I reeled a step back like I'd got punched. No one said a word. It felt like the whole room was holding its breath.

That…that had to be Tarik. He wore Tarik's dark blue suit, with its tailed jacket and silver-buttoned waistcoat, the silver neckerchief in an elegant knot at his throat and the pocket watch tucked in his front pocket. His hair was slicked back and his cheeks fresh-shaven, and he looked for all the world like he'd just left the care of his manservant. But surely his valet would know if it wasn't him…surely the impostor mage wouldn't be brazen enough to *come to the palace...*

Griff shifted like he meant to step forward, but I suddenly had a notion I wanted to see what would happen. If this man, whoever this was...if he *was* the impostor, what would he do? And if, impossibly, it was Tarik... Oh stars, how were we supposed to know? I edged closer to Griff so we were standing shoulder-to-shoulder, and flicked the back of his hand sharply. He stood still.

"Your Highness!" Minister Farro cried, breaking the silence.

The man who looked like Tarik didn't falter, just kept bearing down on us like a thunderstorm, eyes full of rage and fury. He didn't look at Griff or me at all, as if we weren't even there.

"*You!*" he shouted suddenly, coming almost alongside us as he pointed at the Ministers. "Minister Von. Minister Blake. Minister Rigyeri." He swung his hand toward the portly Minister. "Minister Schall." He pointed at one last Minister, a tall, gangly bloke with sallow skin and huge dark eyes, and his lips curled in a feral smile. "Minister Prefanin. I should *hang* every last one of you for what you've done." He swept his finger slowly over the other Ministers. "And all of you should hang for standing by and watching it happen."

"Your Highness, I don't know what you've heard, but..."

The mage turned a dark glare on Minister Von, who looked paler than I'd ever seen him. "Heard, Von? What I've *heard?* What about what I've *endured?* At *your* hands. You, and Kippler, and all the rest of you devils."

Von's hand spasmed on the edge of the table, but he didn't say a word. Griff and I exchanged sidelong glances. I couldn't breathe, not with the way confusion was muddling my thoughts.

"Your Highness," Minister Farro said. "I will be the first to declare my joy and relief at seeing you returned to us safe and sound, but you must understand our caution. After all, how do we know you are who you claim to be? Last any of us recall, there were two of you standing on that dais, both pretending to be the same person."

The mage spun toward him, a stifled laugh lost behind his disbelieving smile. "Oh, *you*, Farro. Don't you dare address me. You're worse than all of *them* put together, and do you know why?" He took two long steps to come face to face with Farro, grabbing him by the necktie and leaning in close. "Because you were the King's friend. *You were his friend!*"

Farro leaned back just slightly from the shouted words, and I realized all at once that the mage had a knife in his hand, and it was pressed hard against Minister Farro's neck. Panicking, I stepped in and laid a hand on the mage's arm. The static charge of an incredibly powerful magic lashed through me at the touch.

"Wait," I said. "Look at me. Please."

He hesitated, then slowly pulled the blade away from Minister Farro's throat. Griff darted to his father's side, dragging him a few steps back, but the mage wasn't paying attention to either of them now. His dark eyes were fixed intently on me, a look both familiar and completely new on his face.

"Do you know who I am?" I asked.

"Hayli," he said. All the wrath had gone from his voice. It just sounded quiet now, quiet and tired, and maybe a little sad. "Of course I know you. You're the only thing I'm certain of."

I let my hand drop from his arm. Derrin told me that Tarik had begged me to come back, but if this were really Tarik, I didn't think this was the reunion I could've expected. There was no joy in the mage's eyes, only confusion, grasping desperately at hope.

I tried to keep the disappointment from my voice as I asked, very quietly, "Who are you?"

"Tarik," he said. His brows drew together. "I'm...I'm the Zealot."

I frowned. Tarik had hated that title, or, at least he'd never wanted it, never claimed it for his own, so those words sounded strange beyond belief falling from his lips. My hands trembled. I tightened them in knots, hiding them in the heavy folds of the long skirt.

"The scion of the mad god?" I whispered.

"No, no," he said. His lips lifted in a faint smile. "*He* is."

"He, who is *he*?" I asked, but he was already backing away from me, his eyes wild, almost terrified. "Wait!"

"He impersonated *me*!" the mage shouted, hands open at his sides. "Why can't you see that? Why can't I make you believe? I'm just the tool in the hands of the craftsman. *He* is the one who will bring chaos on us all!"

And then he was gone.

He just disappeared, like Derrin. Like a Ghost.

For one endless moment, nobody moved. Nobody even dared to breathe. Then, slowly, Minister Farro stepped away from Griff, and

Blake let his hands drop onto the table with a quiet thump.

"Impossible," one of them muttered, while another said, "Stars, it was that impostor mage, daring to invade our halls! How did he even get *in* here?"

Another cursed under his breath and said, "His Royal Highness is no filthy Jixy."

"What the devil is going on here?" Minister Blake asked, flinging his hands at the other Ministers as if they'd have some answer he didn't.

"What were you going to say?" Minister Farro asked me.

I drew a thin breath. "If the anarchists dan' get to you first," I said, loud enough to stop their chatter, not even caring enough to mask my accent, "then that man will kill every last one of you. And if you keep fighting among yourselves, it won't even be a challenge." I took Minister Farro's arm, even though I was sure it was bad etiquette or some such, and drew him away from the table. "Minister Farro, dan' send the Army to the smelter."

I prayed that he would tell me he'd already rejected their request, but instead, he looked dead baffled as he said, "What?"

"I know they've requested orders to go to the old smelter out on the Stad, because the King's assassin is supposed to be hiding there. But he ain't there. None of us was responsible for that. Dan' send them against us. Please. You'll just be putting innocent skitters at risk."

"I've heard no such request," Farro said, frowning first at me, then at his son. "Are you certain?"

A little prickle of alarm spidered down my arms. If the Army wasn't even going to bother asking their Minister for permission...

"Heard they had a squadron on stand-by to move out," I said, carefully. "They were supposed to bring you the report and the request yesterday."

His face darkened and his brows came down in a scowl, and he studied me long and hard like he meant to ferret out the truth of my words with the power of his will alone. "How could you possibly know this information?"

I glanced at Griff, but I hadn't even told Griff about Krigs and his message, so he was staring at me just as muddled as his father. I didn't know what to say. If I told him that one of his soldiers was playing double-agent, would that put Krigs in danger? But if I didn't...how was he to know I was being truthsome?

I swallowed and said, "Minister, dan' forget that the smelter is full of mages who can read minds and dart from one place to another and turn invisible."

He opened his mouth. Then he closed it, and for the space of five heartbeats he just stared at me. I'd a fair notion what he was thinking—if what I said was true, how were any government or military secrets safe? What good were walls when there were folks out there who could walk right through them?

"Well," he said at last, "if such a request comes my way, I will of course need to see substantial evidence proving that the assassin is at the smelter, including the identity of the assassin and the source of the intelligence. And I will call in my general staff this afternoon for a report on their current operations."

I blew out my breath, and nodded my thanks.

NEAR AN HOUR LATER, GRIFF AND I finally gave up on our efforts and left the Ministers still bickering in their Chamber. It didn't seem to matter what we'd said to try to convince them that the anarchists were truly a danger, and not just the ordinary sort of riffraff the city always had—or that the mage appearing as Tarik would likely make good on his threat to hang the lot of them before crowning himself King of Cavnal.

Minister Farro was the only one who seemed the least bit convinced, and even then I wasn't sure if he was just agreeing with us so he'd have a better shot at persuading Griff to come home. Griff was stone-faced and silent as we walked down the long hallway. Me, I couldn't stop my hands from shaking—not from fear, but anger.

We'd almost reached the end of the corridor when I heard the clap of heeled court shoes on marble behind us.

"Wait! Mr. F-F-Farro!"

"Oh, stars," Griff muttered. "This'll be fantastic."

We both turned to see a rather small man with flame-red hair fairly running down the hall on our heels, the wide sleeves of his robe fluttering like pennants behind him. All the powder in the world couldn't hide the bright red splotches on his cheeks or the little trickle of sweat on his temples.

Griff straightened up and flashed the Minister a charming smile. "Minister Batar. How good to see you."

"Mr. F-F-Farro," the Minister said, puffing gently as he stopped in front of us. "Gad, what b-b-beastly business all of this is." He pulled a lace kerchief from inside his sleeve and dabbed his forehead with it. "Who in G-G-God's name was that fellow?"

"You mean you dan' believe it was the Prince?" I asked.

He frowned at me. "Young lady, you have a most p-p-peculiar accent. Mr. F-F-Farro, are you quite sure she *belongs* here?"

"As much as I do," Griff said.

"Hayli," I said, holding out my hand.

He'd started to lift his hand to take it, but suddenly he stopped and drew his arm back, and eyed my hand as if it might bite him. "Hayli, d'you say? But I knew…" He took a scant step closer to me, head tipped to one side. "You're what, sixteen, no, seventeen years old? You're not, by any chance, Hayli *Lorin?* You are the *very* likeness of her Ladyship Vareya."

I flinched, but his statement didn't shock me near as much as when he took my hand and a little spike of electricity stung my palm.

"*Oh,*" I breathed.

"I knew your family, long before I became Minister," he murmured, voice low and suddenly free of its affected stutter. He withdrew his hand and tapped a finger to the side of his nose. "Now, to answer your question, no, I don't believe that man is who he says he is. After all, *he's* a mage. But who is *he?* And what does he *want?*"

"Minister Batar," Griff said, drawing out the words. "*You?*"

"Hush, lad, there's a good fellow," Batar said, waving a pale hand at him. "Beastly troublesome business, keeping your identity a secret from the world, *especially* when you're in my line of work."

I snorted, thinking of Tarik. From what Batar had just said, I gathered he didn't have a clue that Tarik was a mage as well. Guess the Prince had done a better job of hiding his identity than Batar did.

"Minister," Griff said. "I think you ought to have a long conversation with Her Majesty."

Batar straightened up, scowling fiercely. "Why?"

"Just do it. Tell her what happened today. Tell her what we said. And then listen to what she has to tell you." Griff gave him a polite little bow. "Good day, Minister."

"Wait!" he called. "Where can I find you? I may need to know."

We both hesitated, then I gave Griff a faint nod.

"Borokhev," he said.

"Ah, of course. The beginning," said Batar, with a long sigh. "Very well."

"What beginning?" I asked, but Griff was tugging me along after him, and Batar was walking, slowly now, back toward the Court of Ministries. "Minister! What beginning?"

"C'mon, Hayli," Griff said. "Nothing else we can do here."

"He knows something. Let me gan!" I broke free and ran after Batar, not caring if half the palace saw me with my skirts hitched up and my clunky boots beneath. I snatched the Minister's arm, forcing him to turn and face me. "What beginning? What'd you mean?"

He just shook his head sadly. "That's where it all started. At Borokhev," he said. "The impostor. The sedition. That mad and deadly dream, scheming wars to remold the world. Suppose I shouldn't be surprised you lot would end up there." He reached out suddenly and grabbed my arms. "Tarik *has* to reclaim his throne. I know...I know you've got something to do with him, if you're here with Mr. Farro now. He needs to come back and make things right. The situation is unraveling far too fast, and the knot is much more twisted than you know."

"Actually, Minister," I said, "I think it's you who dan' na how tangled it really is. Talk to the Queen. Then come find us if you've still got questions."

"It may be harder than you think for me to have that conversation," Batar said, frowning.

"Why?"

"Because no one knows where Queen Elanar is." Ignoring my shock, he straightened up, smoothed a hand over his court robes, and gently reformed the absurd wisps of his red hair. "Now, if you'll excuse me," he said, "g-g-good day."

# Chapter 19 ~ Tarik

ESPITE AGNIR'S REPROACH, ISKARI MADE NO MOVE TO WELCOME ME. Courtesy, it seemed, was not something Istians understood the same way Cavners did. His gaze just flickered toward me once, disinterested, before returning to his father.

"So the sea spat out another one," he said, and shrugged. "The soup smells good. Is it ready?"

"Not yet. I've only just come in myself." Agnir stirred the cauldron a while without speaking, then, without looking up he said, "We lost the ship."

Iskari froze where he was, his eyes drifting back to me. "Too much baggage?"

"Iskari!" Agnir snapped. "That is Taumir Eyidson. That is our Godar."

Iskari regarded me steadily a moment, cold and remote, then without the slightest hint of emotion he turned back to Agnir and said, "Anything we can salvage from the wreck?"

"We were four days from the coast. Nothing reached the shore before we did. But we'll see if she coughs up any flotsam in the next few days."

I slowly lowered my legs so I wasn't hunched up on the chair like a child, masking the motion by stretching my hands toward the steam vent. It didn't matter; I knew I didn't fool Iskari. More than that, I knew it didn't even matter.

A moment later the door swung open again in a gust of wind that scattered papers around the hut, and Agnir's daughter walked in from the dark. I stared; I couldn't help it. Even dressed from head to toe in fur and leather, she managed to look otherworldly, like a creature of wind and ice. Her hair hung thick and heavy, bound in rope-like knots like Iskari's, but hers was almost as pale gold as mine, decorated with amber and lapis beads. She had the bluest eyes I'd ever seen—the bluest, and the coldest. She took one look at me and shifted her gaze to meet Iskari's, and some shared meaning passed between them that made me feel suddenly small and insignificant.

"Here's the word from the clan," she said, pulling a rolled piece of paper from her courier bag and handing it across to Agnir. She had a rather low voice, as cold and hard as her eyes. "The moot will happen in three weeks."

Agnir glanced at me as she said it, so I asked him, "Is that the moot you were telling me about?"

To myself I thought, *Three weeks? But I can't be here that long…*

He nodded. "We must decide if we will accept you as our Godar," he said. Nika swung around to look at me, but Agnir ignored her as he finished, "Or if we will vote in a new Godar to replace you."

"As if there's a question," Nika said, low, as she passed me by.

"You mean Rigvar? The other claimant?"

She snorted. "At least Rigvar is Istian."

Agnir darted an anxious glance from her to me. I wasn't sure if he thought I'd be offended; I wasn't even sure if I thought I should be offended. Part of me had no doubt the Istians would replace me at their earliest opportunity, and I wasn't sure it bothered me that they might not even give me a chance to prove myself, or try to win their respect. So I met his gaze evenly for a moment, then went back to studying the steam vent, as determined to ignore Agnir's children as they seemed determined to hate me.

I felt Nika's glare still fixed on me, and resisted the urge to smile. *She* at least had expected to offend me. Sometimes I wondered if not caring made me weak, but right then, I knew it made me strong. Or at least it made me feel strong, and that was enough. I folded my arms and braced a foot against the stones of the vent, settling a little deeper into the chair.

"You have to forgive them," Agnir said after a long silence.

"Forgive them for what?" I asked.

"Their...candor."

I smiled, faintly. "Candor is all that matters."

Iskari circled around to the seat opposite me, dropping onto it and leaning onto his knees to study me.

"Candor?" he said with a ruthless smile. "You honestly speak of candor?"

I winced. "What do you mean?"

I wondered if he recognized me after all. Did he know me as Eyid's son or did he know me as the rebel Zealot who had caused such chaos in Cavnal? Or, God forbid, did he know I was Prince Tarik?

He didn't bother to answer me. Instead he reclined back in the chair and crossed his boots at the ankles, folding his arms over his chest. "You can see it in your eyes," he said. "Everything about you is a lie, *Godar*."

I leaned forward, slamming my hand on the rim of the vent. The lamps winked out, not one by one, not slowly, but all of them, all at once.

"Not everything," I said.

I couldn't see them in the darkness; I know I didn't hear them moving. I barely even heard the breath that Nika exhaled, slowly. Satisfied, I stirred my fingers and relit the lamps, one by one, bringing the tiny space gradually back into existence. Iskari finally shifted, sitting a little straighter and glancing sidelong at Nika, who still hadn't moved from her place by the table. She looked like a statue, suspended in a moment of time, one hand grazing the rough wood of the table, the other caught halfway to her heart.

"Is it true?" she asked her father.

"It's true."

I glanced at Agnir. "Is what true?"

I expected him to say something about me, about the stories of the Zealot they'd somehow heard from Cavnal, about my identity. But he only turned away, busying himself with preparing bowls for our soup. I turned to Iskari instead.

"Is what true?" I asked again.

"Not your business, Cavner," he said.

"You know I'm not a Cavner."

One corner of his mouth tugged upwards, cold and humorless—more a grimace than a smile. "And you know that being Istian has nothing to do with your blood."

"*That* isn't true," Nika said.

I glanced at her in surprise but she just favored me with a dark glare; I should have realized she had no interest in defending me, only in speaking the truth.

"Only Istians are Istian, but not all Istians are Istian," she added, turning the glare on her brother.

It took me longer than I cared to admit to parse the grammar of the statement; I knew enough Istian to be technically fluent, but that was a far cry from being *actually* fluent. Before this mad voyage to Istia had begun, I never would have appreciated the difference.

Iskari flicked his fingers in acknowledgement.

Agnir murmured, "It's something Eyid said."

We all turned to look at him, but he still stood with his back to us, his hands still on the edge of the slab counter. Nika's face darkened with fleeting displeasure but she said nothing, and Iskari, tightening his arms around his chest, went back to scowling at the steam pit.

"He said one would follow him who didn't just possess magic," Agnir went on, "but governed it. One would follow him who...who walked in chaos like a reaper through his harvest."

I tried to speak, but my voice caught somewhere in my throat. Finally I managed, "Was he talking about me?"

"Hard to say. He was *thringathstava* not three months later."

I frowned, turning the word over in my head. *Gathstava* meant kill, but I'd never heard it paired with *thrin*...which as far as I could tell, had something to do with a bond of some sort.

"You believe it was at the hands of someone he knew?"

Iskari and Nika exchanged a glance; neither of them spoke.

"There are reasons to believe that, yes," Agnir said. I gave him a pointed glance, and he sighed. "Eyid was stabbed. In the heart."

I arched a brow, out of surprise rather than confusion, but Nika seemed to interpret it as the latter.

"He was the most powerful mage in Istia," she said, with a possessive tone that amused me. "And he was also a warrior."

*Athakurim.* The Istian word for *warrior* intrigued me—it was laden with so much more meaning than simply the Cavnish word. It was weighted with honor and threaded with dignity, and it made my heart burn with something like desire. Growing up I'd never pursued the sorts of military honors that Trabin had been renowned for; my ambitions had never taken that turn—or perhaps I simply had never found anything worth my ambition. But the way Nika described Eyid made me wonder how it would feel to inspire so much pride. I just wasn't sure that my talents disposed me to martial leadership; I'd always preferred battles of a different sort.

I didn't let her see any of that, though. I just held her gaze and kept my silence.

"How does a man that powerful allow someone to drive a dagger into his heart?" she went on, her voice a low hush. "Such a man would never allow an enemy within striking range. The only explanation is that he was betrayed by someone he knew."

I sat back in my chair. "So, are you three the only ones who think that? Or why is Istia claiming that a Cavnish agent assassinated him?"

Iskari let out his breath in a quiet laugh. "I admit it," he said, to Agnir. "He is at least a little smarter than a damn herring."

"It's our speculation," Agnir said to me, ignoring Iskari. "Unfortunately many people only see what they want to see. The rift between Cavnal and Istia has been broadening for some years now. Some *sodthari* in the moot saw Eyid's death as a clear sign of Cavnish treachery. It didn't fit their view of the world to see a traitor's hand in it. And the timing of it, right after Eyid tore up the Accord and...ah..."

"Executed," Iskari promptly supplied, indifferent.

Agnir's mouth twitched. "*Executed* the ambassadors who had brought it to him... Well, let's just say it's easy to see how Cavnal might be blamed for retaliation and a bit of intimidation tactics."

I lifted my brows in surprise. Eyid's death had not been a popular subject of conversation in Brigun Palace—I knew why, now—and I certainly had never heard the report that he had killed anyone, let alone two Cavnish ambassadors. Such an outrage must have been viewed by my father...by Trabin as an insult, if not an act of blatant hostility. Still, Trabin would never have considered it justification for assassinating Eyid himself, and he had always denied responsibility for the act.

"Where did Eyid die?" I asked suddenly.

Iskari gave me a cold look. "He's really his son?" he asked Agnir. "And he knows nothing about his father's death?"

I ground my teeth, meeting Agnir's anxious glance a moment before turning back to Iskari, lifting a hand in expectation.

"It was at his home. Are you going to ask where that is, too?"

"It would probably mean nothing to me if you told me," I said, and gave him my best, most charming Cavnish smile. "I'm not Istian, remember?"

He muttered something under his breath that I realized I probably didn't want to hear anyway.

"Who found him?" The three of them exchanged a glance at that, puzzled. I gave Iskari a reproachful look. "Don't tell me you never even thought to ask?"

"I don't think it was ever stated," Agnir said. "But now that you've asked, I'm curious to know."

Iskari rolled his eyes at the smug smile I threw his way.

# Chapter 20 · Hayli

"WHAT IS IT WITH MEMBERS OF THE BLOODY ROYAL FAMILY GOING MISSING ALL the time?" Derrin asked, scowling like a thundercloud at me and Griff both, as if we'd had aught to do with it. "Batar, he had *no* notion where the Queen might be? Even with him being a mage, too?"

"Not a one," I muttered.

I folded my arms and slouched back against the shell of the smelting pot, avoiding the baffled stares of Tarik's crew. It was late in the evening, and most of the folks had already cleared out of the smelter. With all but a few fires left to dwindle and die away, the place was glacially cold and eerily quiet. A few handfuls of skitters still lingered in the dark corners, piling together the bits and bobs they'd collected like faerie children, stolen treasures of stolen lives. I thought I'd goggled Rivano not too long before, talking to a few of his mages, but I'd not seen him since—not that I minded.

"Well, she has no real reason to stay in the Court, where she might be in danger from whoever assassinated her husband—or those that hoped for it to happen," Griff said. "She's Tulian, not Cavnish. And now, with the King gone—and Tarik too for all the world can tell—she really has no claim to any authority in this nation at all."

Derrin nodded thoughtfully. "But where would she go? Would she stay in Cavnal, or go back to Tulay?"

Nobody had an answer. Me, I couldn't imagine the Queen would go far so long as Tarik was still grounded in Cavnal. Maybe he was off in Istia for now, but he'd be coming back. He had to.

I tried not to let the fear drown me, but I could feel it pressing about the corners of my heart with the voice of a thousand questions. Nobody sailed to Istia in the middle of winter—everyone knew that. What if they'd been shipwrecked? And...what if they somehow survived the voyage, but Tarik found his heart in Istia and decided he belonged there more than in Cavnal? Would he abandon us all to stay there? If he decided he never wanted to see this place again, and never came back... would I ever know the reason why? Would I know if it was because the sea claimed him, or if he'd claimed the sea?

I tapped my teeth, forcing myself to focus. We'd got other problems on our hands much bigger than worrying over Tarik. Worry never stopped the rain from falling.

"Any word about Kor yet?" Anuk asked. "Or *from* him?"

Derrin let out an exasperated breath. Coins shrugged and glanced away, and Jig kicked his heel against the cement step.

"He's been absent since Avnaya Square, right?" Griff asked.

Derrin shrugged. "He'll show up eventually, or he won't. I've never felt too keen about trusting him, anyway. Not sure why Tarik was always so quick to rely on him, but it doesn't matter now."

"Because he's Tarik's uncle," I said softly, and they all gaped at me, except Shiver. "He's the Queen's brother."

Derrin sighed and leaned over his knees, then, with a bitty shake of his head, he straightened up and said, "That certainly explains a lot of things. Well, it's not for now. It's late already—let's get going."

*To Borokhev.*

Suddenly I got to imagining all kinds of things I still needed to take care of at the smelter. I needed to make sure they'd cleaned out Tarik's office properly. Had he left anything in his room? Maybe Luce hadn't got all her fabric packed up, and if I could take care of that, I could save her a trip back...or, hadn't I seen Doc still getting his medical supplies together?

"You jake, Hayli?" Coins asked softly.

I whirled to face him, hands in knots at my sides. "I'm grobbing fantastic," I said. My voice sounded high and shrill, not a bit like me. "Why? Why you goggling at me like that?"

"Because you look apt to sprout feathers out of your beak pot any second, right?" He tried a smile. "Beak pot, yeah? You like it?"

A little laugh bubbled from my lips and I couldn't even help it.

"Yeah," I murmured. "I like it."

Coins made a dramatic victory gesture, and Griff rolled his eyes.

I waved a hand in the lads' general direction. "You lot should gan on already. I'll be along just behind you. Dan' worry about me. I know how to get there."

"Go on, lads," Coins said, mimicking my wave to the rest of the crew and adding a dark glare of his own for extra encouragement.

Nobody made any effort to argue. Anuk touched my arm briefly as he passed, a little knot of worry traced between his brows, but when I gave him a wan smile he trailed on after the other lads without a word. When it was just me and Coins, I sat down on the cement step, and a minute and Coins slid down to sit beside me.

"Can you do this?"

I had my lip clamped tight between my teeth, trying once again to drive away fear with pain. It wasn't working. "Can't you just let me Shift? I dan' wanna gan out there. I know...I know you lot need to, and that's fine, but...dan' make me gan. Please. I'll be fine as the crow."

He didn't say anything. For too long we sat side by side, me hunched small as I could get, him leaning over his knees, his hands clasped loose between them, eyes shadowed.

"What?" I asked finally. "What's on your mind?"

"It's just..." He tipped his head to look at me. "It's so hard, when I know what you need, and I know what the folks need, and those two things don't match, right?" He sighed and went back to staring at the floor. "I know you can't stand the place. I don't blame you. If it were me...and I'd been through what you'd been through there, I'd be halfway to Darbissey by now, just from the thought of going, right? It's just...I also know the skitters and the mages need you. But I don't want to ask you to do this, to go to that place, for *their* sake, as if I didn't care about what you need." He rubbed a hand over his face. "That probably made no grobbing sense at all."

"No...no, it made sense," I murmured. "But how can you say they need me? I'm not anybody. I'm just a kid. We're all just *kids*. Well...I know we're not, not really, but you know what I mean. What would they need *me* for? Rivano's worlds more powerful and smarter than me, and Derrin—"

"They don't need Rivano," Coins interrupted. "Well, maybe they do, but it's not the same. Not the same as why they need you."

I scowled at him. "You keep saying it, and I dan' see why I should believe it. Just because of Tarik? Why?"

"You sacrificed yourself to save the folks in the Bricks' headquarters, back when the Chernayi were rounding up the mages, right?" he said gently. "Then you got them out of Esobor. Saved a lot of people's lives in the Avnaya Square riot. People recognize you—and I don't mean because of what happened in the Avnaya with Tarik at the end. They trust you. Know that you'll look after them. And yes, they know Tarik trusted you, too. That's not nothing."

I shrugged, feeling suddenly self-conscious. "I just did what I had to," I said. "Div'n think aught about it at the time."

"And that's why they trust you." He hesitated. "And maybe... when folks have stood too long on the ground, maybe they need to be reminded that they can fly."

My mouth quirked in a smile.

"But like I said," Coins went on, "I can't tell you to come to Borokhev. I can't do that to you, right? Stars, the place creeps me out." He wrapped an arm around my shoulders, giving me a little squeeze. "Just...whatever you do, don't stray far."

"Give me a night. One more night to get my head sorted."

"Think there are still some skitters hanging about," he said with a faint smile. "I'd hate to leave them here all alone tonight."

He got up without another word and wandered out of the smelter, leaving me sitting uncertain in a swathe of uncertain shadows. I buried my head in my arms. More than aught else, I wished that Tarik were with me. Or Zagger. What would Zagger tell me? Would he tell me to be brave? Would he tell me not to be afraid, to swallow my fears so I could be strong for everybody else? I didn't want to feel strong. I didn't want people to rely on me. Why didn't they see me on the dais, shooting Tarik, and realize I wasn't worth their trust? It would've been so much easier that way.

*Easier.*

Maybe that's what Zagger would tell me. I could just see his solemn, handsome face, always too stern, fracturing in a gruff smile.

*We go through life one choice at a time, Hayli,* he'd say. *And the choice is always the same. Will I do what's easy, or will I do what's right?*

*Funny how those two are rarely the same,* I thought. *Even love is not an easy thing.*

# Chapter 21 ⋅ Tarik

A GNIR SERVED UP BOWLS OF STEW BEFORE I COULD ASK HIM ANY MORE about Eyid's death and the fallout from the Accord. He handed a bowl to me first, then served his children. I half-expected resentment from them on that score, but they didn't even react. It shouldn't have surprised me, though, given what I knew about Istian culture—Istians were stubborn and reclusive and suspicious of every outsider, but they also had stronger traditions of hospitality than any other culture I'd ever learned about. I was a guest in Agnir's house, which meant that, however much any or all of them might hate me, they would see to it that I had the best of everything they had to offer.

Nika pulled herself onto the table to eat, and Iskari left his seat by the steam vent to let his father have the chair. Agnir poured me a shallow cup of some kind of clear liquid from a stone jar and settled into the chair, holding his own cup over the steam vent.

"For *Veka*," he murmured, "and the forgotten gods. Favor and safe harbor."

"Safe harbor," Iskari and Nika murmured.

Agnir tossed the contents of the cup into the deep abyss of the vent, then decanted himself another cupful. I hesitated, wondering if I was meant to repeat the libation, but he just tipped his cup toward me and lifted it to his lips. The first sip of the drink set my mouth burning and my lungs seizing, much worse than any brandy I'd ever drunk, but somehow I managed to swallow without choking. I felt Iskari's gaze fixed on me, though, and I must have made some sort of grimace because he and Nika exchanged a look and a stifled grin.

"What the hell is that stuff?" I asked when I could speak without coughing.

Agnir chuckled and took another long sip from his cup. "*Skatha.* Good, aye?"

I shook my head once to clear my thoughts—one sip was enough to set the room drifting a bit oddly.

"Death in a bottle," Agnir said.

"Why aren't they drinking it?" I asked, pointing my cup at Iskari and Nika.

Nika gave me a rather smug smile. "I prefer keeping my wits."

I looked her straight in the eye and drained the rest of the *skatha* in one swallow. As soon the liquid made it down I realized what a stupid thing it was to do, but, damn my half-mad heart, I was determined to prove I could drink the whole bloody cup and still keep my wits about me. Nika didn't seem impressed by my effort. She rolled her eyes and applied herself to her stew, but Iskari laughed—a harsh laugh, cold as the night wind—and pushed away from the wall. He'd already finished his stew, so he cleaned his bowl and nodded to his father, and disappeared outside. I shuddered in the wind that whipped through the open door as he left and leaned forward, cautiously, to set my cup on the rim of the steam vent.

I was, of course, an absolute idiot. I nudged the cup carefully to the center of the rim, realizing as I did that I was taking entirely too long to do it.

*Why can't Blood magic keep me from getting drunk?* I wondered. *It would be nice if it could do something useful for once...*

*Because...actually healing people isn't useful...*

*What am I even thinking?*

I gritted my teeth and sat back slowly, trying to keep the world from spinning. Agnir was watching me sidelong, some expression caught between pity and humor on his face. When Nika slid abruptly from her place on the table, I focused my thoughts and forced out the clearest voice I could.

"What should I expect from the moot?"

She paused at the washbasin, her empty bowl still in her hands.

"*Veka,*" she muttered. "You're still conscious?"

I gave her a long look, and didn't smile. After a moment Agnir cleared his place and headed out into the dark after Iskari, but Nika didn't seem troubled by their absence. Me, I thought they were both insane, venturing out into the night when it was so bitterly cold—not to mention the sheer thought of standing up made my stomach wrench unexpectedly. Nika turned her back on me, scrubbing out her bowl and stacking it to dry with Iskari's and her father's. I forced myself to eat a few mouthfuls of the rich stew, hoping the food would soften the blow of the *skatha*, but that was all I could manage. Nika swept my bowl away before I could offer to clean it myself.

"You're going to be voted out," she said, just when I thought she would never answer me. She sliced an extra piece of the steam-baked bread for herself and dropped into Agnir's chair, one booted foot propped on the rim of the vent. "You're not Istian. You have no business being Godar."

My head throbbed. I wanted to close my eyes, fall asleep, forget Istia and Godars and ships and death, and just…be. But I couldn't. Not yet. If I was to have any hope of doing what Trabin had asked me, I had to start here, now, with Nika and Iskari and all their suspicion and hatred.

*If you don't hold power over the hearts of the people,* Trabin had told me once, *you have nothing at all. Rule them by awe, or rule them by affection, but either way, you must rule them.*

"Ambassador Eskir thought I did," I said.

Her brows knotted in a frown. "Eskir? How did you know Eskir?"

That was interesting. I wondered if she'd heard the report that Ambassador Eskir had written to the moot before his envoy left Brinmark—before they were murdered on their way out of my city—stating that he had found Godar Eyid's son. Agnir had been familiar with the contents of the letter, but how many other people were? At any rate, even if the Istians could believe I was the son identified in Eskir's letter, it seemed like Agnir was the only one who had figured out that I was actually the Crown Prince of Cavnal.

If I was even that any more.

Maybe I was already King, awaiting my coronation.

Maybe I was a traitor, awaiting my execution.

But I didn't dare tell Nika the truth, not yet. Much as I despised all the lies and deceptions, I knew I could make the truth more powerful if I kept it in reserve, hidden until just the right moment.

I tipped my head back and closed my eyes. "You know nothing about me," I said.

"I know enough."

"Please." I waved a hand in her general direction, or hoped that I did. "Do elaborate."

"You're obviously a Cavnish noble," she said. "That's enough for me."

I frowned, considering the words. Curiously, Istians had no word for *nobility* the way Cavners did. Nika used an odd compound term, *blood-housed*. To an Istian even the notion of hereditary nobility was irrational—irrational, and laughable.

"Cavnish nobility isn't just based on bloodlines," I said. "You should know that."

"What else would it be based on?"

"Merit. Service. Half the *katzpotivyek* I know were elevated because they did something notable in science or industry."

She let out her breath in a sharp laugh. "Oh. That kind of merit. Istians get voted into the *Godartheng* because they've done something worthy of the honor. And I don't mean coming up with some *skatrdrakkeyn* tool or weapon, but something truly honorable."

"What do you consider honorable?"

"My father once sailed out in a maelstrom to save a ship full of sailors stranded off the coast," she said. "That was honorable."

"That *is* honorable," I said, but it didn't keep me from pressing the matter. "Has everyone who sits on the *Godartheng* risked life and limb to get there?"

She gave me an arch look and didn't answer, which meant the answer was *no*. Which meant that perhaps I could do something the Istians would consider honorable without putting my neck on the line just yet. I wanted to tell her that I had saved Agnir's life, but somehow the words felt false. I'd only had to save him because I'd almost been the death of him in the first place.

"What if I can keep Istia out of a war?" I asked.

She laughed aloud at that. When I didn't smile she sobered and braced her foot against the steam vent, tipping her chair back on two legs. She waved her chunk of half-eaten bread at me.

"You can't be serious."

I said nothing.

"You're serious? You think you have the power to do that?" She leaned forward abruptly, the chair legs slamming against the floor. "You think that's what we *want?*"

"I think you have no idea what kind of hell you're about to bring down on yourselves," I said, "if you pursue a war against Cavnal or any of the southern nations."

She stared at me a long moment, eyes narrowed. "You're drunk," she said finally. "You should go to sleep. *You* have no idea what you're talking about."

"I'm not drunk," I said. "You just don't like the idea that I might know something more about Istian politics than you."

Agnir and Iskari returned at that moment, shaking snow off their shoulders like dogs as they came into the hut. Iskari took one look at Nika's face and laughed.

"You look like you just drank a vat of *hukluthn*, Nika," he said. "You letting that foreigner needle you?"

She glared at him and didn't answer.

"Taumir, take the bed, please," Agnir said, waving at the framed bed tucked under the loft. "We'll sleep above."

I nodded and got to my feet, thanking whatever good-humored god was keeping me from falling flat on my face. Iskari and Nika stood shoulder-to-shoulder between me and the bed, which meant that, in that cramped space, I would have to push past them to get there, and I wasn't sure I had the coordination to do so without making a fool of myself. And I was damn sure they knew it, too.

I walked up to them, realizing with a little burn of dissatisfaction that I stood dead-level with Nika, and an entire half a head shorter than Iskari. Even Tarik's lanky body would never have measured up to him. Iskari had his arms crossed on his broad chest, staring a challenge at me, while Agnir stood by apparently content to let the scene play out.

*How do I make him move?* I wondered, my thoughts straying.

I could move him bodily if I wanted, Push him away like an inconvenience; I'd done that much before. But at that moment I had no interest in brute force.

*What kind of magic would I need to bend a person's will to mine?*

*Stars, that's the skatha talking. I don't want that kind of power. I've never wanted that kind of power.*

But I looked at Iskari and, channeling all my energy, all my power, into my voice, I said, "Move."

His face twisted as if he were in pain.

And then he stepped aside.

"*Veka*," Nika said. "What..."

I hated, and savored, the cold thrill of fascination that rippled through me.

Without a word I strode between them and threw myself on the low bed, and fell into a deeper sleep than I'd gotten in weeks.

# Chapter 22 » Hayli

I LET PIPER SPEND THE NIGHT IN THE RAFTERS, PERCHED UP ABOVE THE GROUP of skitters who hadn't cleared out yet, and in the morning I herded them together and did my best to shoo them on their way to Borokhev. As they trickled out, I sat with my back against the reduction pots until the chill in the air got too bad to do aught but think about how cold I was. Tarik's short leather jacket was folded on the step beside me, but I couldn't quite bring myself to put it on.

I'd changed back into my old clothes after Griff and I had got back from the palace, but that coat...it still had Tarik's smell about it, like cinnamon and wood smoke and snow all mixed up together, and being too close to it made my heart ache in the most impossible way. But the air wasn't getting any warmer, so I grabbed it as I stood up and tugged it on before I could let myself think too hard about it. A minute and I just hugged the warm leather close about me, burying my chin in the collar, then I set my jaw and headed for the smelter door.

In the Chamber I spotted Doc still busy in the wide empty space that used to be his infirmary. He was working in that slow, careful way of his, like he was never quite aware of the passage of time. Doc fascinated me that way. Sometimes he was a whirlwind, a chaos of energy and intensity, and other times he just drifted through the world like a spirit. He gave me a small, guarded smile when I wandered over to him.

"Need help?" I asked.

"Not terribly," he said, winding a long strip of bandage around one pale hand. "You've not left yet."

I shook my head, even though I knew he didn't say it to get an answer from me. The old crates were still set up against the wall—they were too heavy to move, and we wouldn't need them at Borokhev anyway—so I hopped up onto my usual spot in the corner and hugged my legs to my chest.

"It's all right to be afraid," Doc said, when the silence had drawn out a bit long.

"I know."

He shot me a sidelong glance, one brow lifted. But if he didn't believe me, at least he didn't argue with me.

"Are you?" I asked. "Afraid of aught?"

"We all fear something," Doc said softly.

He moved even slower now than before, carefully tucking the rolled up bandage into a small wooden crate, as if his mind were somewhere else entirely and his hands weren't quite sure what to do on their own. I chewed the inside of my cheek, hoping he'd add something to that, but it seemed he'd forgot all about my question.

"Would you tell me?"

"It's not your burden."

"Everybody needs someone to share their burdens, sometimes," I said. "Believe me, that's not something I'd ever have said, before. But it's true."

He smiled, but it was a thin, pale thing, haunted by sadness. "I can't tell you. It would..." He paused, staring at his hands. His white hair drifted down over his shoulder, so I couldn't see his face at all as he said, "It would break your heart."

I jumped, then slid off the crate and slipped over to his side. He flinched when I laid a hand on his arm. "You can tell me," I said. "Whatever it is, I promise it can't hurt me too much."

He turned to face me, and I got the sudden odd sense that I'd never stood this close to Doc before. At this distance his eyes were more unsettling than ever, hard and shallow like chips of sea glass, but at the same time, fathomless and utterly unknowable. Even with his white hair I knew he wasn't old, and seeing him this close proved it, because there wasn't a single crease or wrinkle anywhere on his face. This close he barely looked older than Tarik, or Derrin at most. His skin was almost too flawless, until I got wondering if maybe his Blood magic kept him looking so young. It was like his face had been frozen in a moment of time…but his eyes were ancient.

"All right," he said, taking one smooth step back from me. I let out a breath of relief in spite of myself. "You really want to know what I'm afraid of?"

But then he glanced away, toward the smelter door, and abruptly fell silent. I twisted about to see the silhouette of a man standing just outside the doorway, motionless, like he'd been there forever. Alarm prickled through me, warping into fear faster than I could control. My hand snatched out and grabbed Doc's.

"Who's that?"

He tugged his hand gently free of mine. "A friend, I think."

He headed toward the door and I trailed behind, curiosity getting the better of my panic. As we came into the cold morning light, I blinked in surprise. The man wasn't any as I'd been expecting. He looked a proper gentleman, tall and slim, with a sweep of carefully styled dark curls framing an elegant, narrow face. A neat black mustachio punctuated his small mouth and angular nose, and his eyes were dark, almost as dark as Tarik's, and almost as sad. He didn't look a bit Cavnish. Meritian, probably. He wore a leather jacket almost identical to mine, and it took me half a tick to notice that there was a second motorbike lurking just behind him in the factory yard.

"Destri," Doc said, voice tight, caught on a question.

The thin man bowed slightly to me, one hand on his heart, then turned back to Doc. All he said was, "Where is he?"

His voice sounded like a devastation.

Doc said, "I'll show you." He turned to me, some expression I couldn't read in his eyes. "Go on, Hayli. I'll be along."

He left no room for argument, so I nodded to him and tried to smile at the gentleman. But before I left, I couldn't keep from turning back and catching Doc's eye.

"You never told me," I said, "what you're afraid of. What was it?"

Doc's gaze held mine a long moment, then shifted briefly toward the other man. Finally he sighed, and looked me straight in the eye, and said, "I am afraid of Tarik."

# Part Two: Cadence

## Chapter 1 • Jarik

*I* COULDN'T TELL HOW LATE—OR EARLY—IT WAS WHEN I WOKE TO THE LOW murmur of voices. For a few moments I tried in vain to go back to sleep; my head felt thick, pounding with a splintering ache that I knew had little to do with the quantity of *skatha* I'd drunk the night before. The skin over my left ear throbbed with heat, and just the thought of touching it made my stomach churn with nausea. A little Blood magic would surely have soothed the pain and healed the injury, but I hadn't been able to stir that power since I'd saved Mattac.

At least, if I died of a blood infection, I could rest content that I'd saved someone's life who likely deserved it more than me.

As the dull roar of blood in my ears began to taper away, I focused on the voices. I recognized Nika's first, low and cold, then Iskari's, harsh and sharp as the graveled sand on the beach. I couldn't hear Agnir's, so perhaps he was still asleep, or perhaps it was already past dawn and he had gone about his business. With the deep shadows in the hut, it was impossible to tell.

"It doesn't seem right," Nika was saying, "that someone with so little control should have so much power."

"What makes you say he lacks control?"

"Just what Da said, how Taumir believed he caused *Hastol*'s death. How could that happen unless he lacks control?"

"Unless he meant to do it," Iskari said. "Would that be a better explanation?"

Nika didn't answer for much too long, until I started wondering what she was thinking. Did she actually believe me capable of that? Of willfully—intentionally—sending Agnir's ship to the deep, and letting over half her sailors drown with her? What sort of monster did she think I was?

"I don't like him," Nika said finally. My mouth quirked in a grimace. "He's dangerous. If Rigvar finds out…"

"Finds out what? That the Godarson is an archmage?"

"Not just that," Nika said, her voice dropping to a low hush. "More than that."

"*Veka,*" Iskari muttered. "You don't believe that nonsense Rivano and Eyid were going on about, do you? About the Zealot and all of that?"

My breath caught and I turned my head just a little to hear their words more clearly.

"Think about it. You know what Arnthor did in the Scourge. What destruction he was capable of. And he was just an archmage. He couldn't bend magic to his will. *That* is something different. *That* is something more. Something dangerous. And I don't think—"

"What's this?" Iskari asked, laughing softly. "You believe it's possible for someone to have *too much* magic?"

"Look at what he did to you! I don't…I don't even understand how he did that."

Iskari was silent a moment, then he said quietly, "Neither do I."

"Don't tell me you actually respect him."

"That one?" He laughed again, but this time with a harsh coldness that made my insides cringe. "Hardly. But the sea doesn't lie, Nika."

*The sea doesn't lie.* I'd heard the sailors say the same thing, from time to time. It was an Istian expression that I'd never learned from my books, and from all that I could tell, it meant you had to respect the truth—even, or perhaps especially, if you didn't like it.

But the words seemed to mean so much more than that. Or perhaps they only seemed that way to me, because my life had always been nothing but a tangled forest of deception, with none of the sea's honesty. Perhaps it was the Istian blood in me that hated it so much.

*I am the sea…*

*I'm nothing but a lie.*

The contradiction was burning me up inside.

I rolled over and opened my eyes, only to find Nika staring straight at me from her chair by the steam vent. She startled a little when she saw me awake, and Iskari laughed as he glanced at me over his shoulder. I couldn't tell if the laugh was meant for her or for me.

"You're awake," Nika said, voice flat.

"What, were you talking about me?"

I felt wicked saying it. Given their obsession with truthfulness, I knew my taunt was putting them in an awkward way. They exchanged a brief glance.

"Yes," Iskari said. He switched his position on the chair so that he was straddling it backwards, facing me. "What are you, Taumir?"

"That's a rather ambiguous question. Do you want an ambiguous answer?"

"Would you give an honest answer if I asked for one?"

"I'm only half-Istian," I said dryly. "I'll give you half an honest answer. Or a halfway honest answer."

Iskari's mouth tugged into a grudging smile, but Nika's glare only got rather colder at my flippant answer.

"Is it true? Are you an archmage?" Iskari asked.

I shuffled over to sit at the foot of the bed facing them, bracing a hand on the thin mattress as the room swam briefly and a shard of pain lanced through my skull. Everything inside me felt feverish, and I didn't trust my legs enough to stand.

"Neither of you happen to have any healing magic, do you?" I asked, and prodded my fingers over my lips. They felt numb and swollen, but I couldn't tell what state they were in. I only knew it was making it difficult to talk, in a way I couldn't blame on *skatha*.

Iskari glanced at Nika, who was staring at me with some alarm. Perhaps not concern, but alarm all the same.

"I thought you—" she started.

"Not right now."

"Is that possible? Magic doesn't just...come and go."

"And you know that, do you?" I countered, anger putting a sharp barb on the words.

She pursed her lips and didn't answer. Iskari got up without a word and went to the corner of the hut that served as a kitchen. I couldn't see what he was doing in the narrow cupboards, but I heard the clink of stone jars and the slosh of some kind of liquid. Then he returned to the steam vent with a small iron pot in his hands, which he fixed to an ingenious sort of pulley device and lowered into the pit.

The minutes drifted by in silence. None of us spoke, or moved, until Iskari drew the pot out again and ladled some of its contents into a stone mug. I took it with a nod of gratitude that he ignored, and held it up to my face. I smelled the sharpness of alcohol. Willow and hypericum. A trace of honey. The hot liquid tasted like medicinal *skatha*, but all the honey in the world couldn't rid it of the hypericum's bitter taste.

I drank it all.

"Not magic, but it works well enough," Iskari said, taking the cup when I'd finished. "My father said you should stay put and rest until you recover your strength. Why can't you heal yourself?"

"What do Istians consider an archmage to be?" I asked instead of answering him, as the burn in my head began to subside to a dull ache. "I know you think Cavners are fools to divide magic into Gifts. So what is it, in your opinion, that makes a mage an archmage?"

"It's not that the concept of Gifts is foolish," Nika said, voice low, "it's just a gross oversimplification. What you call Gifts are simply examples of proficiency in a specific kind of magic."

"I remember that," I said. "Knacks being proficient in mental powers, Telekines in the manipulation of matter, that sort of thing."

She nodded. "From what I understand, most mages in Cavnal see the one skill where they are adept—their first skill, typically—and stop there. One will stop at moving an object from one place to another by their will alone, and another will stop with the power of willing an object into another shape, and neither of them will realize that the power to do the one is the same as the power to do the other. If they practiced, if they pushed their powers, there would be no distinction between them."

"So, I'm guessing you believe an archmage can use different kinds of magic," I said.

"Precisely. Perhaps with one dominant, but at least three."

"But three is just an Ace…three is common. Or, common enough."

"Ah, but you're thinking like a Cavner," she said. "Would you consider a man who can heal, and read minds, and manipulate people's emotions to be an archmage?"

I considered that briefly. "I suppose so, yes."

"But mind-reading and emotional control stem from the same proficiency."

"So you're saying he would be just a mage?"

She nodded, idly tipping her chair back on two legs. "A powerful mage, certainly, but just a mage. An archmage has three *different* proficiencies."

I dropped my head, bracing my arms, trying to fight off the exhaustion that one night's sleep hadn't been able to cure.

"And what, you think I'm one of these archmages?"

"That's what we're trying to figure out," Nika said.

"What can you do, Taumir?" Iskari asked. There was a gruffness to his voice, almost resentful, but threaded with a subtle respect that caught me by surprise.

Still, I hesitated to answer. My abilities with magic were something I never liked to discuss, or have discussed, or speculated about. There were still moments when I didn't even want to acknowledge them myself; enumerating them for two strangers felt altogether too much like boasting, and a bit like laying my soul bare for their dissection.

"You already know I have Blood magic," I said, quietly. "Sometimes, at any rate."

"Corporal magic, then," Nika said. "Power over the body."

I watched Iskari briefly. He was busy at the steam vent again, making something in a small pot that might have been tea or perhaps coffee, which the *krizanyi* in Cavnal drank like water, but which had only recently become fashionable in high society. Whatever it was, its smell enticed me, rich and complex—sweet and harsh at the same time. My stomach complained, tight with hunger or anxiety.

"What else?" Nika prompted, drawing my attention away from the pot. She was leaning forward now, fingers steepled under her chin, and even though she was still glaring at me I got the feeling that she was at least intrigued.

"I can hide myself. Turn invisible."

Nika glanced across at Iskari. "Turn *invisible*? I've never heard... that is, I'm not sure what kind of proficiency that is. I mean, are you *actually* invisible? You don't just...convince other people that they can't see you? Manipulate their perception of reality?"

"I'm not sure," I admitted. "I can still see myself, but I don't know why, or how."

She pursed her lips in a thin line, then waved a hand. "We'll call it a mental power for now. Like illusion."

"Then I have two of those," I said, "because my first gift was changing my appearance. At least, my mother called it a mental power, but to me it's always felt more like a corporal power, because I *physically* change. It's not just that people see an illusion of the face I want to show them. Believe me, it hurts enough for me to know the difference."

Iskari turned sharply to look at me, studying my face inch by inch as if he suddenly doubted what he was looking at. My fingers tightened on the mattress, and I stared straight back at him in challenge. After a moment the corner of his mouth tightened, and he shifted his attention back to the steam vent.

Nika just nodded and kept her peace, and in the silence that followed my mind turned to Hayli with a little tugging at my heart. Her shape-shifting ability…was that what Nika considered a corporal power? If so…did that mean I could Shift too, if I pushed myself? I wondered, idly, what I would become if I could. A horse? A damn snake in the grass? A bird? An odd little thrill chased through me, dragging into my mind the memory I always kept buried deep, out of sight—of the night two years past when I had stood in the belfry arch, when I wanted to die, when I longed to fly.

On the heels of that memory another thought occurred to me—could Hayli become a Blood? I almost smiled at that, thinking of how much she'd grown to love helping Doc in his infirmary. Being a Blood would suit her. It would suit the caring, selfless side of her she always tried to hide—or protect—from the world.

I sighed, rubbing a hand over my forehead, and pulled my thoughts away from her. If I let myself go on thinking about her, I'd try to find a way to master the power of Ghosting then and there, just so I could see her again. The world always seemed so much darker without her light to guide me.

"Taumir?"

"I'm a Telekine," I said. "I can move objects at will."

"So, manipulation of matter," Nika said.

She peered at me inquisitively, and I felt suddenly small and uncomfortable. Nothing about this conversation pleased me. I wished I could escape it—I rather didn't care how—but I knew they wouldn't stop heckling me until they were satisfied.

"Is that all?" Nika asked. She almost sounded disappointed.

I held her gaze until she looked away. "I can control fire."

"Right," she murmured, glancing toward one of the lanterns on the wall I'd extinguished the night before. "Elemental magic. And of course, you can shape the winds, too." She caught Iskari's eye and they exchanged a long look thick with veiled meaning. "Anything else?"

"I don't know," I said, uncomfortable.

I didn't dare look at Iskari. Was the power I'd exerted over him something new? Or did he just move because, for whatever reason, he had decided to stop being a bastard for that one moment?

"One at least," Iskari said, voice low. "Spiritual power." He folded his arms and scowled at the steam vent, looking almost as unsettled as I felt. His gaze started to drift in my direction but he jerked it away again. "You can command spirits."

My thoughts shifted away from him, wandering back to the dory, when I had silenced the waves that should have torn us apart. Was that elemental magic, or something else? Whatever it was...whatever it meant...I didn't mention it. They knew too much already.

Nika sat back, toying with one of the knotted strands of her hair. "*Veka*," she said. "That's not possible. Iskari, that's not possible, is it?"

He lifted a shoulder in a shrug, and wouldn't look at either of us.

"What isn't?" I asked.

"Five schools of magic, or classes, if you want to call them that. Mental, spiritual, corporal, elemental, material. And you have proficiency in every single one of them."

I winced and looked away. Without even the crackle and roar of a wood fire, the silence in that little space was consuming. I didn't want to go on talking to either of them but I wished with all my heart that one of them would say *something*, just to vanquish the maddening quiet.

Finally Nika said, very softly, "You really don't understand, do you? It's *impossible*. You shouldn't exist."

My mouth tugged into a grimace. Funny, I couldn't bring myself to disagree.

"What are you, Taumir?" Iskari asked again. "You're not an archmage. Are you the Zealot?"

"I honestly don't even know what that means."

The quiet sound of Nika's laughter shattered the silence and startled me from my thoughts. I expected to see mockery in her eyes, but instead she looked genuinely amused.

"Neither do we," she said, waving one pale hand. "No one does, except Rivano, apparently."

"You knew Rivano?"

It made me inordinately glad to have the chance to ask them, so I wouldn't have to betray the fact that I'd been eavesdropping on them. I wasn't sure if the notion surprised me or not—it rather alarmed me, but at the same time I couldn't help feeling a little relieved that they'd known him, as if it gave me some kind of mental context to place Rivano in, to make him make sense.

"Everyone knew him," Nika said. "Or at least of him. He was Eyid's advisor and oldest friend."

"Of course," I said, feeling foolish.

Rivano himself had told me that much, before we had gone to Trabin and Ambassador Eskir—before I'd so impudently demanded peace, as if it had been mine to demand. Eyid was the reason Rivano had come to Cavnal all those years ago—to search for me. To see what manner of man I would become. I let out an unsteady breath and leaned my forehead against my palm.

"Have you ever heard of a book called the *Brigaz Nedash*?" I asked.

Nika shifted her weight. When neither of them spoke for some time, I started to wonder if Istians believed that keeping silent was a way to stay honest when they didn't want to answer a question.

Then Iskari said, "Yes. Rivano had it."

"He and your father…" Nika started, with an uncertain glance at Iskari. "They were always quarreling about that book, at the end."

"Why?"

"Eyid thought it was dangerous. Rivano thought it was the truth."

"Couldn't it be both?"

She pursed her lips, then said with quiet reluctance, "Perhaps."

"Where did the book come from?"

"No one knows for certain," Iskari said. He served up some of the hot liquid into a set of stone mugs, handing one to me first, then one to Nika, and claiming the last one for himself. "Everyone believes Rivano himself brought it over from Cromis."

*Cromis!* I thought, mentally slapping myself.

That would explain why the title didn't sound like Archaic Cavnish. I had never been as proficient in Cromner as I'd been in Istian and Meritian—it was a harsh, enigmatic language, considered to be the most difficult language for non-native speakers to learn. There were so many ambiguities in the grammar that it was almost impossible to translate satisfactorily. In many ways it was the opposite of Istian.

Everything about Istia was straightforward, uncomplicated, and brutally honest (to a fault, some said). Cromis reveled in dissemblance and obscurity. Even its mist-swathed mountains and tangled forests flirted with deception, and it was often said that mortal enemies would happily exchange an hour's pleasantries over sweet wine and cakes before commencing the duel that would claim one, or both, of their lives.

My mind drifted, painfully, to my memories of Zagger. I'd always thought he had inherited the Cromner look, fair-haired and fair-skinned, but none of Cromis's nature—his personality was all Meritian. Restrained, courteous, unassuming, like his uncle Destri Alokin. There was never a deceptive bone in Zagger's body.

He'd always been a better man than I.

"So," I said, dragging my attention back to the *Brigaz Nedash*. "Did Rivano go to Cromis just to get the book, or for some other reason?"

Nika shrugged.

"Where did he find it?"

"If you believe what he said, he got it from Arnthor's cave itself."

"Arnthor! What was Arnthor doing with it?"

They gave me matching blank looks, and I sighed and dropped my head. I knew so little about the last archmage; it struck me all at once that if I wanted to understand what I was going through, perhaps I ought to do a little research into his life and fate. But not now.

Still, if Arnthor was the one who had first possessed the *Brigaz Nedash*...did he himself write it? Was he a visionary?

Suddenly Nika's words sank in, and I studied her curiously. "*If you believe what he said?*" I echoed her. "Isn't he Istian?"

"*Veka*. If anyone could sort out what or who Rivano is..."

"He is Istian," Iskari said, then added, with no little violence, "by blood." He drained his cup and stood. "I'm off to help Da. Nika, get him ready."

And without another word he blew out of the hut like a gale, letting a slant of cold daylight and a gust of bitter wind swirl into the little room in his wake. Nika barely moved to acknowledge his departure. She sipped her drink quietly, reminding me that I'd yet to try mine. I took a tentative taste. It was thick and sweet—some sort of coffee, as I'd guessed. It would have benefited from the addition of a bit of cream, though I doubted cream would be easy to come by in this desolate place.

"What are you supposed to get me ready for?" I asked Nika. "And where is your father?"

"At the beach," she said. "Seeing if anything has washed up." She swallowed down the rest of her coffee and got abruptly to her feet. "We leave today. Make sure you're ready to go."

I threw a hand at her in frustration. "Go where?"

Her mouth tightened. "Bregjarvani, then on to Hejmstrathvir. We'll get you to the city well before the moot begins." She saw my curiosity and shrugged. "My father thinks you need a chance to meet the other sodthari—let them have a look at you, get a sense of who you are. To make sure you have any chance at all of even standing for judgment in the eyltheng, let alone get voted in as Godar."

"But you think it's an exercise in futility."

"It doesn't matter what I think. Maybe I wish it were, but it's not up to me."

I sighed and nodded. I shouldn't have expected anything else from her. After a moment I finished off the rest of my drink, which by then had turned tepid and rather bitter, and got cautiously to my feet. The room didn't tilt nearly as badly around me as I'd feared, but I had to swallow once, then again, to settle my stomach.

"Where are you going?" Nika asked, eyeing me sharply as I picked up my red wool scarf and felt it.

It was still damp—steam not being the best source of heat for drying things out—but it would serve well enough. I wound it around my neck under her fixed stare.

Finally I said, "I'm going to help your father."

"You'll catch your death out there. You're supposed to be resting."

I gave her a feral sort of smile. "I'm supposed to be doing whatever I damn well choose."

She looked at me a long while, eyes hard and cold, until I started to doubt my own words. Then she said, very quietly, "Then you have no business being Godar, Taumir Eyidson."

I turned and left the hut.

## Chapter 2 — Hayli

*I* LEFT DOC AND THE ELEGANT GENTLEMAN IN THE YARD, WANDERING OUT past the gate of the smelter that now stood open and unguarded. I wanted to Shift and let Piper fly to Borokhev, because she was much faster than I could ever be, and because somehow I felt a bit less afraid when I saw the world through her eyes. To her, Borokhev was just a place, and even if she knew what I'd suffered there, she could never feel the fear the way I could. Fear made her strong, made her fast, and part of me hoped that her spirit would change me—as if spending time as the crow could make me brave, even when I would've happily named myself a coward and run away.

*It's now or never,* she whispered in my mind. *You have to go eventually.*
*I don't want to.*

She huffed at that, which got me a bit red, ashamed of myself and the way fear wouldn't let go of me. Finally, giving myself a firm nod, I Shifted.

*HAYLI IS QUIET AS I TAKE to the sky, but I know she is happy to be back in the wind, free on the wing. I stay close to the tree tops, following the river road and the railroad tracks, just to keep an eye out for the children Hayli had just sent out from the smelter. I pass them as they make their way on foot, loaded with rucksacks and dragging a sled behind them laden with belongings. Hayli wants to tell them to wait for a wagon to come back for them, but I remind her that they had a chance to go by train. If they wanted to walk—who would?— but if that's what they wanted, they should be free to go their way.*

As the road sweeps northward, curving around the eastern edge of Brinmark, a line of movement in the distance catches my eye. Dust from the gravel road. It isn't paved, this far out from the city, and something traveling along it is stirring up a white, chalky cloud. Hayli sees it through my eyes, and I feel her heart pattering with fear.

Get closer, *she tells me.* I have to see what that is.

*So I turn and catch a current of wind, and drift closer, and lower.*

Oh, stars, *she says.* No...that's not possible.

*A metal beast inches down the road. It looks like a dull grey slug, plated in iron and steel, with one massive tentacle protruding from its crown. Compared to the men who march behind it, it is massive, likely three times as big as any of the motorcars I have ever seen, and it has neither legs nor wheels, but it slithers along the ground on what I can only describe as two snakes running in tandem. It is the most horrifying thing I have ever seen.*

What is it? *I ask Hayli.*

A steam crawler, *she whispers.* It's...it's the Army. But Minister Farro said...he promised...

*Her voice trails away, crushed by a feel of betrayal. I circle over the crawler, eyeing the ranks of troops marching behind it, armed with heavy guns and weapons I don't recognize. There must be at least a hundred of them—no more, but with that crawler, and those weapons...*

Those kids we saw, *Hayli says.* If the Army captures them, they'll tell everything. They'll tell them we're at Borokhev, and then we'll be in just as much danger as we ever were at the smelter. And, oh, Doc!

*I keep circling, feeling her indecision as powerfully as if it were my own. Where to go? If we go back toward the smelter to warn Doc and the kids we saw on the road, they will never be able to get out in time. But if we go to Borokhev...what good could we do there? Even if we could send Coins out with the coach, or a wagon, he will never reach them before the soldiers do. They will be intercepted on the road no matter which way I go.*

This is so wrong, *Hayli says.* Farro promised...he said he wouldn't let them—

Focus! *I tell her. I say it more harshly than I mean, and she subsides.* What are we going to do?

*Her thoughts stray, and I can't follow the twisting paths they take—trailing through memories, turning over theories and improbabilities. Then I feel her jolt with realization, so strongly that I lose my current and have to beat my wings to seek a new one.*

We need to go back. Go back!

*I wheel about and fly back toward the smelter, abandoning the road to make my way straight across the countryside. But instinctively I know what she has in mind, so I turn my course to intercept the kids still wandering down the road. As I drift to the ground, I let Hayli Shift.*

The skitters all jumped and gaped at me as Piper released me from the Shift right in front of them, but I was in too much a hurry to care.

"Hayli?" one of the girls asked, staring at me through wide blue eyes. She was only eight or nine, and she carried a pack on her back that was almost as big as her. "What're you doing here?"

"You've got to hide," I said. I shook her shoulder, and pointed them all toward the trees. "The Army's coming this way. If they find you, they'll catch you and ask you where we are, where we've gone."

Her eyes got round as moons, but one of the other kids, a stout boy of about thirteen, puffed up his chest with a fierce scowl.

"But that dan' make sense!" he cried, and stomped his foot on the snowy road. "If we gan an' hide in the woods, they'll still goggle our tracks in the snow and follow us!"

I opened my mouth, then closed it again. Couldn't say a word. But dread prickled all over me, cold and nauseating, as I realized he was far cleverer than me in my panic. The little girl started to cry, and I dropped to my knees in the snow to hug her, to buy myself time as I tried to figure out what to do.

It would be no different for Doc and the man called Destri, too. Out in the snow, there was nowhere they could hide.

"Hide anyway," I said firmly. "Dan' be afraid. I'll get you out of this in a jiff."

"How, Hayli?" she wailed.

I gave her my bravest smile, then backed up, and Shifted back to the crow. Somehow Piper understood exactly what I needed and flew straightaway toward Borokhev, chasing the currents, riding the wind. In the central courtyard she Shifted back before she'd even landed, and I staggered on my feet, reeling dizzily.

"Derrin!" I shouted, soon as I got my bearings.

Some of the folks in the yard around me startled, seeing me suddenly standing there where I hadn't been a moment before, shouting as if the world was ending. Then Derrin came running toward me from the gate, mouth pressed tight in anxious lines.

"Hayli!" he cried as he joined me. "Didn't know you were here already. What's wrong?"

I pointed toward the southwest where, from Piper's eyes, I'd seen the crawler and troops again. They'd not made much progress toward the smelter, what with how slow they had to march to keep pace with the metal monster, but they certainly hadn't gotten farther away.

"Minister Farro," I said. "He promised he'd keep the Army away from the smelter...but he lied, Derrin! He lied! They're on their way now, a crawler, maybes a squadron or two."

He gave me a slight puzzled look. "Guess it's a good thing we cleared out."

"Not all, not yet. Doc, and a man named Destri, they're still at the smelter." His eyes widened—I barely noticed. "Some skitters are on the road, too, and they can't hide, what with the snow. Soon as those troops get there they'll see the tracks."

Derrin cussed under his breath and turned a little away, then rounded back on me. "What are we supposed to do?"

"Shiver...Shiver can walk through walls carrying folks with him," I said. "Can you Ghost holding onto someone?"

"I never thought about it," he said, eyes alight with curiosity. I shifted my weight, antsy, as he took his time thinking it over. Finally he gave me a sharp nod. "All right. But if there are kids on the road, I need you to go ahead of me and find them, so I have somewhere to Ghost to. Unless—it wasn't any of the skitters I know, was it?"

"Dan' reckon," I said. "I div'n know their names, for all they knew mine. But I know where they're at."

If only Derrin'd been a Knack too, I thought, maybe he could just hold on to me and let my memory of the skitters guide him. I didn't imagine it would work without him reading my mind, though.

"If I'm the crow, and you try to Ghost to me..." I started, suddenly imagining him stepping out in mid-air, tumbling to his death.

"I won't Ghost to the crow," he said, dark eyes crinkling in a suppressed smile. "If I try to Ghost to you and nothing happens, I'll know you aren't there yet."

I nodded, and threw myself into the wind. Piper flew me straight back to where I'd left the skitters, her little heart pattering like raindrops the whole way. I knew she was pushing herself, flying faster and harder than she ever had before. I only hoped it was enough.

All too soon—not soon enough—we reached the place where the skitters had been on the road, where now there was naught but a wide furrow in the snow heading straight toward the trees. Soon as I'd Shifted, the wee girl came racing out of the woods.

"Thought you'd never come back!" she cried, throwing herself into my arms.

I hugged her, and beckoned the other skitters to come out. "Derrin's on his way—" I started to say, and at that same minute he stepped out of the air beside me.

The tall boy yelped in surprise, and stared up at Derrin in wide-eyed awe.

"He's ganna take you to Borokhev. But you have to leave your bits and bobs. We'll come back for 'em later."

Derrin surveyed the little group—six skitters, all told, most about nine or ten years old.

"How far is the Army?" he asked me.

I swallowed hard. "They've just passed the curve, where the road starts heading north, maybes a mile." I nodded down the road. "You can see the dust already."

The girl started crying again in my arms, and Derrin held my gaze much too long. "I'll take three trips. I don't think I can hold on to more than two at a time."

"I'll stay with them," I said, hoping I sounded braver than I felt.

He nodded, and without wasting a jot longer, he wrapped an arm around one of the younger boys. I pushed the wee girl toward him, and she buried herself against his side with her face all wet with tears. In another moment they were gone. Far as I'd ever been able to tell, Ghosting wasn't quite quick as thought—it was maybe two minutes before Derrin reappeared. We could see the silhouette of the crawler now, and I was fair sure that whoever was driving it could see us, too. Derrin grabbed two more skitters and vanished, and then it was just me and the two oldest boys.

"Hayli," one of them said, tugging my sleeve, and pointing down the road. "Did it stop?"

I narrowed my eyes. The weak sun was setting behind us, and shone off the metal curves of the crawler. That was the only reason I was able to see the long nose of the tank gun inching slowly upwards.

For one second I stood and stared, then I heard, very faint on the wind, a shouted command. Fear exploded through me and I grabbed the lads by the arms and ran for the trees. A terrible *boom!* rang out behind us, then the ground shook, and the whole world rocked.

The force of the blast threw us off our feet. I landed in a heap, half on top of one of the boys, the other lad landing across my legs. I struggled free and tried to get up. The ground still shifted woozily beneath my feet, and there was a spattering of red on the whiteness of the snow. I couldn't tell where it came from. My mouth, probably. I couldn't think. Couldn't figure out what to do. We had to wait for Derrin…

But Derrin had already come back. I saw him when I turned back to look at the crawler, lying sprawled in a black, earthy scar carved from the whiteness of the snow, both arms flung over his head. I stifled my scream for the boys' sake and ran over to him, eyes stinging with tears, fear clouding the corners of the world. Then I was on my knees beside him, shaking his shoulders. Again, again.

Finally he lifted his head, and I covered my mouth to cage in the sobs of relief. "Derrin," I whispered. "Y'a'right? Can you hear me?"

With a terrible effort he made it onto his knees, but he had one arm wrapped tight around his waist, and the ground where he'd been lying was stained dark red with blood.

"Oh, God," I said, over and over.

He said nothing, just waved at the lads with such fierce intensity that they came running at once.

"Warn Doc," he said, gritting the words. "Can't do this again."

"Can you make it with them?"

He nodded, faintly. "I think so. Be careful. Don't let them…don't let them catch you."

Then he reached out and grabbed the boys around their waists. His face was tight with pain as he met my gaze, then he bowed his head and vanished into the wind, and left me standing there by the roadside, alone.

But I didn't give myself a moment to think. That tank gun would fire again any second, and I had no intention of being there when it did.

*I fly all the way back to the smelter, through the wrecked doorway into the main building where I can hear raised voices. In the place Doc used to have his infirmary I see the man named Destri sitting on a low crate, his head in his hands, and Doc leaning against a cement pilaster with his arms folded. He looks angry, or afraid, and the expression on his face is so strange that I catch myself on the rafter.*

*I know I should Shift. I know I need to warn them of the crawler, and the approaching soldiers. But my curiosity—or Hayli's—is too strong.*

*"You can't," Doc says, voice edged like a barb.*

*Destri looks up, and there is something in his eyes that I cannot identify.*

Rage, *Hayli says.* That's the look of a man who has given up control of his rage.

*I am glad that crows know nothing of anger—not anger like that, anger that would take a life without hesitation.*

*"If he were here, I would use it myself," Destri says.*

*"You can't mean that."*

*Destri laughs, bitterly, and shakes his head. "You're never going to persuade me, so save your breath."*

*Doc lifts a hand, then lets it drop back on his folded arm, and says nothing. Destri doesn't seem to notice his silence. He stands up, hands tightening and relaxing in fists at his sides. Everything about him is taut and tense as the wind before the lightning.*

*"I am done with the Court," he says, biting through every word. "I am done with the Crown. I...hate...everything about this place."*

*"Don't be rash," Doc says. "Don't go, not now."*

*Destri stares at him, but Doc doesn't back away from the look in his eyes.*

*"Is there nothing here that you care about?" he asks. "Nothing that would be worth staying for?"*

*"No," Destri says, taking a step closer to him, voice low and edged. "There is nothing Cavnish that I love."*

*I fear he is going to strike Doc, so I slip from the rafter and circle toward the doorway so they will not realize I have been eavesdropping. Then, with a shout of alarm, I plummet toward the ground.*

DESTRI SPUN AROUND WITH A CRY of surprise as I landed in an exhausted heap near them. At least the suddenness of my appearance seemed to have jolted him out of his rage. It was the only relief I felt.

"What—" Doc snapped, but then he saw my face and the irritation flitted away behind a wide-eyed alarm. He pushed past Destri and came to crouch by my side. "Good God, what happened to you?"

I'd no idea what I must've looked like, so I just shrugged and waved away his concern. "Dan' matter. You're in danger. You've gotta… you both gotta get out of here. The Army's coming… They fired on us… and Derrin…"

His hands were on my shoulders, calm, steadying. "Hayli, look at me. Take a breath."

I tried, but couldn't. I gripped the front of his shirt, ignoring Destri, who was staring at me now like my face reminded him of something… or someone.

"I can't save you," I whispered. "They're coming and I can't get you out of here. Derrin was supposed to…but he's hurt, and he can't."

"I need to get back," Destri said, his voice low and smooth, without a trace of the blazing anger I'd seen before. "I have the motorbike." He put a hand on Doc's shoulder. "Come on. I'll take you into the city. You'll be safe from the Army there, at least, and you can make your way out from there."

"Hayli?" Doc said.

"I've got the crow," I said. "I'll be a'right."

Destri's gaze sharpened on my face, and I got that antsy feeling like he was starting to recognize me—and didn't like what he saw. Doc must have noticed too, because he got brisk all of a sudden, and stepped between us.

"Go," he said. "Get out of here. I'll be there soon."

He drove me back, step by step, as he said it, eyes bright and hard with meaning. Bewildered, I gave him a brave nod, and Shifted once more to the crow.

# Chapter 3 ❖ Jarik

As soon as I left Agnir's hut, I regretted my rash decision. The wind buffeted me constantly, first from one direction, then from another, strong enough to unbalance me and cutting straight through the heavy wool of my jumper. I pulled the scarf up over my nose and mouth and shoved my hands deep in my trouser pockets—that meager protection was better than none—but still my skin smarted and burned, and nothing could stop my nose and eyes from watering.

Compared to the weary hike away from the ocean, I barely noticed the distance during the trek back to the desolate beach. I shouldered the narrow ridge that encircled the beach and walked a while along its jagged crest, staring down at the crashing grey surf breaking over the black sands. Closest to me I could see Agnir's silhouette, stooped over some bit of debris. Iskari paced slowly along the waterline a little further away, head bent, pausing now and then to examine something the waves had left behind as the sea foam swirled around his boots.

Guilt gnawed at me as I picked my way down to the beach, my still-sodden boots slipping in the coarse sand. Was Nika right? If I'd had more control…if I hadn't been so broken…could I have saved *Hastol*? Could I have stopped the storm from ever happening? The least I could do was help Agnir salvage what he could of the wreck, though I knew that, for him, nothing could ever take the place of that ship.

I headed farther down the beach from Agnir and Iskari, toward a craggy sprawl of broken rocks and jagged black monoliths shouldering their way into the sea. A frail rain misted over me—rain, or the finest sleet I'd ever seen. A few snowflakes drifted down with it, swirling in the unceasing wind. Even with the endless crash of the waves and the howl of the wind, even with the crunch of my boots in the graveled sand, somehow the world felt dead silent. And though Agnir and Iskari were not a hundred paces away from me, I'd never felt more alone.

*You're never alone.*

The voice drew me up short, then I shuddered and drove it away, deep into the pit of my soul. I reached the crags and climbed up onto the slick stones, my numb fingers struggling for handholds in the jagged rocks, the toes of my boots digging into whatever crevices I could find, until I stood on top of the narrow shelf. Waves crashed endlessly against the rocks, spraying me with sea foam, but in between the sharp ridges was a narrow crevice pooled with still water, untouched and unbroken by anything but the body lying there face-down in a tangle of leather and wool.

I closed my eyes and turned away, drawing in one long breath as I wondered if I ought to call to Agnir and Iskari. But even as the thought occurred to me, I realized that there were three figures on the beach—Iskari, jogging toward his father, and Agnir, helping another man to his feet.

*Alive. One of them survived.*

I bit my lip and lowered myself toward the still pool, picking my way carefully over the rocks slick with spray and frost. Was there any chance at all that the man lying there was still alive?

Or, if he had died...could he be brought back?

Hayli had told me once that she suspected Doc had raised a man from the dead. But just the thought of it made me reel with revulsion, and something like a sick curiosity. Did such a power really exist?

*Only if they're willing,* whispered the voice in the back of my mind, the voice that wasn't mine. *Only if they want to come back.*

*Stars. Is it anyone's right to rob Death? Am I no better than Alokin, daring to usurp the work of the gods, just to see if it can be done? I won't do it. Not ever.*

*Are you certain?*

I shook my head fiercely, driving the heel of my palm against my forehead with a wince of pain. Then I grabbed the man's shoulder and rolled him over. My heart hitched as I caught sight of a familiar brown and orange scarf, draped over the man's face like a burial shroud. I tugged it away, and stared until the face swam in a blur of tears.

That was Mattac. Not Sevnar, or Vaskar, or any of the other victims of *Hastol*'s wreck. It was Mattac, dead pale, eyes wide open and lidless. His lipless mouth hung open as if on the breath of a last desperate prayer. He was utterly gone.

*Mattac...I am so sorry. How did you come to this? Did they cast you off because of me?*

*If I'd let you come with me...would you still be alive?*

I withdrew my hand—it was shaking—and climbed to the outermost ridge of the rocks. There I stood facing the sea, one hand tight on the slick stone of the towering monolith to my right, the other pressed hard against my mouth. The waves snarled as they clawed against the crags, and I closed my eyes against the salt spray. Somehow the bitter cold of the water didn't bother me. I felt nothing at all, nothing but the swirl of the wind around me. I could feel its fingers in my hair, twining around my neck like a living thing, and I stood on the edge of the rocks and the edge of the night.

And I was a part of it, the wind and the sea, or it was all of me. There was nothing else inside of me.

I was as empty as the wind, and as endless as the sea.

Too late I realized someone was shouting from somewhere close by, the voice broken and tossed by the raging wind. I turned, carefully, on my precarious perch, hardly daring to put my back to the treacherous sea.

*Why? What harm can the sea do to you?*

Iskari was calling to me, striding toward me like a tempest in human form.

"Taumir, damn it, get off those rocks!" he cried. Even with his hands cupped around his mouth I could barely make out the words, though I could guess them easily enough. "Do you have a *drakkeyn* death wish?"

I stepped down from my ledge and made my way toward him over the rocks—moving too fast now, reckless, making him wince in anxiety as he watched me.

"The sea's had her fill," I said as I landed in the sand beside him.

I jerked my head toward the pool in the crevice and left him standing there without another word. Farther up the beach, Agnir stood with the other man under the shelter of the mossy ridge. As I got closer to them, my heart sank. Part of me had been hoping with a desperate kind of hope that it would be one of Agnir's crew, but it wasn't. It was a Cavnish sailor from the steamship. Not the boat chief… just a sailor, perhaps in his early twenties, though it was hard to tell past the ragged sailor's beard he wore. I barely recognized him from our brief stay on the vessel.

But if he was here, and Mattac had washed up on the same beach…

*God, they're all dead.*

Did I kill all of them too?

"Any other survivors?" I asked Agnir, in Istian, as I joined them.

I didn't want to look at the Cavner, but at least he didn't seem to recognize us. If he'd recognized me, then…then perhaps he would blame me.

Agnir shook his head. I wondered if his thoughts had reached the same conclusion mine had. I wondered if he thought I was guilty, or just cursed.

I opened my mouth to tell him about Mattac, but couldn't find my voice. All I could do was look at the man sitting wearily on the rocks, body racked with feeble shivers, tattered and bloody, lips chafed and swollen from saltwater, and wonder why he was alive. Why did he survive, and Mattac die?

But Agnir deserved to know.

"I found Mattac," I said.

"What? Where?" Agnir cried, gripping my arm.

I pointed back toward the crags. "He's gone," I murmured. "I'm sorry."

I'd saved his life, and what for? What was the meaning of any of it?

*The sea had already claimed that one's life. All you did was delay the execution.*

Agnir put his hand to his head, gripping the thick wool of his cap as he stared toward the rocks. I could just see Iskari's head there; he had climbed down to the still pool to free Mattac's body.

"*Veka,*" Agnir said. He looked at me suddenly, clasping my arm tight. "It's not your fault, Taumir. I can see that guilt in your eyes. It's not your fault."

I shuddered and pulled away, and offered the Cavner my hand to help him stand. He glanced up at me, frowning faintly, but he said nothing as he got awkwardly to his feet. Maybe he assumed I couldn't speak Cavnish. I had no intention of correcting his opinion at the moment.

"I'll take him to the hut," I told Agnir. "Unless you need me to help with Mattac."

Agnir shook his head. "We'll see to him. He should be returned to the sea."

I had started to turn away, but at that I paused and glanced back at him. "How? Won't the waves just bring him back to shore?"

"Trust me," Agnir said, and that was all. Then he caught my arm again, just above the elbow. "Listen to me," he said. "The sea devours where he will, when he will. There is no reason for it. And it is not in your hands."

I stared at him, distraught, but the only words I could think to say were words I would never admit. Nonsense words. Madness words. But somehow I thought Agnir already knew them, because he had called the sea *him*, when every sailor of every nation I'd ever known called the sea *her*.

He wasn't speaking of the ocean, the vast wildness of water and salt, wind and unknowable depths.

*I am the sea.*

# Chapter 4 ❦ Hayli

*I* SIT IN ONE OF THE LOFTY PINES BORDERING THE SMELTER, PERCHED UP HIGH and hidden, *watching as Doc and Destri come outside. They seem to be arguing again, or at least whatever they are talking about has them both animated, fierce and intent, but they are speaking softly enough that I can't make out their words. They don't stop talking until Destri has the motorbike started. I watch Doc as he climbs on to sit behind him, because his face is cold and remote as a snowstorm.*

*The bike chuffs slowly away toward the north, toward the city, clearing away well before the steam crawler inches up to the gate. I wonder if the soldiers are surprised to find the gate open and abandoned, but they waste no time before they pour into the yard, flooding all through the property like a swarm of ants.*

*Their search doesn't take long. The soldiers begin to congregate in the courtyard again, milling about in small knots, looking perturbed.*

*One man approaches another with more silver on his coat than any of the others, and gives him a smart salute.*

*"No one here at all?" the silver-tasseled man asks.*

*"No one. Obviously there were people living here, but the place is empty, Captain," says the soldier. "I thought our intelligence was sound."*

*The Captain throws up a hand, silencing him, then walks away from a knot of soldiers milling close by. When he stops and glances over his shoulder, the other soldier follows him quickly. If only they knew that they've just come closer to me, where I can hear them both so much better.*

*"It was sound," the Captain says. "They've only just escaped us."*

*"Where could they go so quickly?"*

*The Captain paces a little, and scuffs the toe of his polished black boot against a sooty patch of snow. "Where indeed. With mages like the ones we just saw on the road, there's no telling."*

*"Would the informant know?"*

*"I doubt it. They must have had warning, and our informant gave us the most recent information he had." He draws out a shiny pocket watch that I instantly covet, and examines it briefly. "What a fantastic waste of time."*

*His subordinate shifts his weight, folding and unfolding his hands behind his back. "What will you tell the Minister? If he finds out—"*

*"I'm not going to tell him anything at all, if I can help it."*

*I tilt my head, studying their faces. The Captain, looking annoyed and contemptuous, the subordinate, sly and deceitful. Hayli's curiosity is piqued. Had they gone out without orders? Did Minister Farro even know?*

*"Well, there's nothing for it. First Sergeant, gather your men and take them back to garrison. We'll leave a few more holes in this place though, and maybe keep the rats from infesting it again."*

*I shout angrily at his words, and explode into the air. As I fly away, I see the First Sergeant and the Captain staring up at me, eyes narrowed. Perhaps they know what I am. Perhaps they suspect.*

*Perhaps they should be afraid.*

LONG AFTER I'D GOTTEN TO THE prison town, and hours after Piper had made me Shift back, I sat perched up on top of one of the guard houses—the one that flanked the railway depot entrance where Tarik and the lads, and me sneaking behind, had slipped through the night Andon Vrey had died.

I wondered if Kippler had buried him. Or if maybe he'd taken him to the Mausoleum of State and had him burned to ash as if he were a proper nobleman. Or if he'd left him to turn to bones in that basement room where Tarik had shot him, to keep me from killing Vrey. Or from killing Tarik. I'd never been able to figure out who Tarik had really meant to save, in that moment—his own life, or my soul. Or neither. Maybe it was just he meant to kill Vrey all along.

I sighed and pulled up my knees, hugging them tight against my chest. That high up, I didn't feel quite as skittish as I did down below. Up there I was outside of Borokhev, looking down on it like a scene in a snow globe, safe behind a wall of glass. I knew I couldn't stay there forever—I'd starve, or freeze, or fall asleep and tumble to my death—but no matter how many times I told myself to move, I never could. Instead I watched the folks down below, swarming through the place like a conquering army in the last fading scraps of daylight.

The place was even bigger than I remembered it, but then, I'd only seen it in snatches, in nightmare moments. Straight below me was the wide yard—if Borokhev were actually a town, and not just called one, it would look like a proper plaza. There was a well in the center, nothing as fancy as a fountain, but folks had already set buckets beside it to draw up water with. To the north, there was a burned-out building, long and narrow, its remaining beams stark and skeletal and black against the snowy forest behind it.

There were other buildings scattered around the periphery of the yard—workshops, a huge, low-roofed building with smoke curling from a stout chimney that I guessed was a canteen. A few buildings that reminded me of Red's old office building slouched in the snow closer to me, and straight across from me on the western side of the facility was the big grey administrative building where they'd kept me, close by the wall with its barbed wire crown.

A sudden jolt of terror spiked through me as I looked at it. If the skitters and the folks were exploring inside, looking for a room to claim… If they found my cell, my grey empty room with the madness writing all over the walls…

*No, no, no… Anything but that…*

I let Piper fly me safely to the ground, and soon as I Shifted back I broke into a mad run. I had no idea what the folks had done the night before, because most of them were still milling about in the open yard between the buildings, stacking their belongings and in general being much more efficient than I'd expected. But some of the skitters were flying pell-mell through all the different buildings, wild with the joy of exploring a new haunt. I nearly collided with one wee girl on the ground level of the main building. She yelped and skitted aside, and I dodged the other way, and kept running without stopping.

Derrin, Bridnow, and Coins stood at the top of the steps on the first floor up. I let out a scant breath when I saw Derrin there, hard at work, even though he looked a bit ashen with his waist all wrapped up in a bandage. He had a little notebook in hand and was busy marking down something with a dull pencil. The sight of it set my stomach churning, and for half a tick the world swarmed in grey shadows, and I jammed my fist against my mouth to cage in my fear.

"There are fifteen in this row, and if we find more mattresses or ticking we can fit two to a room," Derrin was saying, but when he heard me pounding up the steps he lurched about, eyes wide. "Oh, Hayli, you made it! We're trying to see if there's enough room in here for everyone... What's wrong now?"

"Dan' gan down there!" I cried, grabbing his arm.

"What, why?" Bridnow asked.

I shoved past them and pelted to the first cell on the left, seized the door handle without looking inside, and slammed it shut. Soon as it was sealed I leaned my back against it, taking deep breaths, swallowing back tears of shame.

A minute and Derrin came up beside me, one hand gentle on my shoulder. "Hayli?"

"Dan' look in there. Dan' ever," I whispered. "Dan'...dan' you remember? Please, dan' let anybody see..."

"See what?"

I bit my lip and glanced away. "Dan' let them see what I wrote there. Dan' let them see how...how broken I am."

Derrin shifted about, catching Coins's eye. Some long, pointed look passed between them, full of hidden meaning that I couldn't sort at all, like dread except somehow sadder. Coins shook his head, very faintly. Derrin let out his breath and closed his eyes.

"What?" I asked. Something about the whole exchange got me feeling terribly fitsy all on a sudden, and I wanted, *needed*, to know why. "What was that about?"

"It's...it's nothing It's all right. We'll seal it up and make sure nobody goes in there. There are plenty of other rooms, I'm sure."

Alarm prickled through me, or maybe anger, and I shoved his shoulder. "I dan' believe you. Nothing wouldn't make you that pale. What aren't you saying?" Then realization hit me, cold and unforgiving, and I stumbled a step back. "You saw it already, div'n you. You already know... Everybody saw it. Oh, stars...everybody's seen it."

"No, that's not—" Derrin started, then took my arms, gently. "We saw it, all right? We did. Just us. Nobody else."

"Then...what?"

My eyes darted past him to the closed door, and I edged a step around him, then another. Then, without a word, I ran back to the door and flung it open.

"No, Hayli! Don't!" Derrin cried, hand flashing toward me, too late to catch me.

I stood blinking in the grey light that pooled into my old cell, and everything came crashing down around me.

Empty.

Bare.

Hollow.

The room was empty…the walls were empty…there was nothing nothing nothing

Nothing but grey stone grey walls grey floor all around me, swallowing me, drowning me

Someone's arm around my waist, pulling me out of the water, pulling me back to light and air and busy walls and Derrin with his eyes wide and Coins with his hand over his mouth and tears in his eyes…why was Coins crying? And Bridnow looking the other way like he couldn't see me…

But then who was holding me? Oh God oh God

Andon Vrey isn't dead

He's here

It's Andon it's Andon

fly away

let me die

"Hayli," a voice said in my ear, not Andon's. Not Tarik's…why couldn't it be Tarik's? And a hand pressed over my forehead, cool and hard, and

DOC WAS CROUCHED BESIDE ME. I blinked against the bright light and twitched my head, only to find that it was his hand I'd felt on my forehead. It was still there, steady, no warmer than it had been the first moment he'd touched me. His eyes were grave as they met mine. A minute and I realized we were alone, alone in that horrible hallway, me sitting against the wall under a wash of grey light, him sitting on his heels beside me, one hand on my head, one hand on my knee.

"Doc?" I whispered. My voice tasted like sand. "What…"

"Come on," he said.

He withdrew his hand from my forehead and at once I felt the panic stirring in the back of my mind, loud and insistent, like a vortex swirling up to drag me in. Doc's arm was around my shoulders, pulling me forward so he could help me stand.

"Make it stop!" I whispered. "Do it again…whatever you did. It made it stop. Please. What did you do to me?"

"I can't Sculpt your emotions to ease your fears. Not anymore. I just put you under for a moment." He glanced away. "I'm sorry. I didn't want to do it, but you were going to hurt yourself."

I rubbed my hands over my arms, trying to remind myself that I was real. "I dan' understand. I *remember* writing on those walls. I can still read every word I wrote, in my mind. I can still *smell* it." I pressed my knuckles against my lips. "I div'n imagine that. A'right? I *div'n.*"

"Can you move?"

"D'you believe me?"

His hand tightened on my knee. "Can you stand?"

"No…I dan'…dan' make me… Doc, please say you believe me!"

Without a word he slipped his arm under my knees and picked me up, cradling me against his chest like I was a skitter. I couldn't figure how he had the strength to carry me. I didn't imagine he weighed much more than me, lean and gaunt as he was. But he carried me all the way to the steps, past that horrid wide room with its water-spraying funnels where Miss Farrady had stripped me down and scalded me with water. I could still smell the lumpy grey soap, feel the slick floor tiles under my feet, and I closed my eyes so I wouldn't see Miss Farrady standing there with her riding crop, smiling so, so coldly at me. Then we were moving down the steps—slowly, carefully, too slowly—and out the front door into the cold and fading light.

"Put me down," I said, soon as we'd left the building. "Dan' let them see me…like this."

Doc complied, though there was nobody nearby. I pressed my own hand against my forehead. Drew a long breath of the sharp, clean air, hoping the chill of it would freeze away my terror. Took two steps away from the building.

I wanted to sit down on the cement step, or curl up in the snow, or fly away forever, but I just paced back and forth, back and forth, and all the while Doc hovered on the top step, watching me.

"Hayli," he said finally. "Stop, please."

I spun to face him. I imagined it was the first time I'd ever heard him say *please* about aught at all, but even that wasn't enough to make me stop my frantic motion.

"Why?" I asked, striding up to him, staring him straight in the eye. "Why? Why'd we have to come to this *vutting* place? Why'd Derrin suggest it? *Why?*"

"Hayli—"

"I div'n wanna come. Not ever. I can't...I can't be here. Dan' make me stay, please. I hate this place! I'll die. I'll *die* here."

He caught my arms, keeping me from flying away. "Pull yourself together," he said, and his voice was firm but somehow kinder than I'd ever heard it.

Still, I laughed, in grief or disbelief. "Pull myself...you dan' get it, do you? You've got no vutting idea what it's like!" I threw his hands off my shoulders, shouting, "You dan' understand anything!"

"I understand," he said, quiet as snow. "Hayli—I do."

He turned abruptly. Planting his hands on the stone bannister of the building's front steps, he stared away at the high wall of the facility, with its crown of barbed wire caging us in, or keeping the world out. A faint line of pain traced between his brows.

I wanted to throw his words back at him, or stomp them into the snow, because how could he possibly understand? But somehow I realized, deep inside, that maybe he did. I'd no ken what he'd seen or endured in his life, but the lost look in his eyes and the emptiness in his voice cut straight to my heart. Maybe he did understand.

Maybe I was the one who didn't.

I passed a hand over my forehead and drew a shaking breath. Every sensible part of me knew that we couldn't have gone anywhere but Borokhev. I knew it was the biggest and safest place we had, and the easiest to defend—not to mention it was the least likely place the Ministers and the Army would ever think to look for us. I *knew* all of that. But somehow the knowing wasn't enough. My heart just wouldn't stop shuddering at the sight of it all around me.

*Look at Doc*, I told myself. *What has he suffered? And he won't tell anybody aught about it. He's got nobody. He's even more alone than you are.*

But Doc was strange, an enigma, and looking at him, I suddenly couldn't think of a single thing to say to him. I wanted to comfort him, but the words skitted away on me.

Finally I managed to say, "That man who came to the smelter."

Doc's gaze snapped back to my face, and I thought he looked more grieved than ever. "Yes?"

"Who was he? Who was he looking for?"

Doc slouched back to sit against the bannister, hugging his arms around his lean torso. "That was Destri Alokin," he said softly. "And he was looking for his nephew, Kalen Zagger."

My hand flew up to my mouth. I felt sick—I couldn't breathe at all.

*It's my fault,* I wanted to tell Destri Alokin. I wanted to shout it from the top of the watchtower, to the whole world, and make them listen. *Blame me. I'm the one who stole him from you. I stole him from Tarik, and from you, and from all of us. It's my fault.*

"I can't reason with him," Doc said suddenly. "And...the worst part about it is, I don't even know if I should try."

"Reason with him about what?"

He hesitated, shoulders hunched, avoiding my gaze. "He blames Tarik. For Zagger. In Destri's mind, it was science that cost Kalen his hand, but it was magic that cost him his life."

"No," I said, biting through the word, surprising myself at my own anger. "It wasn't magic. It was Dr. Kippler. It was Kippler's science, his...meddling. That's what stole Zagger from us. Me. It was *my fault,* Doc, not Tarik's."

"He doesn't see it that way," Doc said. "If he blames you at all, it's nothing to what he holds to Tarik's account—and, I suspect, his own. But you're both wrong, of course. It wasn't Tarik's fault, and it wasn't yours. It was Zagger's."

I choked on my breath, but Doc didn't seem to notice.

"Zagger made his choice," he said. "From his earliest years he was trained to protect Tarik's life at all costs—even at the risk of his own." He reached out like he meant to grip my shoulder, but barely touched me before pulling his hand back again. "He wasn't sworn to protect yours. But he did. He chose that. And no one, not Tarik, not Destri, not you, can lay blame for that on anyone else." I stared at him, shaking all over, though I think it was more the grief in Doc's eyes than his words that hit me so hard. Doc said, "But I can't convince Destri of that. He's swallowed in anger. He lost... Zagger was the only family he had left in all the world."

I turned away as his voice broke, but then I heard a soft noise and glanced back, only to see Doc with his head in his hand. No matter how hard he tried, he couldn't hide how his thin shoulders shook with tears. I swallowed and reached out tentatively to touch his arm. When he didn't move at all, not even to pull away, I wrapped my arms around him and hugged him tight. He tensed briefly, then let me hold him.

"I remember," he murmured, voice thick, "when the last of my family died. I remember it like it happened yesterday. *Nezkhadim vi khola wi shchat...*"

I wondered what language he was speaking—I'd never heard aught like it. More than that, I wondered what he'd said. The words had a keening sadness to them, like a prayer or a poem, with a pain that made my own heart ache as if they were laced with magic.

But in the middle of all that grief, an odd little bitterness tugged at my heart. I released Doc, slowly, and stared at his hands—those long, careful fingers, pale and thin—and the bitterness caught in my throat.

"Why..." I started, and caged in the words.

I didn't want to say them. They were hateful, and cruel, and Doc had never been aught but kind to me, and right now he was caught up in a sorrow just as wretched as mine. But he just waited, quiet and patient, like he knew what I meant to say and wanted me to say it anyway. I pulled my gaze away from his eyes. There was something unsettling about their brightness, that green so sharp and clear against the redness from his tears.

I whispered, "Why div'n you save him?"

And I was angry, so angry, burning and shaking inside, reeling with confusion, and so, so angry.

Doc just nodded very faintly and said, "Zagger was dead long before I saw him."

"That's not what I mean, and you know it."

His eyes widened briefly, his hands listless on his thighs. "What sort of power do you think I have?"

"You told me once..."

It was his turn to be angry. He stole a step away from me, and the only way I knew I'd hurt him was the way he curled one hand into a tight fist, almost behind his back. I watched him, wary.

"I didn't tell you anything," he said, and left me standing alone in the snow.

# Chapter 5 ✦ Jarik

THE CAVNISH SAILOR SAT HUDDLED CLOSE TO THE STEAM VENT IN AGNIR'S hut, wrapped in a wool blanket, much as I had the night before. His eyes had a haunted look about them, and he stared at me for so long I was afraid perhaps he *did* recognize me from when we'd all come aboard his ship. When Nika came back from wherever she'd gone, she took one long look at the man, then turned to fetch him a drink of water. The sailor scrubbed his hands through his sea-tangled mop of dark hair, desperately trying to smooth it into some semblance of style.

"One of yours?" she asked me, in Istian, oblivious to the man's rapt attention as she handed him the cup of water.

I shrugged. It was possible she was asking if he was Cavnish, but I wasn't sure how to answer that question.

Was I Cavnish? It was a question I kept turning back to, a question I could never answer to my satisfaction. Was it blood that bonded a man to a nation, or affection? Could allegiance alone make me Cavnish? Or was it all those things that made the Istian sailors scoff at me, and set me apart—all those mannerisms, beliefs, customs, so natural in Cavnal, so foreign here?

I wished I knew. I was cast adrift; I had no homeland.

Maybe it was better that way. Maybe I had no homeland because no land's laws could bind me.

*I am the sea, ruled by no one.*

"What's wrong with you?" When I didn't answer she folded her arms and leaned back against the stone table, watching me through a faintly anxious scowl. "I know he wasn't one of my father's sailors. He only had one Cavner on his ship, and he was twice this one's age at least."

"Mattac," I said. "He's on the beach. Or was, when I left."

"Dead?"

I nodded.

"Damn," she said. "Then who is this one?"

"He's from the other ship," I said.

I didn't know if she'd heard about the Cavnish steamship that had rescued us; I didn't care to explain. She pursed her lips, but, seeing she wouldn't get anything else out of me, she shrugged and climbed up into the loft to fetch an extra blanket.

The Cavner was still staring at me.

"Are you hungry?" I asked.

He started in surprise. "You speak Cavnish? Thank the stars, thought I'd go barking loony hereabouts with nobody sensible to talk to!" When I didn't smile he waved a hand at me, eyes wide. "Div'n mean aught by that, of course; no offense to your kin. I div'n mean *sensible*, as such, just…understandable. A bit chuffy to get on when you dan' even speak the same language, eh? Sorry, did you get all that? You…do speak Cavnish, right?"

I turned away without answering, and went to the base of the ladder.

"Nika, do you have any food for the Cavner?"

In a moment she appeared at the edge of the loft, giving me a strange look torn between a frown and a grin. "What's this? *The Cavner?*" She climbed down the ladder, stopping too close to me when she reached the floor. I knew better than to read any flirtation in the gesture. Intimidation, more likely. "So quick to give up on your people? Tell me, Taumir, will you do the same to Istia when being Istian no longer suits your purpose?"

I measured her in silence, all the while too aware of the sailor's attention riveted on us.

"What is my purpose?" I murmured.

She snorted and stepped past me, shaking her head as she handed the blanket to the sailor. The silence in the little hut loomed until I thought it would drive me mad—even the sound of her rummaging through cupboards couldn't pierce the metallic whine in my ears. It almost felt like...

It almost felt like someone was trying to read my mind, but the effort amounted to little more than claws scratching at glass. I pressed a hand against my forehead and glanced at the Cavner, but he was staring a little too blatantly at Nika again, oblivious to me, undeterred by how she was oblivious to *him*. When she finally brought him a shallow bowl filled with bread and a few strips of dried fish, he accepted it as if she had laid out a king's feast before him.

She barely even glanced at him.

"What are we going to do with him?" she asked me.

"What usually happens to people who get washed up on the shore?"

She gave me a sour look, then glanced toward the window as if she could see through the heavy pelt curtain. "Never happened before," she said. "The sea usually takes care of them. We can't leave him here, though. He'll die."

"No," I agreed. I studied the man thoughtfully as he choked down the dried fish with an obvious, and unsuccessful, attempt at hiding his disgust. "Where is the moot? Hejmstrathvir?"

"It's the heart of the island," she said. "Well, symbolically more than geographically—the actual heart of the island is a *skatrdrakkeyn* crater that stretches down to touch the very face of the sea."

I waved a hand, more to drive away the mumbling in the back of my mind than her words. "You said we're not going directly there, right?"

"Not directly, no. The only way to reach Hejmstrathvir is to follow the river Stratha up from Bregjarvani."

"The main port city."

She lifted her brows. "Right."

"Then we'll take him with us. He should be able to find passage back to Cavnal in Bregjarvani, shouldn't he?"

"If that's what he wants," she said. "If there's any who would be willing to take him. I'm not sure Istian vessels are particularly welcome in Cavnish ports at the moment."

"Your father had no difficulties."

"He's been trading with Cavnal for decades now. They know *Hastol* in all the major ports. Still, I expect your people were only too happy to see him leave, especially with things so uncertain after Trabin's assassination."

I didn't answer. An emptiness gnawed at my heart as images of the King's funeral flashed into my mind—the black horses with their copper-tassled harnesses, the palace draped in funereal silks. The mourners forming an unbroken line from Brigun Palace to the Mausoleum of State. I hadn't had a chance to offer my farewell. I watched from the shadows, Cloaked, as my mother and my cousins gave their honors to their fallen monarch.

I would have honored Trabin as my King, if only I'd had the chance. I would have honored him as a father.

"Taumir?" Nika asked.

I shook myself out of the memory, only to realize she had a hand on my arm, alarm or worry in her eyes. Interestingly, I felt nothing in her touch. No static charge. No energy. I think I had assumed that she was a mage like her father, and the revelation that she wasn't surprised me. When she saw me staring at her hand she snatched it away quickly.

"Do you always act this strange?" she asked, scowling. "I can't figure you out."

"Don't try. It's better you don't," I said. I turned away and dropped onto the chair across the steam pit from the sailor. "We're leaving for Bregjarvani soon," I told him. "We'll take you as far as the harbor, then you can find passage back to Cavnal on your own."

I made sure to use Shade's Istian accent—on the steamship I'd forgotten, and it had almost cost us dearly. The sailor made an effort at swallowing whatever he'd been trying to chew for the last five minutes—dried herring, I guessed—then gave up and washed it all down with the rest of the water Nika had given him. He looked sore for something a little stronger to drink, but I didn't offer him any of Agnir's *skatha*.

"I'm obliged to you," he said.

"How far is it?" I asked Nika over my shoulder.

"Three days at a hard ride, for experienced riders. With you two to slow us down, I'm guessing four is more like."

I bristled. "He may be more familiar with riding waves than horses, but I've been riding all my life."

She gave me a look, skeptical, but didn't have a chance to argue with me. At that moment Agnir and Iskari returned, their faces and hands chafed from the wind, hair and beards coated with briny frost from the sea spray. Without so much as a word between them, the three started to pack wool rucksacks for the trip. The sailor and I sat in awkward silence by the steam pit, the sailor studying me surreptitiously while I tried to listen in on the others' conversation.

"We have only four horses," Iskari said. "Someone is going to have to stay behind."

Nika pushed past him, hands full of more dried fish packed in brown paper. "Not me. You're both hopeless at navigating on land."

Agnir chuckled and handed Iskari the bag he'd been packing. "I'll stay. See if I can gather anything of use from the wreckage as it comes in. Grethna should be coming by on her way to the city sometime this week, so I can ride in with her. I'll meet you in Bregjarvani, or at least in Hejmstrathvir before the moot begins."

Iskari and Nika exchanged a glance, and Nika muttered under her breath, just loud enough for me to hear, "This should be a delight."

Agnir laid a hand on her shoulder and said something in her ear—I couldn't make out *his* words—but the way Nika glared in my direction it was easy enough to guess.

Iskari finished with the bags and slung one over his shoulder, bringing me another and dumping it unceremoniously in my arms. It was heavier than it looked but I managed to accept it without staggering; I knew they would never let me live it down if I had.

"Ask him if he's ready," Nika said, jerking her head at the sailor.

I relayed the question to him, and for a moment he just sat back and gaped at me like I'd gone mad. His reaction didn't surprise me. He still looked little better than a corpse, his eyes red-rimmed and bloodshot, lips puffy, skin taut and broken from the bitter sea. He was likely on the verge of collapse. I didn't feel ready myself, either. With just one night's restless sleep between me and the sea, I could barely keep my thoughts focused from one minute to the next, and my eyes had a strange tendency to stay closed far longer than I intended when I blinked.

"No," he said finally. "I'm bloody exhausted. I've not slept in four days. I just ate the strangest meal of my life and I'm still skapped enough I could eat a whale on me own. So you tell that ice-eyed *vragyeni* that I'm not going anywhere till I've at *least* gotten some sleep."

I glanced back at Agnir and found him stifling a smile.

"What did he call me?" Nika asked. "I do speak some Cavnish, you know. I know he called me something."

"It's a Cavnish mythical creature," I said. "A sea spirit." My cursory explanation didn't impress her. She waved a hand impatiently, so, staring her straight in the eye in challenge, I said, "They appear on ships sailing near rocky coasts, like specters. They're said to take control of the wheel and freeze it in a bearing that causes the ship to crash."

"Oh," she said. She considered that a moment, then flashed me a cruel, cold smile. "I like that."

"We have time," Iskari said suddenly, surprising me. "Give the man a chance to recover. Both of them, for that matter. Taumir looks like death."

I shuddered.

"*Vragyeni*," the Cavner repeated, emphatically, glaring at Nika. "Bloody ice-eyed *vragyeni*."

I gave Nika a look, half reproach, half mocking. She rolled her eyes, but behind her, I caught Iskari stifling a sudden grin. It caught me by surprise—it was a look of genuine amusement, with no mockery in it, no contempt, and the glance he exchanged with me behind Nika's back felt strangely like kinship.

Given his violent indifference to me at our first meeting, I could only wonder what had changed.

Still, I didn't know if I could count him an ally yet—I still wasn't quite sure of him, and even now I knew he wasn't quite sure of me. Vaguely I wondered what it would take to secure his alliance...but as soon as the thought occurred to me, I shuddered in revulsion. As if it were within my control. As if I *wanted* it to be in my control.

As if I didn't.

I turned away, running a hand over my hair, then, with only a moment's hesitation, I gestured the Cavner toward the bed under the loft. Nika exhaled sharply but I ignored her, and the Cavner ignored us both as he ducked under the loft and threw himself unceremoniously across the bed.

"Where are you going to sleep, *Godarson?*" Nika asked, weighting the title with ridicule.

I gave her a cold smile. "What, do you imagine I've never slept on a floor before?"

Without waiting to see her reaction, I lay down alongside the bed, against the wall. Nika snorted and left the hut, but Iskari surprised me again by tossing me a rough woolen blanket. I nodded my thanks and wrapped it around me, and, with my head cushioned on my arms, drifted immediately into a sound sleep.

# Chapter 6 • Hayli

AS DARK STARTED TO FALL, AND EVERYBODY ELSE HAD GONE INTO THE BIG dormitory building in search of beds, I picked my way around the edges of the prison town, desperate to find somewhere to sleep that wasn't fraught with memories. I wanted to Shift so Piper could sleep safe and sound in a tree outside the facility, but she wouldn't come out, and much as I resented it, I knew why she wouldn't. Sooner or later I'd have to overcome my fear. Sooner or later I'd have to make this place my home.

Finally I found a long, elegant looking building a single story high with the front door unlocked, and I crept inside. It was welly dark, with just the moonlight drifting in through a few windows, and almost too quiet. Then I heard a low murmur of voices and caught the brief flicker of torchlight farther into the building. Peeking into a room just off the main chamber, I found Griff, Shiver, and a few of the other lads claiming beds in what looked like a common bunk room—there were rows of bunks, most empty, with only thin mattresses and nothing resembling blankets.

Griff caught sight of me lingering in the doorway and grinned cheerfully at me, and I gave a feeble wave in return and slipped away down the dark hallway. I came to an open door—a proper bedroom, from what I could see in the frail moonlight. It had a bed, and it was warmer than the hallway, so I threw myself face-first onto the mattress and tried to quiet the nervous chattering of my heart.

Minutes or hours later, I realized I had woken up, and had been laying awake for some time, staring up at the ceiling. Only a little light came in through the high narrow window behind me head.

It was just enough for me to see the edges of the door, the sealed steel door across from me, and the grey walls...the grey walls...

grey walls all around me
grey walls covered in words
top to bottom, end to end
words scrawled everywhere
my hand against the wall
my hand etched with words
my arm scrawled with words
my body covered in words
one word over and over again
**WAKE**
screaming, screaming,
footsteps coming
the door slamming open
torchlight flaring in my eyes
Miss Farrady coming to burn me alive
Dr. Kippler coming to poison my mind
Andon Vrey coming to twist my thoughts
Derrin coming to torment me
Derrin holding the torch
Derrin reaching to grab
**ME**
scrambling back
warding him away
drowning, screaming
"Hayli, it's all right."
but it's not all right
trapped, caged
*Piper, rescue me*
"Hayli, look at me."
Derrin holding my arms,
calm, steady

Then his arms wrapped tight around me, and I could breathe again, and slowly I made sense of the world—the moonlight glancing in through the window, the wooden door standing open, the rug on my floor, the empty, white-stained walls. I clung to Derrin's arms as he cradled me against his chest, and I prayed and prayed for an end to the nightmares.

"It's all right. I know," he murmured, and pressed his lips against my hair. "I understand. We'll get through this."

I woke in the morning curled up on my side, facing the white-washed wall, and wondered if I had dreamed it all.

In the bright midmorning I made my way out to the quiet and lonely rail depot, to get away from the bustle and chaos of folks settling into the prison town. For a long while I sat on the cold cement at the edge of the platform, my legs dangling over the train tracks, and looked out at the winter-lavender slopes of the hills.

I couldn't tell how long I'd sat there alone when I heard a patter of tiny steps behind me, and then Pika dropped down to sit on the ledge beside me. She wrapped her arms around her legs and leaned her chin on her knees.

"Hey Pika," I said, putting an arm around her thin shoulders. "Did you sleep well?"

Her eyes scrunched up in a sudden grin. "I had a bed!" she exclaimed. "Not the nicest one, though. Grown folks all took those ones. You should've seen them…wooden floors and fancy blankets, and linens with little lacy edges on them!"

I couldn't keep from shuddering. In my mind I could see it all too clear—the sunny yellow room, with the proper bed and the chest of clothes, where Miss Farrady had played at being kind to me, as if I were their honored guest and not their hostage. Seeing the old cell was bad enough, as my nightmare had proved. I thanked all my stars I hadn't seen that yellow room too.

If Pika noticed my shivering, she didn't mention it. But she scowled at me like a devil and said, "Where *were* you, Hayli? Div'n see you anywhere abouts last night."

I hesitated, the nightmare and all the terror looming up in my mind again, but I buried it quick in case Pika was feeling nosy.

"Slept in that building over there," I said, pointing at the long building. She nodded and her shoulders slumped, and she was much too quiet for much too long. "Hey," I said. "Y' a'right?"

"Guess so," she said, lifting one shoulder in a shrug. "Just…I keep

 192

thinking, why'd Tarik have to block me out?"

I frowned. "What d'you mean?"

She frowned straight back. "Div'n he ever tell you? Back when I first Woke up, and everybody was screaming in my head, he blocked me out so I wouldn't hear him too. I wish he hadn't, 'cause I know you wanna know if he's a'right. And I can't help you all too much."

She gave a bitter, disappointed little sigh and chewed absently at her lip. I didn't think she noticed my surprise at all.

"You mean you could hear his thoughts at first?" Then, because I was too much of a nosy-beak for my own good, "What did you hear?"

"Div'n really," she said, shrugging again. "Least, not the way I hear other folks' thoughts. It was more like *seeing*. Dan' na if it was a memory, or a dream…but he was younger a few years. And it was like he was looking at himself in a mirror. But it was all twisted sideways, upside down, and I… It wasn't him! It wasn't him. But he thought it was. And someone else was there in the shadows…"

She flinched suddenly and buried her face in her knees, forearms pressed against her ears. I tightened my grip on her shoulders.

"You're a'right! Dan' worry about it now."

"I can't see him no more. But…" She reached out suddenly and clasped my free hand, tears on her cheeks. "I know I shouldn't've, but I did try. And I can see where he's *supposed* to be. So I know he's alive, at least."

I let out a broken breath and ran a hand over my face. Shade was alive. That was enough for me.

"If only I could read folks I've never seen before. I might be able to see him through someone else's eyes. Know if he's a'right like that." She squeezed her eyes shut, forehead crinkled as she concentrated, then she shrugged and curled up against my side. "Can't do it. No use trying. You really in charge now? What're you ganna have us do? We ganna fight the Army?"

I laughed out loud, then shuddered at the memory of what'd happened the day before. "Wake, I should hope not. There's a handful of us, and they've got steam crawlers and aeroplanes and those horrid anti-mage guns. Dan' think we're ganna be taking them on any time soon."

"Then are we ganna join them?"

"Dan' think they'd like that much," I said. "Honestly, I dan' even know who our enemy is any more."

"Meritac and Cromis," she said promptly. "And anybody who's got a mind to sell us out to them."

"Wee skitter! Where'd you come up with that?"

"Bridnow," she said. "He was worrying about it."

I glowered at her. "Were you snooping on his thoughts? Thought we talked about that."

She hung her head and picked relentlessly at a stray thread on her trousers. "I know. Sorry, Hayli. Couldn't help it. He's been so sad lately."

"Sad, why?"

"Dan' na. Couldn't understand. Just a jumble in there. Then I felt bad about snooping so I div'n stick about and try to figure it out."

I ruffled her fiery chaos of hair and shoved myself to my feet. "Thanks for that bit of noodle."

"Noodle!" she snorted. "You hang about with Coins too much."

I laughed and left her sitting there by the tracks, lost in her own thoughts, and went to hunt down Bridnow. Derrin found me first, catching my arm from behind as I passed one of the guard houses, almost sending me straight back into a panic. I shied away from the worry in his eyes, wondering again if he'd really been there last night, comforting me in my terror. I was too afraid, or maybe too embarrassed, to ask.

"Hey," he said, gently. "Are you all right?"

"Dan' wanna talk about it," I said, throwing a hand up between us. Then, subsiding a bit, I nodded toward him. "What about you? You doing a'right?"

For a moment he just watched me steadily, his eyes a riddle, then he shrugged and gestured to the bandage still wrapped tight around his waist. "Fair enough. Can't complain, all told. You did good, Hayli. I don't know if anyone's told you, but you've done some incredible things these last few days."

I blushed fiercely and ducked my head, mumbling over a *thank you*. Derrin laughed quietly, which got me a bit sore.

"I need to find Bridnow," I said. "Know where he is?"

"Last I saw he was setting up a sentry at the front gate with Anuk. You sure you don't want to talk about anything? I know…"

His voice trailed off on an uncertainty. I didn't blame him much. I wouldn't have known how to bring up the matter if it had been somebody else melting down, either. But Derrin knew better than anyone what

I'd been through here. He'd been through his own nightmares within these walls, and suddenly I wondered if *he* needed someone to talk to. I'd never considered that he might be fighting his own panic, his own memories of being trapped, of being turned into a puppet against his will.

I thought of what he'd said last night—or what I'd dreamed he'd said: *"We'll get through this."* Had he been awake because his own nightmares were robbing him of sleep?

But the way he was hesitating, and the way I was hesitating, I thought neither of us were quite ready for that talk.

"Later," I said. "Maybes." I jogged a few steps away before he could say anything else, then turned and called, "Thanks, Derrin!"

He waved, a bemused look on his face, and vanished into the wind. The complex had finally quieted down a bit. I wondered where everybody had got to—if they'd all found places to sleep and were still abed, enjoying the luxury of actually *having* a bed. I wondered how they would all get fed, because far as I knew, Miss Nan had brought naught with her but what she could cart out of the smelter in one trip. She'd been making breakfast in the long mess building first thing in the morning, though I hadn't stopped by to get any myself. I just hoped everyone had gotten enough. Then again, that was precisely one of the reasons I was hunting for Bridnow.

I found him where Derrin had said, standing in the snow out by the front gate of the facility with Anuk and a few of the other lads. Bridnow gave me a guarded smile as I approached, and Anuk wouldn't look at me at all—I wondered if Coins or Bridnow had told him how I'd fallen apart. It didn't surprise me if he was afraid of me. Most of the time I was afraid of me...afraid of my own mind. It was part of the reason I hated Shifting from the crow. Piper was sane. Her mind wasn't a prison. Her body was free.

She was everything I wasn't.

I decided to ignore Anuk just as much as he was ignoring me, and turned to Bridnow instead. "Got a moment, Lieutenant?" I asked, tucking my hands in my trouser pockets.

"Not a lieutenant anymore," he said. "You really should just call me Bridnow."

The other lads scattered at a wordless command from him, leaving the two of us standing side by side. A minute and we both kept staring out at the fields and hills beyond Borokhev's walls—all winter-grey and scattered with snow, like the little frothy waves of a sea I'd never seen except in the Herald's photographs. Bridnow had his hands folded behind his back. I noticed he never put his hands in his pockets, no matter what, not like me and the other street rats. He always stood just like that, head up, back straight, like he was standing ready for a military inspection.

"Do you miss it?" I asked. It wasn't exactly what I'd meant to talk to him about, but I wondered.

"Miss what?"

"The Army. Being a lieutenant. Can't imagine it's been an easy switch for you."

He smiled and bent his head. "Yes," he said. "I miss it. I miss it every day. But…more than anything I miss the belief." When I looked at him, questioning, he went on, "The belief that I was serving something greater than myself. The belief in my mission. All I ever wanted was to be a soldier. Serve in the King's Army. Earn my stars. Offer life and blood for the glory of Cavnal. That's all gone now."

Someone shouted in the yard behind us, and we both spun about to see what was going on. Some of the men were rolling a barrel out of one of the small stone buildings, grinning and laughing as they slipped in the slush.

"What is that?" I asked.

"Whiskey, I don't doubt," Bridnow said, one corner of his mouth lifted in a smile.

"Best not let the skitters get into that," I muttered, and he laughed. "Bridnow—" It felt a bit odd to call him by his family name, the way I'd heard Tarik talk to Griff sometimes—"do you believe in what we're doing here? You said you miss serving. Dan' you think we've got a cause worth fighting for right here?"

"What cause is that?" he asked drily. When I couldn't answer, he shook his head. "I know, Shade is a cause unto himself, isn't he?"

"You dan' believe in him?"

"I do," he said. "And what he stands for. But let's face the truth. Shade left us quite a mess to sweep up. He knows what he's fighting for, and we know what we're fighting for, but what about the rest of these folks? They don't have any idea what they're doing here, besides staying safe and out of the cold. Some of them want to fight alongside

Shade for the rights of mages, I don't doubt, and some of them are probably anarchists who were only too glad to see the monarchy fall. Some are loyalists, like myself, who would rather see him take back his throne."

For a long moment I said nothing, just studied him surreptitiously, wondering how to reply. I knew Tarik had never told Bridnow his identity, but, something about what Bridnow said made me wonder.

"Prince Tarik—" I started.

He smiled faintly. "Shade?"

"You...know they're the same person?"

"I knew who he was as soon as I saw Kalen Zagger at the smelter," he said. "As to them being the same person, though... No. They're really not." He glanced at me sidelong. "But don't worry. I would gladly serve them both. Or either of them."

I frowned a bit and scuffed my boot in the ice. When I'd first realized that Shade was Tarik, I'd been so convinced that they were one and the same, and I couldn't understand how I'd never realized the truth before. I'd believed with all my heart that Shade was the revelation of something hidden inside Tarik. And maybe that was true, but now I couldn't help thinking that maybe Bridnow was right. Maybe they were the same...but maybe they were drifting apart.

Funny thing, if they *did* drift apart, I wasn't sure who I'd be quicker to follow.

"What's on your mind?" Bridnow asked. "I take it you didn't just want to chat."

I had to appreciate that he, at least, wasn't pestering me about how I'd melted down in the dormitory. He watched me earnestly, but openly. There was never any hidden meaning in his eyes.

"*Stravitz*, Bridnow," I said. "I'm promoting you to Commandant of the Patchwork Army."

"The Patchwork—" he started, then both his brows lifted in surprise. "But Shade..."

"Put me in charge," I interrupted, and shrugged. "I know I'm not suited to giving out orders. I haven't got any experience. Never led anybody in my life. Not that I'm not willing to learn, it's just...these folks are counting on me doing something I've got no training in. I'll give a hand any way I can, but if we're ganna survive, we need someone in charge who's got half a ken on what to do. That ain't me. I'll be your second, if you want, but please…tell me you'll do it. We're right on the edge of war and these folks aren't ganna melt back into the city and forget they had a fight of their own. We need someone to lead us who can help us. Help us fight. Help us survive."

I took a deep breath and frowned up at Bridnow, waiting to see his reaction. For a long moment he said nothing, and didn't even move, then he swore softly under his breath and scrubbed a hand over his jaw.

"All right. I accept," he said, turning to me and extending his hand.

I clasped it, shivering at the touch. "Thank you," I whispered, more relieved than I cared to admit. Then, as a little snaking disappointment trailed through me, I asked, "You dan' think I'm weak, do you, giving up command before I even tried my hand at it? Shade trusted me. But… truth is I dan' trust myself."

He laid a hand on my shoulder and squeezed it briefly. "No shame in recognizing your own limitations."

I knew he meant to comfort me, but I didn't feel particularly comforted.

"Were you serious about wanting to help me?" he asked then, clasping his hands behind his back again.

"Course I was," I said.

He smiled. "Then we've got work to do."

## Chapter 7 ❧ Hayli

By the time I realized he'd moved, Bridnow was already striding into the facility, shouting for Anuk, who was sitting on a broken bit of wall with a few other lads not ten feet away. Anuk, beet red like he thought he was in trouble—as if I'd gone and ratted him out to Bridnow for something—immediately jumped down and jogged over to join us.

"Did I do something wrong?" he asked.

Bridnow scowled. "No, why?"

Anuk glanced helplessly at me. I just gave him a sympathetic grin, trying hard not to laugh.

"Report back to the gate with...Lev," Bridnow said, nodding at one of the other lads. Lev was a lanky boy of about eighteen, who'd straggled in with a bunch of other folks after the fire at Minister Von's house. "Stay there until you're relieved."

Anuk had stood plenty of sentry duties with Zagger, so his face cleared immediately and he threw Bridnow a smart salute. Then, shouting for Lev, he turned and disappeared through the tall gate. Bridnow clapped me on the back and continued on, his strides so long I had to run to keep pace with him. In the middle of the yard he stopped and turned a slow circle, his eyes fixing briefly on every building in the complex.

"I don't like where the big company building is situated," he commented, pointing at the grey brick building that we were using as a dormitory. "It's too close to the wall. But there's no helping that. It has enough room for most of the people to sleep in there, and the handful left over will sleep in the guard barracks here."

He swung around to point at the long building attached to one of the guard towers, where I'd holed up the night before. Then he turned and studied me.

"There are sixteen cots in that building and six private rooms, along with a couple of offices and a decent common area," he said. "It'll be our headquarters. We're going to train up a small company who will be in charge of different guard units. Frankly, most of these folks here have no military training, and I can't turn them into anything resembling a military force. But they won't need that kind of training if we do our job, and I *can* train a small group, enough to work as guards and keep this facility secure."

"You need Anuk, then," I said, thinking. "He's a keen eye and a great fighter. And Derrin, of course."

He nodded. "Both good choices."

I chewed on the inside of my cheek. Jig was the best fighter I knew but I'd never in a hundred years see him leading anybody but himself. Coins…somehow I couldn't see Coins in that role either. As a rule he went his own way, and never seemed to think much of anybody's claim to authority over him. He never had.

"Griff!" I said. "He's got somewhat like military training already. Kind of."

"I was thinking the same. Good, then. That settles it."

"But you said four."

He smiled. "Indeed. Welcome to the cohort, Hayli."

"But…" I sputtered. "Div'n we just say—"

"I know you weren't ready to be in charge of the whole operation, but that doesn't mean that Tarik was wrong when he picked you. You underestimate your skills. You're not a leader because you haven't let yourself be a leader. Don't worry. You'll be under my command, and under my orders. But this is your chance to prove Tarik right." He clapped my arm and smiled. "And prove yourself wrong. Now, go pick your four elite guards."

I stood frozen, cursing myself for my hesitation. "Bridnow…" I ventured. "Most of my friends are older than me. Not to mention they're mostly lads. Dan' you think they'll be sore at having to take orders from me?"

"If they are, they'll get used to the idea by and by," he said, indifferent. "And don't think you have to limit yourself to your friends. There are a lot of capable people in this camp."

"Why'd you pick us?" I asked softly. "Me and Anuk, Derrin and Griff? There's grown folks here who must have some kind of skills you could use."

He studied me, thoughtful and quiet, as the grey fur of his hat got dusted with snow and his breath smoked away in the wind. "Let me tell you something about the military," he said. "Yes, there are a few other soldiers here, former policemen, guards. I've already made a roster of them. But I'll be using them for other missions. *This* mission is a training mission. I don't have any trained leaders so I need to make them. And honestly, the younger a person is when I start training them, the better it turns out. Older folks often have too high opinions of themselves. Makes them resistant to being instructed."

I laughed under my breath. "Maybe you should pick someone besides Griff, then."

He chuckled. "Griff's all right. He's got motivation to fall in line, anyway. That's another reason you four are taking up this role. You have dedication, and passion. You're committed to the cause." He eyed me sidelong, humor in his eyes. "Besides, I didn't pick them. I picked you, and *you* picked them. Part of being a good leader is recognizing the qualities that make a good leader. You did well. Now, go pick your squad."

I started to go, but paused as my gaze fell on the guard barracks. "You said there were six private rooms in there," I said. "Figuring that you get one of them, who gets the last?"

"Shade, of course," he said. "When he comes back."

*When he comes back.*

I pushed the thought away—and the nameless fear that followed it—and wandered back out to the rail platform. Pika had gone, so it was just me and the snow and the silence, which was exactly what I'd hoped for. I needed to think over my options. I knew without hesitation that I wanted Shiver on my crew. Anuk would likely pick Jig, but maybe he'd let me have Coins. That was two. But I couldn't decide who else.

Then I realized that maybe I shouldn't be making the decision on my own. I was one of four, not one alone, and somehow I thought Bridnow would be watching to see if I brought the others into the discussion. I sat still a few minutes longer, relishing in the solitude, then sighed and wandered back into the complex. I knew where Anuk was, and it didn't take me long to find Griff—he was in the long, low-roofed building where Miss Nan had cooked us breakfast. At first I thought he was there looking for skappers, then I realized he was helping another man and Miss Nan organize the meager food stores she'd brought over from the smelter.

I beckoned to him and he followed me out of the building, back toward the gate where Anuk and Lev were checking over a horse cart laden with old blankets and tarps. I ran a hand over the top layer of blankets. They were poor stuff, mostly, moth eaten and musty wool, but better than nothing in this frigid cold. Briefly I wondered where the driver had gotten them. From the houses of the folks we'd lost in the uprising? Part of me hated to even imagine it, but the sensible part of me knew that the dead didn't need aught from us any more. They didn't need aught at all. And the things they'd left behind served well enough to satisfy the needs of the living.

With a wave Anuk sent the driver into the facility, then turned to face me and Griff. "Are you two my relief?"

"Nah, your time isn't up yet." He groaned and I elbowed him playfully in the side. "Actually, it is. But hey, d'you know where Derrin is?"

He pointed across the yard, toward the far north side of the prison town past the burned-out building, where I could just spot Derrin's unmistakable silhouette—standing straight and perfectly still in his long trencher, black hat slouched low. He was overseeing some business that I couldn't make out, but when I started walking that way, Anuk reached out and grabbed my arm.

"Wouldn't go that way, Hayli. Not yet. They're proper burying those mages that died here, so."

I froze mid-step, my blood washing away clear down to my toes. *This place is a deathtrap for mages*, I kept telling myself, my heart pattering against my ribs in fear. *We shouldn't be here. We shouldn't. We're all going to die.*

"Did you need me for something?" Anuk asked gently, shaking me out of my terror.

I forced myself to focus on Anuk and Griff. "We'll have to talk to Derrin later, but I wanted to tell you. I put Bridnow in charge. Just div'n feel comfortable doing it myself."

Neither of them looked overly relieved, which secretly pleased me. Anuk just touched my arm, face serious in the long shadows.

"Anyway," I went on, "he's put the four of us as squad leaders over what he thinks is ganna be some sort of elite guard unit. We each get four people under us. Bridnow's ganna train us all. I wanted to talk with you so we can pick the best sixteen folks for the job and divvy them up fair."

"Good thinking," Griff said, then turned and shouted for Coins, who was lingering nearby. "Hey, Coins! Come take Anuk's spot for a quick tick. We need to talk to him."

Coins sauntered over, looking at each of us closely. I bit my lip and didn't say aught, hoping that when Coins found out he wasn't one of the four, he wouldn't be too sore over it.

"Everything fine here?" he asked.

"Yeah, no troubles," Anuk said. "Just need a chat. We'll fill you in later."

Coins shrugged and nodded, throwing Anuk a whimsical salute as he headed out to join Lev. The three of us wandered over to the guard barracks, where we found Bridnow already inside, getting a fire lit in the massive hearth in the common room. He caught my eye as he stood up and nodded, approving, then strode out into the cold without a word to any of us.

I dropped down in one of the rickety wooden chairs around a long, heavy table, which was already scattered with Tarik's collection of maps and documents. I sifted through them a minute, then scanned the whole room, drinking in all the details I'd missed before.

The common area itself was fairly large, stretching back into a narrow corridor that led to the bedrooms and offices, including the big bunk room where the lads had slept the night before. It was well furnished, too, with that huge table sitting near the hearth, a rather fancy looking cabinet on the far wall, and a smaller desk in the corner of the room behind my chair. A few other chairs of cracked and dusty leather sat on the opposite side of the room around a gaming table. With the dark wood wainscoting on the walls, the whole space felt a bit luxurious, if a little utilitarian, and it fit neatly into the gap in my experience between factory basements and the King's palace.

"All right," Griff said. "So, what's this you were saying? We each get a team of four people?"

"Yeah. I thought we should plan it out together, so the squads match up fair," I said. "Make sure each group has a decent mage, such like."

Anuk said nothing a long while, but his silence was so loud that Griff and I both turned to look at him. Then he scrubbed a hand through his red hair and leaned back in his chair.

"Us," he said. "*We're* the four in charge of this group? What was Bridnow thinking?"

"*I* picked you," I said. "Me. Not him. Picked you lot because I think you'll do good. Not interested in arguing my choice, either."

"Fair enough," he said, brows lifted. "Guess I'll take Jig on my crew. Kid can fight, so."

"I want Shiver for mine," I said. "So unless we come up with more than four mages with useful skills, he's my pick."

"I'll take Tam," Griff said. "Even with one eye he's a better watchman than almost anyone I've met."

Derrin blustered into the barracks at that minute, his scarf crusted with ice and face ruddy from the cold. He stomped snow off his boots before coming over to join us, taking the seat closest to the fire and hitching the big leather chair back as near to the blaze as he could get it. He still moved gingerly, favoring his side, and I hoped that Doc had been able to do something for his wound beyond just bandages and whiskey.

"Bridnow sent me over," he said. "He filled me in on the situation." He studied me a minute. "I know that can't have been an easy choice. You know we all support you."

I ducked my head. Then, remembering what Bridnow had told me about how I doubted myself, I looked straight at Derrin and said, "Thanks."

He grinned faintly. "So, what have you decided so far?"

"Not much. Shiver, Jig, Tam," I said, pointing to each of us as I named our choices. "We each get a mage. More if we can think of others who would be good."

"Makes sense. I'll take Aothir for my mage."

"Sounds like an Istian name," Griff said. "Have I met him?"

"He was with us when we came here before, when we got ambushed. Remember? He was the Flint we rescued when we went to get the police wagons. He's half-Istian, at least."

"Right. I remember him now." Griff thought a moment, thrumming his fingers on his chin. "In that case, I'll take that Shard out there who you were standing watch with, Anuk. Was his name Lev?"

Anuk nodded and straightened a piece of paper on the table absentmindedly. "Guess I'll take Scorch."

"I'll take Coins, if I can," I said.

"Oh, come *on*," Anuk said. "I was going to pick him, so. Can we share?"

"Sure," I said cheerfully, and didn't mean a jot of it.

Anuk glowered.

"What about Luce?" Griff asked after a bit.

I thought it over—I'd been thinking of her, too. But Luce didn't strike me as the type who'd care for the kind of training I figured Bridnow had planned for us. Neither, for that matter, would Kite or Gem. Pika would be keen as steel for it, but she was too young yet.

"Dan' think Luce is a good call. She's got other duties," I said. "Like Doc."

"Nobody say Roo or I'll make them rethink it," Anuk muttered.

For a tick there was dead silence, then Griff burst out laughing. "I don't think anyone was thinking of Roo, mate."

"Who's Roo?" I asked, confounded.

"New fellow," Anuk said. He and Griff exchanged a look, both fighting smiles. Even Derrin, to my surprise, was grinning openly. "His name's really Jostim. Maybe twenty, twenty-five? Walks around like so?"

He stuck his hands on his hips with his elbows thrust back and his chest puffed out, and mimed strutting about like a rooster.

"*Bawk*," Griff said under his breath, which got Anuk doubled-over with laughter.

Derrin tipped his chair back on two legs, swiping off his hat and rubbing a hand over his face as if that could hide his own laughter, but it only made things worse.

We talked a bit longer, bandying around names, until finally we each had a crew we were at least mostly happy with. My four included a woman of middling years, Maera, who was tough as nails and reliable as rain, and a man in his twenties, Gunner, who I remembered standing guard with Zagger many a night.

"So, we've got our crews," Derrin said. "What do we do now?"

"Reckon we do whatever Bridnow tells us," Anuk said, "and hope the Army doesn't figure out where we're hiding."

"Farewell, sweet days of freedom," Griff muttered with dramatic lamentation. "I'm far too young for this responsibility."

I snorted and pulled up my knees. "S'pose there's always a place waiting for you in the Court of Ministries."

He jabbed a finger in my direction with a scowl, and I laughed when he couldn't find a single word to say.

# Chapter 8 ✻ Tarik

*I*T MUST HAVE BEEN SEVERAL HOURS LATER THAT I WOKE, COLD AND STIFF, WITH a neck ache that set my head throbbing. The Cavner had already gotten up, and sat near the steam vent chewing on what I guessed was more dried fish, with just one hand escaping the wool blanket he had wrapped tight around his shoulders. Nika and Iskari were both gone, and the hut was strangely silent.

The sailor gave me a faint nod as I took the other chair near the warmth, and for several minutes after I joined him I felt his keen gaze fixed on my face. Finally, annoyed by his attention, I leaned back in the chair and folded my arms.

"Do you have a name?" I asked.

"Mirin," he said. "Mirin Kell. You?"

"Taumir. What's on your mind?"

"Just this feeling I've got, that I've seen you before. But I know I've not." He paused, eyes narrowed slightly as if trying to figure out how much of that I had understood. I lifted a hand in acknowledgment. "She called you *Godarson?*"

"That's right," I said, careful.

"Eyid's son," he said. "Never knew he had one. I'm sorry, about your father's death."

I startled, for a moment caught in that dark memory of Trabin's funeral once again. Then I realized he was talking about Eyid's assassination...or murder. The death of a man I had never met.

"Will you be taking over his title?"

I shifted my weight, crossing my legs at the ankles. "It's not entirely in my power. It's not like the Cavnish monarchy."

Mirin's face fell.

"What's wrong?"

"You've heard word of our King's death, I'm sure." I nodded, grief gnawing at my heart. "And his son, our Prince, is gone missing. Some folks say he run out from his duty, but I dan' believe that. Dan' think he'd do it. Never reckoned he was the rogue the papers painted him up as, just a lad with a bit of spirit. Ah, he'd've made a fine King, that one."

His voice trailed off and he looked away, rubbing a hand over his sparse dark beard. I said nothing. I bowed my head, a war of emotions tearing at me, stealing my voice. The man's confidence in me was humbling, but was he right? Maybe I *had* turned away from my people when they needed me the most. Maybe I'd hid behind my father's final command as an excuse to abandon the duty I should have fulfilled. But my heart called me back to Cavnal with a yearning I'd never known, and never expected. It ached, and I caught myself with my head in my hands, bowed over my knees.

"Are you—" Mirin started.

The door of the hut swung open with a gust of bone-chilling wind, interrupting him, and then Iskari appeared in the doorway like a storm cloud. He paused there with the cold swirling around him, staring at me, then finally came the rest of the way inside and let the door slam shut behind him.

"What's wrong with you?"

I scrubbed a hand over my jaw. "Just thinking." To Mirin I said, "I hope he turns up. I'm sure that's hard for your nation."

He gave me a rather bitter look. "And I'm sure that's no small cake to you."

Iskari glanced between us. I didn't think he spoke much Cavnish, but surely he could understand Mirin's tone. And I was certain he couldn't mistake my rising anger.

"Is he a problem?" he asked, leaning against the black slab table with his arms folded. "Should we toss him back to the sea?"

I lifted my hand, just the fingers, and shook my head faintly.

Mirin leaned forward, unwilling to abandon the subject. "I'm welly sure Istia is keen as rain to see Cavnal in chaos. Did you help with that? Was it payback for what you reckon we did to your father?"

*The irony,* I thought. *If only you knew what you were saying.*

"Now, I swear I've seen you before," he said, when I made no response to his jab.

I turned my head aside, as if it mattered, while a niggling worry crept into the back of my mind. If Mirin had seen Shade's picture in the Cavnish newspapers, and if he knew the story of how Trabin had died...I would never be able to convince him that Istia hadn't been involved—if not responsible for his death.

I studied Iskari briefly, then got to my feet and left the hut without a word to either of them. Outside I stopped and leaned against the stone wall, and a moment later Iskari stepped out behind me, just as I had expected.

"Is there a problem?" he asked. There was no kindness in his tone, but there was something else, something I couldn't quite make sense of.

"I think Mirin recognizes me," I said. Purposefully, I didn't look at him.

"How in *Veka's* name would he recognize you? Were you somebody in Cavnal besides Istia's bastard son?"

I bristled, but when I glanced at him, I saw no hostility or contempt in his face, just honest indifference.

"I led the insurgency," I stated, just as bluntly. "You asked me once if I was the Zealot. Well, that's what they called me, in Cavnal, when I led the mages in resistance to the Court's anti-magic laws."

He rounded on me, eyes wide, muttering a string of obscenities that were all too clear in any language.

"You understand the problem, I'm sure," I said.

He said nothing—I couldn't tell if his silence was agreement or argument.

"I was there, Iskari, when Trabin died. I was under arrest, and standing on that dais."

He jabbed a finger back toward the hut. "So he accused Istia of playing a role in the King's death?"

"Essentially."

A silence stretched between us—long, and tense. Then, "If he returns to Cavnal with that belief..."

"I know."

"Is that why you're really here? Trying to sow discord between Cavnal and Istia? Do you *intend* to bring us into war?"

"What do you think?" I snapped.

"I honestly don't know. I can't figure you out." He kicked the worn heel of his leather boot against a tuft of grey-green moss. "Are you thinking he needs to be removed from the scenario?"

I shot him a cold look. "I'm not talking, or thinking, about removing anyone from anything," I said. "Least of all that poor creature who barely escaped the sea."

"The sea doesn't easily forgive."

I shivered, visibly, and Iskari laughed, as if it were the sudden gust of cold wind that bothered me. As if the wind weren't of my own making.

"I won't see Istia dragged into war against Cavnal," I said.

"Nor I, but who are we to decide?" Iskari asked, but there was a pointed challenge in his eyes. "You can't decide Istia's fate."

"I don't know," I said, staring out at the sea. "I may."

Surprisingly, he didn't contradict me.

WE DECIDED TO LEAVE THE FOLLOWING day, but an unexpected snow storm kept us indoors all morning. The Cavner didn't seem to mind; he didn't get out of bed at all, even for food. Near noon the weather cleared, and Nika went out to see to the horses while Agnir made his way back down to the beach, to continue scavenging for flotsam from the wreck. Iskari disappeared just after Agnir, but I had no idea where he went; he was nowhere to be seen when I left the hut a little while later, aimless and desperate for something to do.

I wandered a while along the beach, but when I couldn't find anything of interest left by the tide, I made my way back to the hut. It was brutally cold, and the snow lay in heavy, wet drifts over the broken ground, much deeper than I'd ever seen in Brinmark. My face was aching with cold when I finally shoved the door open and escaped into the warmth inside the hut, and my hands were so numb that I could barely fumble the knot of my scarf loose.

Mirin was finally awake, and he was staring at me from his seat by the steam vent. Disturbed, I unwound my scarf and drew the wool sleeve of my jumper over my face to mop away the melted snow and sleet.

"You do speak Cavnish," he stated, abruptly, as I took the chair across from him.

"Of course I do," I said, which seemed to take him aback—as if I hadn't been speaking Cavnish to him all along.

"No," he said. "I mean, you *really* speak Cavnish. How else would you have been able to stir up a whole rebellion in Brinmark, *Zealot?*"

I sighed and dropped my head. So, he *had* recognized me after all. "I didn't start the rebellion," I said. "That was brewing long before I came along."

"Does it matter? They believe you did. And they were right. You are an Istian spy."

"I am not," I said, quietly.

"You are the Godarson."

"And?"

"And...what were you doing in Cavnal? Trying to overthrow the monarchy?"

"I had no intention of overthrowing the monarchy," I said, heated, and Iskari's words rang in my ears—*the sea does not easily forgive.*

*What are you going to do with him?* asked the voice in the back of my mind.

*Nothing. It's not worth the trouble. It's not worth my trouble.*

*He could destroy everything. He could destroy you.*

*No,* I told myself, firmly. *He can't.*

"Well," Mirin said, interrupting my inner argument, "whatever you didn't do was pretty damn effective."

I got up and retrieved the clay jar from the kitchen shelf, and poured myself a small cupful of *skatha*. It was too early to drink it, but at that moment I didn't care—I was still numb, inside and out, and desperate for something to warm me. I tossed the whole thing back in one swallow, and didn't even cough at the burn that chased down my throat. For a moment I leaned my forearm against the shelf, weighing my options, as Mirin's stare dug like knife blades into my back.

"I only ever wanted to protect the mages," I said at length.

I wondered why I was bothering to explain myself to the man—he didn't need to know my reasons.

"Protect the mages," he spat.

I glanced at him sideways, then, feeling suddenly claustrophobic under the weight of his hatred, preferring the hostile elements of the

Istian winter, I grabbed my scarf again and walked straight back out the door. I saw Iskari and Nika standing near the horses' pen, but turned my steps toward the sea instead, where the white foam of the receding waves speckled the black beach like the scattering of stars on the midnight sky.

Agnir was still there, sitting on a rough boulder near the water's edge. As I got closer I realized he held something in his hands—a piece of polished but splintered wood, painted with four letters: *stol.*

"I've never been without my ship," Agnir said, his fingers moving restlessly over the letters. "I feel lost at sea, adrift." He finally tipped his head back to study me, and his eyes were rimmed in red. "I think, perhaps, I may understand how you are feeling."

I flinched, and looked away. For days I'd been wondering if I could ever understand *his* grief, and yet, he seemed to understand mine without effort.

"You belong here," he said, "and yet you don't. Your heart belongs to Cavnal—I can see it in your eyes, and every glance you turn to the sea. You don't believe you have any right to your father's title."

"Which one?" I asked, bitterly. "My father in the blood, or in the spirit?"

"Whose son do you think you are?"

I dropped to a crouch beside him, hands clasped between my knees. "I don't know. Both? Neither? Trabin raised me when he might have cast me out. Eyid never claimed me when perhaps he should have. He never even tried to. And yet here I am, trying to bind myself to his legacy. To be honest, I don't think I belong anywhere." A gust of sleet sifted over me, stinging my eyes with the echo of salt spray. "Agnir, I don't know who I am. I don't know...I don't know what I am."

"Iskari told me that they called you the Zealot, in Cavnal. Do you know what that means?"

"No," I said with a sharp laugh. "I have no idea what it means to be the Zealot."

He shrugged. "Well, I don't either, to be honest. But I know it is no title that we, mere men, can give to anyone. Only *Veka* can decide who his Zealot is, if that's what you believe."

"I don't know what I believe, either," I admitted, the words stirring a faint, gnawing ache in my heart that tasted faintly of betrayal.

Agnir stared a long time at the sea, the mist freezing in his beard, hands quiet on the piece of driftwood. When he turned to look at me, I couldn't endure the sadness in his eyes. "Are you saying you don't believe…that you don't believe in *Veka*?"

How could I tell him that I'd been raised despising all talk of gods and daemons and spirits, ridiculing all who professed devotion to the old ways? I'd claimed allegiance to Wake during the rebellion, to unite the mages, but somehow, no matter how hard I'd tried to make myself a believer, even that had felt false. A pretense, just like Shade's face. But I didn't know if Agnir would understand that, or if it would only wound him. I wasn't in a crisis of faith—I'd never had any to begin with.

"I don't know," I said at last. "In some way I think I want to, but I don't know how. I don't know if I can, after everything I've seen. I think…I don't believe in anything."

"I don't think that's possible. You believe in something. You just don't understand what, yet. Maybe you only believe in yourself, but that's something, anyway."

"You're wrong," I said, and stood up. "That is what I believe in least of all."

## Chapter 9 · Hayli

THE NEXT DAY, BRIDNOW WOKE US ALL UP FAR TOO EARLY IN THE MORNING, when it was still dark as pitch outside, and the officers' barracks were dead cold. He had Derrin's Flint Aothir with him, which was actually what woke me up—the mage lit every grobbing lamp and candle in the barracks, even the two lamps in my own room, with a single clap of his hand, sending blinding light dazzling into my sleep-weak eyes. I groaned and twisted onto my belly, burying my face in my coarse wool blanke. The next minute someone was hammering like a blacksmith on my door, refusing to be ignored.

"Fall in!" Bridnow's voice shouted from the hallway.

*Oh, I'm going to regret giving him charge of us,* I grumbled to myself, as I rolled over and fell clear off the low bed. I winced as my knees hit the cold cement floor, and dragged myself to my feet.

Stomping my boots on as I went, I jerked open my door and found Bridnow still outside my room, grinning down at me.

"Dressed?" he asked me.

I blushed and tugged my jumper straight, and ran my cold-stiff fingers through my tatty hair. I'd slept in my clothes, like I always did, but the way he said it got me feeling a bit sheepish about it.

"Yeah, so?" I said.

He lifted a brow and jerked his chin toward the common room, where me and the other lads had divvied up our teams the day before. When I came into the room I found the fire blazing, pouring welcoming warmth all through the barracks, and the mage Aothir leaning over the hearth with one foot propped up on its low step. So far, he was the only one there.

I must have seen him once or twice before then, but for all I tried, I couldn't remember him. He was fair-looking in his own way, with silver-grey eyes and short-cropped hair that might have been light brown or dark gold—I couldn't quite tell in the firelight. Far as I could see, he was taller even than Derrin, lean and muscular, his bare arms etched with countless tattoos. I'd never seen anyone marked like that, with tattoos that didn't seem to mean aught at all, and for half a tick I studied the intricate patterns until I realized he was watching me over his shoulder.

"Good morning, Hayli," he said, flashing me a smile that felt a bit taunting.

"Aothir, ain't it?" I asked, perching up on the long table with my feet propped on a chair. He nodded, and I waved a hand generally over my shoulder. "Where's everybody else?"

"Fighting the good fight, I imagine."

I startled, all my sense perking up, but Aothir just grinned and tucked his hands to one side of his head, miming someone sleeping.

"Oh," I laughed. "And what're you doing here? Did you lot move in last night too?"

He shook his head, rubbing his hands together for warmth. The gesture would've looked perfectly normal, except his hands were full of fire he'd scooped from the hearth. I watched, half-fascinated, half-terrified, as the flames coiled and wreathed about his fingers, and yet all I could think was, *Stars, now we've got two Flints in our group. This is going to be delightful.*

Right on cue, as if to prove my point, the front door slammed open and Scorch walked in from the still-dark morning, trailed by a number of other folks. He gave me a look faintly like a sneer as he came into the common room, and snatched the fire away from Aothir's hands from ten feet away, just by reaching out for it. Aothir bristled at the theft, but Scorch just flashed him a wicked smile full of challenge. When the tips of Aothir's fingers starting to crackle and glow, I flung my hands toward the pair of them.

"Are all you Flints so high and mighty?" I asked. "Stars, if you two can't get along somewhat reasonable, you're both off the squadrons."

For two seconds they both just stared at me, wide-eyed. Then, to

215

my absolute shock, Scorch snapped his fingers and spirited away the flames. He lowered both hands to his sides, but kept his gaze pinned on me, keen as fire. Aothir folded his arms but had the grace to look subdued. And me, I just swallowed, and prayed they couldn't see how fitsy I felt, not just for giving them a rebuke, but for the fact that they'd done the miraculous and *listened*.

The other folks edged their way into the room, joined moments later by the other three squad leaders. I did a mental count-off as each person came into the room, and breathed a sigh of relief when I counted the last one. Everyone was there. That, at least, had to be a good start.

"Hayli," Bridnow said, coming into the room behind me. "All accounted for?"

I turned and nodded, then thought that likely wasn't the best way to answer, so I straightened my shoulders and said, "All accounted for, Commandant."

"Excellent," he said, and waved a hand at us. "Come on, gather around. Get warm. It's brutal out there this morning."

Everyone crowded in a little closer to the fire, taking seats at the long table or sitting on the hearth stones. Griff leaned back against the table beside me, giving me a sleepy kind of smile. Shiver perched up on the table on my other side, looking far more bright-eyed and awake than he had any right to be, that time of the morning.

"Every one of you," Bridnow started, folding his hands behind his back, "is here because someone chose you for this mission. Your leadership abilities, your talents, your dedication have all been deemed valuable to the support of this facility and the people who live here." He paused, his gaze drifting over every face, pausing on a few. "The people here are under our protection. That is a sacred trust, and your first and more important duty. These people are, by and large, defenseless, and utterly dependent on you to protect them. Many of them are no more than children. What you are undertaking is an awesome responsibility. Do not let them down."

I felt a little burn of pride at his words, and my nerves raced with anticipation—part fear, part hope. The doubting little voice that was always in the back of my mind wondered if I was capable of living up to Bridnow's expectations. The pride in me insisted I could do anything I set my mind to, and I'd never let him, or Tarik, down.

*Whatever it takes*, I told myself. *You can do this.*

*Yes,* Piper whispered, nodding approval to me, *you can.*

"That being said," Bridnow went on, "our first order of business is to see to the actual defense of this facility. I don't mean that we're all going to be practicing battle maneuvers and preparing to engage the Cavnish Royal Army any time soon. But it does mean that we will be setting up rotating watches at both the front gate and the depot gate of this facility. You will not be the only ones who are assigned to post, but one of you will be on duty at either location, or standing by as the officer or sergeant of the watch, at all times."

"Sergeant," someone echoed—Lev, I realized. "We've got ranks?"

"Congratulations," Bridnow said, straight-faced, hiding a faint smile. He indicated me and Griff, who were closest to him. "The four in charge of you are my lieutenants. I expect you will treat them with the respect and honor that an officer deserves."

Scorch shifted his weight, his gaze drifting between Anuk and Bridnow. "Does that mean we have to take orders from them?"

Anuk folded his arms, and some of the other sergeants looked a bit uneasy, but Bridnow didn't even twitch. He just stared straight at Scorch and said, "Yes."

"From *him,*" Scorch persisted, nodding at Anuk.

"He is Shade's representative here," Bridnow said, which wasn't what I'd expected him to say at all. I'd thought he would rebuke Scorch for being trucky, or tell him he could leave if he didn't think he could stomach being second to Anuk.

But the far bigger surprise came when Scorch's gaze snapped to Bridnow's face, the color fading slightly from his already pale cheeks. He didn't say a word. He just nodded, once to Bridnow, then to Anuk, and subsided.

I caught a couple of the other sergeants exchanging silent glances, but no one spoke.

Bridnow let the moment hang in the air, then he nodded and planted his fingertips on the table. "Now," he said. "Let's get started."

Later, when Bridnow had finally dismissed us for the day, I lingered in the common room watching the others moving their belongings into the bunk room. Bridnow was sitting at the big table, cleaning one of his revolvers with a slow, methodical process.

"Hayli, I need you to start building up a watch roster," he said, without looking up. "Anyone out there who you think would be reliable and stout on post. We'll assign them watches and you can instruct them in the lessons we talked about today."

For half a tick I just gaped at him. I wanted to question his judgment. Stars, I wanted more than anything to tell him he'd got the wrong girl. I couldn't do what he needed. I could barely write. I wasn't a great judge of character. I didn't know everybody. I could barely remember the First Three Duties he had been trying all morning to drill into our heads. The list of excuses went on forever, growing and growing in my own mind till I thought there was a whole mountain of reasons why I should back down and walk away.

I drew a narrow breath and said, "Yes, sir."

He had his head bent, but not enough that I didn't see how his mouth twitched in a smile. Then he set down the revolver and glanced up at me. "Something else you needed?"

I lifted a hand, indicating the bunk room. "What you said to Scorch earlier," I said, "when he was being difficult. How'd you know what to say to him?"

Bridnow looked pleased that I'd asked the question, and he got up and came around the table to stand beside me. "What do you know about Scorch?"

"He's an arrogant, conceited ba—"

I bit my tongue on the name I wanted to call him, the name I'd heard Shade call him often and almost, it seemed, affectionately. Bridnow laughed aloud, guessing what word I meant to say.

"That's all true," he said. "What else?"

I thought a moment, then tipped my head as the realization hit me. "He worships Shade. I mean, sometimes I think he actually *worships* him. Never seen him so devoted to anybody in all the time I've known him, not even Rivano."

"Well, there you have it."

"So," I said, considering, "you figured if you told him that Anuk stood for Shade, that would make Scorch fall in line?"

"Anuk doesn't just represent Shade," Bridnow said. "As Scorch's commanding officer, Anuk acts in the person of Shade. For Scorch, Anuk is Shade for all intents and purposes. So, insubordination to Anuk is no different than insulting Shade to his face. And for all Scorch may be an arrogant, self-important bastard, he is, as you rightly observed, fanatically devoted to Shade. Any other tack with him would have gone awry. If you understand what motivates people, Hayli, you will be a more effective leader for them. But that requires getting to know your people, because what motivates Scorch is not the same as what motivates you, for example."

I straightened a little at that, puzzled. Did Bridnow not think I was devoted to Shade? Wasn't I just as loyal as *Scorch*, of all people? I was... wasn't I?

If Bridnow sensed my distress, he didn't show it. He just gave me an enigmatic smile and turned back to his revolver. "Go and start working on that roster now, Lieutenant. You'll find paper and a pencil in the command office."

Dismissed, I gave him my best approximation of a salute and went to find the paper.

# Chapter 10 ✦ Tarik

*J* LEFT AGNIR SITTING BY THE BEACH AND MADE MY WAY TO THE HORSE PEN, preferring anything to going inside the hut and facing Mirin with all his doubts and accusations. I found Iskari inside the shelter, saddling the last of the four horses. Nika, I was somewhat relieved to see, had gone back inside the hut; her constant judgment was almost as trying as Mirin's. Iskari glanced at me across the horse's broad back as he tightened the saddle girth.

"You look cheerful," he said.

I glared at him and offered my hand to one of the other horses, letting her snuffle at it in hopes of finding something to eat. Not an apple, surely. I wondered, idly, what sort of treat Istian horses were accustomed to getting. The horse's snow-soft lips slapped at my empty palm, then she, disappointed, snorted and turned away with a shake of her coarse white mane. I caught myself smiling.

"Mirin recognized me after all," I said after a moment.

Iskari stopped what he was doing, barely, then let the saddle flap drop down against the horse's flank. "So," he said. "Do we leave him here?"

"Iskari," I said, exasperated. "What do you think?"

"I think he's a bit more dangerous than you are at the moment, as far as my country is concerned, and that's significant."

"You really think I'm dangerous to Istia?"

He studied me a while, head tipped just a little back, as if I were some kind of text he couldn't quite interpret. I wondered if he could tell how troubled I was at the thought that he might be right.

"I think you're dangerous," he said flatly. "To Istia? Yes, but not only."

I bowed my head. The grey mare butted my arm with her nose, then leaned her broad forehead against my shoulder. I wanted to smile; my throat closed tight instead. Of all things, the damn horse trusted me.

"That isn't what I want," I said. My voice sounded hollow.

"Regardless." He moved to the other side of the tall bay horse, standing with his back to me now as he adjusted the straps and fittings. "Watch yourself, or you may wake up one night with a Cavnish knife at your throat."

"I'm well aware," I said. "Don't worry. Mirin can't hurt me."

I heard him laugh, mirthless. "And you wonder that I say you're dangerous. Your father was dangerous. But even he had a weakness— some kind of human affection. It's what got him killed in the end."

"I have no affection for Mirin, if that's what you're thinking," I said, then added bitterly, "And anyway, I already seem to be following Eyid's footsteps. I let the girl I love shoot me in the heart. Or try."

He turned around at that, that same skeptical, bewildered look in his eyes—half fascinated, half repulsed. "Well, that was a stupid thing to do."

"You wouldn't understand if I explained."

He snorted softly. "Fair enough."

Nika came into the pen behind us, and I leveled a hard look at Iskari, daring him to reveal the nature of my near-untimely death to his sister. His mouth quirked in a crooked smile and he turned back to his work.

"Almost done?" Nika asked, laying a hand on the bony nose of a long-legged gelding. "If I have to endure that sailor's stare one more minute I'm going to put out his eyes."

"Might not be a bad idea," Iskari said. "Cut out his tongue too while you're at it."

"God," I said.

"Oh, poor Taumir. Have I offended your Cavnish sensibilities? I know you people only like polite warfare."

I opened my mouth, trying to think of a retort, failing. He gave me a savage grin, and Nika laughed as she took her horse's reins and led

221

him out into the open to fix her saddlebags. Mirin was already standing outside the hut, waiting for us, bundled up in as much fur and leather as Agnir's family had been able to spare him. I caught him watching me, and looked away.

"Take that horse, Taumir," Iskari said, nodding at the grey mare who was still leaning on me. "For some reason she seems to like you."

At my indignation he threw his head back and laughed, loud and unrestrained, and took the other two horses out onto the moss. Bristling, I led the mare after him, and accepted the saddlebags that Nika handed me. I was just fixing the straps when I felt a hand on my shoulder, and I turned to see Agnir standing behind me with something in his arms—a lump of black leather by the looks of it. Then he shook it out and I realized, with an unexpected flash of grief, that it was Zagger's coat. When I didn't move, Agnir put it in my arms.

"Unlikely as it is, that washed up on shore not ten minutes ago," he said, a smile in his eyes. "Thought you might like to have it back."

I clutched the thing against my chest, not even caring that it was soaking wet, not wanting to admit how much it mattered to me. I wasn't that sentimental, and I wasn't that insecure, but I held onto that coat like a lifeline.

Iskari, looking on, made a noise of disbelief and said, "Was it yours?"

"No," I said, hoarse, hating how badly my voice was shaking. "No, it's not mine."

Iskari and Nika exchanged a glance, then Nika shook her head and swung up onto her horse's back. Iskari held the head of a small, stocky horse for Mirin, who climbed awkwardly into the saddle, then he tossed the reins to Nika before mounting his own bay horse.

I couldn't thank Agnir; I knew I didn't need to. Without a word I turned and tied the coat to the back of the saddle with the saddle bags, then swung up onto the horse's back. She side-stepped, spirited in the cold, and toyed with the bit in her mouth, puffing great clouds of steam from her nostrils. I sat quietly, reveling in the feeling of being on horseback again, and slowly the mare subdued to stand patiently beneath me.

Agnir reached up to clasp my arm. "I wish I could go with you, but I'll join you as soon as I can. I know you're struggling. I see it in your eyes, for all you try to hide it. You've got a stranger destiny than I can even imagine laid out at your feet, but I know it's a terrible thing to face the sea alone." I shuddered and bowed my head. "Just remember, we all travel through this life together. Some of us walk on feet of clay, but some of us…some of us voyage on paper wings, and ships built of starlight."

I held his gaze a moment, then turned the mare's head and cantered after the others.

WE RODE HARD ALL THE REST of the day, just as Nika had promised. Mirin looked almost dead with exhaustion when I finally saw what seemed to be a small hut jutting up like a promise from the barren landscape. As we reached it and Nika slowed her horse, my heart sank. The stone building was barely larger than my own horse's stall at the stables of Brigun Palace, almost half the size of Agnir's woefully cramped hut, and there was nothing at all around it as far as I could see. But it was obviously our destination.

Nika jumped down from her horse's back and the rest of us followed a little more slowly, Mirin almost falling over when his feet hit the ground. I hardly fared better; my legs were still sea-weak, and the long hours of riding had done them no favors. I hit the ground hard, and stumbled half a step back as the muscles inside my thighs threatened to seize in cramps, and hoped in vain that no one had noticed.

"Take off their tack and turn them loose," Nika said, nodding at the horses.

"Loose?" I echoed.

She gave me a cold look. "They need to eat. They have to be free to forage if they're to get enough. Don't worry, they'll come back."

I shrugged and complied, removing my horse's saddle and bridle and then moving over to help Mirin with his horse, because he was staring at the buckles and straps like he had never seen them before. His face was like vinegar as he watched me. I ignored him; I didn't have the energy to confront him. The horses, free of their burdens, trotted some distance away from the stone shelter to graze.

"What is this place?" I asked Iskari, as I followed him and his sister toward the hut.

"Traveler's outpost," he said. "Just a place to sleep."

At the doorway he stepped aside to let me go in ahead of him. It was blessedly warm inside the hut; in the center of the tiny space there was a steam pit just like in Agnir's home. Three pairs of bunks lined the walls, dressed with little more than wool-stuffed mattresses and pillows, and no bedsheets or blankets. There was no other furniture.

Nika tossed her saddlebags onto the top bunk on the left wall, all but a heavy leather sack that carried ground grains and other ingredients for her steamed bread. Iskari claimed the bunk below hers, and I took the lower bunk opposite. Mirin went rigidly to the bottom bed on the wall opposite the door, and without a word to any of us lay down facing away from the room.

"I don't think he likes you," Nika said to me, already kneading a thick dough in her hands.

"I don't care," I said.

She snorted and tied the dough into a linen wrap, then lowered it down into the steam pit. Iskari had taken off his boots and stretched out on the bunk flat on his back, hands tucked behind his head. I grimaced. My feet were cold; I didn't much care for the thought of removing my own boots. The thought of it sent me wandering through a memory of my first night on the streets of Brinmark, when I'd seen Zip's father with his purple feet, trying to steal my boots. I'd eventually given them to Zip for his father, but it hadn't mattered. The winter or the rebellion or some slow sickness had taken his life in the end.

I sighed and leaned over my knees. No one spoke.

Late that night, I was jolted from a troubled, nonsense dream, pricked with the unnerving feeling of being watched. It was completely dark—there were no windows, no lanterns, no soft glow of firelight to break the shadows. I couldn't even see the hand in front of my face. But beneath the constant whining, wailing of the wind that battered the little hut, I could hear the shallow sound of breathing, much too close to my own face.

"What do you want?" I whispered.

"What do I want?" Mirin said, his voice a scant hiss. "What do I want, Godarson? Revenge. That's what I want. I want your blood on this knife."

I'd started to sit up but at his words I froze, suddenly aware of the bite of a knife blade against my neck. Mirin laughed quietly.

"Don't be a fool," I said, and all I could think was, *Well, Iskari was right about the Cavnish knife.*

"What are you going to do?"

"You have gall, anyway," I muttered. "You know who I am, and you still dare to threaten me."

"You're only human," he said.

For some reason his words irritated me, and I Pushed him roughly back. He hit the floor with a grunt, and the knife clattered out of his hand. Then I heard him yelp in surprise amid the sounds of a faint scuffle.

Iskari's voice gritted in broken Cavnish, "What are you doing?"

"What any true-blooded Cavner would do in my place."

"Nika, get a light," Iskari said.

I hadn't realized she was awake too, but then, the room was so small, I couldn't imagine she hadn't heard our quiet confrontation. In a moment there was a spark in the darkness, and a candle's soft glow fractured the shadows, revealing Nika sitting on the edge of her bunk, and Iskari near the steam vent with his arm locked around Mirin's neck, holding him pinned effortlessly. Mirin had stopped struggling, but he was glaring at me with venomous hatred. I stayed where I was, lying on my back, and stared up at the bottom of the bunk above me.

"Taumir?" Iskari said.

"You don't know, it seems," I said to Mirin, ignoring Iskari, "what happened in Avnaya Square, before Trabin died."

Mirin hissed and tried once to break Iskari's lock on his neck, and failed. "Before you killed him?"

I turned at that, rage bleeding through me. "I did not kill the King. Why would I, when he had just proclaimed an alliance with the mages?"

Mirin froze, face pallid, mouth hanging open in disbelief. "What? He didn't—he wouldn't."

"He did. He proclaimed an alliance with me." I lurched off the bed, and Iskari, reading my intent, released Mirin into my waiting hands. I grabbed the Cavner by the neck and dragged him off the ground, driving him back until he hit the post of his bed. "Why would I have any reason to kill him?"

"I don't believe you," Mirin said. His voice was garbled under the pressure of my hand—I held it against his throat, not quite hard enough to knock him senseless, but hard enough to make him uncomfortable. "You're a filthy liar."

"If I'm right? What do you think would happen to Cavnal if

Istia breaks alliance with her, and all because you, Cavner, dared to assassinate their Godarson? Do you think you would escape a war then? Do you think there would be any end to the devastation?"

"If Istia doesn't ally with Cavnal, then Cromis and Meritac will, and Istia will *pay*—"

I tightened my hand on his throat. "You would never know what hit you."

"Is that a threat, Godarson?"

"Taumir," Nika said, very quietly.

I shoved the Cavner away from me, and stumbled a step back. Was it a threat? I didn't even know. If Istia was targeted by Cavnal, would I protect this place, or turn my back on it to ally with the only homeland I'd ever known? The choice was impossible. I only knew I had to prevent that situation from ever developing, no matter the cost—and I would do it, too.

No matter the cost.

I glanced around the room—at Nika, watching me with an undecipherable look on her face, at Iskari, glaring at Mirin with murderous intent. Holding my hand toward him, warning him away, I turned back to Mirin.

"Do not threaten me again."

To my surprise, he subsided. Folding in a little on himself, he picked up his knife and stashed it in his bag, then lay down on his bunk facing the wall again. I rounded on Iskari.

"Leave him alone."

"He would have—"

"He couldn't if he tried," I said. "And I want him alive."

He regarded me a long while in enigmatic silence, then, with a nod of his head that looked curiously akin to a bow, he retreated to his bed. As I lay back down on my bunk, Nika blew out the candle.

WE TRAVELED ANOTHER DAY WITHOUT ANY further trouble from Mirin, and arrived late in the afternoon at a small village—a town, Nika called it, but I saw no more than ten buildings clustered together on one solitary, unpaved road. To me it barely even deserved the name *village*. There was a single restaurant combined with a hostel for travelers, a smithy, a meeting hall, a market, and a mere handful of houses. Nothing else. Nika told me that some of the villagers lived in farmhouses some distance up in the nearby hills, but looking at the barren slopes, I couldn't even imagine what there was for them to farm.

A small crowd slowly drew in as we arrived at the hostel, no more than twenty or thirty people, wrapped in thick coats and scarves. I guessed the oddity of a small swarm of visitors was enough to draw them from their business.

"Eh, Agnirsdatr," an older man called, waving to Nika. "Didn't you just pass through last week going the other way?"

"She's always coming and going," someone else said. "Who are your friends, Nika?"

"No friends of mine," she retorted, with a toss of her head. "That one we rescued from the sea."

She pointed at Mirin, then turned toward me, considering. I imagined she was trying to decide if she should tell them who I was; I wasn't sure myself if I thought she should.

Iskari spoke before she could. "That one is Taumir Eyidson."

A low muttering chased through the crowd. Nika speared a warning glance at her brother, but Iskari gave her a placid, indifferent kind of look in reply.

"The sea doesn't lie, Nika," he said softly, and her lips tightened in a thin line.

"That's our Godarson?" a man of middling years asked, taking a step closer to me.

All of their eyes were riveted on me, now, and I felt suddenly self-conscious. I wondered if they expected me to make a speech, or introduce myself formally; I had no desire to speak to any of them.

"He's young," someone said, as if I weren't standing right there.

Another said, "Rigvar will make a plaything out of him."

I turned to face the man who said it. I didn't speak, but I met his gaze, and held it. He, turning several shades paler, gave me a slight bow and shifted away from the crowd, and in his wake the crowd began to fragment and drift away. When I turned back around I found Iskari watching me closely, hiding a smile.

# Chapter 11 — Jarik

I WAS GIVEN MY OWN ROOM IN THE HOSTEL, WHICH SURPRISED ME WHEN I learned that the others had taken up lodging in the common dormitories. I wasn't sure who had arranged it, but I certainly had no intention of complaining. The room was a tiny space, with one narrow window at the highest point of the slanting roof, the bed tucked uneasily under the lowest part where I'd have to mind my head sitting up. But there were several thick blankets for the bed, woven of grey wool striped with red, and a pumping wash basin that gushed steaming water when I tested it. A vent in the wall close to the floor channeled warm air into the room from somewhere underground.

I had barely freshened up from the ride when someone started pounding on my thin door. When I opened it I found Iskari waiting there, staring away down the hall, one hand on the heavy leather messenger bag he had slung over his shoulder.

"Time for food," he said, and added as he strode away, "It's downstairs."

Bemused, I grabbed Zagger's coat off the chair and followed Iskari down into the restaurant, where a handful of people were already sitting at long tables. There were candles everywhere against the growing darkness outside, but it wasn't bright. I took a seat opposite Iskari, close to a steam vent, and tried to ignore how everyone in the room was staring at me.

Nika joined us a moment later, saying, "Mirin doesn't want food."

"Maybe he thinks it'll just be more dried herring," I said, which brought a faint smirk to her face.

A server came by and dropped bowls of lamb stew in front of us, along with some thick, coarse bread and mugs of ale.

"Did you order—" I started.

"What's to order?" Iskari said, laughing. "This is all they serve. Eat it and be glad."

"Oh, I'm glad about anything that isn't dried fish and Nika's steam bread."

She glared at me, but then, to my surprise, her whole face brightened and she laughed aloud. For a few minutes we ate in silence, while I contemplated the fact that this was the first time the silence between us hadn't felt hostile, or even indifferent.

"Tell me about Rigvar," I said as I finished the last of my stew.

Iskari made a noise of contempt, and Nika gave him a churlish look—if there was anything the two of them disagreed on, I gathered, it was Rigvar. And—possibly—me.

"He's a warmonger," Iskari said flatly.

"He's Istian," Nika countered.

Iskari shook his head. "They're not always the same thing. Rigvar believes Istia stands above all other nations. According to some of the histories, we're oldest, the firstborn nation, the people that all other peoples once descended from. And so he doesn't believe in compromise with any other nation. If it doesn't benefit Istia, he wants nothing to do with it. Even treaties and trade alliances mean nothing to him—I think he would rather see Istia completely unshackled from any foreign ties. Let Istia be Istia, and let the rest of the world sink to the Seven Circles for all he cares."

I picked at my bread, considering. "You don't believe that?"

"What, that Istia is, and should be, supreme?" Iskari asked, and I lifted a hand in affirmation.

"Yes," Nika answered, without hesitation.

"No," Iskari said. "I don't. At least, not to the extent that I would willingly see harm come to our allies. That doesn't mean I don't prefer Istia to every other nation. I do, of course. But I'm a sailor, and if that life has taught me anything, it's that people and nations come and go. Their concerns come and go, and change with the winds. Only the sea is constant, and unchanging." I pursed my lips and looked away, but Iskari didn't seem to notice. He went on, "But Rigvar is something else. He not only thinks Istia is above all others, but that mages are superior to non-mages. In his view, the *aydrding* should never be worn by a non-mage. Mages should never suffer to be ruled by non-mages."

I glanced at Nika—surely that would have given her a moment's pause in her support of Rigvar, since she was not a mage. I'd heard that Iskari wasn't a mage from Agnir, and wondered if that was one reason he, at least, had no loyalty to my opponent.

"Essentially he's the opposite of the Cavnish nobility," I said, "who see mages as inferior, and somehow less than human."

"I suppose so. What about you, Taumir? Do you think mages are superior to non-mages?"

There was a challenge in the question, but I shrugged it off. "Why should I? You're all the same to me."

He drew back at that, studying me with that peculiar look on his face again. "*We're* all the same? What do you mean by that?"

"Hm?" I said, frowning; I couldn't understand why my words had provoked him.

"You said we're all the same to you."

"And so? Mages, non-mages...what difference is there between you, except that some have abilities that others don't—but isn't that true of everything? You can sail, I can't, but I—"

"*Between you?*" Nika echoed, interrupting me, exchanging a look with Iskari. "What, aren't you a mage? Or do you think you're superior to all of us, with your impossibility of power?"

"*Veka*, no," I said, appalled. "That's...that's not what I meant." I looked away, throat tight, and added very quietly, "Nothing could be further from the truth."

I didn't know if they had heard me or not, but I didn't dare look at them to see. No one said anything else for the rest of the meal, until Nika finished the last of her bread and climbed off the bench.

"There's a *kavathika* out in the village court tonight," she said then, "if you want to come."

And with that she headed from the dining hall, leaving Iskari and me in uneasy silence.

"What's a *kavathika*?" I asked.

"A...what would you say, like a party, I suppose? Dancing, music, drinking. A way to pass the time." He shrugged, and I could tell his thoughts were elsewhere. Finally he leaned forward, resting his elbows on the table. "Do you not see value in yourself?"

I jolted, and stared at him. In all my life, no one had ever asked me that. No one had ever dared ask me so bluntly. In fact, I didn't know that anyone had ever even let the thought enter their minds, except perhaps Zagger, who had known all my struggles so well. A bitter ache seeped through me and I leaned my chin on my hand, willing away the hollow grief.

I drew a slow, shallow breath and said, "How long do you have to lie about yourself before it becomes the truth?" He just watched me quietly with no judgment in his eyes. Given his obsession with honesty, that surprised me, and I faltered. But I'd started down that path, and I realized that I, desperately, wanted someone to walk it with me. I asked, "Have you ever found something washed up on the shore, and you can't figure out what it is?"

"Naturally, many times."

"What do you do with it?"

"Toss it back to the sea," he said, shrugging.

"Why?"

"If I've no notion what it is, or what it's for, how could it be worth anything to me?"

I said nothing, and for a moment he just studied me, eyes dark and shamed, and I knew he'd drawn the connection all on his own.

"I don't know what I am," I said. "I'm nothing. I'm a confusion, a cacophony. Everything I thought I was is a lie. Everything I try to be turns to blood and stone, and..." I could feel myself slipping, could feel Iskari's gaze turn sharp with alarm. I pressed my head against my hands. "I'm broken and endless and there's no meaning to any of it. Tell me, what's the worth of that?"

And God, I didn't know why I was saying any of this to Iskari, who had barely gotten over his hatred of me, who would surely realize I was mad and would abandon me without remorse—my one ally, apart from Agnir, in all this barren and empty land. I was a fool, hoping for refuge in someone's friendship, not realizing that all I had to offer was ash and thorns.

"People aren't things," Iskari said, very quietly. "Our worth isn't measured by our use."

"Then what?"

He didn't answer immediately, but he kept studying me, brows drawn, eyes a little narrowed, like he was puzzling me out. And then all at once he dropped both his hands to the table with a bang, startling everyone around us, and sat back.

"*Vingathur thrigun stodadrakkim…*" he stated, drawing out every single syllable of the profanity.

I withdrew, uneasy. "What?"

"I know who you are," he said, shaking his head in disbelief. Then he leaned forward and said, almost in a whisper, "You're the damn Crown Prince of Cavnal."

For too long I couldn't answer. I couldn't even breathe. And Iskari just watched me like he could read the truth of his words in my eyes. Maybe he could.

Finally I said, "How?"

He pulled something from his messenger bag and slid it across the table toward me. "I've been thinking about this since I found it in the bunk room up there."

It looked like little more than a pamphlet, but I realized as I picked it up that it was a newspaper from Bregjarvani, dating from a week or so prior. The story on the front page was all about King Trabin's death. And centered on the spread was a photograph of Avnaya Square, with the mage who looked like me, and me, who looked like Tarik behind the ornate mask I'd been wearing. And there was Zagger, standing behind my shoulder. Everyone else in the photograph was looking at the other mage, but Zagger was looking at me.

My throat tightened and I shoved the paper back toward him.

"Story says that the mage called the Zealot claimed to be Prince Tarik," Iskari said, his eyes never leaving my face, "and was called a liar. But you *weren't* lying, were you. And what you told me about being shot by the girl you love, that's all in this story too." He shook his head. "That mark you wear—you can change your appearance. Is that even your real face?"

"No," I said, very quietly. "But I didn't intend to make myself look like Eyid, if that's what you're wondering. I did that by accident."

He folded his arms on the table. Somehow he didn't seem as surprised or taken aback by the revelation as I'd expected, just curious. Not hostile.

"You're the damn Crown Prince of Cavnal," he said again, as if repeating it could make the truth more palatable. "You're…you should be the damn *King* of Cavnal, now."

"I would need the approval of the Court, and a vote of the people," I said. "It's mostly symbolic, of course, but you realize the problem, when they all think *I'm* a mage, and that other mage looks just like me and could probably fool them all. But he disappeared after Avnaya, and now I've disappeared too. So, as far as anyone in Cavnal knows, there is no Prince, and no King, and it's up to the Court of Ministries to keep everything from falling apart."

Iskari tapped the paper. "That other mage. Who is he?"

I shook my head. "Trouble," I said. "I don't know. But I...I feel like I've seen him before."

"Maybe when you looked in a mirror?" Iskari asked. He said it without humor, but I laughed.

"It's not like that. It's like...a knowing inside. Like his face doesn't matter. It's his spirit I recognize."

"That sounds..." He faltered, an incredulous look on his face. "It sounds strange, you realize."

I didn't think *strange* was exactly the word he was reaching for, but I let it pass without comment.

"So you're the heir to the Cavnish throne," he went on, "and you're in Istia, vying for the *aydrding*. What am I to make of that?"

"If Cavnal accepts that I'm the person they've always known as Prince Tarik, and I'm also the mage known as the Zealot, what do you think?" I asked, bitterly.

"But they don't *know* that the Zealot and Tarik are the same person, do they?"

"No. Well, a few of the Ministers and scientists do. One I'm not worried about. The others...I know they wouldn't hesitate to use that information to blackmail me or undermine my authority. But you're missing the point. If I'm a mage, that means I forsake my right to the crown. Do you understand? I'm the heir to the throne, but I don't have a single drop of Cavnish blood in my veins. I have no place in the Caveni family line, so, in honesty, I *have* no right to the crown."

"So? You could take it."

My gaze edged up to meet his, then, when I couldn't understand the look he gave me, I turned away again. For a few moments we sat in pensive silence, then Iskari slapped the table and got to his feet.

"Come on. Enough. Let's go to the *kavathika*."

I stood more slowly, and before he left the dining hall, I grabbed his arm. I didn't need to say a word.

"Don't worry," he said. "I won't tell your secret."

"What if someone asks?"

"Then it's not a secret, is it?"

I pursed my lips as I pulled on Zagger's coat, then followed him out into the cold and the night. We were met by a din of music, a noise of stomping feet and clapping, from a broad court not far from the hostel. In Cavnal I would have called it the village green, but there was nothing green about this space. It was paved in flat black stones, and a low wall bordering the space held countless oil lamps that stank strongly of fish. Some long tables and benches sat near the wall, but the space in the middle was cleared for a whirl of dancers. Iskari headed straight to an empty table, and sat up on top of it with his feet on the bench. I hesitated only a moment before joining him.

Someone deposited mugs of ale in our hands—he moved so quickly I barely saw him before he'd gone again. On the table behind me sat a long tray of flat crisps and something resembling glazed fish heads. Iskari devoured one of the latter; I pretended not to notice when he offered one to me.

Instead I let myself be mesmerized by the dance unfolding in front of me. I'd never seen anything like it. It was wild, and elemental; everything about it felt chaotic, even when I picked out the simple structure of an ordered dance within its movements. Even north Cavnish folk music was more restrained than the discordant melodies of the Istian flutes and fiddles, and the back-and-forth chant of two men facing each other over a massive drum.

I sipped at the ale and found it bitter, traced with a pungent herbal flavor, and strong enough to take the edge off the sharp night wind. Iskari finished his off in a few mouthfuls and the server came around again, filling both of our mugs before I could turn him away. For a while after he left we both drank and watched the scene, me intent on the dance, Iskari's gaze roving ceaselessly over the crowd. Then he suddenly jumped down, stalked over to a girl sitting on a bench nearby, and without a word he took her by the arm and pulled her into the dance. All my Cavnish sensibilities recoiled at the bluntness of it. But somehow I was more surprised at myself, because I felt drawn to those raw Istian customs in a way that I couldn't quite explain, distant as they were from the rigid manners of the Cavnish Court.

"You don't dance?" someone asked me, close at my elbow.

I turned and found a man leaning back against my table, arms folded. His attention was on the dancers, not on me, but I felt a strange prickling sensation in the back of my mind that instantly put me on my guard.

"Sometimes it's better to watch," I said, carefully.

He tipped his head toward me then, and I could see him better in the guttering lamplight. He was fairly young, perhaps in his mid-twenties, with pale hair pulled back in a tail at the nape of his neck and the hint of a beard covering just the end of his chin. His eyes were grey, like mine—like Shade's—and as cold and incisive as Nika's. He was no taller than I was.

Everything about him felt dangerous.

"Indeed," he said.

He looked me up and down once, slow and calculating. Maybe it was the ale I'd drunk, too fast, but I stared straight back at him without flinching.

He said, "I don't think I know you."

"No," I said. "I don't imagine you do."

His mouth quirked in a faint smile. Then his eyes shifted past me and darkened, and I felt a hand latch onto my arm and pull me forward. Startled, I turned to find Nika in front of me, drawing me after her into the dance. There was no amusement in her eyes. I followed her without a word, stepping out into the midst of a spinning line of dancers where, to my relief, my feet caught the pattern of the dance like I'd been raised into it.

"God, Taumir," Nika said. Her gaze still lingered on the man we'd left behind.

"What?" I asked, taunting. "Jealous, Nika?"

She looked at me, finally, her nose wrinkled in spite or disbelief. But then she shot back, "Of whom, him or you?"

I grinned. "Did you know him?"

She spun away from me as the dance drew us apart, and when she joined me at the end of the line and caught my extended hand, she just shook her head.

"Everyone knows him," she said. "That was Rigvar Karvarson."

235

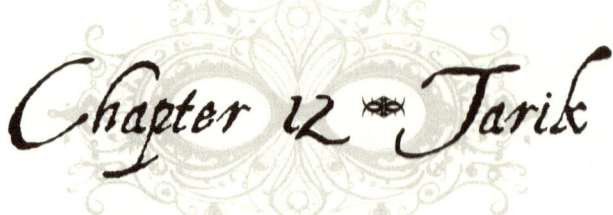

## Chapter 12 · Jarik

"WHAT IS RIGVAR DOING HERE?" I ASKED.

I'd left the *kavathika* after my dance with Nika, and now the three of us were gathered back inside my private room in the hostel. I stood at the window with my back to Iskari and Nika, who were both sitting on my bed.

"Probably on his way to Bregjarvani, same as us," Nika said.

I turned to look at her. "I thought you liked Rigvar. Why not leave me to his mercy and see what would happen?"

She lifted one shoulder in an indifferent shrug. "I could have, but I'm not *that* cold-hearted. I'd at least give you the opportunity of a fair fight. You have no idea what that man is capable of."

"Then tell me."

She hesitated; Iskari said, "He can control people's emotions."

I frowned and took the chair across from them, leaning my elbows on my knees. "Do you mean he's a Whisperer? Or just a Sculptor?"

Nika lifted her hand in annoyance, and I repressed a sigh. I was betraying my Cavnish upbringing again, cataloguing magic into rigid Gifts. Iskari only looked thoughtful, but I doubted he fully understood what I meant by the words either.

"We call mages Sculptors who can manipulate emotions in other people. They can impose fear, hatred, even joy or peace on someone else without their knowledge. A Whisperer..." I hesitated, considering. "I've never met one. I don't know if any exist in the world today. But they're said to be able to speak directly into other people's minds. Give them thoughts, emotions, even memories that aren't real."

Iskari shook his head. "No, Rigvar can't do that. What he does is more the former, if either of them."

I let out a breath, more relieved than I cared to admit. Facing a Whisperer was the last thing I wanted to attempt, if even a fraction of what I'd heard about them was true.

"Is he powerful?" I asked after a moment.

Iskari shrugged. "Well, he never could make *me* give a *viru staga drakk* about him, so..."

Nika stifled a laugh, but sobered when I turned to her. "And what about you?" I asked. "Is that why you're such an avid supporter?"

She blew out her breath and hitched herself back on the bed so she could lean against the wall, her head barely avoiding the low slant of the roof. Iskari lifted a brow faintly at me, hiding a smile.

"No," she said. "I've never been around him long enough or close enough for him to, what would you call it, *Sculpt* me."

"You just think he's attractive," Iskari said.

She glared ice at him. "I do not."

"I don't know, he doesn't look like your typical Istian to me," I said, feeling wicked. "Kind of slight. Not the strong *warrior* type."

"And you should talk," she snapped, which only made me laugh. Her face reddened, surprising me, and she got abruptly to her feet. "I should have asked *him* to dance."

"I'm sure I would've enjoyed that more," I said.

She stared at me half a moment, then flung a hand toward me, thumb extended. Without another word to either of us, she strode out of the room and slammed the door behind her. Iskari got up a minute later, still laughing.

"Get some sleep, if you can," he said. "Leave Rigvar for tomorrow."

I showed him out of the room, then threw myself across the bed with my head in my arms, and tried to forget about Rigvar and Sculptors and dancing under the stars with the wind and the fire.

*BUT THE DANCE FOLLOWS ME INTO my dreams, and the dance floor isn't black stone carved from a hostile land but the bright and endless sky. I feel myself moving, spinning, catching the rhythm of the wind and the currents of the earth. There is no one at all around me. But then from the waning moon a dark shadow steps, and I realize it is Hayli, but her hair is made of feathers and she wears a dress of mourning black and auburn silk. We circle each other once, slow, coming closer and then closer still, until I feel her presence so strongly I could reach out and touch her hand.*

*"They're fighting again," she whispers, turning her shoulder to me, her gaze holding mine as she steps around me.*

*"They're always fighting," I answer.*

*I don't know who we're talking about, but in the way of dreams, I do.*

*Then past her shoulder I see two men locked in a struggle. They are pale and tall, almost identical in every way, and their faces are grim. They have been fighting for years. They began a moment ago.*

*"They'll bring Death to us all," Hayli says. "Won't you stop them?"*

*"How can I? They're fighting on account of me," I say, and I don't mean the two men who stand before us.*

*And as I watch, one of the men staggers and drops to a knee. He is all pale, pale in every detail except the blood that stains his chest and pools around his knees. The other takes a step back, and turns into the wind.*

*"Brother, wait," says the man kneeling, but his brother is gone. Then he bows his head and turns into the sea.*

*"They're always fighting," Hayli says, and she doesn't mean the two men who have gone.*

*I stand on the edge of the night, and too late I notice that Hayli has gone, too. Everyone has gone, and I am alone, tracing the warp and weft of the stars to find their meaning.*

"Well, you look like hell."

I cracked open my eyelids and was met with a glare of bright daylight, and Iskari's broad silhouette framed by my window. Throwing an arm over my face, I focused on taking a few slow, deep breaths to quiet the raging pain in my head.

"I didn't drink that much, did I?" I muttered.

He snorted. "I don't remember. You were fine last I saw you, though. Unless you want back to the *kavathika* after we left?"

"No," I said, darkly. "*Veka*, I feel like…I feel like I've been fighting all night." Seeing his frown I added, "Not physically. With my magic. Or…against it. I don't know. It's all broken."

"You realize that sometimes you sound…"

His voice trailed off, and I tipped my head back to regard him. "What, Iskari, where's your honesty?"

"I've told no lie," he said. He pushed away from the wall as I sat up, and took the chair across from me. "Nika wants to leave before we run into Rigvar again. Are you ready to go?"

"Give me a few moments," I said, and leaned over my knees. He didn't move, so maybe he thought I expected—or wanted—him to stay near. I finally lifted my face to look at him. "Iskari, do Istians put stock in dreams?"

"You mean, attribute them to divine visitation or the like?" he asked. "Some do, I suppose. I've never had a dream that I'd consider a worthy message of *Veka*, but then, maybe I'm just not a worthy recipient of his messages."

He shrugged, toying with the oil lamp sitting on the low table beside him. It was unlit, but at a sudden roguish impulse I gave a slight nudge to the wick with my magic, and it leapt into flame. Iskari snatched his hand back from the knob and stared at it, then at me. When I only laughed, he flicked me an obscene gesture.

"You thought that was funny?"

I grinned in answer, and Iskari surprised me by laughing out loud.

"*Ganthiskur stodadrakkim*," he said, cheerfully, and I didn't feel insulted, even though I gathered he'd just called me mad—among other things. "So, what did you dream that has you so unnerved? You're even stranger than usual this morning."

I sobered with a frown as I tried to recall, but the details were slipping away from me, leaving only an impression of fear and confusion. Hayli had walked through the dream, I remembered, but all I could feel now was her absence. Not for the first time I wished that I had Pika's gift, so that I could see if Hayli was well—if she had ever returned from her sojourn as the crow, if the people in the smelter had welcomed her back. It was the one hope I held fast to.

"Taumir?" Iskari prompted, reminding me of my dream, and how I hadn't answered him.

"There was fighting."

"Well, if that's a sign of divine visitation, then I must be half-god," he said.

I ignored him. "It was two brothers, I think. I don't know who they were, or why they were fighting. I felt like I knew them, though."

"Their spirits?" he asked, blandly, reminding me of what I'd said about the mage in the plaza. I glared at him, and he lifted his hands in an innocent shrug.

"Something like that," I said. "It was nonsense, I'm sure. I just felt so certain that it meant something."

"Maybe it does. Who am I to say? Have you ever had dreams that meant something before?"

"Maybe," I said. "No...I don't know. Sometimes I have this dream, or a memory...I can't tell what it means, or if it actually happened. I used to go out in the city at night, Iskari, all the time. Sometimes with a friend, or a few friends, but mostly I'd go alone. I would just wander the streets...get into little mischiefs if I felt like it, run-ins with the city coppers, that sort of thing, which of course the Herald liked to drag completely out of proportion in their stories. Usually nothing happened, but...then there were nights when...when I would wake up in the morning back in my bedroom, and have no memory of coming home. I couldn't remember anything at all of the night before, except these flashes of memories of sitting in front of a mirror, and talking... talking endlessly...but, it was the strangest thing, and this is where I start thinking it was just a bad dream, because when I spoke, the reflection never moved at all."

"What were you talking about?" Iskari asked, haltingly.

"Oh, I don't even know. I can't remember that. Nothing, maybe. Everything. But like I said, it was always the same, so I'm sure it was just a bad dream, a recurring nightmare." I hesitated, twisting my hands together. "It makes sense as a dream. It makes no sense as a memory."

"Well," he said. "That was insightful." He leaned back and crossed his feet at the ankles, regarding me a long while in silence. I waited, having nothing else to say—nothing else that made any sense. Finally, he said, "I don't know what to tell you. But these dreams, I'm sure they mean something."

I glanced at him in surprise. "Didn't you just call me *ganthiskur*? Maybe it's only madness."

"Maybe," he said, echoing me. It was beginning to feel like the word that defined my life. "But I doubt it. I can't say why. Although, if it really was some message the gods wanted you to hear, I might have thought you'd remember it better."

"*Ethu, ethu*," I said, using a phrase I'd heard the sailors say from time to time, which as far as I could tell indicated reluctant agreement.

Iskari grinned. "Ah, you're finally starting to sound Istian. Just need to make you a little less friendly and you'd almost pass for one of us."

"Friendly?" I echoed, bristling, though I didn't know why. Even as Tarik I'd never been considered *friendly* by Cavnish standards, and most people considered Shade to be positively unapproachable.

"Relax, brother," Iskari said. He got to his feet. "I meant no offense."

He left then, but long after he had gone I didn't move. His words shocked me to my core, and my heart ached in the strangest possible way.

No one, not in all my life—not even Griff, my oldest and dearest friend—had ever called me *brother*.

When I made my way down into the dining area, I found Mirin sitting alone at one of the long tables, staring morosely into his bowl of porridge. He looked even less pleased when I dropped onto the bench across from him.

"Good morning," I said, accepting a bowl of the thick gruel and a cup of tangy yoghurt from the server. The server nodded at me as he poured me a cup of coffee, but Mirin just glared more ferociously at his bowl.

"What's good about it?" he muttered.

"Well, you'll be on your way home today, if you're lucky."

He finally looked at me, a wild little flicker of hope in his eyes. "Really?"

I gave him an impatient gesture, and he shook his head in disbelief.

"I was welly sure you'd be tossing me to the fishes," he said. "Div'n think you'd ever let me gan off free on the wing. Why?"

"I have no quarrel with you," I said. I leaned forward, planting my fingertips on the table between us. "I have no quarrel with Cavnal. I wish you would believe that. There is nothing I want more than the alliance between Cavnal and Istia, and for both nations to stay out of a war."

"Well, you're a bigger fool than I reckoned," he said, "if you ken that Cavnal and Istia being friendly will smooth the knots with Meritac and Cromis. More like as not, it will send us all straight into a bigger war than you'd bargained for."

I sighed and picked at my porridge. "Seems there is nothing we can do to stop war from coming."

"No offense to you," Mirin said, "but if we're bound for war anyway, I guarantee you Cavnal would prefer to be in the traces with our southern cousins than with you lot. You're not so dangerous as them."

I regarded him in surprise, and couldn't quite cage in a faint laugh. "Then you're a bigger fool than *you* seem."

"Oh? And where is Istia's army? Where is your navy? You dan' have aught worth the name. You've got naught at all like our weapons."

"Don't misjudge us just because our military doesn't match your expectations. You have no idea how dangerous Istia can be in war."

He narrowed his eyes, his gaze tracing the lines of my mage's mark. "That scientist was right," he said. "What was his name—Kippler? We ought to rob every last one of you Jixies of your magic. Then where would you be? You would be *nothing*."

I bristled. Memories of Kippler, memories of that horrible blindness to magic traced through me—those endless hours trapped below the Common Court, when I had been robbed of every ounce of my power. I had never felt so vulnerable. I had never wished so ardently for death.

"You've always wished for it."

I jerked my head up. "What did you say?"

Mirin's eyes widened, frightened. "I div'n say aught. Y'a'right, man? You're white as foam."

A hand dropped on my shoulder and I jumped, too violently, my heart rattling like bones. Then Iskari was settling onto the bench beside me, but I couldn't stop the way my hands trembled, the way the room darkened all around me. Still Mirin watched me. The weight of his stare was iron on my soul.

"*Veka*," Iskari said, leaning a little away from me. "What's gotten into you?"

I closed my eyes, but in that dark security I saw a sudden flash of light, like twin lamps, amber gold and terrible—a blindness, and a devastation. It was there and gone, but it shocked me to the root of my mind like lightning. I reeled back, coming to my feet, stumbling over the bench as I tried to get free. Iskari's hand was on my arm but I shook him off. Vaguely I was aware of the stunned silence in the dining hall, but I pushed my way blindly through the thin crowd and into the gnawing, feeble daylight outside.

Nika was in the courtyard outside the hostel with the horses already in hand, saddled and laden with all our belongings. When I joined her, resting my hands against the warm fur of my horse's neck for stability, she gave me a long, narrow look.

"I'm fine," I said. "Don't ask."

She made an impressive noise of disdain and tossed her head back, but to her credit she didn't say a word about it. Instead she asked, "Are you ready to go? Where are my brother and the Cavner?"

I gestured weakly back toward the hostel. "Eating, I think. I'm ready."

To prove my point I gathered up my horse's reins and lifted my foot to the stirrup, but the world shivered strangely beneath me and I lost my balance. When Nika laid a hand on my shoulder, I had my forehead pressed against the leather skirt of the saddle, my hand twined tight in the mare's coarse white mane.

"Are you sick?" she asked. "You're burning up."

I untangled my fingers from the horsehair and pressed the back of my hand against my forehead. It was hot, like she'd said, and dry, while all the rest of me felt clammy and cold.

"You were too long in the sea," she said, when I didn't answer, and jutted her lower lip in a disapproving look. "You push yourself too hard."

"Right on both counts," I mumbled. I tipped my head to look at her. "More than you think."

"You should go lay down," she said. "At least until Iskari is ready to leave. I haven't even seen Rigvar this morning, so, we're not in a particular hurry."

I waved a hand and dragged myself onto the horse's back. "I can't sleep any more," I said. "You don't understand. It's all just shadows anyway."

I turned the horse's head before she could answer, and rode down to the water's edge, losing myself in the scrape of hooves in graveled sand until Iskari came to fetch me.

# Chapter 13 ❈ Hayli

*I*F THERE WAS ANYTHING WORSE THAN ACTUALLY SERVING ON GUARD POST, I discovered, it was being the officer of the watch. Presumably I was allowed to sleep the night in my own room, warm and snug in my own bed, but I was also the person the watchmen would go to if anything happened during their shift.

In the few days since we'd started the round of watches, nothing at all had happened, so on my first night as officer of the watch I'd gone to bed sure that I'd finally get some decent sleep. But of course, right in the very middle of the night, I got jarred straight out of a rare pleasant dream by someone out in the corridor, hammering on my door.

With a rather undignified grumble, I threw off my blanket and got up. Outside the door stood a boy who couldn't have been any older than me, and I shifted my weight as he fumbled over a salute.

"Ma'am," he said, which got me even fitsier than ever. "Um…"

"What's gannin' on?" I asked.

I never felt quite so self-conscious about my South Brinmark accent as moments like this, when I felt dead sure I ought to speak fair and proper like an educated person who actually deserved to be saluted and called *ma'am*. But the boy didn't turn his nose up at me. He just pointed away toward Borokhev's front gate.

"Think we need your help, ma'am. There's somewhat peculiar gannin' on and we dan' see what to do about it."

I tugged on a wool cap and scarf and waved for him to lead the way.

As we left the building the boy turned to me and said, "There's a dog at the gate."

I stifled a groan and the urge to clap my hands around my head. *Of all the barmy things you could've woke me up for, it was a dog?* I wanted to say, but instead I nodded and said, "What's the trouble with it? Rabby?"

"Dan' think so. Just dan' seem right. It won't gan away. We threw it a bitty scrap of meat and everything, and it just turned up its sniffer and kept staring at us! Creeps me out, ma'am!"

I frowned, a niggling suspicion creeping into my thoughts, and motioned for him to pick up the pace. We reached the gate and I let out all my breath, because there, sitting in the snow proper as could be, was a rangy black and tan hound I would've recognized anywhere.

"A'right," I said to the two watchmen. "Stand down, and dan' be alarmed." Then I turned to the dog and nodded. "Hello, Creech."

The dog got to its feet, then there was a flurry of dark shadows, and the man Creech was standing before us.

"Blimey!" the younger watchman exclaimed.

Creech barely glanced at him before turning to me. "Evening, Hayli," he said.

I glanced at the sky, and the sliver moon. "Morning, rather, I should think," I said, and jerked my chin at him. "C'mon in." I paused by the watchmen and said, "Good work, coming to wake me. Stay sharp."

The older watchman eyed Creech with stark suspicion, and he opened his mouth to say something, then closed it again as he thought better of it.

"Relax," I said. "I trust this mage."

He gave me a smart salute and turned back to face the road, but I felt the boy's attention follow me and Creech all the way into the facility until the darkness had swallowed us. I led Creech to the officers' building, and once in the common room, I stoked the fire best I could and indicated the chair next to the hearth for Creech. He nodded his thanks and sat down, warming his hands over the low flames.

"I expect there's a reason you came here in the middle of the night," I said, pulling a chair up to face him. "What's gannin' on?"

"Sorry," he said. His gaze sharpened on my face. "I waited for you three nights ago, where we agreed. You didn't come."

I frowned, trying to remember what day it was, and what day

I'd first met Creech. I remembered telling him I'd meet him again in a week, but stars, I'd completely lost track of the time with the move to Borokhev and all that had happened. My stomach pitched at the thought of my failure, but I swallowed back all the hundred excuses that begged to come out.

I just said, "I'm sorry. I'd never have left you hanging intentionally. I hope you'll believe that."

"I heard what happened with the Army. I think you've probably had your hands full. Anyway, I didn't have much to report the other night."

He paused, and I glanced up at him expectantly. "And tonight?"

"I've got some news I thought you'd want to hear," he said. "Remember how we were speculating about what the Cleavers and Klissen's mages would want with the Chernayi?" I nodded. "Well, now you have a chance to find out. They're meeting tomorrow, though I'm not sure what about. But they all know me there, and know my animal nature, too. I can't get close. You, on the other hand, or one of your mages, might be able to."

My heart jumped. "When? Where?"

He hesitated, just for a moment. "Noon tomorrow, at the Cleavers' headquarters," he said. "The sanitarium, up on Front Street. They've holed up where Vanek Meed used to operate."

"*Used* to?" I echoed. Far as I'd ever heard, he was still in business, running whatever shady affairs he'd been handling since Shade and Coins had gone toe to toe with him, trying to extort Alby Durb's name from him at Derrin's request.

"Yes, used to," Creech said, eyeing me. "He was killed during the uprising. You didn't know?"

I shook my head, speechless.

Vanek Meed was dead. I wasn't quite sure my brain was making sense of Creech's words. Meed had been a fixture on the South Brinmark streets for long as I could remember, for long as I'd been on the streets at least. We'd all hated him—he'd been a crook to put all other crooks to shame, the reason behind every bad deal the Hole rats ever got when we'd tried to find work. Still, it seemed somehow... wrong...that he would just be gone without anyone ever being the wiser. Surely the rumor should have gotten out that someone as powerful as Meed had died. Even if everyone had secretly celebrated, at least that would have acknowledged his passing in some way. But he was just gone.

"A'right," I said. "I know the place. I'll take Shiver, and we'll find out what's gannin' on."

He nodded and got to his feet, pausing one last minute by the fire to soak up its warmth before I showed him out into the snowy dark.

"Just as a point of curiosity," I said as we walked. "How'd you know to look for us here?"

He gave me a hidden kind of smile. "We have a mutual friend," he said, and left it at that, which didn't satisfy me at all. We'd arrived at the gate, and he stopped there to clasp my hand. "Be careful," he said.

"You too," I said. "And thanks."

With a parting smile he Shifted to his dog form and trotted off into the night. Soon as he was out of sight, I nodded my thanks to the watchmen again and wandered back into the officers' quarters. I wasn't even surprised when I found Shiver sitting where Creech had been, leaning back with his ankles crossed and arms folded.

"So, the sanitarium," he said.

"Figured you'd heard all that," I muttered, dropping back onto my chair. "Dan' you ever sleep?"

"Sleep's for the dead," he said, flashing me a crooked smile.

I gave him a look. "Well? What d'you think of all that?"

"Not sure. D'you trust him? He hesitated a tick when you asked where the meet was ganna happen. Think he's set you up?"

"Nah," I said. "Think it just occurred to him that he was actually ratting his clan out, good and proper. I dan' na, I'd hope that would give him a minute's pause."

Shiver lifted one shoulder in a shrug. "S'pose so," he said. "Guess there's nothing for it." He got a sly kind of smile and tipped his head to me, and added, "Ma'am."

I glared at him as I stood up. "Dan' forget it, either," I said. For half a tick I hesitated, scowling at the fire. "He said he knew about Borokhev 'cause we've got a mutual friend. D'you suppose anyone here's been double-dealing with the Cleavers?"

"Besides Red?"

"Red dan' na aught about Borokhev," I said.

"I got no ken, then."

I shook my head, much as to acknowledge him as to nudge the

worry to the back of my mind. "Well, get some sleep, if you can," I said. "I'll talk to Bridnow in the morning."

BRIDNOW WAS ALREADY AWAKE WHEN I left my room the next morning, but then, he was always the first one up and about. Sometimes I wondered if he got any more sleep than Shiver apparently did. He was sitting in the wood and leather chair by the hearth—everyone's favorite chair, it seemed—with his coat and hat already on and his gloved hands resting quiet in his lap.

"Shiver said you needed to talk to me," he said, greeting me with a nod as I joined him.

"Creech came by last night," I said, not bothering with a preamble. Bridnow looked to be in a hurry, and I had no mind to delay him more than I needed to. "He said that Klissen and Red's folks were meeting with Chernayi at their headquarters this morning. Thought I'd take Shiver with me and get a goggle at what's the what."

His brows lifted faintly. "Dangerous?" he asked.

"Prob'ly," I said.

"Where is it?"

"Vanek Meed's old base. The sanitarium, round Front Street."

Bridnow made a noise of distaste and got to his feet. "All right. If you're not back by evening I'm sending someone after you."

"We'll be back by then, sure."

"Hayli," he said, pausing beside me with a hand on my shoulder. "You're a lieutenant of the watch here, but don't make the mistake of thinking you're trained to handle unpredictable situations out there." He jerked his chin toward the door. I opened my mouth to protest, but stopped at the warning look in his eyes. "I know Zagger was teaching you some things too—self-defense, weapons handling—and I'm glad of it. All I mean to say is, you're still green. Don't put yourself into dangerous circumstances because you think you need to prove something." He lifted a finger toward me, but somehow it didn't feel aught like one of Kantian's rebukes. "Whatever you do," he said, "do *not* put your sergeant into danger needlessly. You are responsible for his safety. Don't tell me he can take care of himself, because that is not the point. No matter how capable you think him, *I* will hold you personally responsible for anything that happens to him. You are an officer, Hayli, and he is in under your command. Don't forget that."

I swallowed, but somehow—I wasn't quite sure how—I managed to hold his gaze without looking away. "Yes, sir," I said, and my voice sounded sturdier than I felt.

His mouth twitched in a smile and he released my shoulder. "Very well," he said, and with that he was gone, blustering out into the still-dark morning.

I watched him go, then said, "D'you hear all that?"

But Shiver didn't step out of the wall behind me, and no one answered me. Shrugging, I turned to follow Bridnow outside, but just as my hand reached for the door latch, Shiver stepped straight through the door in front of me. We both jumped in surprise.

"Stars, Shiver!" I hissed. "What're you doing?"

He edged past me into the building, giving me an innocent look with his hands lifted. They were full, which explained why he'd walked through the door instead of opening it like an ordinary person.

"Gettin' skappers?" he said, as if it were obvious. When I just looked at him he said, "Well? I was hungry."

"Miss Nan's already got the breakfast out?"

"Sure. Started early today."

I bit my lip. "Is there enough?"

He held out a small pastry toward me, but I shook my head. "Enough," he said with a shrug. "We got folks out on work crews, dan' we? That should help bring in some more supplies."

I let out a breath and nodded, then went to the door of the bunk room and hammered hard as I could on the wooden frame.

"Time for chow!" I hollered, and couldn't keep a little self-satisfied smirk from my lips as the guards who'd been sound asleep jumped in surprise and groaned in protest. Duty fulfilled, I turned back to Shiver. "Hurry up and eat. I wanna gan soon as we can so we can scope out the place before the Chernayi come."

He shoved every last bite of food in his mouth at once, grinned at me around the mess of it, and darted into the bunk room. A minute and he was back, carrying a heavy coat made of midnight blue wool. I considered going back for the little jacket Luce had made me, but in this weather, it would barely make a difference. Shiver eyed me sidelong as he tugged his coat on.

"Where's yours?" he asked.

I scowled. "My what?"

"Your coat?" I shrugged, and Shiver rolled his eyes and stepped through the wall into my private room, reappearing a moment later with a coat bundled in his hands. "Here. Ma'am."

He said it with that faintly mocking tone he always did, but I didn't have the heart to rebuke him for it. Instead I took the coat from his hands and shook it out.

"Where'd this come from?"

"Dan' na," he said, "but all of us in the unit got one."

"Looks like military issue," I said, turning it back and forth, "but the color's all wrong."

"Does it matter? It's warm. Let's go."

I pursed my lips and pulled the coat on, relieved to find that it actually fit me, far better than I'd expected. Shiver's hung loose and unfitted to his knees, and I'd been dead sure mine would wear the same way, but it was actually cut fine like a proper lady's coat, with two rows of buttons down the front instead of Shiver's one. It also had a faint bit of silvery braid around the wide collar and edging the shoulders where the sleeves were set in. It was warm, too, much warmer than I'd dared to hope, wool on the outside and a soft fleecy flannel on the inside. There was a pair of leather gloves in the front pockets, too, and I tugged them on gratefully.

"We hoppin' a clagger?" Shiver asked, opening the door for me like a gentleman and following me out into the morning's lavender-grey twilight.

"Nah. Is Tarik's motorbike here?" I asked. "It'll be the fastest way to the city."

He waved a hand toward the side of the building, and I found Tarik's bike there along with a few old-fashioned pedal bicycles and, to my surprise, a grobbing great motorcar painted in drab grey.

"Where..." I started, then shrugged and dismissed the question. I'd find out, if it was important.

Shiver wheeled the motorbike away from the wall and fired the engine, watching the gauges as the steam built pressure.

"You think you're driving?" I asked.

"You outrank me," he said with a dazzling smile. "I drive."

I gritted my teeth and climbed onto the seat behind him.

# Chapter 19 ❧ Hayli

WE REACHED THE OLD SANITARIUM WELL BEFORE THE MIDDLE OF THE DAY, AND Shiver parked the motorbike in an alley nearly half a city block away where it would be proper hidden. For a few good minutes we sat on the front stoop of an abandoned building not far from what used to be the sanitarium's gate, which was naught but a tangle of iron and broken stones now.

I wondered what had happened to it. Maybe it got hit by one of those aeroplane mortars, but I'd no notion why or how, when the sanitarium was so far from the center of the city where the main uprising had happened. Unless Meed had been the actual target...

When I asked Shiver, he shrugged and leaned his chin on his fist. "Heard Meed had the police commissioner in his pocket," he said. "Maybe the coppers saw the uprising as a good chance to knock off a problem, quick and neat, so as no one would think odd of it."

"Odd?" I echoed, and waved generally at the mangled gate. "It's the only building on all of Front Street what got hit in the attacks. Ain't that a bit odd?"

"Not if everybody secretly hoped it would happen anyway," Shiver said. He pointed to an upper floor window. "Think that might be a good way in for you. It's broken open, but dan' look like there's any light on inside."

I scanned the tattered building briefly. Far as I could tell, it was all abandoned except the most northerly corner of the lower level, where I could see lamps in some of the rooms, and the movement of silhouettes behind the ragged curtains hanging in other windows. I glanced back at the broken window Shiver had pointed out, which was far on the other side of the building. Going in there I'd have a fair chance to Shift and get oriented without risking facing anybody.

"What about you?" I asked.

He gave me a look. "I ain't Coins. I walk through walls, I dan' squirrel up 'em." He got to his feet. "I can get in anywhere."

"A'right," I said. "Meet me in the room that window opens into. We'll scout together from there. Dan' want us to get separated—neither of us are Knacks, and we'd have no way to find each other if we needed to."

To my relief he didn't question my plan, just nodded and took a step backwards, and melted into the brick wall of the building behind us. I waited a few ticks, then wandered back into the alley where we'd left the bike, and Shifted.

Piper didn't even mutter a word at me as she flew up to the window, but I had too much on my mind to wonder at her silence. Once she landed on the musty floorboards inside, I Shifted back, crouching close to the ground for a tick as my eyes got used to the dim light. The room was empty, all but a rusted metal bed frame tipped on its side and leaning against one wall. I shuddered and tried not to look at it, because imagining it upright and covered with a proper mattress dredged up memories of the Science Ministry, and Borokhev's holding cells.

It was cold in the room, thanks to the broken window, but not so cold as it was outside, and after a minute's thought I took off my fine wool coat and folded it up neat as I could. I left it in a shadowy corner of the room and smoothed my hands over the fresh clothes I'd claimed yesterday from Luce—fitted black breeks that didn't have any bullet holes in them, a dark waistcoat that Luce had tailored to fit me proper, and a black shirt that was probably meant to be a lad's long-sleeved undershirt, because the sleeves hugged my arms all the way to my fingertips without any width to them at all.

My boots were the prize of my collection, though. Knee-high, made of supple leather, they didn't have the clunky soles of the work boots I usually wore. The soles were soft and thin, which was terrible for walking about outside in the snow, but which let me move almost noiselessly indoors, even on the most rickety wooden floors. Shiver had a pair to match. I didn't know where he'd found them, but they were an awful lot like Coins's boots. Thieves' boots, I guessed. I loved them.

I was adjusting my dark scarf around my neck when Shiver walked out of the wall beside me, rubbing his hands together.

"See aught on the way in?" I whispered.

He shook his head. "Just shadows," he said, shedding his own coat and leaving it in a crumpled heap on top of mine.

"You ready?"

He grinned for an answer, and together we crept out into the narrow hallway. As I picked my way over a few broken floor tiles and heaps of fallen ceiling plaster, I couldn't repress a faint shudder.

"Meed actually lived here?" I hissed. "This place gives me the heebies."

Shiver suddenly went rigid beside me, his hand flashing out to grab my arm. I glanced at him in confusion, but his eyes, impossibly wide and alarmed, were staring back the way we'd come.

"Listen," he said.

A minute and I heard it too—a soft, whimpering sound, like someone sobbing. Terror spidered down my arms, threatening panic. I took two sharp, small breaths and clamped my eyes shut.

"It's the wind," Shiver whispered, never letting go of my arm. "Just the wind in the broken glass."

All I could think of was the time Shade had told me he'd stuck his hand in machine oil, to keep me from panicking, when it had really been blood. Mage's blood. My body shook against my will, but Shiver's hand on my arm kept me grounded, kept me from flying away.

"Breathe," he said, his mouth close to my ear.

I took a breath, and then another, and as the fear flickered out, I gave him the faintest nod. His hand dropped away from my arm and he slipped ahead of me, moving like a shadow along the edge of the hallway. I followed close on his heels. Every few feet we paused to listen for voices, but the upper floor seemed completely abandoned. I paused by one open doorway and saw a broad, fine desk inside, like something belonging in the Palace, covered with a neat stack of papers and backed by a massive leather chair on one side and two smaller chairs on the other. There were elegant paintings on the walls and heavy burgundy curtains draped over the windows. In all that wrecked building, it was the one room that looked halfway civilized.

"I'd wager that was Meed's office," Shiver said.

I nodded, but I couldn't understand the doubt that coiled in the back of my mind. Halfway down the hallway, I realized what it was. The front gate and drive had been mangled beyond recognition, but the building itself—and Meed's office—were untouched. If Meed actually was dead—and I wasn't sure now if I believed the report—but if he was, I doubted it had been from an aeroplane's gun.

But we had no time to trouble over Meed's fate. We came to a broad staircase that led down to the ground floor, and already we could hear a drift of voices caught in urgent conversation. Shiver paused, crouched against the wall, the black tattoos of his hand almost melting into the pattern of the wood paneling behind him. He tipped his head back to look at me, green eyes strangely bright in the thick shadows.

"So, d'you want to do this the easy way?"

"Depends," I said.

He held his hand out, reminding me of the first time I'd met him, in the Clan's quarters at the Troyce & Fallon. And just like then, he grinned and said, "Want to see?"

I bit my lip, glancing from his hand to his face. "Is it safe?"

"Oh, I dan' na," he said. "But I brought someone through safe before. Trust me."

"Trust is a lot to ask," I said, but I took his hand.

His grin broadened, then his arms swept around me and shadows washed over me.

The darkness was absolute. I couldn't see a thing, not even Shiver's face or his bright green eyes. But stars, I could hear every bitty thing, like my ears were twice as powerful since my eyes were blind. I could hear the creak of timbers, the scuttle of insects, voices getting louder, then softer. And that was when I realized we were moving. I couldn't even feel how Shiver was holding me, but I didn't get the sense he was walking, at least not in the normal way. It was almost more like swimming, and that bewildered me more than aught else.

Then, abruptly, the sensation stopped, and I could hear a perfectly clear conversation taking place in the darkness right in front of me. But I couldn't move. I couldn't even twitch. For half a tick I was terrified that my chest couldn't even move enough for me to take a breath. I was perfectly trapped in a wall that pressed against every inch of me like air itself.

I was going to die.

"It's a'right," Shiver whispered. "Don't panic. Focus on what they're saying."

"Can't breathe!" My voice sounded tiny, thin as spider silk, barely escaping my frozen lips.

"Yes, you can," he said.

"Inside a wall!"

He laughed, a low, quiet chuckle. "Dan' think about it that way," he said, and suddenly it felt like he'd put me down, though he kept both hands on my arms. "We're inside the wall. Think about it! The wall's what, a foot thick at most? Six inches?" His hands slid down to grasp mine, and he turned me in a slow circle that felt a bit like a dance. "There's no way we could fit inside a wall," he said. "Not if you limit your mind to what you see. Dan' ask me to explain. I just know I can step inside the shell of a smelter pot as easy as I can step into a stone pillar. It's like…becoming part of the matter that exists, not trying to fit me inside of it as I am. Dan' that sound familiar? Or how d'you imagine you can fit all of Hayli inside the body of a crow?"

I stared at him, or where I guessed he was, mouth agape. The curiosity had teased me before, sure, but I'd never sat down and let myself try to think it through. Last time I'd tried I'd given myself a dreadful headache.

Experimentally, I took a breath. Then a deeper one. I laughed, finding that I could, and I started to pull my hands from Shiver's grasp so I could turn about on my own. His fingers tightened on mine.

"Wouldn't do that," he said. "Y' ain't a Rift. Think you can only do what I'm doing so long as I'm touching you."

"Like Derrin," I said, "when he Ghosted with the skitters."

"Exactly."

I said nothing then, but after a tick, when Shiver was still holding my hand—just one, now—I started to get a strange, uncomfortable feeling in the pit of my stomach. I'd never even held Shade's hand as long as I'd held Shiver's now, and the thought made me strangely sad.

"Shiver," I said. "Can you…can you hold onto me arm instead?"

And even though I knew he couldn't see me in the shadowy world we stood in, I turned my face away. Without a word he moved his hand up to grip my elbow, and we stood there like that, side by side, as the voices washed over us from the room beyond.

"When is Davesin getting here?" someone was saying. "He was supposed to be here a quarter of an hour ago."

"Got a worry in your nog, eh?"

That was Red, without a doubt. I bristled, just hearing his voice, and Shiver's fingers tightened on my arm.

"Shut it," the other man said. I guessed it might be Klissen, but I couldn't say for sure. "You do realize what a terrible idea this is."

"I'm sure I've heard you say it some thirty times this morning," Red said, with a lazy sort of indifference. "And I honestly don't give a damn what you think."

There was a faint sound of a scuffle, cloth rustling. I closed my eyes and tried to imagine the scene—Klissen grabbing Red's jumper, probably.

"Do you have any idea what it takes for a mage to be willing to stand in the same room as one of those Chernayi devils?"

"Your hide's safe, Klissen."

"It's not my hide I'm worried about," Klissen said, a little quieter, like he'd moved away from the wall. "Gentlemen," he said suddenly, in a very different voice, smooth and welcoming. "Please, come in."

"Were you followed?" Red asked.

"Why would we be?" a new voice asked, harsh and gravely. "Is there cause for concern?"

"No, certainly not," Klissen said.

"Shut up, Mage. I'm not here to talk to you."

"If you imagine Red has any authority here that I haven't given him, you're sadly mistaken," Klissen said, undaunted. "I'm the head of the Cleavers."

"More like the head of a splinter cell within your pathetic little gang," the newcomer said. "What is it you're calling yourselves these days? The Silver Fog or some such?"

"The Grey Mist," Klissen snapped.

"Right." I heard the man click his fingers, and there was a shuffle of boots on the wooden floor, then the scrape of chair legs as the men sat down. "Let's get this over with. Red, you said you had an offer that would tempt me. So? Spit it out."

*Red is so out of his depth,* Piper whispered in my thoughts. *He doesn't know what kind of power he's dealing with.*

*He never does,* I answered.

After a brief pause, Red said, "You are going to be disbanded."

The silence that followed was longer, tense and full of anger. "What did you say?"

"You didn't know?" I could hear the smirk in Red's voice. I could almost picture him savoring the moment. "The Court of Ministries is going to disband you."

"That is a lie," the Chernaya snapped. I guessed this was the Davesin that Klissen had named earlier. "Why would they disband us, now, after all we did for them?"

"The King is dead."

The anger built until it was so thick I thought I could touch it.

"What does that have to do with us?" Davesin growled. "We did not kill the King. As far as I'm concerned, every *mage* is guilty of Trabin's assassination."

"Bold claim," Klissen said, voice low, "considering the King had just pledged his support for our cause."

"Under what pressure?" Davesin countered. "It seems like perfect timing for the mages to strike, in my opinion—preserving the appearance of the Crown's support while making sure the King could not renege on his promise."

"That—" Klissen started, but Red interrupted.

"That is irrelevant," he said. "At any rate, the accusation is that you allowed the mage called the Rook to escape unharmed."

*Rook*, Piper muttered huffily in my thoughts. *Do they really not know the difference between me and one of those big ugly birds?*

*Shh*, I told her, while my heart pattered a little faster. Even if the name was all wrong, it pleased me more than I cared to admit that I had a mage title all of my own.

"Also," Red went on, "it doesn't change the fact that just yesterday, your precious founders were scheming a way to shut down your operation. Way I heard it, the movement to dismantle your group was headed by Minister Blake, and wasn't he the one directly responsible for its creation? There was even some talk about declaring the leaders among you as war criminals."

"How dare you—" Davesin sputtered. "Why would he want to do that? It makes no sense."

"Maybe they're afraid the dogs will turn on their handlers," Klissen said.

There was a sharp flurry of noises, then Red's voice drawled, "Sit down, both of you."

I was stunned when the noise quieted—I'd never imagined Red would have so much authority over anybody.

"How can you even know all this?" Davesin asked after a moment.

"That's the thing about mages," Klissen said. "You never know what you're dealing with."

There was a brief, hostile silence, then Davesin said, "Let's say, for the moment, that it's true, and Blake's turned on his own. What then?"

"Rather than answer that," Red murmured, "let me ask you another question. Where, Davesin, do your loyalties lie?"

"You dare to ask me that?" Davesin said, a cutting edge to his voice. "My loyalty is first and always to Cavnal."

"And the Court of Ministries…are they serving the best interests of Cavnal right now? Let me lay this on you, as well. They have no intention of looking for Prince Tarik. They have no intention of passing the act that would transfer the Crown to the King's nephew, Horm. They don't *want* a monarch on the throne of Cavnal. What those hidebound greedy knaves want is to rule in their own name. But they can't even keep this city from falling apart, much less negotiate an international treaty that would in any way benefit us. So let me ask you—what then?"

"You're proposing an alliance," Davesin said, slowly. "You want the Chernayi to ally with a bunch of bangers and Jixies—*precisely* the two elements of society we were created to deal with—to do what, exactly? To dismantle the Court of Ministries?"

I sucked in a breath. Shiver's fingers gripped my elbow tighter.

"Your choice," Red said. "Someone's going to get dismantled in the next few weeks. Up to you whether it's your Chernayi or the impotent and fragmented Court that's busy undermining every last bit of Cavnish stability."

There was a harsh, low sound, which took me a tick to realize was Davesin's laughter. "You want to bring down the Court, with what for manpower? A handful of mages and a police force severely outnumbered by the actual city police *and* the King's Army?"

"The Court is rapidly losing control over the Army as well," Klissen said. "Or didn't you hear how they went out against Farro's orders to try to track down and destroy the King's assassin?"

I bit down on my tongue, hard, to keep from gasping.

"That was against his orders?" Davesin echoed, sounding intrigued. "Who gave the order, then?"

"Not sure, but I mean to find out."

A pause, then, "So, if I'm hearing you correctly, you're proposing, what, a military coup against the Court of Ministries?"

"Out with the old," Red said.

"And establish what in its place? Some kind of dictatorship?"

"In with the new."

"It's the only way to bring the stars-forsaken mess in this country into some semblance of order," Klissen said.

"And what of the international conflict?" Davesin asked. "I assume with the White Rain—or whatever you lot are—in tow, that would mean an end to the proposed alliance with Meritac and Cromis?"

"Not necessarily," Red said. I could imagine his smug smile clear as day. "Even though the Hunter experiment failed, we've still got a lot to offer the alliance, not least being that rogue scientist and his pet project. No, Davesin, play these cards right, and the world will tear itself apart around us."

"And leave us the victors," Davesin finished for him. His chair scraped on the floorboards as he stood. "I'd heard about that project—rumors, mostly. Do you know, did he actually succeed?"

"Far as I heard, he claimed he did."

A pause, then Davesin said, "I'll take this offer to my officers. I'll have an answer for you in two days."

There were no farewells, no leave-taking. Just a tromp of boots, and the door slamming shut. The sound of a poker stirring up the fire in a nearby hearth.

"Well, that went astonishingly well," Klissen said after a moment.

"I told you there was nothing to worry about. Now, for the final piece of the puzzle. Are your men going to come with me to the smelter tonight? I won't rest easy until we've got Shade's agreement. If the Chernayi balk, I have a feeling his word will give us leverage. Maybe get them to change their minds. Just hope the cold bastard is willing to listen to us."

"About that," Klissen said, voice trailing off. Red growled a noise of impatience. "You heard what I told Davesin, about the Army going after the King's assassin?"

"Yes...?"

"They attacked the smelter."

"What?" Red cried.

"Well, they tried to. Or rather, they would have, but when they got there, it was already empty. We're not going to find Shade there tonight."

"Damn it!" Red shouted, slamming his fists on a table. "She played me for a fool."

"Yes," Klissen said, blandly.

"Did it never occur to you that this might be something I should know about?"

"Not really, no."

There was dead silence for a long moment, then Red said, his tone acid, "And I don't suppose you know where they went?"

"Not yet," Klissen said. "Even the Army hasn't been able to track them down anywhere. But I've a feeling we'll know soon enough."

"How can you be so sure?"

"Because he's an animal," Klissen said, his voice smooth. "Animals will always seek their own comfort. With the proper amount of pressure, he'll break."

"Creech," I whispered, the thought hitting me like a blow to the stomach. "They must have found out he was playing stoolie. Shiver! We can't leave without him!"

"Well," Red was saying, "as long as he does in the next two days, because we need Shade's answer..." His voice trailed off, then he asked, abrupt, "What's the matter with you?"

"Nothing..." Klissen said. "It's just, for a moment I thought..." There was a frustrated pause, then he finished, "It was fear. Somewhere... somehow. In the room. I don't know. I'm sure it was nothing."

"Bloody Jixies," Red muttered. "Always so jumpy."

Shiver gave my arm a sharp tug, then wrapped his arms around me and pulled me with him through the space between the world.

## Chapter 15 ❧ Hayli

WE TRAVELED THROUGH THE INK-THICK DARKNESS MUCH LONGER THAN I thought we should have, until I started to worry that Shiver was taking us, not back to the upper room where we'd left our coats, but to the alley where we'd left the motorbike. But just when I'd made up my mind to ask him, he stepped through a wall into the world, into the upper room, and released me unceremoniously. I stumbled when my feet hit solid ground, far wobblier than I ever felt after Shifting. Shiver smirked as I got my balance back.

"C'mon," he said, retrieving his coat and tossing mine to me. "Think we'd best be on the get."

I tugged it on, because the building was wretchedly cold, but then I planted my feet where I stood and refused to move. "What about Creech?"

"He knew the risks when he decided to play stoolie," Shiver said, shrugging. "Dan' care much for folks as sell out their clan at a whim."

I frowned, wondering if that was why Shiver never seemed quite so devoted to Shade as the rest of us—Shade, who'd been double-dealing with the Court and the Hole when he first came to us, back when the world still made sense.

"They're ganna torture him," I said quietly.

"I'm sure he'll be fine."

I grabbed him by both shoulders and shoved him hard as I could against the wall. His hands splayed out to catch him, vanishing half into the wall before he steadied himself.

"Dan' you say that," I said, grinding the words through my teeth. "Not ever. Nobody deserves that, d'you hear me? *Nobody*."

He lifted his hands, slowly, and clasped them around mine. I was shaking too bad to pull away. "I'm sorry," he murmured. "I div'n mean that, a'right?"

I didn't want to brush off the outrage, didn't want to accept his apology, as if what he'd said could just be forgotten so easy. But I forced myself to nod, because we had a job to do, and because if Bridnow were to see me now he'd be ashamed of what he saw.

A minute and Shiver let my hands go, but his eyes never left my face.

"He's gotta be here somewhere," I said, turning away.

"You sure?"

"Sure," I said. "This place…it was a sanitarium. Wake knows what they used to do to folks here, but whatever it was, maybe it's still going on."

*It's like the Science Ministry,* I wanted to say. *It's like Borokhev.* But I kept those thoughts close, wrapped up deep in the buried corners of my mind.

We crept out of the room, me in the lead, Shiver close on my heels. I could tell he had a mind to slip through the walls again, but I wanted to move on my own two feet, so I made myself ignore his constant grumbling and sighs. After passing half a dozen empty rooms like the one we'd left, we reached a set of double doors opening toward the inside of the building. I stood on tiptoes to glance through one of the high, narrow windows, but the glass was cracked and grimed and I couldn't see aught at all inside. Biting my lip, I laid my hand on one of the door handles and pressed down. It gave way easily and the door swung open on silent hinges, and somehow, I thought, that was even worse than if it had squealed like a trapped rat.

The room beyond was dim and mote-hazed, with just a few slats of pale grey light drifting and sifting in from a broken skylight high above. The floor along the left-hand wall was a mess of broken tiles and battered furniture, but on the right side of the room it was swept clean—almost too clean. A metal slab of a bed stood in the center with a table beside it. On the table was a large wooden box, full of strange levers and dials, trailing a cord that ended in a leather halo studded with metal dots. It might have looked like a bit like a dog's collar, but something about it made fear twist in my gut like a living thing.

"Stars," Shiver said. "What is that thing?"

I forced myself a step closer. "It looks like…" My hand drifted out, barely touching the cracked leather, and I glanced over my shoulder at Shiver. "Were you there at Esobor, back when the Chernayi took us all hostage and meant to force us through that EMS device?"

He shook his head.

"They were ganna put Shade through first, except—" I swallowed, remembering how Dr. Toma had sided with Tarik against Kippler, helping Tarik get free so he could save the rest of us—Dr. Toma, who'd later got killed by Kippler and Vrey for being too nosy about their experiments with me and Vrey's other mage project. Shaking my head to jostle away the memory, I finished, "This…this reminds me of that thing. The wires. The levers. The crown. It's just…smaller."

"An EMS device?" Shiver said, shying back from table. "But why would they have it here? If Klissen is a mage, and the Grey Mist are all mages…I dan' understand."

"Unless it was Vanek Meed's."

"Meed never did aught with torturing folks, far as I know."

I picked up the halo, gingerly, holding the leather by two fingers. "It's old. D'you suppose it belonged to the asylum?"

He grimaced, watching me with anxious eyes. "Put it down. I dan' want…what if it goes off?"

I wanted to laugh at his fear, but it was my own fear, and I put the thing down a bit too hastily. "Dan' think it would," I said. "Dan' na if it even works any more."

"It works," someone behind me said, and we both spun to find Red standing in the doorway, arms crossed. "Though I'm told the boffins prefer to use some kind of drug to do the same thing these days. How'd I guess I would find you two snooping around here? Creech told you where to find us?"

I swallowed and took a step back as he came toward us, and neither Shiver nor I said a word in answer. Red picked up the leather halo and twisted it in his hands, running his fingers over its smooth metal dots.

"He'll tell us where to find you, too, you know."

"Red, you're better than this," I whispered. "You dan' have to…to torture anybody."

He paused, looking at me with his brows arched in genuine

surprise. "Stars, Hayli," he said. "I know we never much got on, but you don't really think I would…"

I watched him sidelong, wary. If I hadn't just overheard every word he'd said to the Chernaya, I might have believed him. I might have been willing to listen, to give him the benefit of the doubt. But I'd heard him. Heard him propose a military overthrow of the Court of Ministries and a scheme that would bring the world to its knees. I didn't suppose there was any limit to what he was capable of.

"I dan' na if I ever knew you at all," I muttered. "Never thought you'd sell us out, that's sure."

His eyes narrowed. "Sell you out?"

"To the Cleavers," I said, not missing a beat. "Leave our ranks, join them. Why would you do that? And then turn around and try to win Shade over from the other side? If you wanted Shade's help so bad, why not stay in place and try to persuade him from there?"

Red shrugged. "Never could get him to listen when it was just me. Figured he might need some…outside pressure to get him to start looking at the bigger picture."

I laughed at that, shaking my head. "Bigger picture? Stars, you got no idea what bigger picture he's looking at."

Shiver touched my arm, discreetly, and I kept the rest of my thoughts to myself. If Red noticed, he didn't show it. He just stood staring at the warped leather in his hands, turning it back and forth.

"I don't torture anybody," he said finally. "Klissen…that's Klissen's business."

It struck me with a peculiar force how desperate Red was for me to believe him. I took a breath and pointed at the machine.

"Does he use that thing to do it?"

"What, this? Nah, this was here long ago. Don't know how it worked, but I think they used it for the loonies, to try to get them thinking straight again. Way I heard it, it was supposed to jar them out of their delusions."

"What did it do?" I asked, horrified.

"How should I know? Do I look like a doctor?"

"You said they use drugs now, instead?" I asked, my throat a bit dry. "Know aught about that?"

Shiver shifted his weight, and even Red scowled at me a fair bit. "They call 'em salts, I guess. Why? What's it got to do with anything?"

"Just...curious."

He still watched me, perplexed, but I couldn't explain to him my need to know—my fear, my certainty, that Kippler and Vrey had been drugging me somehow, when I'd been their prisoner. I needed to know what they'd done to me. I needed to know what it had made me do.

"You were telling us about Creech," Shiver said, abruptly. I hadn't realized the silence had dragged on so long.

Red gave him a peevish look. "I don't know what Klissen is doing to Creech, all right? But whatever it is, I'd say Creech deserves it."

"Why?"

"Because..." Red started, and saw the trap, and snapped his mouth shut again.

"Because he ratted you out?" Shiver said.

Red gave him a sour look and didn't bother with a reply. "What're you two doing here, anyway?"

"Looking for Creech," I said promptly. "Expected to see him and I didn't, so I came looking. How'd you know he sold you out?"

"I know a rat when I see one."

"Like looking in a mirror," Shiver remarked.

Red didn't even blink. He just knotted his fist and threw a punch at Shiver's unguarded stomach, then grunted in surprise when his hand passed right through him. Shiver gave him a nasty smile.

"Nice try," he said.

Red glared at him for two breathless seconds, then suddenly his arm was around my neck, pinning me back against him.

"Hayli!" Shiver cried.

I struggled until I felt the bite of steel against my throat, then I forced myself to be still, and small as I could be.

"That's right," Red whispered, his mouth close to my ear. "Don't move. Think Klissen would much rather have you than Creech any day, so, maybe we can arrange a little trade."

Shiver took one step back, hands in the air. If I didn't know him, I would've thought it was a gesture of surrender, but I could see the cold glint in his eyes.

"Shiver, it's a'right," I said. Then, to Red, "Where is he? Where've you got Creech stashed away? I'll stay here, quiet-like, but only if you tell Shiver where to find him."

"Really?" Red asked, tilting his head to the side to get a better look at my face. Shiver was staring at me, too, and I just hoped he'd have the sense to go along with me and not start bickering like he usually would. "Didn't think the old gaffer meant that much to you."

"I got him into this mess," I said. "Figure I owe it to him to get him out of it."

"Noble," he said. "It's all rather pathetic."

"Creech, location, now," I said.

"You're not in a position to be making demands, love."

I ground my teeth, wanting to elbow him in the stomach, not daring to with the knife blade against my throat. He laughed as Shiver's face turned a pale shade of anger.

"We'll do this civil, don't worry, Mage," Red said. "Creech is upstairs, at the end of this wing. There's only one room up there. You can't miss it." He leaned to look at me again. "You were almost there, actually. If you'd not been so curious you might have found him already and gotten away clean without ever running into me."

"Well, you know crows," I said, holding Shiver's gaze. "We never can resist shiny things."

Shiver nodded. I felt Red's arm tensing as he shifted his weight, and a little prickle of alarm chased through me. But if Red meant to do something to Shiver, he never got the chance. With dramatic flair, Shiver gave Red a dazzling grin, folded his arms across his chest, and fell straight backwards. Red jolted and even I gasped, but Shiver didn't hit the floor at all. Just melted right into it, and was gone.

"That creeps the hell out of me," Red muttered, after a silence that was much too long. "Now, question is, what to do with you? Maybe I've finally got the leverage to get Shade's attention. Think he'll listen to me now, if I've got you to dangle in front of him?"

"I dan' na," I said, nonchalant.

"You don't know?"

I shrugged, stalling.

"Aren't you and he...that is..."

That made me laugh. "Well, that's the thing about mages, Red. You just never know what to expect from us."

He paused—I realized too late that I'd almost perfectly echoed Klissen, but if he noticed it too, he didn't say aught about it. His hesitation seemed to be all wrapped up around what I'd implied.

He said, "Then you two, you're not...?"

"Maybe...maybe it was always you I cared about."

That got him startled so bad that the knife inched away from my throat. I took the opportunity to twist in his arms and face him, standing far closer to him than I'd ever wanted to. There was only one person in all the world I wanted to be this close to, and he was thousands of miles away. Red's face was flushed a bright crimson to match his tag, and he looked so surprised he didn't even try to get the knife back against my throat. But it wasn't just surprise I read in his eyes. It was hope, too, and for one hair of a second I almost felt bad for tricking him so badly. Almost.

"But that's the thing about mages," I said. I eased my hands up between us like I meant to catch him for a kiss, but instead I wiggled my fingers in his face and gave him my most innocent smile. "You never know what to expect."

And then I Shifted.

I TWIST IN A FLURRY OF *wings right in front of Red's face, spooking him so soundly that he falls backwards, hands flailing, warding me away. With a shout of laughter I wheel about and dart into the narrow corridor, while Red's curses trail after me like smoke in the wind. He is running after me, but I swoop into the room where we first arrived, and make straight for the shattered window. I am out in the open, free on the wing, before Red has even entered the room. I can still hear him calling curses after me but they are no more than empty threats.*

*I make my way to the alley where we left the motorbike, and to Hayli's relief I find Shiver already there with Creech, the motorbike chuffing quietly as it builds up pressure. The older man looks terrible, and he leans on the motorbike's seat like he can barely stand. Shiver watches me as I come into the alley, but I only light on the bike's handlebars and then take to the wing again, hoping he will understand.*

*He does. He climbs onto the seat and pulls Creech on behind him, then kicks the bike into gear. I stay close to them the whole way out of the city, taking the longer route through the mostly abandoned streets in the southwestern quarter, until we come out onto the river road that winds around the city and leads back to Borokhev. As soon as they are well on their way, I turn and catch the currents to carry me northeast toward the facility.*

*Hayli's mind is a cacophony behind mine. I can make no sense of her thoughts—they are a jumble of worry and anger and fear, and behind it all an aching loneliness that I understand perhaps better than the rest of it. There's no form to the tangle of thoughts, but I see Shiver's face and Red's, and against it all are a scattering of memories of Tarik, of Shade.*

He'll be home soon, *I try to tell Hayli.*

*I feel her startle.* How'd you know... *she starts, and then laughs.*

*I laugh too, because we are the same, though we are not.*

*Then her mirth fades and she whispers,* What if he doesn't come back in the end? What if he decides to stay in Istia?

And away from us? *I ask.*

Us! *she echoes, laughing again.*

*I smirk, triumphant that I have lifted her mood.* Why not? Anyway, Cavnal is his home.

Sometimes I worry, with everything that happened with the King, and the Court...he would rather walk away from us. *She sighs, a heavy sigh laden with fear and unspoken doubts.* Cavnal's got no claim on him.

But you do, *I say.*

Do I? *she asks softly.* I shot him, Piper. I shot him in the heart.

Well, that may be something you'll need to work out when he comes back, *I say.*

*I sense her sad smile, and she says nothing else the rest of the way back.*

I GOT BACK TO BOROKHEV NEAR an hour before Shiver and Creech arrived on the motorbike. When they finally chuffed through the main gate, I was waiting in the open yard with Doc and Derrin, and a handful of skitters and other folk gathered behind me. I'd already reported to Bridnow that we'd returned, and now he waited near the door to the officers' quarters for Shiver to arrive so he could get our report.

Derrin walked forward as the motorbike puttered to a stop in front of us, and helped Creech off the seat. I grimaced. Piper hadn't got a very good look at him, and now I was glad she hadn't or I would have made her stay close to the bike the whole way to Borokhev just to make sure Creech wouldn't collapse on the way. His face was a pale and bloody mess, and he cradled one hand close to his chest, his fingers stuck through the front of his shirt between two buttons. I decided I probably didn't want to see what they looked like. He caught my eye and gave me a weak smile and a nod, and I did my best to give him a smile that looked halfway encouraging.

As soon as Creech was on his feet, Doc swept in and took the

 268

Shifter's free arm over his shoulders, and led him away toward the building he'd claimed for his infirmary. Shiver left the motorbike to Derrin and followed me to the officers' quarters where Bridnow was waiting, holding the door open for us. We gathered around the blazing fireplace, Bridnow in the big chair and me on the stool across from him, and Shiver perched cross-legged up on the table.

"So," Bridnow said. "Did you learn anything useful from your foray or just spring that mage?" He gave me an appraising look. "Guess he got caught."

"Somehow. I've not had a chance to talk to him yet," I said. "We overheard an interesting chat."

Bridnow lifted both brows. "Did you."

"It's worse than we thought," I said, and relayed the whole thing, from Klissen's Grey Mist wanting Shade's alliance to the news that the Chernayi were on the brink of being disbanded, to the plot to orchestrate a military coup overthrowing the Court of Ministries.

When I finished, Bridnow swore elegantly and tugged off his fur hat, scrubbing a hand through his short hair.

"I suppose I'll need to get in touch with Krigs, and find out if this rumor about the Army is true," he said. "And what was that about the rogue scientist? Did you get any sense of what or who they were talking about?"

I twisted my gloves in my lap. "Nah. At first I thought they meant Kippler, but then I wasn't so sure. I dan' think they would ever call Kippler a *rogue* scientist, since he seems fair in the traces with them."

"Interesting. Alokin, perhaps?"

I hesitated, my thoughts drifting back to that snatch of a conversation I'd overhead between Doc and Destri.

*"If he were here, I'd use it myself..."* Destri had said.

I hadn't wanted to consider that Alokin was the scientist Klissen and Davesin had been talking about, but I got the sinking feeling that Bridnow was right. Either way, the situation was dangerous. I just wasn't sure whose pet project I'd fear more—Kippler's, or Alokin's.

"Well," Bridnow said, when I offered no comment, "I'll see if Krigs knows anything about that, too. What of the Ministries? Did you get the impression that they were all united now that Trabin is gone, or is there still the old divide?"

"Still divided," I said. "Least, that's how it seemed when Griff and

I went to the palace. Griff's father is the holdout, far as I know."

"Anyone you trust there? Can Farro get word to his father?"

"Might be dangerous," I said. "But I might be able to get word to Minister Batar. He's got…reasons to help us out."

Bridnow gave me a close look. "So, the rumor is true?"

"If the rumor you're thinking of is the rumor I'm thinking of, then yes, it's true."

"What does that even mean?" Shiver asked.

"He's a mage," I said. "No one, or, almost no one knows."

"*Batar?*" Shiver exclaimed. "Well. Dan' think I ever would've guessed *that*."

"Get word to him," Bridnow said, and got to his feet.

It pleased me inordinately that he didn't ask if I thought I could do it. He just said it expecting that I could.

"Yes, Commandant," I said.

"You should brief the rest of the squadron on the situation tomorrow," he said. "You're on watch tonight, Hayli. The fox hours."

I hid a grimace behind a wry grin and said, "Of course I am."

He smiled and clapped me on the shoulder, nodded to Shiver, and retreated back to his private office. It was actually Shade's office, as Bridnow had explained to me, but since he was second-in-command until Shade's return, he had taken to using it himself. I hadn't been in it since the first day we'd come to Borokhev. It had all of Shade's maps and papers tucked away in there now, and most days that made it much too hard to face.

I watched the door close behind Bridnow, then got up from the stool. "I'm ganna gan and check on Creech," I said.

"Any orders for me, ma'am?" Shiver asked, that slightly mocking note in his voice again, the one I hated so much because it made me feel like such an impostor.

"No," I said. "You've got your standing duties. Do those."

I turned on my heel without another word and strode out of the barracks. More than aught else I wanted to slam the door behind me as I went. Instead I took the effort to close it quietly, so Shiver wouldn't see how angry he'd made me. I would never let him—or anyone—see me unstable. Not ever.

# Chapter 16 • Jarik

WE ARRIVED IN BREGJARVANI IN THE LATE AFTERNOON OF THE FOLLOWING day, just as the pale sun was settling toward the horizon against a rack of darkening clouds. I couldn't stop staring as we rode down the main street and through the heart of the city. Like the town we'd just left, Bregjarvani didn't seem quite deserving of the title *city*, but it was certainly the largest settlement I'd seen since we'd set out from Agnir's home. The buildings were tall and narrow as a rule and made mostly of stone and steel, but the people had painted their facades in rakish hues, brighter than I'd ever seen—reds and blues and yellows, as if the riot of color could drive away the grey bitterness of the long winter months.

The sky hung low over the city, breathing down a faint mist traced with snow, and the air was thick with the smell of brine and fish, and—I was sure I didn't imagine it—the hint of wood smoke. But there was nothing green in the city. The little lawns in front of the buildings were covered with mossy stones, and even the lichens were a dull grayish-gold color. There were no trees at all. I supposed that, if my nose hadn't tricked me and there was in fact a proper fire burning somewhere, the wood did not come from Istia.

We passed very few horses on the street. Most of the people we saw were on foot or riding the occasional bicycle; I didn't see anything resembling a motorcar anywhere. Most of the passersby ignored us as we made our way through the city center, which was just as well. I needed time to take in the city before I'd feel comfortable interacting with it, and if the people felt the same way about us—about me—I could hardly blame them.

Nika led us all the way through the city, east to west, until we arrived at last at the wharf. There were few enough boats docked at the piers—most of the fishing vessels would be out chasing the winter migrations, and wouldn't come back until the spring. Some smaller vessels bobbed uncertainly on the water, flocks of terns and gulls riding their masts and rigging, and one fair-sized steamer drifted lazily alongside the southernmost pier. I drew in my horse where the street opened up onto the docks, in the shadow of a port warehouse painted in garish red.

"That steamship is likely your best chance of a voyage home," I said to Mirin, nodding toward the boat.

"Div'n think the Istians had any steamships," Mirin said.

He was squinting at the boat, but it wasn't flying any colors. I could see the name painted on its steel-grey prow, though, and the word didn't belong either to Istia or to Cavnal.

"It's not Istian," I said. "It's a Tulian ship."

Mirin shifted his weight on his saddle and I regarded him in surprise, because his face was etched with utter distress.

"I dan' see how I'll manage," he said, almost moaning the words. "Maybes I'll be stuck here in this forsaken place all winter." I just looked at him, questioning, and he flung a hand toward the ship. "I dan' speak Tulian. I dan' even speak Istian. If they dan' speak Cavnish, how can I ever hope to barter passage?"

I studied him a moment longer, then without a word I nudged my horse forward. None of the others followed me; I hadn't expected them to. When I reached the Tulian ship, I spotted a few sailors working on the deck, scouring the planks, but I couldn't see anyone who looked like they were in charge. I dismounted and tossed the horse's reins over a mooring post.

One of the sailors noticed me walking toward the ship and stopped his work, dropping his brush into a pail and wiping his hands on his trousers as he came to the rail.

"I not speak Istia," he called down to me. "Captain…" His brow wrinkled as he racked his mind for a word, but failing, he just waved toward the stone-and-timber warehouse behind me.

"I speak Tulian," I said. "Can I board?"

His face broke in a broad grin and he waved me up onto the deck. As soon as I joined him there he grabbed my hand and shook it heartily.

"Where are you headed?" I asked, reclaiming my hand from his enthusiastic grip.

He blew out his breath through pursed lips. "Ah, I believe we're heading home after this."

He spoke quickly, but, thanks to my mother, I'd always had an easier time with Tulian than any other language I'd learned. I nodded my understanding, then gestured generally toward the warehouse.

"No trade with Cavnal right now?"

"Cavnal!" he echoed. "Lad, have you been following the news? Tulay and Cavnal are circling like dogs in a pit right now. The only ships we've got anywhere near Cavnish waters are our military vessels, stringing out a defensive blockade in the Grafton Straits, flush up against theirs. No. We're not going to Cavnal."

"Damn," I said.

He eyed me curiously. "You had a mind to go? No offense, lad, but I'd wager you'd be no more welcome in Cavnal than us right now."

"Less, I imagine," I said. "No, it's not for me. I have a Cavnish sailor with me." I jerked my head toward the street where Mirin was waiting. "Washed up on shore from a shipwreck. I brought him with me to see if we could get him passage back to his homeland, no more. But as you see, there aren't many options."

"He may have to stay out the winter, then," the sailor said, and drew up smartly as another man strode past me onto the deck.

"Who's this?" the newcomer asked, stopping beside the sailor to survey me. He was an older man, weathered, with the same warm complexion and dark hair as my mother and myself—or rather, Tarik. "Not hiring any fresh hands, boy."

"He's not trying to hire on, Captain," the sailor said, and tried to explain my request, but the captain waved a hand to silence him.

"I can't go to Cavnal," he said to me. He was a good three inches shorter than me, but he still managed to look down his nose at me, all contempt and impatience. "I'm not a passenger ship, and I'm not a hack service."

I gritted my teeth and glanced away. The wind picked up, salt-scoured and knife-sharp, carrying a cacophony of bird calls from the flocks of northern terns wheeling overhead.

"There's no way I could persuade you? Nothing I could offer that would tempt you to change your mind?" I asked, and the voice in my head whispered, *Why bother persuading him?*

I silenced it.

The captain shook his head, but he was watching me curiously now, his gaze riveted on my mage sign. "Not many commoners here in Istia can speak our language with so much authority," he said, "unless they be traders or merchants. But then, you seem...not like other Istians I've met."

"I'm not," I said, and left it at that.

His mouth twitched in a smile. "What's your name, lad?"

I measured him a moment, wondering if I ought to answer. What did it matter if I told him the truth? What would it matter if I didn't?

The decision wasn't mine, in the end. Just as I decided to hold my tongue, Iskari shouted from the pier, "Taumir! Is there a problem?"

I turned and leaned on the ship's rail to look down at him, but I didn't answer immediately. The captain behind me got a little twitchy; maybe he didn't like the way I was standing, as if the ship were mine.

"He says they're not going to Cavnal," I said finally. "Too dangerous."

Iskari left his horse with mine and strode up the weathered gray plank onto the deck. The captain drew himself up to his full height but Iskari ignored him entirely.

"We can't keep Mirin here," Iskari said. His eyes slid toward the captain, then he added, "I don't trust him, Godarson."

I pressed my lips in a thin line. I wanted to scowl at him, and I wanted to laugh. More than anything I wanted to stare down the captain and see what he thought of my identity now. But I didn't do any of those things. I turned away instead, and leaned my elbows on the rail again, and looked out across the port.

"Godarson?" the captain echoed. "I didn't know—"

"We'll find another solution," I said to Iskari, though what, I had no idea.

Then, nodding to the captain, but not looking at him, I turned and strode down the plank to reclaim my horse, Iskari close on my heels. As we rode away I thought I heard the captain call after me, but I didn't turn around.

Mirin was waiting with Nika where we'd left them.

"They're not sailing to Cavnal," I told him. "There's too much hostility right now with Tulay."

Mirin's face fell, and for a moment he just leaned on the pommel of his saddle, shoulders hunched and head bowed. "I should've known better than hope," he muttered. "I'm sure you're all too happy to keep me far away from Cavnal, though."

I tipped my head, but it was Iskari, riding up to join us, who answered him in jarring, half-broken Cavnish. "He didn't have to try, man," he said. "Be grateful he did." He edged his horse alongside Mirin's and added in a lower voice, "If he'd listened to me, you wouldn't even be here now."

"Peace, Iskari," I said.

Mirin stared at him aghast, but Iskari just gave him a half-wild grin and nudged his horse into a trot. We filed in behind him, me last of all, and followed him a little way from the wharf to a tall tavern, only slightly broader than the buildings around it. It was built in the same half-stone, half-dark timber style as the warehouse—stone from Istia, the timber brought in from Cavnal's northeastern coast. If not for the sign over the door, I would never have known that the building was an alehouse.

"What are we doing here?" Mirin asked, still gloomy, as we left the horses with the stable hands.

"Food," Iskari said. "Ale. What else?"

"It's the best place to get food in Bregjarvani," Nika added.

"It's the only place to get food in Bregjarvani," Iskari corrected.

Mirin scowled and pushed past them into the tavern. I exchanged a pointed glance with Iskari and caught myself grinning as I followed the Cavner into the dark and crowded room. The inside of the tavern was a strange melding of styles, with its walls half made of rugged rust-colored rock and half of carved and patchwork driftwood, and the floor laid with slate-grey stones. Oil lamps hung from the high ceiling and on every wall, but there were none on the long plank tables, which made the whole place feel rather cheerless.

I felt a little thrill of triumph, though, when I saw a massive wood-burning hearth against the inner wall—undoubtedly the source of the wood smoke I'd smelled earlier. Near the hearth the air was wonderfully dry and warm, but around the edges of the room it was almost unbearably cold, and frost rimed the thin glass of the wide windows.

Iskari took the lead once we were inside, directing us to a semi-private table that shouldered up to a chest-high wooden partition, close to the hearth. I sat down on one bench and he took the other, and Mirin surveyed us both with equal distaste before relenting and sliding onto the seat beside me.

"I don't bite," I said, and gave him a savage grin. "Usually."

Iskari laughed aloud at Mirin's discomfort, but my attention was already elsewhere. At the table behind ours sat an older man and woman, dressed all too obviously in high Cavnish fashion, in silk and tawny ermine and far too much lace to be practical. Two men in black uniforms stood against the wall just behind their table, their eyes roving constantly over the dining area. The whole group of them stood out painfully, and, even worse, showed no signs of wanting to blend in.

My gaze rested a moment too long on the silver shield emblem embroidered on the sleeve of one of the guard's coats, and I let my breath out in a shallow sigh.

"Nika," I said after a moment, and jerked my chin toward the man and woman. "Do you know who they are?"

She glanced briefly over her shoulder. Iskari had the sense to stay facing forward, but his eyes held a question.

"Cavners," Nika said, half under her breath.

Hearing the word, Mirin craned his neck to look at them. I elbowed him sharply in the ribs and he slouched back down in his seat.

"Not just any Cavners," I said. "That's Ambassador Vadich and his wife." I nodded toward the two men. "And guards."

"What did you say?" Mirin asked me. "Who're those folks?"

"Apparently that's your new Foreign Ambassador to Istia," I said, "and entourage. What are they doing here?"

"Do I look like I've got half a ken?"

"Maybe you should," I said. "They obviously got here somehow. Maybe you should go introduce yourself. Make a good impression and they might let you slip a ride back to Cavnal with them."

Mirin fidgeted, nervous, and he didn't move to stand up. I hid a laugh by taking a sip of whatever dark beer the server had already set before me. The Cavnish Ambassador's wife was studying me over the rim of her water glass—beer not being at all fashionable for the Cavnish upper class, and the Istians having nothing like wine to offer her. I avoided her gaze.

"Do you suppose they'll recognize you?" Iskari asked presently.

I wondered what made him ask; he hadn't turned around to look at them. But maybe he knew what was happening just by the expression on my face.

"I'm sure they will," I muttered, "if they think about it long enough."

"Can you change?"

I looked at him sharply. "You mean Mask again?" He nodded. "I could. She would see me do it though. If I'm not attracting attention already, I certainly would then."

"Then maybe you should leave and come back. As someone else."

A musician in the corner began playing a set of bone pipes, while another joined him on a soft tabor. The conversation around the tables quieted a little—as if the patrons were simply showing respect to the musicians rather than actually listening to the music. The Cavners watched the musicians for a few moments, the Ambassador's wife looking a bit appalled.

"Stars, look at those men," she said after a moment, putting a proper sh on the beginning s like a good Cavnish noblewoman. "Do they call that *music*? Interrupting everyone's meal with their raucous noise!"

"I think it's quaint," the Ambassador said. "You don't see old-fashioned instruments like that any more. Of course, it's all you'd expect to see in a place like this."

"I *know*. Look at their adorable little costumes, too. All fur and leather... It's absolutely barbaric!" She covered her mouth with a lace kerchief to hide her laughter as she pointed at one of the servers, who was dressed in coarse wool trousers and a leather waistcoat, his knotted hair bound high on his head to keep it out of his way. "Gracious, he looks just like a wild animal!"

"Sweet, don't insult the animals!"

The wife hid another laugh in the kerchief, but Vadich chuckled out loud. Some of the other patrons were watching them now, frowning—I doubted they could hear, or understand, what the two were laughing about, but the Cavners' contempt was plain in any language. Mirin at least had the grace to look uncomfortable.

After a moment the wife laid a hand on Vadich's arm. Her gaze was riveted on me. "Have you noticed? All these atrocious *Jixies* everywhere. Skuddy, dear, what did you ever do to get sentenced to a backwater like this place? Have we not been punished enough already?"

"Hush, there's a dear," Vadich said. "It's only for a few months. We just have to convince these parochial inbred fools what's in their best interest. People like this need to be conquered, if only for their own good."

"Oh, quiet!" his wife said, stifling another laugh. "What if someone hears you?"

Mirin shot an anxious glance in my direction, but I didn't acknowledge him.

"In a place like this?" Vadich asked, and snorted. "I guarantee you, they've no idea who we are or what we're saying."

I met Iskari's gaze. Even though he spoke very little Cavnish, I could tell from the pallor of his face and the tightness of his jaw that he'd understood enough to be insulted. I was insulted for him, for all of the people in that room. My blood was lava in my veins. I picked up my mug of ale, twisting it in my hands as my sanity waged a futile war with my recklessness, then I drew a slow breath.

I said, "Ambassador Vadich." I didn't look at the other table, at the Ambassador or his wife, or their guards. "Your wife is more prudent than you are. You might wish to reconsider your words, and your misplaced contempt."

The guards immediately straightened up, all their attention riveted on me. If Vadich and his wife didn't recognize me, I was fairly certain the guards would if they looked at me too closely, so I kept my head a little bowed, half in shadow from the partition. The Ambassador's wife drew a sharp little breath, and Vadich twisted around in his seat to look at me. I gave him a feral smile.

"Not everyone here is a parochial, inbred fool," I said.

"Well, great *shtars*," he exclaimed, and tried, to no avail, to smooth a smirk from his lips. "Here's one who thinks he can contend with me."

"I have no need to contend with you," I said. "You have no authority I need to recognize."

"I speak in the name of the King of Cavnal!" he protested, cheeks red, chest puffed with indignation.

"Oh?" I asked. I leaned forward on the table, and Nika and Iskari wisely edged to either side of the bench to clear Vadich's view of me. "What King?"

"How dare you!" Vadich cried and jumped to his feet, almost overturning his table.

Mirin seemed to melt into himself as I stood and stepped past him, coming face to face with the Ambassador in the aisle between the tables. The room was dead silent. Even the musicians had stopped playing to watch. Caution whispered impotently in my thoughts; my anger was too loud to hear it, a cacophony in my soul, melting into the colors of the fire.

"Who sent you to Istia, Ambassador?"

He shook a jeweled finger in my face. "Don't you speak so brassily to me, young man. I was sent by the Court of Ministries to oversee negotiations with Istia, on behalf of all of Cavnal!"

"Really," I said, blandly. "And you imagine that insulting the people you came to treat with is going to smooth relations between our countries, especially after what happened last month? Do you really believe that Istia will want peace with a nation whose Ambassador claims Istia should be conquered for her own good?" I knew I ought to stop there; everything sane inside me told me to shut up and sit down, but I couldn't. I said, "I'm sure you were briefed concerning the fate of the last two Cavnish ambassadors."

The words were out before I could cage them in, and I couldn't even silence the little thrill of power I felt as he jerked away from me, his ruddy cheeks blanching a deathly white. For a moment he just sputtered and stared at me, while his wife moaned and fanned herself, on the verge of fainting.

"Who...who are you?" Vadich asked at last. "I *know* you, somehow, I'm sure of it."

I clenched my jaw, then, throwing caution to the waves, I said, "I'm the one you'll be negotiating with, Ambassador."

His cheeks flushed a brilliant crimson at that. "But Istia...but the Godar..."

"Is dead," I finished for him. "And I am his son."

# Chapter 17 ❧ Jarik

AMBASSADOR VADICH DIDN'T SAY A WORD. FOR THE SPACE OF THREE BREATHS he didn't even twitch.

Then he took one step back, turned to his table, and started rummaging through a leather satchel stuffed full of official-looking papers. He was muttering to himself now, probably asking himself why he knew nothing about me, why I wasn't named as a contact in his dossiers and advisements. After a few moments he sat down with his back to our table, and leaned his head in his hands while his wife tried in vain to reassure him. I left him to his panic and nudged Mirin aside, taking the outer seat on the bench in case the Cavners—or anyone else—needed dealing with.

I wasn't sure what to make of the way Nika was watching me—or, for that matter, the rest of the people in the room. Even if they hadn't understood the verbal spar, they had obviously appreciated the sense of it, and they looked at me with open interest that made me strangely uncomfortable. At least the Cavners weren't looking at me now—were making a point not to look at me—which suggested they had some modicum of sense, and an ounce of care for their own safety.

For my part I refused to acknowledge any of them. I leaned my elbows on the table and stared into the fire dancing in the hearth. It was so strange a sight, after so many nights with only the silent, invisible heat of a steam vent; I was captivated by the riot of color, the chaos of noise. For a moment I could almost forget that I was in a room full of people, and all of them staring at me.

"Istiason," a small voice said at my elbow.

I startled—it was more the name that caught me by surprise than the unexpected voice. *Istiason*. It was a name Istians gave to strangers, as a title of respect, the way a Cavner would say *sir* or *Katzpota*. But it meant so much more than that. And I...I felt so unworthy of it.

I turned and found a boy of about ten or eleven standing by my chair, his eyes startlingly dark against the fairness of his skin and hair. Those eyes were wide open, watching me with curiosity scarcely gathered in from fear.

My heart wrenched.

"Bugs," I said, the name catching in my throat.

The boy tipped his head—the word was Cavnish, and he didn't understand it. And he wasn't Bugs, I knew he wasn't, but the knowing didn't matter; every moment I expected to see a ribbon of blood unfurling from his chest, staining his white shirt red. I couldn't breathe.

I said, "I'm sorry."

His eyes widened even further. "For what?"

I shook my head. How could he ask? For everything I'd done wrong. For my weakness, my stupidity, my recklessness. I'd turned their world upside down, and for what? For the dream, for the madness?

How could he look at me like that, like he didn't know, like he didn't understand?

"Taumir," Nika said.

I was standing up—I didn't remember leaving the bench. My hand pressed against my forehead.

The boy asked, "Are you going to save us?"

"Save you?" I echoed, and there was laughter on my lips and my heart was breaking. "All that I touch fractures like glass. I am the right hand of ruin and the air that's broken, saturated in Kudric runes. What is the point...what is the point of cacophony anyway?"

The boy's eyes were white, white like Zagger's in my dreams, white like death. Then I blinked, and they were not, but they were wide and staring and full of fear. That was no wonder. Terror rattled against my ribs like a heartbeat. I backed up a step, then another, shaking my head to drive away the whispers. Then, with the world shuddering around me in senseless mosaics, I turned and strode from the tavern.

Outside in the grey dusk, my feet stumbled and slipped on the slick paving stones, but I didn't slow down my hectic pace. I walked like a blind man all the way back down the long sloping hill to the wharf, past the docks, past the ships and the noisy gulls settling into their evening roosts, to the rocks and the waves and the endless wind. Climbing up onto the tumbled stones, I stared out at the horizon and tried to breathe.

"You hold on too tight," someone said.

I jerked around. A man stood behind me in a wild chaos of light, like lightning and wind barely tamed into human form. There was too much brilliance about him for me to make any sense of him, but he was tall, and I knew he was beautiful, in the way that the moon and the fathomless night were beautiful. His eyes gleamed a white and fire-blue brightness, and I realized I had seen them before, in the depths of the waves when Agnir and I had been cast adrift on the empty sea.

I regarded him without fear, though part of me wondered if I ought to bow before him. For some reason I thought I should. But my perch on the wet rocks was too precarious; if I moved again, I was afraid I would fall.

"I'm not holding onto anything," I said.

"You hold onto guilt," he said, "but you are absolved by blood."

"Whose?"

"The sea's."

I turned, carefully, to see the waves churning against the crags below me, moon-silver foam masking the turbulent dark beneath.

"I'm afraid of the sea," I said. "You don't understand."

"I understand you are afraid of yourself."

I glanced over my shoulder at him. There was no rebuke in his eyes, no condemnation, not even any pity. He just watched me, infinite and remote as the stars. A fisherman standing on the pier close by was staring in our direction, but—I didn't know why—his gaze was on me, not on the other man. He didn't understand either.

I looked at him, and he turned away.

As I faced the waves again, I asked the man still standing behind me, "Who are you?"

"You know who I am," he said, "though you are too stubborn to believe."

For an endless moment I held my breath. Everything inside me recoiled from the name that rattled through my thoughts, but it was on my lips before I could cage it in.

"Wake."

I didn't turn to see his confirmation; I didn't need to.

"You shouldn't fear the sea," he said. "I hold the reins of the waves, and I will never let the sea harm you. Do you doubt me?"

The waves crashed against the stone, spraying me with ice-cold mist, but I didn't shiver; I was on fire. Did I doubt him? Did I trust that what he said was true? I wasn't sure. It made sense the way the waves on the stones made sense, in a turbulent and turquoise way.

"I don't doubt you," I said. "But I don't trust you."

My honesty didn't seem to offend him. I could sense his laughter, and then he said, simply, "Trust me."

"I don't know how."

"Take a step forward."

I stepped forward. I stood at the very edge of the rocks now, where the stone was slick from foam and frost, and the sea opened below me like a breathless dark abyss.

"Now take another."

I swallowed. If I took another step I would fall, and the waves would slam me like flotsam into the rocks.

I said, "I can't."

"I will protect you," he said. "I will always protect you."

I felt his hand like a brand on my forehead and I drew in a quick breath, salt-sharp and cold. Before I could give myself time to think, I closed my eyes and leaned forward.

And then arms wrapped around me, and someone was yelling, dragging me back. We stumbled over the broken rocks and crashed to the sand below in a tangle of limbs as the wind blew and a thin sleet began to fall.

I twisted out of my captor's grip and scrambled to my feet—or tried. Halfway up my legs gave way and I sank to my knees against the crags, and stared at Iskari staring back at me.

"What in *Veka*'s name were you doing?" he shouted, when he'd gotten over his surprise. "Taumir, what were you *thinking*?"

I leaned my head back against the rock and laughed, but it hurt; I must have bruised my ribs when I landed. "Moving forward," I said, "in his name."

"What?"

He didn't believe me. I couldn't understand the look on his face; it made no sense; it was a hawk's look, narrow-eyed and askance, full of fear masked as anger.

"I was testing him. Doing what...what he told me, to see if he was telling the truth," I said. "It's not my fault you don't see it."

"Who told you what?" Iskari asked, picking himself up and brushing the black sand off his pants.

I wondered how Iskari could be so blind; Wake stood just behind him. How could Iskari not feel the hum of his power, or the weight of his stare?

I pointed, and said, "*Veka.*"

Silence, for a moment. Then Iskari tipped his head, like he was waiting for me to say something else.

"What?" he asked. He glanced over his shoulder when I just gestured again, then back at me with a frown. He asked again, "What?"

"*Veka,*" I repeated. I didn't think that he hadn't heard me the first time. His obstinacy in his own ignorance was starting to frustrate me.

Finally Iskari seemed to make the connection, but if anything he seemed more dismayed than before. "*Veka*...told you..."

His voice trailed off, and I groaned and tipped my head back, hands clasped around my head. When I slanted my eyes open I caught Wake's gaze, but he only shook his head in pitying silence.

"He said I just have to trust," I said.

Iskari's face darkened, and he took a step closer to me, pointing toward the rocks. "You were about to throw yourself into the sea!" he shouted. "Any Istian knows you don't tempt the sea! You would have died!"

"No," I said, patiently. I thought, but didn't say, *You fool, I am the sea.* Instead I pointed again and said, "He said he was going to protect me, but that was the test, wasn't it?"

"Who was?"

"Stop *shouting* at me," I said, raising my own voice as I stood up.

Iskari turned a little away, almost running into Wake, then he spun back toward me with a fist clenched at his side. I watched his hand, wary. I watched his feet for the telltale turn, the shift.

"Are you completely insane?" he said. "Look around! There is no one here. There is *no one here*, Taumir! Do you understand?"

I shook my head, feeling suddenly bone-achingly weary. I took my eyes off of him just long enough, and then his hands were on my shirt, throwing me back against the boulders. The stone dug into my spine, sharp and real, and cold. I pressed my hands against the rough surface to find surety. If I'd wanted to I could have fought Iskari off, but I didn't have the energy. I just watched him, quiet, and waited for him to realize the truth.

"You think God is talking to you?" he asked. His face was too close to mine, to the side, so I could hear him over the roar of the waves. "*Veka* isn't talking to you! No one was talking to you!"

"He doesn't understand," Wake said, standing beside me. I could feel his presence there like an ember in the night. "None of them will understand."

"So I'm alone," I said, half under my breath.

Wake nodded.

"What?" Iskari asked, as if I'd been talking to him.

"You don't understand," I said. Then, weighting my words with power, I said, "Let me go."

His hands dropped from my collar, and he took a half a step back. But as I moved to pass him, I caught a movement from the corner of my eye. His arm, tensing. The fear in his eyes.

Then a rage of pain, and nothing.

WHEN I CAME TO, I was still sitting on the beach under the last shreds of silver-blue twilight, and Iskari had gone. Nika sat cross-legged beside me, though, pensive and distant with her eyes on the inland hills, their snowy slopes ghostly against the darkening sky. I gritted my teeth. And then, as I flexed my neck and felt the swollen split in my lip, I felt her glance toward me.

"Iskari said you thought *Veka* was talking to you," she said, when the silence had carried on like the night.

I snorted. Wake had been standing right there, and Iskari still wouldn't believe his own eyes. That wasn't my fault.

"Taumir—" she started, and faltered. I watched her fingers, drifting in the coarse black sand like white feathers. Her eyes met mine, and I thought she looked sadder then than I had ever seen her. "God doesn't…God doesn't *talk* to people."

"I'm not people," I muttered.

Her breath fell in a sigh. "I forgot," she said. "You're the Zealot."

My eyes met hers, and I didn't say a word. To her credit, she didn't smile. Instead she jerked her gaze away from mine, jaw tight and hands still on the sand. I folded my arms and tipped my face back to catch the cold wind on my burning skin.

"Iskari hit me."

She lifted a shoulder. "He was afraid."

I lifted a hand and felt through my hair, gingerly, to prod the skin on the back of my head. It was wet and hot, sticky with blood. "He *really* hit me."

"He was *really* afraid."

"So he hit me?"

"What would you have done?" she asked, glancing at me sidelong.

"Listened?" I offered. "Do you think I was lying?"

Her lips parted, but for too long no words came. Then she shook her head and said, "I don't know what to think. I don't know what's gotten into you. What happened in the tavern? You scared that poor boy out of his wits."

"He was a ghost of my past," I said.

"His name is Alva Anvirson, and he is not a ghost." When I said nothing, she sighed and drew up her knees, resting her hands on top of them. "You can't..." she started, and faltered, and bit her lower lip.

I waited. A faint swirl of snow began to fall.

"Whatever is going on with you, I think...I think you need to step away from the moot."

"You think I'm insane," I said, tipping my head to look at her.

"I don't know what to think," she said again. "You have powers... you have power that I could never have even imagined. Power I didn't think was possible. I don't claim to be able to judge you, but..."

"But you're judging me."

She didn't answer immediately. "I just think that perhaps you need to take care of yourself before you try to confront Rigvar. Whatever it is you're going through...maybe that's more important than chasing after crowns."

"You don't understand," I said, and got unsteadily to my feet. "It's all the same thing."

# Chapter 18 · Jarik

*I* WAS TEN FEET AWAY FROM NIKA WHEN I HEARD HER FOLLOWING AFTER ME, the crunch of her boots sharp in the black sand. She caught up to me in just a few strides, but then, I wasn't walking particularly quickly.

"Come on," she said. "You need to get some sleep. You look like death."

"God, don't say that!" I cried, before I could stop myself. The words sounded panicked, more than I wanted to admit.

She shot me a sideways glance and shook her head, but didn't say anything else. I followed her back into the narrow city streets, lost in my thoughts until I realized we had passed the tavern and Nika still didn't show any signs of slowing down. But when I asked where we were going, she only looked at me over her shoulder and kept walking. After a few moments I realized that Wake was pacing beside me. He was taller than I remembered from the beach, and he walked with hands folded behind his back, head tipped down in thoughtful silence.

"They won't believe you even if you tell them," he said presently. "Don't expect them to see what you see."

"Are you the mad god?"

He stopped, and turned to face me. I stopped too, waiting, holding my breath. His face was inscrutable, but I could sense amusement, and something like pity or contempt in the bright eternity of his gaze.

"You don't know?" he asked.

"Know what? What are you talking about?" I gestured toward

him. "You can't expect me to know anything about you."

"Taumir?"

I jerked my attention away from Wake, and saw Nika standing a few feet from me, watching me in pale alarm.

"What?" I snapped.

"What…" She gestured at me, punctuating the puzzlement on her face. "What are you doing?"

I glanced back at Wake, who just regarded me with a look of sympathy that made no sense.

"It's as I told you," he murmured.

I put a hand to my forehead and turned away from him. "It's nothing," I said to Nika. "But if you don't tell me where we're going, I'm stopping here."

"Honestly!" she said, and, pursing her lips, studied me a moment longer in silence. Then she said, "Iskari and Mirin have gone ahead to the lodging house. It's not far, just about five streets up that way."

She pointed, but I just shrugged and fell in beside her again, indicating the ink-dark road at our feet with a faint wave. Muttering something under her breath, she turned and walked on, driving us at a brutal pace up the hill through the gathering shadows. About fifteen minutes later we arrived at a rather tall building surrounded by a number of small shops, all built into each other as if they couldn't stand on their own. The lodging house was made almost entirely of grey stone, except for the uppermost floor, which was paneled in that dark Cavnish wood. Oil lamps shone brightly in every window on every floor, and a noise of laughter and conversation trickled out onto the street from the ground floor.

It wasn't until I paused to hold the door open for Wake that I realized he had disappeared again, without a word, without a farewell. I frowned and let the door shut behind me.

The ground floor of the lodging house was a common area, with several long tables for dining and a few low couches huddled around a sprawling fireplace. To my surprise, the room was almost packed. I'd never expected to see so many Istians gathered together in one place, and a niggling suspicion crept into the back of my mind. The people were all talking loudly over each other, reminding me of Agnir's sailors, and they ranged in years from about my own to almost ancient. Some were dressed better than others, though all in that half-wild Istian fashion, but I couldn't get any hint of their identities just from looking at them.

I caught Nika's arm before she moved too far into the room.

"Who are all these people?"

"Nervous?" She flashed me a smile that felt rather too cruel. "They're mostly *sodthari*."

"So many?"

She shrugged. "*Sodthari*, their sons or daughters, some assistants. A few guards."

I squelched the rising panic in the back of my mind. These were the people I had to persuade to listen to me—the people Trabin had sent me to lead. Regardless of whether or not they voted to name me Godar, these were the people who could keep Istia out of war, or send her to her destruction. And that was in my hands, one way or another.

*Not now,* I thought. *I can't do this right now.*

Someone hailed Nika from across the room, and without a word of excuse she left me standing irresolute near the doorway, wishing with a childish desperation that I could simply fade into the floor and disappear. Finally I spotted Iskari sitting at a table near the fireplace, alone but for a man dozing over his mug of ale at the far end of the bench. Letting out my breath in a faint sigh of relief, I made my way over to join him.

"Are you going to hit me again?" I asked, standing behind the chair across from him.

He measured me a while in silence, leaning back in his chair, face unreadable. Then he sighed and sat forward with a courteous gesture toward the chair.

"If you don't give me cause to, I won't."

That was as much as I could ask for. I sat down, and dug my fingers against my forehead. The noise in my head was almost unbearable.

"Did Mirin go to bed already?"

He nodded, but he seemed distracted. Then, unexpectedly, he said, "I'm sorry, Taumir. For striking you. I wasn't thinking."

I wondered with idle curiosity how many times in his life Iskari had apologized for anything. When I realized that he was still watching me, waiting for my forgiveness with more patience than I had any right to, I waved a hand generally in his direction and kept my thoughts to myself. Then I realized Iskari wasn't watching me at all, but something behind me, and his face was slowly draining of color.

I twisted around in my seat and saw Rigvar seated at a table not far from ours, with Nika at his shoulder, her gaze lingering on his face with a look almost like rapture in her eyes. My stomach tightened into impossible knots, and I felt the blood in my veins turn to sludge, a mess of dread and rage and contempt. Rigvar was holding one of Nika's hands, but otherwise he was ignoring her.

His attention was all on me.

"Taumir Eyidson," he said suddenly.

His voice carried clearly over the din of the other patrons. I could feel the weight of magic in his words, and silence fell like night over the room. All eyes shifted toward us.

"Rigvar," I said.

His mouth lifted in a faint smile. "So now we know each other, and yet we've never been properly introduced."

"I'm devastated, as you see."

A faint trace of laughter chased through the room. Rigvar caught the eye of a few of the patrons. I caught the glimmer of a smile in his eyes, but it never touched his mouth.

"Well, as you should be. There's a rumor going around that you mean to challenge me for the *aydrding*. Is that true?"

"I have more of a right to it than you do," I said.

Rigvar's brows shot up in surprise, and he gave a fluid gesture toward the people around us. "I think they're the ones who will decide matters of *right*. After all, how are we to know that your claim to Eyid's bloodline is true? Very convenient for you to appear after his death, when he can't confirm that you are who you claim to be."

The smiles of the guests faded into murmured indignation. I got to my feet, standing a little closer to the fire, facing Rigvar across the room. Nika wouldn't look at me. I couldn't bear to look at her. For all she'd confessed to being drawn to Rigvar, I couldn't help but wonder if she was entirely in command of herself at that moment. I could feel Rigvar's magic washing in waves over the crowd, stirring them up with a more effortless control than even the Cavnish Sculptor Lute had ever managed.

I was still trying to formulate an answer, a counter-challenge, when Rigvar went on, "And judging by your mage sign, I'm assuming that isn't your real face, either, is it? Very clever, to make yourself look like

Eyid, to help bolster your claims. Do you always claim powerful men as your father? I heard you just came from Cavnal. Were you someone's bastard son there, too?"

Instinctively I glanced at Iskari, but he wouldn't look at me; he was staring at Rigvar through a red-hot blaze of anger.

"I don't need to claim anyone as my father to have power in my own right," I said, glaring a challenge across the room at Rigvar. "I would've thought that was something you would understand. Or, who was *your* father?"

"A man who at least knew of my existence. A man who could give me a true and proper Istian name. Tell me, *Taumir*, did you pick out your own name? Did you think it was clever, little revenant?" A few people started to laugh. "Isn't that something the urchins in Cavnal do, when they don't know their own parentage? Give themselves clever little names? But perhaps we shouldn't expect any less of our poor friend here," he added, speaking to the *sodthari* and other patrons. "He is Cavnish through and through. Just look at the way he's standing. Everything about him gives him away."

He mocked my pose and a chorus of laughter echoed around the room. I couldn't move—if I moved, I would be acknowledging that what he said was true. I could feel the heat rising to my cheeks; I forced Shade's face to stay quiet, and pale as ever. But I couldn't think of a single word to say. It was all just noise and a dark ocean sadness anyway.

Rigvar rolled right over my silence, giving me a sly smile as he said to the guests, "But I suppose there is at least something admirable in his absolute arrogance, thinking he could come to Istia and prop himself up as our ruler." His voice pitched up absurdly. *"Look at me! I'm Eyid's son, I really am! I've never even been to Istia but you really should make me your ruler!"*

More laughter. Iskari's hands tightened on the edge of the table, knuckles white. Rigvar allowed himself a brief, unrestrained smile as he surveyed the crowd.

"And what claim do you have to the fire crown?" I asked. My voice did not sound nearly as commanding as I intended.

The mirth vanished from Rigvar's face. "I've stood at the helm and kept the ship from crashing in the time since Eyid's death," he said. *His* voice commanded the entire room. "What do you really want here? A place to call home? Is that all you are, boy, a little stray pup looking for a family to call your own?"

He tucked his hands up under his chin, like a dog begging for scraps.

I tried to answer, but my words were lost in the laughter and shouts of the people. Then Rigvar glanced up at Nika, drawing her down to say something in her ear. She hesitated, then whispered something back to him, and all the while she spoke, Rigvar kept me pinioned at the end of his stare. My heart was an anchor in the pit of my soul. I searched the room desperately for some sign of Wake, but he was nowhere to be found. Then, as Nika straightened up, her gaze found mine, and her eyes were full of horror.

Rigvar was smiling.

"Thank you, Nika," he said, stroking her arm as if she were a child. Then, still staring at me, he lifted her hand to place a kiss on it, that same smile hidden in the depths of his eyes. "I think I have been a fool," he said then, and got abruptly to his feet. Everyone's attention was riveted on him, waiting to drink in his every word. "I cannot possibly challenge this man for the *aydrding*."

The people murmured in astonishment, leaning toward him collectively to better hear his voice—it was soft now, more alluring than ever.

He leaned onto the table and said, as if telling each of them a great secret, "Do you know who he is?"

The silence drew out, breathless. I held my own breath, reaching for strength from the fire behind me. What was he going to say? Had Iskari told Nika that I was Prince Tarik? He looked pale with alarm, and his hand, I noticed, was lingering over the hilt of the long-bladed hunting knife he wore on his thigh.

"What will it serve you to tell them?" I asked. The words sounded strangled.

"Tell us!" someone in the crowd called, and the request was echoed by a handful of other voices.

"What don't you want us to know, Cavner?"

"He's not a Cavner!" Iskari said suddenly, slamming his other hand in a fist on the table.

A slow, cold smile spread across Rigvar's face. "Of course he isn't," he said. "He belongs to no land. He's the *Zealot*."

My horror was drowned in the crowd's cacophony of laughter. Rigvar held up his hands, trying to silence them.

"He's not just the Zealot," he said, the smile turning cruel. "*God* talks to him. At least, that's what he claims. Isn't that true, Taumir?"

All the blood sank to the soles of my feet. I felt cold all over, a little dizzy, and I stared and kept staring at Nika, who stood with one hand over her mouth, her other hand trapped by Rigvar's.

It was the truth. How could Rigvar stand there and mock me for something that was true?

"I've seen him!" someone called. "Talking to himself. Arguing with the wind."

"Tell me, what does God say to you?" Rigvar asked.

I could barely hear him. My gaze drifted over the sea of laughing faces, fingers pointing in my direction, tendrils of magic wreathing through the crowd. I wanted to grab hold of the threads and snap them like spider silk, but they slipped endlessly out of my grasp. Nika took a half-step toward me.

"Do you want to know?" I gritted through my teeth.

"You don't—" Rigvar started, and was drowned out by more laughter. "You don't deny it?"

Iskari's hand shot out and latched onto my lower arm, a tight, uncompromising grip. I shook him off.

"Why should I?" I said. "It's true. It's…it's true. Who are you to say it isn't?"

"He really believes it! Look at his face!"

"You see, or, you don't—you don't see… It's the st…it's the stones, and the stones…the stones are…" My hand spasmed in a fist and I looked at Rigvar in horror, but the meaning was slipping endlessly out of my grasp, dragged out in the currents, crumbling like water. "Rigvar! Stop…stop *stealing* the words! You're…you're taking them and you think you know what to do with them, but they're not…they're not *yours!*"

"Oh, so I'm stealing your words now, am I?"

I could feel the fire seeping into my soul from the hearth behind me. But before I could reach into it, Iskari lurched to his feet and grabbed me by the shoulder.

"Let's go," he said in my ear.

"Running away!" Rigvar called as Iskari drove me toward the

staircase at the back of the room.

I jerked away from Iskari and rounded on Rigvar, rage blazing through me.

"Oh no," Rigvar crowed, taking one dramatic step back with his hands lifted. "Someone protect me! I've made him angry. Watch out, *Veka* is going to strike me down!"

Amid the shouts and laughter, Iskari grabbed me again, and this time I didn't resist as he pulled me toward the stairs.

# Chapter 19 ❦ Jarik

ISKARI PROPELLED ME UP THE NARROW, CREAKING STAIRS TO THE MEN'S common bunk room, two floors above. To my relief, no one was there yet except Mirin, who was already asleep, but that was the only comfort I had. I was surrounded by row on row of bunks, and all of them would soon be occupied by the guests downstairs who had just laughed me to scorn. There were no private rooms in this lodging house. Part of me swore I would rather sleep in the barn with the horses than face a single hour in that room when it was full.

Iskari released me once we were inside, and I headed over to the thin-glassed window, which looked out over the night-quiet city streets. After a moment Iskari joined me there, sitting on the narrow window ledge with his elbows on his knees.

"I'm sorry," he said at length.

I looked at him sideways. "That's the second time today you've said that. The second time I've ever heard you say that. You're making me nervous."

He lifted a hand like a shrug. "It's the truth. I *am* sorry."

I gritted my teeth and leaned my forehead against the cold glass. It was still snowing outside, and wind-blown drifts of powdered white softened the edges of the street. A man with a massive dog at his heels walked briskly across the road below the window, ice fringing his hair and beard and gathering in the dog's dark fur. I pressed a finger against the frost-rimed window and traced the rune I read in the man's soul, bright and honest and sharp.

"It's my fault," Iskari said abruptly. "When I found you earlier...if I had just stayed with you, kept what happened to myself, then Nika would never have known about it. Rigvar wouldn't have been able to draw that out of her."

I lowered my hand. "Did you tell her anything else about me?" I asked. "Did you tell her who I am in Cavnal?"

"No," he said. "No, that secret is still safe."

We were silent a little while, then Iskari said, "You shouldn't have had to endure that. Rigvar is a complete *stodadrakkim*. I don't know how he did it either. He isn't that funny, and he certainly isn't that clever."

"It was magic," I said. "I could see it but I couldn't bring it to order."

A pause. Then, "You could see it?"

"Of course. It was the shape of the energy," I said. I tapped my fingers against the glass, all around the edges of the design I'd drawn in the frost. "The rune-patterns tracing the electricals in their souls, shifting the currents." I turned, gesturing to the air between us. "It was there, it was so clear. But it was just water."

He was staring at me. I got the sense that maybe I had said something wrong, but what? He wasn't a mage. How could he possibly understand? Or maybe it was me that was broken. Fractured, like glass.

"You're not broken," a voice beside me said.

I turned and met Wake's gaze—he looked somber, and, I thought, somehow worried.

"I feel broken," I said.

"I told you already," Wake said. "You hold on too tightly. Glass only breaks when it is cold, when it draws back from the fire of the furnace." He came a step closer to me, eyes like lightning blazing into me. "You are resisting my power."

With that last word he drove his hand against my forehead again, and I stumbled back at the ecstatic burn that shot through me, driving fire through every nerve and vein. My hands hit the wall behind me, and I pressed them against it to know it was real.

"God, Taumir," Iskari said.

I shook my head, dazed. Iskari was staring at me, wide-eyed, but when I glanced to the side again, Wake was gone.

"What?"

"Your face," he said. "Were you...what..."

"Spit it out, Iskari," I snapped. I felt unsettled, like my skin couldn't

contain me, like the world couldn't contain me.

"Your eyes, just now. Your whole face." He had his head turned a little away from me now, like he was afraid of looking too closely at me—the way someone might look at the setting sun. I gave him an impatient gesture. "I can't explain it. It was bright. Like...fire. Behind your skin. Behind your eyes. How did you do that?"

"I didn't do anything," I said. My fingers drifted up to touch my forehead, where I could still feel the burn of Wake's touch, and a shudder crept through me. "He did."

"You saw him," he said, flatly. "Again. Just now."

"Just now," I affirmed. "You didn't?"

He turned around to lean against the wall, staring out over the empty rows of bunks with his arms folded over his chest. I pressed my forehead against the glass of the window again, hoping that the cold of it would temper the blaze I felt inside.

"I didn't," he said.

I studied him sideways, curious, but there was no flicker of deception within him. "Really?" I said. "That's interesting."

"It's interesting that I—" he started, and scowled at me. "Taumir, I'm not the one who..."

He faltered again and I said, "I wish you would just believe me. Believe that I'm telling the truth. Believe that I'm not...I'm not mad. Because I'm *not*."

"Has anything like this ever happened to you before? Have you ever seen things that...that other people didn't?"

"No," I said. "Maybe. When I was young, when I was a hundred, and I was a cat. But that wasn't me. That's getting the story backwards, like flipping through a book from back to front. You can't make sense of the pattern when you go that way, but the pattern is still there, inside it, like harmonies and resonances and...and fractions divided into themselves. They just don't see it. They never do. They're blind. That's why they don't understand, why they'll never understand as long as they're in the trees. But it's there, in the stones, and the sea, and the stars, and the pattern—the pattern, Iskari! It's in the music and in the blood, and they would know it if they held it to a mirror, but the mirror is broken and just a window. And that's the secret I mean to teach them, but they'll never listen to me either, because it's all backwards in their heads too. Why are you looking at me like that?"

"*Veka*," he said, and then he just stared at me, fear stark in his eyes. "I don't... When you talk like that, I don't understand what you're saying."

"Of course you don't," I said, indifferently. "Your soul has no runes."

"My soul *what?*"

"It's nothing to be ashamed of. Iskari, please say you believe me."

"I want to," Iskari said, with a fervor that surprised me. "But how can I? The things you say, the things you do... What is a man supposed to make of all of that? You claim that *God* is talking to you. Do you know what that sounds like to the rest of us? I believe in *Veka*, of course I do. We all do. And we believe he's the one who wakens magic in the souls of the mages. Everyone believes that. But that's *safe*. That's...contained. We never really talk about him interacting with us beyond that. Imposing himself on our lives. Stepping into this world and taking part in its events. No, he doesn't *do* that. He's above. Separate. *Other*. But you're claiming to have conversations with him, like we're talking right now. Don't you understand how hard that is for people to accept? Most people...most people who claim they hear God talking to them, we place in asylums for their—and our—protection."

"Do you think I wanted this?" I asked. It wasn't a good response to his protest, but they were the only words I could find. "To feel like I'm always straddling the line, between this world and another, between sanity and madness, between life and death? I don't want it. But... sometimes we have no choice. Sometimes it's the suffering we don't ask for that means the most." I let out my breath in a long sigh and lowered my hand from the glass, where I'd been drawing and redrawing the Kudric runes. "I never wanted to be King, either, and yet I would have embraced that crown for my father...for Trabin's sake, and for the sake of my nation. Is this what's asked of me, now?"

But Iskari didn't answer. He was standing perfectly still beside me, too still, and finally I glanced over my shoulder to see what he was staring at. To my dismay, it was Mirin, laying on his side facing us, his eyes wide open, too wide. And that was the moment I realized that those last few words I'd said, I'd said in Cavnish. In fact, half of the whole conversation had been in Cavnish, that broken meld of languages like my mother used to speak when we were alone, half-Tulian, half-Cavnish. But somehow I knew that wasn't what Iskari had meant when he said he didn't understand me.

"*Thrigun...stodadrakkur,*" I muttered.

Iskari laughed at that, a loud and open laugh. Then he sobered and put a hand on my shoulder, barely meeting my gaze before releasing me and striding over to Mirin's bunk. Without a word, he grabbed the Cavner by the front of his jumper and dragged him off his mattress, and marched him over to stand in front of me.

Mirin's eyes never left my face. I wasn't sure what I read in them—it felt like horror, but it was tinged with awe.

"King?" he asked finally, a hopeful note in his voice. I couldn't tell what he was hoping, though—that I would deny it, or confirm it. "Your...Your Highness? Prince Tarik?"

I sighed and said, "Yes."

His legs wobbled slightly, like they wanted to kneel all on their own. "But...it's not possible..."

"Don't ask me to change my face to prove it to you," I said. "It hurts like hell, and I'm... There's too much noise right now."

"But you're the Zealot."

I hesitated. I knew he meant the name the Cavners had given to Shade, but now I felt keenly that the word meant so much more than that. And I wasn't sure if I wanted to accept all that it meant.

Still, I bowed my head and said, "That's what they called me."

"But..." he stammered again. "You're a *Jixy*. Prince Tarik...the Prince ain't a Jixy."

I glanced over at Iskari, who was watching Mirin with suppressed amusement—and faint impatience. Mirin clutched his arms around his narrow chest, shivering in the cold air that seeped through the thin window glass.

"King Trabin knew?" he asked finally.

"Yes," I said, again.

"He was... Then, it's true, and he was protecting you. But you also said...you're the Godarson. Is *that* true, or were you lying about that?"

"It's true."

"So that means..."

A little sadness washed over me as I nodded, knowing that by doing so, I was confirming his suspicions of my mother. "Things happen," I said. "And life is never simple."

"But he was protecting you," Mirin said again. "He protected you and the Queen both. He...*loved* you."

"Hard to believe?" I asked blandly.

He just shook his head, back and forth, over and over again, then suddenly he reached out and grabbed my arms. Iskari tensed instantly, but I warned him away with a glance.

"What are you doing here?" Mirin cried. I was shocked to see that his dark eyes were glittering, barely blinking back tears. "Cavnal needs you. Why are you here? We need you...we need our King."

"And Istia needs its Godar," Iskari said, sharp.

"The world needs my emissary even more, beyond the need for crowns and kings."

I jolted and instinctively scanned the room, but Wake was nowhere to be seen. Slowly, Mirin lowered his hands, and dropped to his knees in front of me, both knees, a reverence beyond the customary genuflection. I shuddered and tried to make him stand, but he just bowed lower until his head almost touched the floor at my feet.

"Your Majesty," he whispered. "Forgive me. I said things... I *did* things..."

"I'm not your King," I said, shaken to my core. "And there is nothing to forgive. How could I chastise you for your zeal?" I reached down and pulled him to his feet, keeping both my hands firmly on his shoulders. "Listen to me, Mirin. What you know...you are only the third person in Istia who knows it." Iskari glanced at me sharply, but I ignored him. "I need it to stay that way. Before his death, King Trabin commanded me to come to Istia and lead these people, and that is what I am trying to do. But I can only do it as long as my past is my own, and my secrets are my own."

He nodded, then seized one of my hands and pressed his lips against it, like Jig had done once, what felt like a lifetime ago. Pulling my hand free, I nodded him wordlessly toward his bed. He backed away, then went and flung himself on the mattress. He made no sound, but I could tell from the way his shoulders shook that he was weeping.

"Well, that was enlightening," Iskari remarked. I looked at him sidelong and waited for him to elaborate. "Who else knows who you are?"

"Your father. He knew from the beginning, somehow."

"Ah. And...what was that you said, that Trabin told you to come here?"

"It was the last command he gave me," I said, and brushed a hand over my forehead.

"Did he want you to become Godar?"

"I don't know what he meant. I never had a chance to ask. He just said, lead them. What does that mean, Iskari? Take the *aydrding*? Lead them into war, or away from war entirely? But if Rigvar…if Rigvar goes on as he did tonight, I will never be able to convince Istia to follow me in anything."

"Before the moot," Iskari said. "You can make your case to the *sodthari* then, and they will listen to you."

"Why should they?"

He smiled thinly. "Magic is forbidden at Hejmstrathvir. It always has been, and you can see why. With mages who have such spectacular abilities to influence people's thoughts and beliefs, they had to make sure that the *sodthari* were always free to judge with their own minds and hearts. Rigvar's influence through magic is too strong. No one under its sway is free in any sense of the word."

The words were bitter; I knew he was thinking of Nika.

"No," I said. "His power is cowardly."

"Will you forgive her?"

I turned back to the window. "You said it. She wasn't in control of herself or her words. I could see her horror at what Rigvar made her do. If she asks me, of course I'll forgive her."

"Only if she asks you?"

I lifted a shoulder. "How else will I know she did it because of Rigvar, and not because of her own wish to betray me?"

"Fair enough."

I looked at the reflection of the room in the window's glass, still empty but for the three of us. Soon, though, the people downstairs would weary of their cheap ale and talk, and would come up to claim beds and sleep. I didn't want to be there when they did, but when I said as much to Iskari, he just sighed and shook his head.

"This is the only lodging house in Bregjarvani."

I thought perhaps I could ask for lodging at one of the townspeople's houses, but who would give a room to a stranger for no good reason? Even if I claimed to be Eyid's son, would that be enough to demand Istian hospitality? No, I knew what I would do, but I also knew Iskari would never let me do it.

"I'll find my own place to sleep," I said, and turned away from the window. "Don't follow me, and don't try to stop me. I'll be back at the alehouse in the morning."

"Taumir, wait!" Iskari called, but I was already walking away from him. A moment later I heard him jogging to catch up to me, then his hand was on my arm. "Don't...don't do anything..."

"Stupid?" I finished for him. "Rash? Insane?"

He closed his mouth and scowled at me, but at least he released me. "You're your own man," he said. "I'm not your nanny or your bodyguard. Do what you will."

I barely nodded; before he could change his mind, I left the bunk room and made my way down the stairs, and out through the servants' door to the narrow street beyond.

# Chapter 20 ✳ Hayli

I'D LEARNED THE VERY FIRST DAY WE'D DONE WATCH ROTATIONS THAT THE FOX hours of the night were the grobbing *worst* time to stand on post. There wasn't enough time before the watch started to get any proper sleep, and once the shift ended, there weren't enough hours to nap before the day started with its endless march of meetings and duties and drills. Somehow I always seemed to get stuck with that shift, too—sometimes I wondered if it was because I didn't complain about it to anyone but Piper, in the safety of my own thoughts.

A good twenty minutes before I was scheduled to report to the depot gate, I walked into the smallest of Borokhev's three guardhouses to find Coins and Zip both perched up on the thick oak table, cross-legged, with an assortment of padlocks, picks and tension wrenches scattered between them. Zip sat hunched over a heavy lock he had set up on his knee, tongue sticking out just past his teeth as he tried to jimmy the pins. Coins grinned at me in greeting as I joined them, but Zip was too focused to pay me any mind.

"You teaching that lad all your bad habits, Coins?" I asked.

"Aw, hell, he already has more bad habits than a gentleman of leisure," Coins said, mocking a high-street accent on the term. He grinned and twirled a pick through his fingers. "I'm just…helping the little thiefling learn how to refine them."

He shifted back to make room on the table, and I, after just a tick of hesitation, climbed up to sit with them.

"What're you about, Hayli?" Coins asked as I picked up a set of tools and a lock.

It had been a long time since I'd practiced my lockpicking, and a blush warmed my cheeks as I tried—and failed—to slip the lock with Coins watching me. A minute and I didn't answer him at all, just sat like Zip, hunched over my lock, biting the tip of my tongue and trying to feel for the shift of the pins.

"Waiting to gan on watch," I said finally.

"Again? Thought you officers were supposed to get out of the bad watches," he said, "but you lot seem to get stuck with the worst of them."

I grimaced and didn't answer.

"Need company?"

I glanced up at that, frowning. "You already did your round. You should be sleeping, anyway."

"Ah, sleep is for the dead," Coins said through a languid smile.

"That's what Shiver says," I muttered.

"Well, where d'you think he learned that gem of wisdom?" Coins asked, with a little bow from the waist and an insufferable grin.

"I can't do it!" Zip wailed suddenly, throwing the lock onto the table with a resounding *gong*. "It's no use."

Coins just picked up the lock and tossed it back to the boy. As Zip fumbled to catch it, Coins said, "Can't do aught with the pick out of the lock. Go on, back at it."

"Dan' let him rib you too much, Zip," I said. "He prob'ly had just as much a fit of it when he was your age."

"Bah," Coins said. "Lockpicked my way out of my mother's womb, I did. Snuck early into the world and never looked back."

I grinned a little, but flicked a surreptitious glance at him from under my lashes as I kept working my lock. He wasn't looking at me at all—or either of us—but away toward the door with the oddest sort of shadow in his eyes. Then, as if he knew I was watching him, he turned back to us with a quirk smile and a flourish of his hand.

"After all, I am—"

He swallowed the rest of the boast mid-sentence with a hasty glance at Zip.

The boy, without missing a beat and never looking up, finished for him, "The best damn thief in Brinmark."

"Zip, I'm shocked and ashamed to hear you talk like that," Coins

pronounced, fighting a laugh. "How do you even know a word like that?"

Zip paused long enough to glare at him. "'Cause I heard you say it a thousand hundred times, Coins."

"Preposterous. Hayli, can you believe the lies this lad is telling? Think we'd better lock him in irons with a set of picks until he can learn the wickedness of his ways. Or slip his way free." He gave me a broad smile and a wink. "That's how I learned."

"You dan' mean that!" Zip wailed.

I laughed, but that minute the watch bell clanged and I slid reluctantly off the table. "Dan' have too much fun without me," I said. "See you in the morning."

They hollered goodbyes after me as I headed out into the frigid night. Even with my wool scarf and my watchman's cap snug over my ears, the wind still managed to poke its way through every threadbare patch of my coat and every tiny hole in my gloves—my old coat and gloves, since I always kept my fine new ones reserved for daytime duty, when folks could actually see me. Shivering wretchedly, I stomped my way through heaps of snow and slush to the depot gate, where two of the older men were waiting for their relief. Smoke from their cigos and steam from their noses wreathed them like ghosts under the lamplight.

"Evening, Lieutenant," one of them said. "Who's supposed to be on watch with you, ma'am?"

"Damon," I said promptly enough, trying not to squirm at the man's courtesies. I didn't think I'd ever get used to it.

The other man muttered under his breath. I didn't know Damon more than by sight, so the watchman's reaction got me wondering if the man had a reputation I didn't know about. If he did, I guessed I would be finding out more about it in the morning, so I could pass word on to Bridnow. Most of the folks who filled the nightwatch rosters were reliable and stout sorts who took their rounds without muttering, but some weren't so eager, especially on the shifts that stretched through the fox hours.

"I'll go kick him out of his bunk," the second man said, and, flicking his stump of a cigo onto the railroad tracks, strode off toward the barracks without another word.

"Eh..." the other started, and fidgeted. "Lieutenant, don't suppose you'd be willing to release me too? That is, sorry…I wouldn't leave you without a partner normally, I just really…"

He hesitated, shifting from foot to foot and looking a mite uncomfortable, so, stifling a smile, I waved him away. "Gan on. Not like aught's apt to happen tonight anyway."

He gave me a quick nod of thanks and a salute before he disappeared, and I stepped closer to the little brazier they'd set up to keep the watchmen warm, letting the coal smoke sting my eyes and nose. Nights like this I always wondered what made Bridnow so keen to keep the rounds of watches running non-stop. Nobody ever came to the prison town. But I had a notion the watches were less about the folks outside our walls, and more about the folks inside. It was something Bridnow and I had talked a lot about recently—teamwork and discipline, and how they would decide if we would fall apart or survive in the days and months to come.

A thin curtain of sleet sifted down through a heavy shroud of fog, freezing in my hair and the wool of my scarf. The snow from the night before hadn't melted yet, so the sleet just gathered on top of the white mounds and hardened into a slick coat of ice. I watched the frost gather between the rails of the train track, slowly, as the solitary minutes dragged on.

Then, through the dead quiet of the winter night, a rock clattered. Footsteps on the track.

My pulse picked up, every muscle in my body shivering hard. With one hand I reached for the watch whistle hung about my neck, with the other I fumbled for Zagger's revolver holstered at my belt. For a moment there was only perfect silence, long enough that I started to think I'd only imagined the sound. Then it came again, closer this time. I shielded my eyes from the firelight and tried to peer through the fog and the darkness, but couldn't see a thing beyond the edge of the platform and the railroad ties just below it.

And all I could think was, *Creech sold us out to Klissen before we rescued him.* When I'd talked to him earlier that evening, Creech had sworn that he hadn't given up any information, but I wasn't sure I trusted him enough yet to believe him on his word alone. But if it was Klissen and Red and their gang of thugs, me with my one revolver would never be enough to stop them invading my home and putting my folks at risk.

"Who goes?" I called, praying whoever was out there wouldn't hear the sound of my teeth chattering. "Halt and state your business!"

Only silence answered me.

I cast a hasty glance around the platform, but the watchman who'd gone to wake Damon had taken the torch with him. Swallowing, I took a step closer to the edge of the platform and opened my mouth to repeat the warning.

Before I could, a voice whispered through the darkness, "Asylum."

"Who goes?" I cried, my voice shriller than before, laced with fear.

An ink smudge shifted in the darkness, trundling closer, closer. Finally I could make out the shape of a man, tall and thin without the bulk of a coat, arms wrapped tight around his waist. I couldn't tell if he was looking at me. I couldn't tell anything at all.

"Stop where you are or I'll sound the alarm!"

"Don't. Please."

But he didn't stop coming forward. I took one step back. All my instincts screamed at me to run away, to fly away, to bolt back for safety inside the gate…but I couldn't abandon my post. I was sworn to stand and defend it, and I would do it no matter the cost.

*Next time, don't grobbing volunteer…*

"Last warning!" I called.

Still the man didn't stop. Retreating back to the edge of the gate, I dug my whistle out of my coat, numb fingers fumbling useless with the string. I set the whistle to my lips and started to blow, but I'd sounded a bare squeak on the thing when a hand closed around my wrist and wrenched it, hard. The whistle fell from my fingers as a numbing shock arced through me.

I wanted to cry in pain. Instead I twisted around and screamed, loud as I could, *"Alarm! Alarm!"*

"Why?" the voice whispered, close to my ear. "Why did you have to do that?"

I shuddered and tried to pull away. Inside the walls I could hear people shouting, footsteps running toward me. The hand on my wrist released suddenly and I reacted on instinct, grabbing the man's arm with both hands.

"Stop, please. Let me go, let me go!" he hissed, twisting and pulling, trying to wrench free.

"You came to me," I said.

"You, I came to to you. Not them. They won't…don't let them…"

But before he could finish four men burst through the gate behind us, two with torches, two with revolvers. Bridnow was one of them. Light flared in my eyes and I winced, and people were shouting and talking and asking me questions and I couldn't understand what anyone was saying. Someone wrestled the intruder away from me and Bridnow caught me around the shoulders and pulled me back. The man was almost doubled over, turned aside with one arm up like he meant to hide his face.

"Who are you?" one of the men was yelling, over and over again.

Finally someone made a grab for the man's arm and pulled it down, and gasped, "No, it can't be."

And then, through the chaos of flashing light and gun barrels, I saw the man's face.

It was Tarik's.

The next thing I saw was one of the men raising his revolver, hatred and disgust in every line of his face.

"No!" I shouted. I pulled away from Bridnow, and threw myself between the two men. "Dan' hurt him."

The mage who looked like Tarik shrank back toward the wall, breathing hard, and the guard in front of me had an air about him like he meant to shoot the intruder straight through me. Bridnow gave me a dangerous kind of look, but he strode over and clapped a hand over top of the revolver, shoving it down and away.

"Stand down," he told the guard, then to me he said, "Lieutenant? Care to explain?"

I steadied myself and lifted my chin, and said, bold as I could, "I got questions, and it dan' suit to ask 'em of a corpse. Let me talk to him before you do aught to him."

Bridnow studied me a little long while, then nodded once. "Where do you want him?"

"Take him to the dormitory. There's plenty of offices in there where we can talk."

"In there?" the mage whispered suddenly.

He lurched away from the wall and grabbed my shoulder, jerking it so hard that Bridnow raised his revolver on instinct. I waved him back.

"No, no… Don't…don't take me in there," the mage said.

"You asked for asylum," I said, stern as could be. "Where'd you

 308

expect to get it if not inside those walls?"

"I don't know...I don't know. But don't make me go in there! Please...oh please, don't..."

"Come on," one of the guards said, and took a step forward.

I saw the wild light creep into the mage's eyes, and I knew exactly what was going through his mind—I knew exactly what he meant to do. I'd felt it myself, a thousand times or more, but there was no way I'd let him escape me now. Without thinking I pulled the handcuffs free of Bridnow's belt and slapped them around the mage's wrists. I couldn't look at him as I clamped them shut. I couldn't bear to see the betrayal in his eyes.

Instead I turned to Bridnow and jerked my head toward the dormitory. Somehow I found I couldn't speak.

Bridnow took charge without hesitation. He snapped his fingers at the guards and two of them took the mage by the arms and marched him away through the gate, the third following with one of the torches to light their way. For a few moments after they'd gone, Bridnow waited beside me, out on the platform in the sleet and the fog.

"Do you need a relief so you can go deal with that mage?" he asked presently.

"It can wait a bit," I said.

I didn't tell him that, now I had the mage in custody, I had no notion what I meant to do with him. I didn't even know what questions I meant to ask him. That look in the man's eyes haunted me, and my stomach twisted with a sick kind of regret.

The gate squealed behind us and we both snapped around to see Damon coming—finally—to report to his post. Guilt and shame fought a losing battle across his face when he saw Bridnow standing beside me. Bridnow didn't scowl. He didn't even say a word, but the look on his face could have frozen a bonfire mid-blaze.

"Commandant," Damon said.

Bridnow didn't acknowledge him. "I'll send a relief for you," he said, to me. I nodded my thanks and he turned away, but paused beside Damon. "You'll stay on for the next watch as well, and report to me first thing in the morning."

"Sir," Damon said, but Bridnow didn't wait to see his fumbled salute.

## Chapter 21 ❧ Hayli

FOR SOME LONG TIME AFTER BRIDNOW DISAPPEARED THROUGH THE GATE, Damon stood in penitent silence, shoulders hunched, hands in his pockets. I bit my lip on my distaste. Damon wasn't a young man. He wasn't particularly old, either, but surely he was old enough to do his duty respectably.

"Sorry I was late," he said after a bit. "Could not wake myself up no matter what."

I straightened up and folded my hands behind my back, the way Bridnow always did. Since I couldn't think of a single polite thing to say to him, I kept my thoughts to myself and focused on watching the ghostlike drifts of cloud over the surrounding hilltops.

He gave a forced laugh and said, "At least I didn't miss anything, eh?" He faltered, and a second too late he added, "Ma'am."

I gave him my best arched brow and shrugged. "We caught the mage who's been impersonating the Prince."

"You…you're slagging me, right?"

"What do *you* think the Commandant was doing out here?"

"He's here? He came here?"

"Said he wanted asylum."

Damon muttered something under his breath and shuffled closer to the coal brazier. In the light of the embers I could see every etching of fear on his face.

"Bloke gives me the creeps," he said. "I saw him up on the dais with the Prince. Did you?"

My heart faltered a beat but I just kept staring out at the hills. "Div'n everybody?"

"Suppose. Did you see the look in his eyes?"

I finally turned to face him, folding my arms. "What do you mean?"

Damon hesitated, biting the words back. Then he shook his head faintly and said, "He *believed*, Lieutenant. Every word of what he said. He believed he was who he claimed to be."

I shivered and tightened my arms about me. Damon was right. I'd seen it too, not just on the dais, but in the palace when he'd interrupted the meeting with the Ministers. Whoever he was…he really *believed* he was the Prince. And I was determined to find out why.

The gate squealed open again and Aothir slipped out onto the platform, touching his fingers to his forehead in a salute as he joined us. He was bare-armed as always, as if he didn't even feel the cold, and in the low light from the brazier the tattoos on his arms seemed to twist and writhe.

"I'm here to relieve you, ma'am," he said, with a bit more courtesy than he usually showed. "Commandant says you're done for the night."

I nodded my thanks and, muttering a *good night* under my breath, headed back inside the facility. By habit I made my way straight toward the officers' billeting, but halfway across the yard I stopped. The sleet had shifted to thick-falling snow now, and under the red-gold light of the gas lamps the flakes fluttered like embers. The whole facility was dead silent, and all the buildings slouched under a mantle of snow like massive grave mounds. In the dormitory, almost all of the windows were dark. Almost.

I bit my lip and drew a few slow, steadying breaths, then steeled myself for what I had to do. Inside the dormitory I headed to the office whose lamp I'd seen lit from the yard, where two of my guards stood outside the door, still bundled up from the cold.

"He's in there," one of them said as I approached. "Finally calmed down a bit. You should be able to talk to him."

"Need us to come in with you, ma'am?" the other asked.

I hesitated, remembering how Anuk had offered to accompany me when I'd gone to interview Miss Farrady. Somehow I thought it would have been better if I'd let him. If he'd been there, she wouldn't have had a chance to trigger me, and maybe none of this would have ever happened. Maybe Trabin would still be alive, and Tarik would still be here with me, instead of this mage who only looked like him.

But the mage wasn't Miss Farrady, and I doubted he would talk to me at all if I walked in with two toughs at my back.

"I'll be a'right," I said.

They nodded and one of them pushed the door open for me. I twisted my hands behind my back, collected myself, and walked into the room.

Even with the one lamp lit inside the office, it took me a tick to find the mage. He wasn't sitting at the desk but on the floor, in the corner, his knees drawn up and head buried in the crooks of his arms. The metal rings of his cuffs glinted in the light—it was the first thing I saw.

He didn't lift his head, but I heard his voice, muffled in his sleeves, saying, "Why did you do this to me?"

"You were ganna escape," I said. "Ghost away like you did before. I couldn't let you do that. I've got questions, and you're ganna answer them."

I pulled the wooden chair away from the desk and sat on it backwards, looping my arms over its back. Inside the office the air was glacial, but I knew I wasn't shivering from the cold. I only hoped the mage couldn't sense my fear.

He finally picked up his head and looked at me. I half-expected to see him angry, but terror was all I saw in his eyes, mirroring mine.

"How can you be here?" he whispered. "Don't you know what happens here? Don't you…remember?"

I caught in a sharp breath. "How do you know about that?" Then I collected myself and said, "It's our place now. Safe enough for mages, which you had to know if you meant to get asylum here."

"Asylum," he said, a note of laughter in his voice. "Strange word, isn't it? We use the same word…we use it when we want safety…and we use it when we want to lock away the madness. Or are those the same thing? Maybe they're the same."

"Who are you?" I asked, fear making me stern. "Stop wearing Tarik's face. It ain't yours."

"Tarik," he said. "*I'm* Tarik."

I moved before I could stop myself, darting forward and punching him hard in the jaw. My fist screamed pain but it was nothing to the anger that raged inside me like lightning. He reeled back, staring at the blood that spattered on his trouser leg like he didn't know what it was.

"*Shut it!*" I said. "Shut up! You're not Tarik. Show me your real face, now!"

"No, no, no," he moaned. His fingers inched over his lip, and he pulled them away slick with blood. "Don't...don't you see? I can't...I only make sense when I'm Tarik. I'm *Tarik*, damn it! Why don't you believe me?"

"Because I know Tarik," I said, snappish. "And he ain't here right now. So stop lying at me and tell me who you are!"

"Not here," he murmured.

"What?"

"Tarik's here. He's *here!*"

He clapped his manacled hands around his head, again and again, like he would drive out some noise I couldn't hear.

"Madness," I said, under my breath.

But looking at him, I felt my heart twist, sick with bitterness, because I knew every shade of his fear. I'd been where he was, covering my ears to ward away the whispers, laughing just to drown out the rattling noise of the emptiness inside.

"God," he gasped at last. His head rolled back, leaning against the cement wall, and his dark eyes were glassy as he stared up at the ceiling. "I can't be here. Get me out of here! It's all nightmares inside."

"That's another thing," I said. My voice wobbled, but I gritted my teeth and forced it to be steady. "Why is it you keep saying you know me?"

"You don't remember?" He lurched forward, and I, by instinct, pulled back. His eyes were wild and terrible. "It's all gone. It's all lost. I remember. I can't...remember. Don't send me away."

I wrinkled my brow. "But you've been saying this whole time you div'n want to be here! So which is it?"

He just turned his head away, and a minute and I realized there were tears in his eyes, caught on the long fringe of his lashes, and his shoulders shook as he tried to hold them back. Seeing him so distraught caught me off-guard. I sighed and hung my head, trying to come up with some kind of a different tack to take with him.

"Fine," I said. "If you're Tarik, then tell me about your life."

He lifted a hand like a gesture of defeat and shook his head. "What about it?"

"What do you remember?"

"The sea…" His eyes drooped closed, and a little smile touched the corners of his lips. In profile, in the low lamplight, he was Tarik through and through. "I remember the sea, when I was small. My father… We were meant to watch the departure of the newest steamship in Cavnal. But it all went sideways. Zagger…that was my guard, you know, Zagger…he kept me from falling into the sea. And that's when I first felt that I was a mage."

My throat burned, anger and grief and confusion twisting everything inside me into a strangling knot. "You can't remember that," I whispered.

"I do. I remember the taste of the salt air. The sound of the gulls. The smell of the steam from the ship's funnels…"

"What…what else?" I managed to ask. "What else do you remember?"

"Everything, damn it!" he cried, slamming his fist against the floor. "I remember the first *namolo* match I won. I remember thinking, *finally, finally my father will be proud of me.* But he wasn't even there to see it. I remember when Samyr tried to kiss me when we were eight years old and I pushed her away, but I pushed her harder than I meant and she fell in a puddle and wouldn't speak to me for weeks. And I remember standing in the belfry arch of the bell tower in the middle of the night in the rain and the wind and the lightning, and I wanted more than anything to fly and I wanted to die, and I thought, *well, this way, either way I'll get my wish,* only I didn't, because I didn't die, and I didn't fly away. It was just darkness and terror and a voice in my thoughts, and…and that was the day it ended and the day it began."

He stopped abruptly, and I realized all at once that there were tears on my cheeks, that I had a hand pressed hard over my mouth. He shifted into a crouch and shuffled a little closer to me, finding my free hand and holding it in both of his.

"You believe me, don't you?"

I drew a shaking breath and shook my head. "No. *No.*" I tore my hand free of his and stood, so fast that I toppled the chair. He drew back to avoid it, but his gaze never left my face. "One more thing you're ganna tell me," I said. "You tell me how we met."

Grief and a shadow filled his eyes, and he retreated, slowly, back to his corner. For the longest moment I thought he would never answer me, then, with a voice that sounded like a heartbreak, he said, "Don't you remember? It wasn't…it wasn't here, but the other place. The place that felt like here. I thought you were a *thayo*. And, little Hayli, you… you thought I was mad."

"*Oh*," I said. "No…you can't be. You can't be him."

He wrapped his arms around his head, the links of the handcuffs clinking softly, flashing too bright in the lamplight. "I am. I am. Why don't you believe me?"

I swallowed hard and retreated a step, until I stumbled against the desk behind me. Was it possible? That mage, the nutter bloke who'd been in the cell next to mine back at the Science Ministry…he'd told me that his name was Tarik. But I'd been so sure that he had died… how was it I never put two bobs together and realized that the mage standing up on the dais with Shade and King Trabin was my lunatic cell-mate? It made perfect sense.

And it completely terrified me.

"A'right," I said, shaky. "I accept that *that's* who you are, and that's how we met. But you can't be Tarik. You just *can't*. And if you dan' stop wearing his face, this is the last time we're talking."

He just shook his head in his hands, back and forth, slow. "I can't," he whispered. "Don't make me change. I don't know who I am. I don't know…I know…I'm Tarik…I'm not, I'm not. I am!"

He kept on muttering it, again and again, as I edged around the desk and backed toward the door. His nonsense words echoed like terror inside my head. I understood them all too well. I couldn't bear to hear them.

"Then I'm sorry," I said. I could barely hear my own voice. "I can't do aught for you."

"Hayli, wait—"

But I was already out the door, slamming it shut behind me. Soon as I was in the bright hall, with the two guards like pillars of strength on either side of me, I drew a long thin breath.

"Everything all right, ma'am?" one of the guards asked me, touching my elbow.

"Fine," I said. "Keep him secure. Nobody talks to him, clear?"

They both nodded, looking faintly uneasy, but I had nothing else to tell them. I left the dormitory and almost ran into Bridnow, who stood just outside the door in a puddle of lamplight, smoking a cigo that sent smoke twisting away snakelike into the night. He tossed it away as I came out, stomping the butt into the snow. He didn't say anything, just watched me expectantly.

"I dan' na what to make of him," I said, shoving my hands in my trouser pockets. "I thought at first that he really believed he was Tarik, but now…I'm not so sure. More like he dan' na who he is, and being Tarik is the only thing he knows how to be."

"How is that possible?" Bridnow asked.

"I've met him before," I admitted, shrugging.

"What? When?"

"When…when I was here before. Or, not here, but in the Science Ministry, with Kippler and them. He…he was in the cell next to mine for a bit. Then he wasn't. I thought they'd zotzed him. Never really got to see him, so I div'n realize he was that impostor mage from Avnaya until just now. But if Kippler and…and Andon Vrey were mucking about with his head like they were with mine, who knows what they made him believe? Maybe they pushed him so long, so hard, that he started really believing it."

"Is that possible?"

I shuddered, resisting the almost irresistible urge to cover my ears. I wrapped my arms around me instead, my nails pressed into the thick wool of my sleeves. "They made me…they almost…" I shook my head. "Sorry, I can't—"

"It's all right," he said, interrupting my panic, and laid a hand on my shoulder. I jumped before I could stop myself. Bridnow lowered his hand slowly and gave me a small smile. "I'm sorry. Don't tell me anything you don't feel comfortable saying."

I nodded and drew a slow breath. "I remember them talking from time to time—Kippler, and Vrey—when I wasn't supposed to hear them. They were talking about somebody, some mage Vrey was experimenting on as his pet project. Kippler thought the mage was too dangerous for Vrey to handle, but Vrey was sure he could. Back then I didn't know who they were talking about, but now…I'm sure it was *him*." I jerked my chin toward the dormitory.

Bridnow shook his head. "I don't know how those devils managed to do what they did to you lot, but every single one of them should pay for it."

"Vrey already did," I said. "He can't pay more than he has."

"That's one, then," Bridnow said, with a ferocity that caught me a bit by surprise. His face softened then, and he nodded toward the officers' quarters. "Get some sleep, Hayli. We can deal with this tomorrow."

# Chapter 22 ❧ Jarik

*O*UTSIDE THE LODGING HOUSE, IT WAS EVEN MORE BITTERLY COLD THAN I HAD expected, and I suddenly began to doubt my mad plan of finding a place to stay with the city's poor. Surely there were poor in Bregjarvani like there were in my own city, and surely they had some shelter I could use for the night. Surely…surely I wasn't as much of a fool as Iskari feared I was. I should have asked, before I left the lodging house. But I couldn't have asked Iskari—he would only have tried to dissuade me, and I didn't have the energy to argue with him.

I wandered down the narrow side street, staying close to the wall of the lodging house and its meager protection from the wind. My instincts told me that the poor were likely holed up somewhere near the wharf, but I'd already resigned myself to the idea that I might be awake and wandering the city, lost, all night.

"You're playing a dangerous game," someone said.

I drew up instinctively, looking behind me for Wake, but he wasn't there. No one was there. And the voice had, unexpectedly, come from somewhere ahead of me.

I was about to ask what game I was playing when another voice, silken and cold, said, "I didn't know it would be *him*."

Instantly I was on my guard, and without thinking, I faded into a Cloak in the deep shadows of the wall. That was Rigvar's voice—I would know it anywhere, even as it was now, without the weight of magic behind his words. Now that I was focused, I could see his silhouette not fifteen steps away from me, almost invisible against the wall. He was standing with another man near a coal brazier where the narrow street intersected the wider main road.

I stayed perfectly still, willing away the deafening pulse in my ears so I could hear the conversation. There was a sudden, now-expected warmth trickling from my nose, but I resisted the impulse to reach up and wipe away the blood. I kept my mouth closed tight and let the blood run over my lips. But I could taste it in the back of my throat, too, and it was all I could do not to cough, and spit it out.

"You've met him before."

I knew, without hearing another word, that they were talking about me. Part of me wanted to slip closer, but I didn't want to risk discovery if I left the safety of my Cloak. I closed my eyes instead, quieting all my senses so I could focus on listening.

"Once. I didn't know who he was, then," Rigvar said. "Only that he was a mage, and I'd never seen him before—except that he looked almost exactly like Eyid. But then I saw that newspaper...why didn't Eskir tell us that Eyid's son was the one they're calling the Zealot down in Cavnal? It might have been useful information to have."

"I'm still trying to understand why you thought it would be wise to taunt him, publicly, and humiliate him in front of the *sodthari*," the other man said. He was larger than Rigvar, bulkier, and I got a faint glimpse of his scarred and bearded face from the glow of the brazier.

"What would you have done in my place?" Rigvar asked. "That boy is dangerous. If the rumors are true..."

"What *boy*, Rigvar?" the other man asked. "I told you from the beginning not to scorn him on account of his youth, and would you listen to me then? No. Well, listen to me now. Do not make the mistake of underestimating his power. He can *not* be allowed to become Godar."

"Do you think I don't know that? If he *is* the Zealot..."

"I doubt the Cavners know what that even means."

"You were the one who just told me not to underestimate him."

"That doesn't mean I believe he is the fabled Zealot," the big man protested. "You said it—he is dangerous."

"No, no, no," Rigvar said. His voice was thin and tight, and somehow I thought it sounded afraid. "You don't understand. You can't, you're not a mage."

"Then what are you going to do? You've just gone and marked a target on your chest, and why is it I get the feeling that if he aims, he isn't going to miss?"

"Shut up," Rigvar snapped. He hesitated, then said, "I don't know what I'm going to do."

"Just pray he never finds out."

There was a sudden scrape of metal on leather, then I saw the glint of a long knife pressed against the larger man's throat.

"I said *shut up*," Rigvar said, grinding the words through his clenched jaw.

"Steady," the man said. "I'm not your enemy here."

Rigvar sheathed his knife sharply, then scrubbed a hand over the back of his neck. "I feel like I'm being watched," he muttered, only just loud enough for me to hear.

"You're jumpy. And paranoid. Is it any wonder? I would be too if I'd just had the *kalukyri* to insult *Veka's* Zealot to his face."

"I thought you didn't believe he was the Zealot."

"I said I don't know if he is. Don't know that he isn't, either. But you seem to, which makes me question your sanity a bit."

"*Ethu, ethu*," Rigvar said.

The other man snorted and held his hands out to warm them over the coals.

"There's something about him," Rigvar said. "It's not just magic. It's something…"

"Insanity?" the other man said, with a breath of laughter.

"You'd think that, of course. I told you, you're not a mage. You wouldn't understand. It sounds like madness… *Veka*, maybe he *is* mad. But it's more than just that. Did you hear he dressed down the Cavnish ambassador? A man maybe three times his age, with a title and office. And he just reduced him to a blubbering mess with a few words. How did he do that? I'm telling you, it's all part of it."

"Don't tell me you're in love with him like everyone else seems to be, despite your stunning efforts to change that," he said. There was an annoyed silence, then he said, "Please tell me you don't believe that he actually talks to *Veka*."

"No, no," Rigvar said, but he spoke too quickly. "But if he goes on believing it, and if he persuades people he's telling the truth… Because, well, you felt it too, didn't you?"

The big man shifted his weight uncomfortably. I had no notion

what Rigvar meant, and he didn't seem keen to elaborate, since his companion obviously knew exactly what he was talking about.

"But, if there was some way to stop him," Rigvar went on. "Not hurt him, just…take the edge off, as it were."

"You're not thinking about what that doctor was talking about, are you?"

"Well? It might work."

"And if it doesn't?"

"I'll deal with it if I have to."

"Ah, I'm sure you will," the man said, with a quiet note of approval in his voice.

I let out the breath I'd been holding, cautiously. I was so cold I'd stopped shivering, and my legs were so numb that I wasn't sure I would be able to rise from my low crouch even if I wanted to.

*Well, that would be a disappointing end,* the churlish voice in the back of my mind muttered. *Die from cold exposure and Rigvar will never have the need to face you again.*

I ground my teeth and remembered, suddenly, the scorching fire I had felt from Wake's touch on my forehead. Carefully, I stirred the corners of my soul, searching for a remnant of that heat. When I found it, I gave it the slightest nudge with my magic, and a peaceful warmth inched through me, thawing my cold-locked muscles one by one.

"Do you feel that?" Rigvar asked, reminding me that the two men were still there, close by. He shivered violently, and his hands ran restlessly over his arms. "*Veka, Veka,*" he said. "What is that? It's like being in the heart of a thunderstorm."

"You mages all sound half-mad when you start talking about magic," the bigger man said.

I stilled my magic immediately, and just as quickly the numbness rushed back over me, worse than before, coming so close on the memory of warmth.

"Come on," the other man said. "It's cold as hell out here. And you're making me nervous."

He spun away and Rigvar turned to follow him. But he hesitated, and glanced over his shoulder, his gaze sweeping over the darkness of the narrow street. Then he shook his head, and, muttering under his breath, followed the older man back into the lodging house. I suddenly had the mad desire to find out what would happen when Rigvar came into the bunk room and discovered I wasn't there. Then I decided I didn't want him guessing that I'd been eavesdropping, so, untangling my numb and shivering limbs, spitting blood into my sleeve, I swallowed my pride and buried my fear, and crept back through the servant's door, up the narrow staircase, and back into the bunk room.

A few other people had come in and were already sleeping soundly—too soundly, by the noise of it. Iskari was still awake, reclining on a lower bunk near the far wall and whittling something with a thin knife. When he saw me come in he sat up so sharply that he almost hit his head on the bunk above him. I flashed him a taunting grin and reached to pull myself up onto it, but he shot off his own mattress and grabbed my shoulder.

"Good God," he said, tilting his head to look at me closer. "What happened to you? Get in a fight with a lamp post?"

"Magic," I said. I drew my sleeve over my mouth and nose, and stared grimly at the dark stains on the wool. It was more blood than I'd expected. "I'm fine."

"Taumir..."

I pulled myself onto the upper bed without answering, and rolled over so I was facing the wall. After a moment I felt the bunk shift as Iskari sat back down.

"So, I take it you changed your mind?" he asked.

"Cold as hell out there," I muttered, echoing Rigvar's companion.

"You don't say."

I closed my eyes and listened as some number of people filtered into the room, claiming beds with the general noise of creaking springs and rustling blankets, and hushed conversations. I wondered if Rigvar was one of them, but didn't savor the idea of letting them know I was awake by rolling over. The noise in the room was just beginning to taper down when I got the eerie sense that I was being watched.

Then someone made a crooning noise just beside my head, and said in a silken, mocking voice, "How sweet. He looks even younger when he's sleeping."

Someone else hissed, "What are you—"

I didn't bother opening my eyes. I just coiled my magic and Pushed out in the direction of the first voice as hard as I could. There was a surprised cry and a sharp crack, and I propped myself on my elbow to look down at Rigvar, who was on hands and knees on the ground beside my bunk. Someone across the room was trying too hard to stifle a laugh. The rest of the room was deadly silent.

I didn't say a word, just watched as Rigvar staggered to his feet, one hand nursing the back of his head. Past him I saw the larger man standing in the aisle between the rows of bunks, studying me through a dark and ferocious scowl. I gave him a feral smile, and watched his frown fade as his face turned a perfect shade of white. Then, hardly knowing what I was doing, I slid off the bunk and landed right in front Rigvar, much too close to be safe. Behind me, I could sense Iskari tensing, rigid, his eyes boring holes in my back.

I gave Rigvar my most charming, most Cavnish smile. "I feel like we've gotten off on a poor tack," I said. "Let's start over."

I held out my hand, and he, studying me with faint suspicion, reached out to take it. As soon as our palms touched, I drove the full weight of my power into the static charge. He tore away from me with a cry of pain, stumbling against the bunk beside mine, hugging his hand to his chest. I thought—but I might have been mistaken—that I caught the faint stench of charred flesh. For one endless minute he just stared at me, eyes impossibly wide, brow creased with anguish.

"How..." he started, then backed a step away from me, shaking his head.

The larger man dropped a hand on his shoulder, dragging him into the aisle, and for a moment he looked like he had half a mind to push Rigvar out of the way and come after me himself. Then Iskari shot to his feet beside me, still holding his whittling knife bare in his hand.

For the space of three breaths no one moved or dared to speak. Then, of one accord Rigvar and the larger man both turned and strode out of the room without a word or glance at anyone. Keenly aware of the almost palpable fear in the room, I climbed back up onto my bunk and lay flat on my stomach as if nothing had happened, hoping the other lodgers would take the cue.

The bunk creaked as Iskari returned to his bed, and gradually, after several tense moments had passed, a low hum of conversation crept in to fill the silence.

"That was either brilliant," Iskari said, so softly I could barely hear him, "or dead *drakkeyn ganthiskur.*"

I snorted and pulled the coarse woolen blanket over my head.

WHEN I WOKE IN THE MORNING, cold daylight was already spilling through the window, and the room was empty except for Nika, who perched cross-legged on the upper bunk next to mine, her elbows on her knees and her chin resting on her hands. She was watching me, and I got the uncomfortable feeling that she had been for some time.

"I thought this was the men's bunk room," I muttered, wrapping both my arms over my head. Then, although I knew well enough what she wanted to say, I asked, "What's bothering you, Nika?"

"You hurt Rigvar," she said.

That was not what I had expected.

"I only enlightened him," I said, and rolled onto my side to look at her.

Her mouth twitched. "I'm glad," she muttered. Her gaze lingered on my face, her eyes blue and cold and etched with sorrow. "Taumir..."

"What?" I asked, then realized that it sounded unnecessarily harsh, so I tried again, "What's wrong?"

"What's wrong?" she echoed. "I baited you for Rigvar. I told him..." She shook her head. "I wanted to please him. I felt this intense...*loyalty* to him, and it made me want to say anything to impress him."

I lifted an eyebrow, and she flung both her hands toward me.

"I didn't want to! Don't you understand? I didn't want to say anything, to do any of it. I couldn't help myself."

That made me curious, so I sat up and shifted around to face her, leaning my forearms on my legs. "When you say you couldn't help yourself," I started, and hesitated. "Was it...was it like what...with Iskari, when..."

*Damn*, I thought. *I never struggle with words like this.*

Nika didn't smile at my mumbling, though. She picked at a stray thread on the edge of the blanket she was sitting on, twisting it around her fingers and then letting it unravel again.

"When you made Iskari move?" she asked then, lifting her gaze, barely, to mine. "No, I don't think so. That was...that was something else entirely, something... I've never even heard of a power like that before. But Rigvar's not that strong. What he did to me would never have worked on Iskari, I think." She didn't blush, though I thought she might—instead, her face got colder and stiller than before, and her eyes flashed. "Rigvar was playing on the respect I already had for him," she said, and gave a bitter laugh. "As a result, he lost all of it. How could I possibly respect him now, after he did that to me?"

She lowered her head and rubbed a hand idly over her arm—the arm that Rigvar had touched, last night. I had a feeling I understood what was going on in her mind, so I didn't press her. Instead I jumped down from my bunk, pausing next to her.

"It's not worth your sorrow," I said, and turned away.

I had almost reached the door when her hand caught my arm, but when I turned to face her, the last thing I expected was the look of fear in her eyes.

"Taumir," she said. "Iskari told me..."

She shook her head, edging to the side, angling away from me, and her fingers worried over her lower lip. I took a breath and forced myself to wait quietly, but she must have sensed my impatience because she dropped her hand and glanced back at me.

"You keep seeing...someone, and you think it's *Veka*. Are you sure...are you sure it's *Veka*?"

"Of course," I said, but doubt suddenly curled at the corners of my mind.

"How do you know?"

I racked my thoughts, trying to recall that first time I had seen him. I had named him Wake; he had never said whether I was right or not.

"Who else...who else could he be?"

"Is it possible that he is the mad god?"

I grabbed her by both arms, so fiercely that she yelped in surprise. "What does that mean? I've heard...someone else said something once..." I shook my head against the fragmenting memories. "Aren't they the same—*Veka*, and the mad god?"

She just stared at me. "You don't know?"

I flung a hand at her in exasperation.

"No," she said. "No, they aren't the same, no more than the night is the same as the day. *Veka*, you never knew?"

It was my turn to stare. My mind couldn't process the confusion, as I turned over and over the words of the *Brigaz Nedash* when it said: *The Zealot, the scion of the mad god.* Was it possible I had misunderstood that

325

line? Or, had Shiver? After all, he had been the one to recite it to me in the first place, late one night before everything had fallen apart.

And if it was possible, then what did it mean?

"Is the mad god…"

"Not a god, even," Nika said, shrugging. "At least, we don't believe he is. Just a powerful spirit, the most powerful of the *thayoi*."

"*Thayo!* He's a daemon?" I asked. An instinctive shudder ran through me, in defiance of the doubt and skepticism that had been drilled into me from my youngest years.

"And the sworn and eternal enemy of *Veka*," Nika said.

"The *Brigaz Nedash* makes it sound like the Scion and the Zealot are the same person."

She gave a dramatic shrug, flourishing one pale hand in the air. "It's a Cromner text," she said. "Are you surprised it's ambiguous?"

I cursed under my breath and rubbed a hand over my eyes, racking my memory for lessons on the Cromner grammar, but I'd buried them under years of other language lessons and I couldn't dredge up the energy to recall anything useful. More than anything I wanted to get a look at Rivano's book, because by now I was certain that Shiver hadn't remembered the line correctly.

Vaskar, before he died, had asked Agnir if I was the scion of the mad god.

The Cavnish captain said it was true.

And I wanted to shout my objection to the sky, to reject the very idea that I could be thinking about Wake and the mad god as if they were real, as if I believed they actually existed. And yet I couldn't deny what my own eyes had seen, the words I had heard. I couldn't pretend away the power I felt—the fire I still felt coursing through every single vein in my body, no matter how hard I tried to will it away.

"Who are they?" I asked Nika, with one last desperate attempt to find clarity. "The Scion, and the Zealot? *Who are they?*"

She shook her head.

"Nika," I said. "What am I?"

She just shook her head again, and took a step away from me. Then another. And before I could call her back, she turned and fled from the room.

# Part Three: Echo

# Chapter 1 ～ Hayli

I COULDN'T SLEEP ALL NIGHT. WHENEVER I CLOSED MY EYES, ALL I COULD SEE was the mage's face—Tarik's face—ghastly in the low lamplight, and the haunted look of betrayal in his eyes. I kept imagining him huddled on the floor in the corner of that office, cold and wretched, more uncomfortable than Kippler had ever made me when he'd imprisoned me here. But where else could I have put him? I didn't know anything about him. I didn't know how dangerous he was, but if I put my people at risk by setting him among them…I would never forgive myself.

When the first glimmer of daylight crept through my window, I groaned and rolled onto my stomach. A gnawing pain throbbed behind my eyes, as an endless list of jobs and worries unfurled in my mind. I didn't want to get up.

Still, better to get up on my own than have Bridnow catch me sleeping in, and send someone to wake me up, because waking folks up as rudely as possible was one of the horrid things we'd all taken to delighting in. I tumbled off my bed and fumbled into a clean shirt and trousers, and stomped my boots onto my feet on my way out to the common room. Halfway there I caught a drift of conversation—Bridnow's stern voice, and he didn't sound happy. It sounded like a proper dressing down, and suddenly I got to thinking about Damon, and how Bridnow had meant to have a chat with him this morning.

But then I heard another voice answering, and it wasn't Damon's, but Griff's. Always too curious, I sidled forward a little more until I could hear more clearly, my heart in my throat at the thought of Griff getting rebuked for anything.

"I *thought* you said you had military experience," Bridnow was saying. "Of all my lieutenants, you were supposed to be the one who understood military procedures, and the demands and expectations of a unit like ours."

"Yes, sir."

"I cannot understand how you could so completely fail in the one, simple mission I assigned to you. Did you not grasp the importance of that order?"

"I did, sir."

"Well, apparently you didn't, because if you'd had any real military experience you would understand that no operations are possible without the addition of this single element. This one, simple thing that I entrusted to you. Is that clear?"

"Yes, sir."

"Now, do I have to hold your hand and walk with you to the mess hall, or do you know where to find the coffee on your own?"

"I can find it, sir."

"Then why isn't it here?"

"Because I'm a vutting worthless lieutenant, sir!"

He said something else, but his words were lost in a sudden chorus of laughter. I stood where I was, in the shadows, in the hallway, so bewildered I couldn't make sense of what I'd just heard. When I finally made up my mind to walk into the common area, I found Bridnow perched easily on the edge of the big table, Anuk in stitches by the hearth, and Griff halfway to the door, rosy-cheeked and laughing.

He caught sight of me and broke out into a fresh gale of laughter. "Poor Hayli looks like she just walked in on a public flogging."

Bridnow glanced at me over his shoulder, and I startled at the broad grin on his face, because I'd never seen him look so cheerful and comfortable in all the time I'd known him.

"Don't mind us," he said.

"I thought you were proper scolding him!"

Griff laid a hand on his heart. "Oh, were you coming to rescue me?"

"Shut up or *I'll* give you a scolding," I laughed.

With an exaggerated cry of dismay, Griff threw both hands in the air and ducked for the door. "Coffee. Right. Be back soon."

"All that was about *coffee?*" I asked as he left.

"Have you ever *had* coffee?" Anuk asked, appalled. I shook my head. "That explains it. If you'd ever had it, you would know how vitally, crucially, infinitely important it is, so."

Bridnow chuckled. "I told him to see if we could get some coffee brought in to the facility on a regular basis. I'm sick to death of that Meritian swill Nan makes us drink. And if I recall correctly, part of that instruction was to have coffee available for us here when everyone gets up in the mornings. Lubricate the machine of war, as it were. Or..." He waved a hand generally at the building around us and shrugged. Then he stood and nodded to Anuk, and made his way toward me. "We need to talk, Hayli."

He seemed serious now, and I followed him back to Shade's office feeling a little gloomy, sorry to see his good humor faded.

The office was meticulously clean—completely different than the first, and last, time I had ever seen it, when we'd carried all of Shade's things into it. Some of Shade's maps were tacked up on the wall, and his papers, I guessed, were tucked away into an archive box that stood on a corner table. The desk itself was spotless except for the watch roster and another paper which I guessed was a roster for other duties.

Bridnow went to stand at the window, hands folded behind his back. "We have to talk about that mage," he said at length. "We can't just hold him prisoner without cause. As far as any of us know, he has done no actual wrong. It is criminal to keep someone chained just because we don't know what to do with them."

My face flushed hot and I bowed my head, unable to even look at Bridnow through the weight of my shame.

"I know," I said. "I div'n want to chain him up. At least..." I took a breath, then forced myself to meet Bridnow's gaze. "Least I think it was justified, last night when he wouldn't halt when I asked, when he grabbed me and tried to keep me from calling in help. Far as any of us could know just then, he meant us harm. So I dan' think we were wrong to take him into custody for that. And then question him."

Bridnow's mouth twitched, barely, hiding a smile. "Sound reasoning, Lieutenant," he said. "But going forward, we need to either establish the fact that he's a threat—in which case he should be turned over to the Brinmark officials—or not. And if he's not, we need to release him."

I hesitated. I wasn't sure if Bridnow was suggesting that I be the one to talk to the mage and find out. If he wasn't, I didn't want to assume, but if he was, I didn't want to look foolish and ask. Bridnow must have understood my silence, because he moved to sit at his desk and folded his hands on top of it.

"You'll take one of your sergeants and question him," he said. "I don't care which one. I'd say you should take someone who is not a mage, though, to give some balance to the interview."

I had just opened my mouth to acknowledge the order when someone rapped on the open door behind me. Bridnow lifted a hand and a young woman I didn't know stepped into the office, but she wore a dark blue wool coat and scarf, so I guessed she was one of our watchmen. She gave a nod to Bridnow, but then turned to me.

"Lieutenant," she said. "Someone is waiting at the front gate to see you."

I frowned and met Bridnow's gaze briefly, then gave him a smart salute and followed the woman outside.

"Did he…or she give a name?" I asked.

"No, ma'am," she said. "He's a bit bundled up, too, so I couldn't see if he was anyone I might recognize."

We reached Borokhev's main gate and found a small figure wrapped thick in wool and fur standing in front of two other gate guards. On the road was a smart shay drawn by a tall grey horse, standing patiently as another guard held its reins.

I stopped in front of the stranger. More than aught else I wanted to cross my arms, but I stood the way Bridnow always did instead, hands folded behind my back. At least it made me look confident, even if I didn't feel a jot of it.

"What business d'you have here?" I asked.

"Lady…Oramay," the stranger said, and pushed back the hood of his dark wool coat slightly, just enough that I caught the glint of watery sunlight on his flame red hair.

"Oh," I breathed. Turning to the guard who held the horse, I said, "Bring the shay inside and give the horse some grain, if we've got any."

Then I turned on my heel and strode back inside the facility, waving Minister Batar along behind me. Once we'd gotten to the officer's quarters, I showed Batar to the seat by the hearth. I could've asked him to sit at the table, I supposed, but it was too wretched cold outside to stand on ceremony like that. Batar was shivering like a mongrel dog.

I watched him peel off his damp gloves and carefully remove his fur cap, his trembling fingers trying to smooth the tufts of his hair delicately back into place.

"Gad, I never wanted to be back at this town, that's for certain," he said after a while. "Love what you've done with the place, though."

I leaned back on the thick table and finally allowed myself to cross my arms. "I take it you got my message, Minister?"

He sighed as he looked up at me, sounding like a fellow who'd completely run the luck. I got the distinct sense he wouldn't be within five miles of this place if he felt he had any other choice.

"I did."

"You could've sent a letter, if you div'n want to come yourself."

"No," he said. "Can't trust the post."

I straightened slightly. "D'you suppose my message to you got seen by anybody?"

"No, I doubt it. You were clever enough not to put anything incriminating in it, so, even if someone saw it, I assume it would have made no sense to them." He sighed. "No, I came because, if you claimed you needed to see *me*, then the situation must be worse than I even imagined. Is it so? The country gone to hell, and frankly I don't see how we're going to crawl out of it. Hayli, my dear, have you heard anything at all from Tarik? Where is he? What has become of him? Is he in danger?" He patted a lace-edged handkerchief over his forehead, then tucked it back into the sleeve of the checkered suit jacket that poked just past the hem of his coat sleeve. "Please tell me you have heard something from him."

I frowned and shook my head, wondering if I ought to tell him that we had the mage impostor in custody. I just wasn't quite sure what good that would do.

"No," I said. "I haven't seen Tarik in weeks now."

Batar's face crumpled and he pressed his forehead against his hand. For a moment I got the odd sense he might be weeping, but then he lifted his chin and his cheeks were dry.

"We're lost without our monarch, my dear," he said. Somehow I found I didn't quite mind the endearment when it came from him—

and at least it was better than the affected stutter he put on for high society. "I just don't know what is to become of us all. Where is Kor, I might add? Do you…know Dreyden Kor?"

"Yeah, I know Kor," I said, scowling harder than ever. "You mean he's gone missing too? With the Queen?"

"I see you know more than I might've expected," he said. "Well, that's good at least."

"I know more than you, I wager," I said, a challenge in my voice.

His brows flew up in surprise. "Well!" he exclaimed, then, when I didn't say aught else, he leaned forward conspiratorially and added in a low voice, "Anything you'd care to share?"

"Not sure," I said. "Tell me, Minister, why do you want Kor?"

For several long moments he just sat still, shaking his head slowly back and forth in a perfect picture of misery. I waited with every last scrap of patience I could scrounge up. The front door opened behind me, and I glanced over my shoulder to see Doc drifting in, his head bare as always, his hair like ice against the black leather of his coat.

He took one look at me, then one look at Batar, but the expression on his face never changed. Without a word to either of us, he wandered over to the high wooden cabinet and took out a crystal decanter full of some kind of amber liquor. I watched him in surprise, because I was dead sure I'd never seen Doc drink aught at all—or eat, either, for that matter. But Doc didn't drink the glassful of liquid he poured out. Instead he brought it over to Batar and handed it to him without comment.

Batar nodded his thanks, but he was staring at Doc like he'd seen a ghost. We both watched as Doc moved away to the smaller desk tucked in the corner, on the other side of the hearth, where he busied himself with poking through a sheaf of papers like he was looking for something in particular. I shrugged and turned my attention back to Batar.

"You were going to tell me why you're looking for Kor," I said.

Batar took a long sip of the liquor. "The situation is unraveling faster than any of us can weave it back together. As you know, or may know, the Court of Ministries is perilously close to making a dangerous and—dare I say—downright treasonous alliance with Meritac and Cromis."

"Cavnal's been toying with that alliance a long time now, Minister," I said. "What's new?"

"No, no, no, my dear. This is much, much worse than that. You don't *understand*. The Court isn't supposed to have the authority to make foreign alliances—"

"But there's no King," I interjected.

Batar made a soft moaning noise, leaning his head in his hand. "I know, and so the Court *can* claim emergency powers. And so the Ministers who favored the insurrection while Trabin was alive are now very busy drafting a treaty far more dangerous to Cavnal—and especially us mages—than anything Trabin ever considered. If you think the Accord was bad, with its half measures of restrictions on mages, the situation will be a hundred times worse for us under the new alliance. And right now we are dead evenly split between those wanting the alliance and those opposing it."

"Minister Farro is still holding out?" I asked.

Batar nodded. "And he has to, now. His hands are *tied*."

"How d'you mean?"

"You know the Army attacked the smelter without his permission, of course."

"I'd heard something like that. I'd thought for sure he betrayed us, but it's true? They actually went out against his orders?"

"Precisely, my dear. He never gave the order. But he can't rebuke them for it, because they made the public claim that they were hunting the King's assassin. If Farro chastises the Army, he will look like he is conspiring with the assassin. And Von and the others will certainly run with that accusation to bring him down. So, to appease the *people*, Farro can't do anything. He has to pretend that he authorized the attack. But we loyalists are also in a bind, because, well, you saw that impostor mage who came into the Assembly! He looks like Tarik, talks and acts just like him, but he is *not* our Prince. And so unless Tarik himself comes back and sets things aright, we cannot publicly push for the monarchy, because the only person the people will believe has any right to the crown is *not*, in fact, the Prince."

By the time he finished, my head was swimming. From the corner of my eye I noticed Doc's hands had stilled on the stack of papers, but his head was down and I couldn't tell if he was reading something, or covertly listening to us. I pushed away from the table and took the stool close to the fire, hoping the warmth would drive away my violent shivers.

"So, lemme get this straight," I said. "When you say loyalists... does that include Farro?"

"Yes, yes, privately a loyalist. Ever since Avnaya. I think he repented after what happened to Trabin, who, after all, *was* his friend."

I nodded. "So what you loyalists want is for Prince Tarik to come back and take the throne."

"Precisely, yes, but where *is* he? All we have is an impostor." He sighed and added gloomily, "We are all monarchists at heart, but this impostor makes us all have to play the part of parliamentarians. Gad, it roils the stomach."

"But if the Army was going after the King's assassin—or so they say—dan' that make *them* monarchists?"

"Not so clearly," Batar said with a little sigh. "It makes them anti-mage and pro-alliance, is what it makes them, since everyone assumes the King's assassin was a mage."

"But that makes no sense—"

"Regardless," Batar said. "It's what they say."

I folded my hands between my knees, my gaze searching the bright shadows of the fire. "So tell me what this alliance means, if it goes through."

"It means, my dear, that everything Trabin tried to do right before his death—declaring support for the mages of Cavnal, and so forth—will be undone. The three-way alliance will put pressure on Istia and Tulay to sign the Accord, or whatever new variation to that horrid document they'll come up with now. But they will never bow their necks to the Accord, and damn the consequences. And now Alokin has gone back to Meritac, taking all his knowledge and experiments and inventions with him, which means the southern alliance will have complete military superiority in any war to come, no matter how many mages Istia and Tulay can muster to their defense. And that puts pressure on Cavnal, because I guarantee you we'd rather be allied to the nation who's got Alokin's doomsday weapons at hand than opposed to them."

"What?"

Batar and I both startled and turned to Doc, who still stood behind the desk, one hand barely touching the stack of papers. His eyes were on us, and his face, if possible, was paler than ever.

"What *what?*" Batar asked, flustered. He darted a glance at Doc, but for some reason he avoided looking at him steadily.

"Alokin is gone?"

"Yes. You...you know him? He went home to Meritac. Said his duty to Cavnal was fulfilled."

"No, no," Doc said, the word trailing away. "No, he can't have done that. I told him..." He rubbed a hand over his forehead. "The foolish idiot, what is he thinking?"

Hand still pressed to his brow, he skirted around the desk and strode out of the building like a snowstorm, and slammed the door behind him. We both watched him go, stunned speechless.

"Who...em, who was that?" Batar fumbled, after much too long.

"That's Doc," I said. "Our Blood mage. D'you know him?"

"I just...I swear I've seen him before. His face. I know his face from somewhere." He shuddered suddenly. "It's nothing. Just my imagination, I'm sure."

"Minister," I said, after giving him a moment to compose himself again. "I sent word to you because the situation isn't just about which Ministers are loyal and which aren't. Not anymore."

He looked honestly puzzled by that. "What do you mean?"

"Some folks are plotting a coup to overthrow *you*. The whole Court. The Chernayi got word that Blake wants to disband them, and the Chernayi aren't willing to roll over for it. There's a group of mages and anarchists in the city, and some rogue elements of the Army—I'd guess the same ones who went out against Farro's orders—all with a mind to set up a military state in your place."

A minute and he just gawped at me, his already pasty face a deathly shade of white. "Dear *God*," he whispered at last, and lifted his hands, fingers fluttering in agitation. "The throne sits empty and the whole damned country crumbles apart."

"I thought you should know," I said, a bit feebly, not knowing what else to say. "But we support you."

He got to his feet. "I should be going. I need to speak to Farro about all this, though Wake only knows what we can do about it. And thank you...I do thank you for bringing it to my knowledge. But, my dear, if you know anything, *anything* at all about the Prince's whereabouts..."

"He's in Istia."

I almost whispered it. Batar almost missed it. He faltered a step and looked down at me, eyes wide.

"I beg your pardon?"

"I said he's in Istia. Where Trabin told him to go, before he died."

"Istia! But...sweet stars, whatever *for*?"

"To lead them out of a war," I said. "To sue for peace with Cavnal."

"But if the alliance goes through, he will never succeed. Istia will see Cavnal as their immediate threat and make a preemptive strike in self-defense. They'll attack *him* first of all! He cannot stay there. If he keeps trying to spread that message, they will only believe he is double-crossing them."

I wondered if it would change anything if Batar knew that Tarik hadn't gone to Istia as Cavnal's Crown Prince, but as their own Godarson. Either way, the Istians wouldn't listen too keenly to him if word got out about this treaty. And if Tarik found out about it...would he stand with Istia? Would he forsake the mages in Cavnal as a lost cause, and join Istia's forces with his grandfather's in Tulay? I couldn't bear to imagine it.

And then there was the impostor mage. For whatever reason he'd chosen to look like Tarik, but why? Did he have his eyes on the throne, or did he care about the Cavnish crown at all? I wasn't sure...but I was determined to find out.

I got to my feet and walked with Batar toward the door, both of us silent, both of us lost in our own thoughts.

"I pray every day for his safety," Batar said suddenly, stopping at the door and facing me. "We are lost without him. What was Trabin thinking, sending him there? And where is Kor?" He shook his head woefully again, and laid a hand on my shoulder. "If there is any way you know how to get word to Tarik...he *has* to know what is happening here. If he's in Istia he may not have access to news from home. And if you see Kor...send him to me. We need to know where Her Majesty is. We need something. Some stability. *Something*."

"I'll let you know if I learn anything," I said, "or if I hear from Kor or Tarik." He nodded, but just as he reached to open the door I stopped him with a hand on his arm. "Minister, do you know a man named Creech?"

Batar's face crinkled with a sudden smile. "Ah. Heard you'd sprung him from the madhouse. I do thank you most kindly for that."

"So, that's a yes."

"We're cousins, yes. Second cousins, or some such. I never can

 338

keep it straight."

"He's a Shifter," I said. "What is your Gift?"

He tipped his head to regard me, brows lifted in an almost comical expression. "Trade secret, my dear. Good day."

With that he stepped out into the cold, calling for the guardsman to bring up his shay.

# Chapter 2 ~ Tarik

ISKARI FOUND ME AN HOUR LATER STANDING AT THE WINDOW IN THE COMMON bunk room. I heard him coming, by now recognizing his stride—a solid, determined pace that never seemed to hesitate or slow down. I listened to his footsteps all the way across the long room, and when he stopped beside me, I didn't move to acknowledge him.

"Taumir, have you eaten?"

I lifted a shoulder, and pressed my fingertips against the glass. Iskari watched me through a dark scowl until he realized I had no intention of answering.

"You can't stay up here forever, you know."

"I can try," I muttered.

"Don't be such a child," he said. "So, you got humiliated. You humiliated Rigvar too. It's all part of the game."

"I'm not worried about that," I said. "I don't care in the least what Rigvar says about me."

His brows shot up in surprise, but he just leaned his shoulder against the wall to get a better look at me. "Then, what?"

"Nika…she asked if the person I've been seeing might be the mad god, and not *Veka* at all. I don't even know how I would know the difference. But the worst thing of all is that…I don't really care."

I could feel his uncertainty, his alarm, but still I refused to meet his gaze.

"What do you mean by that?" he asked finally, and when I kept staring out the window, he dropped a heavy hand on my shoulder and jostled me. "Taumir? What does that even mean?"

"I mean I don't care who it is," I said. Iskari growled at my non-answer, his fingers tightening on my arm. I shoved him off and turned to glare at him. "Look, I don't want anything to do with him, whoever he is. I don't *want* what he's offering me."

"Do you imagine you can survive without me?"

I shuddered and bent my head, pressing my forehead against the cold glass and closing my eyes so I couldn't see the storm-terrible figure lingering behind me.

"Leave me be," I whispered. Iskari took a step back, but I reached out and gripped his upper arm. "*Him*. Not you. Don't leave me alone, Iskari, please."

Iskari's face softened slightly—more sympathy in his eyes than I'd ever seen before. "Come on. Come downstairs, get some food. Maybe it'll distract you. Maybe it'll help."

Suddenly weary, I nodded and followed him toward the stairs, elbowing past the luminous figure who waited for me without even looking at him.

"Tarik."

The name fell like a hammer stroke in my mind, or in my soul, reverberating against my bones like the stroke of a tower bell. I stumbled and almost fell to my knees. Iskari didn't notice—he was halfway to the door already, and he never turned to wait for me before heading down the steps. I gritted my teeth and turned to face the figure whose presence I felt like a lightning bolt behind me.

"Well?" I said.

"You doubt me, still?" he said. "You named me Wake, and you named me well."

He was right in front of me, towering over me, so close I could feel a static charge crawling all over my skin. I hadn't felt that peculiar sensation when I'd seen him before, or maybe I just hadn't been paying close enough attention to notice it. His eyes were like firebrands, so bright that my own watered just to look at them. Without warning he reached up and clasped his hands on either side of my head, thumbs pressed against my cheekbones, index fingers driving into my temples.

He said, "I am not the being you call the mad god, though I have seen his handiwork in your life. And the longer you resist my power, the greater his hold on you."

I flinched back, aghast, and tried to bend my head away from the power of his stare, but his grip prevented me. "How do I know *you're* not part of that handiwork?" I whispered. "Nothing but an illusion, a figment of my madness?"

"By the fact that you can ask that question," he said, and there was pity in the wildness of his eyes.

My heart faltered, stumbling over a beat, and my soul blazed, saturated with a fire far more intense than any flames my magic had ever harnessed. Every instinct in me wanted to fall down before him. But I could not. Maybe I was a fool, maybe I was cursing myself by my idiotic stubbornness, but no matter the consequences, I would not allow myself to move. So I Commanded myself to stand steady, imbuing my will with as much power as I'd once used to make Iskari move.

Without a word Wake took his hands away from my head and held them out between us, inviting me to place my palms against his. His skin was threaded with filigrees of light, rippling and flashing and fading like sunlight on waves. When I didn't move, his fingers curled slightly and then straightened again, renewing the invitation. I was painfully aware of my lungs failing me; I couldn't recall the last time I had drawn a breath. My arms twitched against my sides, almost by their own will. I gritted my teeth and clamped them against my body, shuddering in every muscle with the effort.

"Why are you so afraid?" Wake asked, his voice gentle, but so unexpected that I wondered how long we had been standing there, face to face, silent.

"I don't know…" I faltered. I took a single step back. "I don't know what you are asking of me."

I turned away, but almost collided with someone standing directly behind me. I couldn't see who it was—if it was Wake, or someone else—before a hand drove against my forehead, and the world went black. I felt no rush of power. But a chaos of color and light and shadow unfurled before my eyes, flickering over a rush of images so fast I felt dizzy. I couldn't make sense of what I saw; it was all too terrible.

I saw a city laid waste, razed in ruin. Fires billowing so high they licked the crown of the sky, in plumes of red and ash-black smoke. The dead unburied in the streets in numbers beyond count, bodies rotted, faces twisted with decay. A black swathe of devastation across a countryside, as far as the eye could see.

The smell of char and burning flesh filled my nose, and the sound of screams filled my ears. My throat burned and burned until I realized that I was screaming too.

I was on my hands and knees, and Wake was gone, but Iskari was there beside me with his arms around my shoulders. He was yelling too, calling my name. Blinking wildly, trying to banish those nightmare images from my mind, I suddenly realized I couldn't see anything at all. My vision was a dark and churning mass of shadow. Vaguely I felt my forehead pressed against the wooden floor, Iskari's hands tightening on my arms as he tried to steady me. There was a patter of footsteps on the stairs behind me.

"Nika, close the door!" Iskari cried. "Don't let anyone in here."

The door slammed shut.

"*Veka*," Nika breathed, and my whole body shook at the name. "What happened to him? Who did that?"

"I don't know, I don't know!" Iskari said. "The room was empty when we were leaving, I swear it!"

"Someone stabbed him? Oh, God...all that blood..."

Iskari's grip on me shifted, and I felt him trying to drag me out of my curled-up position. I couldn't make myself cooperate. My body felt rigid, trapped in stone, broken. But at least the darkness was beginning to retreat from my vision. All I could see now was red, but that was something besides shadow.

"Taumir, what happened?" Iskari asked, practically shouting in my ear. "Was it Rigvar?"

I coughed, hollowly. A hot coppery taste filled my mouth, and I shuddered and spat. And that was when I realized the red I saw was a pool of blood—my own blood. It was all over the backs of my hands, too, and I shifted dizzily when I saw how far the pool spread beneath me. But I didn't feel any pain, except that somewhere deep inside, deeper than I'd ever felt anything, I felt raw and scorched.

"No," I whispered. "I don't...I don't know."

I tilted my head so that I could see Nika paralyzed by the door behind me, her face chalk-white and eyes terribly wide. Iskari looked no better, but there was anger in his eyes, too, and not just fear.

"Don't try to get up," he said. "All right? Just lay down!"

"Here?" I said, inanely.

343

His hands were pushing down on my shoulders with gentle but insistent pressure, and finally I gave up and collapsed, rolling onto my back. I suffered him to examine me, his hands drifting in perplexed circles over my torso, my head.

"I don't understand," he said at last. "There's blood everywhere, but...he's not wounded. Just—"

I cracked my eyes open long enough to see him looking at Nika, gesturing at his mouth.

"What did you say?" I asked, hoarse.

"Your mouth and nose are bleeding—"

"No," I interrupted, and swallowed against the ache in my throat. "What did you *say*?"

He frowned down at me and sat back on his heels. "I said there's blood everywhere, but you're not wounded. I can't find a single wound anywhere on you."

The words had barely left his mouth when my body seized tight, my fingers digging knife-like against my thighs. I could feel myself shaking all over, and no matter how I tried to will myself to be still, I couldn't stop trembling. The blood was in my mouth again, and now I couldn't breathe without choking on it. I stared at Iskari in terror, begging him to help me. I didn't know what was happening. The fluid trickled into the back of my throat and my chest convulsed with a feeble cough. I was going to drown in my own blood, and Iskari was just staring at me, frozen.

Suddenly Nika was on her knees beside me, shoving me over onto my side, holding me steady as I vomited blood. Tears scorched my cheeks but I didn't even care.

"Shh," she said. "It's all right. It's all right."

Her hand was stroking my head like a child's, her cool fingers brushing back the fringes of my hair. I could feel her hand trembling, and that terrified me almost more than my own tremors.

"Iskari, get water," she said. "Now."

He scrambled to his feet and disappeared from my line of sight. When he had gone, I closed my eyes, reached down deep into my will, and forced myself to move. I rolled away from Nika's grasp, back onto my hands and knees, and tried not to grimace as my palm slipped in the pool of blood. Gingerly I leaned my weight onto one hand, and with the other I felt over my own chest and stomach. Iskari was right. There

344

wasn't a wound anywhere on me. But I knew that much blood hadn't come out of my mouth.

"What happened?" Nika murmured.

It took me a moment to realize her hands were still on me, resting gently on my shoulders. I shook my head. My throat burned so badly I wasn't sure if I could force my voice out again.

"*Veka*," I managed at last.

Her fingers stiffened, then all at once she was on her feet, her hands sliding between my arms and my torso, dragging me off the ground. I did my best to move with her help, staggering to my feet and stumbling beside her to the nearest bunk. When she had me sitting down, she knelt in front of me, her hands on my knees. Her eyes were bluer and colder than I'd ever seen.

"*He* did this to you?" she said, voice low as the sea wind. "The person you've been seeing, the one you said was *Veka*?"

I couldn't answer; my thoughts still churned in a jumbled mess that understood nothing. All I could comprehend were those flashes of images I'd seen, but the memory of them roiled in my stomach like nausea. I leaned my forehead in one hand, but then Nika's arms were wrapped around me, and I dropped my head on her shoulder as the horror brought me crashing down in tears.

"I don't know," I said, as steadily as I could. "I was talking to *Veka*. And then…I turned…and someone touched me. It was like how *Veka* has touched me before, but it felt nothing like that. There was no power. I just saw…I saw such terrible things, Nika. Oh, God. I saw such ruin. It's coming. The darkness. The devastation."

"Shh," she said again, stroking her hand over my head. "Let it go."

I squeezed my eyes shut and focused on my breathing, centering all my thoughts, all my will on the inhale and exhale. After a few moments it struck me that Nika still had her arms around me, that I was still leaning into her embrace. A moment ago it had meant nothing at all, but now… She had to know it meant nothing still.

I withdrew from her grasp as gently as I could, and passed a hand over my burning eyes. I couldn't look at her, or face the worry in her eyes—or whatever tangle of emotions she had hidden there. Instead I glanced back at where I'd gone down, where Iskari was now trying to mop up the blood with a sad heap of rags. There was a bucket of water on the floor beside him, and I gestured at it feebly. Nika left me at once to fetch it, bringing it back to me along with a clean rag. The water was bitterly cold, but I plunged my hands as deep into the bucket as I could, as if the chill of it could burn away the memory of all that had happened.

When I had washed my face and hands to Nika's satisfaction, she left me to help Iskari clean up the rest of the blood on the floor. I collapsed back on the bed, suddenly and strangely weak.

No wounds.

*Wake.* I spoke the name in my thoughts in a breath of frustration before I realized I'd said it, and I ran my hand over my face again. *Was this what happened to Trabin at the end?*

I narrowed my eyes, then slammed them closed and retreated into the quiet chambers of my mind.

*Wake!* I shouted there, like a summons, as if I could dare summon Wake like I might call my valet.

And yet he came and stood before me, more formless in my thoughts than he was in the flesh.

*Did you do this to me?* I growled, pacing toward him. *Did you do this same thing to Trabin? Did you kill my King? Is that how he died, all his blood spilled, and not a wound on his body?*

Wake circled closer to me in turn, and his eyes, so fire-bright in the shadows of my mind, were full of sorrow. *I did not,* he said. *I did not give you that vision, and the loss of your lifeblood was not by my hand. But as I told you before, the longer you resist me, the worse it will get.*

*He was here?* I demanded. *Was it the mad god, and you let him in here? You let him get to me? I thought you said you would protect me.*

*I protect my Zealot,* he said, and I heard, for the first time, a note almost of anger in his voice. A moment passed, then he said more quietly, *In answer to your question, no. He was not here.*

I spun away, rage tremoring through me.

*Then who...* I started as I turned to face him again, only to realize he had gone.

With a groan of frustration I forced my eyes open and dragged my body into a sitting position. I felt lightheaded in a way I hadn't felt since I'd stopped the rain of bullets at Borokhev...only to have them all find their mark in my body in the end anyway. My hands, planted on the mattress, were almost as white as my shirt, and my gaze drifted against my will toward the heap of red-soaked rags between Iskari and Nika.

How much blood had I actually lost?

Suddenly and irrationally nervous, I scraped a splinter of the wood from the bed frame and drove it hard into the flesh of my fingertip, then jerked it out again and clamped my hand into a fist. No bead of blood formed at the puncture. No matter how I kneaded my finger, I couldn't squeeze out a single red drop. I looked at Iskari and Nika, saw them looking at me, and the world gave way around me.

# Chapter 3 ~ Hayli

I WATCHED MINISTER BATAR DRIVE OFF IN HIS SMART SHAY UNTIL HE WAS out of sight, then wandered back into the yard. For once I had no morning drills or duties to attend, but I knew Bridnow meant for me to use the free time to deal with the impostor mage. I just couldn't conjure a single thing to do or say to make the situation right. I didn't want to talk to the man again at all, but I knew he was my responsibility, and if keeping him locked up was cruel, well, that was my cruelty to blame. And *cruel* was the last thing in the world I ever wanted to be.

A sudden gust of unnatural wind tousled my hair and nearly unseated my hat. I clapped both hands on top of my head and looked up, staring in astonishment as the old aeroplane from the smelter glided overhead. The plane was low enough that I could see the cockpit and Griff's familiar ruddy face, his dark curls sticking out every which way from under the edges of his aviator's helmet. Below his round goggles he was grinning like a fiend.

A small crowd knotted around me to watch as Griff swooped once over the prison town, then brought the plane down easy as a sparrow on the road outside. It sped along for some distance, churning up a spray of muddy snow, until finally it came to a slow crawl. Then it nosed around back toward the north, bumping over the grass alongside the road as it went, and finally sputtered to a standstill outside the gate, the airscrew wobbling like a top as it slowed to a stop.

I ran out to meet Griff as he climbed out of the cockpit.

"Well," he said, through that mad-cat grin, clinging to the outside of the cockpit like a squirrel for a tick before dropping down beside me. "Guess she can fly after all."

"And land," I said.

He laughed and nodded, slapping the nose of the aeroplane fondly, like a favorite horse. I ran my fingers along its sleek shell—it was warmer than I thought it would be, and little traces of steam curled away into the cold air.

"I was dead sure the Army would've destroyed it, when they went to the smelter," I said.

"Ah, well, she did look rather worse for wear," Griff said, tugging off his helmet and goggles and wiping his sleeve over his forehead. "Anyone who isn't a pilot probably would've taken one look at her and thought she'd flown her last. They probably didn't think they needed to waste their time on her."

"Lucky for us," I said. "You ganna leave it out here?"

Griff shrugged. "Can't get her through the bloody gate, unless there's some way to open half the wall up for her wings. I don't *want* to leave her out here, but there's no room for a runway inside the walls, either."

He headed toward the gate with ground-eating strides, chin high and a mad gleam in his eyes, all full of that cocky modoc swagger that everyone always talked about. When he found the little crowd gathered in the yard to watch, he grinned bigger than ever and waved his helmet at them. The skitters whooped and cheered, jumping up and down, which only made Griff laugh as he blustered past them.

"What's got your mind?" he asked then, walking backwards to look at me as I hurried to catch up. "You look more worried than usual."

"Do I usually look worried?" I asked, scowling.

He laughed and shook his head. "These days, yeah." He studied me sideways a minute. "Heard there was some kind of ruckus at the gate last night. What happened?"

I stopped there in the middle of the yard, in the middle of the snow, twisting my hands together. "Something I need to talk to you about. You gannin' anywhere in particular?"

"Somewhere we can talk, I'm guessing," he said. "I've got nowhere to be just now."

"I want the crew. I need to talk to everyone."

349

He lifted his brows, curious. "I'll help find them. Where are we meeting?"

I scanned the scattered buildings, chewing my lip. I wasn't used to Borokhev, not yet. I didn't know all its hiding places, all its best spots for secret meetings. All I knew was that I wanted to stay as far away from the dormitory building as I could, where the impostor mage was waiting for me to decide his fate.

"Rookery?" he offered.

I frowned. "What?"

He got a sly grin at that and pointed to the officers' billeting. "The Rookery. Are we meeting there?"

"The Rookery?" I echoed, completely flustered. "Why'd you call it that?"

"Everyone calls it that," he said. "Well, since yesterday."

"But..." I sputtered. "But why?"

"Oh, I don't know, maybe because the Rook herself lives there?" I gaped at him, but he just laughed and threw an arm around my shoulders. "Shiver told us. You can blame him."

I shook my head and said, "Fine, yeah. Send 'em to the...Rookery. No one's apt to be there right now anyway, except maybe the guards who were on watch last night, but I guess they'll all be asleep."

"Like you should be?" he asked, gentler than I expected.

I shrugged and waved his concern away. "I'm fine."

He peered at me closely another minute, then nodded and sauntered off toward the western half of the facility. That left me to search the eastern side, where the dormitory was. I tamped down a surge of displeasure and tromped through the drifting snow toward Doc's infirmary, to see if anyone was there.

As I'd halfway expected I found Derrin inside, letting Doc examine the wound on his stomach. He nodded a greeting to me, but Doc was too focused to acknowledge me. On a bed nearby lay Creech, wrapped in heavy blankets and sound asleep, but other than the three of them, the building was empty.

"Morning, Hayli," Derrin said. "You need something?"

"You, when you're done. Something I need to talk to you about."

"I've got to organize a supply run after this," he said, frowning. "Can we talk now? Is this about last night?"

"What'd you hear?"

"Heard someone came to the facility while you were on duty. Is it true?"

I waffled a bit, watching Doc's steady hands as they moved, almost glass-clear, over the angry red wound on Derrin's torso. He glanced up at me, but his face was expressionless, all but the single line of concentration between his brows.

"Ten minutes," I said. "That's all I need."

"Fine," Derrin said. "Where?"

"Rookery," I said, barely stumbling over the name, and ducked back out of the infirmary.

I found Jig and Scorch sitting on the front steps of the dormitory and rounded them up, and across the yard I spotted Griff with Coins and Anuk already heading toward the officers' building. The only one I figured was still missing was Shiver, but I doubted I'd find him even if I looked for him—he was probably hiding in a wall somewhere. But when we walked into the Rookery he was already there, along with Derrin, the two of them lounging in the chairs closest to the hearth.

"I should've known," I muttered, as Shiver gave me an impish smile.

"No secrets," he said.

I waved him off and gestured for the others to pull up chairs. Most of them complied, but Coins perched up on the table instead, and Anuk leaned against the wall next to the hearth with folded arms.

"So what's this about?" Derrin asked. "What exactly happened last night?"

"Heard you got attacked," Jig said. "That so?"

I glanced at him in surprise. "Nah, I div'n get attacked. But it's true, someone came to the facility last night. Walked in on the tracks just like we did. We've got him in custody now."

Anuk gave a low whistle, but Scorch leaned forward, saying, "Really? Must be someone important if it's got you so worked up."

"It's the mage from Avnaya." I glanced at Griff. "The one who came to the palace and threatened the Ministers. The one who's been wearing Tarik's face."

All of them were silent, and all of them were staring at me—except Derrin, who was looking absently toward the back of the room. I frowned at the fire, chewing the inside of my cheek.

"I dan' na what to do with him," I said.

"He was impersonating the Prince," Griff said, with a savage

351

bite to his voice. "He should be turned over to the palace guard and imprisoned, if not executed."

"I dan' think he knows what he was doing," I said.

"How could he not—" Anuk started.

"He was here with the Science Ministry, like me and Derrin. Under Kippler's thumb. Wake knows what they were doing to him, or for how long."

"He was there when Trabin died," Coins said. "How do we know *he* didn't do it?"

"He's scared!" I said, almost shouting it. "I dan' think he even knows what's real any more!"

"That makes him *less* dangerous?" Griff countered, just as loud. "I don't know much about mages, but if he can disappear *and* change his appearance, that seems pretty powerful already."

"He can disappear?" Derrin asked, startled.

"He's a Ghost like you," I said.

Derrin said, "Damn," and rubbed his hand over his face.

"What should we do with him? I dan' trust him on the loose and I dan' na that I trust him hereabouts, but I ain't ganna keep a mage imprisoned for naught but that he's a mage, and unlucky at that."

"Not unlucky."

I muttered a curse under my breath that might've made Anuk proud, and we all turned to see Doc standing in the shadows behind us, near the cabinet where he'd fetched Batar a drink. I had no idea how long he'd been there. Certainly I hadn't heard—or felt—the door open, but there he was, staring at us. His face was bone white, and if I didn't know any better, I would've said he was dead terrified.

"He's not unlucky," he said again. He took two steps forward, planting his thin hands on the table and leaning toward me. "You let him in here? What have you done, girl?" he said. "Do you know? Don't you understand…he *cannot* be here. You have no idea…you have no idea what you're dealing with."

"And you do?" Griff asked. "Who is he?"

Doc tore his gaze from my face to look at Griff, but somehow I thought he didn't see Griff at all.

"Doc!" I said, sharp. "What do you know? Tell us who he is, so I can deal with him proper!"

Doc glanced back at me, shaking his head, silent. "It's a disaster," he said at last. "First Destri, now this…" He rubbed his hands over his arms. "I knew it… I should have known, last night, when… Oh, God. You have no idea what you've done."

He turned away, and I felt like I was watching an echo of what had happened not three hours ago, with Batar. Only this time Doc didn't storm out of the building in an icy rage. He retreated a step at a time, then, without another word, he…*fled*. I stared after him for the space of three troubled breaths, then ran to the door and threw it open to call him back. But he was nowhere to be seen, and the snowy, muddy mess in the yard was so rutted with tracks that it was impossible to tell which way he'd gone.

I sighed, feeling strangely anxious, and wandered back inside where the others were waiting for me.

"He left?" Derrin asked, frowning, thoughtful.

"Dan' na where he lammed off to."

"What do you suppose he meant by all that?" Anuk asked.

I sighed and shook my head. "Got no ken. But I'll have to gan and talk to that mage again. If I get the sense he's dangerous, then I'll need some of you lads to take him into the city. Griff, you think you could handle that? We'll turn him over to the palace, just like you said."

He nodded, and I prayed it wouldn't come to that.

I sat on the edge of the table as the lads wandered off, one by one, to other duties, and other amusements, until Derrin was the only one still sitting by the hearth. For some time after the Rookery emptied out, neither of us spoke.

Finally I sighed and slumped my shoulders. "What's got into Doc lately? I've never seen him so cagey before. I mean…he's always been a mystery, but it's different now. I dan' na what's wrong with him."

"It's like before, his secrets were all well and buried," Derrin said, "and now, it's more like he's trying desperately to keep them that way."

"I dan' like it," I muttered.

"We all have secrets, Hayli," he said gently.

"Yeah, but why do I get the feeling that his are a bit more worrisome than yours or mine?"

He gave me a look. "Ours have been fairly worrisome."

That much was true, anyway. I waved a hand and tucked it back between my knees. "Guess we'll find out. Or not. But for now, s'pose I'd best gan and have a chat with that mage."

"Do you want me to go with you?"

I did. More than aught else, I wanted Derrin with me, but Bridnow had told me to take a non-mage instead. Even when Kantian used to tell me what to do or how to do it, I'd never felt all that bound to listen. I'd mostly gone my own way, and dealt with the consequences if I had to. It was different with Bridnow. I couldn't *not* obey him. I didn't even want to try.

"I'm ganna take Griff with me," I said. Then, so he wouldn't get sore over it, I added, "Bridnow told me."

He nodded at that and got to his feet. "Good luck. And if you need me for anything..."

"I'll ask," I said. "Dan' worry."

I watched as he left the Rookery, and for five solid minutes I sat and stared at the flames, and tried to find the courage to do what I needed to do.

# Chapter 4 ~ Hayli

WHEN GRIFF AND I OPENED THE OFFICE DOOR WHERE WE WERE KEEPING the mage, we found him still huddled in the corner where I'd last seen him, knees drawn up, arms wrapped around his head. Griff startled when the mage lifted his face, just as I did. No matter how many times I saw him, I could never get used to seeing Tarik's face as part of someone who wasn't Tarik. I remembered how Tarik had always sworn he'd never rob another man's real face—he told me he'd had to do it just once and hated every minute of it. Looking at the mage in front of me, I could understand why. There was a cruelty to that kind of theft that made my blood boil.

"You came back," the mage said, watching me. "I thought you said you wouldn't."

I gave him a solid glare and climbed onto the heavy desk that sat against the inner wall. "You have half a minute to change your face to someone who's not Tarik, or I'm walking back out."

"And do what with me?" he asked, eyeing me bitterly. "You're just like *him.*"

I flinched. "Who?"

"Kippler," he spat. "Or did you forget how he held you prisoner here? Look at you. Look at what you're doing. You're no better than he is. Hayli! How could you do this to me? Caging a fellow mage, robbing him of his power…"

He lifted his cuffs with the last words, shaking them until the links jingled. I stepped back, stricken, words and thoughts escaping my grasp like puffs of smoke. Under the weight of his accusations I could scarcely breathe.

"Fifteen seconds," Griff growled.

"I've seen you before, too, at the palace."

"Right," Griff said. "When you threatened my father. Which you would know if you were really Tarik. Ten seconds."

"Farro?" the mage said, brow knotting. "You've changed...I didn't recognize you."

Griff's hands knotted in fists. I got off the desk again to make a point, and the mage finally got a little panicky look about him.

"All right," he said. "All right!"

He buried his face in his hands and I heard the low sing-song of his voice as he chanted something to himself, reminding me of the first time I'd met him, across the wall of my cell in the Science Ministry, when I'd been dead sure he was completely cracked. I still wasn't convinced he wasn't.

Griff leaned against the desk beside me, arms folded, and we watched as the mage's hair lightened to a warm honey-gold color above his hands. Then he lifted his face and looked straight at me. I drew back, not quite sure what to expect. The mage looked barely older than Tarik now, with a faint trace of a beard on his pale jaw, and eyes that were a dark moss green flecked with amber. His face was narrow, handsome in a puzzling kind of way, framed with the wisps of hair that hung just a little longer than Tarik's.

He looked oddly familiar, and yet for the life of me, I couldn't figure out who he reminded me of. At least—I breathed a sigh of relief—it wasn't Tarik's face any more.

"Good," I said. "Now, you dan' get to use his name any more, either. So give me something to call you."

"Little Hayli," he said, a plaintive note in his voice that would've broken my heart if the words hadn't made me so angry. "Little Hayli, you're robbing me of everything I know."

I licked my lips. "You're a Mask," I said. "And this is—I'm guessing—a Masked face. Dan' wanna know whose face it is, either, so dan' tell me. But just pretend you're ganna give this face his own name, like you'd make him his own person."

"Like Tarik did with Shade?" he said, those baffling green eyes settling on me with a keen, savage light.

Beside me Griff jolted, and I heard him mutter, "*Tam,*" under his breath.

"Don't you remember?" the mage said, his gaze never leaving my face. Then, in a voice that sounded strangely like my own, he said, "Shade's got a secret could destroy the world. *Cursed the crown.*"

"Oh, *Wake,*" I muttered, closing my eyes. "That...that really happened?"

"What's he talking about?" Griff asked.

I ground my teeth. "I'll tell you later. But Tam will be glad to know he div'n spill Tarik's secret." I looked at him sideways. "*I* did. I thought...I thought it was just a dream."

"It was all dreams," the mage murmured, and I shuddered.

Griff measured me in silence, then shook his head. "You're right. You can tell me about it later. Meanwhile." He fixed the mage with a stern look. "You, spit out a name."

The mage glowered at him, but he at least seemed to be making a halfway honest attempt at conjuring up a name. His brow furrowed and he dropped his eyes closed, fingers thrumming restlessly on his knees.

"There's a name," he said after a tick. "But whose? Who is the mage? Who? Ar...Aro..."

His voice died, and I offered, "Arrow?"

"I could be an arrow," he said, tipping his head, birdlike, to the side. "But you're the one with the feathers. Arrow. Aro...Ah, I can't remember. Can't think. It's all lost in stone and mist."

"Stars, he even sounds like Tarik," Griff muttered, and I elbowed him hard in the ribs. He grunted and didn't say anything else.

Suddenly the mage straightened up, his eyes flashing back to mine, and a bare smile lifted the corners of his lips as he said, "Aroden."

"Aroden," I echoed. "Is that...is that your real name?"

He slouched back against the wall, waving a hand in my general direction. "Don't know," he said. "Don't care. It's a name. It's locked away up here, but it's a name, and he can use it." He tapped his head with one long finger and leaned his head back. "Now that that's settled, I imagine you want an account of me."

"That would be helpful," I said, "for starters. Why did you come here?"

"I wanted to see you," he said, so earnestly that my stomach fluttered in spite of myself, then he shot Griff a peeved glare. "Not *him*. Not anyone else. *You.* You're the only one who can make sense of me. Because…you understand."

"Understand what?"

"The chaos," he said. "The fear. Not knowing…knowing not knowing…" He closed his eyes, brow creased and lips tight, everything about him taut and tense as lightning. Then he wrapped his arms around his chest with a low moan and whispered, "Oh God, *thayoi* in the walls, all around me…can't you hear them? Can't you hear the whispers? Always in my head, behind my eyes, lips against my ears… *Take it, take it, take it.* And I can't take it. I can't. I tried, but it just won't *die.* All that power, all spilled out. So *pointless.*"

"What were you taking?" Griff asked.

For half a tick Aroden just stared at Griff, his lip curled and eyes narrowed with revulsion, as if Griff were a dead rat in the kitchen. Even Griff seemed startled by the rawness of that look—most folks, even in the south streets, were simply too polite to show their feelings so plainly.

Then Aroden muttered, "You wouldn't understand," and flicked the fingers of his cuffed hand in Griff's direction.

Griff reeled back, cracking his head back against the wall before he could stop himself. He swore, loudly, and lurched to his feet. But I was already standing between them, holding a hand toward each of them to keep them apart.

"What was that?" I cried. "Did you just do that to him?"

Aroden blinked in genuine puzzlement. "Was that…was that wrong?" he stammered. "Should I not…I mean, I didn't mean…"

I glanced back at Griff, who was rubbing his head and glaring murderous daggers at Aroden. "Are you a'right?"

"Fine, I suppose, but—"

"Are you *hurt?*"

"No."

I gave him a warning look, pursed my lips, and turned back to Aroden. "Dan' do aught like that again, savv?" He ducked his head and nodded, which was more than I'd hoped for. When I was sure they wouldn't spring at each other the second I stepped back, I lowered my hands and leaned against the desk. "How'd you do that?"

He turned his head stubbornly and waved a hand. It was a careless, dismissive gesture, but that didn't stop Griff from flinching like he expected to be flung against the wall again.

"I don't know," Aroden said. "The same way I do any of it, I suppose. It's just there, and it happens."

I chewed on the inside of my cheek, a faint curl of fear gnawing at my stomach. Aroden was *powerful*. I'd guessed he was from the beginning, but now it was so obvious I couldn't ignore it if I wanted to. He was a Mask, certainly, and a Ghost, but now it seemed he was a Telekine too, by the way he'd shoved Griff without even touching him. But that wasn't the most troubling thing about it. All I could think—and I hated to think it—was how every time Tarik used his power it seemed to drain him of something...his life, maybe, or maybe his sanity. But Aroden seemed to wield his power effortlessly, almost whimsically, like he wasn't even aware of himself as he did. And he did it with his hands bound.

It bloody *terrified* me.

I drew a cautious breath and folded my arms. "I got a question for you, and I need a straight answer." Aroden didn't move, and didn't look at me, but I could feel all his attention riveted on me. "If I take those cuffs off of you, what will you do?"

He startled, visibly, and shifted around to face me again. "You mean, will I go?"

"That's what I mean."

"Depends," he said. His mouth lifted in a pale kind of smile. "Are you going to give me a reason to escape, or a reason to stay?"

"If we let you stay, can you promise that my people will be safe from you?"

His eyes widened. "Safe!" he echoed. "From me? What do you think I would do to them?"

"I dan' na. That's why I'm asking. Got no reason to trust you, but I'm willing to try if you dan' give me a reason not to."

"You're defending yourselves here," he said, nodding generally at the building around us, at Borokhev. "You're afraid. You're isolated. Believe me, I know how that feels." He held his bound hands toward me. "So I will do what I can to help you protect these people from whatever dangers you fear. That I promise."

"Why?" Griff asked. His hands tightened on the edge of the desk—I wasn't sure if it was because he was angry, or because he was bracing himself against another Push from Aroden.

"Because, idiot, we have the same enemies," Aroden snapped.

Griff flushed a deep red at that, and when I put a hand on his shoulder he shrugged me off. "Stars, would you stop *defending* him? Making excuses... This person, whoever he is...he is a crown-standard *bastard*."

Aroden gave him a vicious smile that looked a bit more like a snarl, and Griff's hands curled into fists. I rounded on the mage.

"He's right about one thing," I said, jabbing a finger in his direction. "*Dan'* press your luck with me. I will sooner defend him than you, every single time. Him I trust with my life. You, not at all. Got it?"

The smile vanished, snuffed out, and a bleak darkness crept into Aroden's eyes. "Got it," he muttered. "I'll win your trust, Hayli. I promise that, too. I'll do whatever it takes."

Griff gave him a look of supreme disdain at that, but I just shrugged and turned toward the door. "I'll be back in a couple of ticks. I dan' have the key to your cuffs with me."

"Don't bother," Aroden said.

He bent his head and eyed the cuffs thoughtfully, then I heard a soft click and he shook the open links from his wrists. Griff and I stared, speechless, at the manacles lying like a dead thing on the floor.

"You could've done that at any time," Griff said. "Why'd you stay?"

Aroden got carefully to his feet, one hand braced on the wall for support. Now that he was standing, I realized he was taller than he had been before, though he was still as whip-slim as Tarik. He gave me an odd smile as he answered Griff.

"Call it a show of good faith."

I turned without a word and opened the door to the office. Griff went out ahead of me, and then Aroden. The two guards standing outside the door jumped a fair bit when they saw Aroden, which I supposed was only natural. They'd seen one man get taken into that room, and now a different one was coming out.

"Oh," Aroden said, and gave the guards a disarming smile. "I didn't even know I had company."

"Lieutenant," one of the guards said. Griff and I both turned to look at him. "Who is this?"

"Aroden," I said. "He'll be staying with us. For now."

The guard's jaw clenched visibly. I could see a million and one questions trapped behind his eyes, along with a fear and suspicion too powerful for him to hide. And doubt. That doubt, I realized a second too late, was aimed not at Aroden, but at me.

"Griff," I said. "Show Aroden where he can find a bunk. Anywhere but that room."

He nodded understanding. I didn't know who was responsible for word getting around, but *that* room, the one that still haunted my dreams, had got roped off that first day I came to Borokhev, and nobody ever went in it. I guessed most of my lads knew why, and they never raised a question about it, and the rest of the folks never had a reason to care.

Aroden looked like he had a mind to say something to me, but Griff took him by the arm and marched him off toward the stairs at the end of the hall like he was a disobedient skitter on his way to a walloping. Soon as I was alone with the guards, I pulled my Bridnow imitation—chin lifted, hands folded behind my back, gaze steady on the face of the guard who seemed the most disturbed.

"Speak your mind," I said.

He looked fair surprised at that, and exchanged a brief glance with his fellow. "Apologies, *Lieutenant*, but I'm trying very hard to understand why that man is on the loose, and I'm trying very hard not to be angry about it."

"I understand—"

"You *don't* understand, or this wouldn't be happening!" he cried. Then he flushed deeply and said, "I'm sorry...ma'am. That was out of line."

"Your worry's not for no reason," I said, quietly. "But listen. That mage has done nothing wrong that we know of, but I *do* know he was trapped by Kippler and had his brain meddled with like I did." The guards shifted at that, uneasy, but I forced myself to ignore the suspicion in their eyes. "Anyway, from all I know, his loyalties are in the same place ours are."

"Then why was he parading about looking like the Prince?"

"Honestly I think it's all he knew how to be." The guard opened his mouth to protest again, but this time I held up my hand. "My decision stands," I said. "If you've got concerns, take them to Commandant Bridnow."

They both saluted as I turned away, but somehow, I got the sinking feeling that I hadn't convinced them in the least, and that by the time I turned the corner at the end of the hallway, they would already be whispering, murmuring complaints and accusations against me. I ground my teeth. I'd done what Bridnow had asked, but somehow I thought it hadn't solved our problems.

Instead, I got the sinking feeling it had opened a whole pit of new ones.

# Chapter 5 ～ Tarik

"TAUMIR, ARE YOU WITH ME?"

Iskari's voice, thin and taut with fear, was the first thing I was aware of. The next was the fact that I was aware of nothing else.

With a profound effort I dragged open my eyes and looked at him, as I tried in vain to make sense of his words. I was lying on the bed again, and it took me a moment to remember—I had tried to draw blood from my finger, and nothing had happened. Shoving Iskari back, I lurched upright and lifted my hand. My heart was hammering in my chest, and that, I told myself, had to be at least somewhat of a good sign. I clutched the finger that I had pricked with the wood splinter, and squeezed it as hard as I could. After a moment, a bead of dark red blood seeped from the narrow wound, and I let out all my breath in a shattered sigh of relief.

"I thought…" I started, and met Iskari's gaze. "It was nothing. I was just a bit lightheaded."

"You passed out."

"Just a little."

He gave me a narrow look and I knew he didn't believe me, but at least he didn't try to contradict me, or ask how it was possible to pass out *just a little.* When I felt a bit steadier, I waved him away and got to my feet.

"Are they still serving breakfast?" I asked.

That made Iskari laugh, at least, even if it sounded a bit strained. Nika, still on her knees near the last remnants of my spilled blood, was watching me steadily while she pretended to work.

"I think so," she said. "Are you sure—"

"I'm starving," I muttered. I watched her a moment, then, stomach tight with fear, I pointed at the heap of rags and said, "Burn that."

She didn't even argue.

I took a step away from the bed and faltered, as the room swam around me in inky shadows, pitching under my feet like a ship's deck. Then the floor steadied, and the color returned to the world, and I moved forward a little more surely. Iskari stopped me at the door and gave me Zagger's coat—to hide the bloodstains on my shirt, I realized. Even after I'd pulled it on, he followed me like a shadow all the way down the stairs, reminding me so much of Jig and Scorch that I half-expected to see one of them walking beside him when I turned around.

"I'm *fine*, Iskari," I snapped. "You don't have to sheepdog me."

His mouth quirked in a grim smile. "I will until I'm sure you're not going to start screaming or bleeding again," he said, and pushed past me to open the door to the dining area for me.

There were, to my dismay, maybe two dozen people still crowded around the long tables, talking and eating and poring over papers. Some of them looked up at me as we came into the room, and those that did eyed me strangely, like they weren't quite sure what to make of me. As if what they saw confused them. And some of them ducked their heads and looked sheepishly away from me, as if they remembered something that shamed them.

I exchanged a glance with Iskari and sat down at an empty table, casting a cursory glance over myself as I did to make sure none of the bloodstains were still visible. The coat was clean, at least, but I still felt strangely like I had blood on my skin, somewhere. I could still smell it in my nose, and taste it in the burn at the back of my throat.

I was halfway through a now-familiar breakfast of porridge and tangy yoghurt when an older man I had never seen before sat down across the table from me.

"Taumir Eyidson," he said, without waiting for me to acknowledge him. He folded his hands on the table between us. "What is it you mean to do for Istia, as her Godar?"

The spoonful of yoghurt in my mouth turned oddly dry at his question, and it was all I could do to force myself to swallow. Beside me, Iskari shifted his weight.

"Taumir," he said, before I could speak; I guessed he was giving me time to gather my thoughts. "This is a friend of my father's, Thane Grivson." He looked at the older man with a smile. "You already know Taumir, apparently."

"I do," he said, bluntly, and then went back to staring at me.

"Istia has had a long-standing alliance with Cavnal," I said, carefully. "An alliance that has been somewhat strained in recent years, true, but an alliance all the same. Peace between these countries has always been beneficial to both, and with all the chaos in the world today, that hasn't changed."

I faltered; I knew without looking at either man that I was showing my Cavner upbringing with every word I said. There was nothing wrong with my statement, but it was diplomatic, measured, saying little through well-spoken platitudes. I set down my spoon with a sigh and met Thane's uneasy gaze, all too aware of a handful of other *sodthari* at the nearby tables obviously listening to the conversation.

"If things continue as they are, unchecked, there is going to be a war in the coming months that decimates this world," I said. I closed my eyes as those horrible visions of the charred earth swept over me again. "It will bring every nation to its knees, and *Veka* knows if any of them will ever rise from those ashes. The only way to prevent it is to preserve the old alliance between Istia, Tulay, and Cavnal. So, you asked what I mean to do for Istia? I will not stand aside and let some upstart usurper drive a stake through that friendship for the sole purpose of proving his own superiority. I don't care if I'm elected Godar or not. I will do everything in my power to stop Rigvar Karvarson from driving us into war."

Thane's brows lifted and he sat back, a speculative look on his weathered face. "Spoken fair and sound, Eyidson," he said. "But you realize that an alliance goes both ways. Are you sure Cavnal is willing to preserve that peace? With all that happened in recent months, even before the death of Cavnal's King…"

I assumed he was talking about the Cavnish ambassadors and Eyid's subsequent demise—and, more recently, the deaths of Eskir and his entourage.

*Cavnal will be willing, if I can just get back and repair the damage done by the sedition,* I thought, but I couldn't say that.

Instead I said, "I believe that Cavnal is just as unwilling to go to war right now as we are. She just lost her King, and her government is trying to maintain stability in an astonishingly volatile political situation. War with anyone would only destabilize her further, if not bring her utterly to ruin."

"Then what should we make of the alliance that Cavnal's Ministries want to make with Meritac and Cromis?"

I faltered. I knew Trabin had been contemplating such an alliance when he'd been pressured by the Court, but as far as I'd known, the aftermath of the Avnaya incident had put all those talks on hold.

"The Cavnish Court of Ministries doesn't have authority to make foreign alliances," I said, carefully. "They are still subject to the will of the monarchy, even when, for the moment, the throne sits empty."

He tipped his head, and from the look on his face, I got the strange feeling that he knew something I didn't. Iskari, beside me, was thrumming his fingers on the table.

"Thane, spit it out," he said finally. "There's something you're not saying."

"I have...inside information," Thane said. "There is talk that, not only do the Ministries have no intention of finding Prince Tarik, or of settling the crown on the former King's nephew—oh, what was his name..."

"Horm," I said softly, without thinking.

"Horm," Thane echoed. If he thought it was odd that I knew the name of the Cavnish King's nephew, he gave no sign of it. He was watching some of the *sodthari* at a nearby table, almost absent-mindedly. "The Ministers seem to be angling themselves to take over the government and abolish the monarchy altogether. But that's not the least of it. Apparently there are also elements in Brinmark who want to stage a military coup and bring down the Court itself."

I let out all my air in one shattered breath. "How do you know this?"

"I told you, I've got ears to the ground in Brinmark."

"Well-positioned ears," I said, not even bothering to mask my alarm. "Where is your informant, that they would have access to that kind of information? And how is it you know this before anyone else? As far as I was aware, there isn't much by way of travel between Cavnal and Istia right now."

"Ah," Thane said. "I can't give away my informant's secrets, but I will tell you that his messages don't come on paper. It's not unlike how our foreign ambassadors report intelligence back to the *sodthari* and the Godar, but my informant isn't an ambassador."

I sat back, astonished. The only explanation I could think of was that Thane and his informant —and the Istian ambassadors—were using the kind of mental communication that I thought I'd invented with Pika and Luce.

"You're a mind-reader?" I asked, careful not to use the Cavnish term Knack.

"We can talk at a distance, if that's what you're asking. Up here." He tapped his forehead with a wry smile.

"And..." I hesitated, cursing my curiosity. "Has your informant told you anything about me?"

His grin widened. "Ah now, that's a curious thing. I have indeed heard a great many fascinating things about you. In fact, my informant recently shared a very interesting rumor." I gave him an impatient gesture, fighting to subdue my alarm. He leaned forward, conspiratorial, and said, "Very few mages have ever existed, as far as I know, who have the ability to bend time to their will. Isn't that so?"

"*What?*" Iskari gasped.

I cursed under my breath and rubbed a hand over my face. Somehow, when I'd been rattling off my list of bizarre talents to Iskari and Nika, I'd completely forgotten about the incident at Borokhev when—for that one, near-fatal moment—I had stopped time.

"That's hardly a well-known fact," I said, holding Thane's gaze.

"But a most interesting one." He sat back again, clasping his hands. "Some people believed, or maybe hoped, that Eyid would prove to be an archmage. Rule by someone that powerful could only boost Istia's standing in the world, they said. He never reached that height, though. Gave up his power to save his sanity, some say. But you?" He tilted his head, studying me as if I were a bit of ancient text he needed to translate. "Is it true? Are you the Zealot?"

"I am not," I said, firmly, and I didn't even hesitate.

Thane smiled. "Well, I'm a bit relieved to hear that, I admit. An archmage I would gladly see crowned with the *aydrding*, but the Zealot has no need for earthly crowns."

I braced my hands on the edge of the table, trying to steady the whirlwind chaos of my thoughts. "What do you know of the Zealot?"

"Enough to know I'd rather not live to see his coming."

"Why not? He's supposed to…he's supposed to be *Veka's* emissary in the world. Is that a bad thing?"

And I regarded myself with bemusement, wondering why I was feeling so defensive of the Zealot's reputation all of a sudden. What did it matter to me if people thought ill or well of him? He was no one I would ever be.

Thane laughed, low and long, and shook his head. "Oh, lad, if you're asking that…go back and brush up on your histories." He got to his feet, nodding first to me, then to Iskari. "I've taken enough of your time. Good day, Eyidson."

I was too distracted to do any more than give a faint nod in return. As soon as he'd gone I shoved my bowl of now-cold porridge away from me and turned to Iskari.

"What the hell did all of that mean?"

He lifted his hands. "Don't look at me. I don't know any more about the Zealot than you do."

I ground my teeth and glanced away, pushing Thane's enigmatic comments about the Zealot out of my mind. My far greater worry was what he had told me about the state of affairs in Cavnal, in Brinmark. Which people in the city could possibly be wanting to overthrow the Court? Had any of my lads gotten swept up in Red's idiotic anarchist schemes? Stars, I'd left them rudderless. If Hayli hadn't come back…

I desperately needed to know the truth of the situation. All of the truth.

I pushed away from the table and started for the front door of the lodging house, Iskari practically nipping at my heels as I went. He followed me all the way out onto the street before I finally turned to face him.

"Iskari, go back inside before I make you."

He laughed at that, but it was all disbelief. "Oh, no. Every time I leave you alone, you end up in stranger circumstances than I can possibly explain, and every time I find you, you're in worse straits than you were before. I am *not* leaving you."

"I need somewhere to be alone, and think," I said. I didn't tell him what else I wanted to do—he certainly wouldn't leave my side if he knew that. "And I can't *think* with you watching me. Show me a private room in that lodging house where I can have a few minutes' peace and quiet, and I'll gladly stay here. Otherwise…"

"There's nowhere inside that's private," he said through a black scowl. Then he cursed under his breath and turned aside. "Look, I can take you to a place, but only if you let me stay in the building with you. I won't follow you into whatever room you use…just let me stay near."

I glared at him for a few solid moments, then shrugged and folded my hands in my pockets. "Fine. Lead on."

He hesitated, glancing back at the lodging house; I suspected he was anxious about leaving without telling Nika where we were going. But when I made a quiet noise of impatience, he shrugged and strode out onto the street, beckoning me to follow him.

"It's not far," he said.

For once, it seemed, that was true. We turned a corner down a narrow side street angling north, and at the next broad avenue it intersected, he led me straight up to the second building on the opposite side of the street. It was tall and narrow, a good three stories in height, not painted like the other buildings but almost completely paneled in the dark Cavnish wood. The upper stories had a few sliver-thin windows frowning down at the street, but I couldn't see any lights on inside, and the door, when we climbed the front steps, was inauspiciously unbolted and hanging slightly ajar.

"What is this place?" I asked at the threshold, for some reason reluctant to move forward.

"This," Iskari said, "was your father's home." His gaze drifted over the building's facade, a strange, drawn look on his face. "This is the place where he died."

I swore under my breath. "Oh, that is bloody fantastic," I muttered.

"Or we can go back to the lodging house and you can do your thinking in the women's bunk room," Iskari said, half-mocking.

I glowered and pushed the door open, and stepped inside.

For a place that had been abandoned for months, it was disturbingly warm within the house, apparently from the steam vents that never needed fuel or tending. I eased my way into the front hallway, feeling like an interloper, like someone desecrating a burial site. The air crawled over me, so close and oppressive that I was sure I couldn't be the only one who felt it, but Iskari stalked behind me as if we were walking on the ocean shore, or a ship's deck, or some other godforsaken place where he felt at home.

He paused at the narrow doorway into a small sitting room that opened off to our left. "I'll wait here while you do your thinking," he said, leveling a hard look on me that felt somehow taunting.

I flicked my thumb at him and continued on by myself, making my way toward the narrow staircase that led to the upper floors. My gaze roved over everything as I went. The wood-paneled walls were bare, with neither paintings nor portraits to fight the gloomy emptiness, not even any moulding to soften the severity of the hallway's angles. There were no ornaments or curios on any of the shelves. I wondered if thieves had picked the place over after Eyid's death, because it looked not only abandoned, but like it had never been inhabited. On the second story the scene was much the same. I found what must have been Eyid's bedroom; I glanced in, and stayed out, feeling the intrusion into his privacy was too great even if he was no longer alive to care. But what I saw gave the same uninhabited impression, and more than anything, that made me uneasy.

At the end of the short hallway I came to a small study. My feet moved toward it like magnetism, while the hairs on the back of my neck prickled strangely. The door was ajar; I pushed it open and stepped inside.

For one moment, for just one single moment, I stood face to face with a man. He looked like me, like Shade, but older, with short, fair hair and a stern face, and eyes as wild and desolate as a storm at sea. And then I saw the trickle of blood at the corner of his mouth. The hand pressed against his chest, blood slipping between his fingers. The look of betrayal in his eyes.

I reeled back with a gasp of shock, tearing away from the gruesome sight, and when I blinked and looked again, the room was empty. Grief-stricken and shaken, I crept into the room and stirred my fingers to light the oil lamps on the walls and the corners of the broad empty desk. In the flickering light, I could still make out the bloodstain on the floorboards where Eyid had died. Someone had tried to clean it, but poorly; there were still flecks of dried blood in some of the cracks. I knelt without thinking, running my fingers over the stain.

"I'm so sorry," I whispered, to no one, to the emptiness, to a past that wasn't mine.

But maybe it would be my future. Would that be the end I would come to, one day? Stabbed in the heart by a friend, an ally... My gaze drifted against my will toward the door behind me, toward the stairs and the front room of the house where Iskari waited for me. Would Iskari betray me one day? If he did…if any of my friends did…would I be any more capable of stopping them than my father had been?

I shook my head and sat down hard on the floor, tugging off Zagger's coat in the comfortable warmth and leaving it folded beside me. I couldn't let thoughts like that distract me now. Right now I had only one task that I cared about—only one mission I needed to accomplish.

I needed to unlock one more power in my soul. I needed to learn how to Ghost.

# Chapter 6 ～ Tarik

I WASN'T SURE HOW LONG I SAT THERE ON THE FLOOR IN EYID'S OFFICE, NEXT TO the place where my father had died. I had my head on my drawn-up knees, but my thoughts were caught deep inside my own soul.

My mind kept turning over the truth Nika had once told me: *"One mage will stop at moving an object from one place to another by their thought, and another will stop with the power of reshaping an object, and neither of them will realize that the power to do the one is the same as the power to do the other."*

I was convinced her words held the secret I needed to understand the intertwining of magic—but for all I *knew* what I needed to do, I could not wrestle my power into obedience.

*I can move objects from one place to another,* I told myself. *What is the difference between that and moving myself?*

But I knew that when I used my Telekine gift, I was only moving objects within their normal environment. I could Pull a gun across the floor, or Push someone out of my way, but I couldn't Pull a weapon from Cavnal and have it appear before me here in Istia. The object never changed state, only location. But as far as I could tell, Ghosting had to involve moving out of physical existence in one location and back into existence somewhere else.

I wrapped my hands around my head, stifling a groan of frustration. The power was more like being a Rift, like Shiver, than anything else. But Shiver seemed to move through the material of the world, using it as his personal pathway, while Derrin seemed rather to move *in spite of* it. I'd never even heard anyone suggest the concept before, but it was almost like Derrin moved himself through the spiritual world instead of the material one when he Ghosted. If Shiver made his body part of the matter of the world, it was as if Derrin made his whole being into spirit. And just as thoughts could fly from one place to another without effort—just as my thoughts right now could be with Hayli in Brinmark as easily as they could be with Iskari downstairs—so too, Derrin could move to any place he already held in his mind with just the movement of his thoughts.

I couldn't help grinning a little at the realization. But even so, it didn't please me in the least, because I didn't have a Rift's powers any more than I had a Ghost's. I drew a breath and refocused my concentration. What was the power undergirding them both? Was it simply manipulation of matter, or was it manipulation of the fabric of reality itself?

Still feeling a bit weak and disoriented from my loss of blood, I lowered myself down to lay flat on the ground, with my head cushioned by Zagger's coat. My thoughts drifted of their own accord back to Brigun Palace. I held a memory of the time I'd gone home after Hayli had been captured, when I'd faced Trabin and he had asked for my allegiance, and I had lost control of the fire. My mother had used her Blood magic on me, then left me alone in that parlor—left me broken, worried sick about Zagger, terrified for Hayli. I remembered standing in front of the gilt mirror, where I had scried Hayli sitting in the Science Ministry's cell just before my reality fractured around me.

I'd *seen* her, as clearly as if I'd been looking at her through a window. And somehow I knew that, if I'd managed to keep my wits about me, I could have gone one step further. Instead of fracturing the glass, I could have stepped through it like an open window, and crossed straight from Brigun Palace into Hayli's cell. I knew without anyone telling me that that was, in fact, the essence of Ghosting.

So why couldn't I do it?

True, I didn't have a mirror here to look in, but I shouldn't need a mirror. Derrin never did—and I could imagine one in my mind perfectly well. I closed my eyes and wandered into that mental chamber where I'd called on Wake earlier, and placed a mirror in front of me, tall, set in a gilt frame, exactly like the one in Brigun Palace. And then I stood in front of it and focused my thoughts, and tried to *see* Hayli on the other side.

God knew that, if longing were all that mattered, I would be with her in the space between one heartbeat and the next, but for endless moments I stood and regarded myself in the polished steel. What I saw made me strangely sick. I looked like death, just like Nika had said. There were bruised rings under my eyes and my cheeks were hollow, with faded stains of blood on the too-pale skin around my mouth and nose. And my eyes... I couldn't recognize myself at all in those eyes.

*I'm imagining all of this,* I told myself. *This isn't a real mirror. I don't know what I actually look like right now. This is just the face of my fears.*

I closed my eyes and pressed my hands against the smooth glass, reaching deep into the sea within the pit of my soul where my magic pooled and rippled.

*Hayli...where are you?*

"You know that all my gifts would be yours if you asked for them," Wake said behind me, a little sadly.

I opened my eyes to look at him in the mirror, but the mirror was empty. Even my own reflection was gone. There was nothing in its surface but the endless night.

"No," I said.

"The more you push, the more you will fracture," he said. He reached past me and laid his fingertips against the glass, and I watched in dread as the spiderweb cracks rippled out beneath his touch. "You are killing yourself like this."

He pulled his hand back, and the glass shattered.

I shook my head and squeezed my eyes shut tighter, plunging my hands back into the dark pool of my magic. I could feel the threads there, all colors and shapes of energy, and my fingers drifted over each one, searching for understanding. But the threads kept slipping through my fingers, and I couldn't trace the pattern. Electricity crackled over my knuckles, sharp and stinging.

"It's there," I said. "I can feel it."

"Of course it is there," Wake said. "I placed it there. But take care lest you delve too deep."

"It's in my soul," I said, "so it's mine for the taking."

He said nothing; I could feel his disapproval like the weight of thunder, but I forced him out of my awareness. Wind whipped around me, and my feet faltered. I was no longer in my empty mental chamber, but standing on the edge of my sea, the frigid surf tugging the sand around my bare feet. My hands were in the water, grasping after the currents, fighting the moon for the tide. But the water was rising, and rising, and the current swept my feet out from under me. Then I was kneeling in the waves, the water drifting ever closer to my mouth as I scoured the depths.

"This sea is mine," I whispered. The water slipped over my bottom lip and I choked on the taste of salt, and the liquid wasn't cold, but warm and thick. "It's mine. Why can't I subdue it? Why can't I bend it to my will?"

"The sea is mine. *You* are the sea...and you are mine."

"No," I said again, coughing against the fluid in my throat. "I can find the truth."

"You hold on too tightly."

I pulled my head back from the water, and slammed my hand on the surface of the waves, shouting, "*Hayli!*"

But it did no good. Ripples cascaded out beneath my hand, shuddering all the way to the horizon. Inside I felt a deep and horrible humming vibration, as if my heart had struck a wrong chord and sent my blood into dissonance. I dragged myself back, trying to escape the water, but my feet were tangled in the currents, and the blood was flowing from every inch of my skin to mingle with the water of the sea.

Above me I saw Wake, looking down on me with pity, or maybe contempt.

"Why do you fight so hard?" he asked. "You don't have to do this on your own."

I couldn't answer; the sea was drowning me. But when Wake held a hand out toward me in invitation—or summons—I closed my eyes and plunged my hands down into the sand beneath me. The waves crashed over my head. Panic surged inside me, memories of the night sea swallowing me, the wreck, *Hastol* in ruins, Vaskar sinking to the deep. I cried out, or tried to, and fought for the surface.

"Damn it!" someone was shouting above me. "Damn it!"

And then I felt the hands on my shoulders, dragging me up from the waves. I cast out my arms, desperate to stay afloat, only to find myself sprawled on the floor in Eyid's office. I was soaking wet from the sea—no. My white shirt was stained red, wet and hot with fresh blood.

"God!" I screamed through my teeth. "It burns...oh God, it burns!"

I curled onto my side, clutching my arms against my chest. Fire sheared my heart to ribbons, scratching at the edges of my soul like bitter needles. I couldn't breathe.

Iskari was kneeling over me, his hands rigid on my shoulders. *"Skatrdrakkeyn akla drakk!"* He shook me violently, and I couldn't pull away. "You *ganthiskur...stodadrakkim!* What did you do this time? What have you done?"

I uncurled my fingers from their tight fists; they were bone white, but the backs were all streaked crimson from the blood that trickled from the bases of my fingernails. They trembled, and they felt numb, but not numb in the way of coldness. I simply couldn't feel anything.

When I didn't move, and didn't answer, Iskari staggered to his feet, his hands, wet from my blood, tugging through his knotted black hair in desperation. I watched him from the corner of my eye; I never would have believed it, but he looked like he was on the verge of tears.

"Don't move," he said suddenly. I wanted to inform him that moving was highly unlikely, but I couldn't make a sound. *"Veka, Veka...* just don't do *anything,* do you hear me? I'll be back..."

And with that he stumbled out of the room. I heard the deafening clatter of his feet pounding down the stairs, then the door slamming shut behind him. As silence fell over the room, I let my eyes drop closed.

*I AM STANDING IN FRONT OF a blond man—Eyid, I realize—here in this very room. He is still blood-stained, just as I am, but he is sitting on the edge of his desk with a small knife in his hands.*

*"I couldn't accept it either," he says. He hasn't looked up at me yet, but he seems to know I am there in the room with him. "The promise. The power."*

*All of a sudden I desperately want him to see me. What would he think of me, seeing me for the first time? Would I show him Shade's face, or Tarik's? Would he be proud of the son he has never met?*

*"I gave it all up instead," he finishes after a moment.*

*"They say you stopped the fracturing," I say softly. "You saved your sanity in the end."*

*"I did. Maybe I was a coward. Maybe I was weak, but I held out, and that was my prize—my sanity. For all the good it did me."*

*He looks at me then, and I flinch back, because his eyes are white, white*

 376

*like Zagger's, like death.*

*"Don't let him have you," he says. "You don't understand the cost. He will take everything from you. He will rob you of all that you are, and all that you have. He will drain you and leave you empty to serve his will, and all that you have and all that you love will be lost. You have no idea what you will lose. You have no idea what it means to lose so much."*

*"Father—" I say, but the room is empty again, all but a bloodstain on the floor that is wet once again.*

I SHOOK MYSELF OUT OF THE dream, pressing the heels of my palms against my eyes. For a moment, for an eternity I lay still like Iskari had asked me, but when the wind picked up, I shivered in the cold and forced myself onto my knees. And then, when I opened my eyes, I found I wasn't in Eyid's room any more. My heart cried out in futile protest, because once again I was standing on the shore of the sea. Wake wasn't there, but still, I was not alone.

There at the edge of the water stood a woman, wrapped in shadow, her skin like starlight. She was facing the darkness, the hem of her black gown trailing in the sea foam. Livid red light spilled from the tips of her fingers, and the wind never touched the crimson hair that coiled down her back like blood in water.

I drifted a step toward her before I realized I'd moved. My feet made no sound on the black sand, but she must have heard me, because suddenly she was facing me. A chill washed over me. That was no woman, or no mortal woman. She was young but ancient, and I couldn't tear my gaze from the strangeness of her eyes—they were gleaming black where they ought to have been white, and her irises were amber gold from edge to edge, without the normal dark of a pupil to interrupt the ring of color. If anything they seemed brighter at the center, as if they would shed light instead of drink it. There was no color in her face except the deep bruises beneath her eyes, and her lips...her lips were as black and void as the night.

She was the most beautiful and terrible thing I had ever seen.

"You have finally returned," she said, and her voice was sorrow and hatred and the loneliness of the stars.

I cast a glance around. The water was black and the sand was black, the moon overhead rimmed in red, and though it all felt somehow familiar, I knew with bone-deep certainty that I was not standing on the shore of my own sea.

"How can I return somewhere I've never been?" I asked.

She smiled, knowing a secret.

I was closer to her now than before, moving in the way of dreams, effortless, without thought, though through it all I felt impossibly awake. My legs carried me closer to her while everything inside me cringed away, powerless but longing to flee.

"Are you...are you the mad god?" I asked.

She only laughed as if I had said something clever, and shook her head. I stood directly in front of her now. She was tall for a woman— or whatever she was—and this close the amber glass of her eyes enthralled me.

"Are you the Zealot?" she asked. Her mouth tipped up, but showed no teeth behind her smile. "Or are you the Scion? Do you even know? Have they done with fighting over you yet?"

"What do you mean?"

"Stupid," she said, but the word had a fondness to it, and she lifted her hand to touch my cheek.

Livid light washed over me, staining my vision in crimson hues. Her touch burned like fire, like Wake's, but colder, and I shuddered and gasped and tried to back away. I could not. Her gaze lowered to my chest, and her hand followed, pressing against the skin over my heart.

"You push yourself too far," she said. "Stubborn. If I didn't know better, I'd almost believe you were trying to find me."

"Who are you?" I asked. My voice was weak and thready, burning in my throat.

"You were mine long before you were theirs," she murmured. "Either of theirs. They stole you from me." She paused, studying me through those empty, cold eyes, then she leaned in to me, her other hand slipping behind my neck, her lips close to my ear. "Don't you remember? You tried once to escape into my embrace but they prevented you. But you've never forgotten me, have you? Couldn't you hear me, through all the years, calling out to you?"

I stumbled out of her grip and turned my face away. "I don't know who you are," I whispered, hoarse. But it was a lie, because I knew her voice, woven in the sadness of the moon. I had heard it a thousand times or more. "Magic? Is magic your domain?"

"Magic is the fabric of reality," she said, with a brisk sharpness as if I'd annoyed her. "And it is Wake's province. He is the origin, the wellspring, and the end of all the roads. I…I stand only and always at the edge. At the crossing of the ways, the bounding wall. I stand here at the unraveling of things."

She drew her hand away from my chest and pointed toward the sea behind her, and in the bloody light I could see the waves pulling apart into a tangle of currents, formless and void. My gaze drifted down toward her feet, but they were hidden in shadow there at the edge of the sea, caught in a swirl of sea foam and night-dark sand. I drew a sharp breath.

"I know you." Fear and grief and darkness and longing tore at my heart, tore my mind to tatters like the black ribbons on a funeral pyre. My eyes found hers. I said, "Death."

She caught my face in her hands and pressed her fire-cold lips against mine. Everything inside me burned with ecstasy or devastation, pain or rapture. I was falling or coming up from drowning. I thought I was dying.

I pulled away from her and stumbled a step back. For an endless moment she stared at me, one hand hovering in the air between us, her face etched with anger or contempt.

"You are mine, still," she said. "You have no love for Wake, so would you serve me instead?"

My lungs felt close, caving in, empty. I fought for a breath, and managed to whisper, "I belong to no one."

Her hand lifted, fingers stretched, reaching toward me. Blood-red light streamed from the tips of her blood-red nails, but the rays of it did not touch me now. Her lip lifted in a bitter curl, and she dropped her hand to her side once more.

"A pity. You belong to him, and you can't even see it yet," she said. "He has you under his protection. But not forever. One day…one day he will give you back to me."

"I belong to no one," I said again, desperate.

Her smile grew crueler, but already she was fading into the crimson moon. "Then no one will save you," she said, and with one sweep of her hand, she cast me from her shore.

# Chapter 7 ~ Hayli

I DIDN'T SEE GRIFF OR ARODEN AGAIN UNTIL NAN SERVED DINNER IN THE mess, just after the winter-early night had fallen. Anuk and I were waiting along the inner wall for our sergeants to go through the food line, and the big crowded room was full of chattering folks and the clank of silverware somebody—Coins, I assumed—had nabbed from a high street hotel. Then, as if on cue, the noise in the hall quieted, and everybody's gaze turned the same way. I leaned around Anuk for a view of the front door just in time to see Griff walking in with Aroden on his heels.

He still *looked* like Aroden, to my relief—half of me had feared that everyone had got quiet because they'd seen Tarik walk in instead. Still, I got the sense that, even with Aroden looking like Aroden, word had somehow gotten around that he was the mage who had impersonated the Crown Prince, and suddenly, nobody knew quite what to do.

Griff ignored the sudden attention and made straight for the chow line, but Aroden faltered by the door. Then, just when I wondered if I was going to have to go over and rescue him, he held up his hands and came a few steps into the mess.

"I know you're afraid of me," he said, and his voice, soft though it was, seemed to command the whole room. "I'm sorry for that. I mean none of you any harm. Please, give me a chance to prove myself before you turn on me."

*Stars, he just wants somewhere he can belong,* whispered the voice in the back of my mind. *Like you did. How long was he trapped in that cell all alone? Remember…he thought that room was the whole universe when you first talked to him.*

"What do you want here?" someone asked from the far side of the room—a stout older man that I knew by sight, though not by name.

"Asylum," Aroden said, lifting his hands a little higher so the man could see them. "I just want somewhere safe to stay."

"It's what we're all looking for," my sergeant Maera said softly, turning to face the older man. "None of us had to prove *our* loyalty before Hayli and Shade made us welcome."

I barely caught the slight tightening of Aroden's mouth—it was there and gone in a flash, then he gave Maera a shy sort of smile and lowered his hands. Most everybody else had turned back to their meals, if not satisfied by Aroden's claim, at least indifferent to his presence. I let out the breath I'd been holding and slouched back against the wall.

"I don't like him."

I glanced up at Anuk in surprise. He was glaring across the room at Aroden, and even with his arms crossed he couldn't hide how tense his muscles were, as if he were barely holding himself back from a fight.

"Why not?" I asked. "You div'n like Shade at first either."

"Shade made sense," Anuk said, belligerent. "Even when I didn't like him, I could respect him. I could play him at his own game. Even when he was playing two sides, there was something honest about him. I don't feel that with *him*."

He jerked his chin toward Aroden, who was now trailing Griff through the food line, picking at the different food options like he didn't much know what they were. Somehow it reminded me of the first time I'd met Shade, out in the rain and the cold, when it seemed he had no clue how to survive on the streets. Like he was experiencing the world for the first time. But Aroden knew so much of the world, of Brinmark and Court politics, of Tarik's past. Had Kippler fed him all that information? How else would he know it, if he'd spent years locked up in the Science Ministry?

I sighed and pushed away from the wall, seeing the food line dwindling to nothing. "C'mon, let's get skappers," I said. "And if you dan' like Aroden, just avoid him. No one's telling you you have to be friends with him or aught."

Anuk touched my arm suddenly and nodded toward the door.

Aroden was making his way toward the one empty spot he'd been able to find, close by the front door where the draft was too chill for most folks to bear. But the door was open, and in the doorway, as though frozen to the spot, stood Rivano. My stomach clenched. I couldn't make sense of the look that passed between Rivano and Aroden in that one fraction of a moment. Aroden looked apt to panic and Ghost, and Rivano...Rivano was smiling.

"Oh, stars," I said under my breath. "What is that about, now?"

"Gives me the heebies when Rivano smiles like that," Anuk muttered. "Usually means he's got some scheme up his sleeve, so."

I swallowed my uneasiness and made my way to the food line, making a point to take the path that led directly between Rivano and Aroden. Rivano looked a bit startled when he saw me coming toward him, staring at him the whole way. I stopped in front of him.

"Were you getting in line?" I asked, waving toward the food.

His face softened and he shook his head. "Please, go ahead."

I drew myself up. "I'll wait till you're through."

"She won't eat till everyone else has gotten food," Anuk said, coming up behind me.

Rivano's brows lifted and he gave me a curious nod that felt almost like a bow, or a salute. "Of course," he said, and moved past me to get in line.

Anuk's hand squeezed my shoulder gently, and I gave him a smile that I knew didn't express half the gratitude I felt. Anuk had no love for Aroden, but if he saw me protecting Aroden from Rivano, he'd never let me stand alone. I wasn't sure what I'd ever done to deserve a friend like that. I pushed him ahead of me and followed him through the food line, scraping up the last shreds of canned beans in gravy and winter tubers. There was naught left of whatever meat Nan had scrounged up, which meant there would be no seconds for anyone either. I frowned and made a mental note to talk to Bridnow about adjusting how much food we needed for each meal.

I was scanning the rows of tables and crowded benches for a place to sit when Maera waved me over. "Lieutenant," she called. "I'm just finished. Please, sit."

Smiling my thanks, I beckoned Anuk to follow me, and we both crowded onto the bench in the little space she gave us. Anuk didn't even grumble at the lack of elbow room, and when I apologized for crowding him, he just laughed and put his arm around me, then tried to use both hands for his food with me squashed against his side. I was laughing too hard to do my dignity any favors, as I tried, and failed, to wriggle out of his grip.

"Lemme gan!" I hissed, punching him in the stomach.

Anuk cheerfully shoved more food in his mouth, saying to no one in particular, "Hm, thought I heard a mouse."

"Anuk! This ain't...*becoming*...for officers of the Patchwork Army!" I protested, but my voice lost all its power in the wool of his jumper.

He released me then, still chuckling to himself, and I shoved him once for good measure. Then, eyeing the table, I cried, "Hey! Where'd all my food gan?"

"What, was that your food?" he asked, eyes wide with horror.

I opened my mouth for a lament but he just grinned and, with a dramatic flourish, retrieved my plate from where he'd hidden it on the other side of him.

"You oaf," I laughed.

"Hey! I'll have you kindly remember that I'm a *great big* oaf."

"That's for sure."

I shoveled food into my mouth, keeping half an eye on Aroden, who was finishing his own meal down the long table from me. He was by himself—I wondered where Griff had got to, since he seemed to have abandoned Aroden as soon as they came into the mess. The kids sitting across from Aroden seemed to be making too big an effort to ignore him, with their heads bent together as they chattered in hushed whispers. At least Aroden didn't seem too sore at being ignored. He just ate slowly and quietly, and finally cleared his place like all the rest of the folks and shouldered his way outside without so much as a glance at anyone.

I shoveled in my last spoonful of beans and climbed off the bench.

"You on watch tonight?" Anuk asked around a mouthful of potatoes.

"First watch," I said. "Gotta scram."

He nodded and let me go, even though we both knew there was still a solid hour between the end of dinner and the start of the first night watch. I was glad he didn't question me. I wanted to keep an eye on Aroden, make sure he didn't do aught wrong or rash, but doing that meant I had to know where he was.

383

Soon as I'd cleared away my plate, I hurried out of the mess and into the crisp night. It was clear, for once, with a scattering of brilliant bright stars over the ink-dark sky, and my breath hung in a ghostly cloud around my mouth in the still air. I stopped outside the mess to pull on my gloves, and startled like a spooked cat when Aroden stepped out of the shadows beside me.

"*Stars*," I said, "dan' do that to me."

"I'm...sorry?" he said, looking perplexed. He shifted his weight and said, "I was hoping you would come out."

I gave him a sidelong glower and finished tugging on my glove. "Dan' try to be charming with me, Aroden. I got a job to do."

I struck out toward the main gate, my mind swirling with uncertainty. Even though it wasn't near time for me to go on watch yet, the only other place I had to go was the Rookery, and Aroden had no place there. I'd already decided that the easiest way to keep an eye on him was to keep him with me, but that meant finding someplace to go where we both belonged.

He followed me quietly all the way to the gate, hanging back in the shadows as I stepped out to address the guards.

"Did you lot get dinner yet?" I asked.

They shook their heads, and I pursed my lips in annoyance.

"Then gan on and see what they've still got left over," I said. "But I'm afraid it won't be much. I'll take the watch from here."

"Are you sure, Lieutenant?" one of them asked.

"Sure," I said. "Gotta show our newest guard the ropes, anyway. Figured I'll keep him busy with that until Jostim comes on."

They left with an endless stream of thanks and salutes, and soon it was just me standing outside the gate. Aroden finally left the shadows to join me near the coal brazier.

"I wish you would trust me," he said. "What could I tell you that would make you believe me?"

"You can't *make* someone believe you, or trust you," I said, then hesitated and added under my breath, "Unless you're Kippler."

His jaw tightened and he turned a little away. At first I thought he was turning away from me, then I realized it was the sight of the dormitory behind me that he was avoiding.

"I don't want to hurt anyone," he said, after a long, thin silence. "I never did. I'm a healer, Hayli. I don't hurt people. You of all people should understand that. But I can help you."

"You're a Blood?" I asked, startled, and wondered, *Stars, how many Gifts does he have? If I hadn't seen them both standing on the same dais at the same time with my own eyes, I really might believe he's Tarik.*

Aroden jumped, wiping his hand on his trousers, then holding it toward the fire to look at it in the light. "Just a little blood?" he said, perplexed.

For half a tick I didn't understand, then I waved a hand in annoyance and said, "No, I mean *you*. You're a Blood."

Aroden regarded me keenly, the firelight turning his green eyes an almost tawny shade of gold. "Oh. Call it that if you must," he said. "But aren't you?"

"Aren't I what?" I asked, stupidly.

"A…Blood. A healer."

"Nah," I said. "Sorry, mate. I'm a Moth, shape-shifter."

He frowned and drew his shoulders up against the cold. "You don't know, then. You've never even tried." When I just looked at him he took a step closer to me—almost too close—his hands drifting between us like he'd meant to lay them on my shoulders, but thought better of it. "You have corporal magic. You can turn into a crow. Don't you see? Don't you understand? Your magic weaves through the fabric of the body. What do you think being a healer is except using that same magic to mend the ways the body is broken?"

"You're saying I could be a Blood," I said flatly, "if, what, I just think about it hard enough?"

The smile that lit up his face was like the sun after a thunderstorm. "That's exactly what I'm saying."

"You're cracked," I said.

I hugged my arms around myself, trying not to think about what he was suggesting. It didn't make sense. I was a Moth. My magic bound me to Piper. I couldn't do what Aroden thought I could. If I tried, I knew I would fail, and then Aroden would only think I was weak, and nowhere near as powerful as him.

*Maybe he's only powerful because he set aside doubt and embraced his magic,* the voice in the back of my head whispered.

"You should try it," Aroden said. "Just for fun. Just to see."

"Maybes," I said, and refused to look at him.

If Aroden was a Blood, I felt I ought to take him to Doc, and let Doc have a look at him. Would Doc reconsider his fear and anger if he knew Aroden was a healer like him? Would he maybe give him a chance? At the very least, Aroden could help him out in the infirmary, where Doc always seemed stretched too thin.

"How many powers have you got?" I asked quietly.

I was watching his hands, feeling slightly queasy, because his fingers were dancing through the low flames in the brazier like he didn't even realize what he was doing. The flames licked at his palms and teased the hem of his coat sleeve, but the fabric never caught fire, and his skin never burned.

"I don't know," he said. "I was a Mask first. That was the first one I ever used, on the train, coming back from Ridgemark."

My breath hissed out. "That's Tarik's memory."

"No," he said, pulling his hand away from the fire to press it against his forehead. "It's mine. I *told* you. How many times do I have to tell you? The person you think is Tarik…he's impersonating *me*. I've been trapped…so long. Ever since the bell tower, when he walked in from the night. He *robbed* me. Stole everything that I am. Made me a stranger in my own city." He dropped to a crouch, hands clasped around his head. "Do you know…do you know what it was like? He used to come to the Science Ministry. Sit across from me. Me, my own face, sitting across the table from me. And he would… Oh God, it hurt. It hurt. Drag his claws through my memories. Dredge the depths, just so he could learn what it meant to be me. That's all truth, Hayli! That's the truth, the truth. I don't remember…these last few years. I don't remember any of them, except what I gleaned from him, as he walked through the life *I* should have been living!"

"You were reading him?" I asked. My voice was a bare whisper, hoarse and shaking. "I thought you said he was reading you."

"He said once that it was like reading a book, but it's more like a window. The moment he touched my mind, I had a link to his. Do you know what a torture that has been? Trying to stay…trying to stay sane. Losing it…little by little. Nothing but grey. Grey, always, grey all around me…"

*Grey stone grey walls grey floor*

I didn't realize I'd said those words out loud until Aroden wrapped his arms around me and pulled me close. I was shaking all over, fighting with every scrap of my will to banish the fear, the emptiness, the hollow pain. I wanted to pull away but I was trapped by the scent of wood smoke and cinnamon, and when he released me, it was Tarik standing there beside me, with Tarik's face, Tarik's hands on my arms, Tarik's eyes lingering on my face like a caress.

"Stop it!" I shouted, shoving him away. "Just *stop*."

He pressed the back of his hand against his mouth, staring at me like a betrayal.

"Go," I said. "Please, just gan inside."

"You can't watch alone—"

"I bloody well can!" I cried, and jabbed my finger toward the dormitory, but my voice had skitted clean out on me, and I couldn't say another word.

He bowed his head and brought his features back to Aroden's, then, avoiding my gaze, he slipped through the gate and disappeared into the shadows. I bit back tears as I hugged myself against the cold, wishing with every breath that I could Shift and fly away to some place where the world made sense again. Part of me wished Shiver would step out of the wall behind me, or Coins would drop down from a precarious perch on top of it. But neither of them came, and the minutes dragged by in endless, solitary silence.

I pulled out my knife as I walked, and turned it over in my hand, letting the low ember light from the brazier catch on the blade. Then, before I had a chance to doubt myself, I drew the tip over my palm in a quick flick, hissing in pain as the blood welled up from the shallow cut. I closed my eyes and tried to *feel* the cut with my magic, but I couldn't feel aught at all except the wound stinging as the cold air nipped its edges.

*What am I even doing? This is completely bodgy. I'm not a Blood.*

*Why do you doubt yourself?* the voice in the back of my mind answered. *Tarik knew it was true. He could see the connections in the magic. Seeing magic as Gifts just stifles your own power.*

I curled my hand into a loose fist and tried again, but still, naught at all happened.

*What am I doing wrong?* I asked Piper.

*You're thinking about it too hard,* she answered.

*You believe Aroden, then?* I asked. *You think I could be a Blood?*

*I think you don't understand half of what there is to know about your magic,* she said, sounding smug.

I was about to ask her to explain herself when I heard a scuff of footsteps in the snow behind me, and I turned to see Scorch, of all people, standing at the threshold of the gate.

"You're all alone?" he asked.

I shuddered, and wanted to deny it in hopes that he would go away... but why? For all he was terrifying and arrogant and deadly, Scorch had never done aught to me. When I nodded he came out to join me.

"Who's your watch partner?"

"I relieved the guards who were here, since they'd not had skappers yet," I said. "I was with..." I waved my hand, then gave up hiding the truth and said, "I had Aroden with me. But I sent him back inside. Just waiting on Jostim to come out, now."

"Aroden smells like trouble," Scorch said.

*And you don't?* I wanted to ask, but kept my peace.

"Well? You must have had a good reason to send him away."

I ground my teeth, then turned to face him. "Look, he claims that he's Tarik. The *real* Tarik. Says the Tarik we know is an impostor, impersonating him. He's got all Tarik's memories...and the things he's said... What if it's true?"

"You're not seriously thinking about believing a single word he says, are you?"

"I dan' na," I sighed. "Shouldn't we at least be willing to see it as a possibility?"

"I respect you, Hayli," he said, "but that is the damn stupidest thing I have ever heard you say."

I winced and turned away, but didn't take back the words. Scorch reached out suddenly and took my hand, holding it palm up between us. I curled my fingers closed, but his eyes, ember bright in the firelight, were on my face, not my hand, and I couldn't meet his gaze.

"What happened?"

I shrugged. "Just cut myself."

His lips tightened in a thin line, but he just put his hand on my shoulder, more gently than I expected. "You're exhausted. You push yourself too hard. Find Jostim and send him out early, and I'll stand watch with him for you."

I shook my head, baffled, because I'd never known Scorch to do a kind thing for anybody but himself in all the time I'd known him. "Why would you do that?"

"Stars," he said, the firelight snagging on his pallid scar as he tried a small smile. "We're comrades, aren't we?"

At least he hadn't tried to suggest we were friends. Comrades I could accept.

"Thank you," I said softly. "Think I'll try to track down Doc before I turn in. Aroden says he's a Blood too, so I wanted to get Doc's thoughts on having him help in the infirmary."

I turned to go, but Scorch stopped me halfway through the gate. "Don't bother trying to find Doc," he said. "He's gone."

"What do you mean, gone?"

"I mean, gone. Derrin went to see him about his wound, and he was nowhere to be found. Coat, gone. Bag, gone. Everything. He's *gone*."

"Doc..." I faltered, trying desperately to make sense of his words. "Doc wouldn't do that. He cares about us. He takes care of us!"

"And yet the fact remains," he said.

"D'you...d'you got a ken where he went?"

"No one does. Rivano was smoking angry when he found out. And why wouldn't he be? Doc was the only healer we had."

I nodded and turned away, chewing on my lip as I went.

*Maybe Aroden can be useful after all*, I thought. I scowled down at my hand, then watched in baffled silence as the edges of the wound knitted slowly together. A smile tugged the corners of my mouth. *And maybe... maybe we have two Bloods now, not none.*

Then, suddenly nervous, I clamped my hand in a fist and shoved that thought aside, and hurried toward the dormitory to find Jostim.

# Chapter 8 ∽ Hayli

I'D BARELY WALKED INTO THE DORMITORY WHEN A SHORT, WIRY MAN STRODE up to me, fists planted on his hips and thin chest puffed out, wearing naught but his white sleeveless undershirt tucked into a pair of long flannel undertrousers.

"Evening, Lieutenant," he said, giving me a smart nod, as if he were dressed in the full ceremonial uniform of a King's Army officer. "I'm looking forward to the opportunity to serve with you on watch tonight."

"Jostim," I said. "Can I ask a favor of you?"

He cocked his head to one side, sharply, and took two small steps away from me, then back. "Of course, Lieutenant," he said. "Anything you ask."

It was all I could do not to laugh, as every move Jostim made got me thinking about the lads, and how they'd called him *Roo*, and mimicked his habit of strutting about like a banty rooster.

"You're actually ganna be on post with Scorch tonight. Think you could make it over there a few ticks early?"

"Not you?" he asked, thrusting his chin out. I clamped my mouth shut hard to wrestle down the grin.

"It was s'posed to be me," I said. "Dan' feel so well. Scorch took my slot."

He reached out and clasped my arm. "Feel better, ma'am. Of course I don't mind. Scorch, is he out there already? I can go any time. I'll go out there right now. You get some rest, ma'am, and don't worry about a thing. Scorch and I will watch that gate like nobody's ever watched a gate before."

He disappeared into his room, an office that he and a few other folks had made into a bunk room, and returned a moment later, dressed, tugging on his coat. Soon as he had his wool cap snug on his head, he gave me a smart nod, strutted past me, and headed out into the cold night.

I watched him go. Every instinct I had drove me to follow him out the door and head back to my own room in the Rookery, but now that I was standing in the dormitory, I felt a draw strong as magnetism rooting me where I was. No, not rooting me, but pulling me, dragging me toward the room on the second floor, *that* room.

I wanted to walk away. Stars, I wanted to escape more than anything. But almost without realizing it, I turned my steps toward the staircase. My fingers drifted over the splintered bannister as I climbed the steps. A smell of oil and lard soap stung my nose, and I was shaking so bad I nearly vomited. Step by step I climbed until at last I was standing in front of the roped off room. My heart was a flutter of bird's wings in my chest.

"Wake," I whispered. "I dan' wanna be here."

*You need to know the truth. You need to face it.*

Swallowing hard, I laid my hand on the latch and pushed it down, letting the door swing open on silent hinges. The cell was completely dark, without even a glint of moonlight to banish the shadows. I crouched to slip between the two ropes one of the lads had strung up over the door, and stepped into the room.

Empty...it was all empty, just like I'd feared.

*Breathe.*

A noise of laughter echoed from somewhere down the hall, and I jumped and spun to face the doorway, fear pounding in every vein. A light was bobbing closer down the hall and I wanted to scream and I wanted to run away because Miss Farrady...Miss Farrady was coming with that oil and that lamp to light me on fire and watch me burn burn burn

"Hayli?"

A strangled whimper escaped my lips, and I backed up and up until I hit the wall behind me. Then I was on my knees, and my arms were pressed to my ears but I couldn't drown out the noise the sound the fear the emptiness

"It's me, Hayli," the voice said, a stranger's voice, not Miss Farrady, not Andon, not Kippler, not Shade.

Aroden.

He was kneeling beside me, a candle on the cell floor beside him, throwing his face in light and shadow, casting monsters on the bare and empty walls.

"It's all right," he said, gently. "Look at me. Look at me."

I couldn't. Couldn't look away from the door, where my nightmares entered in. His hands were on my face, turning my head toward him. Finally I blinked, forced myself to look at him. He was all Aroden, golden hair and moss-green eyes, but somehow I couldn't look at him without seeing Tarik's face, and how he'd tried to comfort me, and how I'd driven him away. And the odd feeling in the pit of my stomach—I couldn't tell if it was from anger, or something else, something I didn't even want to name.

"Why did you come in here?" he said, his voice soft and soothing. "Why would you do that to yourself?"

"I had to know," I said. "I had to see if...if it was real."

"If what was real?"

I planted my hand on the wall beside my head, running my fingers over the stone. "It's a lie. It's all a lie. Dan' you remember when I wrote those words on the wall? You were here. You were *here*, with me, weren't you? I thought I dreamed you there, but you were really there."

"I was really there," he said. He brought his hand up beside mine, laying his cheek against the cold wall. "And I remember. You wrote it all down."

"Then where is it?" I slammed my hand against the wall, voice pitching up, louder, shouting, "Where?"

His hand darted out, pressing lightly against my mouth. "Don't alarm the others," he said. I shoved his hand away and bent my head, but stayed quiet. "Did you think that perhaps Kippler and Farrady painted over the walls before they abandoned this place? To leave no trace of what they'd done here?"

I made a noise of disbelief. It couldn't be that simple. It couldn't make that much sense. But Aroden was smiling through a look of pity and understanding and encouragement all wrapped up in one, and I closed my eyes against the threatening tears and leaned my head against the wall.

"It was the only thing I had," I whispered. "Writing it down. That was the only way I knew they were lying."

"The only way to save your sanity," he said, resting his head against the wall too, so we were sitting there face to face, our heads mere inches apart. It felt dangerous, being that close to him, but I didn't have the energy to move. He was looking down, though, not at me but at his hands drifting over the pocked stone. "I understand," he said. "When the world is breaking apart around you, you write it all down, and you can begin to see the pattern, see the shape of the mosaic come clear. The words show you the meaning and the truth, when you think it has slipped beyond your reach."

"Sounds like the fracturing," I said.

"What fracturing?" he asked, frowning.

"With Tarik..." I hesitated, flicking an uncertain glance at him, but he made no reaction to the name as I'd feared. I swallowed and tried again. "That's what they said Tarik was going through. A fracturing, because of his magic. Div'n you...div'n you ever have aught like that happen?"

He tipped his head back to look at the ceiling, eyes darting back and forth over nothing at all. "Only here," he said. "Only under the meddling of Vrey and Kippler. God...they pried and they pried...don't you remember? The lies, the promises, twisting everything sideways... You know. You understand. But they...they hurt me, too, as if the pain could put me back together. *Who are you, who are you, what do you know... tell us the truth of you and all the pain will stop...*" His shoulders convulsed and he pressed his hands against his head, digging his fingers into his scalp. "And when...when it didn't work, they...there was something, they put it in my food...did they do that to you?"

"I dan' na," I faltered, whispering. "Sometimes I was sure they drugged my food, but I never knew..."

"They did...but it didn't work either. They needed a weapon and they made a coffin instead, a shell for hiding a dead thing. I'm dead... I'm dead...I don't know what I am." His fingers clutched at his hair and he moaned softly, drawing his knees up to his chest. I stretched a hand toward him, uncertain, but he batted it away, hissing, "Don't...don't touch me. I'm a whisper, I'll break like winter. Hands full of needles... eyes corrupted with lies... *What do you see when you look at me? Empty empty hollow...*"

He jerked back suddenly, pressing the heels of his palms against his eyes, shaking his head back and forth, back and forth. Watching him in anxious terror, I couldn't help wondering if this was what my own friends felt when they saw me trapped by the nightmares—helpless, powerless, pitying but never quite understanding. Aroden's shoulders shook with sobs, and without thinking I reached out and gripped them fiercely, then pulled him toward me. This time he didn't pull away.

*Stars, what am I doing?* I wondered. *I don't trust him. I don't. I don't believe a word he says.*

*Why not? Look at him. Does that look like a man who wants to deceive you?*

He leaned into me, hands still covering his face, but at least his shuddering had quieted. Then, seconds or minutes later, he scrubbed a hand over his face and pushed away from me. He wouldn't look at me at all.

"I'm sorry," he said.

"For what?" I asked. "You got naught to be sorry for. *I'm* sorry, for what you've been through."

"What we've been through," he corrected, gently, then gave a strained laugh and said, "Maybe I should write it down."

"You never did?"

"I tried…it was nonsense. It just smoked away like embers and left me empty."

I sighed and shifted around so I was leaning my back against the wall. "D'you suppose it would help if you tried again?" I hesitated. "If you *were* suffering from a fracturing, from your magic, d'you s'pose writing would help…help save your sanity?"

"You're thinking of *him*, aren't you?" Aroden asked, his voice bleak and tired.

"Yes," I said, and didn't even shrink from saying it.

"I don't know. It wouldn't hurt, I don't think. Maybe…maybe if it can't heal his mind, it could at least help him remember who he really is. He wouldn't be the first."

I tipped my head to look at him. "Someone else did it?"

"Arnthor," he said. I gaped at him, but he seemed more puzzled than me. He frowned, kneading his forehead with his fingers, then shook his head back and forth against the wall. "Why did I even think of that? I don't…I don't know what made me think of it."

"He wrote something down?" I asked.

"His story," Aroden said. "How could he do that? After all he did, after all he destroyed, and he just wrote it down and walked away, as if none of it had ever happened. How? It isn't right. He should have suffered. He should have..."

He growled low in his throat, and his fingers flexed, making the candlelight flare upward in a sharp burst.

I reached out and gripped his hand. "Stop," I said. "It's in the past. It dan' matter any more."

"But don't you see? It's all bound together. No beginning and no end, just the same battle, over and over again."

"Hayli?"

I jumped, almost knocking over the candle, while all the blood rushed clear to the soles of my feet, because Anuk was standing there in the doorway of my cell, behind the crisscrossed ropes, holding a torch in one hand with the beam trained on the ground. My stomach roiled and I felt my cheeks flush hot, and I didn't even know why.

"What are you doing here?" Anuk asked. He flicked the torch beam at Aroden's face, making him duck his head aside to shield his eyes. "What's going on?"

I shoved myself to my feet and pushed my way out of the room, tearing down the ropes as I went so I wouldn't have to climb between them. Without a word to Anuk I stalked past him and down the hall, back toward the stairs, back toward the night and the clean cold air.

Too late I realized Anuk was close on my heels, but I ignored him until I'd left the dormitory and escaped out into the moonlight.

"Hayli, stop!" Anuk shouted after me. He barreled down the steps behind me and grabbed my arm, strong enough that I stumbled to a stop and couldn't do aught but turn and face him. "What the hell was that?" he growled, pointing back toward the building.

"What, that I was in that room, or that I was talking to Aroden?"

"Take your pick," he said. I flinched away from the blazing anger in his eyes, suddenly unsure of myself. "You gave Scorch your watch and told Roo it was because you weren't feeling well, but were you in your room? No. I've been searching this whole bloody complex for you. I even climbed up the damn *trees* looking for the crow. And you were there the whole time, talking to *him*?"

"I div'n gan up there to talk to him, if that's what you're suggesting,"

I snapped. "He found me there same as you did."

"That's not what it looked like to me."

I clenched my hands in fists, glaring up at him, but I couldn't bear the look in his eyes. It almost looked like...betrayal. With a hiss of exasperation I threw my hands in the air and turned away from him. I should've known I wouldn't get clear of him that easily, though. He overtook me in two strides and planted a hand on my shoulder.

"Why're you so angry?" I asked, swiping his hand away. "Because I was talking to Aroden, or because I wasn't talking to you?"

He just gave me a baffled look, hurt and disbelieving. "I'd always hope that you would talk to me if you need to, but that's not... I don't even know how to explain this to you, since you don't seem to be comprehending of it on your own. Don't you know what that looked like?" I didn't say a word, and he rubbed a hand over his face. "*Stars.* Aroden...don't you see that there's some kind of history between him and Shade? I don't pretend to understand it, but even if all I knew was Avnaya Square, I'd say those two were as close to enemies as I've ever seen two people be. And you're... Hayli, you can't flirt with the enemy of the man you love."

"What?" I gasped, staggered. "*Flirt*, with Aroden? Me? How...*dare* you!"

His jaw spasmed, and he jabbed a finger at my chest. "Take care, because I'm finding it very hard to believe you don't think that's what you were doing." He grabbed my hand, eyes soft and pleading, and cooed, "*Oh, Aroden, stop!*"

"Shut up!" I said, snatching my hand away. "That's not what I was doing. That's not what any of this is about!"

I realized too late that there were tears scorching my cheeks. My heart ached with a numb, sick pang, like it was quietly being strangled, and I couldn't make my lungs remember how to breathe.

"Anuk," I sobbed, and pressed a hand against my mouth. "Dan' you know how I miss Tarik? Have you got any grobbing clue? Every single day. I worry...and I pray and I...I miss him. How could you ever think I'd turn on him? How *could* you?"

His face softened, and he wrapped his arms around me and pulled me close. "All right, girl. It's all right. I'm sorry. We all miss him, and none of us..." He leaned his cheek against my head. "None of us want harm to come to him. From the world outside, or from within his own walls. Just take care. There's something…something I don't understand about Aroden. And I don't like things I don't understand, so."

"Me either," I said.

He released me and held me at arm's length, and heaved a great long sigh. "Stars, you really do look tired. Go to bed. *Actually* go to bed this time."

"I will," I muttered. "None of this would've happened if I'd not gone to find Jostim." I giggled suddenly, before I could stop myself. "You should've *seen* him."

Anuk gave me a lopsided grin and puffed his chest out, scraping at the snow with one boot. "*Bawk,*" he said.

# Chapter 9 ~ Tarik

CAST FROM DEATH'S SHORE, I HURTLED ENDLESSLY THROUGH NOTHINGNESS, then slammed, hard, back onto the floor in Eyid's office, landing in a heap on my stomach. Gasping, coughing, I tried desperately to gain my feet. Everything inside me felt like ice, or fire—it burned all the same, numb and prickling, tattered with fear and loss. Even the air felt charged, rich with an energy that clung to my skin like a humming electrical film. A constant noise roared in my ears, deafening me until I realized it was just the sound of my own pulse.

I gave up trying to stand and forced myself to lay still, to breath slowly and deeply, and gradually the sound receded to the corners of my consciousness. In the quiet that followed, I heard a stomp of footsteps outside the room, and a murmur of voices slowly getting louder. Three voices—two I recognized, one I did not. Iskari and Nika, and someone else.

"I don't care if you believe what he claims or not," Iskari was saying. "Something is happening to him, and it's nothing that can just be explained away as..."

"Madness," Nika murmured.

"I'm not judging his claims," the unknown voice said.

The footsteps came up alongside me, and I slit my eyes open just enough to see three pairs of boots close by my face.

"*Veka,*" the stranger breathed. "You told me...but I never even imagined..."

"Iskari..." Nika's voice hitched with panic. "Taumir? What—"

"I don't know. *Veka*, I don't know," Iskari said. He sounded just as frightened as his sister. "He wasn't like that when I left him, I swear it."

Nika crouched beside me, one hand hovering uncertainly in the air near my shoulder. "I don't understand."

"I can hear you, you know," I muttered.

Her hand snatched back, then flashed out and gripped my shoulder. But as soon as her fingers touched me she gave a little cry of pain and scrambled back.

"What *was* that?" she gasped.

The stranger was hanging back, I noticed, his weight shifting uneasily from one foot to the other. "Are you a mage, Agnirsdatr?" he asked, very quietly.

"No!" she said. "No, I'm not."

The silence dragged out, and still the man stood withdrawn. Finally he shook his head and said, "I'm sorry. I can't help him."

"You have to," Iskari growled. "You're the only mage I could find with healing powers. Get over here and do what you can for him."

"You don't understand," the man said, pleading. "Nika felt it when she touched him, and she's not even a mage. I can't...I can't get near him. It's too much."

"What's too much?" Iskari asked.

I took a shallow breath and pushed myself up onto my hands and knees, groaning with a pain that seemed to come from somewhere much deeper than the innermost recesses of my body. The stranger hissed faintly and backed toward the door.

"He'll be fine on his own, I'm sure of it."

"Halvir, please," Iskari said.

"You don't understand," Halvir said again, and threw a hand toward me. "I can't...I can't *heal* that. There is nothing there to heal."

I lifted my head and looked at him, but I never got a good view of him. As soon as our eyes met, the man cried out and threw his hands over his face, and stumbled blindly out into the corridor beyond.

"What's wrong with him?" I asked.

Iskari was staring at me, speechless. I finally turned to him and gestured for him to say something.

"I don't know what it is," he managed. He shifted, twisting his hands in the folds of his wool jumper, though I doubted he realized he was doing it. Everything about him radiated fear. "Something's wrong.

I can't say what. It's just...your eyes. There's something wrong with your eyes."

I grimaced, wishing for a mirror, and covered my face with my hands.

As I closed my eyes those twin amber lamps flashed into my thoughts again, only this time I saw them for what they were—the eyes of Death.

*I'm not hers,* I told myself. *She has no claims on me.*

*Death,* a voice whispered in the back of my thoughts. *You've always longed for Death.*

*Shut up. It isn't true. It isn't. I...I don't want to die.*

I took three deep breaths and lowered my hands. And that was when I saw the strands of unruly hair hanging in front of my face. I blinked, and reached up to run my fingers over my head. That was definitely Tarik's head, Tarik's hair, not Shade's. Had I let my Mask slip, then? But...

But the hair hanging in my eyes was bone white, and the hands I held up were much too pale—pale as Shade's skin, not the warm copper of Tarik's.

"What the hell," I whispered.

"I know," Iskari said, and dropped into a crouch in front of me. "What happened to you? Is that...is that your real face?"

I ignored him. It was all I could do to wrestle down the panic rising in my chest.

"You've lost more blood," Nika said. "What... Iskari, what was he doing up here?"

"He was supposed to be *thinking,*" Iskari growled. Then, to me, "What were you doing?"

I pushed myself into a sitting position. "It's strange how every time I find myself like this," I said, "you're with me."

The look of betrayal in his eyes was so deep it cut my heart. "Taumir," he said. "Are you accusing me of something? I'm not...I'm not a mage. This reeks of magic however you look at it." He grabbed me by both shoulders, failing to hide a slight grimace of pain as he did. "I would never raise a hand against you," he said, and he said it with such a force that I took it for what it was—a proclamation under oath, a solemn vow.

I bent my head. My chest felt hollow and empty, and for a few

 400

breathless moments I sat perfectly still, desperately trying to feel my own heartbeat. When I caught its faint, fluttering pulse, I let out a shallow sigh and clasped Iskari's forearm.

"I'm sorry. I know. It was...it was fear talking. I just want this to be something I can..." I faltered, struggling not for words, but for the humility to say them. "I want it to be something I can explain. Something I can understand. I can understand betrayal. I can't...I can't understand this."

I gestured at the pool of blood with my too pale hand. Iskari's hands tightened on my shoulders briefly, then released me, but he said nothing.

"Eyid..." I started.

"Was stabbed," Nika said, guessing the line of my thoughts. "The wound was obvious, and there wasn't nearly..." Her voice faltered, and she swallowed as her gaze drifted to the floor beneath me. "There wasn't nearly that much blood. He didn't die like...like Trabin did."

I jerked my head up. "You thought of that too."

"When we found you earlier, I just kept thinking of that story in the Post," she said, "about Trabin's death. How they never found any wounds on him, but somehow he had bled out."

"There's someone else you're forgetting about," Iskari said, very quietly.

We both turned to look at him.

"He was executed, but a single stab wound doesn't explain complete exsanguination. Archmage Arnthor died like Trabin did."

I jolted, and my mind instinctively flashed back to the painting called *The End of the Scourge*, which hung in the library in Brigun Palace. I'd always thought it a macabre piece for a library, showing Arnthor, pale and broken, his body striped with wounds and pierced with a sword. The pool of red blood spreading beneath him. The blood that the Cromners had collected and used for a century to anoint the breasts of their royal infants.

My body shuddered, and Iskari's hands were immediately on my shoulders again, as if he expected a repeat of whatever had happened to me earlier. I feared it myself, but I waved him away and staggered to my feet, and found myself face to face with a poor-quality mirror hanging on Eyid's wall.

I stared, and my reflection stared back at me.

I was Tarik...but pale as Shade in every way, like some strange melding of the two faces into something new. My hair was as pale as Shade's but longish and unkempt like Tarik's, and my skin was as fair as Shade's but the lines of my face were all Tarik's—Tarik's nose, Tarik's somber mouth, Tarik's dark eyes—and there was no sign of Shade's white mask tattoo. I stumbled a step closer, pressing my fingertips against the glass. Then I closed my eyes and tried to change, tried to consciously unMask to Tarik, but when I opened my eyes, nothing had happened. The same haunting face, the same haunted face, watched me in sullen silence.

"No," I whispered. "I don't...I don't understand."

Desperately I bowed my head and tried to bring my features back to Shade's. When I looked at the dingy mirror again, relief flooded through me, because at least the face staring back at me now was Shade's, ordinary as ever. I rather didn't care for the hostile way he was watching me, but I was just glad to see something familiar...not warped and twisted like that other face.

I heard Nika let out her breath behind me, and turned to face them. "I don't understand this," I said, pointing at the mirror.

"Well, whatever happened, you fixed it—"

"No," I said, and pointed more emphatically. "The mirror. There is nothing hanging on any other wall in this building. So why the mirror? Why here?"

Iskari shifted his weight and exchanged a long, somber look with Nika.

"Taumir," he said then, very quietly. "There is no mirror."

I put my hand to my forehead and stumbled past him, out into the corridor and away from the ghosts. I didn't want to believe him, because I'd touched the mirror with my own hands, seen into it with my own eyes...but why would Iskari lie to me, now, when I was already so broken? For all his faults, Iskari wasn't that cruel.

And I couldn't trust anything that came from me.

# Chapter 10 ～ Tarik

Nika caught up to me as I stumbled down the front steps of Eyid's house. She didn't just fall into step with me, though—she moved in front of me and grabbed me by both arms, and shoved me back against the door frame.

"Stop."

"Nika, let me go," I said, wearily.

Her eyes widened and her fingers relaxed, bit by bit, until she finally dropped her hands from my arms. "I'm sorry," she said. "We're just worried. You've got to stop…whatever it is you're doing to yourself."

"You think I'm controlling this? You think this is what I want?" I said.

"What *do* you want?"

I wrapped my arms around my torso, clamping the blood-soaked cloth against my skin even as it started to freeze in the brutal air. Nika noticed me shivering and scowled, but when she advanced a step toward me, meaning to drive me back into Eyid's house, I held my ground.

"I'm not going back in there," I said. "Don't even bother trying to persuade me, and *don't* make the mistake of trying to force me."

Her mouth twitched, but she nodded and retreated a half pace from me. "But you're going to catch your death out here. Will you go back to the lodging house at least?"

"And do what? Sit by the fire and let Rigvar mock me a little more?"

Iskari joined us on the step, shifting a glance between us. He must have heard what we were discussing, because he said, "At least Eyid's house is private."

"I will not go in there again," I gritted. "Too many ghosts. Death is in every room in that house."

"Eyid—" Nika started, but I cut her off.

"You've never seen her. You don't know what you're saying."

"Her?" I'd pushed past her, roughly, but she barely missed a beat before jumping down the stairs to step in front of me again. "What are you talking about?"

"God, Nika!" I cried, driving her out of my way. "Leave me alone!"

"We've tried leaving you alone," Iskari said. "Every time we do you promise you'll be fine, but look what happens."

I glanced back at him. I felt like I was on the brink of bursting, or shattering. There was no sense to the fog of my thoughts, no bridle for the agony that thrashed against me. Even through all the darkest moments of my life, I'd never felt this close to the gnawing heart-ache of despair. I couldn't escape. I couldn't get free. I couldn't break the shackles and find clarity—it was all broken, clinging to the knees of my soul like a supplicant with nothing left to lose. There was nowhere I could turn. No solitude, no quiet.

I was trammeled by a chaos of my own making, and for one moment, one fraction of a moment, I remembered the allure of Death's eyes and almost called out to her in my mind.

An icy wind gusted over us, making Nika stumble and Iskari duck back into the shelter of the doorway. I didn't move. I held my hands open at my sides and let the wind wash over me. Let it freeze the tears on my lashes before they could fall and turn traitor on me. My hands tightened slowly into fists, and I knew without looking that they were wreathed in fire.

"Stop," Iskari said. "Please, stop."

The wind picked up and I squeezed my eyes shut, desperately searching for calm. I thought I felt the stones beneath my feet shift, and suddenly Nika's arms were around me, her voice shouting in my ear.

"Taumir! *Stop!*"

I slumped down onto the step and listlessly regarded the empty street. A crow was wandering along the sidewalk across the street from me, and I watched it for long while and wished with a desperate sort of hope that it might be Hayli. But it was a northern crow, with the telltale white streak at the corner of each eye, not the pure black of Hayli's crow.

Iskari sat down on the step beside me, looping his arms over his knees. "You can't sit here forever," he murmured.

"I have nowhere to go," I said. "Send me to the sea, to the depths where I belong."

"Hush," he said, so sharply that I regarded him in surprise. "Don't say such things when the gods are listening."

I lifted a brow. "Wouldn't you say they're always listening?"

He pressed his lips in a thin line, but it was Nika who answered. "Yes, but you don't tempt the gods' messengers."

"What are you *talking* about?"

She nodded her head, barely, in the direction of the crow. "He's the voice and the ear of the gods," she murmured.

"It's a crow," I said.

"Of course it's a crow, idiot," she said. "In the beginning, when the world was born, the crow was the least of all the birds, ignored by gods and men alike. Because they paid him no heed, they spoke their secrets in front of him, and he learned all the mysteries of the world. He was the one who told Wake of the betrayal of the mad god, and so Wake blessed him and made him his messenger, and gave him the veil between the living and the dead as his private kingdom. The crow whispers Wake's words into the ears of men, and takes all the secret thoughts of their hearts to Wake's ears."

I clutched my arms tighter around my stomach and leaned back against the doorframe, fighting a wave of nausea. "Why did you tell me that?" I whispered. "Why did you have to tell me that right now? I can't... Why?"

It was a myth. It was as foolish and farfetched as the myths of *thayoi* and *tazimy* and Wake. Wake...who was standing across the street from me now, with the crow resting contentedly near his feet, running his heavy black bill through his feathers. I pressed my forehead against my knees and shook my head back and forth.

*I can't make sense of this right now. It isn't true...it's just a myth. Just a myth.*

When Iskari got to his feet and lifted me up beside him, I didn't resist; I barely noticed the walls of Eyid's house enfolding me again. Iskari shouldered his way into the front sitting room and pushed me, gently, down onto a low couch. I lay down without protest, and turned onto my side to face the wall.

For hours I drifted in and out of sleep. Sometimes I heard the low cadence of Iskari and Nika's conversation, but more often there was complete silence when I woke—silence, and the perpetual feeling of being watched. When I started to shiver, in spite of the steam vent close by my head radiating the earth's warmth, someone covered me with a rough wool blanket.

"What can we do?" I heard Nika ask at one point, when my thoughts clawed close enough to waking for me to make sense of her words. "This can't go on, can it? If he loses any more blood…"

"I honestly don't see how he's still alive," Iskari said, so quietly I almost couldn't hear him. "He can't have much blood left in him."

"But how? I just can't understand…"

"It's like…it's like he's being torn apart," Iskari said, "from the inside."

I pressed my hands tighter against my chest and buried my face in the musty wool fabric of the couch. Iskari was right—more than he probably knew. That was exactly what it felt like. Like my soul was being picked apart, piece by piece, and left in bloody ruins by a sadistic tormenter.

I slipped into dreams again, or out of the realm of the living, and found myself standing once more on Death's shore. She was waiting for me there, her feet in the waves, her hands spinning moonlight into blood.

"What do you want from me?" I said. Here at least I felt no pain. Here my thoughts were clear, and my own. I moved to stand beside her, ankle deep in the low tide. "Do you want my death? Is that what this is about?"

"Why should I want your death?" Her lips curved in silent, mirthless laughter, and her fingers never stopped moving. "What would your one death give me, when the nations of this world are fit to topple, and glut me to satiety?" She looked at me a long while, and there was pity or hatred in her eyes. "What," she said. "Do you imagine you can stop them? Do you think to pit yourself against them, one boy, against their madness machines and their lust for destruction? I am all that awaits you at the end of that road, my poor dear one. Neither Wake nor the mad god in all their might could protect you from that end, if you choose to face it alone."

"If you think I need their protection," I said, "you don't really know me at all."

She laughed—out loud this time—and shook her head. "Your arrogance has some charm, though. If only you could see yourself through my eyes… What a vain little private war you're waging. If you keep battling them, do you imagine you'll have any strength left to save your precious humans?"

She reached out one pale hand and placed the ridge of her thumb on my forehead, then pulled it away again with a little disappointed sigh.

"Ah, more's the pity. He's already marked you for his own. I wonder if the miscreant knows. Is it all just a formality now?"

"Who has marked me?" I asked, the words clinging to my throat like frost.

She only smiled, and placed her hand on my chest, and pushed me away. "Wake," she said, and I fell like lightning back to my senses.

I groaned and rolled onto my back, and found the sitting room empty but for Wake, who stood at the window gazing down onto the dark street outside. He didn't turn at my movement. Lifting a hand, he traced a pattern against the glass, the light from his skin rippling through the room, like sunlight glancing over the sandy bed of a quiet pond.

"She said you marked me," I said. "I told you I didn't want your power."

"Marked or not, you are always free to refuse me," he answered. He turned at last to face me. "But you should know that the sigil of my will is the only thing keeping you alive right now."

"Maybe it would be better if you took it back," I said, more boldly than I felt. My heart shuddered with fear and dread, and I stared in shaken horror at myself and the words I'd spoken.

"Is that what you want?" he said. "Do you truly believe the world would profit from your death?"

I closed my eyes, and when I opened them again I found not Wake, but Mirin kneeling beside my couch. His face was far too pale, and I startled when I saw the tears on his cheeks.

"What are you doing here?" I asked.

I'd just been talking to Wake, so how was it my voice sounded so weak, so hoarse? Mirin clasped his folded hands against his forehead with a little moan and didn't say anything. I glanced past him and found Nika sitting on one of the other chairs in the room, a thin ribbon of lamplight from the corridor falling across her hair. There was no sign of Iskari.

"He wanted to see you," Nika said. "He was worried."

There was no mockery in her voice. I almost wished there was.

"Your Majesty," Mirin whispered. "Who did this to you?"

I pushed him back from the couch, gently. "I told you, Mirin, I'm not your King."

"You're the only King we have," he said. "You can't abandon us."

He kept his head bowed, but one of his hands crept out and clasped mine where it rested on my blood-soaked shirt. I shivered, but found I didn't have the strength to pull away.

"What are you doing?" I hissed. "What is wrong with the both of you? It's like..."

*It's like you're waiting for me to die,* I thought, and a shudder seized my body.

It was just like when King Geyn had died. I'd been just a boy at the time, seven if I remembered rightly. Geyn hadn't been an old man—he'd passed the crown to Trabin shortly after Trabin and my mother had married, but he'd fallen into poor health not four years later, and over the next three, a slow sickness had whittled the strong man I knew to a mere shadow of himself.

I could still remember the long vigils the servants kept around his bedside, the midnight visits from Dr. Besdin, the court physician, the endless march of days when I was paraded past the former King's sick bed to pay him my respects. And finally, the day when the servants came running to tell us that he had gone, in one rare moment when he'd been left alone. No one, not even his own valet, had been with him when he'd died.

I grimaced at the memory and tried to ignore Mirin, who was still kneeling beside me just like I'd been made to kneel beside Geyn's bed. It was all too much.

"Where is Iskari?" I asked Nika.

"Trying to reason with Halvir."

"The Blood," I said, but when she wrinkled her brow, I realized I'd said it in Cavnish. "The healer," I tried again, and she nodded. "Why?"

"You need help," she said, a pleading note in her voice that alarmed me.

"I'm fine," I said.

"You're dying."

"I'm *fine*."

"*Veka*," she muttered. "You really are Istian."

I glared at her and rolled over again, desperate to block out the weight of their concern.

I knew that my mind would take me to Death's shore as soon as I closed my eyes, but I couldn't help myself. For all I insisted I was fine, I was so tired, weary to the very marrow of my bones, and somehow I found I didn't care if I faced Death again or not. If I had a reprieve from the pain that ate at my soul, however brief, it might even be worth it.

This time I was at her side as soon as I was aware of being in her realm, walking with her as she paced the edge of the tide.

"Wake said his mark is keeping me alive," I said. "Is it true? Is he holding you back?"

She walked in silence for several paces, then tipped her head to look at me. "I told you once already, foolish boy, I don't want your death. It would gratify me, but it wouldn't serve my needs. And anyway, I am almost more interested in seeing the outcome of their war over your soul."

"What?" I asked, startled.

"Wake," she said, "and the mad god. You know they are fighting over you. And well they should. It has been far too long since either of them had an emissary in the world." Her night-black lips lifted in a mocking smile. "What would the world do with you then? They barely know what to do with you now—now, when you are yourself, and so weak."

"Wake said he's seen the mad god's handiwork in my life. What does that mean? I've never known... You would think I'd be able to feel that."

"Stupid," she said. "You would think, indeed. And haven't you felt it? You suffer it every day. First it was just in your mind. Now you feel it in your body, too. They are tearing you apart like maddened wolves."

"The fracturing?" I asked, swallowing against the dryness in my throat. "The madness?"

"The madness belongs to the mad god," she said, "obviously. But the fracturing belongs to you. You do that to yourself, and you have the power to stop it."

"How?"

She stopped pacing and turned to face me. "You are fracturing because you insist on resisting Wake's claim on your soul. I told you once. Magic is his domain. Most humans are content with the little pool of magic they have been given, but you are an abyss."

I frowned. "What do you mean?"

"You consume and you consume. You are like the sea, devouring all the waters of the world, yet always thirsting for more. And what you need to understand about yourself is that your soul *could* consume more, so much more, whereas most mages...they would drown in the depths of the power that you've absorbed. But you don't—*won't*—drown anymore than the sea could drown itself. Yet you must understand what I mean when I say that magic is Wake's domain. You are bound to his laws, and his strictures, when you choose to walk the path of magic. Souls like yours, Tarik, are a sea like glass. You can empty yourself, or you can shatter under the weight of your own power, or you can become liquid to be shaped by the hands of Wake. But you cannot survive as you are. As long as you resist Wake, the mad god will feed on your weakness, and drive you closer to breaking. Closer to madness."

"Is there no way out, then?" I asked, fighting back a wave of despair. "Am I destined to belong to one of them?"

Her lips lifted in a smile so cruel I couldn't bear to see it. As I turned my head away she said, "Well. You could serve me instead. That is what Arnthor chose."

I staggered like she'd struck me and whirled to face her. "*Arnthor* did? How? What happened?"

Her smile widened, and she reached out to stroke my face, her fingers drifting over my cheeks and the edges of my hair like a blind man desperate for the face of a loved one. She said, "At his request I gave Arnthor power over life and death. Well, to...a certain degree. Of course, he tried to escape his oath to me in the end, but I had my justice."

I thought I was going to be sick. I pulled away from her, shaking my head as if that could make her words less true. "You mean the Scourge? The genocide? That was because of you?"

She gave me a look of rebuke. "Honestly, Tarik," she said. "Tens of thousands dead, and you think that was done without my knowledge? But if you think it was all so simple, it's because you understand so little of the past."

"Then teach me."

"It is not for me to teach, but for you to learn."

I looked down at my feet, at the swirl of sea foam snagging around my bare ankles. "If I serve you, what will you do to me?"

"It's your choice, love," she said. I cringed at the endearment. "I will not make you into something you're not, and it is up to you how you will use my gift. Stay my hand, or bring it down on your enemies— that is your choice."

"There must be a catch."

"No catch. But I do offer you an enticement. You long to forget the bitterness of your past, don't you? You always have. So many choices, so many mistakes, so many lies. So many times you hurt the people you love. It's why you sought me from the belfry arch. It is also why you sought refuge in the haze of Branigan's drug."

I winced, wondering how—why—she had to know so much. "What about it?"

Her smile became sweet as honeyed wine, almost coy, and she turned a little away from me. "I can help you forget, with no knots to tangle you," she said, watching me over her shoulder. Even in the still air, her hair drifted around her face like a blood drop in water. "The drug had its complications. I'm sure you would be the first to agree with that. My gift has no such consequences, just forgetting, pure and unhindered. Whatever good things you want to remember are yours to remember. Whatever causes you grief, causes me grief, and I will cast them into my sea forever."

I folded my arms and regarded the blood-red moon, Death's words trailing through my thoughts, weaving through all my most deeply-buried desires.

"You said you wouldn't make me into something I'm not," I said then, carefully. "What did that mean?"

Her eyes narrowed, but it only made the amber light from the center of her irises more intense, like sunlight reflected off plated gold. "I mean you will stay who you are. Do you think that if you become Wake's Zealot, or if you become the mad god's Scion, you will be allowed to remain Tarik? You will be an emissary. You will be refashioned to do their work in the world. There will be nothing left of Tarik Eyidson when they are done with you. And don't make the mistake of believing that *Zealot* is a title of honor. You believe it must be something good, because it belongs to Wake. I assure you, good has nothing to do with it."

I drew away from her, or tried to, but my legs felt strangely numb. "I can't move. God, everything hurts. Even here, it hurts."

"What did you expect would happen when you told Wake to withdraw his sigil?"

"But you're *Death*," I said, panic making my voice shake. "Wake's sigil couldn't be the only thing keeping me alive."

She laughed; the sound harrowed my soul. "Ah, there's that glimmer of cleverness I've always cherished in you. In many things I am subject to Wake as much as you are, and I withheld my hand from you by the power of his sigil. But that's not the only reason I can withhold my hand."

"You can save me?"

"Oh, dear boy. I cannot save you. As you so astutely observed just now, I am Death. But I can give you back to life, for now. Your friends are mourning you even as we speak. Should I let you surprise them with a miraculous recovery? Should I let them have you back?"

"Would it make me your servant?" I asked, hesitating, feeling the undercurrent of the sea tugging ever more insistently at my ankles. "Would it bind me to you in some way, if I let you do this?"

"Always the politician," she said, and pursed her lips. "No. I will give you a reprieve. You can taste how sweet my gifts can be, but your choice remains ahead of you. But the next time we meet, your decision will be final."

She took my face in her hands and pressed her lips against mine one more time. Then she planted a hand against my forehead, and pushed.

# Chapter 11 ～ Hayli

JIG WAYLAID ME ON MY WAY OUT OF MY ROOM THE NEXT MORNING, STEPPING clean in front of me before I could even get through the doorway. He had his arms crossed tight over his narrow chest, and the lamplight threw his face in severe lines. Grimacing, I tried to rub the sleep from my still-tired eyes, but I had no patience for figuring out what he wanted.

"Hayli," he said, jerking his chin at me in greeting. "Got a question for you." He leaned closer to me, planting his hand on the doorframe beside my head. "What the *hell* is that mage doing loose? Heard a rumor he was mucking about in the mess hall last night, but I'd never ha' believed it if I hadn't seen him myself this morning. I thought we had him in bloody chains for safekeeping."

"We did," I said, watching him carefully. That was all he said, though, so I hoped Anuk hadn't said aught about the quarrel we'd had the night before. I shrugged and added, "I released him."

"*Why?*"

I lifted a hand and shoved past him into the corridor. "Dan' need to explain my reasons to you. Dan' you got somewhere you're s'posed to be right now?"

"Yeah," he said. "S'posed to be fetching you for Bridnow."

I glowered at him. "Why div'n you say that at the first?"

"Because I wanted a word first," he said. "Commandant's in the little guardhouse."

He fell in step beside me as I made my way out of the Rookery. I didn't get the sense Bridnow had asked him to escort me all the way, so maybe it was just he had something on his mind that he still wanted to chat about. For all he was one of Tarik's crew, though, I had no burning interest in jawing with him, so I did my best to ignore him.

"I'm worried about Shade," he said, all on a sudden.

I stopped short at that, and frowned at him. "We're all worried about him."

"Yeah, but..." He shook his head, brushing his wind-blown hair out of his eyes. "I dan' na. Rivano's afraid he might lose track of his mission up in Istia."

"Rivano is?" I asked, scowling all the fiercer for it. "Istia *is* Shade's mission right now."

"Is it, though?" Jig hunched his shoulders and scuffed his toe in an icy puddle. "Pika's got a bit fitsy about him, too."

I grabbed his arm, making him jump. "What's that supposed to mean? Why's she worried?"

"Dan' na. Maybes you should ask her, like. Found her like that in the mess hall, but she'd barely say two words to me. Maybes you'd get her to chat up."

"Found her like what?"

He just waved a hand toward the long building and didn't favor me with an answer. I bit my lip, torn between reporting to Bridnow and going to find Pika myself. Jig must've sensed my thoughts because he gave me a wry kind of smile.

"Bridnow div'n say I should hurry," he said.

I gave him a puzzled grin and squeezed his arm briefly, then made my way fast as I could toward the mess. It was almost empty, with just a few knots of folks enjoying a meal of canned peas and near-black toast. I'd almost given up hope of finding Pika there when I spotted her fiery red curls bowed over one of the long tables, in the far corner of the mess hall. Stomach in knots, I hurried over and laid a hand on her shoulder.

She didn't even jump when I touched her. It was just the bare rise and fall of her thin shoulders that kept me from a full-out panic.

"Hey Pika," I said gently. "What's bothering?"

She lifted her head, and my blood turned to lead in my veins. Her ruddy cheeks were streaked with tears, and her eyes were wide and red and glimmering behind their swollen lids. For a long moment she just looked at me, lips quivering, then suddenly her face crumpled and she buried her head in her hands.

"Oh, *Hayli*," she sobbed.

"Stars, what's wrong?" I cried, dropping onto the bench beside her and wrapping her tight in my arms. "Did you...have you seen something?"

"N-no, not really," she said. "But Aothir...he did."

I put her at arms' length. "Aothir! The Flint?"

She closed her eyes and shook her head dramatically. "Nooo," she said, as if I ought to have known better. "That ain't all he is. He's a Knack too. And he *knows* someone in Istia."

"Oh," I breathed, and tamped down hard on a sudden surge of indignation. "Well, what? Did he say something?"

"Um," she said. She twisted away from me and propped her elbows on the table, leaning her head in her hands. "Not 'zactly."

"Did you read *him*?"

"Couldn't help it! He was crying."

"Aothir was crying?" I asked, bewildered, as the knot of dread settled even deeper in my stomach. "Why?"

"It was the strangest thing! I slipped in his mind and it was like...it was like he was watching the world through someone else's eyes. Like it was all happening right when he saw it. Oh stars, I'm so scared...I'm so scared for Shade."

Her voice dissolved in tears again, and she dropped her head on the table as sobs wracked her tiny body. I wrapped an arm around her again, trying to be patient, trying so hard to be a comfort to her when I desperately needed answers.

"Tell me what you saw," I said.

"I saw this big room...lots of tables, a bit like this place but brighter and...higher." She waved generally at the ceiling, then shook her head again. "Strange clothes on all the folks. Guess that's Istian fashion. Fur, and leather, and you should see their hair..."

I gritted my teeth and tamped down the impulse to tell her to hurry up and skip the details. She had to tell me as she saw it. I had no right to demand aught else of her.

"There's an old man sitting across the table. I guess it's whoever Aothir's friend was talking to. And there's a handsome man in the background. I div'n get a sense of what he was talking about, but it was so strange...I just wanted to look at him and listen to him. It's peculiar, too...I think because I was in Aothir's head, I could understand what all the folks were saying, though I'm dead sure they weren't gabbing in Cavnish! And then...and then I'm looking at the door, and this big man comes in. He dan' look too old, maybe Derrin's age. He's got long dark hair, long, long, all bound in thick coils. I can *feel* the alarm everybody feels when he bursts in. His eyes are red. He's got blood all over his shirt."

She sat bolt upright suddenly, eyes wide as she lost herself in whatever memory she'd gleaned from Aothir.

"Halvir!" she cried, her child's voice pitched absurdly low. "I need Halvir!"

"Why? What's wrong?" she went on, in a different voice. Her hands tightened, bone-white, on the edge of the table.

In her own voice she said, "He's coming toward me. There's...oh, a *beautiful* girl rushing in behind him. She's tall, and her blonde hair is all in those long knots like the man's. And a smaller man...he looks a bit Cavnish, actually. He's standing inside a doorway, and he's looking at the two people, and...stars, he looks apt to pass out. The black-haired man comes close, leans on the table so only I can hear him."

"It's Taumir," she said, in the low voice. "*Veka*...he's..."

"He's what?" I asked, at the same time that Pika said the same two words in the other voice.

"He's dying."

I snatched my hands away from Pika's shoulders. "Pika!" I cried. "That's a lie!" My voice broke, and the world was caving in around me. My hands tangled in my hair, trying to drag the pain from my lungs. "No...it's not...it's not true!"

Pika just buried her face again, sobbing quietly. "Taumir," she said after a moment, the word thick with grief. "It's Shade, ain't it?"

I had my hand pressed hard against my mouth now, but it did naught to stop my tears. I tried twice to answer her, but I couldn't even conjure up a voice till the third try. "It's his...it's his Istian name," I said. "Oh, stars, what happened to him? What was the blood? Pika! Do you know aught else?"

"I dan' na, I dan' na," she wept. "That was all I saw. I couldn't bear any more after that...I just couldn't."

As she buried her head in her arms again I squeezed her shoulder, then got to my feet and fled from the mess before she or anybody else could see my grief. Outside I went straight for the burial mound where Derrin and the others had laid the slaughtered mages to rest—it was a quiet spot, still shrouded in snow, a place nobody went if they didn't have a reason. When the world blurred too bad for me to see aught at all, I dropped to my knees in the snow and covered my face with my hands, and wept until I had no tears left to cry.

"He's not dead," I told myself, a hundred times or more. "He's not dead. They'll save him. He'll...he'll save himself. Oh, *Wake*. What happened? You'd never...you'd never let yourself fall so far..."

I was still muttering prayers and rebukes to the snow when someone laid a hand on my shoulder. The touch was gentle, but the lash of the static charge was powerful enough to jar me out of my grief. I glanced up, half-expecting to find Doc standing there, but Doc was missing, and instead it was Aroden. He had an anxious kind of air about him, and as soon as he saw my face he dropped to his knees in the snow beside me.

"Hayli! What's wrong?"

I shied away from him, bewildered, too distraught to know what to say. How could I explain, without bringing up Tarik? If the mention of him sent Aroden into a fit, I didn't think I had the patience to talk him out of it just then. And echoing deep in my thoughts were all the terrible things Anuk had said to me, all his doubt and grief.

Still, I heard myself saying, "It's Tarik. Pika said...he's..."

"Dying," Aroden said, twisting away from me, curling over his knees with his head in his arms. "Dying!"

"You *knew*?"

"I felt it. Why...why won't it just stop?"

"You can feel it? Why'd you never say aught about that before?"

He just rocked back and forth for a few moments, then slowly he lowered his arms and straightened up, and turned to face me again. "Would you have believed me?" His fingers drifted in the snow, tracing lines and swirls as if he were drawing some kind of pattern.

"What do you feel now?" I asked.

His brow creased and he tipped his head back, a little to the side, as if he were listening for something far, far away. "Pain," he said. "Confusion."

"He's alive, though?"

"If you can call it that."

I grabbed his shoulder and shook it, hard. "What's that supposed to mean?" Aroden bent his head, refusing to answer. "Aroden? You said he came and stole your life. If it's true…who was he before? What was he before?"

He jerked his gaze up to meet mine. "Before he was me? I don't know. Maybe he was a *thayo*. Maybe he is a *thayo*. Or…" He hissed suddenly, as if in pain. "The mad god…he…he almost has him enthralled."

"But—"

"The mad god, Hayli! Don't you understand? His deceit knows no bounds. He is subtle, a trickster. He knows exactly how to play on people's fears and doubts." He paused, then added, voice rising, "He's a master of illusion. He'll show Shade exactly what he wants to see. He will convince Shade of whatever he wants Shade to believe! And God help us when he does."

"Tarik wouldn't listen to the mad god," I said, desperately, but even I could hear the doubt fraying my voice. "He's stronger than that."

Aroden turned toward me, his face grave in the long shadows under the snowy pines. "Not right now he isn't."

"He has to be," I whispered. "He's all we have."

Aroden's lips pursed in a thin line, then he got to his feet and helped me to stand. "Hayli…you don't know—"

I jabbed a finger toward his face. "No. Not right now. I know what you're ganna say and I dan' wanna hear it. Keep your thoughts about him to yourself, savv?"

I heard his breath escape in a long sigh as I turned away, but I didn't wait to see if he had a reply to that. Jaw clenched, eyes gritty and burning from my tears, I stomped back through the snow to the warm sanctuary of the Rookery. Inside I found Anuk leaning over the big table, poring over a supply list. As I swept in on a gust of chilly air he glanced up, and his whole manner changed the minute he saw my face. He dropped the papers he was holding and skirted the table, and I threw myself into his arms.

"Hayli! Stars, what's wrong?" he asked, tightening his arms around me. "Did Aroden…"

I shook my head against his chest, but I couldn't bear to tell him what Pika had told me. Instead I said, my voice muffled in the wool of his jumper, "Where is Aothir?"

"Aothir!" he exclaimed. "Why? Did he do something I need to know about, so?"

"Nothing like that. Just need...just need a word with him."

Anuk released me and jerked his chin toward his right, which I took to mean the depot gate. I gave him a shaky smile and patted his arm.

"I'm a'right. Trust me," I said, and headed back outside.

But Aothir wasn't at the depot gate when I got there. Two other guards were, and neither of them had seen Aothir at all that morning—one of them told me sourly that he'd gotten stuck taking Aothir's watch, which I guessed explained his bad mood.

My mind was a tangle of worries as I left them. The notion that Aothir would shirk his duty surprised me, but not as much, I realized, as the thought of him crying. Arrogant, cocky, sarcastic Aothir, whose heart always seemed like it had been molded from the unfeeling ice and snow...I couldn't imagine anything upsetting him enough to bring him to tears.

I searched the facility a good twenty minutes without finding word or whisper of him, and finally gave up and headed to the guardhouse where Bridnow was waiting for me. Both the Commandant and Griff were inside, organizing a supply of small firearms on the long table. Bridnow glanced up and smiled as soon as he heard me coming in, and Griff gave me a nod of greeting as he examined a long-barreled revolver.

"Good morning, sir," I said. "Morning, Griff."

"Feeling better?" Bridnow asked. "Scorch told me he offered to stand in for you last night."

I startled, and waited, but he said nothing else. Apparently Anuk hadn't said anything about finding me in the dormitory, talking to Aroden. But I really shouldn't have been surprised—it wasn't in Anuk's nature to be a tattle. I gave Bridnow a noncommittal kind of nod and joined them at the table, picking up a glossy black revolver with a strange, squarish barrel.

"Got a job for me, Commandant?" I asked.

"I do, in fact." He sat down on the edge of the table. "I told you once that I'd made a roster of the folks here with former military or police experience, and that I've been using them for their own missions."

I nodded, but it surprised me how prickly I felt at the thought—

when we'd first talked about it, the notion that Bridnow had experienced folks to do the tricky jobs for him had been a relief to me. Now, more than aught else, I wanted him to put me and the other lieutenants on those hard jobs. I wanted him to believe we could succeed.

"I've also been relying a bit on Derrin, simply because of the unique nature of his Gift," Bridnow went on. "We've been doing some reconnaissance at the palace and in the various Ministries, and I'm preparing a report to share with all of you on what we've learned. But before it's finished, I want to make sure I haven't missed any sources of information."

I set the gun down on the table and waited, patiently, for him to finish.

He sighed and said, "We can't find Dreyden Kor, nor any hints as to his whereabouts."

"Lemme get this straight," I said. "You've got folks infiltrating the palace, and you want me to find Kor?"

"Precisely." He leveled a hard look on me. "I've heard that you are personally acquainted with Kor, perhaps more than anyone else here now that Shade is gone to Istia, and Zagger…is no longer with us."

"What about Rivano?" I asked.

"I'm not sure that Rivano has the…ability to find out the information we need."

"You could just say you dan' trust him," I said bluntly.

"I could, but that wouldn't be entirely true. I don't know him well enough. I know he's a wanted man, so, asking him to go into Brinmark in search of information is rather…difficult."

"And you think I'll be able to do what these other folks can't?" I asked, puzzled enough that I didn't realize I was questioning Bridnow's orders until the words were already out.

"I do." He turned back to the guns. "Take the motorbike, if you like, but you might find it faster to just fly."

Griff grinned faintly at that, and I nodded my acceptance and showed myself out of the guardhouse, because if Bridnow hadn't been able to spade up a scrap of intelligence about Kor yet, then there was nothing left for him to tell me.

# Chapter 12 ~ Hayli

**H**AYLI LETS ME TAKE OVER AS SOON AS WE GET OUTSIDE, AND *I* TAKE TO THE CLEAR *air while she grumbles in the back of my mind. The wind is cold and the currents are strong, and my heart soars as I climb higher and higher into the sky. These are the days I live for.*

Where do you suppose we should look for Kor? *Hayli asks, finally letting go of her annoyance.* I've got no idea where he could be, and Brinmark's a grobbing huge place.

Not that huge, *I tell her.* People know people who know people. It seems all very connected when you get right down to it.

What would you know of that? *she grumbles.*

More than you, apparently. You forget, I'm always paying attention, even when you're distracted.

Distracted by what?

*I laugh, and say,* Tarik.

*I can sense her embarrassment, but she just mutters at me and can't find a word of argument.* All right, then. What have you noticed?

Do you remember when you followed Shade to the palace, when you first started suspecting him of double-dealing the Hole? *I ask. She gets a little uneasy at this, probably at the memory of Shade's troubled early days with the crew, but then she nods.* He went to talk to Kor, didn't he?

Yeah, after Alby Durb kicked, *Hayli says,* and Kantian told him to go to a meeting that was never going to happen. I remember. Kor told him to go to the meeting anyway to save his cover. Stars, feels like that happened years ago.

I know, but keep thinking. Kor told him a way for Shade to get in touch with him, outside of the palace.

*Hayli says nothing. I can sense her scouring her memories, searching for whatever it is I've remembered that she has forgotten. I blame the way human minds work, and the messy way they organize their thoughts and memories. My way is so much more sensible.*

No, it's not, *Hayli grouses at me.* Your way makes no sense at all.

Should I tell you what you're missing, then, or should I just let you wait and see?

Just tell me!

Fine, *I say, though I rather wanted to show off what I knew by taking her there directly, and surprising her.* Kor told Shade that he could contact Astel if he needed.

Astel! *she cries.* Blimey, I almost forgot about Astel.

Well, there you go. Guess we'll be paying a visit to her diner.

*I'm over Brinmark's rooftops by now, and I turn my path toward the strange in-between stretch of city that lies south of the Oval Wall and the high streets, and north of the slums of South Brinmark. I've never flown to Astel's diner, but I know the way easily from the memories in Hayli's mind, which she picks out and holds up for my observation as we fly. Soon I reach the broad avenue where the diner sits, its open door spilling greasy light and laughter onto the sidewalk below. I land in the alley behind, where Shade once kicked a box to splinters in a rage over Alby Durb's death, where Astel gave bowls of soup to him and Hayli, and Shift.*

Soon as I'd gotten my brain straight from Shifting, I picked my way around to the front entrance of the diner and made my best impression of a confident entrance. Halfway toward the bar I realized I was wearing my fine officer's coat, which, even without an insignia of any kind on it, still made folks look twice when they saw me. That time of day, there were naught but twenty-odd people in the diner, but it was enough to make me self-conscious. Blushing under the weight of half a dozen stares, I walked straight up to the counter and waited for Astel to notice me.

She was turned away from me at first, dusting the shelves where the liquor bottles sat, but when one of her rowdier patrons called her name with a request for another drink, she tossed down her dust cloth in annoyance and turned around. Then her gaze fell on me, and her mouth dropped open.

"Hayli!" she exclaimed, softly. "Not seen you about for ages! Where you been hiding, doll?"

"Here and there," I said.

"Astel! I wan' anotha bloody ale!" called the man sprawled a few stools down from mine.

"Clap that trap, Hinkly!" she shouted back at him. "You get one when I give you one, not a dot sooner! I got a new customer to deal with an' I like her worlds better than you, so shut it!" I swallowed my surprise as she turned back to me with an apologetic smile. "Now, doll, what's brought you through my front door today? Care for a drink? Beer? Cider?"

"I'm good, thanks," I said.

She regarded me a moment, eyes a little hooded, then brushed back a stray strand of red hair from her narrow face. "You want something. Maybe not a drink, but you got something on your mind, I can tell. Can't help you if you don't spill it, though."

"Astel," I said, leaning over the counter toward her and lowering my voice. "Got a question, and hope you can give me an answer."

"Sure, ask," she said.

I drew a breath and said, "Where is Kor?"

Astel didn't answer for much too long. She served up the rowdy patron's ale, then turned back to the liquor shelves and took her time straightening and re-straightening every last bottle that slouched up on the high shelf. In the dim light of the restaurant her face looked a bit more gaunt than usual, the circles under her eyes a bit darker. If I hadn't known better, I might've thought she'd recently been crying.

"Hey," I said. "What's bothering?"

She finally turned to face me again, jerking her chin at the man she'd served the ale to. With naught more than a grumble he slid off his seat and ambled away, beer mug tipped woozily in his hand. Astel watched him go, then leaned on her elbows across from me.

"What's the deal? Why d'you want to know about Kor, doll?"

I shrugged. "Not seen him in weeks. Maybes I'm just worried about him."

She narrowed her eyes a bit, tipping her head to one side. "What're you going to do to him, if you find him?"

"What am I going to do to him?" I echoed, baffled. "What *could* I do to him?"

"I know you're a mage. You mean to hurt him? Y'know he never threw in with those insurgents in the Ministry, don't you? Not really."

Apparently Astel didn't know that Kor was a mage too. Figuring it wasn't my place to spill his secret, I just shrugged up my shoulders again and gave her my best innocent look.

"I know. I got no quarrel with Kor," I said. "And actually we could use his help about now."

She chewed on her lower lip and studied me a good long tick, until I got a bit fitsy and glanced away. Then she sighed and dropped her head.

"There's things happening in the city right now," she said. "Don't see that I really get all the ins and outs of it. Who's on whose side. Who stands for what. Who's a threat to me and the ordinary folks who don't want to get in anybody's way. You think Kor can help make sense of it all?"

"I wouldn't be asking you about him if I didn't."

She heaved another sigh, still hunched over the bar. After a minute she glanced up somewhat, just enough to catch my eye. "I don't want anything bad to happen to Kor."

"You care about him a lot," I said.

"Sure I do," she said. Her mouth twitched in a sad, funny little smile. "You know, he's the only one...he's the only one who's ever looked at me like...like I was worth looking at. *Me.* Looked right past this odd little face and saw deep inside to really *me.* Like I was something special. Like...I was worth caring about."

My heart tugged strangely at her words, and I reached out, for no good reason why, and laid my hand over hers.

"Think I got a ken what that's like," I said.

Her smile warmed. "Thought you might. Where is that boy of yours, anyway? Not seen Shade about in a good long while."

"You...you know about what happened in Avnaya Square, right?" I asked, hesitating.

"Well," she said, and flicked her fingers. "I know what the newspaper said about it, but Kor always said it was a bunch of lies and propaganda anyway." Her eyes searched my face—I wondered what she saw. "What happened, Hayli? You were there, weren't you."

"Sort of," I said. I didn't know how to explain that I'd not been entirely myself, that I'd done things that I, Hayli, would never do. "I know Shade was arrested, and…he got shot…and his folks snatched him away. And the King died." Hoping to keep her from pestering more about it, I said, "But Shade, he's…he ain't here. He's alive, far as I know. Just not with us." I picked at a bit of fraying wood on the countertop. "We got no rudder right now."

"Ah," she said. "Makes a bit more sense now. So you say you want to find Kor. Need to find him, even. I wish I could tell you for certain, truly I do. But I only know as much as he told me. And all he said was, 'I'm going home, Astel. Just for a bit.' And he said he'd be back soon as he could. That's all I know, honest. I…don't even know where he calls home."

*Tulay*, I thought. *Did he take the Queen back to Tulay with him?*

"How long ago was that?" I asked.

She pursed her lips. "A month ago, maybe? Not long after that horrible day at Avnaya." She sighed, tracing the whorl of the wood in the counter. "What's gonna happen to us? You think there's gonna be a war?"

"I dan' na," I said. "Wish I did."

"I'd move out if I could. Go back home, away from this sorry place. But I don't think my home town is much safer than the city. Too close to the sea."

"Dan' na where you could go and be safe right now," I said. "Lest maybes up by Marag, in the mountains."

"Ugh," she said, with a shudder. "This place is too cold already. I couldn't last a day in the mountains."

I smiled, trying my best to hide my disappointment. I'd pinned all my hopes on getting information about Kor from Astel, but she was just as much in the dark as I was—and worlds more worried.

"Thanks," I said, squeezing her hand. "Stay safe, a'right? I gotta lam off for now, but I'll let you know if I find out aught about Kor."

"If I see him first," she said, "where should I tell him to find you?"

"Tell him to go about his business," I answered. "We'll find him."

Her face paled and she gave me a wavering smile and a nod, but as I turned to go, she reached out and snatched my arm.

"There was one thing he said." She kept her face a little aside, as if she could hide from the truth. "He told me…if things worked out the way he hoped, there'd be no more need for kings and crowns in all the world." She glanced back at me then, face pale and drawn. "What did

425

he mean, Hayli? Why's it that makes me feel all knotted up inside in the strangest way?"

I couldn't answer. I felt knotted up, too, queasy and anxious. Whatever Kor meant…I wasn't sure I wanted things to work out his way in the end.

I GOT BACK TO BOROKHEV LATE in the afternoon, after spending a few hours in the city letting Piper scour the streets from above for any sign of Kor—with no luck. Feeling miserable at my failure, I steeled myself to face Bridnow, but after hunting for him for a good quarter of an hour through the whole vast sprawling complex, I still hadn't managed to track him down. It wasn't like Bridnow to leave without a trace, without leaving any kind of message for us in the Rookery as to where he was going. Anxious, and more than a bit worried, I finally made my way out to the front gate to see if either of the gate guards had any information for me.

What I found there drew me up short. Coins was on post, which I'd expected, and Lev was his watch partner. What I hadn't expected was to see Aroden perched up on one of the low boulders that edged Borokhev's walls, laughing at something that Coins was saying.

Lev saw me first and gave me a smart salute, then Coins and Aroden both turned to face me. Coins grinned and tipped two fingers to his forehead, which half made me want to grab his shoulders and shake him, but Aroden glanced toward me, then away again, and then back, and a small smile touched the corners of his lips. I ground my teeth and rounded on Coins.

"Where's the Commandant?" I asked.

Coins opened his mouth, then closed it again. "Last I saw he was out talking to Derrin," he said. "Down near the east guardhouse." I nodded and turned to go, but he stopped me with a hand on my arm. "Hayli…I was looking for Kite earlier."

I just looked at him, waiting for him to say something I needed to know. I knew Kite had finally started tolerating Coins's unflagging devotion, and if Coins wasn't on duty I was fair sure I'd find Kite somewhere nearby. But it was true—the last few days, I hadn't seen her at all, with or without Coins.

"I couldn't find her. *Anywhere*," Coins said. "Not even Gem knew where she was."

"Maybe she's on a job? Work crew went out yesterday, div'n they?"

"She didn't go with them." He shoved his hands in his trouser pockets, looking more anxious than I'd seen him in ages. That softened me a bit, and I put a hand on his arm, but he only gave me a small, tense smile. "She's not been herself lately, right? I'm just worried."

"I'll ask around," I said. "But I wouldn't worry too much, Coins. She can handle herself."

He didn't look happy, but at least he nodded and turned away, letting me go. I acknowledged Lev's wave with a nod and turned to leave, my gaze snagging on Aroden as I did. He slid off the boulder, and my heart sank.

"I'll walk with you," he said.

Coins tossed me a glance over his shoulder, but with Aroden's attention riveted on me I couldn't do aught but give him a silent, meaningful look. Then I gave Aroden an indifferent nod and headed back into the complex. Aroden fell into step beside me, hands tucked in his pockets, chin up and staring at the whole world in challenge.

"Seems you're settling in a'right," I said as we walked.

"Most of them are still afraid of me," he said. "Coins is kinder than most."

"Coins always was good at making folks feel welcome," I said.

He nodded, and we walked a while in silence, then suddenly he said in a rush, "I hate being feared. I hate it. Is it because I'm a mage? Is it…is it because of something I did? I don't even know. I just want…" He pressed his lips in a thin line and shook his head. "The worst thing of all is that I'm…" His voice broke again, then he took a deep breath and finished, "I'm afraid of myself."

My steps slowed of their own accord, and I frowned up at him. "Afraid of your power?"

"I don't know. Afraid of what I am. What I'm…capable of. Afraid I won't be able to stop myself, or control what's buried inside of me. The magic, the devouring sea…"

"What d'you suppose you might do?" I asked carefully.

He shrugged, and picked up his pace. "I don't know. I don't even want to think about it."

I hurried to catch up to him, my heart aching in the worst possible way. Everything he'd said gnawed at my mind, wrapping words around my own fears, echoing the fears Shade had once spoken to me in secret. I understood exactly what he meant—and I didn't want to understand. I didn't want Aroden to make sense.

*You're the only one who could say Aroden makes sense,* whispered the voice in the back of my thoughts. *Because you've walked through the same darkness. You've been lost in the same wilderness.*

"Doing things helps," he said, drawing me out of my confounded thoughts. "Helps distract me." He started to glance toward the northern wall of the complex, then shuddered and turned his face away. "I have memories of this place," he said after a while. "Things…I think I did. Things I didn't mean to do. You asked me once how I can do things, how much power I have. The truth is I don't know. Sometimes it's like I have no control over it. It's just inside me and it comes out and things happen and I don't mean any of it. And sometimes I hear your brother's voice in my head, whispering, over and over and over again, and I don't know if any of it was real."

I stopped dead in the middle of the courtyard. "My *what?*"

He shifted to face me, the biting wind scattering his hair across his forehead, drawing a ruddy color to his cheeks. There was a faint line traced between his brows, and he was frowning at me like I'd been speaking the wrong language.

"Your brother," he said, helplessly.

"I dan'…" I started, and faltered. "Aroden, I dan' have a brother. Who the devil are you talking about?"

"The devil indeed," he said, "in the flesh." His hand stretched out, catching mine before I could pull it away. "I'm sorry. I thought you knew. I thought Luce told you."

I jerked my hand free and knotted it in a fist, taking one step closer to him when more than aught else I just wanted to fly away. "*Luce?* How d'you know Luce, and what's she got to do with aught?" I put both hands on his chest and shoved him, hard. He didn't even blink. "You spit tips on what you know, *right now,* or so help me—"

"I don't want to hurt you," he said. "If you don't know…it's better it stays that way."

"Aroden," I growled.

He took a step closer to me, catching my face in his hands. "Hayli, sometimes it's better not to know, believe me. Sometimes it's best just to let the past's secrets stay buried. Is any of it worth remembering, anyway?" He suddenly bent his head, brow knotted with tears, and he released me to point away to the north. "I want you to know, Hayli. I want you to know all the truth of me. I did…I did that. I didn't mean to. He lied to me. But I'm so afraid it will happen again, and I won't be able to stop it. I want to know I can stop it."

For a moment I just frowned at him, baffled, not understanding. But he kept pointing, his other hand covering his face, and finally I shifted to look to the north…to the snow-shrouded mound where Derrin and the others had buried the mages. Drop by drop, all my blood seeped out of my heart. I stared, numb, refusing to believe. It couldn't be true.

"You killed them," I whispered, and spun back to face him. "You killed those mages. I thought Kippler did it, but it was *you!*"

"I didn't see mages," he wept. "Not mages. They weren't mages! They were just…they were just facts. They were only numbers and figures, and Kippler told me…and he said…and then I solved the equation for him. But they weren't mages then, I swear it. I didn't know. I didn't."

I covered my mouth with my hand, trying to cage in my anger, my grief. Stars, if I didn't know what it was to be so broken, broken down, broken apart, and all the cracks filled in with lies. Over and over again I relived that terrible scene on the dais in Avnaya Square, lifting the gun, pointing it at Tarik, firing, all the while believing he was the enemy, believing I was doing the right thing. Kippler had done that to me. Twisted my world into a nest of lies. What had he done to Aroden? What had he made him believe?

But even that thought couldn't ease the horror raging through my mind. What Aroden believed didn't change the fact that he'd slaughtered all of those innocents, just like my belief didn't change the fact that I'd tried to kill Tarik.

"Please," Aroden said.

He didn't say anything else, but I knew all the things he was asking with that one word—*don't hate me, don't turn on me, don't drive me away. Believe me.*

*Save me.*

Then he stepped away from me, and vanished into the brightness of the winter sunlight.

# Chapter 13 ～ Hayli

FOR WHAT FELT LIKE HOURS I STOOD AT THE PLACE WHERE, MOMENTS AGO, Aroden had been, my mind too baffled to even begin to know what to think. I didn't want to forgive Aroden but my heart ached for him, for his torment, for the guilt and shame of what he'd done—I understood all of it only too well.

With a sigh I shoved my hands in my pockets and picked my way over the puddles and icy patches, heading toward the east guardhouse near the depot gate, where Coins had told me I'd find Bridnow.

But I found Aothir first. I didn't know it was him straight away—I saw naught but a dark shape hunched against the guardhouse wall, close to the ground. When I got closer I recognized Aothir's fair hair and bare, tattooed arms, and I let out all my breath in a sigh of relief.

I stopped across from him, but even though I wasn't trying to be quiet, he never moved to acknowledge me. He had his head leaned back against the wall and his eyes were closed, his brow creased with concentration or worry. I wished vainly that I had Pika's gift, because I was sore to know what he was seeing with his mind's eye.

"I know why you're here," he said suddenly, making me jump. He still didn't open his eyes. "Shade...he's alive. For now."

I slumped down against the wall beside him, drawing a shaky breath. "What happened to him?"

He held up a hand to quiet me. For near five minutes he sat perfectly still, and I sat perfectly still next to him, while the snow seeped through my pant legs and numbed my skin until it ached.

"No one knows," he said then. "There are rumors, though… Rigvar says he's gone mad."

"Who is Rigvar?"

Aothir slitted his eyes open and looked at me sideways. "Shade's opponent for the title of Godar."

*Shade's fighting for Istia's crown?* I thought, startled. I knew he'd gone to Istia to salvage the alliance with Cavnal, and I knew he was the former Godar's son, but somehow I'd never believed he would actually attempt to claim rulership there.

*He's not supposed to rule Istia. He's supposed to rule Cavnal.*

*You still believe he wants anything to do with Cavnal?* the bitter voice in the back of my mind whispered.

*He's got no claim to rule Cavnal,* Piper said, sharp. *Maybe he thinks that ruling Istia is the next best way to keep the alliance alive.*

I grumbled mentally, then whispered, *Do you think it's true? Do you think he's gone mad?*

But Piper refused to answer me. I could almost see her in my mind, tucking her beak behind her wing, doing her best to ignore me.

"That dan' explain how Shade almost died though," I said.

"No," Aothir said, and sighed. "It doesn't."

He leaned forward and rubbed his hands over his face. I hadn't noticed before but he looked dead weary, with dark rings beneath his eyes and a strange drawn look to his mouth. All his movements were listless, too, with none of their usual intensity. He wasn't even making an effort to mock me, and that alone said a lot.

"Are you a'right? You look grobbing horrid," I said.

He lifted a shoulder in answer.

"You're a Knack," I said. "You never told us that."

"Was I supposed to?" he asked, a bit acidly. "My gifts are my own."

"We're supposed to trust each other," I said. "Hard to do when someone doesn't spill the fact they're a bloody *mind-reader.*"

"It's not like that, quite so precisely," he said. "Thane and I have a different connection than most mind-readers. He can see through my eyes. I can see through his. I don't have that connection with anyone else. And it's not my strongest power, either, so using it is never easy."

I glared at him, trying to figure out why I felt so overwhelmingly angry. It hit me all at once, and my hands curled into tight knots.

"How long have you known?" I asked.

He startled at the venom in my voice. "Known what?"

"That Shade was alive. Anything. Whatever. How long have you known about him and what he was doing in Istia?"

"A...day? A day and a half? Thane spoke to him just yesterday. *Veka*, I'm not trying to hide anything from you. I honestly know only what Thane knows."

"And when Thane was talking to him? Was he a'right then?"

"Pale," Aothir said, carefully. "Very pale. He looked tired. But he spoke fair enough. Then Thane shared some of what's been going on here, and that alarmed him somewhat, naturally."

"You've been sharing with him," I said. "With Thane."

"Naturally," he said again.

"Are you an Istian spy, Aothir, or are you honestly on our side?"

"I'm on the side of mages," he snapped. "Brinmark is my home. Istia is my homeland. Do you understand?"

"No," I said. "You never explained why you're here in Cavnal."

"I was born here," he said. "I'm only half-Istian, like Shade."

"But you said—"

"I said Istia is my homeland." He shrugged. "It's what it is."

I got to my feet and dusted my pants off. "I still dan' understand, but I'll let you have your reasons. Dan' ever hold out information about Shade again, though, d'you hear? If you hear aught at all I should know about, *aught at all*, you tell me."

He held my gaze, steady, intense, as he said, "Yes, ma'am."

And for the first time, I didn't feel that he was mocking me.

I left Aothir and headed into the guardhouse, where I found Bridnow still talking with Derrin in the main room. Bridnow was leaning over the table when I walked in, pointing at something on a map that showed the whole world, while Derrin stood beside him, arms folded, looking thoughtful. When he saw me, Bridnow straightened up and favored me with a welcoming smile.

"Ah, you're back," he said.

"Where've you been?" I asked, before I could check myself. "I looked everywhere for you. Swear I even looked in here."

He exchanged a glance with Derrin, then gestured to the map. "Derrin Ghosted me out to meet with Krigs in his bivouac. I'm sorry I didn't leave a note. Did you find out anything about Kor?"

I shook my head. "I talked to his sweetheart, but she div'n na

 432

where he'd lammed off to, either."

"Kor has a sweetheart?" Derrin asked, incredulous.

"I know," I said. "But yeah. She just said he meant to gan home for a bit. I figure that means Tulay, and maybes he and the Queen both skipped out together."

Derrin rubbed a hand over his face. "Tulay, of course. No wonder I've not been able to Ghost to him."

"I was ganna ask if you'd tried that. But why's it matter that he's in Tulay? You know him, right? Can't you just Ghost to where he is?"

"Ah," he said, with a funny kind of smile. "Not so easily. Some places in the world still have wardings. Places that have a longer and closer history with magic. The Grand Duke's Palace in Tulay is one of those places—it's warded against all use of magic."

"Even Blood magic?" I asked, frowning. "Seems that'd be a useful one to keep about."

"Especially Blood magic," Derrin said. "Or didn't you ever realize that someone who knows how to heal is equally capable of knowing how to kill? What better assassin than a Blood mage?"

I scowled, and rubbed my thumb over the palm of my left hand.

"Anyway," Derrin said, "it just means that I can't get to Kor right now, until he moves away from wherever he is. And…" He studied the table, briefly. "I'm sorry, Hayli. But wherever Shade is, I can't Ghost to him, either. I tried."

I looked at him, startled, but he just gave me an apologetic smile. "Thank you," I said softly. "I appreciate you trying, honest."

He nodded and bent his attention back to the map. I watched him surreptitiously, my memories drifting back to the days when I'd been held prisoner by Kippler, when Derrin had been under the scientists' thumb much as me and Aroden had been. He'd called himself Samrick, and had helped Kippler torment me, and break down my reality. Aroden…Aroden had said something about my brother. Was it possible? What if Derrin was truly my brother, and I'd never even realized it? And if he was…did he know who I was?

"How are things in the complex?" Bridnow asked me, shaking me out of my troubled thoughts.

"How d'you mean?" I asked blankly.

"With Aroden being given liberties. How are the folks taking it?"

I shrugged, suddenly nervous. If Bridnow started asking me about

Aroden…would I have to tell him what Aroden had told me? He would never let Aroden stay if he knew the truth about the slaughtered mages, but somehow I knew that Aroden was less of a threat here within these walls than he would be if we turned him away.

"Some folks dan' seem to care. Some are a bit fitsy about it," I said, trying to sound neutral.

"And what do you think?" he asked.

"About Aroden?"

"About the mood in the complex. Should we be concerned about the people who are complaining?"

I frowned. I hadn't said aught about folks complaining, but Bridnow was watching me with a curious, closed look, like he knew something I didn't. Like he knew I'd drawn an answer for him out of thin air, and we both knew it.

"I div'n know anybody was complaining," I admitted.

Bridnow sat down on the edge of the table, moving the map out of his way. I glanced down at it as he did, my gaze snagging on the little island nation to the northeast of Cavnal, much too far away.

"Here's the thing, Hayli. Word's gotten out that, not only did Aroden make the mistake of wearing the Crown Prince's face, but he actually believes that he *is*, in fact, the Crown Prince."

"But Aroden is a mage, and most people still think Tarik isn't."

"Except the people here," he said, "who'd already accepted the notion that Tarik and Shade were the same person. See where this gets complicated? They already were willing to believe the Prince might be a mage, and now, here is Aroden claiming that the revolutionary who was leading the uprising in Brinmark wasn't the true Prince, but someone with chaotic motives who is a threat to the true heir to the Cavnish throne. Most of the people here aren't anarchists. That's why they're here and not trailing the Cleavers. They wanted to work with the monarchy. They want a monarchy to work with."

"You mean…some folks here actually believe Aroden?" I asked, the thought turning sickly in my stomach.

"He can be quite charismatic," Derrin said quietly. "I told you I remembered him from my time here at Borokhev. He would tell me stories of his childhood. Stories only someone could know about themselves."

"Do *you* believe him?"

He lifted one shoulder in a weary shrug. "I don't know."

I swallowed hard. Aroden had told me those stories, too, in a desperate effort to convince me that he was who he claimed to be.

Remembering something else Aroden had said, I asked Derrin, "When…when you were in the Ministry before, and Aroden was too… was there ever anybody else? I mean, did Kippler ever bring in someone else to talk to Aroden?"

"Besides Vrey?" Derrin shook his head. "Not that I recall."

I frowned, tucking that puzzling information away to consider later on, when I had half a moment's quiet to think.

"You're getting sidetracked," Bridnow said, stern. "What you think about Aroden is immaterial. I want to know what you plan to do about the people who want to see him gone."

I avoided his gaze. Derrin stared fixedly at the map.

"Well, I think…" I stammered, racking my mind for something useful to say. "I guess, as long as folks are disagreeing civilly, they can believe what they want."

"This isn't like they're disagreeing on whether Darbissey is a finer city than Brinmark, or what wine goes best with broiled duck!"

"Are *you* concerned?" I asked, eyes widening at his outburst.

Bridnow laughed and rubbed a hand over his face. "Yes, I'm concerned," he said. "I want a King on the throne of Cavnal, but I certainly don't want the *wrong* one on it. What do you think is going to happen when Tarik comes back?"

"He'll…convince them that Aroden was misguided?"

"How?"

My mouth opened, then closed again, speechless. How, indeed? What proof did either of them have but their own word? Somehow— impossibly—they shared the same memories, the same face, the same personality that could sway a whole crowd if they put their mind to it.

"Maybe…maybe we should do what Shade said, when he was up there on the dais," I said, my voice a bare whisper. "When he told Von to shoot him with a Chernayi gun."

Derrin's look of horror was enough to make me want to disappear through the floorboards. "You want to rob them of their magic?"

"Both of them," I said. "Reveal the real face underneath."

"You can't be serious! The two most powerful mages in the world and you want to just flip a switch and…*break* them? To prove a point?"

"I dan' na," I muttered, but Bridnow cut over me—

"The two most dangerous mages in the world."

We both turned and looked at him. "Cavnal doesn't need a mage on her throne, she needs her King," he said. "These two...they defy what is supposed to be possible for magic to achieve. Maybe...I'm not convinced of this myself, yet, but maybe the world would be safer without that much power in the hands of two..."

"Madmen," Derrin supplied, almost under his breath.

Bridnow pursed his lips as he and Derrin exchanged a glance, and neither of them would look at me. I was boiling with anger, my hands clenched in fists, but I was angriest at myself because there was a little part of me that knew they were right.

All three of us jumped in surprise when Shiver suddenly stepped out of the wall behind me, bringing a draft of cold air with him as if he'd left a window open.

"Would you please learn to use a door?" Derrin snapped, which just earned him a glare from Shiver.

"You're one to talk," he said, then turned to Bridnow. "Apologies for the interruption," he said, and looked at me. "There's something going on you need to see."

Bridnow dismissed me with a nod, and I took the normal human way out of the guardhouse as Shiver stepped back through the wall. He met me outside but didn't pause to wait for me.

"What's gannin' on?" I asked, jogging to catch up to him.

"It's bad. Rivano...Rivano's questioning Aroden."

The way he said it made all the hairs on the back of my neck stand up, and a chill of fear spidered down my spine. There was no way he just meant they were having a chat, and I suddenly got a sick, twisty feeling in my stomach as I tried to imagine what was happening.

"Where?" I asked.

We were both in a full-out run now, slipping across icy patches of pavement and splashing through puddles.

"Dormitory basement," Shiver said. "You wanna see or did you wanna go the hard way and interrupt?"

We'd reached the dormitory, and Shiver stopped near the wall, not the door, holding his hand toward me. I hesitated—I wanted to stop Rivano quick as possible, but Piper's nosy-beak curiosity was in the back of my mind, wanting to spy and see for myself what was happening before my presence made it stop. Finally I gritted my teeth and took Shiver's hand, and he pulled me with him into the walls.

I held my breath for about ten seconds before I remembered I could breathe, but I still did it cautiously, trying to keep it steady so Shiver wouldn't hear how nervous I was. Little by little I caught a drift of voices, and little by little they came louder and clearer until I could hear every word being said. Shiver stopped then, and I felt like we both had our ears pressed against the barrier between Shiver's world and the real one.

"I told you," Aroden was saying. "I don't *know* you."

"Are you sure? You've never seen me before?"

I could hear a low sound of footsteps, pacing back and forth.

"How is he keeping Aroden there?" I whispered to Shiver. "Aroden...he can unlock handcuffs with his *mind*. He can Ghost. Why isn't he getting away from Rivano?"

"Dan' na," Shiver hissed.

"What do you want with me?" Aroden asked, then there was a strangled cry of pain, hoarse and shuddering.

I jumped, and almost fell through the wall—and would have, if Shiver hadn't stopped me.

"I just need some answers," Rivano said. "Why are you being problematic? If you didn't fight me I wouldn't have to fight you back. What was Kippler planning?"

"Kippler!" Aroden spat. "He's not the one you need to worry about any more."

"Farrady?" Silence. "Then who? Shade?"

"You never knew what you were dealing with, with Shade," Aroden spat. "But no, he's not the one I meant."

"I'm losing my patience."

"Wait, wait, please. Don't. Not any more—" The words were cut off in another agonized cry.

I hissed and Shiver tightened his grip on my arm. "Stars, lemme gan... What is Rivano doing to him?"

"Alokin!" Aroden cried suddenly, the name falling at the end of his scream, thick and shaking. "Destri Alokin."

"Alokin is gone, from what I understand."

"Yes, and he took the blueprints with him."

"What blueprints? The Hunter? The EMS device?"

Aroden laughed, a cold, hollow, bitter laugh. "Those were toys compared to the project he finished since. You can thank your so-called Zealot for that. It targets magic. Latches onto it like a magnet."

"And you know about this how?"

"Because they told me about it," he said, his voice tight with pain and irony. "As if the threat of it would be enough to control me. They made it for me, you know."

"Why would Meritac, or Cromis, or anyone besides Dr. Kippler and Miss Farrady care about a weapon whose sole purpose was to destroy *you?*"

"Because Alokin changed his design!" His voice pitched up. "I saw it...I saw what he did. Don't ask—I wanted to destroy it before he used it, but I couldn't reach him. He was already gone. I only saw the designs he left in his laboratory. You think it'll just destroy me but it won't. It will cause a devastation you've never even dreamed of. It will bring us utterly to ruin."

There was a tense silence, then Rivano said, "One of you has the power to reshape the world," he said. "You've done a marvelous job in a few short days of throwing everyone's convictions into confusion—mine included. Are you Tarik, or are you Aroden?"

"You don't even know," Aroden laughed. "I remember you now. I do. You were there at the beginning."

"The beginning," Rivano echoed, mocking. "You remember nothing of what happened before?"

"I only remember my life."

"Tarik's life."

"That's what I mean."

"I don't know if you're a madman, the world's most brazen thief, or a pathetic victim," Rivano said. There was a thoughtful silence, then he said, softer, "And nor, I think, do you."

"I don't know," Aroden said. "I know I don't know. I know I know. Please don't hurt me again. I'm just trying to help. You don't understand. You don't understand...Shade. You don't know what he's capable of. You think you know what you're dealing with, but he will destroy you, and he won't even feel sorry for it. He's been under the thumb of powers far greater than yours for a long time now, Rivano."

"And you haven't?"

"I don't know...I don't know what you're ta—*aghh!*"

"That's it," I hissed. "Get me out of this wall, Shiver. Put me in the hallway outside that room."

Shiver moved without complaint, guiding me a few steps to the side before stepping through the wall. I stumbled when my feet hit solid concrete, then I straightened up, gritted my teeth, and marched up to the room where I could still hear Aroden's scream.

I threw open the door, and stared in horror. Rivano stood in the middle of the room, frowning faintly at the figure curled up against the wall. My heart wrenched. Aroden was doubled over his knees—or not Aroden, but *Tarik*. That was Tarik's face, Tarik's hair, Tarik's body. His hands were rigid in the air on either side of his head, but that made it only too easy to see the leather crown circling his skull, and the wires that dragged across the floor to the wooden box that sat on the desk beside Rivano.

"Rivano!" I shouted.

He jumped and spun to face me, his face turning a perfect shade of white. I just wished I knew if it was fear or anger that I was facing.

"What in Wake's name are you doing to him?" I cried.

I stormed past him and jerked the wires out of the box, flinching as a faint electrical charge stung my fingers. Without waiting for Rivano to make up an answer, I dropped to my knees beside Aroden and tugged the leather crown off his head. There was a faint trickle of blood trailing from his ears and nose, and even when I released him from the device, he just sagged over his knees. I left him there to recover and jumped back to my feet.

"You were torturing him," I growled. "He is under my protection. How *dare* you raise a hand against him?"

"My," Rivano said, his shock fading into a look of mild annoyance. "You've certainly become quite confident in the last few weeks. I'm impressed. Kantian never realized what a treasure he had in you."

"Stop dodging the question."

"That mage you're protecting is not who you think he is," Rivano said. He frowned, and for a moment he looked dead baffled, like a man waking up from sleep-walking.

"Where did you get that thing?" I asked, pointing at the box.

"It was here," he said, still vague. "It was Kippler's. I...I'd heard that this therapy could be useful in unlocking the minds of lunatics. I thought I would see if it would be of use here."

"You thought…" I started, and failed. It was so far beyond belief that, for half a minute, I couldn't think of a single coherent thing to say to him. Then I flung my hand toward the box again and said, "Whatever that *thing* has been used for, you have no idea what you're doing with it. Even if it did help some folks, look at him! Look at what you've done! That ain't…that ain't therapy, Rivano! You can't just grab a scalpel and forceps and think that, since doctors use them to cure people, you can cut someone's heart out to make them better!"

Rivano pursed his lips, and his gaze drifted past me. I guessed Shiver was standing in the doorway behind me, but at least he was keeping his peace. I didn't need him distracting me, not this time.

After a minute Rivano sighed and lifted his hands, then sat against the edge of the desk. "I'm sorry, I truly am," he said, and his voice was thick with an earnest plea. "I had no intention of going behind your back, and I honestly had no intention of causing undue harm. But I warn you, don't be too quick to judge that creature sitting over there. You have no idea who he is or what he's capable of."

"And you do?"

"I know more than you do," he said, then nodded toward Aroden. "And more than he does, apparently. My only hope is that Shade comes back before this situation spirals any more out of control."

He pushed past me and then Shiver, stalking out into the corridor without another word. I ran back to Aroden.

"Shiver, give a hand," I said.

Shiver came at once, and between the two of us we managed to lift Aroden into the wooden chair that sat behind the desk. He shuddered, and a minute and he reached up to wipe the blood from his nose.

"Hayli, thank God," he whispered. He glanced up at Shiver and clasped his arm, then took my hand and held it much too long. "Thank you, both of you. I don't know…how much more of that…"

"Hush," I said. "I can't *believe* Rivano would do something like that to you. To anyone! That's not like Rivano at all."

"Don't ever try using that thing," he said with a wobbly smile, nodding at the device on the desk. "Hurts like hell."

I ground my teeth and slouched against the desk, arms crossed. I was so skundered at Rivano I didn't even have the heart to ask Aroden to change his face back.

"What'd he want with you?" I asked after a moment, so he wouldn't guess that we'd been eavesdropping on the interrogation.

"He wanted to know about Shade, what I know about Shade. I'm terrified, Hayli. I'm terrified of what Rivano means to do with him, if he can get him under his influence. Rivano doesn't know what he's dealing with, and the most frightening thing about it is that the mad god could use Rivano's ignorance to wreak ruin on the world."

"Shade...Shade dan' want to wreak ruin on the world," I said, feebly. "He wants to stop the war."

"Does he?" Aroden asked. "Really? What do you think he will do once he wins the *aydrding* of Istia? Will he stop there? He could make a claim for the Grand Duchy of Tulay, you know, and if he comes back here and presents himself to the Court, do you think he would hesitate to receive the crown of Cavnal? That would be three of the most powerful nations under his domination, and do you think the rest of the world would stand a chance against him?"

"He dan' want that much power," I said. "He never has. He dan' wanna be King or Godar."

"Then why is he pursuing the *aydrding* of Istia, when he was never meant to? When he doesn't need to?"

"Maybe the situation there made him rethink his plan," I said. "Maybe he reckoned it was the only way."

"Really," he said, bland. "And you think having *him* in power will make Istia roll over and show its belly to the Accord? Will he ever agree to a treaty that would circumscribe his own power?"

"But if Cavnal stands with Istia...surely Meritac and Cromis will see it ain't worth a fight! They'd have no chance of winning!"

"Alokin's weapon might be enough to tip the balance in their favor," Aroden said softly. "And the way things currently stand, Cavnal isn't likely to ally with Istia, is she?"

"*Stars,*" Shiver said, speaking for the first time in ages. I'd almost forgotten he was there, hovering ghostly in the background.

"And what does Rivano have to do with all this?"

"Rivano wants to remake the world," Aroden said, holding my gaze. "And he wants Shade to do it for him."

# Chapter 14 ～ Tarik

"*STODADRAKKEYN GANTHISKUR DRAKK!*"

That was Nika's voice, shouting somewhere above me. Her hands on my shoulders. When I opened my eyes I found her bending over me, her face streaked with tears, eyes blazing with anger or relief or fear.

"What, Nika," I said. My lips were numb, and the words came out mumbling, but I forced a lopsided smile. "Were you worried about me?"

"*Veka,*" she said. She pounded a fist against my shoulder, though not hard. I winced a little anyway, just to rib her, then laughed when she lifted her hand as if she had half a mind to slap me too. "Taumir, how could you do that to us? We thought you were dead. Mirin's in despair over there and Iskari…"

I sobered at that, and tried to roll over and face her. My body felt strangely heavy but I was more light-headed than ever, and for a few long moments I just rested on my elbow and tried to gather my thoughts and my fragile breath.

"What happened?" I asked.

"I don't know," she said. She dropped onto the couch beside me, shoving my legs out of her way unceremoniously. "Mirin said you just…" Her face grew very still, and very pale. "When you were talking to him, he said you were shaking. Burning up, like a fever. Then you just…stopped. Like you had just decided not to fight any more."

I lifted a hand to cover my eyes; the light coming in from the windows was almost painfully bright. A streetlamp, I realized, hanging just outside Eyid's house, though the light it shed felt as sharp and white as if it were fueled by magic, and not by whale oil. It was after dark, then, and the day had escaped me. Had I been unconscious for that long?

"It's night," I said.

"Not quite," she said. "But the sun is down." She tipped her head to look at me, then, plucked at the blood-soaked front of my shirt. "I don't understand this," she said. "What's happening to you?"

She said it quietly, on a musing note—a question for the air, as if she didn't expect me to answer. I was glad of it, because I had none to give her. I clawed my way to a sitting position, pressing a hand against my chest where my skin still felt hot, where it still felt like I had a hundred tiny knives carving lacerations between my ribs.

"I need a new shirt," I muttered.

She gave a faint laugh and nodded. "Mirin!" she called. "Get in here!"

She said it in Istian, but her meaning must have been plain enough to Mirin, because the Cavner appeared immediately in the doorway of the sitting room.

"Nika," I hissed under my breath.

She patted me on the shoulder and got to her feet. "I'll find you a shirt."

"Not…one of Eyid's. Please," I said.

She studied me a moment longer, then left without a word, shouldering her way past Mirin who still stood frozen in the doorway.

"Oh…*stars*," he said when she'd gone. Both his hands were around his head, tearing at his hair. "Your Majesty…you're…you're *alive*."

He looked caught between wanting to run to me and wanting to faint, his knees wobbling unsteadily, face contorted with grief. Deciding that having him dote on me would be easier to cope with than having him pass out in front of me, I lifted a hand and beckoned him forward. He came at once, stumbling at a half-run, and threw himself at my feet with his forehead touching the tops of my boots.

I grimaced. As Crown Prince I'd never had to deal with supplicants; I'd never had to share Trabin's responsibilities of riding out into the boroughs and villages to meet with the common folk and receive their homage. Cavners had never been very fond of the abject obeisance some cultures showed their monarchs, especially among the *katzpotivyek* and the nobility who lived in Brinmark, but even so, the commoners were always rather more excessive in their show of honor than they needed to be by the rules of etiquette.

Seeing Mirin bowed so low before me made me strangely uncomfortable, but I knew that rebuking him for it would do no good. Knowing my luck, it would probably just make the situation worse. After a minute of sitting frozen with him weeping at my feet, I swallowed my discomfort and laid my hand on top of his head. I couldn't say a word.

"I thought you were lost to death," Mirin said, picking himself up to clasp my hand and kiss it reverently.

I shuddered, as much from the kiss as from his words, and looked away. "I'm fine," I said, "for now."

"For now?" he echoed.

"Do any of us know the time appointed for us to die?" I asked quietly.

"It isn't your time, yet," Mirin said, the words fierce. "You have to get back to Cavnal. Receive your coronation. Lead us out of this hell!"

I pulled my hand free of his grasp and got unsteadily to my feet. Mirin sat back on his heels and watched me, hawklike, as I moved to the window. The only rational thought I could conjure and hold onto was the desperate hope that Nika would return soon, or Iskari. Someone to distract Mirin from his all-consuming absorption with my well-being.

I leaned my forehead against the cool glass of the window and looked out at the night-dark street, with its inky pools of amber light that felt much dimmer now than the white-sharp light I'd seen before. Presently I saw Nika and Iskari's familiar figures coming up the street toward the house, Nika with her arms full of cloth that I suspected was not just a new shirt, but possibly an entire set of new clothes. The Blood, Halvir, was trailing some ten paces behind them, his face white and drawn with fear. I sat down on the window ledge when they reached the house, and waited for them to come into the room.

Nika took one look at Mirin, still crouched beside the couch, then met my gaze with a shake of her head, resignation mixed with pity.

"Here," she said, and held the clothes out toward me. "Enjoy. Don't bloody these ones up, all right? It cost me five *fenniks* to get them."

As soon as I took the pile from her, she turned and prodded Mirin with the toe of her boot and jerked her head toward the hallway. He got up obediently and scuttled from the room with Nika stalking out on his heels, leaving Iskari and Halvir with me.

"I don't need help," I said as Iskari came toward me. Then I looked straight at Halvir, smiling a little when he jerked his head aside. "Halvir, wasn't it? Is there still something wrong with my eyes?"

He glanced back, cautiously, and studied me. "No, *avlaskayd*. Not any more."

"But you still won't come near me."

Iskari was standing beside me, trying to wrestle the blood-soaked shirt over my head. Being helped with my clothes brought back a stabbing ache of nostalgia, as I remembered Liman's endless fussing over me every morning and evening. Idly I wondered what had become of him. I wondered what had become of all of them, in the vacuum that was left by Trabin's death and my disappearance. Perhaps my mother was holding the reins in my absence, and keeping the wheels of government firmly in the ruts. I could only hope, but what Thane had told me made me doubt.

Iskari finally got the soiled shirt off my shoulders, but before he gave me the new one, he snapped his fingers at Halvir.

"I don't care what you say you feel, come here and help me," he growled.

Halvir ducked his head and came forward. I saw now that he wasn't an old man but roughly middle-aged, with sparse blond-and-grey hair and a beard that didn't quite know which way it wanted to grow. His face was calm enough, given what Iskari was asking of him, but he had none of Doc's careful, ever-thoughtful movements.

"What am I supposed to do?" Halvir said, stopping right in front of me, but nothing could mask the fear that lingered behind his eyes.

"See if he's all right."

Halvir shot a sideways glance at Iskari and pressed his lips in a thin line, then gestured to me. "Please, *avlaskayd*, sit down."

I moved back to the couch and sat, holding my arms a little away from my sides so he could examine me. He frowned at me under lowered brows, then, very gently, placed his hands on my torso, one in the front over my heart, one directly opposite on my back. His breath escaped in a hiss and his hands jumped, ever so slightly, when they touched my skin, but to his credit he didn't back away, just closed his eyes and focused. I could feel the fingers of his magic probing through my veins, cold and sharp, almost painful. The magic seeped from my heart all the way to the tips of my toes and to the base of my skull, but when he tried to push farther than that, a stabbing, shearing pain tore through me and we both cried out.

Iskari glared at Halvir as he steadied me. "What did you *do* to him? I brought you here to heal him, not to hurt him more!"

Halvir was kneeling beside the couch, his hands cradled against his chest like he'd been burned. "I told you once, Agnirson, I can't *heal* that!" he shouted. "I don't know what's wrong with him. Nothing's wrong with him. *Everything* is wrong with him. But whatever's wrong with him, my magic can't touch it. Do you hear me? I *can't* do anything for him." He turned to look at me, horror and fear now stark in his eyes. "*Avlaskayd,*" he whispered. "What…what are you?"

I held his gaze, and felt a cold, harsh smile tugging at my lips. I said, "I am the sea."

He stumbled a step back from me and staggered to his feet, then, shaking his head, he turned and fled without another word.

"What does that mean?" Iskari asked. "That meant something to him, didn't it? What?"

"I don't know what it meant to him," I said, wearily. "I don't know what it means to me either, but it's always in my thoughts."

Iskari's jaw tightened but he just helped me pull the clean black shirt over my head, and change into a pair of black woolen trousers that were two sizes too large for me at least. Iskari handed me a woven belt, and I grimaced when I looked down at myself.

"Black, really?" I asked.

"Bloodstains won't show up as easily," Iskari said, with a forced smile and a careless shrug.

As I pulled my boots back on, I said, "Halvir kept calling me *avlaskayd*. I've never heard that word before. What does it mean?"

Iskari sat down on the couch beside me. "I don't know how to translate it into anything you'd understand," he said. "But it is the title of honor we give to the Godar."

I made a sharp noise of displeasure and leaned back against the couch cushions. "First Mirin calling me *Your Majesty*, now Halvir calling me this. God, I wish they would just stop."

"Do you think you don't deserve those titles?"

"I know I don't," I snapped. "I'm not the King, and I'm not the Godar. Not yet. And…don't you see what choice I have to make? I can't be both. I *can't*. But either way I choose, people will suffer, and I'm fairly sure that war will break out in either case. I can't win. And why…"

I let the silence swallow the words I meant to say, and shook my head.

Iskari said softly, "Why should it be you?" I nodded, and he got to his feet. "Because, Taumir, there is no one else." Halfway to the door he glanced back and said, "I'm going to fetch you some food. Don't die while I'm gone."

I flicked him an obscene gesture, which made him laugh, and then wandered back to the window to watch as he strode off in the direction of the lodging house, disappearing quickly into the deep shadows of the narrow side street. I wondered where Mirin and Nika had gone; I'd not seen or heard any sign of them since Nika had ushered Mirin out of the room.

Taking a deep breath, I turned to face the center of the room, and closed my eyes.

# Chapter 15 ～ Hayli

"D'YOU THINK ARODEN WAS TELLING THE TRUTH?" COINS ASKED. He was sitting up on the long table in the Rookery next to Griff, while me and Derrin sat in the chairs and Shiver leaned against the wall by the hearth. It was quiet, late at night when everyone else had either gone to bed or was out on a watch. Even Bridnow was—miraculously—asleep.

"I don't know if Aroden was telling the truth," I said. "I don't know if Aroden *knows* what the truth is. I think he was telling us what he believed the truth is, but who knows what that is?"

"I've always had my reservations about Rivano," Derrin said softly, "from the first day he showed up here in Brinmark and started his Clan. Just...never felt quite right."

"But you were one of his best mages," I said, and jerked my chin at Shiver. "Both of you. How could you follow him if you div'n think he was fair and proper?"

"It was exciting at first," Shiver said, quietly. "Being part of something arcane like that. But Derrin's right—Rivano's got secrets. Rivano's secrets've got secrets. I dan' na if I believe every word Aroden said quite so precisely, but...he makes a good point."

"Which is..." Griff prompted.

"Shade div'n have to go after Eyid's title," Shiver said. "He div'n have to look to rule Istia. So why is he?"

I chewed on the inside of my cheek, willing away the suspicion with all my power. I didn't want Shiver to be right. I didn't want to doubt what Shade was doing.

Derrin sighed and leaned back in his chair, hooking one ankle over the other. "I want us to keep an eye on both of them. Aroden, and Rivano. And when Shade comes back, well, we'll keep an eye on him too for good measure. I'm a mage too, but even I don't pretend to understand what's going on here. Here's what I do understand—war. If there's anything we can do to... Oh, what am I even saying," he said, and dropped his hand on his thigh in a gesture of defeat. "We're a couple hundred scarecrows banished outside one city in Cavnal. What do we imagine we can do anyway, except keep ourselves safe?"

"Day by day," I said, and got to my feet. "There's naught else to do but keep going."

Everyone stood up as I did, and drifted off to their respective beds. I picked up my coat off the table and balled it in my arms, waiting for Derrin to join me before I headed down the hall.

"I feel like I dan' na who to trust any more," I muttered. "Too many secrets, Derrin. Everybody's got too many secrets."

"I know." He clasped my arm and gave me a thin smile. "But don't worry about it any more tonight. There'll be time enough for worry tomorrow."

I watched him disappear down the hall, then, with a small sigh, I turned to go into my room. But not one step through the doorway I drew up short, and dropped my bundled-up coat on the ground at my feet, because there, sitting on my cot in a wash of pale moonlight with a bloody handkerchief pressed to his nose, was Shade.

"Oh, God," I whispered.

He tipped his head back, and I drew a step away. I couldn't process the sight of him sitting there, now, without warning, with that wild look about him—laughter on his lips and terror haunting the depths of his sea-storm eyes. Dressed all in black, his body melted into the shadows, making it look eerily like he wasn't entirely there.

"Shade...is that you?"

It was the only thing I could think to say. I had to know if it was Tarik, *my* Tarik, or if it was the mage who only looked like him—even if Aroden had never once tried to take on Shade's face. More than anything in the world I wanted it to be Tarik, but my Tarik wasn't a Ghost. Aroden was.

"I...think so?" he said, pulling the cloth away from his nose.

His lips still held the echo of a laugh, traced in blood like a livid halo.

I drifted a step further into the room, suddenly and irrationally angry. "Are you *drunk?*"

"No."

I swallowed. "Are you…"

I couldn't finish the question, but somehow I thought he knew what I meant to ask, because he got a darkish look about him and the smile got a bit more dangerous, but all he said was a quiet, "No."

"Then why…"

*Then why are you laughing?*

And maybe he'd added mind-reading to his list of powers because he leaned forward, elbows on his thighs, and said, "I figured it out." When I didn't say aught at all he closed his eyes, mopping a trickle of blood from his nose. "I figured out how to Ghost."

I let out a scant breath. The way he said it was so strange, as if he'd done nothing more remarkable than work out a sum. I wanted to ask him how he'd done it—how it was possible to simply *figure out* a Gift like Ghosting—but I couldn't.

Instead I asked, "Why are you bleeding?"

"Hell, I don't know," he muttered. "Seems I can't do anything these days without…without feeling like…" He stopped abruptly, physically recoiling like he'd been slapped. "It's nothing."

I pressed a hand against my mouth, then lowered it again, slowly, as I drew a deep, steadying breath. "You're a'right. I was so worried… Oh, Wake, I've been so worried."

For some reason he flinched a little at that and turned his head aside, but then he glanced up at me and that laughter was teasing his lips again. "If you call this all right, sure," he said.

I hovered there in the doorway, torn between running for Derrin and running to Shade. But I couldn't force myself to go to him. I couldn't say why. It was *Shade*, and not a single day had gone by that I hadn't wished to see him, to beg his forgiveness, to be with him…even to rebuke him, and ask him to explain all the mysteries away. So why was it, now he was here, I only felt afraid? Maybe it was the sound of Aroden's warnings still ringing in my ears. Or maybe it was the hum of power I felt all around him like a coming thunderstorm, charging the air so that I imagined I couldn't get near him without getting hurt.

If I thought Aroden's effortless magic was terrifying, the raw power of Tarik's made all that look like naught but a child's game.

"You're really Tarik?"

A minute and he just stared at me, eyes wide. "Who else would I be?"

I bit my lip and forced myself a step closer. "Why…what are you doing here? Are you back for good? You ganna stay?"

He contemplated the red stains on his handkerchief, and shook his head.

"Then why'd you come?"

*How can you do that to me?* I wanted to add, but kept that thought to myself.

"I had to talk to you."

If he'd said he had to see me, I might've slapped him, because that was just what Aroden had said. But *talk* to me? That was different. Maybe he meant that he wanted to talk to all of us, that he needed our counsel… I glanced over my shoulder. I had half a mind to call Derrin back, but suddenly the door slammed shut in front of me, all on its own. I startled and spun back, only to see Shade staring at me with a strange cold light in his eyes. When my gaze drifted down to his extended hand, he slowly curled his fingers against his palm as if that could hide what he'd done. I swallowed, hard.

"You," he said. "Not them. I don't want them knowing I'm here." He sighed and added, "They would try to make me stay, and I can't."

I drifted a step closer to him, then another, until the static hum in the air got so strong it felt dangerous.

"Are you sure you're a'right?"

"Why?"

"It feels…jumpy around you."

"Jumpy?" he echoed, one brow lifted.

I waved a hand, wishing I could explain how everything inside me felt jittered—and not just because it was Shade, and he was here.

"The air. It feels like when…when you touch me, but it's in the air all around you."

"Really?" he asked, straightening up and looking genuinely intrigued. "Fascinating."

"It's horrible," I said.

"Why?"

"Because." I wondered if he could hear the desperation in my voice. "Because it makes me want to stay away from you."

That darkness crept back into his eyes and he bent his head, holding the bloodied cloth in a loose fist.

"I'm sorry," he said.

That wasn't at all what I'd expected him to say. I forced myself one step closer, my skin crawling with the electric charge.

"No," I said. "I've been wanting to tell you for weeks how sorry *I* am. I'm so..." I tried to draw a breath, but it caught in my throat. "Oh, stars, I'm so sorry."

"For what?"

I couldn't answer, just pressed one hand over my mouth to cage in a sob.

"Oh," he said. The life seemed to wither up inside of him, and he put his head in his hands.

I sat down gingerly on the cot next to him.

"Can you heal yourself?" I asked him, nodding toward his bleeding nose.

"What's to heal?" he muttered. "Anyway, I can't. I can't seem to find my Blood magic." He lifted his head suddenly, his sea-storm eyes lighting up in the most impossible way, with a joy and excitement that got my own heart racing. "Hayli!" he said. He looked like he had a mind to take my hand, but he just waved his own hands between us like a mime. "I almost forgot...I've been hoping for a chance to tell you. You're a *Shifter*."

"Yes...?"

"The magic you have...it's the same power as Blood magic. You could become a Blood!"

"I know! I already have," I said, so eager to tell him that I almost missed the disappointment in his eyes, and the way his shoulders slumped, all the energy fizzling out of him. I tipped my head to look at him, the blood flowing freely from his nose, and reached one hand cautiously toward his face. "Could I..."

He swiped my hand away, the pulse of power from his touch so strong I bit my tongue on a cry of pain.

"Don't," he growled. "Don't even try."

"Why...why not?"

"There's nothing your Blood magic could do for me."

He bent his head, kneading his fingers over his forehead, and wiped the handkerchief futilely over his nose again. I studied him sidelong, noting all the ways he had changed since the last time I'd seen him. His hair had grown out a bit, hanging in fair shaggy wisps around his face, and he had the faint scruff of a beard on his jaw. I knew he could Mask his face and his hair to look however he wanted, but I'd never imagined that, if he left his Mask alone, it would change over time like any normal body.

"Shade..." I said, and suddenly didn't know how to ask him what I wanted to ask. I fumbled for words, but at least he still had his face buried and couldn't see how fitsy I'd got. Finally I managed, "D'you... d'you think you could unMask?"

"Why?" he asked.

I sat back, caught off guard by the sharpness of his voice.

"Am I not good enough for you?" he added, and sighed, leaning his forehead against his palm.

Something about the whole exchange struck me as peculiar, and I'd a devil of a time trying to figure what. It just didn't make sense. Why was Shade being so odd about unMasking? A strange thought occurred to me—was Shade *jealous* of Tarik? Was that even possible? Or...did he not want to unMask because Tarik's face was just as much a lie for him as Shade's?

*I can't think that. I won't. I don't believe it.*

"Please?" I said. "Then you can change back if you like. I just need to see...*both* of you."

He shook his head against the palm of his hand. "You don't want to see Tarik right now," he said. "Trust me."

"Why not?"

"He's broken. You...you won't understand."

He tipped his head just enough that he could meet my gaze, holding it a long moment until he realized he hadn't put me off the notion at all. If anything, he'd just made me wilder than ever to see him, sure that something terrible had happened to him. Then he lifted his other hand and buried his face in both of them.

And then he unMasked. Only...only at first I didn't realize he had, not until he shifted his hands and looked at me again. My breath caught in my throat.

"*Oh*," I whispered.

Because he was definitely Tarik. The dark eyes, the fine mouth that always looked like it was hiding a secret, the line of his jaw, even the way he sat there, it was all Tarik. But...but the unkempt hair that spilled through his fingers was pale as Shade's, and his skin was pale as Shade's. And my mind couldn't make sense of what I was seeing. It was like somebody had taken all the features that made Shade, Shade, and all the features that made Tarik, and mashed them up together to make something new. He looked like a ghost of himself.

Somehow he reminded me of Doc.

I pushed past the prickling pain and shifted to kneel in front of him, taking his hands in both of mine and trying not to wince at the touch. Touching another mage always felt like a bond, a warm welcome, but this felt more like a warning, and the thought pained me even more than the static charge. He let me draw his hands away from his head. My heart fluttered in my throat at being this close to him, with the smell of smoke and cinnamon all about him, the moonlight reflecting weirdly in his eyes.

I let go of one of his hands and touched the shaggy fringe of his hair. It should be dark, the voice in my mind lamented. His hair was supposed to be dark. Dark like the midnight sea, to match his eyes.

"What happened? You look like Shade, but...not."

"I look like Tarik, but changed," he said sharply. "Shade looked Istian. I look..." He twitched his head aside and didn't finish the thought. "Hayli," he whispered. "I told you you wouldn't understand."

My heart jerked strangely, and I was just glad he was staring at my hand, still holding his, so he wouldn't see how my cheeks burned.

"What can I do?" I asked, tightening my grip on his hand. "What do you need?"

"Will this ever leave me?" he asked suddenly, pulling his hand free and tugging his fingers through his hair. "I hate it. I feel like a lie. More than I ever did."

I grimaced, Aroden's doubts rearing their heads in the corners of my thoughts.

"It looks...nice...?" I offered.

He glanced up, startled, then suddenly the pain in his eyes fractured and he laughed, and curse him, his laugh was always infectious—that impish, boyish laugh, just like when he'd tricked me in the old Troyce & Fallon and made me believe he'd got eaten by a *thayo*. I laughed with him, and before I could stop myself I threw my arms around his neck and hugged him hard as I could.

454

"You're *alive*," I whispered. "You've got no ken…weeks now we've not even known if you'd made it to Istia. I've been so afraid…What if you'd got swallowed by the sea?"

He shuddered in my arms and I loosened my grip on him, just enough that I could get a look at his face.

"What's wrong?"

"It's nothing."

"Dan' ever lie to me," I said softly. "You know I know what it's like to live with the nightmares." I cupped my hand against his cheek, forcing him to look at me. "You've been through one yourself. I can see it in your eyes."

He measured me quietly a moment, then he put a hand between us and pushed me, gently but insistently, away from him.

"Then you won't try to make me talk."

"Fair enough," I said. I pulled myself back onto the cot beside him, sitting cross-legged with my chin in my hands. "Something happened recently, though, div'n it? Aothir said…"

"Aothir?" he interrupted, looking at me sharply.

"Yeah, the Istian Flint…remember him?"

"Of course. He's a good friend."

"Well, a good friend with secrets. He ain't just a Flint. He's a Knack too. He said he knows someone—"

"Thane," he interrupted, and rubbed a hand over his head. The motion brought all his features back to Shade's—I wasn't sure if he realized he'd done it. "I wondered who his contact in Brinmark was."

"Aothir said you were dying," I said bluntly.

He froze, then very slowly he relaxed, until he was leaning his elbows on his knees. "It's not important."

"You dying is important!" I cried, and he gave me a look warning me to keep my voice down. "But it's true. We were all so worried."

"I'm sorry for that," he said, softly. "And glad I could come and ease your mind somewhat on that score. Though Iskari and Nika are going to kill me when they can't find me."

"Who…are they?" I asked, but I could guess, from what Pika had related to me about the dark-haired man and the blonde-haired girl.

"The captain of the ship I sailed to Istia—they're his children," he said. "We traveled together to Bregjarvani. I've…made them a bit anxious lately too."

455

I pursed my lips, feeling oddly irritable. "Well?" I asked. "You're here, so, what was it you wanted to talk to me about?"

"I need to know what's going on here," he said. "I've got no sources of news about Cavnal in Istia, except what little Thane was able to tell me, and that was enough to worry me. Anarchists, in Brinmark? Not my crew, is it?"

"You're not ganna like the news," I said, trying not to feel sore that that was what he wanted to talk to me about. "No, it ain't us that's gone anarchist. Red, and some mages who want to see our kind in power. Red ain't with us now."

I eyed him surreptitiously as I said it, remembering how Red had wanted to put Shade in charge of his coup, and how Aroden claimed Shade would want to take over Cavnal after he was done with Istia. But Shade made no reaction. Instead he was looking around, up at the ceiling, at the walls, at the door.

"Of course," he said, then, under his breath, "Idiots."

"They've got the Chernayi welly in their pockets, and seems like they've a mind to try to get the Army on their side, too. The Court's so trupped they're fit to fall, and Red's folks know it, too."

"God," he said. "The Chernayi *and* the Army? What is Red thinking?" It was a question he didn't want an answer to, so I just held my peace. A minute and he gestured to the room and said, "Where are we? This isn't the smelter."

"Had to clear out of the smelter. We're...we're at Borokhev."

His eyes widened, and he, hesitating, reached out to touch my cheek. It was the barest whisper of a touch, and even the static charge of his power was nothing to the way my heart jumped in response.

"Hayli," he said. "Are you doing all right?"

"Most days," I said, trembling. From the very first time I'd met him, Shade had always reminded me of a barely-tamed thunderstorm, full of wind and fury even in his quietest moments. But there was a gentleness to his voice now that I'd never heard before, and it set all my blood fluttering in my veins. "It's not always easy, though."

"I'm sure," he said. He left his fingers against my cheek a moment longer, then lowered his hand and bent his head. "I'm sorry it's come to this. I was only trying to do what Trabin asked, but it seems the harder I try to do what everyone needs, the more everything falls apart." He sat very still, his only movement the flickering of his eyes over nothing at all, and the scant rise and fall of his shoulders with his breath. "My mother…is she managing the government or have they gone mad for power without Trabin there to stop them?"

"I'm sorry," I murmured. "She's gone missing. We got no ken where she's lammed off to."

Oddly, the news didn't seem to alarm him. He just made a soft noise like a laugh and said, "And Kor?"

"Not seen him since Avnaya, either," I said. I studied him curiously. "You're not surprised?"

"No. I figured she wouldn't stay, though I hoped she would."

"Do you know where she went?"

He hesitated, then shook his head slowly. A minute and he shrugged, the pain in his eyes fading away, and he said, "I'm not surprised about Kor, either. He'll be around eventually. Or not. I imagine they've gone to Tulay." He tipped his head to study me. "What about you? I'm sorry I left such a mess for you to deal with."

"I put Bridnow in charge," I said flatly, hating to admit it, but wanting him to know the truth.

He regarded me a while in silence, then, when I was dead sure he meant to rebuke me, he just nodded and said, "Good choice."

I couldn't decide if he meant Bridnow was a good choice—which pleased me—or that it was a good choice for me to give up command—which stung a bit—but either way, I was at least happy I hadn't disappointed him.

"Shade…the Ministers want to make an alliance with Cromis and Meritac," I said.

"I know. I heard that much from Thane." He narrowed his eyes suddenly, head tipped to the side, scanning the confines of the room like he'd heard something that troubled him. "What… Is there…" he started, then shook his head faintly, dismissing whatever worry had troubled him. His hand drifted over his chest again, feeling his black shirt, then he let out his breath in a sigh and planted his hands against my thin mattress. "Anything else I need to know about?"

I hesitated much too long, my mind locked in a bitter war. Then I shook my head. "Just getting by a day at a time," I said.

He nodded. "Then I should get back. Don't want those idiots panicking again and thinking I've run off to die somewhere."

But he didn't move when he said it, and for a few ticks I just sat and

457

watched him, trying to make sense of the darkness in his eyes. Then it came to me, sharp and unexpected as a gunshot.

"You're scared," I blurted.

For endless long moments he just studied me, one faint line between his brows. Then he bowed his head and murmured, "No, Hayli. I'm terrified. I'm terrified of this darkness inside me, this craving, this...this thirst. If it came from something...from someone else...it wouldn't frighten me so much. But it's mine. Every corner and shadow of it. I hate it. I hate how much...how much I love it. How much I need it. Because I do. I need it, more than I ever needed Branigan's drug."

I could barely convince my lungs to keep breathing. Deep in my mind I heard Aroden's words over and over again, spinning a web of doubt in every shadowy place in my thoughts.

"What...darkness?" I managed.

"The long sadness," he said.

I reached out, cautious, and touched his hand. "I've heard rumors," I said, hating to admit it. "Folks saying such horrid things, like that you've...that you've gone..."

"Mad?" he guessed, his voice acid. "I've heard them too."

"Why? Why do they say that?"

His gaze was on the far side of the room—I looked that way, to see what was holding his attention, but there was naught there but a blank wall.

"Why not?" he asked.

I frowned, thinking he was answering my question, but suddenly I got the peculiar sense that he wasn't talking to me at all.

Then his breath hissed out and he waved a hand near his head, muttering, "No, no. I don't care. I *don't*...care."

"Shade?" I whispered.

He looked at me, and maybe he read some kind of fear in my face because his paled slowly, and his eyes widened with dismay.

"I'm sorry. Hayli—don't...don't pay attention to me. It's not madness, I swear it. It's bright and breaking and his promises...the things he promises..."

"Dan' do it!" I said suddenly, gripping his hand so tight he startled. "Whatever it is...it ain't worth it, d'you hear? Dan' listen to...to whoever it is."

He was looking at the wall again. In the shifting moonlight I

 458

thought—but I might have imagined it—that I saw the glimmer of tears on his lashes.

"I don't know," he murmured. I didn't know if he was talking to me at all. "I know what I have to do, but I'm so afraid…" His shoulders slumped as he finished, "I'm so afraid of what will happen if I do."

"Will you come back?" I asked quietly, hating the fact that I was even asking the question. "When you're done in Istia, d'you mean to claim your place as Trabin's heir?"

"Would it matter if I did?" he said. "Would it matter if I didn't? What good is the crown of Cavnal? I don't know what I'm saying. Don't listen to me." For a moment he didn't speak, didn't move except to trace a pattern in the palm of his hand, over and over again. "In the end Trabin was a failure, you know," he said. "Bound by the laws that he swore he stood above. He always said that justice and truth existed by his word, that right and wrong were such by his decree, but I don't think he really believed it. He certainly never acted like he did, so ultimately he never could accomplish what he intended. He couldn't stop the war. He never could have stopped the war. His hands were tied."

I swallowed. "And what about you?" I asked, dreading to hear the answer. "Are your hands tied?"

In the low light his smile was ice, terrible to see. He said, "Who could tie them?"

# Chapter 16 ~ Tarik

HAYLI WAS LOOKING AT ME LIKE SHE'D NEVER SEEN ME BEFORE. Of all the pain I could have felt—of all the pain I *did* feel in that moment—that somehow felt worse than all the rest of it put together. She had been shying away from me from the first moment she'd seen me; even when she'd touched me, I could feel what an effort it was for her; she was forcing herself with every ounce of her will to come near me.

It was not at all the reunion I had imagined.

But she was alive, she was Hayli, and she at least seemed to have overcome her fears enough to do what she needed to do, for herself, for my crew, for the people who had followed her to Borokhev. Still, it was *Borokhev*, and just sitting in that room made my skin crawl with memories. Almost against my will I remembered Andon's face, the blood blossoming from the hollow where his eye had been, the expression of surprise and dismay frozen on his face as he stared at me, sightless, down the length of a gun's barrel. My hand spasmed, and my mind skittered away from that memory and lighted on another—when, moments before that lethal encounter with Andon Vrey, I'd stood in the hallway outside Hayli's cell, face to face with myself.

*"Are you going to save me?"* the other me had asked.

At the time I'd thought it was madness, an illusion, a figment of my shattering mind.

I wasn't so certain any more. Ever since I'd seen the other mage, the impostor, on the dais in Avnaya Square, I'd wondered if it was actually the second time we'd met. He'd been *here*. I could still feel a trailing remnant of his power in the air all around me; it was what I had sensed earlier, like a remembered pain, an echo of a nightmare.

I sighed and tipped my head to look at Hayli again. She carried herself differently now, I'd noticed. Straighter, more confident, chin high and a challenge in her eyes for the world to see. She was even more beautiful than I remembered. And yet she couldn't look at me without something like fear in her eyes.

Fear, and doubt.

My heart stung at the thought, and I was just glad that, for the moment, she *wasn't* looking at me. I didn't think I'd have the strength to take my leave of her if she was looking me in the eye. More than anything in the world I wanted to take her in my arms, lean on her strength, taste the sweetness of her kiss...just once, before I lost her forever. But I couldn't; I couldn't bring myself to intrude on her doubt and brush away her hesitation, as if I didn't notice or didn't care.

So I closed my eyes and bent my head, and let myself fade away into the space beyond the physical world. For a moment I stayed where I was, having not quite decided where I meant to go. Ghosting was much like Cloaking, I'd finally realized. In the past I'd never comprehended what it meant to Cloak, but I saw now that they were sister powers, and so closely intertwined that I couldn't understand how I'd never seen it before. When I Cloaked, I was fading out of the material world and into the spiritual world, though staying, essentially, in the same place. To Ghost I needed only to fix my thought on a destination, and a few short steps would take me to it.

But the realm was the same, which I would have realized long ago if I'd learned how to see beyond the physical world, with the eyes of my soul. It was a bright and windless place, like a tunnel of glass carved between trees made of stone, with a million paths leading in a million directions, and each one as short or as long as I imagined it to be. That was where I stood now, at the crossroads of an infinite choice, but my gaze was not on my destination, but the place I had left behind. I stood motionless and watched, aching with loneliness, as Hayli looked up, and realized that I had gone.

"No," I saw her whisper, mouthing the word. Her hand stretched out, resting on the spot beside her where I'd been sitting. Her next words I could hear. "Shade, please...please dan' go."

Burying her face in her hands, she laid down on the bed and twisted away to face the wall, and I stood outside the world and watched her weep until sleep came to calm her. Then I turned, heavy at heart, and fixed my focus on the Troyce & Fallon, and the answers I hoped I would find within. In fourteen steps I made it to the hallway below the old factory where the storage room was, where I'd Cloaked to hide from Derrin that first night I'd come to the Hole, so long ago. At the end of the hall, the strange magical lights of the Clan's wing still glowed on the walls, casting the corridor in a spectral blue glow.

I stepped out of the void and into the corridor, and made my way, cautiously, toward the Clan's wing. I'd been there only once before, and then only to the common room where Derrin and Doc had confronted me about becoming a Blood; beyond that, I only knew what Shiver had told me, and what Hayli had shared, in fragments of conversations. It was in one of the deep-buried rooms in the east wing of the factory that Rivano had built the Clan's Sanctum, and that, as far as I'd ever learned, was where the *Brigaz Nedash* was kept.

There was no one else there. The whole factory underground had a cold, clammy feel like an unearthed grave, long-abandoned and forgotten, protesting the intrusion of time. I passed a number of small rooms, mostly studies and a few bed chambers, until I came to a strange double door of wood carved in arcane patterns. It was locked—I knew that before I even reached out to touch it. But the locking mechanism was on the inside of the door only, barring anyone from entering who could not magically unfasten it from the outside— or Rift the door itself.

I laid my hand on the door and tried to feel the lock, and found a series of tumblers and pins like any ordinary lock. Smiling, I bent my magic to tap each pin into place, then, when they were all lifted, I gave a slight twist of my hand and was gratified by the sound of a muffled clang as the lock released.

The door swung slowly open, and I found myself face to face with Doc.

For the space of three breaths we just stood and stared at each other. Then Doc slammed shut the book he was holding and drifted a few scant steps closer to me.

"Tarik," he said. "I thought you were in Istia. What…what are you doing here?"

I stepped past him into the room, looking around curiously. The strange bronze lighting gave the wood-paneled space an eerie kind of feel, and my skin crawled when I glimpsed a brass basin set on a marble stand in the middle of the floor, its hollow stained a red so dark it was almost black. A wooden lectern stood beside it, holding an old book with a cracked leather binding. I knew what book it was without even glimpsing the title.

"I could ask the same of you," I said, walking slowly around the periphery of the room, letting my fingers drift over the dusty shelves of the bookcases lining the walls. I stopped in front of the *Brigaz Nedash*, painfully aware of Doc's attention riveted on me. "You're not at Borokhev with the others?"

His jaw spasmed, and he took three quick steps to stand across the lectern from me. "I had to leave," he said. "It's too dangerous there, now. I couldn't risk… You didn't go, did you?"

"Yes," I said, frowning. "I had to see Hayli."

His breath slipped out in a hiss and he turned a little away from me. "That was a foolish thing to do."

"What, you believe the Istian lore about crows?" I said, bitter. "Is Hayli the reason I'm going mad? If I recall, all this started after I met her."

"Well, love is a peculiar kind of insanity, I suppose, but no, that's not what I meant." Doc lowered his gaze toward the book between us, his thin shoulders tense, hunched, like he was awaiting an attack. "Don't tell me you approve of her letting him stay there."

"Letting who stay where?" I asked, baffled.

"Aroden," he said, as if I should have known. "Did you see him, or was he staying out of sight?"

"Who is Aroden?" I shook his shoulder. "I didn't see anyone but Hayli. Who is Aroden and why should I care about him?"

"Because he's been having quite a romp playing at being the real Prince Tarik."

I staggered. "What? The mage…*that* mage…he's at Borokhev?"

"You really didn't know?" Doc's eyes widened, darkening under a look of horror and dismay. "*Oh*," he said. "Oh, no. Did she…tell you?"

I didn't know what to say. My gaze tore from his, falling on the worn Cromner titling on the cover of the book between my hands. I didn't even know what I ought to feel. I felt nothing at all but a vast and numb emptiness.

"She gave him asylum," Doc said, very quietly. "I'm sorry. I am. I tried to warn her. I tried to tell her he was dangerous, but…Aroden is very persuasive. And I think she probably felt she couldn't turn him away, not with all they'd both been through at her brother's hands."

I leaned over the lectern, my mind churning like the heart of a maelstrom. *I must be inventing this conversation,* I told myself, *because none of this can be real. It's just madness. It'll pass.*

"I'm not…making any sense of anything you're saying," I said, carefully. "Did you just say *her brother?* What the hell, Doc? Hayli doesn't have a brother."

"Well," he said, the word trailing on a note of reluctance, "not any more, she doesn't."

I tipped my head to look up at him. The realization was so obvious, so painful, and yet it sank over my mind like a weighted funeral pall. "Andon Vrey," I said, choking on the name. "Her *brother?*"

"He was away at school when their parents were executed. He went to Meritac afterwards, changed his name to avoid being caught up in the family scandal, studied under the most brilliant Meritian scientists, then decided to come back and claim what remained of his fortune and offer his services to Kippler, whose work was so closely aligned with his own—solving the mage problem that cost him his family."

I sighed and ran a hand over my forehead. "Her brother. The last living member of her family. And I shot the bastard," I said. "Did he know Hayli was his sister?"

"I have no idea," Doc said. "I only know what I just told you from what I gleaned from Luce and a few other mages at Borokhev. Luce had the most to say, naturally, since she's the one who hoped to marry him."

I lifted a hand in a gesture of defeat. After all he'd told me, I didn't even have the strength left to be surprised.

"Damn," I said at last.

"Indeed," Doc said. He leaned a little closer to me. "Did she happen to tell you about Destri?"

"Dr. Alokin? No, what about him?"

He pursed his lips in a thin line and turned aside, folding his arms over his thin chest. "He went back to Meritac, not too long ago."

"He had no real reason to stay in Cavnal, I suppose," I said, but my words didn't seem to please him.

"Listen. I don't know how to tell you this kindly, so I'm just going to tell you. Destri blames you for Zagger's death. And I have a feeling he won't disappear quietly into the night. He's scheming something. And I wouldn't be surprised if it was retribution against all of Cavnal for the death of the last surviving member of *his* family."

He spoke it bitterly, hands tightening to fists against his ribs.

"What are you saying?" I asked, frowning. "I destroyed Alokin's EMS device. I destroyed the Hunter. Do you mean…there's another weapon?"

"He told me once about a prototype he'd been developing in cooperation with Miss Farrady. I don't know if it ever amounted to anything. I always told him it was too dangerous, that the idea was too catastrophic even to put it on paper. But if he did it anyway—and it wouldn't surprise me that he did—and if he got the cursed thing to work… Tarik, if Meritac uses that weapon against Cavnal, there won't *be* a war, because there won't be a nation left to fight it."

I provided him with a stream of Istian obscenities to tell him exactly what I thought of that news. Even if he didn't understand the words, I was sure he got the gist of them. His mouth twitched.

"I know, don't argue," he said. "He's being irrational, and he knows it, but that makes no difference. He's even-tempered to a fault until something pushes him over the edge, and then his passion knows no bounds." Doc flicked a sidelong glance at me. "He won't *stop*."

"What am I supposed to do?" I asked. "I thought I understood the situation but every time I look up, it's so much worse than I imagined. I see a hundred paths laid at my feet and all of them seem to lead into ruin."

He studied me a long while in silence, as if debating some weighty matter in his mind. Then he closed his eyes briefly, and reached out to grab my hands. His were cold, almost bone thin, but they gripped mine with intense strength and wouldn't let go.

"You have to come back," he said. "Claim the crown of Cavnal. Silence the Court of Ministries and end this foolish pandering to Meritac and Cromis. Secure the alliance with Istia and Tulay and the other nations will have no choice but to back down. As far as I know Alokin only has one of those weapons, and he won't use it if he knows two other nations will retaliate as soon as the dust has settled, and reduce his homeland to a pile of rubble."

I let out my breath in a long sigh and shook my head. "I wish I could do that. I do. I would do it in a moment if I thought I could succeed. But I can't, not now. Not any more."

When he glanced back at me in surprise, I closed my eyes and, slowly, carefully, unMasked to Tarik, with my pale hair and pale skin, and every way my face was wrong. Doc made a low noise like a hiss.

"I can't go to the Court of Ministries," I said. "If I leave Shade, this is the face I'm trapped in, and do you imagine the Court would ever listen to me if I came to them looking like this? They will never believe I am who I say I am. I *can't* unMask. I can't undo…whatever this is." I let out a breath and said, "This is all that is left of Tarik."

I never expected the look of pain on Doc's face. He watched me askance, brows knotted, lips parted. He was breathing hard too, I realized, thin shoulders rising and falling in the thinnest semblance of control, and his hand was tight on the edge of the lectern.

"Tarik," he whispered. "I'm so sorry. Is it…is it because of her?"

# Chapter 17 — Tarik

IN THE BACK OF MY MIND, I COULD HEAR A FAINT RING OF PANIC, LIKE THE LOW sonorous clang of the palace alarm bells. In the silent moments that dragged out in the wake of Doc's words, it was the only thing my mind could make sense of.

"*Her,*" I said at last. "You…"

And suddenly I looked at Doc as if seeing him for the first time—his white-pale hair, his too-fair skin. He was watching me closely, watching my mind work through the equation.

"I didn't always look like this," he said softly.

"You've…you've seen Death. Did she—"

"Kiss me?" he asked, wry. "Yes. Unfortunately."

"Does she do that…often?"

He met my gaze, a drift of humor behind his eyes that caught me by surprise. "What, kiss people? Ask for their service?" He shrugged. "Not often, I don't think. Or at least, most people aren't…*aware* enough to know that is what is happening."

I grimaced. My thoughts kept trying to drag me back to the memory of Death's shore, but I refused to give in to the impulse; she was the last being I wanted to confront at the moment. I looked at the book instead, my fingers tracing the ornate lettering—hand-written—on the leather cover.

"Did you listen to her?" I asked softly.

"Listen to her promises, you mean?" Doc asked. His attention was on the book, too. "Take care. All her words are honeyed lies."

"I've no intention of serving anyone."

Doc straightened up slightly at that, eyes narrowed as they fixed on me, and I could feel the weight of a hundred questions on his soul. But whatever he was thinking, he kept the questions to himself, which both relieved and infuriated me.

Gritting my teeth, I tapped my fingertips against the book cover. "What do you know of this book?"

He glanced down, his body shying a little away from it as he did. "It's nonsense," he said. "Dangerous nonsense. Rivano was a fool to bring it here. He has *no idea* how dangerous it could be."

I lifted the corner of the cover. "But if it's just nonsense—"

"Words have power, Tarik," Doc said, clapping his hand down over mine, sealing the book again. "Words have the power to heal, but they also have the power to destroy. Sometimes the same words are capable of both. Never underestimate the power of the written word."

I looked at him steadily, the coppery lamplight tracing livid shadows over his narrow face. He still hadn't released my hand, and I got the strange sense he would do anything to keep me from reading that book.

"Is it a prophecy like they say?"

He snorted, and finally lifted his hand away from mine with a little wave. "You tell me," he said. "You speak Cromner, don't you?"

"Barely," I muttered. "I read it better than I speak it, for what that's worth."

"What do you remember about the grammar?"

I frowned a little, racking my mind for some tenuous memories of my lessons in Cromner linguistics. It had been a nightmare trying to learn the language, because it wasn't constructed anything like Cavnish, especially—

"Damn," I said. "They don't use conjunctions, do they? That's why Shiver didn't understand the text."

"Why the *translator* didn't understand the text," Doc corrected, tapping a finger on the book. "Shiver read the Cavnish words correctly, but it was a poor translation. It's perfectly clear in the Cromner."

"*The Zealot, the Scion of the mad god,*" I recited. "The Zealot, *and* the Scion. They're not the same person. I'd thought for certain they were."

"Indeed," he said, a strange, drawn look on his face. "Do you remember anything else?"

I thought a moment longer, then swore under my breath and said, "The verbs?" Doc grinned faintly. "They don't conjugate their verbs like we do. There's no difference between past, present and future verbs except context."

"Precisely. And context might be social, not written, mightn't it? So some ignorant non-native speaker trying to translate a Cromner text… do you suppose he would know how to parse a phrase like *skrizhakarin nal tribviasch?*"

I mouthed the words to myself, then said, *"In those days he rose up?"*

"Rises up. Will rise."

"A prophecy and a historical account at the same time," I mused.

"Or one man's journal of his trivial daily existence," Doc said, with a thin smile.

"I understand a fair bit of Cromner," I said, "but I don't understand *that.*" I gestured to the title. *"Brigaz Nedash.* It doesn't make sense."

"No." Doc's gaze fell on the book's cover, but he eyed it like a piece of dung, like it was beneath his notice. "It doesn't mean anything. It's just…madness." He shrugged and glanced up at me, a shadow in his eyes. "Do you see yet how a text like this could be dangerous?"

"Rivano…"

His breath escaped in a sharp exhale and he turned away, pacing a few steps across the floor with his arms folded tight over his chest. "Rivano knew it was dangerous, but that man has a habit of trying to control things that are more powerful than he understands, thinking he is the mastermind who can bring his vision into actuality by manipulating forces far above him."

I said, "You mean me."

"Well, if you're going to be Istian about it—yes. To put it bluntly, that is what I mean."

"Rivano has no control over me."

"I'm glad to hear it," he said. "But take care, and don't underestimate *his* power."

"He's just a Wind."

"And not all power is magical," Doc said, with a sharp warning note in his voice.

I lifted a hand in agreement, then dropped it again onto the cover of the book, toying with its lower corner. "I need to think."

"The time for thinking has passed. You need to act."

"And do what? I don't have all the information. I'm like a blind man walking a cliff's edge."

Doc's gaze was riveted on my hand, watching me lift and lower the corner of the book's cover. I wondered vaguely what made him so afraid—if he thought I would be led astray by the ambiguous text like Rivano had been, or if he feared something else. The more he watched me, the more I wanted to flip the book open, just to see what he would do, but my heart wasn't in the fight. I sighed and lowered my hand to my side instead.

"What should I do?" I asked, quietly.

It had been so long since I'd asked for advice, I almost didn't know how to form the shape of the words. Doc regarded me in surprise, as if he knew how hard it was for me to swallow my pride and ask.

"You said you don't have information. So, find it." He leaned his forearms on the lectern, bringing his face almost too close to mine. "You're going to have to make a choice, and it won't be an easy one. I know...I know how you're struggling. Believe me, I understand. I pray..." He faltered, then finished, "I pray you have the strength to do what I never did."

I nodded, knowing better than to press him for an explanation. His words moved me strangely, and as he backed away again, I found myself studying him with new interest, wondering how many secrets he had hidden behind the sea glass of his eyes. I didn't imagine I would ever understand all of them.

"Thank you," I said, taking a step back.

"For what?" he asked, startled.

I shrugged. "The illumination. The support. The...understanding, I suppose."

His mouth curved in a small smile, bemused, and he shook his head as he turned away. As I slipped into the void, I heard him say, half under his breath, "Godspeed, Tarik."

As I stepped into the world beyond the world, I found myself standing not at the heart of a web of tunnels like I'd begun to expect, but instead in a single long corridor without branches or turnings, gleaming with the faint light that seemed to come from within the tunnel itself. Wake was standing beside me.

"So you can follow me here, too?" I asked.

He smiled at that. "This, Tarik, is my realm," he said. "I give you safe passage through it, you and all mages I've opened its doors to."

"Where are all the passages?" I asked. "Usually there are so many, leading every direction, more than I can ever count. Is this your way of trying to show me I have no choice?"

"You always have a choice," he said. In this realm, I could barely make out his form, just the impression of light and wind and power, far more daunting than even his overwhelming presence in the flesh. "Only have a care that you make the right one."

"And how do I know what that is?"

He only favored me with a smile, then he was gone. I ground my teeth and faced the long brightness ahead of me. I could go back to Iskari and Nika, who were doubtless in a panic over my disappearance. But going back to them would not answer any of my questions. I wanted—needed—to confront Dr. Alokin about the weapon Doc had told me about, but when I reached out to find him in my mind, a wall seemed to fall over the tunnel before me, opaque and cold, solid as milk-crystal glass.

I placed my hands against the face of it, trying to see Alokin on the other side, but it was like slamming my fist against a brick wall. There was a faint, ice-white gleam in the surface of the barrier, like an etched pattern that seemed somehow familiar to me.

"What is that?" I asked, knowing Wake was still with me.

"A warding," Wake said. The voice came from behind me, or above me, formless and infinite. "It belongs to the man himself, shielding him from the view of mages like you."

"A warding," I echoed. "Alokin has access to a mage capable of making something like this?"

But no answer followed my question, and I glanced over my shoulder to see the tunnel still empty, without even the hum of Wake's power to betray his presence. I traced the rune pattern on the glass, but I couldn't comprehend its pattern. But I understood all too well what it meant—Alokin was barred from my interference.

That left only one option if I wanted answers. If I couldn't reach Alokin, I could reach his associate. Tamping down a surge of displeasure, I closed my eyes and found my destination. Beneath my fingers I felt the glass barricade fall away, and I passed through the veil to the world beyond.

# Chapter 18 ⚘ Tarik

**I** STEPPED OUT OF THE VOID INTO A SMALL OFFICE, CLUTTERED WITH STACKS OF books and laboratory equipment, sharply illuminated in cold white light from an electrical lamp that hung on the wall just behind me. The close air in the tiny space was laced with a faint, acrid smell that made my throat seize. Two tall bookshelves leaned toward each other like slightly tipsy revelers, and in the space between them was a low table holding a half-eaten and long-abandoned plate of food, quite possibly the source of the stench.

A long narrow desk occupied most of the center of the office, and sitting behind it in a rigid chair, staring at me in horror and abject fear, was a thin, severe woman I had met only once and had hoped never to see again.

"It's late to still be working," I said, "Miss Farrady."

Her mouth opened, then closed, and she started to pull her hands off the desk to fold them in her lap until I gestured sharply for her to keep them where they were, where I could see them.

"A little paranoid, Zealot?" she said, lips curved in a faintly mocking smile.

"Don't call me that," I said. "I see you managed to slip your chains. Should I be hiring you to teach my thieves your tricks?"

"Shocking for a prince to be keeping company with thieves."

I had the presence of mind not to startle at her words; it shouldn't have surprised me that she would have learned that secret. I wondered if Kippler had finally told her, or if she had connived her way to gleaning it from some other source.

"Thieves, politicians," I said, shrugging. "I'm not entirely sure I can tell the difference."

Her smile broadened into genuine amusement for a moment, then she pursed her lips and leaned back in her chair. "I assume you have a reason for so dramatically intruding on my privacy at this hour, which, as you correctly noted, is so very late."

"I want to know about Alokin," I said. I sat down on the edge of her desk, turning a tidy stack of papers into a scattered mess as I did. Her lips thinned in a scowl of annoyance, which I answered with a malicious grin. "You worked together in the past. I've heard a rumor you worked together more recently, too."

The scowl vanished from her face. For a moment she just studied me, eyes wide, hands frozen on the desk. The only sound was the ticking of a small clock on one of the shelves and the occasional rattle of the window pane behind her, jarred in its casing by a stiff wind. I waited, semi-patiently, for Farrady to shake herself from her surprise and answer me.

"You know I parted ways with Destri some time ago," she said, carefully.

"But he asked you for advice, didn't he? Recently?"

"Not so recently," she said. "I worked with him a little when he was developing the Hunter, and…" Her hands spasmed suddenly. "No," she whispered. "This isn't about…this isn't about his doomsday weapon, is it?"

I swallowed. "Doomsday weapon?"

She got to her feet, taking a few short, quick paces to the window and holding the drab green curtain back to look down at the scene below. From where I was I couldn't see what she was looking at; I had no idea where we were. A chill draft, unshackled from the heavy curtain, drifted across the office, dropping the temperature in the cramped space just enough to be uncomfortable.

"It was an idea he had," Farrady said. "I told him he should leave it alone, but you know Destri. Once he got an idea in his mind, he would never let it go until he could make it work or abandon it as impossible. It was based on some of the research Vrey brought back from Meritac, which he and Kippler brought to Destri's attention as a possible solution to the mage problem."

I bristled at the term *mage problem*, and, somewhat sternly, corrected her, "And you." She lifted a brow, questioning. "Vrey, and Kippler, and you. Don't try to claim that you were uninvolved with what happened at Borokhev."

She pressed her lips together. "Yes, and me," she said, coming back to stand behind the desk. "Anyway, Kippler and Vrey commissioned Alokin to use the knowledge to develop a new weapon in case their pet project got out of hand."

She lifted her thin brows and watched me expectantly, waiting for me to say something that would indicate that I knew what she was talking about. I delved deep into my mind, trying to piece together everything I knew about Borokhev, about Kippler and Vrey's experiments. Everything, too, that Doc had just told me.

"Aroden," I said.

"Is that what the little nuisance is calling himself these days?" she asked, and shrugged. "Alokin's weapon was supposed to be a failsafe. A kill switch, designed to target the mage if Kippler and Vrey lost control of him. But after the disaster with the EMS device, Alokin went back to the drawing board. He said he had to rethink the weapon's purpose and design. How it functioned. How it destroyed."

"You said it was based on Meritian science," I said. "What, exactly, does it do?"

Farrady gave me a long, narrow look. "I don't expect you would understand the science, Your Highness."

I slammed a fist down on her desk, toppling a jar of ink and startling her so badly that she stumbled and nearly upset her chair. Then she rushed back to snatch up inkwell, blotting the spill with a linen handkerchief, but her eyes were on me with a look torn between anger and fear.

"Do *not* call me that," I hissed. "And answer the damn question."

For a few moments we glared at each other, Farrady's hands in tight little balls like she was trying very hard to control her temper.

"Do you know what an isotope is?" she asked finally, and gave me a look of contempt when I shook my head. "In Meritac they had found that certain minerals they mined in their southern regions had very...dramatic properties when rarified, but the process of separating these elements is still being investigated. One of the processes the scientists were experimenting with was a way to use electromagnetism to divide the elements into these specific *isotopes*, which they could then use for various…interesting purposes. It was that research that first led Alokin, along with Kippler and Vrey, to imagine they could use electromagnetism to separate *you*—or mages like you—into your component parts. Isolate the magic, and then use electromagnetism to excise it from your body. The whole idea behind the EMS device and the Hunter was to leave you a shell, devoid of magic, but capable of resuming a normal human life in normal human society—with, of course, the proper application of a little constructive reeducation to make sure you didn't go insane over your lost identity."

"Because they believe we are broken," I said.

"Aren't you?" she asked, dry, her gaze scalpel sharp on my face.

I winced and looked away, but said, "You still haven't answered me about this new weapon. How is it different from the EMS device, or the Hunter?"

"The Hunter was designed to interrupt the electromagnetism that linked you to your magic," she said, "which, as I said, would destroy the magic but save the mage. As far as I know, this weapon… Well, it simply *targets* that electromagnetism."

"I don't understand."

"I only know the details from the prototype, but its application was all brute force. In the case where it would be used, there would be…no intention of saving the target." When I said nothing, she lifted a hand and said, "Honestly, I have no wish to hide any information from you. What good would it do me? Especially since you seem to have figured out a way to resist the EMS device, as well as our magic-suppressing guns."

"It was a clever try," I said.

She gave me a resentful look and sifted through some of the papers on her desk.

"And what does it have to do with these isotopes?"

She smiled bitterly. "One of their applications is to create an explosive power this world has never known. I think Alokin always toyed with the idea that someday he could use Meritian science combined with his invention to make something the likes of which the world has *never* seen."

I shuddered and looked away.

"Listen," she said. "I lost touch with Alokin after Avnaya Square. I have no idea what he's doing now, or even where he is. I don't know if he shelved the idea for his weapon or if he's developing it into something new. I just know that Avnaya nearly destroyed him."

"He's in Meritac," I said, "and word has it he's been working on that weapon with the intention of targeting Cavnal, in retribution for what happened to his nephew. Zagger."

Her lips parted, and her hand reached out and snatched my arm; I don't think she was even aware that she'd done it.

"Targeting *Cavnal*," she echoed. "Then he did it. If that's true, then he actually made it work."

"The...isotope?"

She nodded, eyes wide, then hissed, "Oh, stars. He *can't*. If he gives it to the Meritian government..."

"Is his anger that violent?" I asked. "Would he betray this country, his safe haven and refuge for the last thirty-odd years, for...for something that no one wanted to happen?"

My voice faltered over the words, and when I glanced back up at Miss Farrady, I was surprised to see a look almost of pity in her cold eyes. I ground my teeth, reminding myself of every way she'd hurt Hayli, refusing to be placated by whatever apparent compassion she had for me.

"I don't know," she said. "I truly hope not, but Destri was always a man of complicated affections and attachments. I don't know what a man like him would do, with as much power as he holds in his hands, and a world of anger burning in his heart."

"Is there anything that would stop him from using it, do you think? Or of keeping it to himself, and not giving it over to his government?"

She regarded me thoughtfully, then got to her feet again, this time pacing the narrow breadth of the office to one of her bookcases. But she just stood there irresolute, not looking at any of the books or instruments, simply running her fingers back and forth over the smooth dark wood of the shelf.

"The alliance, possibly?" she said. "If Cavnal declares for Meritac, the Meritian government would never target us with a weapon like that."

I stifled a groan and leaned over my knees.

"You're beginning to understand the magnitude of the situation," Wake said.

I turned to glare at him, finding him standing just behind me along the wall, arms folded as he watched me.

"Why are you bothering me right now?" I asked.

He never looked annoyed when I overstepped my bounds. I almost wished he would, but just as quickly I wished he wouldn't, because I had no idea what would happen to me if he lost his tolerance for my foolhardy temerity.

"You weren't...talking to me, were you?" Miss Farrady asked, staring at me in bewilderment.

I cursed under my breath and rubbed a hand over my forehead. "No," I said. "I'm sorry."

She looked at me another long while, not believing me, not understanding what she read in me. Then, to my dismay, I saw her confusion fade into fear.

"Shade," she said, her harsh voice a bare whisper. "What is wrong with your eyes?"

I tipped my head back and looked away, staring fixedly up at the ceiling as I tried to find calm. "What's wrong with my eyes?" I asked, turning the question back on her.

"I can't...I don't know. I can't explain it." She started forward, all alight with scientific curiosity. "Will you look at me again? I've never seen anything like it...can I make a few notes?"

I turned to glare at her before I could stop myself, and she peered closely at me. The excitement faded, leaving dull disappointment in its wake.

"Oh," she said. "It must have been a trick of the light. I apologize."

"Noted," I growled.

"Now, dear, don't be so testy," she said.

I lifted a finger, aiming it at her throat, but I couldn't find a rebuke to carry its weight. She smiled when I stayed silent, and seated herself gracefully behind her desk.

"I suppose the next thing you will want to know is where Vrey's pet project disappeared to."

I bit my tongue on telling her I already knew; I was more curious what she would tell me if she thought I didn't.

When I said nothing she thrummed her fingers on the edge of the desk. "He vanished after Avnaya," she said. "You'd think that someone running about with, well, *your* face on would be fairly easy to spot, but no one has seen so much as his shadow in weeks. I always told Vrey and Kippler they were madmen for thinking they could control him.

But, perhaps without them meddling with his brain, he will forget all that they were trying to make him into."

"What were they trying to make him into?"

She looked me straight in the eye and said simply, "A weapon."

"Is it possible that Aroden is dangerous not because of what Vrey and Kippler did to him, but in spite of it?" I asked.

She didn't answer for a long while, just tapped her fingers on the desk until I could barely restrain the impulse to grab her hands and make her stop.

"Do you know something about him I don't?" she asked.

"I don't know anything about him," I admitted. "Except that he was, as you mentioned, very inconveniently wearing my face. Did the three of you make him do that?"

She stifled a smile, one brow faintly lifted. "No, no. He came to us like that."

"What?" I asked, stunned.

"Just what I said. He came to us looking like you—that is, like the Prince. Claiming to be the Prince. It was all very fascinating, especially since anyone who worked inside the Oval Wall knew you were perfectly alive and well *outside* the confines of the Science Ministry."

"How did he arrive? Did he just, I don't know, walk in and ask to be your experiment?"

"No, of course not," she said. Her eyes narrowed slightly, and she leaned back, savoring the moment in a way that made my skin crawl. "Dreyden Kor brought him to us, of course. He brought us most of our best experiments." I must not have hidden my rage very well, because her smile grew smug. "You seem surprised."

"I knew what he was doing for you," I said, my voice a low growl, "but why did he never tell me about *this?*"

"And what would you have done, if he had?"

I leaned toward her, all the blood in my veins kindling with rage. "If I'd known before that they were holding some mage imprisoned in the Science Ministry who had *stolen my face*, I would have gone there and killed him myself before any of this could have happened. And then I would have found out just how good of a Shard Kor really was."

She drew back, a little pale, and gave me a tentative smile. "No need to take it out on me, dear," she said. "I was against the project from the beginning. But if you think you could have killed him that easily…well, none of *us* managed to do it."

"You tried to kill him?"

"Hmm, yes," she said. "Multiple times. Particularly after he suffered a breakdown and slaughtered the rest of our experiments. He just…wouldn't…*die*."

I shuddered. It didn't surprise me to learn that Aroden had been responsible for the slaughter of the mages, and yet…almost against my will I felt a pang of dismay for whatever tortures the scientists had contrived for him, in a vain and foolish attempt to bring him down. If I knew anything about them, they would not have made their efforts kind.

Thinking of that, my thoughts drifted of their own accord to Andon Vrey, and, dreading to know the answer, I heard myself asking, "Did Andon Vrey know that Hayli was his sister?"

"What? *I* never knew. Are you certain?"

I nodded; she frowned and swiped restlessly at the ink spill with the black-soaked kerchief.

"That young man…" she started, and faltered. "I don't know what he knew or didn't know, but all I can say is—it would not surprise me if he knew, and did what he did to her anyway. There was a cruelty to Vrey that made me look like an Anointed. It's probably a mercy that he's gone."

My hand twitched, fingers spasming, and I tried to stop the motion by pressing my palm against my forehead. Then, with a heavy sigh I got down from the desk, fighting back a wave of weariness. My legs shook and stumbled when I stood, and I leaned a moment against the desk until the world steadied around me. Farrady's gaze riveted on me, hawklike.

"Are you well, Shade?" she asked.

I gave her a look, askance. "Don't tell me you're getting sentimental about me," I said.

She lifted her hands from behind her desk, giving me a cold, thin smile. "Not at all, dear, not at all. I'm simply an opportunist," she said, and pointed a coal black revolver straight at my heart.

I heard it fire as I threw myself backwards into the void.

I wasn't fast enough.

# Chapter 19 ∽ Hayli

WHEN I WOKE UP, IT WAS STILL DARK IN MY ROOM, AND THE SKY OUTSIDE my little window hadn't even begun to lighten with the coming of morning. I'd no notion what time it was, and I didn't even care. Bridnow would come and hammer on my door sooner or later, and we'd have our morning ritual of meetings and plans and divvying up the watch schedule, and then everyone would scatter for skappers and the day would go on just like the day before. I pressed my face against my pillow a moment, then pushed myself upright.

For much too long I sat and stared at the edge of my bed. Had I just imagined Shade coming to see me? Had it been naught but a dream? My hand drifted over the rumpled sheet, wondering why I felt so sad— it was something far, far worse than just the fact that Shade had been here, and that he had left again.

The worry dogged me as I got dressed and stomped on my boots, and when Coins found me in the common room some ten minutes later, it was still troubling me. I shifted uneasily as he dropped onto the chair across from me.

"Stars," he said. "You look like you just came from a funeral, right? What's going on?"

I shook my head. I wanted to tell him that I'd seen Shade—more than anything I wanted him to know. But what would Coins say if he found out Shade had been here and hadn't stayed to talk to him? Would I tell him about how Shade had tried to unMask, and Tarik had looked nothing like Tarik? Would it be wrong of me to keep it a secret?

*Secret.*

It hit me all at once, the shape of that formless worry in the back of my mind, and I choked on a breath that came out like a sob.

I'd kept a secret from Shade. I should've told him about Aroden—I'd had plenty of chances to do it...but I'd hidden the truth as if I were ashamed of it.

"Hayli?" Coins said gently.

I waved a hand to brush away his worry, knowing it wouldn't work. "It's naught important," I whispered. "Just worried about Shade is all."

"Yeah, aren't we all," he said with a sigh. "Any particular reason why?"

I hesitated, then shook my head. Bridnow appeared that moment with the other lieutenants and half the sergeants—the ones who hadn't been on duty overnight. I drifted through the morning meetings in a fog, giving my reports by habit, hardly hearing a word of what Griff and Anuk and Derrin had to say.

"I have some news," Bridnow said, as the morning call was dwindling to a close. That finally snapped me out of my daze, and I glanced up to find him watching me closely. "The Chernayi agreed to work with the Cleavers and the Grey Mist yesterday afternoon, and from what my contact told me, a delegation from the Army was present as well."

"So they're going to go through with it," Anuk said. "The military coup."

"There isn't a timeline yet, but there are two ways they could proceed. Either they could wait for all the Ministers to be together and overthrow them at once—"

"You mean massacre them," Griff said, voice thin and tense. "That's what you mean by *overthrow.*"

"Yes," Bridnow said. He held Griff's eye a moment, then went on, "Or they could begin by picking off the loyalist Ministers one by one, in the hopes of persuading those with more...parliamentarian leanings to give up their power."

"Bloody unlucky day to be a Minister," Jig said.

"Watch it," Griff growled. "That's my father we're talking about."

"Can't pick your family," Jig said with a shrug.

Griff jumped off the table he'd been sitting on, but Bridnow snapped, "Lieutenant!"

Everyone subsided at the tone of his voice, and Griff leaned back on the table and contented himself with glaring murderous death at Jig. Jig seemed all too happy to ignore him.

"For what it's worth," Bridnow said, quieter now, when everyone had settled down, "I'd much rather the former. If they go for a big massacre like that, it will require planning and preparations. More chances for them to make a mistake. More chances for us to intervene and try to persuade the Ministers to listen to us and defend themselves. More chances for us to take the element of surprise and throw a counter-coup against Red and his lot. If they pick off the Ministers one by one, there's no way to know who they will strike first, or where."

"I could try talking to Batar again," I said.

Bridnow nodded. "Derrin, maybe you could make her trip a little quicker than usual, so she doesn't have to waste time looking for him."

Derrin nodded, and Bridnow dismissed us after telling Derrin and me that we were off the duty roster for the day. I was halfway back to my room when Derrin caught up with me. He eyed me closely, but to my relief he didn't ask me if I was doing all right.

"When will you be ready to go?" he asked.

"Give me an hour," I said. "Just got to get a few things in order before I gan."

He nodded and headed on to his own room. I watched him go, then slipped into my room and found a sheaf of scrap papers I'd claimed from Bridnow's waste bin and a short, dull pencil. Hoping to avoid interruption by anyone who had a right to ask my attention, I left the Rookery and made my way to the dormitory, hesitating only a moment before going up to the second floor cell. The ropes were back up, but this time I made sure to shut the door behind me when I crept in.

Sitting on the floor in the corner of the room, I wrote down every single thing I could remember from Shade's visit. Everything he had said. Everything I'd said. I needed to know if it was real, or just a figment of my dreams. I was just scribbling down how Shade had vanished, without a word of goodbye, when I realized I wasn't alone. Aroden was sitting in the corner of the room opposite me, knees drawn up, eyes strangely bright in the room's thick shadows.

"I thought you might come back," he said.

I glared at him under lowered brows and kept writing. He was half the reason I felt so sore this morning, and I wasn't feeling particularly kindly toward him at the moment.

"What are you writing about?"

I finished and folded the papers up, tucking them into an inner pocket of my fine officer's coat. "Naught you need to worry about," I said.

"Something you need to remember," he said softly. "Something to make sense of the darkness."

I startled and stared at him, and he stared straight back at me, so intent I could feel a little warmth creep into my cheeks. I couldn't understand the understanding in his eyes. I wished that he didn't understand so well.

"I thought if I wrote it down," I murmured, "I'd be able to tell if it was a dream, or if it really happened." He waited, head canted, and didn't say a word. I sighed and hugged my knees to my chest. "Shade came to Borokhev last night."

"I know," he said.

I jumped a little, and he laughed at the expression on my face. "How could you *know* that?"

"I could feel his presence. It's not something I can easily forget, not after…" He shuddered and shook his head. "You would have felt it too, if you hadn't been face to face with him. I think every mage in the complex knew something was going on. They just couldn't tell what."

I thought of the hum of power I'd felt surrounding Shade, wondering if that was what Aroden was talking about. That raw, terrifying power.

"I was afraid of him," I admitted, hating myself for saying it.

"Anyone would be," he said, in a bare whisper. "Did you…did you tell him about me?"

I eyed him surreptitiously, then, slowly, shook my head. I almost missed the ghost of a smile that flitted over Aroden's face, like relief— there and gone again.

"Anyway, that's what I was writing down. All I could remember. S'pose I could've just asked you if it happened."

He smiled genuinely then. "Better for you to write it down and make sense of it in your own way. Do you…do you suppose I could have some paper? I've been meaning to write down what I remember, too. I can't tell where the fracturing from Kippler's hands ends and where my magic's fracturing begins—I never would have known there was a difference if you hadn't taught me that. But if I could write it down like Arnthor did, maybe it would help me salvage my mind."

"Of course, I can get you some paper," I said, and frowned. "You've mentioned that before, about Arnthor writing down his story. What do you know about it?"

He shrugged, tapping his fingers restlessly over the wall beside him, gaze intent on his hand. "Only what I told you. But ever since I heard about that book, I've thought about going to Cromis and seeing if I could find it. Seeing if it could heal my mind." He closed his eyes, brow knotted with pain. "I'd give anything to be free of this madness. I'd give anything to know what I am."

*Cromis...* I startled, my mind jumping back to something Scorch had said about Rivano, in a late night conversation not so long ago: *Just like he's using that damn Cromner book.*

"Arnthor's book," I said. "Did it have a name?"

There was a hollow light in his eyes as he met my gaze across the cell. "I...I don't know. I never heard tell of one."

I bit my lip and got up. Was it possible that the *Brigaz Nedash* was Arnthor's journal, his musings and half-mad rantings? It seemed so farfetched, and yet, it made so much sense. It even made sense of the fact that Rivano would have it.

I nodded a farewell to Aroden and slipped out of the room before he could stop me, making my way back to the Rookery with my thoughts in an even messier jumble than before. Soon as I got done with Minister Batar, I was going to go back to the Hole, and I was going to have a good long look at that book.

DERRIN GHOSTED US STRAIGHT INTO THE palace, where Batar, as Minister of the Court, had his offices. I'd never Ghosted with anyone before—I remembered even less of the journey than I did when I Rifted with Shiver. Just a rush of brightness and a feeling of spinning, and then we stepped out into a richly-appointed office of dark-paneled walls and fine tapestries of hunting scenes in autumn and garden parties in spring. In the center of the office was a wide desk covered with meticulous stacks of papers, with a crystal decanter of some kind of liquor sitting precisely two inches from both edges in the upper left corner. A cut-crystal glass half full of amber liquid sat on a little square of etched stone near the center of the desk.

As I got my balance back I took a good goggle at the room, but I kept coming back to one of the hunt scene tapestries, with its vibrant depiction of horses and hounds and a fox trying to give its pursuers the slip. Looking at it, I suddenly remembered something Doc had told me once, and I reached out and delicately lifted up the bottom corner of the tapestry. Just like Doc had said, the backside of it was a chaotic tangle of knotted threads, with no sense to any of it, and no hint of the orderly picture on the other side. I grinned a little and let it go.

"Where's Batar?" I asked Derrin, dragging my attention away from the tapestry.

Derrin just pointed toward a pair of glass doors that opened onto a narrow balcony. Batar stood against the bannister with a cigo in one hand and a teacup in the other, wrapped in what I thought looked a bit like a dressing gown of gold and dark blue silk. He was staring into his office, straight at us. After the initial shock faded, he tapped out his cigo and pushed the glass door open, carrying a gust of chilly air and a whiff of smoke into the room with him.

"Minister," I said.

"Lovely to see you, my dear," he said, setting his teacup on a sideboard and removing the silk wrap, shaking it out thoroughly before hanging it on a peg near the balcony door. "Please, come in. Oh, you already have."

He gave me a taunting smile and settled himself into his desk chair, then waved us forward to sit in the chairs across from him.

"Now, to what do I owe the pleasure of your company, not that your company itself is not sufficiently satisfactory?"

Derrin's hand twitched on the arm of his chair. I smiled at Batar, but I was too anxious to put much warmth in it.

Then I said, flatly, "You're in danger."

"My dear, if I had a kip for every time I'd heard that in my long career, I'd be funding a kingdom of my own in the Shark Islands."

I leaned forward and planted my hands on the desk. "I told you before that folks were plotting a military coup with you—the whole lot of you—as the targets."

"But surely that was just rumor. We've heard nothing else…"

"It's happening," I said. "The coup is underway. The anarchists, the Chernayi, and half the King's bloody Army are involved. We dan' na how it's ganna happen or when, but your life is in danger."

485

"You need to take precautions," Derrin said. "If the Court gets overthrown…"

"Damn," Batar said. "Damn, damn, *damn*." He leaned his elbows on his desk with his head in his hands, then he drew a deep breath and swallowed all the liquor in his glass in one gulp. "What is the point, my dear? We're doomed either way."

"Care to explain that, Minister?" Derrin said, snarling the words a bit.

Batar rolled his head from side to side with a serious of sharp cracks that made me cringe. "Thwart the coup and the Court will abolish the monarchy for good, and bind us to an alliance that will bring us inevitably into war. Let the coup succeed and watch the Court fall, the monarchy fall, and Brinmark's defenses wash the gutter, leaving us easy prey for any international vulture who covets our resources here."

"What can we do?" Derrin asked.

Batar let his hands drop on the table and gave Derrin a long, weary look. "Find the bloody Prince and plant a crown on his head and his posterior on the throne, and maybe that will put an end to all this nonsense."

Derrin's mouth twitched. "I wish it were that easy."

I chewed the inside of my cheek and said nothing.

"You might want to put some of your…informants on this issue," Derrin said after a bit. "Isn't this something the Intelligence Committee should be keeping you abreast of?"

"Well, if the IC could be counted on not to follow their own private agenda, of course," Batar said. He thought it over a moment, then waved a hand in a florid gesture and said, "How is Creech doing?"

"Fine," I said. "He's up and about, though he dan' like to talk about what Klissen did to him. Spends most of his time as Howler helping out the gate guards."

"Howler!" Batar sputtered. "Pity's sake, couldn't he call his damn dog something a bit cleverer than that?" He fluttered his fingers in annoyance. "Well, tell him I want to see him. If what you say is true, then it may be I could use a watch dog."

"I'll tell him," I said. "And we'll let you know if aught else comes up. Meanwhile, you might wanna let the rest of the Ministers know. Who can say? Maybes having a common enemy will make you lot stop squabbling like skitters and work together for once."

"Indeed," he said, musing, regarding the empty depths of his crystal tumbler despondently. "You'd best be going, friends," he said then, with a glance at his wall clock. He smoothed up the tufts of hair over his ears and gave us a beatific smile, slipping into his public affectations like a comfortable pair of gloves. "I do b-b-believe I have a meeting in mere moments."

Derrin nodded and I smiled in farewell, then Derrin wrapped an arm around me and we left the world behind.

# Chapter 20 ~ Tarik

I STAGGERED AS I SLIPPED INTO THE VOID, PAIN EXPLODING BENEATH MY RIBS, seeping out in burning arcs through every vein. Before I could catch myself I fell, sprawling on my back as the white vault of the tunnel soared away above me. The glittering light of its walls dimmed beneath a livid crimson glow that throbbed in time with every frantic beat of my heart.

I lay perfectly still, hands pressed against my chest as the hot blood pulsed through my fingers, and with all my willpower I forced myself to breathe slowly, shallowly, in a vain effort to tame my panic. The walls of the tunnel drifted lazily away from me, retreating farther and farther into the night-red shadows. My hand dropped from my chest and landed on the cold floor of the nothingness around me, my fingers scrabbling uselessly at the ice-smooth surface.

"If I die here," I whispered, knowing Wake was nearby, "what happens? Will anyone ever find my body?"

"No," he said.

"I'll just be gone." I thought about that a moment, and let my breath out in a shuddering sigh. "Well, that's not so bad, I suppose. There would be worse ways to go."

"But you aren't going to die," Wake said.

"If you think I'll accept your power to save my life, you're mistaken," I said.

I felt a wave of patient pity from him, but he only said, "Death won't find you here." Then he was crouching beside me, the tips of his fingers drifting through the fringes of my hair. "Do you imagine the world's problems will right themselves if you are gone?"

I shivered and rolled onto my knees, coughing as the burn in my lungs seeped up into my throat. "Maybe they would."

"Then I will find another Zealot," he said, and I felt his presence drifting away from me.

*No, wait,* I wanted to say, but the words stuck in my throat.

I closed my eyes, trying to focus. Could an ordinary Blood heal this wound for me? It was a natural enough bullet, not tainted with magic, so perhaps someone…perhaps Hayli…

A pain deeper than the bullet hole spasmed in my heart and I pressed my head against the cold surface beneath me, pushing the thought away with a firm nudge of my will. I could always go back to Doc, but I'd gotten all the answers from him that he could give me. There was only one other Blood who might be able to help me, and I needed to talk to her anyway.

Staggering to my feet, I focused my thoughts on my mother, and tried to find her in the mists of the world. After a bewildered few moments of searching, I glimpsed her in a strange land I had never seen before. She was on horseback, with Kor beside her, framed by the rising sun, out on a wild and desolate plateau that edged the sea. With a thin smile of triumph, I stumbled forward and pushed through the veil, and stepped out directly in front of the horses.

And fell face-first in the grass.

"Tarik!"

One of the horses whinnied, and I watched from much too close a distance as the hooves shuffled in the scrubby grass, toying with the earth in alarm. Then there was a pair of ladies' boots in the grass among the hooves, running toward me. I rolled onto my back and gave my mother my laziest, most charming smile.

"Good afternoon, Your Majesty," I said. "Enjoying your ride?"

She dropped to her knees beside me, dragging me onto her lap and cradling my head in her arms. "Stars, Tarik," she whispered, face chalk-white, eyes glittering with tears. "What have you done?"

"I got shot," I said, gesturing at my chest. "Can you fix me up?"

She drew a hand back, bewildered.

It was Kor who spoke first, as he strode up beside us with the two horses in hand. "The first time you've seen your mother in how long, and all you can ask her is if she'll heal you?" he growled. "Hell, kid, if I were her I'd leave you here."

"It's a good thing you're not me, then," my mother said, giving him a warning glare. "Tarik, darling, hold still."

I stopped trying to sit up and let her hold me, watching through slitted eyes as she laid her hand over my bloodied chest. Her fingers plucked and coaxed the air over the bullet hole, like a lutist plucking his instrument's strings, and a burning, tearing pain tore through me. I screamed through my teeth, sweat pouring down my face and back, then, as soon as it had started, the pain vanished, and my mother held up a small bullet for my inspection.

She tossed it into the grass and placed her hand back over my chest, and instantly I felt the soothing prickle of her magic weaving through the ragged edges of the wound, the faint tugging ache as the hole began to close. I breathed a sigh of relief without meaning to; part of me had feared that, if she tried to heal me, she would find the same impediment to her power that Halvir had found.

Her hand withdrew after a moment, but then hovered in the air over my torso, uncertain. "Is that all?"

I nodded, and she helped me to sit up.

"What happened to your Blood magic?" she asked softly.

"I lose control of all my Gifts from time to time," I muttered. "Sometimes they come back."

I eyed her sidelong, wondering if she could feel whatever it was that Hayli had described, when she said the air around me felt *jumpy*. She certainly hadn't hesitated to come near me, or to touch me.

"Did you…have any difficulty?" I managed to ask. "Healing me?"

She pursed her lips and stroked my hair back from my forehead until I pulled out of her reach by standing up.

"No, but…" She faltered, and folded her hands in her lap. It struck me suddenly that I was standing but she was still on her knees, sitting on her heels; with her hands folded, it looked like a pose of reverence. I shuddered and turned away. "You've unbridled your power."

I glanced back in her direction, then away again. "My power has bridled me," I countered. "I'm in a prison of my own making."

"Well, then," she said, with a rather wry smile. "You should be able to make yourself an escape route."

A million questions pressed at the corners of my mind, begging to be asked, but the only one that came out was, "Mother, why are you here?"

She got to her feet, dusting the dead grass and frost from her skirts. "Here? I knew you needed to talk to me, which meant I had to be away from the Palace of the Grand Duchy, or you'd never find me."

"Warded?" I asked, bitterly, and she nodded. "But you know that isn't what I meant. Why did you leave Cavnal?" I turned to Kor to include him. "Why did either of you leave?"

She took her horse from Kor but didn't mount again, just led the gelding by the bridle at a gentle walk, expecting me to follow. I trailed her at the horse's shoulder.

"The situation in Brinmark was too volatile," she said presently. "I was a foreigner. What good could I have done by staying?"

"Given the people some sense of stability?" I said, heated. "Foreigner or not, you are their Queen, and they love you. But you abandoned them when they needed you the most."

She turned to face me, a sharp, icy look in her eye that I'd never seen before. "I did?" she asked. The horse snorted and tossed his head, sensing his rider's agitation. "I was not the one next in line for the throne, darling. Whose disappearance do you think was the harder for them to endure, mine or yours?"

"That isn't fair. Even if they don't understand it, what I'm doing right now is for *their* sake, because their King asked me to do it."

"Go to Istia?" she asked, incredulous.

"How did you know I was in Istia?"

She waved a hand dismissively. "A merchant ship's captain who arrived in Tulay yesterday. He sent a report up to the Palace saying he'd met Eyid's son in Bregjarvani, which naturally raised everyone's hopes that Istia would honor her old alliance with Tulay."

I let out a bitter breath. "I know you never cared about Cavnal, and I know you're probably pleased as a fox in a henhouse to see what that nation is suffering right now. But if you think I am going to follow your lead and turn my back on her now, you're sadly mistaken."

She pursed her lips and exchanged a look with Kor. "I'd rather see Cavnal in alliance with Tulay than standing on her own, and I'd certainly rather see her in alliance with us than with the southerners. But what do you mean to do about it, *Shade*?"

I winced and scrubbed a hand over my hair, but I couldn't unMask and show her what Death had done to her son.

"What is it you want?" she persisted. "Who will you follow?"

I circled away from the horse to stand facing her, my hands loose at my sides, feeling the currents of the wind around me, the charge of energy in the air, rising to my call.

"I am sick to death," I said, "of being other people's pawn. I will not be a pawn in anyone's schemes, not any more."

"Then what will you be?" she asked. Her voice was quiet; it was the only thing that saved it from sounding like contempt. "The Admiral? The Fortress that cannot be moved?"

"I will be King!" I shouted.

Thunder shook the ground around us, and her horse shied, almost careening into Kor's as it pranced beside him. Kor grabbed both horses' reins and walked them in tight circles, while my mother watched me, open-mouthed, the wind snagging in the silk scarf that covered her dark hair.

"Well," she said. "You can stop that now, darling. I heard you."

I closed my hands into fists, and the wind immediately fell still. My mother shot a quick glance at Kor, then nodded him over to join us. The horses had calmed so he led them toward us, his face fixed in a stern scowl that completely failed to mask his fear.

"What is Tulay's plan?" I asked.

Kor laughed aloud. "You want us to just tell you the Grand Duke's tactics, his battle plans, his strategy, just because you want to know?"

I gave him a feral grin. "If I'm not mistaken," I said, "by the Tulian laws of heredity, since my uncle Alster died *I'm* next in line for the title of Grand Duke. Not you, Kor."

"Bastard," he said.

"So it seems," I said. My mother gave us both a cold glare, but wisely didn't say a word. I kept my attention fixed on Kor. "So, if there's something I need to know about, I'd appreciate it if you would tell me so I can be on my way. Either that, or I'm taking you with me back to Brinmark, and you can tell those poor devils holed up in Borokhev what kind of hell is about to rain down on them if war breaks out." I took a step closer to him. "Do you have no care for Cavnal at all? No affection for any of the people there?"

"Of course I do," he snapped. "But duty comes before affection, and the handful of people I might *possibly* tolerate on a good day is not a compelling reason for me to shirk my responsibilities to my homeland. Remember that little chat we had about duty the first time you tried to back out on Trabin, or did you conveniently forget about that?"

With one more step I was face to face with him, measuring him coldly. "Fine," I said. "I don't care what you do going forward. I'm finished trying to make up reasons why I should trust you. But I just want one answer."

He leaned, fractionally, away from me. "What's the question?"

"I heard from Miss Farrady that you took that impostor mage to Kippler and the Science Ministry," I said, my voice frigid. "I want to know… I want to know everything. How? Where did he come from? Why would you do that? Why did you never tell me? And finally, what the *hell* were you thinking?"

"Tarik, darling," my mother said. Her voice was, if possible, even colder than mine. "Don't make me regret coming out here for you to find us."

"Did *you* know too?" I asked, rounding on her.

"Don't be a vutting fool," Kor snapped. "Of course she didn't know."

"You told me once that you'd never met a Mask before."

"I lied."

I ground my teeth. "Was *he* the reason you asked me if I could impersonate another person?"

"Yes," he said, "for what it's worth. I never really doubted…but I decided to test you anyway."

"Doubted what?"

"That I'd taken the right mage to Kippler. It was either that or take him to Rivano, and personally I would have preferred Rivano, but if you happen to have forgotten this too, there was that little problem of Kippler having vutting control of my *mind* at the time."

I frowned. "Rivano wanted Aroden too? What for?"

"Well, in the likely chance that you would live up to your reputation of failing people's expectations—"

"Kor," my mother said quietly. "That's enough."

I held up a hand. "I've heard enough in the last few hours to baffle my mind for ten years," I said. "I'm done. I'm sorry to have wasted your time." I turned as if to go, then paused and said over my shoulder, "Rivano's ambitions are petty, you know, as were Kippler's. I suppose

I'm not all that surprised they drew you in so easily."

I saw his hand clench the split second before he swung.

I spun toward him and said, "Stop."

He froze, face contorted with confusion and wrath, while I tried desperately to drown the thrill of satisfaction that pulsed through me, seeing him snared so completely in the web of my power. My mother watched me, standing as motionless as if I'd Commanded her to stop too. I turned to face her.

"I don't care whose side you are on," I said. "I don't care what cunning schemes you've hatched, what private alliances you've made, what secret plans you've woven for me over these last long years. You're my mother, and I love you. But I will never let you bring this world to the brink of war by anything you could contrive to do. I *will* bring peace if it's the last thing I do, but if I fail and war breaks out, I swear to you I will end it. So, perhaps you might rethink whose side you claim to be on."

"Darling," she said. Her voice was shaking. "I have always, and only, been on your side. When did you ever begin to doubt that? All I have ever done has been to raise you up. You don't need Cavnal. You don't need Istia, or Tulay. Just listen to what Rivano has in mind—he will see you triumphant, and the world at peace at your feet."

"Rivano! Rivano doesn't want peace," I said, the words wisping up on a note of question.

"He wants your peace," she said. "He knows what your father knew, that you would be the only one who could bind the nations of the world into unity. *You*, my son. At your will all this talk of war could end."

My stomach churned, and I clenched and loosened my fists. Kor was still frozen where I'd left him, but the anger had faded from his eyes, so, with barely a look at him, I released him from the hold. He stumbled and dragged in a deep breath, though I knew well enough that my binding hadn't robbed him of air.

"The Zealot?" I asked my mother. "Is that what you mean? Rivano...he was the one who first started the rumor in Brinmark that I was the Zealot, wasn't he? Do you mean he actually wants me to embrace Wake's power?"

She laughed softly. "Wake? Have you fallen into those Istian superstitions in your time there? This has nothing to do with Wake.

It has to do with you. Your power. *Your* magic. Your will to triumph."
She took a step closer to me, taking my hand and pressing it against my
chest, where the bullet hole had found its mark. "Just imagine it, love.
No blood, no pain, no suffering. No death. Just the grateful obedience
of the peoples of the world to follow your will."

"That's madness," I whispered, hoarse. "That's…an abomination.
I could never…"

"You could never?" she echoed, and lifted one hand gracefully to
gesture to Kor. "What, use your power to control the will of another
person?" I ground my teeth and stared out across the empty plateau,
the wind stinging my eyes. "Do you have another solution?" she asked
then, with an almost haughty lift of her chin as she looked up at me. "If
you do not take up the mantle you were born to wear, this world will
tear itself apart. And every city that burns, every child that dies, every
mage that suffers will be because you failed to act."

I closed my eyes, the vision of the ravaged city, the unburied dead
thundering through my memory, and my knees buckled. My mother
caught me and lowered me gently to the ground.

"It's all right, love," she soothed, stroking my hair back from my
forehead. "You will find your strength. It's already within you. You just
have to reach out and take it."

"And go mad in the process," I whispered.

"Your father…your father saved his sanity, you know. In the end."

"You don't understand what happened," I said. "He gave up his
magic. And in the end, he failed anyway."

I staggered back to my feet, leaving her staring after me as I walked
to the edge of the towering cliff. It stood brooding over a choppy
turquoise sea, its copper-brown face as smooth as if a massive hand
had carved a half-moon from the edge of the continent. The drop was
sickening; it had to be several hundred feet to the water below; I could
barely even hear the crash of the surf against the rocks. The wind raged
around me, twining its fingers in my hair.

"This doesn't mean I accept your power," I said, to Wake, knowing
he could hear me, "but I suppose it means I am willing to listen."

I glanced over my shoulder at my mother and my uncle, who were
watching me in puzzled curiosity, and favored them with a cold smile
of farewell. Then I threw my arms wide, and let myself fall.

# Chapter 21 ~ Hayli

As soon as we'd Ghosted back into the Rookery, Derrin released me and strode a few steps away, taut as a tug-war rope. I watched him warily as he paced, wondering what had got him so thoroughly skundered.

"Where the hell is Tarik?" he asked suddenly, rounding on me. "Why can't I reach him? We need *someone* to get a message to him, persuade him to come back here and do his duty, or we're all in the mucks. Can Pika do it?"

I shook my head, guilt gnawing at my insides. "Nah, she's never been able to read him, or contact him in any way. But Aothir…maybes he could get a message to Thane, who could get a message to Tarik…"

"Brilliant," he said. "Do it."

"You do it," I snapped. "Aothir's *your* sergeant."

"True," he said.

He turned to storm off, but I stopped him before he could vanish. "What message are you ganna tell Shade?"

He said simply, "*Come home.*"

Then he was gone.

I checked the watch roster, then, grabbing my hat from my room, I ran to the depot gate where Shiver and Zip were on watch. Zip was sitting on the edge of the platform, his legs dangling over the railroad tracks, and Shiver was hunched in a crouch next to him, idly letting a pebble slide through each of his palms—literally *through*, like water dripping through a strange kind of mesh.

I'd asked Bridnow once if he thought Zip was too young to be sitting sentry duty, but Bridnow had just waved me off and told me it was good training for the boy's self-discipline. And of course, Zip had been soaring high ever since he'd heard the news that he was being groomed for the guard squad. Sometimes I thought he did his duty with more zest and zeal than half the grown folks we had.

"Good morning, ma'am," he called when he saw me, giving me a cheerful smile along with a sharp—if a bit misplaced—salute.

Shiver nodded in my general direction.

"I should demote him and make *you* my Sergeant, Zip," I said, "since you're the only one who knows how to show an officer courtesies."

Zip beamed, but Shiver just scowled.

"What's got you so sore, Shiver?" I asked, kneeing him in the shoulder, making him lose his balance.

"Nothing so much," he said, getting up and facing me. His gaze drifted down toward Zip, and I caught his meaning all too clear—he needed to talk to me about something, but at least he had the kindness not to do it in front of the skitter.

"I need your help with something, after your watch ends," I said. "Meet me by the front gate."

He tossed his head but nodded, and I left him to stew over whatever he had on his mind. I filled the two hours till he was finished by helping Miss Nan in her scullery, cutting up slabs of brined meat along with Gem and Lev. I watched Gem sidelong as we worked, wondering at the notion of seeing her without Kite somewhere nearby.

Thinking of what Coins had told me, I finally turned to her and said, "You seen Kite lately?"

Gem pressed her lips in a thin line. I half-expected her to ignore me, or maybe tell me it was none of my business, but after a moment she peeked at me under her sweep of hair and I realized with a touch of surprise that she, who always looked so flawless, had dark circles under her red-rimmed eyes.

"Kite hasn't come out of her room much lately," she said. "I don't know why. She won't talk to me at all. *Me.* At first I was afraid maybe... maybe she'd..." She glanced sidelong at Lev and bit her lip. "Maybe something had happened to her...?" she tried, looking at me expectantly to see if I got her meaning.

My eyes widened a little.

"But then I saw her once and…she didn't look any different. Maybe a little thinner than usual, but she's not been eating much."

"Should I send—" I started, and then remembered that Doc had lammed out on us, and me and Aroden were the only folks resembling Bloods here now. "Should I go see her?"

"What makes you think she'll talk to you if she won't talk to me?" Gem asked, with a haughty toss of her head.

"Because I'm a Blood, and I might be able to help her if something's gone wrong."

"You're a Blood?" she asked, forehead wrinkling—I couldn't tell if it was from surprise or distaste. "That figures, I suppose. Try talking to her if you want. I doubt it'll do any good. Her room's on the second floor up, third from the end of the hall."

"Thanks," I said, but she just looked at me in bland silence. I gritted my teeth and focused on carving up the meat. "This looks good," I said after a while. "Who scored this treasure?"

"Just the humble folks here who have to work to keep everybody else fed," she said.

"We're grateful to you, more than any of us can say," I said softly.

Her brows arched at that, then she smiled reluctantly and glanced away. "If you can…if you *do* manage to help Kite, I wouldn't know how to thank you."

"It wouldn't be necessary," I said.

I finished the last of my heap of meat and handed it over to Miss Nan, then, murmuring a goodbye to the three of them, I headed toward the dormitory. I'd no notion what I meant to say or do to Kite—if there was even the slightest chance that I'd be able to help her if she needed a Blood. I'd somehow mended a tiny cut on my hand, and I still hadn't figured out how I'd managed to do that. Could I pretend that I'd have the skill to go mucking about with someone else's health? What if I did more harm than good?

I made my way to the second floor up, but halfway down the long hallway I heard someone say my name, and I froze. Backtracking a few steps, I peeked through an open door and found Aroden sitting cross-legged on a bed, fingers pressed against his temples.

"Did you call me?" I asked, pausing in the doorway.

He lifted his head to look at me, and scrambled to his feet. "You're upset about something."

"Not upset," I said. "Worried." I chewed my lip and studied him thoughtfully. "Nobody's given you any duties?"

"I offered to stand on guard duty," he said, shrugging, "but no one will put me on the roster. And they won't let me help in the kitchen either, but I don't know why. I don't know what else to do. I've got no skills to help anyone here, and if I can't help them…" His voice trailed off, and he shook his head.

"Well," I said, "I got a duty for you. Come with me."

He hesitated just a moment, then nodded and followed me down the hall. The third door from the end was closed, and when I knocked, no one answered.

"She's ill," Aroden said suddenly, his palm pressed against the smooth door. His eyes were wide and dark. "She's dying."

I staggered, and reached to try the door latch. It wouldn't give.

"Kite!" I called, leaning my forehead on the door. "Please let us in. We can help you!"

"She's too weak—she can't get up," Aroden said.

He snatched his hand away from the door, then, without a word, he touched the handle and pursed his lips in a thin line. In a moment I heard a soft click, and the door swung gently open. I rushed in ahead of him, my heart stumbling against my ribs when I saw the low bed where Kite lay wrapped in a thin blanket, ghostly pale.

"Kite," I whispered, and knelt by her bed. "It's me, Hayli."

Her purple-bruised eyelids fluttered open, and her gaze drifted listlessly over the room, the ceiling, the walls, and finally toward me. She looked at me a moment, then shifted her attention past my shoulder, where Aroden was standing.

"Hayli?" Her voice was faint as a rustle of summer grass, and her lips were cracked and bleeding. "Go away."

"You need help," I said, tears stinging my eyes. "You're sick."

"Leave me alone," she whispered. She struggled to turn away from us. "I'm dying, Hayli. Just let me do it in peace."

"People are worried about you," I said, laying a hand on her arm. It was thin, so thin, and her skin was like paper. "You dan' have to suffer alone. Let the people who love you take care of you."

"I didn't want anyone to see me like this," she said. She tilted her head back to look at me again, her golden hair falling across her cheek. "I didn't want them to know."

"Let us help you."

"Can't," she said. "Doctor said it's the end. There's something inside me...like I'm being devoured from the inside. That's what he said. And now Doc's not here...I thought he might help me but he's gone. So just leave me alone and let me die, or..." She broke off, taking a few shaking, shallow breaths. "Or if you really care about me, you'd carry me out of Borokhev, so...so Coins never has to see me dead. Tell him I found a new life somewhere else. Stupid boy. Stupid, beautiful boy. It's his fault he...cares so much."

"Aroden is a Blood, like Doc. Will you let him try to help you?"

Her gaze shifted past me to Aroden again, eyes a little narrowed. "Who is he? Never seen him before. Do you...trust him?"

For one awful moment I hesitated, then I turned and glanced at Aroden. He was looking at Kite, not at me, a dark pain in his eyes and a sad tilt to his mouth that, even though he wore Aroden's face, reminded me all too much of Tarik. His gaze drifted toward me, but his expression never changed. There was no hope, no expectation in his eyes, but somehow...it felt like he was begging me to let him help. And there was only one way I could do that.

"I trust him," I said, quietly.

He didn't smile, but bent his head. There was a silence, as Kite studied him through a faint frown, then her fingers stirred in a weak gesture of indifference. "Not like he can make anything worse. I can feel it. Fading slowly around the edges. God! It's easier than I thought it would be."

I scrambled away from the bedside to give Aroden room, and he sat down gently on the edge of the bed.

"I'll try not to do anything that will hurt you," he said softly, "but I can't guarantee this will be comfortable."

She lifted a thin shoulder in a shrug and closed her eyes. Aroden reached out and placed his hands on either side of her head, letting his own eyes drop closed. A minute and he released her, and his hand drifted down to her heart, hovering in the air just above the blanket. Then again, a little further down to her stomach.

"The disease has spread all through your body," he said softly. "It is no wonder the doctor told you what he did. There is no medicine, no science that could cure you."

A tear gathered at the corner of her closed eye, and trickled down into her tangle of hair.

"But I'm not a doctor," Aroden said. "I'll do my best."

He placed his hands over hers where they rested on her stomach and bowed his head. A minute and his skin took on that same strange clarity I'd seen in the working of Doc's magic. His breathing grew faint and shallow, and a thin line of concentration gathered between his brows. I watched, holding my own breath, and Kite ground her teeth as the sweat began to stand out on her forehead.

"Stars," she gritted. Her hands spasmed beneath his. "It burns... what're you...what're you doing?"

Aroden didn't answer.

Kite suddenly gave a sharp cry of pain and her back arched, but Aroden never let go of her hands. "Stop!" she wept. "Just let me...just let me die!"

"Shh," I said, stroking her sweaty hair off her face.

"Hayli," Aroden said. His voice was very thin, almost a whisper. "I need your help. Just find my magic and do what I do."

"I can't—"

"You can. Trust yourself."

Swallowing hard, I dropped to my knees beside the bed and cupped my hands around her head, and closed my eyes. I had no idea what I was doing. The way some of the powerful mages talked about their magic, it almost sounded like they could feel or see their power in a way that made me feel completely blind. But still I tried. Tried to concentrate, tried to empty my mind of expectations. And then, slowly, I saw a flickering light behind my eyes.

Sure I was imagining it, I just kept concentrating, but the light began to spread, and suddenly I realized it was not just spreading, but moving—and, strangest of all, I could *feel* Aroden's presence in every bit of it. I wasn't sure what the light was doing, but all around its brightness were patches of broken shadow, and wherever the light touched, the fragments seemed to melt into wholeness. Then I realized, with a shudder of horror, that the whole vast spread of my vision—where the light didn't touch—wasn't just like the blankness behind my closed eyelids, but more of that horrible dark brokenness. And compared to it, the tendril-thin curl of Aroden's light was so, so small.

I reached out, tentative, and tried to find my own magic deep inside me—tried to feel it the way I thought Shade could feel his power. A little blossom of violet light unfurled before me, and, feeling my heart pattering—distantly—with fear and excitement, I pushed it out into the shadows.

I don't know how long I stayed absorbed in that strange focus. I guided my light alongside Aroden's for a while, letting his work teach me what to do, then I moved away and drove my power into the darkest pits of shadow I could find. I lost myself in the rhythm of the work, the seeking, the mending, putting chaos into order. Nothing else mattered.

Then, slowly, I grew aware of hands on my shoulders. A voice in my ear, saying, "Hayli, Hayli, let go."

I thrashed, trying to pull my magic back to me, but I felt so far away from myself.

"Hayli, focus. Listen to my voice."

I tried. Slowly, slowly, I drew my power back into my soul, and suddenly a glaring light blazed into my eyes. Daylight. I came with a jolt back into my senses, and reeled away from the bedside. If not for the arms around me, I would have collapsed, but someone was holding me tight, one arm around my waist, one hand cradling my head against his shoulder. I tried to make sense of the world I was looking at, but all I could see were my hands, glassy, shaking.

Then Kite. She lay perfectly still on her bed, pale, her eyes closed, face peaceful.

"Kite!" I cried. "Oh no…"

"Shh, shh," Aroden's voice whispered in my ear, and that was when I realized that he was the one holding me. "Don't wake her up. She's needs her sleep."

"Sleep?" I whispered. "Then she's not…she's not…"

He released me, but only so he could look me in the eye. He looked dead exhausted, harrowed, but he was smiling.

"We did it," he said. "I couldn't have done it alone—there was too much sickness. But you were amazing. A natural. How did it feel?"

"Exhilarating," I whispered.

His smile widened, then he reached up and rubbed his thumbs over my cheeks, a little crease between his brows. Part of me wanted to pull away from his touch, but I didn't have the strength.

"You pushed yourself hard," he said. "Almost too hard. You're still

 502

new. You need to pace yourself, but, I don't know that that's in your nature. Go and get some rest."

"She's ganna be a'right? Really?"

"Eventually. Just because we got rid of the disease doesn't mean her body is healthy. She needs a lot of rest and nourishment." The corner of his mouth quirked in a little smile. "Assign Coins to that duty, and she'll be better in no time."

I laughed, weakly, and got to my feet. The world wobbled around me but Aroden was right there, holding my elbow to steady me. We left Kite's room together, and by the time we reached Aroden's room, I felt strong enough to walk without help, and my skin had finally got its normal color back.

"Thank you," I said, clasping Aroden's arm.

He smiled and ducked his head, and turned to go into his room. But halfway through the door he paused and glanced over his shoulder. "Did you mean it?"

"Mean what?"

"When you told her you trusted me."

I looked at him a long while, searching his moss green eyes, seeing the wild, desperate hope trapped in their depths. Was it just my trust he wanted? I didn't know, but just the question made my stomach tighten in a little queasy knot, and I swallowed hard.

"Aroden," I said, quiet, knowing I had to speak now before it all spiraled out of control. "I *do* trust you." His eyes lit up; I looked away. "But I love Shade."

I turned without waiting to see his reaction to that, and made my way, stumbling and exhausted, down the hallway, down the stairs, and out into the chill daylight. My heart ached and the world blurred a bit around me. I sat down hard on the front step of the dormitory, and buried my face in my hands.

A few minutes and I collected myself, drawing a deep breath to clear my mind. Then, because I had no idea how long I'd been up in Kite's room, I made my way toward the Rookery, and the motorbike parked in the shadow of its wall. Shiver joined me not ten minutes later, eyeing the motorbike as he strolled up alongside me.

"We're ganna gan for a ride?"

"To the Hole," I said. "Need to get inside the Sanctum again."

"You want to look at the book again, dan' you," he said. "Div'n you hear what Doc said last time? It's dangerous. Not worth our notice."

"So what's he hiding?" I asked, grinning wickedly—if a bit shakily—as I climbed onto the motorbike.

Shiver rolled his eyes and got on behind me. He didn't say a word the whole time we rode into the city, nor after we'd parked the bike in the abandoned yard outside the Troyce & Fallon, or crept down the cold staircase to the underground tunnels we'd used to call home. He led the way back to the Sanctum, and when we got to the door, instead of stepping through to unlock it, he just grabbed my hand and tugged me through with him.

"A'right," he said. "You're here. Do what you need and let's get out of here."

I shivered, rubbing my hands over my arms in the cold, closed space, letting my eyes adjust to the brassy light. Everything was just as it had been the last time, with the book on its pedestal and the basin empty and stained beside it. Ignoring Shiver's restless pacing, I went straight to the book and laid my hands on the cover.

"Aroden was telling me about Arnthor's journal, the one he wrote to heal his fracturing mind. D'you think this might be it?"

He came up to stand beside me, his fingers tracing over the lettering on the cover. "If it's his, how would it be written half in Cavnish, then, and half in…whatever language the rest is in?"

I flipped open the book, rifling through to the page where the Cavnish language started. I'd never gone back to the very beginning, I realized, though it should've been the first thing I did. There, above the top line of text, was written a fancy scripted *"One."* I turned back to the very first page of the book, where, in a completely different hand, above the top line of text, was written the word, *"Aktu."*

"I'm so stupid," I whispered, going back to the Cavnish. "Why div'n we notice that? It ain't a continuation. It's a *translation.*"

"Maybes that's why it dan' make too much sense sometimes," Shiver said, frowning. "If it *was* Arnthor's, and he was gannin' off the ropes a bit, maybe what he wrote was a lot of jibberish nonsense."

I nodded, then took the book off the pedestal and carried it over to a few low stools sitting against the far wall, which didn't look the least bit comfortable but had to be more pleasant than standing up to read. Shiver sat next to me and I held the book between us, and for a while we read in silence. I got annoyed after a bit, though, because

Shiver read so much faster than me, and he kept trying to turn the pages before I'd finished with the one we were on.

"I dan' get this," he said suddenly. He'd been holding up a page so he could read the back of it while I read the front, but now he flipped it over on top of my hand and jabbed a finger at a line of text.

"I seen this now ten times. Started counting after the fourth. Firstborn? Secondborn? I dan' get what it means."

I scanned the passage, then read it aloud for good measure.

"*Then the firstborn will return and sow chaos where he walks, and the secondborn will follow, walking through chaos like a reaper through his harvest. The harvest will be a harvest of blood and the firstborn will drain the blood of the wheat, and the secondborn will follow behind him and undo all the madness of his works. But the firstborn will have a harvest of blood from the secondborn, and the secondborn will rise up and strike down the firstborn. And he will rise up, and he will be free of his shackles, and the secondborn will be shackled.*"

I scowled at the page as I came to the end of the passage.

"What a lot of malarkey," I said after a few minutes. "How's anybody s'posed to make sense of that?"

"I just want to know who these people are that he's writing about. If Arnthor *did* write the text…was he one of them?"

"Maybes it's talking about Wake?"

"Wake, and who? Arnthor? But for this to make sense, Wake would have to be the secondborn, but no one would say Wake is younger than Arnthor, because…Wake is forever, and Arnthor was just a man."

I blew my breath out through pursed lips and shoved the book into Shiver's lap. "I've read all I can. My eyes are going funny."

He nodded slowly and carried the book back to the pedestal. "Was it worth it?" he said. "Did you learn what you wanted?"

I hesitated, staring at the pedestal, my thoughts straying. If anything I was more confused than ever. If this *was* Arnthor's mysterious journal, I couldn't make heads or horns of how it could possibly have healed his mind. It was bloody well making mine want to crack, just from trying to make sense of it. But then, I'd never suffered the fracturing like Tarik had, and some of the words did sound an awful lot like the things he said sometimes. I wondered if reading it would heal *his* mind. I wondered if it would heal Aroden's.

"I dan' na," I said at last. "I div'n na…what I wanted to learn in the first place. I wanted answers...but all I got is more questions."

"Funny how that happens," he said, sharp. "Like how, when I realized Shade came to Borokhev last night, I thought we'd all get some answers about what's been gannin' on with him, and instead, we hear mum about it. What'm I to make of that?"

"Shiver, you grobbing horrid *monster*," I snapped. "You gotta stop snooping on folks, especially in their grobbing *bedrooms!*"

His mouth twitched. "I div'n snoop on you, if it matters. I just...I felt a power in my bones that I've not felt before, and it had all the feel of Tarik about it." He waved a hand. "That dan' make sense, but I can't make it make sense."

"I felt it too," I said quietly. "It's like...recognizing his voice."

He nodded, and for a minute we faced each other in silence, in the dim shadows. I sighed and leaned over my knees.

"I div'n want to say aught because...I thought it would just upset everybody. Because he div'n stay. He div'n want to see anybody else." I glared, not at Shiver, but at the world in general. "Not that he seemed to care much about seeing me, either."

His face softened at that, and he raked a hand through his tangle of dark hair. "I'm sorry," he murmured. "Dan' imagine that was easy for you."

"He said he's not coming back. Not yet. Not...any time soon."

"He knows how much we need him, though, dan' he?" I nodded, and he said, "Selfish bastard. S'pose it's all part of his grand scheme to rake up as much power as he can get."

I picked forlornly at a stray thread on my coat. I didn't want to agree with him, but somehow I found it hard to argue, too.

*"Are your hands tied?"*

*"Who would tie them?"*

Whatever else was happening in Istia, Shade was slipping into some kind of shadow. I didn't know if any of us would know how to stop him.

# Chapter 22 ～ Tarik

I PLUMMETED ENDLESSLY IN SICKENING FREE-FALL, STARING AT THE CLOUDLESS blue expanse soaring above me as the noise of the wind melted into the roar of the waves. Then my vision bleached white and something warm and soft embraced me—not the bitter sea cold, not the blaze of Wake's power. Just a sense of drifting, cocooned in light, not numb but feeling nothing at all. How long I stayed like that I didn't know; time was immaterial. I gave up trying to fight my way free of it and let myself rest, my mind, for once, clear and empty of worry.

I thought I heard Wake's voice, patient and amused, murmuring, "You always did have a flair for the dramatic."

And then I slammed into the floor of Eyid's sitting room, and bit my tongue so hard it bled.

The room was dark, and the window was dark; I must have been caught in that strange white rest for longer than I realized. I pushed myself onto hands and knees, then carefully to my feet, sure I would find Iskari and Nika pouring out a stream of obscenities at me from somewhere nearby, but no one was there; I was all alone. Prodding my tongue against the roof of my mouth and trying to staunch the trickle of blood, I stumbled out of the sitting room and out the front door.

The street was empty, too. The whale oil lamps swung creaking in the stiff breeze, dripping pools of amber light on the uneven cobblestones, and a misting sleet curtained me as I made my way back toward the lodging house. At least it was easy enough to remember the way—and at least it was no great distance. In the alley my steps faltered, but only for a moment, and only because I was suddenly cast in pitch darkness with the buildings on either side of me leaning over me in a rather claustrophobic way. A few steps later I came out onto the broad main street of the city, and found the lodging house almost directly across from me. The lower rooms were still aglow with light, and in a few of the upper rooms a single lamp seemed to be burning, but the building was quiet.

Resigning myself to whatever welcome I was bound to receive, I made my way up the steps and pushed open the front door. A handful of people were still awake, sitting around the hearth in the common room, and when I came in with a gust of a cold air, they all turned to see who had arrived.

"*Veka,*" one of the men breathed. "Geddir, go get Iskari."

A slight, wiry boy leapt to his feet and ran past me, gaping at me openly as he did, then took the stairs to the upper rooms three at a time. The man who had sent him beckoned me forward, a wary light in his eyes.

"Eyidson," he said. "Come, come. Get warm."

I moved toward them, trying not to notice how the other men shuffled their chairs back to make way for me, and turned their faces away as I got closer. Vaguely I wondered if there was still something wrong with my eyes, so I just kept them lowered and took the seat Geddir had vacated, close to the fire.

A few moments later there was a clatter of steps behind me, and then Iskari was storming across the room straight toward me. I got up before he could say so much as a word, and grabbed him by the front of the shirt.

"Iskari," I said, shoving him backward. "We need to talk."

He stumbled a step, but recovered quickly and swiped my hand away. Eyes blazing with anger, he just turned sharply and strode back toward the staircase. Halfway there he realized I wasn't following him. I waited, patiently, as he turned to look at me, then I went without a word to the front door and stepped out into the cold night beyond. A moment later he joined me, stopping on the top step under the ring of lamplight.

"You're insane," he said. "It's too cold out here to talk."

I shrugged. "It's too crowded in there, so, take your pick."

"Taumir, where the *bloody hell* have you been? Do you know...do you have any idea—"

"Unfortunately, yes," I said. "Listen. I had no choice. There were things I had to learn, and I couldn't learn them from here."

"So you just left without a word to any of us. We had no idea what had become of you...if you'd gotten lost in the city, or if you'd..."

"Thrown myself into the sea?" I asked blandly.

He glared at me and didn't favor me with a response.

"If I'd told you, would you have let me go?"

He took the last few steps down from the porch to stand in front of me. "Could we have stopped you?" he asked. "Taumir, you *stodadrakkeyn* idiot, you know we can't keep you from doing whatever you want to do. So you could have at least done us the kindness of telling us beforehand that you meant to disappear for a *whole bloody day*, so we wouldn't have to worry!"

I glanced away, thoroughly chastised. "I'm sorry. I honestly didn't mean to give you grief."

"No, but sometimes I think you just don't give half a *drakk* what other people feel, especially if it inconveniences whatever *schemes* you're concocting."

"That's hardly fair," I said.

"But it's true."

I took a step closer to him. "Maybe I don't particularly choose to care what people feel about me at any given moment," I said, "but you can be damn sure I care what happens to them."

He regarded me quietly, then gave a slight shake of his head. "That's not all that matters in life," he said. "Caring about people in generalities, in the abstract—that's not what friendship is. That's not what makes life worth living. And it certainly isn't what makes your sacrifices, and all that you've been suffering, meaningful. It *matters* what people think. It *matters* that you care."

I clenched my jaw. "Does it, truly?"

"Yes," he snapped, gripping my shoulder and giving it a firm shake. "I don't care if you think you're above the rest of us or beneath us. You don't get to stand outside all our petty quarrels and rivalries and friendships, like some heartless god watching the drama of humanity from his throne of wind."

I said nothing.

He released me with a string of muttered obscenities, and for a while we stood side by side, arms crossed, doing our best to ignore each other. Finally Iskari let out all his breath in a sigh of frustration and turned back to me.

"So, where did you go?"

"Brinmark," I said. "And Tulay."

His brows shot up in surprise. "Quite a lot of travel for one day."

"I had to go to Tulay," I said, one hand drifting up to feel the bullet hole in my shirt, "for several reasons." He watched me sidelong, his gaze riveted on my hand, but I was just glad that he kept his thoughts and commentary to himself. "The situation is so much worse than we thought."

And then, against my will, my thoughts turned to Hayli, and a bitterness seeped into my heart until I couldn't think of anything else. I sat down on one of the steps and leaned my head in my hands.

"You want to know why I don't care?" I said, my voice muffled. "Why it's better to be the heartless bastard you're accusing me of being? Because at least when you don't care, it doesn't hurt so much when people betray you. Because they will, always. Even the people you love. Especially the people you love—that is, if they don't get stolen from you first. If they live long enough, sooner or later they will turn their back on you."

Iskari sat down on the step beside me, but it was some time before he said, "Your girl? Did you see her? What happened?"

I let out a breath and lifted my head, pressing my fingers against my cheeks as I collected my thoughts. "The impostor mage," I said. "She's giving him asylum."

"Your enemy," he said flatly.

"Well, for all I know he was just a victim of some rather vicious mental tortures, like Hayli was." I shook my head. "It's not the asylum I care about. Hell, I might have done it myself if I'd been there. It's that... she didn't tell me, Iskari. She kept it a secret. I learned he was there from someone else."

"Damn," he said.

"Why would she do that? Did she think I would be angry?"

"Would you have been?"

"I don't know. Maybe." I kneaded my forehead and said, "The worst thing though is that it's just eating away at my thoughts, and I can't focus on what I know I should be focusing on. Between that and my mother's schemings...do you wonder that I have a hard time caring about anyone?"

"Your mother...?" Iskari asked, wisely choosing not to answer the question.

With a sigh, I told him everything that had happened. All that Hayli had told me, all that Doc had told me. Meeting Miss Farrady, and how she had shot me. How my mother and Kor had tried to persuade me to follow Rivano, and how they dismissed the concept of Wake's Zealot.

"Well," Iskari said, as I ended with that confusion. "If they are truly followers of Rivano, it doesn't surprise me."

"But Rivano...he founded the Clan in Brinmark. Revived worship of Wake in Cavnal. What are you saying?"

"Is that what you think he did?" he said, regarding me sidelong. When I didn't speak he went on, "What I'm saying is, Rivano was always an agnostic. It's one of the things he and your father used to argue about endlessly. Your father *believed*, but Rivano..." He shrugged. "My father said that Rivano always advocated the usefulness of a shared piety."

"Usefulness!" I echoed. "So the Clan was just a sham? A false religion?"

"A tool," he said, indifferently, "to unite people."

I ground my teeth and dug the heels of my palms against my eyes. "Stars, I am *tired*," I said. "I can't make sense of any of this. And I feel so useless, because I'm supposed to be persuading the people to listen to me, to be willing to follow me, and *look* at me. I can't do a jot of good when I feel like I'm always hovering on the edge of insanity—or death. Especially because I'm seeing Wake constantly, or Death, and I can't even tell if they are real or just figments of my madness."

"Wake...or the mad god," Iskari offered, tentative. "That was the worry, right, that you didn't know which one he was?"

I lifted a hand in defeat.

He was quiet a minute longer, then he asked, voice low, "Death?"

"She's in my thoughts too."

He laughed out loud at that, then sobered. When I eyed him sidelong, questioning, he just said, "Of course Death is a *she*." He chuckled under his breath again and shook his head. "Well, maybe there's something we could do to help you. Magic is Wake's province, right?" I shuddered, hearing Iskari unwittingly echo Death's words. "And the heart of magic in all the world is at Hejmstrathvir, where the *Vekahratha* is. That's why the moot takes place there. It's supposed to be the closest thing to the divine that man can reach, and the idea is Wake's justice will guide the *sodthari* in their affairs." He jostled me slightly, trying to shake me out of my dark mood. "It's worth a try, don't you think? If we go there, maybe you will get some insight and clarity into who's been talking to you. Maybe it will help you understand if it is just because you're dead *drakkim ganthiskur* or actually touched by the hand of God."

"I can't think of any way I'd rather spend my time," I muttered, "than purposefully throwing myself in Wake's path."

"That's settled, then. We'll leave in the morning. We can leave Mirin here this time, unless you prefer him groveling at your heels the whole way."

"God, no," I said, and got up, wincing at a faint residual pain in my chest—either from the bullet wound or from slamming so hard into Eyid's floor. "But I'd rather have groveling than a gunshot wound any day."

He snorted, his mouth tightening into a crooked line that was half smile, half grimace, and followed me into the lodging house.

LATE THE NEXT MORNING, AFTER NIKA had finally gotten tired of berating me for my disappearance and Mirin had finally convinced himself that I was actually alive and still mostly in possession of my sanity, Iskari, Nika and I left Bregjarvani on horseback for the two-day ride to Hejmstrathvir. We followed the river Stratha inland for hours, winding our way into foothills of hardened lava and moss-grey scrub, scattering flocks of mountain goats and sheep as we went.

By nightfall we had reached a small river village, where a fisherman and his wife put us up for the night in his goat shed with profuse apologies for the smell. I didn't even notice the smell; I only noticed that the animals were warm, and the wind couldn't reach us in that little turf-shrouded shelter. The couple gave us fish stew and fresh goat milk for the strangest breakfast I'd ever eaten, and we left the village before the sun had even risen.

Midway through the morning, we turned north and headed straight toward the mountains, whose wicked black slopes jabbed like a remonstrance into the throat of the sky. The wind clawed our faces, stiff and bitter and numbing, and even the sun hanging low on the horizon gave nothing that resembled warmth. If Iskari and Nika noticed the cold, though, they showed no sign of it. I envied them their defiance, bare-armed and fierce, as if daring the winter to break them.

Me, I hunched over my horse's neck without shame, swathed in wool and leather, my eyes watering and crusted with frost. I thought of Scorch, and the way he always seemed to burn with an internal flame, but I didn't dare trust my power to keep me warm. Knowing my luck, I would catch my heart on fire and that would be the end of me—inglorious failure, desperate for comfort, too weak to face even the simplest hardship. And I certainly had no intention of trying to dredge up the warmth I'd felt from Wake's touch, not here, this close to the Wakestone at the heart of the island.

The air thinned as the rugged slopes marched up around us, and the horses slowed to pick a careful path between rocks and ghostly formations of ancient lava. Nothing green grew here, not, at least, at this time of year; it was all cold and dead, black stone and wind. I hadn't been willing to believe that any part of the island could be colder than the coast, but when the snow started swirling down around us in a blinding fog, I realized I would have to reevaluate my judgment.

I'd lost track of time when we left the dangerous slopes for a broad and broken plateau, rimed with frost and ice. All at once I felt that something had changed—something fundamental to the pattern of things, something beyond what I could see and smell and taste. My skin prickled, tingling with a sudden rush of energy. I bit down on my tongue so hard that I split it open again and tasted blood, and beneath me my horse snorted and skitted aside.

Nika drew her horse to a walk and glanced over her shoulder at me. "Taumir?" she called. "What is it?"

"You can't feel it?" I asked.

The world rocked beneath me, sky caving in above me, stars like ice. I gasped for breath. And the noise of it, murmuring, lilting, singing, now loud, now soft, driving out my thoughts, trapping me in my mind. It wasn't Death's voice weaving a lamentation in my thoughts, but a sharp and gazing brightness. I dug the heel of my hand against the side of my head.

Nika nudged her horse and cantered back to me, leaning over without a word and snatching up my horse's reins. "Come on," she said. "You'll understand in a moment."

"No, no. Not closer," I said, snatching at the pommel as the horse moved obediently forward. "Let me go."

But she didn't, and I couldn't make myself move. I watched the ground drifting below and longed to be swallowed into stone, but we never stopped moving. The noise pitched to screeching cacophony, a string out of tune, discordance in the web of things, and when I couldn't bear it any longer I threw myself from the saddle, hitting the ground hard. But still I couldn't escape the wrongness of it.

"What is this place?" I gasped.

My hands were planted on the spongy turf, breaking the crust of frost that filled every gap in the grey moss. I dug my fingertips into the earth and tried to breathe.

Nika was standing beside me. "We've reached Hejmstrathvir. The heart of the island. See the cairn there?" I looked, and found the small stone she was pointing at. "The Wakestone marks the center of all things. That is where magic is the strongest in all the world."

She said it with pride but I only laughed, a harsh and cruel sort of sound. The cairn was nothing remarkable. It was nothing but a dull grey rock shaped like a bullet, less than a foot high, ringed by white stones that stood out stark in the bleak landscape. And it was all wrong.

"Why are you laughing?" Iskari asked from somewhere behind me, still on horseback. He was watching me thoughtfully, eyes bright and intense.

I staggered to my feet and forced my way toward the cairn. It felt like walking through a wall of water, and my skin crawled. I bent and let my fingers graze over the rough stone. The hairs on the back of my neck stood straight on end.

"Don't you see?" I asked.

"Don't *touch* it," Nika snapped. "It's sacred. It's a holy thing."

"It's *wrong*," I said, glaring at her over my shoulder. "Couldn't you tell it was out of tune? Can't you *hear* it? This…this isn't the heart of the island."

I bent and wrapped my arms around the rock and lifted it gently, like a child. It was strangely light in my arms, vibrating against my bones like an electrical charge.

"*Taumir!*" Nika shouted.

Her rage was nothing. None of it meant anything.

I walked a few paces toward the north, listening as the discordance shifted, narrowing. Then, feeling the stone's hunger like the magnetic draw of a lodestone, I carried it a little to the west, and again a few paces to the north.

"Here," I gasped.

And the song came true, and the cacophony came silent, and the stone fell from my hands as the world gave way to midnight and the weeping sea, and moonlight traced like tears on wet sand.

I stood still.

I was not facing the dark abyss of my own sea, nor was I on the now-familiar strand of Death's blood-limned shore. I stood on a tiny island in the midst of the vastness of the ocean, and I was not alone. Perhaps twenty feet from where I stood, two men circled each other, locked in ancient battle; I thought I recognized them, but they were not the fighters from the dream I'd had before.

Then, as I stepped closer, I realized that one of them was Wake. He was taller here than I'd ever seen him before, shining with the sharp, cold brightness of lightning, his eyes like suns. The figure facing him was only slightly shorter, wrapped in chaos like a cloak. The first moment I saw him, I thought I was looking at Wake's reflection, but then I saw every way the image was distorted, every way it hung in mockery from the figure's body like ill-fitted clothes.

I let out my breath and dropped to a crouch on the wet and gleaming sand, praying that neither of them would notice me. But the smaller figure saw me immediately, and faster than I could process, he was crouching in front of me.

"Ah," he said. "I wonder, what must you be thinking, trapped here at our caprice, a spectator watching the duel that has for its prize his own life?"

I tore my gaze from the wrongness of his eyes, and glanced at Wake, who stood motionless in the background, watching. I shifted my weight.

"What, did you think you would see some hint of shared memory from him?" the figure before me asked. "You know in your heart. You've known all along—you have never seen him before. You have only, ever, seen *me*."

"You're the mad god," I choked, my mind desperately trying to throw a barrier against his words.

Still Wake stood motionless, content to look on.

"You're the mad god," I said again. "Do you expect me to believe a word you say?"

He gave me a faintly chiding look and stood up, beckoning me up with him. "He claims he wants you for his Zealot," he said, conspiratorial, but his voice was loud enough that Wake could surely hear it. "But the truth is he doesn't care about you. He doesn't care if you live or die. He doesn't care about anything except seeing his justice reaped on the world. Is that what you want to be? Do you imagine the world will tolerate you then? The world hates what it cannot understand, and above everything else, it cannot understand *him*."

"But it understands you?" I asked.

He smiled. "Clever," he said. "He will bring the world to ruin. I seek the path of peace."

"Chaos," I said.

"Peace," he repeated. "And only a little blood. A little blood is always necessary to bring about peace."

"Is that what you told Arnthor?"

He tipped his head to regard me curiously, then his gaze flicked toward Wake. I might have mistaken it, but I thought I saw a ghost of a smile touch his mouth. "I always forget that humans have such short memories," he murmured. "So limited, in so many ways."

"I suppose you mean to tell me that if I join you, I won't be limited any more?"

"Hm," he said, the sound a stifled laugh. He reached up to brush my hair off my forehead, the wild chaos of his amber-gold eyes fixed on mine. I shied away from his touch. "Essentially, love, you have a very simple choice," he said. "A little blood—" he gestured to himself—"or a lot of blood." He pointed to Wake. "Peace and happiness and a long, boring life with your bird girl as *my* emissary, or hatred and darkness and ruin as the right hand of Wake." He gave me a faintly mocking smile. "Your choice."

I took a step closer to him, driving him a step back. "I am not an emissary," I growled, "am I? I am the altar on which you would sacrifice the world."

"Now, now," the mad god said. "That's a bit extreme, don't you think?"

"But isn't it true?"

He walked a few paces away from me; without meaning to, I followed. "I find it curious," he said, "that you sound so sure about this, and yet you don't have the first idea of who you are. What you are. Just a bit of flotsam tossed onto a foreign shore, aren't you?"

"Don't you throw my words back in my face."

"Fiery," he said, smirking. "I can understand why Wake has had his eye on you." He leaned closer to me. "Come now. You really didn't think he was walking in and out of your life, did you? As if *God* would speak to you? Visit *you?*"

I turned to look at Wake, silently pleading him to speak, to step in and reveal the truth—whatever the truth was. But he just watched me, stern and remote, fathomless.

I didn't recognize him at all.

My stomach churned, and I dropped to my knees in the sand. "It wasn't you," I said to the mad god. "You're nothing like him."

He crouched in front of me again, and I jolted when I glanced up and found myself face to face with Hayli. "Stars, Shade," she said. "You dan' think I could be whatever I want?"

"Shut up," I said, scrambling back to my feet, throwing a hand toward her—*him.* "I've heard enough. I'll take my chances with Rigvar and Aroden. I'd rather face Destri's weapon myself than listen to another one of your lies. I *will not* be anyone's emissary!" I took a step back, stumbling, and rounded on Wake. Just the sight of him made my knees shake, and I knew I ought to kneel, but I couldn't. "Are you just going to stand there and watch?" I shouted. "Aren't you going to make me stay? If you're Wake, why don't you just *make* me your Zealot and be done with it?"

He was directly in front of me, faster than thought, looming over me, his lightning-bright eyes riveted on mine. "I don't desire your subservience," he said. The sound of his voice shook every bone in my body. "I desire your cooperation."

The mad god stood back—pressed back, I realized, by the weight of Wake's power. I was glad of it; I didn't imagine I could face both of them at the same time. It was all I could do to hold fast where I was, electricity arcing all around me as if I stood in the heart of a storm.

"Was any of it real?" I murmured, surprising myself as I realized that I, desperately, wanted it to be true. "Were you ever with me? Was it ever you I saw?"

He reached his hand toward me. "It was always me," he said, and planted his palm against my forehead.

# PART FOUR: SILENCE

# CHAPTER 1 ~ TARIK

I FELL TO MY KNEES, MY HANDS HITTING THE FROSTY, MOSS-SHROUDED GROUND, and Nika was shaking my shoulders and screaming for me to wake up. But I had never been more awake in my life.

"Taumir!" she shouted. "*Veka, Veka...*"

"I'm all right," I gasped, shuddering as the trailing remnants of Wake's power ebbed away. I felt naked in the cold without it, as if the biting wind were coming from somewhere inside of me.

Nika sat down hard on the ground beside me, pulling her knees up to her chest. Iskari joined her a moment later, his face drawn and strangely pale, and he reached out wordlessly to help me sit upright.

"I'm so sorry," he murmured. "I thought for certain that coming here would help you. If I'd imagined—"

I waved a hand to brush away his concern. "No, no. You were right to bring me here. If I'd waited for the moot, I'd have been helpless." I glanced at each of them in turn, Iskari watching me intently, Nika with her gaze fixed on the Wakestone. "What happened?"

"You dropped the cairn," Nika said. "And then you froze. We couldn't get your attention. You just stood there with your eyes wide open and..."

"They were changing," Iskari said softly. "Your eyes. They turned gold, first, then silver blue, and at the end..."

"So bright," Nika said, hugging her arms around her chest. "Everything about you was bright like lightning. And it felt...it felt like before, when I couldn't be near you. It drove us both back. And then you fell."

The last few words she said flatly, almost reproachfully, as if she'd expected me to stay trapped in some kind of divine translucidity forever. I gave her a peevish look and rubbed my hands over my head.

"It's damn cold here," I muttered.

Neither of them said a word. Iskari got to his feet and helped me up, while Nika fetched the horses. When I managed to clamber onto my horse's back, I sat a few long moments staring at the cairn, my mind a tangle of memories and fears and confusion. At least the song at the heart of the island had come into harmony. The discord was gone, and the pain and the wrongness. Maybe, if I could be remembered for doing one good thing in my life, it was fixing the Wakestone where the wellspring of magic really was.

I turned my horse's head and led the way back across the plateau, toward the perilous path out of the mountains.

WE REACHED BREGJARVANI BY NIGHTFALL THE following day, and left the weary horses with the stable boys behind the lodging house. When we got into the common room, Iskari shoved me gently into a chair near the fire, and went to request hot meals for all of us from the cooks. I leaned over the table, my fingers tracing Kudric rune patterns in the wood, painfully aware of Nika's covert attention following my every motion, and the furtive glances of Halvir and Thane and a handful of others sitting at the tables around us.

"What happened to you up there?" Nika asked finally, when I was about to tell her to speak her mind or leave me alone.

We'd spoken no more than strictly necessary the whole journey back to Bregjarvani; I had hoped that, now that we'd arrived, that wouldn't change. I hated being wrong.

"I don't want to talk about it," I said. "I wish I could forget the whole thing."

"Did you see—"

"I said I don't want to talk about it," I said, flattening my palm against the table so sharply that she jumped at the noise.

She was quiet a while, then she leaned toward me, shaking her blonde hair off her shoulders. "I told you before that I thought you were a madman, when you first started claiming that you were seeing something...*someone*. I even asked Iskari if he thought you were safe

522

to be around. If it was safe to let you be free, and on your own. I know there are some people who still wonder that, who say that an asylum and the best drugs science has to offer are the only cure for people who…" She shook her head. "But after what I've seen, I can't believe that any more. Not only does insanity not explain the…the blood, and all you've suffered lately. It also doesn't explain *you*. You really are touched by the divine. You have so much power." There was a note of awe in her voice that I wasn't sure I liked. "It's wonderful."

I laughed, cold and bitter. "Wonderful? It isn't wonderful. It's a bondage, Nika. I'm enslaved to my own magic. And every time I grasp at a power out of desperation, it breaks over me and binds me a little tighter, and wears down my mind until there's nothing left but a hollow light. And I can't escape it, because I need it. I hate how it grows like a hole inside me, worse than a drug, always needing…always devouring…" I pressed my head in my hands, trying to drown out the echo of Death's words in the back of my mind. "God, I wish I were free of it all."

"How can you say that?" she asked. "You wouldn't be able to stand living without magic."

"Yes, I could," I said, the ferocity of the words startling us both. "If it meant I could be free of this madness, I could. I would rather be sane and whole, and an ordinary man, than broken like a shattered sea. Can't you understand that? My soul is a battleground for the gods, Nika, but I want nothing to do with either of them. I want no part in their cosmic war. I'm not their weapon, and I'm not their arbiter."

Her gaze faltered from mine and she looked at the fire instead, her hands listless on the table between us. "But our fate is shaped by the battles they wage. Sometimes standing back, refusing to take a side— it's as good as turning your back on all of us who cannot act on our own behalf."

"Who laid the fate of the world on my shoulders?" I asked, standing up—too fast. The chair clattered to the floor, and the room around us fell silent. "I never asked for it. This is *not* my burden." She was on her feet too, and I took a step closer to her, lowering my voice. "Give me the crown of Cavnal," I said. "Give me the *aydrding* of Istia. I would gladly be King, or Godar, in my own right—I would rather shoulder either of those mantles alone to the day I die—if it meant I could be free of this madness."

523

"You don't mean it," she said.

I said, "Every word." Then something inside me crumbled, and I bent over the table, cradling my head in my hand. "No, I don't mean it." I drew a long, thin breath and said, half in whisper, "If I thought by my suffering I could save them, there is nothing I wouldn't endure. I would gladly die for them."

She looked at me quietly. "Would you?"

Iskari returned that moment, balancing three bowls of lamb stew precariously in his arms. He looked at us standing across the table from each other, my chair still toppled on the floor behind me, the room around us still caught in watching silence, and muttered a few colorful obscenities under his breath.

"What'd I miss?" he asked, carefully depositing the bowls on the table.

"Taumir wants to abandon us to the whims of gods and daemons."

I snorted and pulled my chair upright, and sat down to the bowl of stew Iskari pushed toward me. "Think about it, Nika. They're battling over me to be their emissary in the world, but if I can just hold out and not agree to cooperate with either of them, then what will they do? If I side with either of them, it will bring their battle into our world and you all are going to be the ones who suffer the consequences of that. But if I don't, it keeps their fight confined to their own realm, and we can make a *skatrdrakkat* of this world in any way we like."

Nika laughed under her breath, but Iskari just looked more anxious than ever. He set down his spoon and planted his fingertips on the table. "Do you imagine the mad god only works in this world through emissaries? Don't you think half the mess we're facing right now might be due in some way to his interference? He is chaos."

"Men I can deal with," I said. "Even misguided ones." I stabbed my own spoon in his direction. "I am *not* going to add oil to the fire."

He gave a long, unhappy sigh but subsided, focusing his attention on his stew. Nika polished off the last of her own meal and shoved the bowl away.

"Wake and the mad god fighting over you," she said. "Let me guess. That's what you saw when you picked up the *Vekahratha*."

"Damn, you saw right through my cunning bluff," I said blandly.

She gave me a peeved look. "Well?"

"Well what?"

 524

"What did they offer you? I assume they offered you something, to entice you to side with one or the other of them."

"Yes," I said. "Blood, death, ruin, destruction. Sounds charming, doesn't it?"

Nika and Iskari exchanged a glance, then Iskari said, "Did you ever stop to think that, if you were to become the Zealot, you could stop this war once and for all? Isn't that what you *want*?"

"More than anything, but I will never agree to be the Zealot. There is a price for that power that I am not willing to pay."

"Stubborn bastard," he said.

I sighed and got to my feet. "Work the problem out," I said, "to its logical conclusion. Use your imagination, Iskari, and consider the consequences, and then tell me if you still think I should become an emissary for either of them. For any of them."

"Any?" Nika asked.

"Death," Iskari said, carelessly. "She offered him a bargain too."

"Death's a she?" Nika said, and flashed me a mocking smile. "I like that."

I rolled my eyes and kicked my chair back under the table. "I'm going to bed."

"Don't disappear again."

I hesitated beside the table, then caged in the words I wanted to say and headed toward the staircase.

*I have nowhere left to go.*

# CHAPTER 2 ~ HAYLI

FOR TWO DAYS AFTER SHIVER AND I HAD GONE BACK TO THE SANCTUM, I'D been mulling over what we'd read in the *Brigaz Nedash*, but I never got any more clarity about the words than I'd had before. I knew what I had to do if I ever hoped to make sense of it—and I was running out of reasons to put it off.

Still, I paced for a good twenty minutes in the courtyard, under a feeble mid-morning sun, before I finally made up my mind. The courtyard was quiet, with just a few knots of folks trailing between the dormitory and the other buildings, and a handful of older men sitting by a can fire with an empty barrel between them for a table, locked in a game of Adurac. None of them paid me the least mind as I made my way to the front gate of the facility, where Scorch was on watch with Lev.

"Got a question for you, Scorch," I said, answering their salute with a nod of greeting.

"Fire," he said, with a wicked smile.

"Got any ken where Rivano holes up these days?"

"Never cared too much to find out," he said, "but if I were to guess, I think I've seen him loitering around some of the basement offices in the dormitory."

I grimaced. The basement offices—too many of my memories of Borokhev lingered in those rooms. Still, I had questions that Rivano needed to answer, and if that was the only place I could count on finding him, then that was where I would go.

As I turned to go, Scorch said, "What do you need Rivano for?"

"My business," I said.

"Heard you went toe to toe with him over that impostor mage."

"He has a name, y'know," I said, glaring at him over my shoulder. Scorch's face got very dark and very drawn at my words, his eyes snapping fire-bright. "And yeah, I did. What of it?"

"Just take care. You think you know who Aroden is, but you have no idea."

"And you know better? *He* dan' even know who he is."

"Like hell he doesn't," Scorch snapped. "You really believe that?"

I took three steps to face him again, blood burning in all my veins. "Have *you* ever known what it's like to have your brain played with? To have folks telling you the sky is green and up is down, and somehow making you believe it's true? Dan' pretend you understand what he's been through. Dan' ever."

His eyes narrowed, very slightly, but he didn't say aught in answer. And yet, when I turned and stalked away, I couldn't even feel that I'd won the argument. My heart hung heavy in my chest, worry and fear churning and burning in the back of my mind. Then, with as much will as I could muster, I shoved the whole tangle of thoughts into a mental box and slammed the lid closed. If I meant to face Rivano, I needed all my focus.

I found the Clan Master just where Scorch had suggested, down in one of the basement offices—the one, I realized too late, where Shade had shot and killed Andon Vrey. My stomach churned as soon as I pieced together the memory, and for half a tick it was all I could not to turn on my heel and walk away. But Rivano was already watching me expectantly from the desk, from the very chair where Andon had died. I wondered if he knew.

"Hayli," he said. "Stars, girl, are you well? You look a little pale."

"I dan' like this room," I admitted, the words escaping in a rush. "You know somebody died here, right?"

"Somebody died in many of the rooms in this place," he said, carefully. "It has a long history. But I take it this was a bit more of a personal experience for you." He studied me through hooded eyes, then he nodded. "Ah, yes. Shade killed someone here. Jig told me about that."

I glared at him and folded my arms over my chest. "That's not why

I'm here. I wanna know about the *Brigaz Nedash*."

I expected him to be surprised, maybe even angry to learn that I knew about the book, but he barely even glanced up at me. He didn't move a jot, and his expression never changed.

"Arnthor's book," he mused. "Delusional ravings of a dangerous man."

"It *is* his book?" I asked, flabbergasted, and then, without waiting for an answer, "If you think it's delusional…why would you put it on a pedestal in your own Clan's ritual room? That dan' make the least kind of sense!"

"It's perfectly sensible," he said, finally looking up at me, his fingers toying with the end of his long braid. "I suppose you have a reason you're asking about it? What do you want to know?"

"If it's Arnthor's, how'd you get your hands on it?"

"I heard a rumor of where it was in Cromis, and I went and took it," he said. "It wasn't safe where it was. Arnthor had left it in his cave, unprotected, unsecured. I figured it would be better under the seal of the Clan, where at least we could keep it from falling into the wrong hands."

"And whose hands would those be?"

He sighed and ran his fingers along the edge of the desk. "That text is a mystery. If you've looked at it, I'm sure you've drawn that conclusion yourself. I'm a competent scholar of Cromner but there are elements of the text that simply defy reason. As I told you, they are no more than delusional ravings. But there is enough substance to the text to make it a useful tool for gullible fools who are eager to believe anything that tastes of hidden things."

I frowned, troubling over his words, trying to pick out why they had me bothered. Then I understood, and said, "Is that what you're doing with it? Are your Clan members just gullible fools you've a mind to trick?"

"Is that what you think I'm doing?"

He almost sounded hurt, and I wavered. "I dan' na what I think," I said.

*Is it true what Aroden said about you?* I wanted to ask. *Do you mean to goad Shade into remaking the world?*

"Who is the Zealot?" I murmured.

"Shade," he said, without hesitation. I glared at him and he lifted his hands. "You mean, *what* is the Zealot. Arnthor believed the Zealot to be the right hand of Wake. But what is the Zealot, really? He's someone who can unite the world, someone with enough power and charisma to redefine all of our washed-up and worn-out ideas, our faded beliefs, our tired and broken definitions of archaic things like *right* and *wrong*. Don't you understand? All this conflict, this brewing war…it's all because we've failed to bring our morality into time with our changing world. The old standards don't hold true any more, and the longer we cling to them, the more narrow-minded, the more stagnant we become as societies, as peoples. But we could have *unity*. We could elevate ourselves to a higher state of being. We could reach the very summit of human possibility under the guidance of someone like Shade, and leave behind petty quarrels and rivalries once and for all."

"All that," I said. "You'd lay the burden of doing all that on Shade's shoulders? Why? What can he do to change the world?"

Rivano smiled, and my stomach crawled to see the gleam in his eyes. "The question, Hayli, is—what can't he do?"

I looked at him a long moment in shaken silence, then turned and strode out of the office without another word. Aroden caught me as I was coming up the stairs, but seeing him was almost as bad as seeing Rivano, and I held up a hand as I stalked past him to try to ward him away. If anything, it just made him more intent on following me.

He trailed me all the way out of the dormitory, all the way to the can fire that the card-players had now abandoned. I sat on the barrel they'd been using for a table and folded my arms. Aroden stopped in front of me, mimicking my pose and my glare.

"You were talking to Rivano," he said.

I gritted my teeth and looked away. For one irrational moment, I almost called on Piper to come and fly me away, somewhere far, far away where folks weren't constantly snooping in my business. I was so sick of mages who knew too much. And behind Aroden's words I heard another accusation: *You were listening to Rivano.*

And that thought scared me more than I wanted to admit, because I'd gone to Rivano angry, I'd gone convinced he was doing something wicked, and I'd meant to catch him in his own lies and denounce him once and for all as the right and proper enemy of us all. Instead, I was horrified because I caught myself wondering if, in some way, he was right.

529

What if Shade *could* stop all this talk of war, all this division and hatred, just by embracing his own power—not just his magical power, but his power to inspire and lead folks? If he just accepted what he was—what Rivano knew he could be—could he end our suffering? But I knew what Shade would say. He'd say he didn't want that power, that he didn't believe he could do aught that Rivano was claiming. He'd *refuse.*

In fact, he already had.

Aroden shifted his weight, drawing me out of my thoughts, and I heaved a long sigh. "I know what book you were talking about," I said. "Arnthor's book."

"What?" he said, eyes widening. "You do?"

"It's here in Brinmark," I said. "They call it the *Brigaz Nedash.*"

He tipped his head, frowning at the words. "That doesn't…mean anything," he said.

"You speak Cromner?" I asked, baffled. He looked at me, face inscrutable, and didn't say a word. I faltered and added, "So they're not Cromner words?"

"No, they are, but you don't put them together like that. *Hope Ruin.*"

"That sounds like it means something."

"But what?" he asked, flicking his hands up in annoyance. "It could mean anything. It could mean nothing."

"Kind of like the whole text."

He took a step closer to me. "You've seen it?"

"Yeah, couple times. Dan' make much sense to me, but maybe because it wasn't written for the likes of me."

*A tool for gullible fools…*

"Hayli," he said, very softly. "Can you take me there?"

I hesitated, suddenly wishing that Shiver were with me, or Derrin, or somebody else who could tell me if I was a fool for wanting to say *yes.* At any rate, what harm could it do? If the words meant anything more to Aroden than they meant to me, maybe they'd do what he hoped, and heal the brokenness in his mind. And if I could do that for him…just that much…

If someone knew a way to patch together what Kippler had torn apart in *my* mind, and didn't tell me, what kind of person would that make them? If I didn't do whatever I could to help Aroden…that would make me no better than Vrey. No better than Miss Farrady.

"We'll need to get Shiver and the bike," I said, "or get Derrin to take us, because I dan' na how to get inside the Sanctum on my own, and it's a fair trek from here."

"No need for them," Aroden said, with a shy kind of smile. "If you let me…if you give me permission…I could see the place in your mind and take us there myself."

I chewed the inside of my cheek, scanning all the yard around us, waffling in the worst possible way. Aroden took a step closer to me, holding out his hand.

"Please? You trusted me once. Won't you trust me in this?"

"It's not that," I said. "I just…"

"You're afraid of what will happen if I read it?" He smiled faintly. "It's just a book. If it doesn't help me, it certainly can't hurt me. But it *might* help me."

I swallowed, then reached out and slipped my hand into his, wincing at the touch. His smile widened briefly and he came close to me, resting the fingertips of his other hand gently against my temple.

"What're you doing?" I hissed. "You dan' need to touch me to read my mind."

He laughed under his breath and whispered, "No, I don't."

Then he wrapped an arm around me and pulled me out of the world.

We stepped out of the bright and blazing light into the Clan's long hallway, not twenty feet from the sealed doors to the Sanctum. I rubbed my arms, trying to banish the creeping chill I felt from Ghosting, and started toward the doors. A few steps and I glanced back at Aroden, realizing he hadn't moved at all. He had his head tipped to one side, both hands poised in the air in front of him, looking for all the world like a hound tracing a scent.

"Aroden? It's this way, c'mon."

He followed me, slowly, but the closer we got to the doors, the more puzzled he looked. "This place," he said. He canted his head to the other side, eyes narrowing. "He's been here."

I frowned. "Who has?"

A minute and he didn't move at all, just grimaced like he'd tasted something sour, or heard a note in a song sung out of tune. Then he looked at me again, brow furrowed. "*He* was. I don't know. It's a confusion, it makes no sense. I know…but I don't know. It's too far away." A pause, then, "It's in there?"

"You mean Shade? Yeah, it's in that room."

His jaw tightened but he said naught at all, just laid his hands against the doors. Then he shuddered and took a step back.

"Of course he did," he muttered.

I flung my hands up in frustration. "Who did what? You're not making any sense."

"He's warded it against me. He doesn't want me to see what's inside. I should have known he would. But who? Who is *he*? Who is the mage? I don't remember…" With a sharp gasp as if something pained him, he pressed the heel of his hand against his temple and screwed his eyes shut. "Just out of my reach," he whispered.

I gritted my teeth. Why would Shade ward the Sanctum against Aroden? How would he even know to do it? My stomach pitched suddenly, and I caught at the doorframe for support. What if Shade had sensed Aroden's presence at Borokhev, the way Aroden had sensed *his*? Did Shade know I'd kept that secret from him? Oh, stars…if he did…

Tears stung at the backs of my eyes and I shook my head, willing them away.

"Why would he do that?" I said, finally asking the question out loud.

Aroden gave me a long, bitter look. "I imagine it's because he wants to keep me broken. He always did. Because he's…because he's afraid of me." He grimaced again and pushed his hand harder against his head.

Fighting down a surge of anger, I nodded at the door. "Can you open the lock? Like you did with your handcuffs?"

The corners of his mouth tipped faintly upward and he placed his hands against the door again. After a moment I heard a series of low clunking noises, then one louder clang. Aroden twisted one of his hands, and the door swung silently open.

"I can't get inside," he said, "but this is the least I can do."

I studied him a moment, then, steeling my resolve, I marched into the Sanctum, grabbed the book off the pedestal, and carried it out to Aroden's waiting hands. He held it gingerly a moment, staring at the cover through wide eyes.

"I've been looking for this for so long," he murmured. "It's his…it really is. That's his writing." He glanced up and shook his head. "Can you believe it? Arnthor himself wrote these words."

I swallowed, and watched as he cracked open the book and began to read the Cromner text from its very beginning. His face never changed as he read. He flew through the pages, much faster than I or even Shiver could read, and the flit of his eyes over the pages as he scanned the text was the only thing about him that moved. I didn't move, either. I stood frozen in front of him, fearing at every moment that someone would find us standing there, but no one came, and nothing happened. Aroden read, and I waited, and prayed with every breath that I'd done something good.

Aroden stirred suddenly. He had the book cradled in the nook of one arm, and the fingers of his other hand were tapping one of the pages. "This is all of it?"

"Stars, you're already done?" I muttered, shifting my weight. My knees ached and my back was stiff, making me realize how long I'd been standing there motionless. "That's all there is." I peered at him curiously. "Well? D'you feel aught different?"

He looked up at me then, and I startled a step away from him, because his eyes were bright with tears.

"I understand," he said. He clapped the book shut and clasped it to his heart, then covered his face with his other hand and bent his head. "I remember...I remember all of it. What did he *do* to me? You don't... you have no idea who he is. What did he do... *Why?*"

He spun away suddenly with an animal cry of rage or pain, slamming his fist against the wall, then sliding down to a crouch with his head buried in the crook of one arm, the book in the other, clutched to his chest. For much too long he didn't move. His eyes, wide and wild, stared out at nothing, as if he were trapped in some kind of waking nightmare.

My stomach clenched in pity to see so distressed, and I stepped forward, cautious, to lay a hand on his shoulder. "Tell me what you learned."

He shuddered and glanced up at me, his gaze searching mine until I had to look away, uncomfortable. I couldn't make sense of the riddle in his eyes.

"Tarik..." he said finally, scrubbing his sleeve over his eyes and turning his face, embarrassed-like, away from mine. "The mage you know as Tarik? I told you I was afraid the mad god was toying with him. But it's so much worse than that. He *is* the Scion of the mad god.

533

He always has been."

"But you said you were the Zealot."

He shook his head. "They aren't the same. You knew that, didn't you? Wake, and the mad god. The Scion, and the Zealot."

I swallowed, and couldn't find a word to say.

"Don't you see?" Aroden said. "Ever since Shade first came, he's been sowing discord. The Accord. The assassination of Eyid. The assassination attempt on King Trabin. The Chernayi. Esobor. Kippler and his schemes. The rift within the Hole, and Kantian's death. The sedition in the Court of Ministries. The revolution in the streets. You getting trapped by Kippler. Your brother's death. Avnaya Square and Trabin's *actual* assassination. The alliance, the constant looming threat of war." He shook his head, horror in his eyes. "It all started two years ago, when he came out of the night, and took my place."

I knew I should've listened to all the words he said. I should have been horrified by the revelation as he was. But my mind had shut down, and all I could think, over and over again, was, "My brother's death?"

I said it out loud, and Aroden winced as if I'd slapped him.

"Oh, Hayli," he said, reaching out to touch my cheek. "I'm so sorry. I didn't mean…"

"Who is my brother?" I growled, swiping his hand away. "*Tell* me."

"Adde," he murmured. He wouldn't look at me. "Adde Lorin, by birth. But that's not the name he chose for himself, after your parents died, though I suppose he was sentimental enough to keep part of your mother's name—Vareya." He met my gaze. "Vrey. Andon Vrey."

I couldn't breathe. Couldn't think. Couldn't process his words. It didn't make sense, none of it made sense. It was nonsense nonsense nonsense

Lies

A cruel joke

Aroden's arm was around me, but I pulled away, grabbing the book from his hands, slamming it back on its pedestal, shutting the doors of the Sanctum behind me, walking away from Aroden, from the memories, from the nightmare.

*Andon…Andon was my brother? Is that why I thought I recognized him the first time I saw him? Why he wanted to know my last name? Oh, stars, if I'd told him, would he have realized his only sister was being held captive?*

*Maybe he knew. Maybe he found out. Maybe he really was trying to get me out of Borokhev...maybe he knew the truth about Shade and wanted to warn me... and that's why Shade killed him.*

*Shade killed him.*

*Shade killed my brother. He knew Andon was my brother. How could he not? He knew all the families of all the nobles. He knew I wasn't my parents' only child. Why didn't he tell me?*

*He lied to me.*

*What if he didn't know?*

I startled in surprise, because that was Piper's voice, contradicting me, sounding worried—and I'd never known Piper to sound worried about aught.

*How can you say that?* I snapped at her. *Of course he did.*

*Hayli...* she whispered. I could taste her fear, but it made no sense to me, so I shoved it away. *This isn't right. This anger...it's not like you. How can you think so bad of Shade without even letting him explain himself? For killing Andon! Andon, who tortured you—in case you forgot. Who tried to break your mind!*

**Shade had a chance,** I said. *He had a chance to explain himself and he didn't. And look at what he did—he tried to keep Aroden away from the Sanctum because he knew what would happen if Aroden read the book. He knew Aroden would learn his secrets!*

*It's not Shade's secrets I'm worried about,* she said.

*You're just a grobbing bird. You don't understand people at all.*

She didn't say anything in answer.

# CHAPTER 3 ～ HAYLI

IT TOOK ARODEN A GOOD HOUR BEFORE HE'D COLLECTED HIMSELF ENOUGH TO start halfway making sense again, and even then he was oddly quiet as he wrapped an arm around me and pulled me with him to Borokhev. As soon as we stepped back into the world, I knew something was wrong. The ordinary folks were nowhere to be seen, but the courtyard was crawling with people—mostly older people, men and women who went openly armed, and who wore midnight blue coats rather like my own. Bridnow was in the middle of them, talking in close conversation with three men. One, I realized, was Creech.

I exchanged a glance with Aroden, then of one accord we both moved toward them. Bridnow cut off whatever he was saying in mid-sentence when he saw us coming. He didn't greet me either, just leveled a scowl at us that seemed aimed a bit more at Aroden than me. I suppressed a sigh. Bridnow had made it clear from the first day that he didn't trust Aroden—that he *wouldn't* trust him, no matter what Aroden said, no matter what I said on his behalf. He hadn't even been impressed when I told him how Aroden had saved Kite's life.

About ten steps away from him I faltered, then, feeling strangely low, I turned, prodded Aroden's arm, and walked away. As we went I heard the murmur of their conversation start again.

"Wonder what's going on?" Aroden said.

I glared at him. "You're a bloody Knack," I said. "Dan' try to pretend you couldn't find out if you wanted to."

"I—" he started, regarding me in surprise. "I *could*, but I know you don't approve of Knacks prying in where they're not wanted."

*Of course, now I get stuck with a decent, upstanding kind of Knack,* I muttered to myself.

"Gan on," I said. "Find something to do. I'll find you later when I figure out what's gannin' on around here."

"What do you want me to do?"

I thought it over a minute, then jerked my head toward Doc's infirmary. "See if anybody's there looking for healing," I said.

"The other Blood," Aroden said, hands in his pockets, eyes oddly bright. "He never came back?"

I shook my head. I couldn't read the peculiar look in Aroden's eyes at that, but he just gave me a nod of agreement and headed toward the long, low building.

*Thank the stars there's at least one person here who does what's asked without pitching a fit,* said the voice in the back of my mind.

I sighed and headed to the Rookery, where I built up the fire in the common room and sat down beside the hearth, and waited. Likely half an hour later or so, the door swung open and Bridnow came in with a swirl of brisk wind. He tugged off his gloves as he came close to the fire, stretching and curling his fingers to work the feeling back into them.

"Vitresk is dead," he said as he sat down, without a word of greeting, without a word of explanation.

A minute and I just stared at him, baffled. "Who's Vitresk?"

He measured me in silence, the disapproval so thick in his gaze that I felt near an inch tall. "I suppose you've been too distracted the last few days to read the dossier I gave you."

My cheeks flared hot, and I sank deeper into the chair, as if that could hide me, as if it could erase the magnitude of my failure. I didn't even know what dossier he meant. Before I could even fumble my way to an excuse, the door slammed open behind Bridnow, and Anuk blustered in.

"Anuk," Bridnow said, making room for him by the fire. "If I said, *Vitresk is dead,* what would that mean to you?"

Anuk stopped short, his ruddy cheeks paling. "What? You're slagging us, right? He's *dead?*" Bridnow nodded, and Anuk answered with a string of emphatic cuss words and rubbed his hand over his face.

Bridnow just looked at me.

Even when I'd failed Kantian in the past, I'd never felt so thoroughly crushed. Tears prickled my eyes, and my whole soul felt like it was caving in, horrified at the notion that I'd disappointed Bridnow, that I'd somehow failed the trust he'd shown me. I wanted to hide, I wanted to Shift and fly away, part of me wanted to argue and pretend that I'd done something far more valuable than read some bodgy dossier I probably wouldn't have understood anyway.

"I div'n read the dossier," I heard myself saying instead. "I got no excuse."

To my shock, Bridnow's face softened a bit at that, and he shooed Anuk away with a wave of his hand. When we were alone again, he leaned back in his chair and regarded me thoughtfully.

"That wasn't easy, I know," he said. "Thank you for being honest. Vitresk was Minister of External Affairs. Of all the Ministers, he was the one who came closest to having any real influence over Cavnal's foreign policy, though his concern was primarily in trade." He paused. "They found him this morning."

"Someone murdered him?" I asked, cold clawing dread creeping over me. "The coup? One of Red's followers?"

"It doesn't seem likely. He…ate his own revolver. As far as we can tell, he took his own life."

"But that dan' make sense," I said, though I couldn't say why.

"He may have been under pressure from the other Ministers, and it just got to him in the end. He was a loyalist. Servant of the Crown forever."

"What'd Creech have to say about it? Saw him here earlier."

Bridnow's mouth twitched. "Batar is understandably spooked. The two of them are convinced foul play was involved, but it's hard to point a finger at someone in these circumstances."

"I wanna talk to Creech myself," I said. "If they're spooked, there's gotta be a reason why."

Bridnow nodded. "He's still in the yard. You might hurry though. I'm not sure how long he meant to stick around."

I was on my feet at once, grabbing my coat off the table and shrugging into it as I headed outside. Creech was standing near one of the many can fires lit around the edge of the yard, holding a mug of something hot close to his nose. I could see its trails of steam all the way across the yard, and as I got closer I caught the enticing aroma of coffee.

He gave me a feeble smile as I joined him.

"You the one who brought news about Vitresk?" I asked, and he nodded. "Sorry to hear about it."

"Serro is the one who found him," he said. At my puzzled look he said, "Batar. Serro Batar. He found him in his office this morning."

"Stars," I breathed. "He must be pretty shaken up."

"He is. It could have been him, after all. He could be next. God knows."

"Bridnow said it looked like suicide."

"Looked like it, sure, but how hard would it be for an assassin to stage a death like that?"

"You think that's likely?" I asked.

He hesitated, then shrugged. "I got a look at the scene myself. It's hard to say." He held the cup close to his face again, breathing in the fragrant steam a minute before taking a slow sip. Then he sighed and said, "Of course, it doesn't bloody matter if he did it himself or Klissen and his cronies got to him somehow. Even if Farro decides to get off the fence, the loyalists in the Court of Ministries can never outnumber the parliamentarians now. If they lose even one more of their number, it's over. The southern alliance will be arranged, and that'll be it."

"Istia and Tulay will declare war," I said.

"And the Accord will come into effect here in Cavnal, which means you and I will no longer be welcome."

"But Klissen's got half the Army in his pocket—"

"Which means Cavnal will likely be torn in half. Half siding with Tulay and Istia for the preservation of magic, and half siding with Meritac and Cromis. It will be a bloody free-for-all."

I gave up trying to mimic Bridnow. I stuck my hands in my pockets and shrugged up my shoulders against the wind, and closed my eyes, as if blocking out the world could somehow make all its problems disappear.

"I'd best be getting back," Creech said. "I'm doing my best to protect Serro, but I don't even know what I'm protecting him from right now." He drained his coffee and held the mug toward me, questioning. "Where should I—"

"I'll take care of it," I said. "Thanks for bringing us word. And take care of yourself."

"Yes ma'am," he said with a faint smile, and next minute a black and tan hound was loping toward the front gate of the complex.

I returned the mug to Miss Nan's kitchen, then headed back into the yard. Minutes dragged by as I paced, my mind in a tangle, indecision nipping at my thoughts.

*You know what you need to do,* whispered the voice in the back of my thoughts. *You've been toying with the idea for days now.*

*I can't. It's too much. It's wrong in every possible way.*

*Is it though? You know there's no other good solution. It's just temporary. You could at least ask. You could at least find out if he's willing. Because it's possible he wouldn't be.*

*I can't,* I protested again, but feebly. *It can't be the only solution.*

I turned on my heel, as if I could turn away from my own thoughts, and almost careened into Derrin. He grabbed my shoulders to steady me, regarding me with surprise.

"Stars," he said softly. "What's troubling you? You've been pacing like a prisoner for ten minutes now."

I shivered and shook my head. "You heard about Vitresk," I said.

"Yes. Bloody unfortunate business."

"Do you believe he killed himself?"

He hesitated a good long tick. "Not sure," he said. "We've both seen people driven to do things that they didn't want to. Compelled, against their will. I guess all I'm saying is, even if Vitresk pulled the trigger, I'm not persuaded he did it of his own free will."

I heaved a sigh and chewed on the inside of my cheek. That was a possibility I hadn't even considered, and it was more horrifying than the idea of an assassin trying to stage the death to look like a suicide.

"We need Tarik," I whispered.

Derrin's face fell, and he caught me by the arm. "Aothir got word to Thane, like we asked." He paused, and I waited, breathless, hating the darkness in Derrin's eyes. "Shade isn't coming back. Aothir told Thane how desperate our straits are here, and Thane told Shade. But Shade said…it wasn't his concern. We're on our own."

I bit my lip, trying to cage in a sob, failing. Derrin wrapped his arms around me and held me tight, rubbing my back as if I were a wee skitter in need of comfort. I took two deep breaths to steady myself and untangled myself from his grip, and swiped the traitor tears from my cheeks.

"A'right," I said. "Then it's time we took control of our own fate."

I left him staring after me as I stalked across the yard toward the dormitory. Without thinking, I headed straight toward the second story cell, only to find the door already open, and Aroden sitting on the floor inside. He just watched me in silence as I climbed between the ropes, like he'd been expecting me to come.

"Minister Vitresk is dead," I said, "and there's only one thing that can stop this madness from tearing us apart."

"What is that?"

I leaned against the wall across from him and folded my arms. "Cavnal needs her King," I said. "We've got to have Prince Tarik take up the crown."

His eyes narrowed slightly. "You were able to get word to Shade, persuade him to come back?"

I drew a long, slow breath, and let it all out. "No," I said. "Shade's not coming back…" I faltered, and because I simply couldn't accept that Shade's decision was final, I added, "yet." Then I looked at Aroden long and hard, and said, "But Prince Tarik is."

# CHAPTER 4 ~ HAYLI

FOR ENDLESS MOMENTS ARODEN WAS SILENT, HIS FACE AN ENIGMA IN THE cell's heavy shadows. I waited, fitsy, heart hammering like lies against my ribs, and prayed with every ounce of my strength that I hadn't just made a terrible mistake.

"I don't want to presume," Aroden said, carefully, when I was near to bursting, "but...are you asking me to..."

"You already did it once," I said, more snappish than I meant. "You already persuaded half the city that you were him, without hardly trying." I let out a broken breath. "Will you at least think about it?"

"You don't believe me—I know you don't. I know you still think that Shade is the real Prince Tarik, and I'm nothing but an impostor. So, what you're asking me to do is usurp Shade's crown, usurp his authority, and fraud my way into rulership over his country. How is that possibly a good idea?"

"Because we're fit to fall to ruins if we dan' have someone on the throne as can unite us," I said, all in a rush. "If Jig could convince me *he* was Prince Tarik, I'd be willing to send *him* to do the job. Savv? I still believe...I still believe Shade's ganna come back and do right by us. I have to believe that. But we've got to buy him some time. Make it so's he can be in two places at once until he's ready to take the throne himself."

Aroden considered that quietly a moment, head tipped down, his thumb pressing out a crease in the leg of his trousers. "And you trust me enough to believe that I would retreat gracefully when he is?" He glanced up at me without lifting his head. "You know what he did to me."

"I know—" I started, and bit my tongue on arguing with him. I needed his help; this was not the time to quibble about the past. "I know you would," I said instead.

"I have no desire to be King," he said softly.

"And that's why I think you'll be more than happy to step aside when the time comes."

"It's a lot to ask of someone, you understand," he said. "That is a heavy mantle to wear, no matter how long you have to bear up under it. You really think I would be able to navigate us out of this morass? *Me?* I've been imprisoned in the Science Ministry for two years. I've had my brain picked apart and kneaded into mush. I've slaughtered...I've slaughtered innocents I thought were clay soldiers."

"But you're not broken any more," I said. "At least you've got that going for you."

*Unlike Shade,* whispered the voice in the back of my mind.

"Unlike Shade?" Aroden murmured.

I flinched. "You reading my mind, Aroden?"

"It was written all over your face."

That, at least, I could believe. I sighed and slid down to crouch against the wall, my arms hooked over my knees. "Sometimes folks just need to be reassured that they've got somebody looking out for them," I said. "Even if you dan' do aught before Shade comes back but show them their Prince's face, you'd give them some peace. And that's something."

Aroden leaned forward slightly, spearing me with a sharp look. "And what, do you suppose, will Shade think when he finds out I've been coronated in his stead?"

I swallowed hard. "Well, if he's skundered about it, then I've got two things to say to him. First being, *you div'n want it, remember?* And second being, I*t's yours whenever you want it back.*"

"And you imagine he'll listen to that?"

"He'll listen to me!"

Aroden didn't say aught to that, and I jerked my gaze away from his.

"He has to," I added, in a bare whisper.

Aroden pushed himself to his feet and paced back and forth

across the cell a few times, cradling his chin in his hand, while I toyed with a loose thread on my breeks and watched him out of the corner of my eye.

"There's a slight problem, though," he said presently. "Last time I was in front of the Ministers, I Ghosted away. If they think I'm a mage, they will never accept that I'm Prince Tarik...except the ones who already know Tarik is a mage."

"Ah, but they only think *you're* a mage—you, Aroden, the mage that Kippler and Farrady had hold of. If you go back as Tarik, and dan' do aught, and I mean *aught at all* that smells of magic...if you denounce the impostor mage, deny that you ever showed up at the palace, tell them you've been held captive somewhere since long before Avnaya, or whatever you want to tell them...how would they ever know you aren't who you say you are?"

*This is a terrible idea,* Piper whispered suddenly in my thoughts.

I slammed a mental door on her, and buried the gnawing guilt deep down inside.

"They have those EMS weapons," Aroden said. "Don't you think they could jar me out of the Mask?"

I stood up to face him, giving him a smile that felt much too cold. "Well, that'll be an interesting event," I said. "If you *are* Prince Tarik like you claim to be, well, there won't be a Mask for them to jar you out of, will there?"

His mouth inched up in a smile. "I might ask them to prove me by fire, as it were, if it meant I could persuade you once and for all."

"So..." I took a step closer to him, tossing my head back. "Will you do it?"

He looked down at me a long while in silence, a hundred emotions and a hundred worries flickering behind his eyes. Then he bent his head and said, "I'll do it."

I let out all my breath and turned away, one hand pressed hard against my forehead. "A'right, then. We gotta proceed carefully. Bridnow would never stand to see this plan carried out..."

The thought wrenched my stomach unexpectedly, and I froze where I was. Could I go behind the Commandant's back? Could I intentionally go against his wishes, even if I thought I was doing the best thing for Cavnal? Oughtn't I try to persuade him first?

*You know you won't persuade him,* whispered the voice in the back of

 544

my head. *He's loyal to Shade—to Shade, whom he ardently believes is Prince Tarik. He would never stand to see an impostor on the throne, no matter what motive, what end you claim.*

Aroden touched my arm briefly. "His loyalty to Shade is honorable, and a great credit to his strength of character," he said, "but right now, it could be the ruin of his nation. If you edge around his notice, it's not because you dishonor him, or wish to deceive him, but because the situation demands it."

"You think so?"

He nodded. "Remember, this isn't supposed to be permanent. I'm just stepping in, like you said, to buy Shade the time he needs. To push off the inevitable fall of war. But if we're going to do this, we need to act quickly, or more Ministers are going to die mysterious deaths."

I could hear the murmur of Piper's voice trying to get my attention, but I did my best to ignore her.

"A'right. Then here's what we need to do…"

I found Luce in one of the storage buildings, where she'd set up a bit of a workshop for fixing skitters' jumpers and mending coats. She even had a few rows of the blue military-style coats like I was wearing, all hung up proper like at a high street shop. When I came in she was trying to fix the shutters over one of her narrow windows—it was half-shut, and the light that slipped in past it was poor and dim. Finally she managed to wiggle the slats a bit more open, and stepped back in satisfaction as a stream of grey daylight washed across the warped floorboards.

"It'll have to do," she muttered, and turned to me with a warm smile. "Morning, Hayli. Not seen you about for a few days. What's the bother?"

I pulled myself up onto the heavy table that slouched against the far side of the room, among a heap of fabric scraps and scattered buttons. "When you sent me and Griff to the Palace, you gave me a lovely dress to wear, but said it wouldn't make me a noblewoman. Well…have you got anything on hand that would?"

She set down the jumper she'd just picked up, eyeing me curiously. "Now, what scheme have you got hatched up in that head of yours?"

The door inched open behind her, and a moment later Pika scampered into the workshop, slamming the door behind her. Her cheeks were bright red from the cold, and her hair was sticking out under a thick wool cap, frizzling in a million directions at once. When she saw me she squealed and ran to give me a hug, then picked up a few scraps of cloth and a rather large sewing needle, and carried them over to Luce.

Luce bent to help her set up her sewing practice, keeping half her attention on me. The last thing I wanted was to go gabbing my plans in front of Pika—talking to one Knack was bad enough, and Pika was even less apt than Luce to mind the privacy of people's minds.

"Got a need to go to the Palace," I said carefully. "And I need to look the part this time. We've got to tell the Court that…that Prince Tarik's on his way back, and I need to make sure they'll listen to me."

Luce straightened up, one hand on her hip. Beside her, Pika was stubbornly jamming the needle in and out of the fabric, her tongue stuck out between her teeth in a way that reminded me of Zip when he was working on his lockpicking skills.

"Is he?" Luce asked, quietly.

I hesitated a fraction too long, but then I gave her my most hopeful smile and said, "Yes, he is."

I waited, breathless, as she studied me through a faint frown, then she shook her hair back from her face and waved me to follow her into a back room. I jumped off the desk and trailed after her, sneezing once when I came into the little chamber that was even dustier and gloomier than the main room of the workshop. At the back of the room, Luce knelt in front of a massive old wooden chest, pulling out articles of clothing and laying them aside, one by one.

"Do I want to ask what you're planning to do?" she asked, very quietly, as she worked.

I glanced over my shoulder at the open door to the main workroom, then dropped to my knees beside her. "Just a sleight of hand," I said. "A bit of well-timed trickery. You know Aroden came here looking like the Prince? But Shade, he…he can't come back just yet…but if we wait for him, it might be too late. Savv?"

Luce drew a length of cream cotton from the bottom of the chest—I realized as she pulled it out that it was wrapped around something else. In the gloomy light, her face looked drawn and thoughtful.

"It's a good plan," she said. "Shade's been on my mind, lately. I'm worried about him."

"Me too."

 546

"You know what they're saying about him, in Istia?"

"That he's…gone mad?"

She eyed me sidelong. "Is that all you heard? Aothir said…he said that Shade claims that Wake is talking to him. Visiting him."

"What?" I asked, alarm prickling through me. "That's…that's…not possible, is it? Wake dan' do that kind of thing."

But it made me think of how Shade had acted when he'd come to see me, how he'd stared at the corner of the room like he saw something that wasn't there, how he'd said things that I knew weren't meant for me. I shook my head, desperate, as if I could unmake the memory.

"I know," Luce said. "But if he believes it…what might he do, claiming that Wake commanded him to? I know how much you love him, and I care about him too. Honestly. But I can't help this niggling feeling I've got that…maybe Aroden is *safer* to put on the throne anyway." She winced and bent her head. "I feel like such a traitor for saying it."

I bit my tongue. I didn't know what to feel, much less what to say. Part of me wanted to argue, to protest, to defend Shade and demand to know how she could ever turn on him like that. And yet…

*She's right,* whispered the voice in the back of my mind, *and you know she is. You've been thinking the same thing.*

I covered my mouth, struggling to steady my breath, and nodded.

"Don't cry," Luce said. "You don't want to get tears on this dress— you'll ruin the fabric."

She gestured me to my feet and stood herself, shaking the cotton cover away from the most exquisite garment I'd ever seen. It was like a long jacket in plum-colored silk, with cream lace cascading beneath the hems of the sleeves, and ruched trim in a deeper purple all along the edges of the flared, split skirts. Underneath was a skirt of cream silk, beaded from top to bottom in gold and crystal over an embroidered pattern of filigreed gold.

"It's a common enough style for a day dress," she said. "The lady who ordered it never came to claim it, so I…relieved the shop of it. It'll do for most Palace functions during daytime, but if it's an evening function you have in mind, we'll need to get more creative."

"No," I said. "No, we'll be going during the day, I think."

She laid the garment across my arms and bent to retrieve a pair of black, pointed-toe ladies' boots with a small, delicate heel, and from somewhere in the depths of the chest she drew out a lovely little black hat trimmed with black netting and a single dark plum-colored rosette. When we carried the goods back into the workroom, I realized with a little relief that Pika had gotten bored with her sewing work and left the shop. I didn't want to try to explain to her what I meant to do.

"Step behind that screen and put the dress on," Luce instructed, pointing me to a wood and paper partition that stood a little taller than me, hiding the back corner of the room. "And then we'll see how to fix it up to fit you proper."

Like most of the buildings in Borokhev, Luce's shop was frigidly cold, so I hurried as fast as I could to slip out of my own clothes and into the plum silk. It weighed a grobbing ton, I realized, as I tried to fasten as much of the bodice as I could reach, and the skirts were near four inches too long for me, even with the heeled boots. I held up the lengths as best I could and stepped out to get Luce's help with the rest. She worked quickly, fastening up the back of the bodice and then working to pin in the sides and mark up the hem to a proper length.

"It's a lovely color for you," she said, smiling up at me as she knelt beside the little stool she'd made me stand on, so she could hang the hem. "You will look exactly right."

The door swung open and we both startled and looked to see who had come in, but while I stifled a groan of dread, Luce's face brightened in a dimpled smile. Scorch stood in the doorway, holding something in his hands that I couldn't quite make out across the room.

"Is that my lamp?" Luce asked.

Scorch's face softened—it was the kindest I'd ever seen him look. He held up the tangle of black metal in his hands like a child presenting a crumpled flower to his mother, and the faintest smile toyed at the corners of his mouth. The thing was a wrought-iron lamp, I realized, complete with a hurricane shade.

"I hope it serves," he said. "On this wall, right?"

She nodded, and he set the thing down on the desk to examine the wall where she wanted it hung. I watched, bemused, as he made himself busy. Of all the people in the facility, the last person I would ever have imagined doing a common laborer's work was Scorch.

He glanced at me over his shoulder as he climbed onto a chair. "You're looking very fancy, Hayli," he said. "What's the occasion?"

"None of your business," I retorted.

Luce looked at me, aghast, and I gave her an apologetic smile.

Scorch just laughed under his breath and turned back to his work. "If I didn't know better," he said, carefully marking a spot on the wall with a piece of chalk, "I'd think you had an appointment with a Prince."

"We both know Shade ain't here," I snapped.

He gave me a look so cold I felt it like a burn on my skin, and said, "No, he isn't, is he?"

# CHAPTER 5 — TARIK

I WOKE TO A STRANGE, HEAVY FEELING IN MY HEAD, A VAGUE SENSE OF WRONGNESS. My eyelids felt gummed closed; my tongue cleaved to the roof of my mouth. None of my limbs wanted to function, and in the back of my head, I felt a sharp, throbbing pain like a pen knife jabbing repeatedly into the base of my skull. I couldn't see at all; I had no idea where I was. My skin was too numb to even make sense of the surface I was lying on.

"He's waking up," someone said.

At least my ears still worked.

My mind churned, sluggish, trying to create explanations for what I was experiencing. I'd gone to bed after dining with Iskari and Nika. Had I perhaps been drugged? Poisoned?

Had they?

I fought for a breath but the air stuck in my throat, and when I tried to cough I found my stomach heaving instead. Someone did me the kindness of rolling me onto my side; I vomited and choked, and couldn't even lift my head.

"Are you sure this is a good idea?" the voice asked, closer now.

"They're having fantastic results with it in Ceruvay," said someone else, and I made a noise of irritation when I recognized the Blood Halvir's voice. "It's the only thing I can think of that will help him. We don't have the kinds of therapies they have in Cavnal, but I've heard they've begun using this, too."

"It smells terrible."

"Hopefully it won't taste as bad."

A hand lighted on my shoulder, shaking me gently. If these men had poisoned me, they were the damned most considerate would-be assassins I'd ever met.

"Taumir, wake up," Halvir said. "Wake up."

I shuddered, and finally managed to crack my eyelids open, but the world beyond was blurry, ringed in faintly yellow hues. I closed my eyes briefly, then tried again. This time I managed to make some sense of my surroundings—I was in a small dark room, lying on a threadbare couch, and leaning over me were Halvir and another man I had never seen before. Halvir had a dark amber glass bottle in one hand, and a metal tumbler in the other. The table beside my head held a single oil lamp—the source of the dingy yellow light. Behind them both, near the door, Wake stood looking on.

I looked at him in panic, but he didn't move, so I fixed my attention on Halvir instead.

"What are you doing to me?" I gritted. My mouth tasted foul; my thick tongue could barely form the words. "Where are Iskari and Nika?"

"Sleeping," he said. "Now, I understand you've been experiencing some…hallucinations. Is that true?"

I tried to edge away from him, but my body wouldn't obey. To my annoyance, I realized my wrists had been bound, tight enough to cut off the blood flow to my hands. I could hardly move my fingers at all.

"No," I gritted. "It's not true."

"Do you see things that other people don't see?" When I just glared at him, he sat down on the edge of the couch and gave me a patient look. "I'm not just a healer in the magical sense. I went to medical school in Ceruvay. I'm a physician. I can help you."

"I don't need help."

He exchanged a glance with the other man, then said gently, "You keep looking at something in the corner of the room. What is it?"

I'd been looking at Wake, silently pleading him to step forward and reveal himself; now I fixed Halvir with a dark scowl.

"It's not my fault you're blind," I said.

"That vial is dangerous," Wake said suddenly. "It is not meant for the likes of you."

"What will it do to me?"

"This?" Halvir said, lifting the bottle in his hand. Then he frowned a little and said, "Were you talking to me?"

I hesitated, then growled, "Answer the question."

"If you feel imprisoned in your mind now," Wake said, "if you felt imprisoned and cut off from your magic when they used the Hunter on you, that is nothing to the chains that drug will wrap around your mind and your will. If they put you under its influence you will be reduced to a passive, malleable state, and they will be able to do anything they like to you. Persuade you of whatever they choose. Make you do their bidding." He took a step forward. "Do not let them give it to you."

"What am I supposed to do?"

"Taumir, who are you talking to?"

"If they persist," Wake said, "do whatever you must to escape their control. You must escape it."

"Are you hearing a voice right now?" Halvir asked.

I looked at him, perturbed, and nodded faintly.

"What is it telling you?"

"That you mean to harm me," I said, struggling to sit upright. Halvir edged a few inches away from me. "That I can't let you give me whatever is in that bottle."

"It's a simple medicine," Halvir said, lifting it toward me. "It calms the mind, restores your mental balance. It has proven very helpful for people in your situation…"

"There are no people in my situation!"

"People who see things that aren't there. Who hear voices telling them things. It's for your own good. You can't function in society if you go on like this, talking to yourself, claiming to have visions of God. We need you as a functioning part of society. I believe you can do many good things for Istia, but only if you let me help you through this disease."

"I am *not* diseased."

"You're suffering delusions. Hallucinations."

"You're Rigvar's crony, aren't you? Or did Aroden send you? For all I know, maybe you *are* Aroden."

"Come now, Taumir," the other man said. "You're suffering a nervous disorder of the brain."

"You think I'm insane!" I shouted. "Don't you?"

"We don't like to use that word," Halvir said carefully. "You're…

suffering from altered perceptions of reality. You've been hurting yourself, and I'm worried that one day you're going to go too far, and—"

"You think I did that to myself?" I asked, aghast. "I didn't do that. *He* did."

"Who did?"

I ground my teeth and leaned my head against the low back of the couch. "You wouldn't understand if I told you."

"I told you they would not understand," Wake said.

"You look like you're listening to someone," Halvir said, his voice aggravatingly calm. "What is the voice telling you?"

I gave him a malicious grin. "That you can both go *drakkethe sala dak*."

Halvir pursed his lips in a thin line, then poured a tiny trickle of fluid from the amber bottle into the cup and swirled it gently. "Is the voice telling you to hurt us, or anyone? Yourself?"

"You, if you bring that cup anywhere near my face," I said, lifting my tied hands between us. They were bound with wire, I realized, not rope that I could burn, or cuffs whose lock I could unfasten. The sides of my wrists were trickling blood.

"I didn't want to take chances," the other man said, noticing my attention. "Now, be a good lad, and take your medicine. I promise you'll feel better on the other side. It might take a couple of doses, but then there will be no more madness. No more confusion. And a chance to actually defeat Rigvar at the moot. You'd like that, wouldn't you?"

"Stop *patronizing* me," I gritted.

Halvir lifted the cup toward me again and I edged back, but I was trapped in the very corner of the couch, my back pressed against its wooden arm, the oil lamp burning dangerously close to my elbow. Halvir saw my gaze drift toward it and jerked his head at the other man, who hurried over and blew the lamp out. I gave him a feral grin and focused my power on the wick, and stirred it back to life as soon as the man's hand had withdrawn from the base. He swore and tried to blow it out again.

In the half-moment of darkness that followed, a hand clamped on my jaw, squeezing hard. "Just drink. It's for your own good," Halvir gritted.

I tried to swing at him with my bound hands, only to find them pinned against my stomach by the other man's iron grip. Desperate, I thrashed, twisting my head to get my mouth away from the cup.

"Listen to me," Halvir hissed, bringing his face close to mine. "I'm on your side. I hate that knave Rigvar, and I want to see him brought down in shame and ruin. Won't you save us? You're the only one who can do defeat him, but no one will even let you into the moot as you are. Do you understand? I *need* you to be better. All of Istia needs you to be better."

"Then don't push me," I tried to say, the words garbled by his hand still clamped hard on my jaw.

The cup came closer, shaking. Halvir's associate grappled me more firmly, trying to keep me still. Behind them, Wake watched in silence, and if I didn't know better, I would have thought he looked anxious.

"Why don't you do something?" I mumbled, glaring at him.

"Because I don't need to," he said.

I looked at Halvir and said, "Stop."

He froze, his face contorted with confusion.

"Let me go."

His hand yanked away from my jaw, like it was being torn back against his will. But I'd failed to consider the other man; I didn't remember him until I felt the sharp poke of a knife tip under my arm, between the ribs, sending a burning pain shuddering through me.

"Let him go, or I'll make you," he hissed. "Don't be a fool."

"You think that can stop me?" I asked, turning to look at him.

In that one moment of distraction my Command slipped. Halvir jerked like a marionette at the same instant the other man twisted the knife point a little deeper into my skin. Halvir dropped the cup and the bottle; at the last instant I saw that the hand he was stabbing toward my neck held a syringe instead.

I closed my eyes and choked out a single word.

"*Die.*"

# CHAPTER 6 — TARIK

I WAS ON MY FEET BEFORE THE TWO MEN HAD HIT THE FLOOR. MY LEGS SHOOK, and my vision blurred and focused in a spasm of red light as I tried to make sense of the bodies at my feet. They couldn't be dead. They couldn't.

*God*, I thought. *I didn't want...I didn't want them to die.*

My knees buckled and I fell, bracing myself on my still-bound hands as my stomach tried to empty itself of whatever contents it still had. My whole body shook like a fever. The wire around my wrists cut into the tender flesh like a garrote, and hot blood trickled from the laceration over the backs of my hands and between them, staining my palms.

"I didn't want to kill them," I gasped. I pressed my knuckles against my forehead, my body folding in agony. "Why...why did you make me do that?"

Wake stood beside me, charging the air around me like a lightning storm. "I made you do nothing," he said, and there was a gentleness to his voice that surprised—and infuriated—me. "I gave you the end. You chose the means. It was your free choice, and now you must accept the consequences." He reached out and briefly touched the wire around my wrists. "You should remove that before it cuts you any more deeply."

"How?" I muttered.

"Look at it," he said, and vanished.

I turned my hands over, examining the length of the wire until I found where the two ends joined—they were simply twisted together, ending in a rather sharp point. Grimacing, or smiling, I nudged the two strands of wire with my magic and mentally unwound them, and watched as the wires obediently uncurled and loosened, and finally fell to the ground. I massaged my torn wrists, trying to work some feeling back into my cold and numb fingers, as if the same motion could knead my heart into numbness.

Could I have gotten free sooner? If I'd been able to think…if I'd had the presence of mind…could I have done this while the men were still alive, and then found some other way to defeat them that didn't involve…death?

I bent over Halvir, rolling him gently on his back. His face was perfectly calm, almost peaceful. I'd Commanded him to die, and his body had simply given up living. It was the most horrific feeling I had ever, could ever have, imagined. Everything inside me reeled with revulsion.

"I'm so sorry," I whispered, clasping his cold hand. "I'm sorry."

"For what?" someone asked behind me, and I shuddered even before I turned around, because I would have recognized Death's voice anywhere. "They meant you harm. You defended yourself."

I wiped my hands on my pant legs, trying to rub off the drying blood. "I suppose you're going to tell me that I've used your gift, so now I'm bound to you?"

"Charming as that would be," she said, tipping her head to one side, "that was all you, my dear. That was all magic. That had nothing to do with me or any gifts I could give you. I admit being a little jealous—I don't like the thought that someone can usurp my power so effortlessly. But you do see the advantages I could give you."

"If this is what using your gift feels like," I said, and pointed at Halvir, "then I want nothing to do with it. It's a nightmare."

"A nightmare?" she echoed. "I think you enjoyed it far more than you let yourself admit. It belongs to all of your dreams, love."

I stayed perfectly still a moment, sitting on my heels, the blood slowly clotting around the cuts on my wrists. Then I looked up at her and said, "Leave. Just leave."

"Ordering Death around?" she said with a teasing smile. "Brazen, even for you."

"I don't want…I don't want to see you any more. Either of you. Any

 556

of you. Just leave me in peace."

"Peace is the one thing you can never lay claim to, Tarik Eyidson. You were born to war."

I picked up the syringe that Halvir had dropped, turning it over in my fingers.

"You think Branigan's drug made you useless to the people who depended on you?" Death asked, watching me narrowly. "That drug will make Branigan's look like a harmless pastime."

"You would want me to believe that, wouldn't you," I said. "If Halvir was right, maybe this will make you shut up and leave me alone once and for all."

"And leave you empty," she said, "and helpless, and weak. Rob you of your will, your passion, everything that makes you human."

I closed my eyes, tightening my fingers on the thin amber glass of the syringe. "You have my answer. I will not be the hand of your harrowing."

"Shade!"

I flinched so violently that I dropped the syringe; it rolled away into the shadows before I could grab it.

"What the hell?" I said, looking around.

The room was empty. Not even Death was with me now. And yet I'd heard that voice, that high, childish, desperate voice, as clearly as if whoever had spoken was shouting in my ear. Then, gradually, I felt a faint scratching at the edges of my mind, and panic surged up inside of me.

Someone had reached me, somehow, within the boundary stones of my thoughts. I'd let my guard down...or I'd been too weak, too distracted, to keep it up, and someone had broken through. Someone, I realized with a little sadness, whom I'd once deliberately blocked from my thoughts.

I closed my eyes and let a calm settle on my mind, and focused all my attention inward. Then, very carefully, I opened the book of my thoughts just a fraction. "Pika?" I said.

"Oh, Shade!" Her voice sounded strained, thick with tears. "I div'n think I could reach you. I've been trying, and trying..."

"Why were you trying to reach me?"

"You gotta...come back. Please. Doc...Doc wants...see you."

The words were fragmented; I knew that if I opened my mind

the rest of the way to her, I would hear her clearly, but I didn't want to risk it.

"What's going on?"

"I dan' na...so many things. I...understand all of...but...say you're not coming back."

"Who did? Why would anyone say that?" I asked, alarmed. "Of course I'm coming back."

I could feel her weeping as if her broken sobs were my own. My heart wrenched, and without thinking I reached out in my mind to try to soothe her.

"Tell me what's going on," I said gently. "Whatever you know."

"Can't," she whispered. "It hurts too...trying to talk to...like this. Can't keep it... Just come...please. Doc said...be waiting where he saw... last time. He—"

The mental link broke off, abruptly, and frantically I tried to reach her again. But I sensed nothing at all where I'd felt her presence before.

*Poor kid,* I thought. *Stars, what have those idiots done now?*

I sighed and tried to find the white-walled tunnel, Wake's realm, the infinite web, but my mind was dark and closed. I frowned. Was it my mind that had broken the connection with Pika, not hers? What was wrong with me? I tried to stand up, but my legs felt strangely weak. My thoughts...my thoughts were getting muffled.

A hazy sort of calm washed over me, from fingers to the tips of my toes, and I slumped over my knees.

"That's good," someone murmured behind me, patting my head in a pleasant kind of way. "Just rest now. You've been through a lot."

"I know," I said. My hands rested listless on my thighs.

*Something is wrong.*

*Something...*

The panicked whisper reminded me of the first time Branigan had drugged me. So long ago. So...so long ago. But I couldn't understand why. How could something be wrong when I felt so peaceful?

I canted my head to the side and found Thane smiling down at me. He held a strange glass syringe in his hand, with a long, cruel needle affixed to it. It reminded me of something...but it didn't matter what.

"Shame about Halvir and Kima, though. How'd you manage that?"

I just looked at him, not understanding the question.

"Well," he said, with a small smile. "At least you could plead insanity if they bring you to trial for it."

"I didn't do anything," I said, fear surging in my heart.

"Of course not. You just stay here now, Taumir. Get some rest."

"I'll just stay here," I said, contentedly, and dragged myself onto the couch.

It wasn't very soft, but the wool coverings on the cushions were warm, and I pressed my cheek against the coarse fibers. Thane patted my shoulder and plucked up a glass bottle off the couch near where I'd stretched out my feet, and tucked it into his coat pocket.

"You'll be good as new in a few days," he said. "I'll be back soon to check on you."

"Thank you," I said, and rolled over to face the back of the couch.

"You don't want to go anywhere, do you."

"No," I said. "I don't want to go anywhere."

I listened as the sound of his footsteps faded away, and let myself drift toward tranquil sleep. But just as the dreams were creeping up to take me away, the silence shattered under the sounds of a scuffle—footsteps, many footsteps stomping on stone floors, someone crying out. I blinked and listened with mild curiosity, wondering what was happening elsewhere in the room. There was a louder grunt of pain, then a resounding crash and shattering of glass. I tipped my head back but didn't hear anything else, so I turned onto my side again and hugged my arms a little closer around me.

Then someone was shaking my shoulder, hard. I shrugged away from the hand with a mumbled protest, and for a moment the shaking stopped.

"Taumir. *Veka*, what've they done to you?"

I wrinkled my brow at the voice. "Agnir?" I said, twisting onto my back. Somehow, impossibly, the sea captain was standing beside my couch, watching me in stark terror.

*It must be a dream,* I told myself, and tried to turn away again.

Agnir reached out and planted a hand on my shoulder, pinning me where I was.

"What happened?" he asked over his shoulder.

I followed his gaze and found Iskari and Nika behind him, Iskari with a death grip on Thane, and a knife pricked against his throat.

"Tamed the beast," Thane wheezed around Iskari's choke hold.

Agnir left me, striding straight up to Thane and slamming a fist into his jaw as hard as he could. Thane slumped in Iskari's arms, blood pouring from a split in his lip. I watched the scene, curious. Nika was staring at me like she'd never seen me. There were tears on her cheeks.

"You gave him salts," Agnir said. I'd never heard him sound so angry.

"With obvious success," Thane said.

Agnir shook out his hand; it must have stung after striking Thane so hard. "Look at him. He looks like a *drakkeyn* sheep. Why would you do this? *Why?* Do you think that...*creature*...is going to be able to stand up against Rigvar?"

"Once he stabilizes, certainly," Thane said. "We're on the same side, brother. Neither of us wants to see Rigvar wearing the *aydrding*. Let the salts work a little bit, and he'll be fit to take on the whole world. *Without* going around claiming he talks to *Veka*."

Agnir looked at Iskari, who grimaced and gave a faint nod.

"He said he's seen *Veka*? Talked to him?" Agnir asked, glancing at me over his shoulder. "I believe it," Agnir said then. "If you'd seen what I've seen..."

"And what we've seen," Nika added, very quietly.

Thane struggled briefly against Iskari's grip.

"What have you done?" Agnir said. "*Veka, Veka,*" he groaned, turning away from the three people, his head in his hands. "Don't abandon Taumir now. Please, pity him."

Wake watched him from beside my couch, a thoughtful look on his face.

"Aren't you going to tell him?" I asked.

All four people turned to look at me.

"Isn't who going to tell whom?" Agnir asked.

I tipped my head back to study Wake. "It was supposed to make you disappear, wasn't it? I remember...I remember now."

Agnir paced two cautious steps toward me, as if I were a rabid animal cornered in a burrow. "Taumir...who are you talking to?"

I dragged myself into a sitting position, fighting back a wave of nausea. My stomach was wretchedly empty, I realized, and I vaguely recalled the reason why.

"*Veka,*" I said, and on a sudden impulse I gave Thane a slow smile. "Not...not the result you expected?"

"You still think you see him? That should be impossible. The medicine… Maybe I need to increase the dose…"

I got unsteadily to my feet, took a moment to find my balance, then stalked straight up to Thane. "I am not," I said, "insane." I swayed, feeling light-headed, but Agnir gripped my elbow to steady me. I nodded my thanks to him and went on, "Whatever that was, whatever you dosed me with…" I licked my lips; they were dry, and my mouth felt sticky. "You can take the rest of that bottle and shove it down your throat."

Iskari swapped his knife to his left hand and tightened that arm around Thane's neck, and with his right hand he reached down and felt at Thane's coat pockets. A moment later he withdrew the amber bottle, held it front of Thane's face, then smashed it on the floor at their feet.

"God, Iskari!" Thane cried. "Do you know how much that was worth? That is the most expensive—"

"It is not worth the price *he* paid for it," Iskari said, jerking his chin in my direction.

"He needs *help!*"

"He doesn't need help, he needs your allegiance."

"He already has it," Thane said. "Why do you think I want him staying here? Why do you think I would do anything to see him become Godar?"

"Then why are you *drugging* him?"

Thane thrashed again, eyes wide and—strangely—full of fear. Shining and red with tears. "Because the world can't survive the coming of the Zealot," he wept. "Be our Godar and be content with that, please."

I wanted to agree with him. More than anything, I wanted to nod and back down, go and lay on the couch again, and be content. My body tugged me earthward, my will curled up in a corner of my mind like a dog with its nose buried in its tail. My mind invented a thousand reasons why I should agree with Thane. I didn't want to be Godar but it was infinitely preferable to my other options. And yet…

And yet Wake was still standing by the couch, watching me, eyes blazing with expectation.

I half-wished Halvir's drug had worked, and banished Wake, and the mad god, and Death from my thoughts forever.

561

"I have a duty," I said, very quietly. "I will see it done, and then I'm going back to Cavnal to mend what I left broken there."

"Don't bother," Thane said, mouth twisting in a smile. "I told my contact that you weren't coming back."

"*What?*"

"I told him to tell your followers that they were on their own. There will be no welcome for you if you go back."

Iskari didn't even hesitate. He drew the knife across Thane's throat with one smooth motion, and let his body fall in a heap to the ground in a pool of spreading blood.

# Chapter 7 ~ Hayli

THE DAY AFTER I COMMISSIONED LUCE TO MEND THE DRESS FOR ME, EARLY IN the morning when the sun was just rising, I headed out to serve my watch on the depot gate. The air was a bit warmer than it had been lately, and the ice was thawing all around the facility under the long-slanting sunlight. The wind still nipped a bit, but I was just glad that, for the first time in near a week, I had a daytime shift.

Coins had already gotten to the post by the time I walked up, and he was chatting amiably with soft-spoken Quickly and another man I only knew by face. I didn't often serve watches with my own sergeants, but I whispered a prayer of thanks that our shifts had fallen together today. Coins was the missing element of my plan, and two hours posted alone at the gate with him was a perfect time to chat.

Soon as I showed up and got the report from Quickly, the two guards took their leave of us and sauntered off toward the mess in search of a hot drink. Coins amused himself with walking back and forth along the edge of the platform, balancing effortlessly on its very edge.

"I was thinking that guard duty would be much improved if we could persuade Miss Nan to send out mugs of coffee to the guards on post every shift," he said. "Right? Wouldn't that make it so much better?"

"Yeah," I said, smiling. "Except I dan' think Miss Nan's got enough coffee for all that. Every guard, every shift, and so."

Coins waved a hand so dramatically he wobbled mid-step, but he recovered at once. "Bah," he said. "I'll get her some more. I know a place."

"Been thieving again?" I asked, fighting a smile.

He tipped his head back to eye me, mouth quirked in a lopsided, cocky grin. "Again? Stars, my dear girl, do you think I ever *stopped?*"

"Do I wanna know?"

"Likely not," he said. He reached the end of the platform and came over to join me at the coal brazier. "Brr," he said. "I'll be glad when winter finally scoots the boot. Scoots the boot, yeah? You like it?"

I rolled my eyes, stifling a laugh, then I turned to look over my shoulder at the prison town behind us—*our* town—and a strange little ache tugged at my heart.

"What d'you suppose will happen, when all this is over?" I asked. "If we escape a war…if things ever get back to normal…what do we do? Do we keep on living here? Does everybody drift apart, go their own way, never looking back on these days?"

"Stars, you're in a mood," he said cheerfully. "You mean if Tarik becomes King and you…well, whatever you do…" He wiggled his fingers at me and I laughed, and blushed, and wanted to curl up in a hole. "Me, can't I just keep being a thief?"

"If Tarik is King, I dan' na if he'd approve of that very much."

"Maybe I can be his royal thief. They have those, don't they?"

"Yeah," I said. "Think they're called tax collectors."

He laughed gleefully at that, and I shook my head. "It'll be a fine day," he said. "And don't fret. It'll be here before you know it."

"Speaking of that…" I said, and waffled a bit, stabbing a stick into the brazier to stir up the coals.

"Yes…?" Coins prompted.

"You ever driven a motorcar before?"

His grin got even wider, if possible. "Well, I'm probably not supposed to tell you this, but…ahh…some of the lads and me *may* have taken the motorcar out one night on the old road and I *may* have popped behind the wheel to give it a go. And it *may* have happened on…multiple occasions."

I laughed. "Sneak-thief," I said. "Well, I got a plan I want to run by you. It's dangerous. It sounds…wrong, if you think about it the wrong way. But honestly, it's the only fix I've come up with to make sure we ever get that fine day you were talking about."

"I'm all ears," he said.

I took a deep breath, and told him everything. The whole time I laid out the plan, I watched him closely. He looked more serious than I'd ever seen him, a faint line between his brows, mouth tugged down in a scowl. More than that, though, he looked *upset*, and I suddenly got to wondering if he was the wrong person to try to get on board with my scheme.

"You *want* Aroden to usurp Tarik's crown," he said when I finished, and shook his head slightly. "Stars, that's bold, even for you."

"D'you think…d'you think there's any chance that Aroden's telling the truth? About…Tarik, I mean? That maybe—"

"That Aroden is really Tarik and Tarik is…someone else? It sounds nutter." He took the stick from me for his own turn at jabbing the coals. "I mean, I *like* Aroden. He saved Kite's life, right? But as for him being the real Prince Tarik…" He shook his head. "How can we ever know who's telling the truth? Trouble is, someone's pulling a confidence game on us, and we can't figure out who. Both of them, let's face it, are masters of deception. We already know Tarik—let's say Shade—can pull a con on all of us. We know that Aroden's capable of doing the same thing. So either one of them is lying, or they both are. Or…" He waved the stick, making it wobble as if the stick were bending in impossible ways. "Or one of them is insane, or they both are."

"Or neither are," I said softly.

"D'you believe that?"

"There's a second possibility," I said. "The Zealot, and the scion of the mad god."

"Oh, wonderful. That's so much more reassuring. One is a force of divine retribution and the other is a force of chaos. *Perfect*."

He wobbled the stick again and I watched closely, trying to figure out how he was doing it—if maybe by sleight of hand he'd switched the stick for something bendy. But then he tossed it back to me, and it was just a plain stick.

"When do we embark on this madness?" he asked.

"Luce said she'd have my dress done later today. You still got that fancy livery you wore to the Palace last time?" He nodded. "Then we'll go tomorrow morning."

He started to nod again, but suddenly he perked up and his gaze darted past me to the gate. I turned and found Aothir standing there, looking dead pale.

"Hayli," he said, not even bothering to call me *lieutenant*, not even to taunt me. Something had to be wrong. He stumbled a step, and caught at the iron bar of the gate to steady himself. "My contact...I can't reach him. I'm afraid...I think he's dead."

I licked my lips, which were suddenly dry. "Dead?" I echoed. And then, dreading the answer, I asked, "How...?"

He shook his head, passing a hand over his forehead, his eyes. "It was a stupid idea from the beginning," he said. "They should have known better than to try." He gripped the bar again, pressing his forehead against the coldness of it. "Just before I lost touch with Thane, I saw...I saw through his eyes. Two of Thane's friends were trying to help Shade. Trying to...*heal* Shade. I don't know how, but they said it would make the hallucinations go away." His face turned a ghastly white, and he winced like he was in pain. "Shade killed both of them."

"He wouldn't—" I started, but at the same moment I saw him in my mind, revolver in hand, the cold, calm look in his eye as he'd shot Andon...as he'd shot my brother in the head.

"That's not the worst of it though. I thought I knew him. I trusted him. He was a friend. But...what do you do with someone who can... *command* his enemies to die, and they die?"

Coins muttered a stream of obscenities under his breath, but me, I just felt numb, understanding nothing.

"He...what?" I managed at last.

"He commanded them to die," Aothir said, "and they died." He shook his head again, like it could settle the facts into something like sense. "I lost touch with Thane just after. I'm afraid...he did the same thing to him."

"Aothir," I said. "I'm so sorry."

It was the only thing I could think to say. No other thought made sense. Every part of me recoiled from the news, and no matter how hard I tried, I just couldn't make sense of it. I couldn't accept it; I couldn't deny it. My mind was a chaos of argument.

*Shade would never do that unless he had no other choice. Something must have happened...maybe Thane was mistaken.*

*But how is it even possible? What kind of power must Shade have, to do such a monstrous thing?*

*Is he really the person you want sitting on the throne of Cavnal? Someone who would slaughter his enemies with a word?*

*That's not Tarik. That's not my Tarik. He would never...*

*But he already did.*

Aothir moved suddenly, drawing me out of my internal quarrel. "I'm sorry," he murmured, turning to go. "I didn't want to be the bearer of such wretched news. But I thought you should know."

"Thank you," I whispered, and watched him trundle back into the facility, head hanging, hands shoved deep in his pockets.

"Stars," Coins said, when he'd gone. "What a damned mess."

# CHAPTER 8 — TARIK

"I'M SORRY, DA," ISKARI SAID, IN THE LONG SILENCE THAT FOLLOWED, AS WE all looked at Thane's body lying lifeless at his feet. "I know he was your friend."

"*Friend*," Agnir echoed. "Once, maybe. We drifted apart a long time ago." He regarded the body quietly a moment longer, then his shoulders lifted in a sigh. "If you hadn't done it, I would have."

My legs shook, and I stumbled a step, and before my mind could catch up, Nika had helped me sit back down on the couch. She brushed the back of her hand over my forehead, her lips pressed in a thin line.

"He's burning up," she said, over her shoulder.

"It might be the salts," Agnir said. He came over and took a long look at me, brow knotted and mouth turned down in a faint frown. "Taumir, how do you feel?"

"I feel fine," I said, and shuddered. "That's what scares me. I know I shouldn't. I just feel so…content. And it's all wrong." I could feel panic beating at the corners of my mind, muffled and weak, but insistent. "There are three dead bodies in this room, two of them by my own… hand. And *Veka* standing there, and you're here and I didn't even know you were in Bregjarvani."

"I arrived last night," Agnir said. "Found my son sleeping so soundly I couldn't rouse him no matter what I did. That was my first hint that something had gone terribly wrong. I'm sorry…" His voice trailed off, and he swiped his wool cap off his head and twisted it restlessly in his hands. "I'm just sorry we didn't get here sooner. I'm sorry we couldn't have stopped him from doing this to you."

"It's all right," I said. I rubbed my forehead. "I remember now...I was distracted. Someone was trying to contact me in my thoughts, and I was so focused on that...I must not have heard Thane come in."

"I can't believe he would stoop to this," Agnir said, swinging a hand toward Thane's body. "What a *fool*."

"And Halvir," Iskari said. "I'm ashamed to say I trusted him."

I slouched against the back of the couch, hating the peaceful indifference that numbed my thoughts, not knowing any way to drive it away. I just didn't give care about any of it, and I was perfectly happy to let it stay that way.

Only, deep inside, I wasn't. I closed my eyes and looked inward, trying to dredge up my Blood magic in hopes of nudging the drug out of my veins, but I couldn't stir it at all.

"I've told you countless times," Wake said. "You would have no trouble using any of my gifts if you embrace the power I'm offering you."

I jabbed a finger in his general direction. "*No.*"

I heard a faint gasp and opened my eyes, only to find them all watching me warily, Agnir with eyes wide and horrified.

"Did you just tell *Veka*... Did you just tell him *no?*" he asked. Then, almost breathless with anticipation, "What's he telling you?"

I tipped my head to the side to glare at him. "How I could find my healing magic again if I become his Zealot."

"And you won't?" he asked.

I looked away at the disappointed rebuke in his voice. "Never," I said. "I don't have *that* much of that damned drug in my system."

Agnir exchanged a glance with his children. "Well," he said. "Be that as it may. We should get you out of this place. It's...not fit for staying in."

I eyed the bodies, the blood, the vomit, the musty couch, all combining to create a stink that—now that I was aware of it—threatened to turn my battered stomach all over again.

"I can't go back to the lodging house like this," I said. "I'll agree with whatever Rigvar says."

Iskari looked faintly amused at that, but Nika just scowled at the floor, arms tight across her chest.

"The salts will eventually fade from your blood," Agnir said. "It may take a day, maybe two, and I can't guarantee it will be a pleasant feeling, but at least you've only had the one dose."

"Believe me, I've been through worse," I muttered. "What do you know of it?"

"The drug? I know they developed it in Ceruvay, and some scientists and psychiatrists in Cavnal have been experimenting with it as a way to treat diseases of the brain. I don't know if they've had any success. Didn't know they were starting to use it here, either. Thane's right, the stuff is bloody expensive. I wonder how Halvir came by it."

"Probably Ceruvay," I said. "Since he said that's where he studied." I heaved a sigh and leaned over my knees. "Well? Let's get out of here. I suppose there's only one place to go," I said, and met Iskari's gaze.

He nodded and, without a word, stooped to help me to my feet.

"I'm not sleeping in there," I said.

Iskari had half-dragged, half-carried me the whole ten minute walk to Eyid's house, then marched me all the way up the stairs to stand in the doorway of Eyid's bed chamber. I planted my feet, stubbornly refusing to let Iskari move me another step forward. I felt inordinately proud that I had enough of my own will left to do that.

"It's the only *drakkeyn* bed in this house, Taumir."

"There's a *drakkeyn* couch downstairs," I retorted.

Iskari let out a breath I realized was laughter, and gave in. "Fine, if you really want to walk down the stairs again..."

I muttered something impolite to him under my breath and he laughed out loud. But he helped me down the stairs without complaint, and soon I was ensconced in the corner of the couch, shivering wretchedly, wrapped in a thick woolen blanket. Iskari took the chair, dragging it across the floor with a horrible scraping noise until it was positioned closer to where I was sitting.

"I need to go back to Brinmark," I said after a few minutes, and told him, as best as I could, what I remembered of Pika's frantic message to me. The memory was a bit blurry, but I recalled enough to make me worry all over again when I related it.

"And Thane told his contact you wouldn't be coming back."

"Aothir," I said, musing. "Aothir was a good friend. I wonder if he believed Thane. Stars, what will Hayli think? I hope it doesn't..." My voice trailed off. "She's suffered so much, Iskari. It's hard for her trust any more. If she thinks I've abandoned her...I hope to God it doesn't wreck her."

I closed my eyes, fighting off memories of Hayli crouched, broken and terrified, in my room at the smelter after Derrin had brought her back to me, struggling to reclaim her mind from the nightmares that haunted her. I didn't want to exaggerate my own importance, but I was terrified of what the news of my imagined betrayal would do to her.

"I'm surprised you haven't just disappeared then," Iskari said, "like you did last time."

I waved a hand in his direction. "She has a lot of support," I said. "They'll get through this. I'll go back...in a few days. Once I can find my magic again. It's somewhere... I put it somewhere...I don't know where." I smiled and tipped my head against the back of the couch. "How much trouble can they get into in two days, anyway?"

"You must really be strapped," Iskari muttered. "For one thing, you're asking that question, and for another...didn't she *lie* to you? I thought we were angry about that. Weren't we angry about that?"

"I'm sure she had a reason," I said. Not worrying about it was so much pleasanter than the agony I could faintly remember feeling before. "Hayli always has a reason."

"Must be some girl," he said.

"She's beautiful," I said. "She's a crow."

Iskari, who had been leaning his chair back on two legs, slammed it forward and looked hard at me. "Did you just say your sweetheart is a *crow*?"

I gave him a lopsided smile. "She's the voice of the gods, Iskari," I said, taunting, and he just flicked me his thumb and kicked his chair back onto two legs again.

"I'm still trying to make sense of the part where your sweetheart is a bird."

"She's a Shifter," I said. "She turns into a crow."

"Of course she does," Iskari grumbled. "That figures. You keep some rather strange company in Cavnal, don't you?"

"My dear freaks," I said. I felt strangely tired; my eyes wanted to close on their own; my thoughts drifted in a whirl of color and sound. "Keep an eye out, will you?" I murmured. "I feel the pressing need to... pass out."

# CHAPTER 9 ~ HAYLI

COINS AND I TALKED THE REST OF OUR WATCH ABOUT HOW WE OUGHT TO get Aroden to the Palace, but between the two of us, we couldn't conjure up anything resembling a good plan. It wasn't until Derrin and Griff came to relieve us that an idea occurred to me, and for five minutes after the changing of the watch, I paced back and forth just inside the depot gate, gnawing on my lip. Coins leaned against the wall, arms folded, and watched me with a puzzled smile.

Finally he said, "You know we're off duty now, right?"

I nodded and went to stand beside him. "What d'you suppose Derrin would say if we told him our plan? Think he'd rat us out to Bridnow?"

Coins's face got a bit pale at that—I think it was the first time he considered that we were going behind Bridnow's back. "I don't know. Hayli, are we *sure* this is the best plan?"

"Dan' waffle on me now," I muttered. "Unless you come up with a better scheme, this is the best one I can think of. Aroden said he dan' wanna be King. I got no worry that, soon as Shade comes back, this can all get set right."

"I don't know about Derrin, though," Coins said.

"Maybe you should just ask him," Derrin said suddenly, and we both spun to find him standing just beyond the gate. "You realize you were standing on the other side of the wall from me, don't you? We could hear everything you were saying."

I blushed bright red at that, and Coins scrubbed a hand through his hair self-consciously.

"Well?" I asked. "You heard it. So, what d'you think?"

"Think? I think you're as vutting insane as Tarik is rumored to be right about now," he said. My heart crumpled, but then, before I could try to explain, he added, "I also think you're canny brilliant. Having Tarik take the Crown is the one thing anyone can think of that would set things right, or at least put a stay on all this madness. Well? We might not have him right now, but we've got someone whom everyone can believe is him. That might have to be enough."

"Did…did Griff hear all this too?"

Derrin glanced over his shoulder, and a minute and Griff stepped off the platform to stand beside him. He had one hand pressed over his mouth, and my heart wrenched unexpectedly, because in the bright sunshine there was no way he could hide the glitter of tears on his lashes.

"I've heard what Aroden's been claiming," he said. "Not saying I believe any of it. Still…you haven't known Tarik as long as I have. You haven't seen him these last few years. He changed a lot. Sometimes… there were days I thought I didn't even know him any more. I'm *not* saying I'm turning my back on him. But, stars, I don't even know what I'm saying. I just want things to make sense again."

I went to him and wrapped an arm around his shoulders, and he let me hold him for a minute before dashing a hand over his eyes and pushing me gently back. Derrin had his arms folded, kicking at a bit of gravel unearthed by the melting snow.

"I think we have to try," he said. "Griff, what is the best way to do this?"

Griff took a deep breath through his nose and cleared his throat to compose himself, then scrubbed a hand through his curly hair. "Well, the Court has to offer the Crown to him, and if he accepts, word goes out across Cavnal for the gentry to cast a vote for him or against him. I imagine they'll radio out the news—it won't take long. It's mostly symbolic, of course, but once that vote comes in, they'll have the coronation. Of course, Tarik technically became King the minute Trabin died, but there's a formal procedure. There's always a damn formal procedure, and if it's not followed, he'll never see the inside of that crown."

"So we need to prepare the Court for the news that Tarik is coming back," Derrin said. "We can say we found him, held hostage just like the papers were suggesting, and negotiated his release. But he's on his way home right now, and will be arriving in Brinmark tomorrow."

"A'right," I said. "How do we break that news?"

Derrin's face brightened with a slow smile. "Get word to the Ministers of the need for a public announcement? I know just the man for the job."

"Batar," I said, and he nodded. "Go now, Derrin. He'll need time to get everything ready, and to tell the other Ministers. We'll stand your watch for you while you're gone."

He nodded, and clasped my arm with a sudden serious look, and vanished. None of us said a word while he was gone. We paced, and paced, all looking nervous with our arms folded. Me, I was dead sure Derrin would come back and tell us that Batar had mysteriously died, or that the coup had happened without anyone expecting it, or *something* had gone wrong. But then, some fifteen minutes after he'd left, Derrin stepped out onto the platform beside me.

"He'll do it," he said.

Coins whooped in relief, but when we all looked at him in alarm he subdued, and peered through the gate to make sure nobody had heard him.

"He took the news well?" I asked.

"Excited as a hound pup when I told him. He said he'll make all the necessary arrangements for a public announcement tomorrow, and he wants you to know that he *knew*, he p-p-positively *knew* you would find him."

I smiled, but deep inside, my heart felt strangely sad.

THE NEXT DAY, HALFWAY THROUGH THE morning, Coins drove the motorcar out the front gate with the claim that the horse cart was taken and he needed to haul goods out of the city. I changed into the plum-silk gown in Luce's workshop, then Aroden came to fetch me, wearing a suit that looked a bit worse for wear. When I was ready, he Ghosted us to a spot on the road some two miles outside of Borokhev, where Coins, dressed in his fine chauffeur's livery, was waiting with the motorcar. Aroden changed his appearance to Tarik, and I, shuddering in spite of myself, climbed into the back seat of the motorcar after him.

As we drove, I realized that Aroden hadn't just made himself look like Tarik. He'd given himself bruises and half-healed cuts—making sense of the bedraggled suit he wore—and his face was thinner than I remembered Tarik's ever being.

"I was in captivity," he said, his voice slipping effortlessly into Tarik's rhythm of speech, the quiet, refined shape of his words. "Lady Oramay, thank you for your ceaseless efforts to find me, to negotiate my release."

My mouth twitched. We'd agreed to gloss over that part of the business as much as possible, lest people start to look too closely at me and find out what a sham *I* was.

For a few miles we rode in silence, then I tipped my head back and said, "Aothir told Luce that Shade's been claiming to see Wake. Saying that Wake is talking to him, telling him what to do."

For one briefest moment, Aroden froze, then he sat up straight and the warm copper of Tarik's face paled drastically. "Not Wake," he said. "Wake doesn't... Wake doesn't come among us like that. He simply doesn't. If Shade thinks he's seeing a deity... Stars, Hayli. The mad god is just stringing him along. The scarier addendum to that is, Shade may be fully aware of it."

"You mean, you think Shade knows it's the mad god, but he's claiming it's Wake, as if that would—"

"Bolster his claims," Aroden finished. "Make him a figure of awe and power that no one wants to oppose." He kneaded his forehead and sighed. "I don't like where this is going. We have to..."

*Stop him,* whispered the voice in the back of my thoughts.

I nudged the words away, and tapped my gloved fingers against my lips. *One thing at a time.*

We arrived at the Oval Wall almost before I was ready. My stomach was a mess of fluttering wings, and I could hear the rapid *tap-tap* of my pulse in every corner of my body. Coins maneuvered the motorcar up to the gate, and the guard took one look inside the vehicle and sprang into the sharpest attention he could manage.

"Your Royal Highness," he said, rigidly, and concluded his smart salute.

As Coins took the car up the long drive, I peeked out the back window and saw the guard run into the gatehouse.

"Oh, *stars,*" Aroden muttered beside me, and I shifted back around to see the whole long palace road lined with people.

Newshawks stood with their cameras, the bulbs flashing as they photographed us passing by, and countless people were waving tiny Cavnish flags. Almost all of them were crying. Aroden looked every bit as bashful and self-conscious as Shade ever had as Tarik, as he lifted a hand and waved at the crowd blurring by.

"I expected a reception, not a bloody parade," he said. "Your friend Batar must have spared no effort."

The next few moments passed in a blur. The motorcar drew up in front of the palace, where countless guards in ceremonial regalia stood arrayed in parallel lines all the way down the stairs, pennants flapping from the tips of their long pikes. All ten of the surviving Ministers were lined up on the top step in their official robes. Half of them looked pale, I thought. Half just looked ecstatic.

"Batar will shake your hand," I whispered suddenly.

Aroden gave me a lopsided smile. "Don't worry about a thing," he said.

One of the palace footmen stepped forward to open Aroden's door, while another circled around to open mine, his face a bare mask of suppressed excitement. We stepped out together, and one of the Guards waved Coins toward the carriage house. As the motorcar drifted away, Aroden took a few steps up the broad staircase to stand in front of the gathered Ministers. Behind us, the crowd had pushed all the way up to a rope the Palace Guard had strung across the road, near where a podium and microphone had been set up, facing out toward the crowd.

"Your Highness," Minister Batar said. "Is it really you?"

He met my gaze briefly, and I—I felt like such a liar, as I smiled, and gave him a faint nod.

Aroden stepped forward and embraced him. I watched Batar's face, hawklike, and suppressed a faint surge of triumph at the look of relief that flooded his eyes.

"Minister Batar," Aroden said, voice choked. "My father...is it true?"

Batar's face shifted instantly to compassion, and he clasped Aroden's shoulder. "I'm s-s-so sorry, Your Highness. He was...he was taken from us, b-b-brutally, almost two months ago now."

"I wasn't here," Aroden said, his voice a taut mixture of disbelief and horror. "I should have been here. I should have been at his side when... Oh, God..."

He bent his head, ducking a little aside, as if he could hide his tears. Some of the Ministers shifted their weight, some exchanged sidelong glances.

"Your Royal Highness," Batar murmured. "In these sad t-t-times, we are so g-g-glad to have you safely returned to us. I d-d-dare say, you find us *united* in our joy and hap-hap-happiness to welcome you home. You are well, we trust? Should we...send for D-d-dr. Besdin to attend you?"

Aroden passed a hand absentmindedly over his bruises and shook his head. "No, no need, Minister. I'm fine. It's not important." He scanned the row of Ministers, a frown crossing his brow. "Where is Vitresk? Where is Younger Bell?"

Batar's face fell, and he tightened his grip on Aroden's elbow. "Dead, Your Highness. I am sorry to bear the ill news."

"Dead!" he echoed. He gave a very good impression of looking terrified, overwhelmed, suddenly unsure of himself.

My crow-sharp ears heard Minister Von whisper to the Minister next to him, "Bloody fantastic. Now we get to be ruled by the incompetent rogue Prince."

"Hush," the other Minister said, looking faintly puzzled. "He's our monarch."

Von pursed his lips and said nothing else. I saw Minister Farro shift his weight—he looked uneasy about something, and suddenly my throat closed, and I prayed and prayed that nobody had said anything that would raise his suspicions. The story about the Prince's captivity... surely Farro would understand the necessity for that ruse, if he really did know about Tarik and Shade.

"Please, Your Highness, if you would," he said suddenly, stepping forward and indicating the podium behind us. "Let us announce your safe return to the people. Your nation has been rudderless too long."

Tarik—Aroden—bent his head, stricken with grief and regret. "I'm sorry. If only I'd known..."

Farro just squeezed his arm briefly and the whole company of Ministers, all the Royal Guards, Tarik—*Aroden*—and I marched across the circular drive to the podium with its microphone. When nobody questioned my presence beside him, I wasn't quite sure if I was more relieved or annoyed. Farro stepped up to the microphone first, tapping on it a few times to silence the pressing crowd.

"My fellow Cavners," he said, his voice ringing across the palace grounds. Camera bulbs flashed. "It is my great delight and privilege to announce to you that our Crown Prince Tarik Trabinis has been safely returned to us from his captivity. In our hour of need, he has come back to us, and it is my singular honor, no, my *deepest* honor, to speak on behalf of the entire Court of Ministries, and on behalf of all of you."

He turned to look at Tarik, a smile on his lips that didn't quite reach his eyes. "Your Royal Highness, it is with great hope and great humility that the Court recognizes you as the heir of our late monarch Trabin Geynis, our beloved and fearless monarch who sacrificed so much for the good of our nation. We recognize you as the rightful claimant of the Crown of Cavnal. It is with great pride that I now ask you—will you, Tarik son of Trabin, accept the offer of the Crown, and submit yourself to the burden of rulership, taking on your shoulders the safety and well-being of all Cavnish peoples—to hold in trust the power of the King to rule us in all fairness and justice, to govern our affairs abroad, and keep us united, prosperous, and peaceful all the days of your life?"

I could feel the collective breath everyone held as Tarik stepped up to the microphone, clasped Farro's hand with a slightly bashful smile, and turned to the crowd. I stood just behind him, hands folded tight to keep them from shaking.

"I was not with you in your hour of greatest tragedy, in the hour of our greatest national mourning, and my own..." He faltered, and bowed his head, and the crowd surged in as close as they could to drink in his every word. He tipped his head back, collecting himself, and then spared an uncertain smile for the people. "I regret that more than anything," he murmured, and even though he said it quietly, the crowd was so dead silent that the words seemed to echo endlessly. He drew a deep breath and squared his shoulders, and said in a loud clear voice, "It is with gratitude, and deepest humility, that I accept my father's Crown, the Crown you have offered in all faith."

Farro leaned in front of him, and, as the crowd erupted in cheers, he shouted, "Peace and triumph to His Majesty our King!"

# CHAPTER 10 — HAYLI

AFTER THE ANNOUNCEMENT HAD BEEN MADE, AND THE CROWD HAD FINALLY begun to fade back into the city, the Royal Guard and the Ministers walked Tarik and me back to the palace. As we came into the soaring vestibule, Tarik stopped short, tipping his head back and letting his eyes drink in the sight. One of the Ministers clasped his shoulder as he passed him, giving him a sympathetic smile that Tarik didn't manage to return.

*Aroden,* I heard Piper's voice hiss in my thoughts, shrill and sharp, refusing to be ignored.

*What?* I asked her, irritable.

*You keep thinking of him as Tarik. He is not Tarik.*

*And you know that, how? How are you so sure?*

*It's the darkness,* she whispered. *You can't see it. You won't see it.*

*What darkness?* I asked, moving aside as one of the other Ministers passed us. I was desperately trying to figure out what was supposed to happen next, and it was bloody difficult trying to do that with Piper chattering in my thoughts.

*Inside him. It's all chaos inside. It's broken and faceless and emptied out and put together again.*

"Lady Oramay," someone behind me said—the butler, Pont. "Will you be staying with us? I can have a room made up."

"No," I said, trying to focus on what he was asking, trying to make my mouth form a proper high-street accent. "No, I won't be staying."

Tarik...Aroden looked at me in alarm, and silent pleading.

I lifted my chin slightly and added, "I'll stay to the end of the day, but then I should go."

"Very good, *katzpotim*," Pont said. He bowed to Aroden. "Your Majesty, welcome home. I believe you'll find Liman waiting to attend you in your chambers."

He turned and disappeared into the little office opposite the cloak room, and suddenly Aroden and I found ourselves left entirely alone, with only a handful of watchful servants in full livery, posted at various places along the entry hall. Aroden set off, confidently enough, toward the main body of the palace, but when we came to the end of the vestibule, he stopped abruptly. A second later I realized why.

"Kor?" I whispered, choking the name in my surprise.

Because Kor was most definitely standing there in the hallway opening off to our left, like he'd just stepped out of one of the offices on purpose to intercept us. And he was staring straight at Aroden, his face set in a blank mask.

"The hell is this?" he said. "Did I really just hear what I think I heard from my office?"

"I'm...not sure what you heard," Aroden said. His voice was frigid, his hands curling into fists at his sides.

"You're *here*?" I interjected. "You're in Brinmark, and you didn't come to see us?"

"I looked for you at the smelter," he said, peeved, "and found the place all burned to ruins. What was I supposed to do? Look, kid, I didn't have to come back at all. It was a damn inconvenience." His gaze shifted back to Aroden. "You were just so bloody insistent."

"I appreciate you coming," Aroden said smoothly, after only the barest hesitation.

Kor's eyes narrowed, then he laid a hand on Aroden's shoulder and marched him a little way down the hall. When we'd left the servants far behind, he stopped and shoved Aroden away from him, and rounded on me.

"What have you done, girl?"

"What do you mean?"

He jabbed a finger at Aroden's throat. "That is *not* Tarik."

I swallowed hard. "Are you so sure?"

He didn't answer me. Instead he turned back to Aroden, stepping so close to him that Aroden had to lean a little away from him. That just made Kor laugh. "Tarik knows better than to back down from me," he said, over his shoulder, to me. Then, to Aroden, "Well? Have you thought more about what your mother and I were telling you?"

Aroden shifted away from him, pacing a few steps down the hall, then back again. I could see his thoughts working like mad, and had no doubt Kor could see it too. Kor's question just puzzled me, though. Had Shade found Kor and Queen Elanar since Avnaya Square? If so...how? Even Derrin couldn't find Kor, and I had no doubt he was a more skillful Ghost than Shade could be, having just discovered that gift.

"I'm just doing what seems best," Aroden said at length.

"Best," Kor spat. "You can drop the act, Aroden. I know that's you."

"How do you know that name?" Aroden asked, genuinely shocked.

"Because the man whose face you're stealing told me."

"How did *he* know?" Aroden turned to face me. "You said you didn't tell him about me!"

"I div'n!" I said, which got me a sharp, cold look from Kor. I fumbled and looked away, and said, "I swear, I div'n tell him."

Kor glanced from me to him, then swore and rubbed a hand over his face. "Fine, this is pointless. Just tell me one vutting thing, and tell me honestly." I nodded, hesitant, and he said, "Where is Shade?"

"Still in Istia," I said softly.

"*Damn*," he said. "And do you have any way to get in touch with him?"

"What for?"

"Because, girl, I don't care what this mage has made you believe, but he is *not* Tarik and he is *not* a statesman, and I want to know exactly what I should tell the damn *butler* to say to the ambassadors from Meritac and Cromis who are waiting for an audience with *someone* in this vutting government who knows what the hell is going on!"

"Ambassadors?" I said, in a bare whisper.

Aroden thought only a moment before shaking his head and saying, "Please, have them put up in comfortable rooms in the Palace. Tell them that I've only just returned home, and I need to be briefed on all the news and strategies before I will be able to discuss anything with them. Tomorrow. I will meet with them tomorrow."

Kor snorted. "Well, that's halfway sound strategy. Fine." He started to go, then turned and came back to Aroden. "Here's a piece of news to apprise you of the situation, in case you missed the report. Meritac's fleet is encroaching on Cavnal's waters, and their foremost battleship is hauling a weapon that is like to wipe this city off the map if they decide to fire it." He backed a few steps. "And Tulay's fleet just sank one of your ships that strayed into their waters."

"Are you going to tell me to refuse the coronation?" Aroden asked, softly, before Kor could walk away.

Kor's mouth twisted in a terrible smile. "No. You can keep the crown," he said. "Tarik won't stoop to a prize that petty."

With that he turned and stalked away, leaving us in stunned silence, watching him go.

"Stars," Aroden said. "Explain to me again why I agreed to this scheme?"

ARODEN MADE HIS WAY SLOWLY TOWARD the longest wing of the palace. I still followed close behind, desperately trying not to notice how uncertain he seemed to be in deciding where to go—or how to get there. We were halfway down a long, gold-carpeted hallway, wide enough for some fifteen people to walk side by side, when a servant approached Aroden and gave him a formal bow.

"Your Majesty, the Advisors to the King have requested an audience with you at your convenience," he said, "to discuss the question of the foreign ambassadors."

"Yes, of course," Aroden said. "Where can I find them?"

The servant bowed slightly again, so I couldn't see the look on his face. "That is typically left to the discretion of the monarch, Your Majesty."

I watched Aroden close enough to see his jaw tighten, then he said, airily, "I'll receive them in the Leaf Hall."

The man simply bowed again, and said in a voice entirely without expression, "Very good, Your Majesty."

As the servant walked away, Aroden rounded on me, eyes alight with anger. "Why did you do this to me? Did you just *want* to see me suffer?"

"What good, *Your Majesty*, would that do anyone?" I snapped, meeting him with a step forward of my own. "But now I've gotta leave you to suffer without me seeing it. Your advisors would never let me sit in a meeting with you, and besides, I've gotta get back to Borokhev.

They need to know what Kor said."

"I'm scared," he said suddenly. "It's been so long, I...I don't know what I'm doing."

"Stars, you think I do?" I said, backing away. "We're all just pretending, and hoping the world dan' notice."

I headed slowly back the way we had come, feeling Aroden's gaze follow me until I rounded the corner into the front hallway. As soon as I came out onto the steps, one of the guards stepped into the guardhouse to speak into his radio relayer. Moments later, Coins brought the motorcar up and a footman escorted me down the steps, and handed me wordlessly into the back seat. Coins didn't say a word the whole way down to the Oval Wall gate.

I stared at the wall as we passed by, an odd little pang tugging at my stomach. There, maybe fifty feet down the road near the covered hack stand—that was where Jig and I had tried to get up the wall, where the guard had spooked me, where Piper had flown away and nearly got killed by Prince Tarik's motorcar. Where Zagger had found me, and thought I was a boy, and Tarik had laughed at him. Where I'd felt the bond of touching another mage for the first time.

"Stars," I muttered. "That was so long ago."

"Talking to yourself, Hayli?" Coins asked from the cab. "Should I be worried about you, too?"

"I'm fine," I said. I leaned forward and braced my arm on the back of the seat in front of me. "D'you think we did right?"

He drove a few minutes in silence, taking the motorcar out of the city by its eastward road, which was much faster than going west and south past the smelter.

"It's a bit late to be wondering that," he said.

"I saw Kor."

He glanced at me over his shoulder, almost sending the motorcar careening onto the sidewalk too. "He's here?"

"Apparently Shade saw him and the Queen at some point. He knows, Coins. He knows Aroden ain't Shade."

"Notice you didn't call either of them *Tarik*."

I leaned my head against my forearm. "'Cause I got no ken. None at all." I sighed. "There's ambassadors from Meritac and Cromis at the palace, too."

Coins swore elegantly under his breath. "Really? And...you trust

Aroden enough to just leave him there alone to deal with them?"

"Naught I could do about it," I muttered. "If they started looking too close at me, they'd realize there never has been a Lady Oramay. Certainly not one who should be allowed to sit in meetings with the King and his Advisors."

He didn't say aught to that, and we rode the rest of the way back to Borokhev in silence. When we pulled in through the gate, I got a horrid sinking feeling in my gut, because, for all my planning, I'd never once stopped to think what would happen when Bridnow heard the news about the upcoming coronation. Because he *would* hear about it, sooner or later. Word traveled fast in Brinmark.

To my relief, he was nowhere to be found when we arrived, and I left Coins to park the motorcar and went to return my fine gown to Luce. I found her standing by her window under the warm halo of light from Scorch's lamp, hands twisting nervously in front of her.

"Did it work?" she asked as I came in, and immediately left the window to help me unfasten the back of the gown.

"Yeah," I said. "It worked. The coronation'll be in four days, assuming he gets the vote of the *katzpotivyek*."

"Don't sound so cheerful," she said, shooing me toward the screen partition. "We won."

I laughed, bitterly, as I tugged off the gown and pulled my own comfortable clothes back on. "Oh, Luce. It's so far from over."

I carried the things back into the room and found Luce by the window again, looking out just as anxiously as she had before. Frowning, I set the gown and shoes down on the long table and went to join her. I'd been sure she'd been waiting to hear our news, but if anything, she seemed fitsier than ever.

"What's bothering?" I asked.

"Have you seen Pika lately?"

I frowned. "Just the other day, when she was sewing over there. Why?"

"Not seen her since either. She's usually here three or four times a day. And...I can't even reach her. You know, like I used to."

I caught in a sharp breath. "D'you think she's a'right?"

"I don't know. I've looked everywhere for her, too, and I just can't find her. It's not like her at all."

"Maybe she went for a romp in the city?" I offered. "Skitter's not used to being cooped up in one place for a long time. Maybe she just needed some air."

"Brinmark's not safe for skitters like her right now," Luce said, and lowered her hand from the window shutters with a sigh.

"Where is?" I asked, and she just met my gaze in silence.

# CHAPTER II ~ HAYLI

AFTER I LEFT LUCE, I TRIED TO SNEAK BACK INTO THE ROOKERY, BUT IT WAS no use. No one could come or go without everyone inside realizing it, if only because of the wind that somehow managed to find its way into every cranny of the building every time the door opened. Apparently news from the city hadn't made it out to Borokhev yet, because Bridnow was standing at the long table when I crept in, and he just gave me an amiable nod of greeting.

I tried a smile in return, then looked at the man standing beside him, then at the device sitting on the desk in front of them.

"Krigs!" I exclaimed, and the grenadier lifted his hand in a wave. "What're you doing here?"

"It was high time for me to cash out and walk out. My entire battalion turned on the Court and took sides with the Chernayi and the coup. I got out with this little beauty before I got roped into something I'd no wish to be a part of. Figured it would be useful to get information from the other battalions and companies that are still loyal."

"A radio relayer!" I cried, suddenly recognizing the little case with its knobs and dials, identical to the one we'd had during our own little insurgency. "So there are some parts of the Army that aren't going along with the coup?"

"A handful. Vitresk turning up dead just bolstered the resolve of the coup, and those who were on the fence. With one less Minister to worry about, I think they started believing their chances of success were a bit better."

I nodded. Then, so they wouldn't get too suspicious, I asked, "Have we got a plan for how to stop the coup?"

"We can't take on the Chernayi and half the Army," Bridnow said quietly.

"But the mages who are in tow... Can't we reason with them? They've *gotta* see that if the coup succeeds, they'll be next on the block. Chernayi'll never stand to see them proper members of society, not to mention leaders of their new government."

"Does Klissen seem like the kind of man who would see reason?" Bridnow asked.

"No." I chewed my lip, staring at the relayer like it was a sleeping snake, afraid that any minute it would wake up and bring news of Aroden's appearance at the palace. "Least, I think he knows how risky it is to work with the Chernayi. If we had some way to prove that the Chernayi mean to stab them in the back as soon as the coup succeeds, he might listen. If we can't do that, though, maybe the individual mages in the Grey Mist? If we talk to them one on one, maybe they'll be more apt to listen. Creech was."

"Creech is also a high society cast-off with family in the government."

"So was I," I said flatly.

"A long time ago."

He said it gently, without rebuke, and the compassion in his eyes burned a gnawing hole of guilt in my stomach.

"Damn," Krigs said after a moment, and leaned over the table with his head bowed. "I hate feeling useless."

Suddenly wanting to be anywhere but the Rookery, I nodded to Bridnow and headed back outside, not even caring that I'd just apparently gone inside for no reason at all. And then, since I didn't have a watch until the next evening, I decided to let Piper spend the night in one of the high pines edging Borokhev, and wait for the world to come crashing down around me.

*I DON'T WANT TO TALK TO Hayli, not after she has so stubbornly ignored me for so long now. She keeps calling my name, trying to get my attention, but I can be just as stubborn as she can. With the wind wreathing in the pine branches around me, I pull up a foot into my downy feathers and hunch close to the branch for warmth, and try to go to sleep.*

Piper, *she says.* Piper, please, I'm sorry. Why won't you talk to me? I didn't mean to be rude, I swear, you were just distracting me.

I was trying to warn you! *I say finally.*

About what?

*I snap my beak, then bury it in the feathers behind my wing.* Aroden is dangerous.

Shade is dangerous, *she retorts, bitterly.*

There's dangerous, and then there's dangerous, *I say, hoping it makes sense.*

*Shade is not dangerous the way Aroden is dangerous. Aroden—I am sure I am not mistaken—Aroden is the type of man who would kill an innocent without remorse, and then effortlessly make everyone believe that he was the victim. If Shade has taken a life, I know that the remorse would be eating his heart from the inside.*

*Hayli doesn't say anything for a long while, and I begin to drift to sleep, rocked by the gentle swaying of the tree boughs.*

I only wanted to help, *she says suddenly.*

*I tuck my beak a little more snugly under my wing and force her voice from my mind, and go to sleep.*

*In the morning, Hayli doesn't seem eager for me to Shift back, so I focus on scrounging for a bite to eat. There's little enough carrion around Borokhev, but near the Rookery I find an overturned plate of food, like someone had dropped it in a hurry and forgotten to go back for it. I land beside it and hop closer, inquisitive, to see what they abandoned. Some creamed corn, now half-frozen, and a bit of over-salted ham smothered in thick, tasteless gravy. It's a feast, and I dive in, picking up each individual piece of corn and keeping half an eye on the comings and goings around me. Someone stops nearby, leaning against the wall, and I cock an eye up to see Anuk watching me.*

*I wonder if he knows it is me. I call a greeting to him, and his mouth twitches, and I resume my meal in peace.*

*And then darkness.*

*A weight settles over me like wings; I panic, and try to escape. I'm pinned to the ground; I don't know what is happening. Then the darkness presses closer and the world lurches—someone is carrying me. I fight and I fight, and I scream at the world, but the darkness never ends.*

*Exhausted, I finally lay still, and that is when I realize that the motion has stopped, too. The darkness tugs around me, and a stream of light suddenly dazzles my eye. I stagger, stunned, and find myself sitting in a heap of fabric, on a desk inside the Rookery. Inside Bridnow's office, no less. I explode into the air and make straight for the window, but the world outside is trapped away where I cannot reach it. I hit the glass hard and fall like a rock to the office floor, and suddenly there are hands around me, pinning my wings, trapping me.*

*I have to get away.*

*I never understood Hayli's fear until this moment. I am sure my heart will burst with it.*

*"Hayli," says a voice, deep and booming, somewhere above me. I jab my beak against the fingers holding me, and am rewarded by a hiss of pain—but the hands don't release me. "Hayli, be still."*

I am not Hayli! *I want to scream.* Don't punish me for what she's done!

Traitor, *Hayli sobs.* Don't Shift…please don't Shift. Don't make me face him.

Well, I bloody well can't talk to him, *I say,* so if you want to know what this is about…

It's about Aroden, I know it! *she cries.* They've found out. Oh stars, they know…

*"Hayli," the voice says again, very calm and soothing. "I need you to come out. We have to talk."*

*I tip my head and see that it is Bridnow holding me. Anuk stands in the background, his face drawn and pale, etched with regret and fear. When I don't move, and don't try to nip his hand again, Bridnow sets me down, gently, on the floor. And then, even with Hayli screaming at me in the back of my mind, I close my eyes and retreat.*

"Piper!" I screamed, hitting the floor of Bridnow's office hard on hands and knees. Sobs racked my body, and my head splintered with stabbing pain, as if Piper had physically torn herself from my mind when she Shifted. "How *could* you?" I whispered into my hands, curling over my knees, trying, wishing, praying to disappear.

"Hayli," Bridnow said. His voice was calm—dead calm. That scared me almost more than if he'd started out shouting. "Stand up and look at me."

I swallowed back my tears and brushed the edge of my sleeve over my face, and got slowly, shakily to my feet. I didn't want to look at him—stars, anything but that. Anything but seeing the disapproval and…*disappointment* in his eyes.

589

*I did what I thought was right,* I told myself, over and over again, as if repeating it could somehow make it true.

With a shuddering sigh, I squared my shoulders and lifted my chin, and met his gaze. He just looked at me for a long, long while, his face as expressionless as Shade's old mask.

Then he said, "What the hell have you done?"

I choked on my breath, and said nothing.

Bridnow's jaw tightened, then he turned away and moved a few papers idly on his desk. "Imagine my surprise when Krigs and I got a report late last night that Crown Prince Tarik Trabinis had returned to Brigun Palace, and accepted the Court's offer of the Crown of Cavnal. Imagine my even greater surprise to get a copy of the Herald this morning and see no one other than my very own lieutenant standing behind this aforementioned Prince Tarik at the podium, at an event that took place yesterday morning. Imagine my utmost surprise when I discovered that Aroden is nowhere to be found on these premises, and that Prince Tarik is very much still in Istia."

"How d'you know that?" I asked before I could stop myself—of all the things Bridnow had just said, that was likely the least important.

His face darkened into a genuine scowl, and my stomach turned and squirmed in a mess of crawling nerves. I suddenly wondered if the food Piper had eaten would come up if I retched.

*Don't cry, don't cry,* I commanded myself, but I felt my lips trembling and pressed them together with violent effort. When I lifted my hand to cover my mouth, Bridnow drew himself to his full height.

"Did I tell you to stand at ease?" he thundered. I dropped my hand immediately, but my body was shaking, and I couldn't breathe against the well of sobs drowning my lungs. "Hayli, I'm not sure you understand the gravity of this situation. I don't know if you understand how utterly and completely you've bodged up. But what I really want you to understand is how disappointed I am in you. Not only for what you did—which was foolish, dangerous, and potentially catastrophic—but that you *lied* to me. You hid this from me, knowingly, and then, when you realized I was bound to find out, you hid *yourself* from me." He sighed. "I know you've got a loyal heart, and I imagine you're punishing yourself enough right now for the both of us. Just explain it to me. *Why?* Why did you do this?"

"Because," I said.

The word escaped on a broken sob, and I was dead sure I would start weeping and not be able to say a single sensible thing. I drew a breath through my nose and let it out again, and steeled myself, pushing the whole nightmare of grief and regret deep down inside.

Then, speaking all in a rush so I wouldn't lose my nerve, I said, "Because the coup was going to overthrow the Ministers, and if they failed, the Ministers were ganna sell us out to Meritac and Cromis, and if they did, we'd be at war with Istia and Tulay, and the only thing that anyone ever said would put it right was for the Prince to come back and take up the Crown. But Shade is in Istia and he dan' wanna come back, and so…I thought this was the only way to save us all."

"What makes you think Tarik doesn't want to come back?" Bridnow asked, frowning.

"That's what Aothir said. He's got a contact in Istia…or had one, anyway. He tried to get Shade to come back, but Shade wouldn't have aught of it."

"And you're sure that's what Tarik meant? Messages can get terribly convoluted when they get passed from person to person." I said nothing, and he sighed and ran a hand over his forehead. "I don't accept that he has no intention of coming back, but we'll set that aside for the present. I do accept that you had sound motives for what you did. But trusting Aroden with the Crown? And then proceeding to deceive me about it? *That* was not sound judgment. And I honestly don't know how we're going to clean up this mess now."

There was a knock on the door, and as Bridnow turned away to greet whoever had come, I scrubbed my hand over my eyes again. I couldn't look at Anuk at all.

To my dismay, it was Krigs standing behind the door when Bridnow opened it, with a sheet of paper in one hand. He handed it wordlessly to Bridnow, whose face paled visibly while he read it. My blood turned to a strange sluggish mess, and I realized after a minute that I hadn't even been breathing.

"Damn," Bridnow said.

"What is it?" Anuk asked, speaking for the first time.

Bridnow and Krigs exchanged a look, then Bridnow turned, tapping the paper against his hand. "The call for a vote on the King's accession went out by radio this morning. But King Tarik," he said, with a hard look in my direction, "has just dismissed the Meritian and Cromner ambassadors."

"Dismissed them," Anuk echoed, flatly.

"Apparently he extended them a courteous invitation to take their terms of alliance and shove them...somewhere dark and...tight."

Anuk's mouth twitched. I didn't quite get what Bridnow was saying, though I got well enough that it wasn't appropriate, but Anuk seemed to understand it the way boys always seemed to understand such things. But I got the sense of it plain enough. Aroden had tossed out the alliance—and the alliance's ambassadors—in the most brazenly disrespectful way he could have. Wake only knew what would happen now.

"We...didn't want the alliance anyway, did we?" I whispered.

"Only if Istia and Tulay are at our backs," he said. "Tulay is not feeling particularly congenial toward us at the moment, since she just saw fit to sink one of our damn battleships because it got close enough to make her twitchy. And from what I understand, the other claimant to the *aydrding* of Istia has sworn to establish complete Istian independence—Istia versus the world, if you will. So unless Tarik manages to defeat him and pledge support for Cavnal, we are on our bloody own." Bridnow took a few steps to stand in front of me again. "You thought Aroden would only hold the crown temporarily, didn't you? Back down, retreat quietly when Tarik came back to claim it?"

I nodded, my throat impossibly dry.

"Well, he has just thoroughly bodged your plans, I'm afraid, by making Tarik's goal for peace *only* possible if he stays in Istia as her Godar. Tarik may be many things, but the one thing neither Cavnal nor Istia will ever tolerate is having him be *both* King of Cavnal *and* Godar of Istia at the same time."

For endless minutes I couldn't think of a single coherent thing to say. All I was aware of was the rapid flutter of my pulse, and the tick of a mantle clock, pushing us always and eternally onward. I wished vainly that I had Shade's Gift—I wished I could freeze the whole world in that one moment, as if just stopping time could make all the jumbled pieces of this mess fall into place.

"Stars," I said. I darted a glance at Anuk, but he wasn't looking at me; he was staring fixedly at the floor instead. "You think there's any chance that...that Shade could just convince Rigvar to side with us?"

"It would be the only way out," Bridnow said, "that is in any way satisfactory. Otherwise...I don't know what is going to happen. With our military divided and in shambles right now, I just pray your *King* can put down this coup and reestablish order, or we won't be able to muster a single squadron to our defense, let alone a corps."

"The Meritian fleet was dispatched a few days ago, as a precautionary measure," Krigs said quietly, "with a weapon on board designed by our very own Destri Alokin. What we need is the navy."

"I dan' think that will help," I said, just as quiet. I fiddled with the cuffs of my sleeves and added, "That weapon dan' need to be delivered into Cavnal, or dropped on her from an aeroplane like one of those mortars. It's meant to fire from a long way away. I guess Alokin called it a guided bomb." I met Bridnow's gaze. "And it's supposed to be drawn to magic."

"How...how do you know that?" Krigs asked, wide-eyed.

"Because I talked to someone who knows," I muttered. "It's drawn to magic, but that dan' mean it won't destroy everything where it hits. It was never meant to be all as specific as the Hunter was."

"So we stick Aroden on a boat by himself and send him toward the fleet," Bridnow growled.

"Commandant!" I cried, horrified. "You can't mean that!"

"Well?" he said. "With Tarik away in Istia, who do *you* think that bomb will fixate on?"

"There's got to be another way," I said. "Some other way to stop them."

"When you figure it out, be sure to let the King know. It seems you have his ear."

I glared at him, and didn't have a single thing to say in answer.

# CHAPTER 12 ~ TARIK

Aᴛᴇʀ ꜱʟᴇᴇᴘɪɴɢ ᴘᴇᴀᴄᴇꜰᴜʟʟʏ ꜰᴏʀ ꜱᴇᴠᴇʀᴀʟ ʜᴏᴜʀꜱ, I ᴡᴏᴋᴇ ᴛᴏ Aɢɴɪʀ ᴀɴᴅ ʜɪꜱ children's raucous company. Agnir and Nika had brought baskets of food and bitter beer from the lodging house—or some restaurant nearby—and when I clawed my way out of the thick-headed sleep, they were all crowded into the small parlor around me, Nika sitting on the couch by my feet, Iskari still in his chair, Agnir in the other, heavier chair which he'd also pulled closer to the couch. They were laughing and talking, dividing up the beer into tin mugs, and it took them several minutes to realize that I was awake.

"You lot are in a disgustingly cheerful mood," I said.

Iskari, grinning, took a mug from his father and passed it to me. "And aren't you the picture of a man served a bowl of *hukluthn*. What's wrong with you? Thought the salts were supposed to put you in more or less a cheerful mood yourself."

"Oh, I'm fine," I said. "I'm…" I eyed the mug of beer. "Is it a good idea for me to be drinking this?"

Agnir reached over and snatched the mug out of my hands again. "I'll be happy to take care of that for you, Eyidson, no need to worry."

I shook my head faintly and sat up. "Seriously, what's gotten into all of you? Did Rigvar miraculously die while I was asleep?"

"If only," Iskari said. "But he hasn't caused any more mischief while you've been out, and no one's asked about Thane and the others, so, it's been a good few days."

"Days."

"Days. You've been asleep for two days."

I swore and kneaded my fingertips against my cheekbones, under my eyes where I felt a dull ache. "I thought I'd slept no more than a few hours."

"Oh, you've been in and out this whole time. Mostly *drakkeyn* delirious. Making even less sense than usual, if that's possible."

"Sounds like a damn useless drug, if it destroys a person's ability to function that much," I said.

"I wondered about that, too," Agnir said, "but I figure it was the salts combined with whatever they slipped in your meal to knock you out. The salts themselves wouldn't do that much damage. But combined with something else... Well, they were idiots to try it, not knowing what would happen. Especially for Halvir, who always went on about being some kind of officially trained physician, or whatever he said he was. It could have killed you."

I lifted a hand in acknowledgment, and accepted the brown bread Nika passed to me. It was still warm, the top smeared with a generous layer of lard or butter, with a few thick pieces of smoked herring folded inside a slit that ran down its length. I ate it as slowly as I could; my stomach had been worse than empty for a long time now, and the last thing I wanted to do was lose the first meal I tried to eat. When I'd finished the bread, she handed me a tin jug.

"Water," she said. "None of us need it, so just take the whole jug. We've been trying to get you to drink it all day anyway."

I drank until I ran out of breath, then wiped my mouth with the edge of my sleeve. As I did, I noticed that my wrists had been bandaged, and the blood had been washed off my skin.

"Thank you," I said, lifting my hands a little. "Whoever did this."

Nika ducked her head, then pulled her knees up to her chest and focused on her own slab of bread.

"How are you feeling?" Agnir asked. "Better?"

"Not sure," I said. "I still feel a bit...placid."

Iskari looked at me askance.

"I know," I said. "It's a horrific way to feel. I *know* I should feel differently but I just...don't...care. But I care a little more than I did before, so, hopefully that's something."

"And your magic?"

I shrugged. "No. I feel like...my mind is trapped in this tiny, padded room that's safe and warm and peaceful, but I know there's this endless sea just outside my reach."

"Well, try to find it soon. The moot is coming up, and we need you fit to face Rigvar."

"I thought magic wasn't allowed at the moot," I said.

His mouth twitched. "That's true, but as long as you're cut off from your power, you're not…*you*. I don't know that you'll be able to defeat him if you're not fully present, if you know what I mean."

"I do," I said.

The three of them seemed to sober a bit after that conversation, and I regretted the loss of their banter. And in the quiet that followed, I suddenly became aware of another noise, faint at first, slowly getting louder.

"Shade? *Shade!*"

I slammed my eyes shut, diving into the depths of my mind, scraping and pulling at the barriers around my thoughts. "Pika?" I called. "I'm here!"

"Oh stars," her voice wept. "Been trying to find you… Where you been, Shade?"

"I got drugged," I said. "Poisoned. Right when I was talking to you last time."

There was a moment of pure silence, then her little voice asked, "Are you a'right?"

"Getting better," I said, wondering if she could sense my smile. "I lost touch with my magic though, so I haven't been able to reach you, or come back to Brinmark. Is everything all right?"

I didn't hear an answer. Terrified that I'd lost her again, I called her name.

"I'm here, Shade. Dan'…dan' ask me to 'splain it. Please just come and talk to Doc."

"I'll try," I said.

"Hurry," she said. "I gotta…I gotta gan now, Shade."

The connection with her faded. For a few moments I sat motionless, my eyes still closed, aware of the press of silence all around me.

I slit my eyes open to look at the others, who were all staring at me, frozen, like actors in tableau. "Well, I found my magic," I said. "And something's wrong, in Cavnal. I have to get back and find out what's going on. I just…don't know if I'm strong enough to Ghost yet. Stars.

If Thane and Halvir hadn't protested so *violently* that they were on my side, I would've believed they purposefully set out to destroy me. They could not have picked a *worse* way to hamstring me right when I needed all my wits and all my strength."

"Was that my ears fooling me, or did you sound a little angry just now?" Iskari taunted.

"Damn right I did," I growled.

"Fantastic."

I glared at him, but then I couldn't help smiling; it felt good to feel something running through my veins besides placid indifference.

"What can we do to help?" Agnir asked.

I thought that over a minute, then said, "Bring me Mirin. It's time that poor fool got to go home."

Agnir got up at once; of the three of them, his Cavnish was the best, so it made sense that he be the one to go and persuade the sailor to come back with him. I threw off the woolen blanket and sat on the edge of the couch, eyes closed, curling and uncurling my fingers as if the motion could help me focus my thoughts. I could feel Iskari and Nika's attention riveted on me, but I forced myself to ignore them. If I was going to Ghost—and, certainly, if I was going to Ghost with Mirin in tow—I needed all of my concentration.

Agnir and Mirin returned not fifteen minutes later, Mirin instantly rushing in and throwing himself at my feet. I looked up at the ceiling and drew a long breath to find patience, then touched Mirin on the shoulder and gestured for him to sit with me on the couch. Gingerly, he sat on the very edge of the couch, as far away from me as he could with Nika sitting on the other side of him.

"Mirin, did Agnir tell you why you're here?"

"No, just that you had summoned me, Your Majesty," he said, with an anxious glance up at Agnir.

For my part, I leveled a dark glare on the captain; he answered with a smirk.

"Are you familiar with Brinmark?" I asked Mirin.

"Ahh, I've been there once, sure, but it was welly ten years ago. I dan' think I remember much of it."

"There a train station," I said. "Wherever you're from, you will be able to find a train to get you there."

"But, ahh, how'm I to get to Brinmark?"

"That part's easy," I said. "I'm going to take you there."

He leaned a little away from me, eyes wide. "Jixy business?" he said.

"It's your chance to leave Istia," I said.

"You're sending me away."

I took a subtle breath, willing myself to be calm. "No, but I would much rather see you safely at home, among our people."

"Our people," he echoed. "Your Majesty, if you...if you wish me to go with you, I will do whatever you ask."

I gave up trying to persuade him I wasn't his King; it wasn't worth the effort. "I know you will do whatever your King requires," I said instead, "and that is why I am trusting you to come with me."

He lifted his thin shoulders up and nodded fiercely, and I suppressed the impulse to roll my eyes.

To Agnir I said, "Make sure Rigvar doesn't destroy the country while I'm gone."

"We'll see it done, Godar," he said.

I favored him with another glare and got to my feet, beckoning Mirin up beside me. "Hold on, and don't let go," I said.

"I could not presume to—" he started.

I grabbed him around the shoulders, closed my eyes and plunged my hands deep into the sea of my magic, and pulled us both into the realm beyond.

Mirin clung to me like a child. I wondered vaguely what he saw, if he saw anything at all, in that bright-walled place. I stood just for a moment at the crossroads, then focused on Doc and stepped straight through to the factory yard of the Troyce & Fallon. When I opened my eyes, it was sleeting, and a dank wind was blowing in from the north, and Mirin still had his arms cinched tight around my waist. I shoved him gently back.

"You can open your eyes. We're here."

"Bloody hell," he said, stumbling to his knees. "Bloody *hell*. That was...fast." He got carefully back to his feet, studying me sideways as he bent his head from the wind. "What about you, Your Majesty? Have you come back to Cavnal for good? Are you going to take up the Crown?"

"Not yet," I said. "As soon as I find out what my people needed to talk to me about, I'm going back to Istia. I've still got work to do there. But I'll come home soon, I promise you that."

*Home.* The word felt strange in my mouth, but Mirin's face flooded with relief.

"You're a free man, Mirin," I said. "If you follow that road south, you'll come to the South Brinmark Station."

I held out my hand, intending for him to shake it, but he grabbed it and kissed it instead. "Godspeed, Your Majesty," he whispered. "I will pray daily for your safety and your victory over your enemies."

I shivered and pulled my hand free. "Thank you," I said, and meant it. "Goodbye, Mirin."

"I hope I will see you again one day, Your Majesty," he said.

"If we cross paths again, I'll make sure you're given approach."

He bent his head, then folded his whole body in a deep bow, and headed out the factory gate and into the city of Brinmark. I watched him until he had disappeared around the corner. Then, kicking aimlessly at some stray, sodden papers, I made my way down into the basement of the Hole, and from there, to the Clan's eastern wing.

Doc was waiting for me at the door of the Sanctum, and I drew up short when I saw him.

I had never seen anyone look so afraid.

"Doc?" I asked, hurrying the last few steps to join him. "Good God, what's wrong with you? Did someone die?"

"If only," he said. "I'm so sorry, Tarik. I am...so sorry."

"For what?" I asked. "What's going on? Pika wouldn't say..."

He just lifted his hand, and I realized he was holding out a copy of the Herald. I took it, frowning, and opened it to the first page.

### CROWN PRINCE TARIK RETURNED SAFELY FROM CAPTIVITY
### CORONATION TO BE HELD ON 17 VORATHEN

I couldn't force myself to read any further; I was aware of nothing; the paper slipped from my fingers. Without a word, Doc bent and retrieved it, and for endless moments he just stood there with it held in both hands, his gaze steady on my face. But I couldn't focus on anything at all.

"Is it... It's him, isn't it?" I managed at last. "Aroden. He's gone and usurped my *damn throne.*"

Doc nodded.

"How...how did he get out of Borokhev with a plan like that?" I asked. "Hayli would never let this happen."

He just held up the paper again, and his silence was worse than anything he could have said. I forced myself to look down at it, at the photograph that took up the lower corner of the page. There I was, in all my royal trappings, standing before a microphone, with a bruised eye and split lip; the mummery of it all made my blood boil. And behind me—behind Aroden—was a lovely young woman in elegant dress, a small hat pinned on her head, just barely slanted forward on her brow. And even though I'd never seen her in a dress, and I'd never seen her with her hair done up in high society fashion, there was no mistaking it.

That was Hayli, watching someone who wasn't me accept the Court's offer of my Crown.

# CHAPTER 13 ~ TARIK

"I WILL *KILL* HIM."

Doc watched me pacing, a sad, weary look in his eyes that made him look suddenly much older than I imagined he was.

"Tarik," he said at last. "What good would that do? You would only throw this nation into instability *again*, and this time there wouldn't be any chance of salvaging it. Or do you think you could march up to Brigun Palace and persuade them that *you* are the real Prince? Would they believe you?"

I swore and tugged a hand through my hair—it was Shade's hair, but I was thinking of Tarik's death-white hair and cursed death-pale skin, make me a liar of myself.

"Why...why would she do this?" I asked, shaking the paper in his direction. "Doc, please, *please* explain this in some way that makes sense. Explain it so it doesn't make her a traitor."

"She knew you were busy in Istia," Doc said, obliging me, "but things were so unstable here that she took what she knew was a desperate measure to keep the nation from plunging into ruin. A temporary fix only, until you could return and take the Crown yourself."

I looked at him a while in silence, mulling that over. Finally I nodded, and dropped the newspaper on the nearest chair. "Fine," I said. "I'll accept that. It doesn't...make complete sense, but it's better than any reason I was coming up with. Still, it doesn't give me any notion of what to do from here on out. As you just so kindly reminded me, I *can't* go back and take the Crown. I certainly can't come back before the coronation—that's going to be the day before the moot. Even if Hayli meant it to be temporary, how can I ever rule as Tarik if I can't bloody *look* like him? And she knows that, too."

"If it were anyone besides Aroden, I would say you might try to broker a deal with him, where he rules publicly, and does whatever you tell him, while you hold the real power behind the scenes."

"But it's Aroden," I said.

"But it's Aroden," he affirmed. "And you have no idea the hell this situation has just opened up for us."

"I'm getting a fairly good idea." I chewed on a ragged fingernail as I thought, then, grumbling, I said, "We could lure him into doing something fantastically stupid so the people and the Court force him to abdicate. It's happened before."

"But in those—what were there, two?—instances, there was always another heir to keep the Caveni line on the throne," Doc pointed out.

I turned to face him. "I don't know if you noticed, Doc, but the Caveni line is already broken."

"But the people don't know that."

"Doesn't make it less true."

"Tarik," he said, sounding exasperated. "I'm not sure what it will take, but you must get Aroden off the throne. He is far more dangerous than you can imagine. You *cannot* allow him to rule."

"I thought you just told me I couldn't kill him."

"I don't have the answer for you," he said, lifting a hand in a gesture of defeat. "I honestly don't. But whatever you do, do it soon. The Meritian fleet is encroaching on Cavnish waters south of Ridgemark. Whatever happens has to happen soon or they'll get tired of waiting and use that damn weapon."

"Alokin's bomb," I said.

He nodded faintly.

"If I'm in Istia, it will target Aroden. He's the most powerful mage in Cavnal, isn't he?" He nodded again, almost wincing as he did. "But it will destroy the whole city."

"If he's made the changes to the weapon's design that he told me about, then…yes."

I squeezed my eyes shut, those visions of the devastated city rearing in my thoughts again, the smoke and ash and the dead unburied.

"For my part," Doc said, very quietly, "I am heartily sorry that it

 602

has come to this. It's my fault, in the end."

"Doc," I said. "How could it possibly be your fault?"

He opened his mouth, then closed it again as if he'd thought better of what he'd meant to say. Then he lifted his shoulders in a shrug and said, "I couldn't reason with Alokin. Couldn't make him stay, or give up his mad invention. And I abandoned Hayli when she most needed guidance. If I'd stayed, I might have been able to persuade her of the danger of trusting Aroden."

I eyed him curiously. "You know an awful lot about that mage," I said. "How is that?"

"I've been looking for him for...a long time," Doc said, hesitating. "Chasing him is what first brought me to Brinmark."

"But when he came across your path you ran away," I said. "Why?"

"I couldn't let him know that I was there. If he'd realized I was in Borokhev, if he remembered..." He shook his head violently, pressing his fingertips against his forehead. "I was looking for him, yes, but I meant to trap him, to render him powerless so I could confront him. I couldn't do that if he already knew I was coming." He hesitated again, then swore softly under his breath and went to the lectern, his fingers lingering over the cover of the *Brigaz Nedash*. "The situation is worse than you can imagine," he repeated. "Can you feel it?"

I looked at him askance, then, slowly, at the corner of my consciousness I felt it again—that prickling, needling sensation in the back of my thoughts that I'd first felt in Borokhev, when I'd gone to visit Hayli.

"He's been here?" I said, startled.

He pursed his lips and nodded. "I tried to protect it from him," he said. "I put the strongest ward I could weave on the door of this Sanctum. There is no way he could have bypassed it unless..."

"Unless he had help?" I asked, my heart sinking.

"Yes."

"What were you trying to protect from him? This room? The book?"

Doc traced the script of the title, eyes shadowing. "The book," he said. He seemed to come to a decision then, because he swiped the book from the lectern and carried it to me in two long strides. "Take it," he said. "Read it. There's something you need to understand. Now, get out of here before I change my mind."

603

I took the book gingerly from him, searching his face for understanding, but he just flung a hand up between us and moved away. Sighing, I turned to leave—I didn't even know where I meant to go—and found myself face to face with little Pika. She stared at me for one long moment, then she burst into tears and barreled toward me. I stooped and caught her in my arms, and she buried her face against my chest as she sobbed.

"Shade," she wailed. "Dan' be so sad. Your poor heart!"

I flinched but said nothing; I patted her unruly red curls in the best effort I could make at comforting her.

"It's all right," I murmured.

"Hayli dan' mean to hurt you, deep down, I *know* she dan'...but Aroden just...he needles and he needles and... Stars, she won't even talk to *Piper* now!"

"Who's Piper?" I asked, baffled.

"Her *crow-w-w*..." she said, the word drawn out on another sob.

I let out a breath and set the book down on the ground beside me, then shifted Pika away from me so I could look her in the eye. "You've been bringing messages and news to Doc?" I asked. "Focus. I need information."

"Y-y-yes..."

"She's been my eyes and ears since I left," Doc said, softly, from the other side of the room. "She keeps me informed of what's going on at Borokhev, and carries what news I've got to Bridnow."

I nodded and caught Pika's eye. "Can you keep doing that for me?"

"A-a-aothir said you...killed his friend."

I closed my eyes. "I did not. But his friend nearly ruined me. Remember how I told you I was poisoned?"

Doc shifted around at that, fixing me with an alarmed gaze.

Pika's lip trembled. "Thane did that to you?"

"I'm afraid so. One of my friends rescued me, but...it got ugly. Things happened. No one wanted Thane to die."

"Wish I could tell H-h-hayli that," she said, tears springing to her eyes again, "but she'd never b-b-*believe* me."

I let out a thin breath and sat back on my heels. "Aothir told Hayli I killed his friend?"

She nodded. "He div'n know. He was just so sad. And dan' be angry at Hayli, Shade, *please*," she said. "*Promise* me."

"I'm not angry at her," I said, very quietly.

That just seemed to make it worse; she burst into tears again, both hands clapped over her mouth, then she dropped them and said, "Oh, *Shade*...my poor Shade!" and flung her wiry arms around my neck.

I exchanged a glance with Doc over her head and patted her back. "Pika, listen to me very closely," I said. "Things are going to get a little strange, I think. I need you to promise me something."

She wiped away her tears and nodded, lower lip jutted out.

"Don't try to read anyone for a while, all right? Not me. Not Aroden. Not Hayli. Not anyone. Do you understand me?"

"Why, Shade?"

"Just trust me. If you need to reach me, or if Doc needs to reach me, you can do that, just don't try to do any more than that."

"A'right," she said, sounding a bit forlorn for it. "I promise."

"Good kid," I said. I picked up the book and the newspaper and got to my feet, squeezing her shoulder briefly as I did. "Take care of yourself."

"You too," she whispered, and ran over to where Doc stood among a small stack of books.

She curled up in the chair he was standing beside, her head buried in the crook of her arms, and closed her eyes. I met Doc's gaze, and he tried a smile that I tried to return. We both failed.

I LEFT WAKE'S REALM AND STEPPED out into Eyid's sitting room. I could hear a low murmur of voices from an adjoining room—Iskari's, and Nika's. A moment later I heard Agnir's familiar, sea-rough voice, and I smiled to myself. Outside the street was dark, a swirl of snow drifting down like ash in the oily lamplight. I didn't think I'd been gone so long, but I'd wandered a while in Wake's realm, not wanting to face the inevitable, wishing I could stop time until the world started to make sense again.

With a tired sigh I set the book and the newspaper down on the table beside my couch, and dropped onto the low cushions with my head in my heads. Tomorrow. Tomorrow I would read the book, and try to discover what Doc wanted me to know. For the space of a breath I wondered if I ought to tell the others that I was back; I nearly decided to let them find out for themselves in the morning, but then Iskari's rebuke chased through my thoughts and drove me back to my feet.

605

I walked down the narrow hall to a room that might have been another parlor or a dining room, making no effort to soften my steps. The voices fell silent when I was three steps away from the room, and when I pushed open the door, they were all sitting around a table, staring at the doorway expectantly.

"You're back," Iskari said.

"You look like hell," Nika said.

Agnir, more circumspect, said, "Taumir, what happened?"

"Aroden is going to be crowned King of Cavnal next week," I said, and left them staring after me.

I dreamed of the bell tower again. It had been a long time since I'd dreamed of it—not since the night before my birthday—but this time it was different. It was a nightmare drawn more precisely from my memories, starting long before the dream usually began, reliving the whole thing in the frightening clarity that dreams often bring.

*I'm sitting in my study, with my private tutor K. Trubek standing across the desk from me. He holds a slim book in one hand and a pointer in the other, which he holds habitually, even when he doesn't need to use it. His expression is puzzled; I remember that it is because of the question I have just asked him.*

*"Why did Count and Lady Lorin get executed?"*

*He is instructing me in the names, titles, and histories of the current and recent aristocracy, and I've gotten stuck on the Lorins, because I know their daughter was Griff's friend when we were much, much smaller. Before the execution.*

*"They were found to be Jixies, Your Highness," Trubek says, waving his pointer in my direction.*

*"So, just because they were mages, they got killed? By my father?"*

*"By the State," Trubek corrects. "Not because they were mages, but because they knowingly concealed that fact from the Crown. They knew it was against the law for their kind to hold office, and yet they persisted. They lied to your father the King, and to all the Court, and pretended to be something that they were not. They were given a trial, and asked to renounce their titles and offices, and all their honors with an offer of clemency in exchange, and yet they refused. In fact, they had the gall to rebuke the whole government for its laws. Publicly. And so, they were found guilty of high treason against the Crown, and the punishment for high treason is death."*

*I can't eat a thing at dinner that night. I keep staring at my mother, fear and dread roiling in my stomach. I am fifteen; I know what death is, I know the absolute finality of it. I fear it with all my heart. And yet…I am a lie. I am nothing but a lie. I should be dead, like Count Lorin. My mother should be dead. Everything in my life is a lie, and I hate what I am more than I hate the law that makes me ashamed of it. My mother watches me in concern; my father is indifferent, as always. Of course he is. I understand why, now.*

*I am a plague he cannot cure.*

*I am the knife at his back, waiting endlessly, patiently, for him to stagger. To be weak, for one moment.*

*I leave the house before dessert is served. Deep in the city there is a bell tower, an old monument to a bygone age. My tutor has taught me all of its history, but I only care that it is my favorite place to climb. I crave the thrill of fear and triumph as I scale up its rugged face, digging out handholds among broken masonry and grilled windows. At the top I stand in the belfry arch, where I have stood a hundred times or more. But tonight I can't see the lights of the city below me. They are a blur, swimming in my tears. I feel the wind stirring around me; at that height it rages, and it twines like fingers in my hair, around my neck, tugging my arms and teasing my grip, daring me to let go.*

*I can't make sense of the ache in my heart. It seeps all the way to the pit of my stomach and clutches at my lungs, so sharp and longing that now I can't even weep. It is all so vain, so pointless. The lies are burning me up inside. I am nothing; I am worse than nothing. I am a blight on my father's house; I am the disappointment of all his hopes. I am the shame of my country. If I die, they will mourn me. If I live…if I live, then one day they will inevitably come to hate me. It is the way of all history.*

*I stare down at the pavement far below. The night calls to me; I hear sorrow in the voice of the wind, in the broken moonlight, luring me out. I long to fly away. I can imagine with too-keen clarity the movement of the air around me—the wind under my control, serving my needs, not trying to drag me to ruin. I close my eyes and wish with a mad and breathless wish that I might sprout wings and lurch from the belfry and conquer the sky. I long to fall. I long for an end. I want never to face the world again.*

*I let go of the belfry arch, feeling the wind tugging around me, gleeful, taunting. I spread my arms wide to the night.*

*At least this way, either way I will get my wish. I will fly, or I will die; either way, I will be free.*

*I lean, and catch my breath, and before I can think, before I can change my mind, I throw myself forward.*

THE LANDING AT THE BOTTOM OF the fall always used to wake me up. Tonight, it didn't. I tossed and turned, wanting to break out of the nightmare, feeling trapped in its boundaries. I remembered the drift of falling, slower than I ought to have fallen, without any of the control of flight. Now I knew why; it was because Rivano had been there, watching me, and had used his Wind's power to save me.

I remembered the feel of hitting the ground—even though I'd fallen slowly, gently, I still landed on the pavement much too hard. I sprawled on the ground, spitting blood from a split in my cheek as the wind stroked my tangled hair.

That was where my memory went dark if I pushed it too far, but this time I woke myself up with that last moment caught in my mind, and forced myself to examine it from every possible angle. It was just darkness. All I could recall was the press of cobblestones against my cheek, a drip of dim, sodden lamplight from over the bell tower door. And there...in the very corner of my rapidly darkening vision, I saw a pair of feet, walking toward me.

A hand on my shoulder.

A static charge as if I'd been struck by lightning.

It was that—and not the fall—that had knocked me unconscious.

# CHAPTER 14 ~ TARIK

WHEN ISKARI CAME INTO THE SITTING ROOM THE NEXT MORNING, HANDS full of bread and a crock of yoghurt, I was sitting on the edge of the couch with the *Brigaz Nedash* open in my lap.

"Damn," he said, when he saw me. He deposited the food on the table beside me and sat down in his usual chair, and stared hard at me. "How long have you been up?"

I let my fingers drift over the page facing me; it was the last page in the book, and it was blank. My eyes were as weary as my mind.

"Too long," I said.

"May I?"

I shoved the book toward him, and he flipped pages for all of two seconds before pushing it back at me. "Well, that's useless. I don't read Cavnish *or* Cromner." He eyed me a moment. "I take it you probably read both."

"I read the whole bloody thing," I said. "The Cromner, and the rather shoddy Cavnish translation."

"And?"

"And what?" I asked. "It's so ambiguous. Even the Cromner is. It's amazing whoever made the Cavnish translation was able to do as much as he did with it."

"Rivano," Iskari said.

I rolled my eyes. "Figures that Rivano translated it. Take this for example. He keeps translating the words *gridekh* and *anudekh* as firstborn and secondborn, but that's not what the words really mean."

"Siblings?" he asked.

"More than that. It's rather like, *first-birthed* and *second-birthed*."

"Twins."

I nodded. "This is Arnthor's journal. His account of the days leading up to the Scourge. Rivano translated the whole thing as a bloody prophecy, but I don't think that's how Arnthor meant it. He was just trying to make sense of what he had experienced."

Iskari straightened up, his eyes flickering as he considered that. "Was there someone else? I've never heard anything like that. All the accounts of the Scourge…they just talk about Arnthor, the archmage."

"But depending on what account you listen to, he either started, or ended, the Scourge."

"So, are you saying…"

"I don't know what I'm saying. I don't even think it matters any more. But all of it is tied up with this talk of the Zealot, and the Scion of the mad god."

"Do you think one brother was the Zealot, and one the Scion?"

My mind flitted back to my dream of the two men fighting, and the mad god's taunt when I had asked him about Arnthor and the Scourge. I nodded faintly.

"Arnthor never answered my call to be my Zealot," Wake said, appearing beside me, "though he could have. If he had, he could have stopped the Scion's blood harvest, but he held back. He knew what it would mean. He knew what retribution he would be asked to deliver to the Scion, and it was too much for him. Even after all his brother did, Arnthor still loved him. So he turned to Death for a favor instead."

"But the Scion was actually the Scion?" I asked. "He *did* answer the mad god's call?"

Wake nodded. I was keenly aware of Iskari trying not to pay attention to me conversing with the air.

"There is no more battle for your soul," Wake said. "The mad god has found his Scion. Take care lest you make the same mistake that Arnthor did, and leave your world to be reaped in blood."

I held the book a moment longer in my hands. The smell of the warm bread tickled my nose, making my stomach grumble fitfully, but I pushed aside the desire for food and set the book on the table.

"I need some time to think," I said to Iskari as I got to my feet.

 610

"Don't try to follow me. Trust that I'll be back soon. I'm not in any danger of...drowning."

He just regarded me in silence, and didn't move to stop me as I passed him by. I took the long street straight down toward the harbor. It curved a little away from the main street that the lodging house was on, and didn't open out directly on the docks like that road did. Instead it ended at a long pier jutting out into the wild and ice-crusted sea, where, maybe a quarter of a mile off the shore, it curved to form a breakwater. I followed the pier all the way out onto the mole, and walked to its very end, where the waves crashed against the sea wall in a spray of frigid foam. The grey stones were slick where they weren't crusted with barnacles, and I had to place my feet carefully to keep from slipping.

Ahead of me, the sky was a churning grey fraught with storm clouds, and the sea beneath it was troubled.

"Wake," I called, tipping my head back. "I'm not promising anything. But if I'm to move forward, you have to tell me what you expect of me. You have to tell me what I can expect."

Wake was in front of me, like he was part of the waves and part of the wind, and his face was a wildness of rapture that tore my heart with longing.

"Then look, and take your fill," he said, and reached out, and planted his finger and thumb against my forehead.

I was swept up in a cacophony of wind
A chaos of light, a sunrise like fire and a dust-scarred earth
A face like thunder and eyes ablaze like lightning
Power surging electric through every corner of my soul
An endless abyss reaching before me,
Like my skin couldn't contain me
Like the world couldn't hold me
I was reeling with strength and intoxicated with joy
The world below me swirled in a wild ecstasy of color
The breathless infinity of the stars
The blood-song of the moon
The sweep of an endless sea on an endless shore
And life was everywhere around me, and within me
Bright and glorious
I hurtled back to my senses, and for minutes or hours I stood

with my arms open to the cold wind and the spray of foam and every beautiful color that shattered off the broken waves from the half-shrouded sun. Every nerve in my body hummed, alight with power and rapturous fire. The whole world spread before me in endless possibility; if I just held out my hand, I could do anything. I could achieve anything. I was alive and I was strong and nothing in the world could break me. For that one moment, I was the master of my sea.

If this was what joy was, I never wanted to let it go.

I staggered a step, suddenly, as the burn of fire faded from my veins. The world darkened, and the wind sighed over the broken rocks, and that old, sick pang settled deep in the pit of my stomach. I turned a slow circle, careful with my back to the waves, and saw nothing but the sea behind me, and the sea in front of me. The churning dark abyss beckoned to me, seducing me with whispers of quiet and the old promise of an end to all the madness. There was nothing…nothing at all. Nothing but the deepness, and the long emptiness. I shuddered and dropped to one knee on the sea-slick stones as the truth crept over me like a slow sickness.

I was alone.

*I am nothing.*

I blinked, suddenly aware of light and energy pulsing around me, and when I looked up I found Wake kneeling in front of me. He reached out and took my face in his hands, his gaze searing into mine.

He said, "You are Tarik."

NIKA WAS WAITING FOR ME ON the front step of Eyid's house when I got back; or at least, she was standing on the step, arms folded, staring stubbornly the opposite direction that I was coming from, as if she hadn't been watching me walk all the way up the street. When I stopped in front of her she finally looked at me, mouth set, a faint line traced between her brows.

"You've been gone for hours," she said, then added flatly, "I wasn't worried about you."

"Of course not," I said, stifling a faint smile. "Is there any of that bread left, or did Iskari eat it all?"

"There's some," she said. "I brought some stew up from the lodging house, too, if you want that."

I nodded my thanks and stepped past her and into the house. Iskari was, inauspiciously, standing at the window in the front room. He nodded to me as I came in, and waited in silence for me to speak.

What I said caught him by surprise. "Iskari, would you be so kind as to bring Rigvar to me?"

"The hell?" he said.

"Just what I said. I want to talk to him."

"You're *drakkeyn* kidding me, right?"

"I wish I were."

"Did…Wake tell you to talk to Rigvar?"

I gave him a bland look. "I am somewhat capable of making my own decisions most of the time, Iskari. This one I think he's pretty indifferent about."

"Your funeral," he said, and stalked out of the room.

Precisely one minute later, Nika stalked in.

"You sent Iskari to do *what?*"

"You know exactly what I sent him to do," I said, favoring her with a dark glare, "so if you don't like it, I suggest you go sit upstairs for a while until Rigvar leaves. I'd rather not put you or Iskari in his way while we're talking if I don't have to, anyway."

She pursed her lips in a thin line and shook her hair over her shoulder, but then, apparently figuring it would do no good to argue with me, she turned on her heel and left the room. I heard the sound of her marching up the staircase, then the slam of Eyid's office door, and I suppressed a smile.

I didn't have to wait long before Iskari flung open the house's front door. Holding my breath, I listened to the sound of his footsteps coming in, and then, just when I resigned myself to the idea that he'd failed, I heard another, lighter tread following his.

"He's in there. If you try anything, I will gut you."

"Thank you, Iskari. I'm well aware of your inclinations," came Rigvar's smooth voice. "Bring your sister with you and it might even get interesting."

"You leave her out of it," Iskari growled.

Rigvar only laughed, but even from the corridor I could hear the faint lace of fear in it. A moment later his shadow fell across the sitting room door, and then he himself stepped in. He took one look at me—I was helping myself to the stew Nika had brought—and hesitated. I saw his fingers curl briefly, then he brushed one hand over his arm with a faint shudder. He was remarkably pale. For a moment I wondered if he would just turn and walk away, but then his jaw tightened and he circled a few steps into the room, still staying as far from me as he could.

"You're a dangerous man to be around, they say," he told me. "Should I be nervous, coming here in front of you, all by myself, unarmed?"

"Only if you wish me ill," I said.

"How do I know you didn't call me out here—" He took the room in at a glance, and his face grew paler still—"to kill me?"

"Honestly, Rigvar, you should know that if I meant to kill you, I could have done it any time, from any where."

He swallowed visibly and took the chair, trying to make a show of sitting back casually.

"Look, I just want to talk," I said, "but if that doesn't suit you…"

"Talk to me about what?"

"What will you do for Istia, if you become Godar?"

He startled, lurching forward in his chair. "*What?*"

"Do I need to speak more slowly? What is your plan, if you become Godar? I don't know if you noticed, but there's an international war brewing right now, and Istia is a lynchpin."

"Which is just as it should be," he said. "What Istia decides *should* alter the course of the world."

"Don't be so short-sighted," I said. "You realize that some of the countries involved in this aforementioned crisis are in possession of a weapon that could wipe out half the population of Istia in one blow."

"Our mages—"

"Would draw the weapon straight to you," I said. "It targets magic."

"*Skatr,*" he swore.

"Yes."

"If this is true—and I'm *not* saying I believe you—what could we possibly do to stop it?"

"That's what I'm asking you. You want the *aydrding*. So, convince me that you deserve it."

He frowned, leaning a little away from me. "You would…let me have it? You'd step away from the moot, without a fight?"

I finished off the last of the stew and reached for the bread, pulling off a hunk of it and slathering it with some of the creamy white butter Nika had provided. Rigvar shifted his weight.

"I never give up anything without a fight," I said. "But I want you to convince me it's worth my time." I felt a faint pressure buzzing at the corners of my mind, like a moth beating against a glass lampshade, and I tipped my head to look at him. "Don't even bother trying," I said.

His face paled, and he shook his head. "I'm not trying anything."

"And don't lie," I said. "Or aren't you Istian?"

His head snapped up at that, and he glared at me with a dark blaze of hatred. "Fine," he said. "I was *drakkeyn* manipulating your feelings to be more favorable toward me. What of it?"

"It was a pathetic attempt is what it was," I said. "You really should know better."

"What do you *want* from us?" he asked. "Why are you here?"

"What I want, Karvarson, is to preserve peace between Cavnal and Istia," I said. "Reaffirm Istia's commitment to our old trade agreements, and your commitment to defending mages no matter what country they hail from. I want to stop you from doing something so fantastically stupid as antagonizing your allies. I want Istia and Cavnal and Tulay to take a stand against those two wretched, hateful countries that want to see everything unique about us destroyed. Clear enough?"

"*Our* commitment," he echoed. "Our superiority. Are you admitting that you're not Istian?"

"What I am is of little importance," I said. "You know what I stand for."

"You came to Istia to become Godar, but no self-respecting Istian would vote a foreigner into that office, even if that foreigner has some claim to Istian blood."

"You make some bold assumptions," I said, "like the idea that my intention in coming to Istia was to become Godar."

"It wasn't?" he asked, after a rather strangled pause.

"I only made that decision when I realized what a dangerously incompetent idiot was laying claim to the title."

His face reddened, and his lips twitched, but language seemed to have pulled a vanishing act from his faculties.

"You are an absolute *stodadrakkim*," he said at last, which may not have been the eloquent reply he was reaching for.

615

"Well," I said mildly, "you would certainly know."

He shoved his chair back as he stood, sending it clattering down on the bare floor. Whatever silken composure he'd carried the first few times I'd met him had completely disappeared, and I almost felt a bit uncomfortable for him, for the way he was sweating, and the way his hands were trembling.

"I will cast you into ruin if it's the last thing *Veka* sees fit to let me do," he said. "I swear it."

"He won't," I said, buttering another piece of bread. I glanced up at him when he didn't move. "*Veka*. He won't see fit."

"We shouldn't have bothered trying to medicate you," Rigvar growled. "We should have just put a bullet between your eyes like a rabid dog."

"Ah," I said. "I was wondering if that was you."

"I didn't say—" he started, then cursed and flung a hand between us. "It wasn't my first choice, believe me, but it was all I could persuade them to do. They were…surprisingly loyal to you."

"Not so loyal to me," I said. "Just very unhappy with you."

I polished off the bread and took a long drink of water from the mug Nika had left me, then sighed and got to my feet. Rigvar shied back from me as I stood in front of him, all the haughtiness gone from his features.

"We both want the same thing," I said, quietly. "We want peace for Istia, and prosperity. We want safety for people like us, and the freedom to be what we were born to be." I took a step back and turned toward the window. "I want you to remember this. I could have killed you at any time while we were talking. It wouldn't even have been difficult. It might even have given me a bit of satisfaction. But I didn't. You can go."

For a few moments he stood rooted where he was, and I could feel the weight of his stare. I wondered if he was calculating his odds of success if he should try knifing me in the back; I certainly wasn't giving a show of defending myself. But fortunately his good sense seemed to outweigh his hatred, because he let out his breath in a quiet hiss and left the room. I listened as his steps retreated, then watched as he descended to the street and stalked away toward the lodging house, one hand gripping the edge of the hunting knife he had slung at his hip.

"Were you trying to completely antagonize him?" Iskari asked, coming into the room a few minutes later.

"No," I said, softly. "Just driving home a very particular point."

"And...what point would that be?"

I turned to him with a thin smile. "Whatever happens from here on out, happens because I allow it."

The next morning, it looked like the whole city of Bregjarvani was emptying. Wagons drawn by particolored horses carried entire families out of the city, heading north along the river Stratha, while individuals rode rickety bicycles or their own stocky horses. Many people seemed content to make the journey on foot—I wondered how long it would take them.

Agnir and I stood with Nika and Iskari in Eyid's doorway, watching a trickle of people winding their way up the street. All of them were carrying bundles of food and blankets, shouting back and forth to one another while a few people tried to drown them out by singing raucous folk songs.

"They're all going to the moot?" I asked.

"Eh," Agnir said, shrugging. "The moot is for the *sodthari* and their attendants and guards. But there'll be feasting and music and games for the rest of the people while the *eyltheng* is taking place."

"Even in this weather?"

Iskari laughed. "Istians would never forgo the chance for a festival," he said, "even in the dead of winter, in the heart of the mountains."

"You're all dead *drakkeyn ganthiskur*," I said cheerfully. "I'm a picture of impeccable sanity by comparison."

"And you're in a frighteningly good mood," Iskari said.

I flicked my thumb at him and Nika grinned, stooping to pick up her leather rucksack. "Well, are you ready? We should try to get there early, so we can get the best campsites."

"Campsites," I echoed, grimacing. "Let me guess, the best spots are close to steam vents in the earth?"

"He's catching on," Iskari said, and slung his own bag over one shoulder. "Come on, then. There's stale beer and dried fish waiting for you at the end of the day."

I muttered a few choice obscenities under my breath and picked up my bag, and followed them back to the lodging house to claim our horses. As soon as we all had our belongings stowed behind the saddles, we mounted up and followed the migration of Istians heading for Hejmstrathvir.

"I just hope nobody's touched that bloody rock," I growled as we left the city behind, "because I am *not* fixing it again."

# CHAPTER 15 ~ HAYLI

THE VOTE OF THE *KATZPOTIVYEK* CAME IN TWO DAYS AFTER THE RADIO announcement of the Prince's return, declaring almost unanimously in favor of Aroden's coronation. Even the Court of Ministries had voted nearly of one accord—though the vote was anonymous, the numbers were reported over the radio: nine *ayes* to one *nay*. I wondered who the holdout was, but I remembered the Ministers standing on the Palace steps, and guessed it was Von.

The mood at Borokhev in the days after I took Aroden to the Palace was tense. It reminded me of the days leading up to the insurgency, when everyone was fit to erupt, and petty quarrels sprang up everywhere that had naught to do with anything except the situation I'd created. I had done what I thought I had to, to keep my people safe, and the only thing I felt like I'd accomplished was proving that I never deserved the leadership Shade had entrusted to me.

And the worst part of it was that I had nowhere to go. I couldn't stay at Borokhev, and face the doubt and judgment of so many people—especially Bridnow, who'd trusted me just as much as Shade ever had. I couldn't bear to see the way everybody eyed each other sideways, doubting each other's allegiances. But I couldn't go to the Palace either, where I had no place, where there was nothing Aroden could say or do that would make me belong.

Instead I let Piper stay at Borokhev, keeping to the trees and rooftops, and sometimes the windowsills to eavesdrop on conversations, but she insisted on blocking me from her mind as much as I'd ever blocked her from mine. No matter what I said, she wouldn't accept my apology. It hurt worse than when I'd been cut off from her by Kippler's meddling.

She released me unexpectedly in the middle of the day when she'd been foraging for scraps near the mess hall. I spooked a handful of skitters when I appeared suddenly against the wall near where they were playing at knuckle-bones, and for half a tick I just crouched there, looking around, trying to figure out why I'd been so unceremoniously dumped back into my senses.

Then I saw what Piper must have seen—Creech, or rather, Howler, trotting across the courtyard. I jumped up and went to meet him, and with a flurry of wind and color, Creech was there in front of me.

"Afternoon, Hayli," he said, clasping my arm. "Where's Bridnow?"

I looked away, flustered, and pointed toward the Rookery. "My guess is there. Div'n you check?"

He headed immediately for the building, but he spoke to me over his shoulder as he went, which gave me no choice but to walk with him—even though the Rookery was the very last place in Borokhev that I wanted to be.

"I had to get away from the Palace," he was saying. "Bloody chaos there, what with the preparations for tomorrow. I thought we might be seeing a bit more of you there, since you were the one who brought the Prince back. No?"

"I've…had other duties," I stammered, and hated the lie as soon as I said it.

Creech nodded and picked up his pace, chattering at me about nothing at all—nothing I could make sense of—the whole way to the Rookery. He knocked on the door, though he didn't need to, and I almost got away as he stepped inside, but then he turned and held the door for me. I steeled my nerves and followed him in.

I saw Krigs first, sitting at the smaller desk tucked in the corner near the hearth, cupping something that looked like metal and leather earmuffs against his ears. He had the radio relayer in front of him, so I guessed he was listening to some sort of transmission. Bridnow appeared a moment later at the mouth of the long hallway. He took one look at me, and his jaw tightened, then he turned to Creech and came forward with hand extended.

"Creech," he said. "What brings you out here today? Aren't they keeping you busy at the Palace for the big event?"

He leveled me with a stern look as he said it, and I looked away. I half-expected him to tell Creech that the man about to be coronated was not the missing Prince at all, but he apparently decided it would do more than harm than good at this point.

"You have no idea," Creech said. "Will you come to the coronation? It's a public event." He glanced at me. "I'm sure Lady...*Oramay* is planning to attend?"

"I'll be there," I said, barely loud enough for him to hear.

Bridnow showed Creech to the big chair by the fire, and settled into the chair across from him. Because I couldn't very well escape now without causing a scene, I leaned against the wall and crossed my arms, and tried as best I could to be invisible.

"I wanted to tell you," Creech said, "I got word from a contact I left within the Cleavers. The Army backed out of the coup as soon as Tarik's return was announced, and His Majesty issued a statement yesterday morning that he was giving his blessing to the Chernayi."

I let out my breath in a thin hiss that neither man noticed.

"That means—" Bridnow started, and Creech nodded.

"Chernayi were only involved in the coup because they felt backed into a corner. They don't want instability any more than the Army did. And now that the Ministers have declared for Tarik, the Chernayi can't be seen to publicly oppose *them*, or they will look like traitors to the Crown."

"So the coup failed."

"Not sure what Red and Klissen and their lot mean to do, now, but apparently Red is being oddly close-lipped about the whole thing. Whatever they meant to do, they're sitting tight for now. Now we only have Meritac and Cromis to worry about."

"And that's enough," Bridnow muttered, wiping a hand over his face. "They're pushing us for an explanation for why their ambassadors got dismissed. I think they're getting a bit twitchy."

"I'd heard as much," Creech said.

"What is the mood in the Palace?" Bridnow asked.

Creech hesitated much longer than he should have. "Generally ecstatic," he said, carefully. "The machine of government is running smoothly again with the foreman back."

"But..."

Creech met Bridnow's gaze. "There's something wrong, and I just don't know what it is. Serro is worried. He won't say much about it, but…that's what he tells me. *'It's just wrong, Creech.'* It's something about Tarik. Captivity changed him, maybe, but…even him being in captivity doesn't explain some of the things that have been happening. Things the Crown Prince—the *King*—oughtn't be doing. Just little things. Facts he gets wrong. Holding meetings in the wrong rooms. Going the wrong direction in the palace. Some of it we might attribute to his recent trauma, but…Serro is understandably concerned."

"It's odd," Bridnow said flatly. "But there is a lot of pressure on him right now."

Creech nodded. "That's what I tell him. He told me once that he missed the Prince's brightness, but when I asked him what he meant, he wouldn't explain. Does it mean anything to you?"

"Can't say that it does."

"Well, that's all my news," Creech said with a sigh, and got to his feet. "I hope to see you at the Palace tomorrow."

He shook Bridnow's hand and gave me a nod of farewell, and was gone. For an endless long minute, Bridnow didn't move. Then he let out his breath and got to his feet, and turned to face me.

"I've been worried about you, Hayli," he said.

My heart caught in mid-beat. "You have?"

He nodded. "Well, it looks like your sleight of hand bought the Ministers some time, anyway, and forestalled the coup."

"You still dan' approve of what I did."

"It doesn't matter. It's done. I can accept that something good has come of it, without changing whether or not I approve of it. I just hope…" His voice trailed off, and even when I prompted him to continue, it was some time before he did. "I just hope you will be willing to accept the consequences of what you've done."

I HAD NEVER, IN ALL MY wildest imaginings, dreamed of anything as splendid as the Throne Room of the Palace on the day of the coronation. It was the single biggest room I'd ever seen apart from the smelter, with a ceiling that soared away to the sky as if the towering marble pillars were there to hold it down. The whole room glittered in white and gleaming gold—white marble pillars, white marble floor, gold adornments on all the carved and sculpted trim. Banners in green and gold fluttered down between every pillar, and massive clerestory windows let in broad swaths of shining sunlight.

The front of the Throne Room was divided from the back by a marble bannister—the common folk could crowd in as thick as they pleased in the back half of the chamber, where there was only room to stand, but the front had benches in beautifully stained darkwood, and that was where the Ministers, their families, and the *katzpotivyek* of Brinmark were invited to sit.

At the top of ten marble steps was the throne itself. A seat for a giant, I thought. The stories said that the first King, Caveni, had it made just to fit him, but as big as it was, I was sure that was just a legend. In all that chamber of bright white marble and shining gold, the throne was almost plain. It was darkwood, carved from a single tree trunk—though I wondered if that was just a myth, too. But it had no adornment on it except what subtle figures the craftsmen had worked into the wood. It was the most impressive thing I had ever seen.

In front of it stood a marble pedestal, which held the ceremonial crown of the King. I'd never seen it with my own eyes, before. I didn't think I'd ever seen it in pictures, either, since the King rarely actually wore it. It was crafted in silver with a rounded mitre in embroidered white silk, with emeralds set in filigreed gold all around the band. Looking at it from my spot close to the front of the chamber, I couldn't even imagine how heavy it was.

I swallowed and smoothed a hand over the front of the front of the green silk gown Luce had spent the last few days making for me. I could feel dozens of gazes on me, uncertain, skeptical, wondering why someone they'd never seen before had got a place so close to the throne, right next to Minister Farro and Griff. In the bench behind me was Minister Batar, who smiled beatifically at me, and Creech, dressed in the uniform of a bodyguard, who nodded silently when I caught his eye. Across the aisle I spotted Minister Von and his children— Risiya and Samyr, and both of them were staring at me openly. Risiya, I thought, looked a bit pale, and when I flashed them both a wicked smile, he turned almost white.

*Good*, I thought. *Let him fret. Let him wonder.*

My vengeful thoughts were interrupted by a clarion trumpet call from a man in spectacular, old-fashioned regalia standing behind the throne—he looked like he'd walked out of a historic play, with his long fluttering sleeves and particolored tunic. At the trumpet blast everyone stood of one accord, and peered toward the back of the chamber. I did too, my heart fluttering recklessly, and something buried deep inside weeping at the wrongness of it all.

First came the Royal Guard in ceremonial uniforms, marching in to line the wide aisle. When they were all in place, they turned as if at an unspoken command, and faced the aisle with their pikes held rigidly at their sides. I didn't know quite what to expect next. Griff had told me that the ceremony usually had the former monarch processing in first, followed by his heir. At the throne, the monarch would demand an oath from the heir, and then would place his own crown on the heir's head. But that couldn't happen here. The former monarch was dead, and the Queen was missing, and so the crown sat waiting on its marble pedestal.

There was a moment of pure, breathless silence, then I caught movement at the end of the aisle, and Aroden appeared. He was dressed in a long, gold-embroidered black coat that looked almost as ancient as the trumpeter's, with a long sash of gold silk draped across his chest and looped over his wrists. In one hand he carried a scepter. His head was bare. His hair had been trimmed and slicked back, but as he came closer I almost smiled, because one little lock of hair above his temple was stubbornly refusing to stay put. Always a little unkempt, I thought. Always a bit of a rogue.

Then I reminded myself it was Aroden I was looking at, not Shade. Not the only man I'd ever known to be the Prince.

He was almost halfway down the aisle when I caught the sounds of a faint scuffle—some kind of commotion in the crowded public area at the back of the Throne Room.

Then someone shouted, "You're a liar! Fraud! I know my King and you ain't him!"

Aroden's pace fumbled, just barely, and his face paled, but he just lifted his chin and kept walking forward. Guards were moving into the crowd, but the man kept shouting.

"You're not Tarik! I kissed the hands of my King and you ain't him! My King is in Istia, and you're a bastard and a thief! Fraud!"

The whole chamber buzzed with distress. Some of the Ministers' wives were crying openly. I didn't even see Aroden walk past me— my attention was still on the crowd, where the guards had dragged a young man in sailor's trousers and a heavy wool jumper into the aisle. He was weeping as he fought against the guards, then one of them struck him in the back of the head with the butt of his revolver, and they hauled him, unconscious, silent, from the Throne Room.

Batar was staring at me.

*My King is in Istia.*

I'd told Batar that Tarik was in Istia. Oh, stars. Did he know what I'd done? Did he suspect? He didn't say a word, and he didn't move, just looked steadily at me. But the betrayal in his eyes was loud as a shout, and suddenly I couldn't meet his gaze. I glanced over at Griff, who looked back at me in stricken silence, his face terribly pale.

I turned, shaking all over, just in time to see Aroden stop in front of the marble pedestal, facing the crowd. A man in a fine suit who I guessed was the Master of the Ceremonies stood behind his left shoulder. When the noise in the Throne Room dwindled, and a silence so pure it was deafening filled the space, Aroden pressed his right hand to his heart and lifted the scepter in his left.

"I solemnly swear, in the sight of all men," he said, his voice ringing through the vast chamber, "that I will uphold the laws of Cavnal as long as the crown is mine to wear. I will honor her allies, and fight her enemies tirelessly with all the energy I have been given. I will be the voice of the *krizanyi* in the Assembly, and suffer no harm to come to them while I have the strength to defend them. For the sake of all my people, I will pursue the path of justice and peace." His eyes drifted, fractionally, toward me. "I will honor the oaths of my father. This I swear."

He handed his scepter to the man behind him, then lifted the heavy crown from the pedestal. For a moment he held it in his hands, then, looking straight at me with something like resignation, he settled it firmly on his head. No one breathed or moved as he walked up the ten steps to the throne, not until he had seated himself and the Master of the Ceremonies handed the scepter back to him.

"Peace!" the man shouted, and the whole assembly shouted the word back to him.

"Triumph!" he cried, and received the crowd's echo.

"Honor!"

And all the people dropped to a knee, and gave their new King fealty, and I knelt with them.

# CHAPTER 16 — TARIK

WE ARRIVED AT HEJMSTRATHVIR BY MID-AFTERNOON THE FOLLOWING DAY. To my relief, the hum of magic in my bones was true—a ringing, resonant chord that settled deep in my soul and smoothed a hand over the rough waters of my sea. I breathed deeply, letting the cold, thin air prickle in my lungs and cleanse my thoughts, and nudged my horse after Nika's as she headed straight for a plume of white steam curling from the earth. Someone else was riding toward the same spot as we approached, but he took one look at us and held up a hand, and turned his horse away.

Nika gave me a faint smile of triumph and swung off her horse's back. "A perfect spot," she said. "High up, so we can see everyone else, and we even have a hot spring behind that rock."

"If you imagine for one moment that I'm going to—" I started, and Iskari laughed, interrupting me.

"Poor baby-skinned Cavner, never bathed in a hot spring before. Let's toss him in, Nika, shall we?"

At my sheer horror they both laughed, and I exchanged a long-suffering look with Agnir as I sat down on my folded woolen blanket. As Nika set to making a bit of bread, Agnir poured a trickle of *skatha* into a small tin cup, and held it out over the steam vent.

"For *Veka*," he said, his gaze locked on mine, "and the forgotten gods. Favor and safe harbor."

"Safe harbor," I murmured, and watched him pour out the libation.

He handed me a cup of my own after that, and I sipped cautiously at the fluid—more cautiously than I had the first time I'd had it. Nika watched me sidelong with a smile toying at the corners of her mouth.

"Not going to gulp it this time?" she taunted.

"I have nothing to prove," I said simply, and leaned back against a rough rust-and-black boulder that was at least twice as big as me.

"I don't suppose you do," she said softly.

We sat in companionable silence while the crowds slowly gathered into the bowl-shaped hollow of Hejmstrathvir, and the sounds of music and laughter filled the space and echoed off the bare rocks of the surrounding slopes. Two teams of men formed up in a wide empty space and started a game of tug-war, while, far across the hollow, I glimpsed a group of people goading each other to jump into a small, ice-crusted pond.

"*Ganthiskur*," I muttered.

"Ah, a time-honored tradition," Agnir said, sipping his *skatha*.

I shook my head and accepted a hunk of steaming hot bread from Nika, topped with a few slivers of raw fish that Iskari had caught earlier in the day, at one of our breaks along the Stratha. I eyed the raw fillets skeptically, then shrugged and stuffed the whole thing in my mouth. For a meal composed of bread, butter, and raw fish, it was shockingly delicious, and Nika laughed as I cleaned my fingers and looked expectantly at her for more.

"You should go down this evening," Agnir said, "and find the *sodthari*. Talk to them. I know you've not been well, and had a hard time mingling with them and letting them get to know you, but it can't hurt to do it now. They know you by reputation, anyway, and what the three of us have been able to do."

"Thank you," I said, strangely moved. I hadn't been aware that they'd been campaigning on my behalf among the *sodthari*; the thought that they would, without my asking, was something I never would have expected.

Agnir lifted a hand, dismissive, and applied himself to his own meal. Some minutes later he said, "You may find them more open to you here, anyway."

"The ban against magic at the moot," I said, guessing what he meant. "That's already in effect?"

"As soon as we crossed into Hejmstrathvir."

All four of us went down to mingle with the crowds as the low-hanging sun sank down behind the mountains, and oil lamps came out to dot the hollow with warm flecks of amber light. I had never sympathized with Trabin so much as I did in the hours that followed, moving from one knot of people to the next, exchanging coarse pleasantries with strangers, answering brutally honest Istian questions with equally honest answers.

I was almost asleep on my feet when I heard a smooth, cool voice somewhere behind me saying, "Taumir Eyidson, so glad to see you made the journey."

I sighed and turned, slowly, to face Rigvar. After I'd summoned him before me to talk, I had hoped he would be a little more reluctant to confront me in public, but apparently prudence was not one of Rigvar's virtues. Still, I was curious to see what he had to say to me, especially since his golden tongue would be effectively tied by the ban against magic. Wishing idly that Iskari or Nika were still with me, I put on a show of confidence and made my way over to where Rigvar sat in a ring of lamplight with the large man I'd seen before and a handful of other people I didn't recognize.

"Rigvar," I said, pleasantly, and sat down across from him as if we were old friends meeting in a tavern. His eyes shadowed, and I allowed myself a faint smirk of triumph. "Always a pleasure to see you."

"Well," he said, "I know."

That raised a laugh from a few people gathered around us, and even I couldn't help grinning at the man's absolute arrogance. His mouth barely suppressed a smile, but it crinkled the corners of his eyes. Then he reached behind him and pulled out a cup and leather sack.

"*Skatha?*" he asked, pouring some and offering it to me.

My hesitation was all internal; I took it without missing a beat, while my mind offered a feeble protest that I should be careful. Not only had I already had one cupful of the hellish stuff, but I had no doubts that Rigvar would stoop to poisoning me himself if he thought it would do any good.

As I sipped—cautiously—at the ice-cold fluid, Rigvar leaned forward and said, "I've heard a most curious rumor, Taumir. Forgive me...I can't recall who told it to me, but *someone* told me that, not only are you not really Istian—though conniving your way to the *aydrding*—but that you actually already have a foreign title hanging over your head."

He paused, watching me carefully; I took another sip and then slanted a glance at him. "Well?" I asked, taking care to sound bored.

"They say you are none other than the missing Crown Prince of Cavnal."

The people around us erupted in a chaos of accusations and mad speculation, some staring at me, some at Rigvar. I drained the *skatha* and tossed Rigvar the cup, giving him a tolerant smile.

"Please," I said. "Your so-called *informant* needs to check their facts before spreading such absurd theories around."

"Well?" Rigvar said, heated. "Can you prove it? Can you offer any defense for yourself other than your words? Coming as they do from a madman, we already know those mean nothing."

"Just because we disagree, Rigvar, does not make me a madman," I said, and held out my hand.

I didn't have Coins's flair for legerdemain, but I'd apparently been subtle enough about reaching into my inner coat pocket that no one expected me to be holding anything—and yet, there was a folded up page of a newspaper in my hand. Rigvar snatched it from me, his face settling into a sullen scowl as he read.

For the sake of the others, who probably wouldn't have been able to read the Cavnish anyway, I said, "Crown Prince Tarik Trabinis was welcomed back to Brigun Palace four days ago, where he received the Court's offer of the Crown. And since today is the seventeenth of Vorathen, I presume his coronation has already taken place."

I hoped my voice didn't betray the deep bitterness I felt inside. All day I'd been tempted to Ghost to Brinmark to observe the ceremony, but I was sure I wouldn't have been able to endure it in silence. I would have done something foolish, and turned all the chaos into fresh madness.

"How did you get your hands on this?" Rigvar cried.

"I have a friend who's a Ghost."

"Your friend is a ghost?" someone asked, and another whispered, *"Ganthiskur."*

I leveled a hard look on both of them. "It's a kind of mage. In Cavnal they're called Ghosts. They can move from one place to another at a thought." I looked at Rigvar. "I have to have some way of staying abreast of what's going on abroad."

"And how do I know this isn't you?" he asked, tapping the paper, and the photograph of Aroden and Hayli standing at the microphone.

"How did I get there?" I asked. I let the question hang in the air a minute, while the other people watched Rigvar with new skepticism. Then I shrugged and added, "Besides, while this was going on in Cavnal, you may recall that I was trapped in a drug-haze that *you* arranged—a drug-haze that, I might add, completely locked me from my magic."

"What?" gasped a woman sitting next to Rigvar, looking at him in horror. "You tried to poison your opponent?"

"It wasn't—" he started to shout, then dropped his voice to a more polite volume and finished—"poison."

"But combined with the drug they used to knock me unconscious, it nearly was," I said, shrugging. I got to my feet and nodded amiably at the people still sitting. "It's been a pleasure. Rigvar, I'll see you tomorrow."

He gritted his teeth and nodded, and as I walked away, I heard him give a sharp dismissal to the little crowd he had gathered.

*Let them do my work for me, now,* I thought as I made my way back to the steam vent.

The others hadn't come back yet, so in the peaceful solitude I rolled myself in my blanket under the star-embroidered sky, and watched the strange shifting, swirling streams of light dance high overhead until I fell asleep.

# CHAPTER 17 ~ TARIK

I WOKE WITH AN ACHE IN MY NECK THAT FELT LIKE SOMEONE HAD SKEWERED me from ribs to skull, and one entire side of my body was numb with cold—the side, naturally, that faced away from the warmth of the steam vent. It was near bloody miraculous that I'd slept at all on the bone-hard ground, I thought, and even more miraculous that I hadn't died from the cold.

Nika and Agnir were already awake when I sat up, but Iskari lay sprawled out on the other side of me, one arm flung over his face. With the sun starting to rise it had to be late morning already, but Nika just laughed when she saw me looking at Iskari.

"He was up late," she said. "And probably had more *skatha* than was good for him."

"When does the *eyltheng* begin?" I asked, accepting a cup of hot coffee from Agnir.

It was bitter, without anything to sweeten it or tame its flavors, but it was almost scalding hot and I savored every sip of it. Nika held her own mug up close to her face, little puffs of steam curling up from its rim with every breath she took.

"Around noon," she said. "The time for you to speak is done, so, I hope you made a good impression last night."

I didn't answer; I didn't think she expected one. My stomach was a knot of nerves, and I wasn't even sure what I feared more—that the Istians would vote me out, or that they would vote me in. I wasn't sure which would be the greater catastrophe. In the back of my mind

I couldn't stop thinking about Aroden wearing the crown in Brigun Palace, parading around with my face on, making decisions and policies in my name. If I was Godar, could I do anything at all to stop him? But if I wasn't, would it even matter?

"You hold on too tightly," Wake said. This time he wasn't behind me, but standing in front of me, a little farther from me than Agnir. "When will you learn that no good can come from limiting yourself to earthly crowns?"

"No," I said, jabbing a finger in his direction. "Not right now. I can't deal with this right now."

Agnir glanced up in surprise, and I, flustered, tried to wave him away. Wake turned and looked out over the crowd gathered on the gentle slopes below us, but I watched him, some corner of my soul yearning to taste again that ecstatic joy I'd felt on the breakwater. Jaw clenched, I tore my gaze from him and focused on the mug of coffee instead, praying for an end to it all.

We stayed where we were on the moss-shrouded slope until the crowd began to separate. Most of the people wandered toward the southern sweep of the hollow, while a smaller number began making their way toward the north, where the Wakestone hummed with it s sleeping power. I took a deep breath and got to my feet. Iskari, finally awake, stood up as I did.

"You're not coming?" I asked Nika and Agnir, hoping they couldn't hear the panic in my voice.

Nika shook her head, and Agnir said, "I named Iskari my proxy for the moot two years ago. Only one of us can go, and I'd rather it was him."

I looked at Iskari. "You sure you can make it down there without me carrying you?"

He flicked his thumb at me and slung his fur wrap over his shoulders, then clapped me so hard on the shoulder as he passed me that I almost lost my balance. Grumbling under my breath, I followed him down and across the broken turf to the cairn, where the *sodthari* had gathered in a wide ring.

As soon as the last few people had straggled up, a number of uniformed men who I guessed were Istia's police positioned themselves outside the circle, and then one man stepped into the center of the ring. He wasn't an old man, but probably in his early forties, with a completely bald head and a thick black beard that covered his entire neck. His scalp was etched with tattoos, but I didn't get the sense they meant what they did in Cavnal—they were simply adornments, stylized patterns of waves.

"*Sodthari*," he cried, opening his arms and turning a slow circle. They responded with an enormous shout that caught me entirely by surprise. If I'd been expecting civilized government proceedings like I knew from Brigun Palace, that shout thoroughly disabused me of the notion. "The *eyltheng* has begun. Who are the claimants for the *aydrding*?"

Rigvar, dressed head to toe in elegant black, stepped up beside the officiator. I, realizing too late that I was also dressed all in black, nodded once to Iskari and left the security of the circle to stand across from Rigvar.

"You know these two men," the officiator thundered. "Rigvar Karvarson, who has managed our affairs with fairness and passion in the months since Godar Eyid's untimely death. And the Godarson himself, Taumir, recently arrived on our shores."

*Thanks for the generous introduction,* I thought bitterly.

"Stand, then, and be judged according to your merits."

The officiator stepped back, holding his hands above his head. I knew what would come next, from what Agnir had told me. The *sodthari* had been asked to judge us, and they each would have one opportunity to offer their opinion. *The time for you to speak is over,* Nika had told me. But now it was time for everyone else to speak.

Still, knowing what was going to happen didn't do anything to calm my nerves. I had no idea what the people would say about me. I wasn't even sure I knew what I wanted them to say.

Then one of the men stepped forward, holding up a hand to silence the chattering of the other *sodthari*. "Taumir Eyidson," he said, "claims to speak to God."

With that he faded back into the circle. I frowned, trying to catch Iskari's gaze, but he was staring at Rigvar through narrowed eyes.

"Taumir Eyidson," a woman said, coming forward, "killed Halvir and Kima in cold blood."

Her attention wasn't on me, either, but the crowd, daring them to deny her judgment. Even if I wanted to protest the woman's accusation, I had no right to say so much as a word. Part of me wondered if Iskari would speak up in my defense, but I realized he was waiting; if I knew Iskari, he would play the game wisely. He wouldn't give up his one chance to speak so early in the proceedings.

"Taumir Eyidson," someone else said, "usurped the authority to address the Cavnish ambassador before being duly elected."

The accusations kept coming. Person after person stepped forward, at first saying things that were mostly true, if somewhat warped, but eventually even my real failings and mistakes ran out.

"Taumir Eyidson," said a woman, spearing me with a hateful look, "killed three Tulian merchants with their own fishhooks, and strung up their guts to weave into nets."

A murmur rumbled through the crowd, and I gaped at the woman, mostly in awe of the creativity of her accusation. And the *sodthari's* muttering wasn't the sound of skepticism or ridicule, but horror. They *believed* it.

"Rigvar Karvarson," a small voice said. The whole crowd seemed to churn in on the speaker, a lovely young woman with hair as red as Pika's and a face covered in freckles. "Rigvar Karvarson arranged the poisoning of Taumir Eyidson earlier this week."

I regarded her in surprise, but the other *sodthari* erupted in a chorus of denial, stomping their feet to signal their displeasure. Only Iskari remained unmoved, though from my distance I could see the muscle of his jaw working. He was the only one of the *sodthari* who hadn't spoken. Every eye turned to him in expectation, with some people muttering insinuations and speculation to each other.

He tossed his head back and strode into the center of the circle, not stopping at the periphery like the others, but walking up until he was five feet away from Rigvar—close enough that the officiator got a little twitchy.

"Rigvar Karvarson," he said, his voice crashing over the crowd like the waves on the rocky Istian coast. "You are using magic within Hejmstrathvir."

Rigvar stared at him. No one else dared so much as breathe.

"I am *not!*" he shouted at last.

"Rigvar Karvarson, you will be silent!" the officiator thundered. He strode back into the center of the circle, planting himself between Rigvar and Iskari. "Iskari Agnirson, this is not just a judgment of worth but an accusation that this claimant has violated the most sacred law of the moot. What is your evidence?"

"Weren't you listening?" Iskari said, flinging a hand toward the crowd. "One person. One. Of all these people gathered here, only *one* person had the *kalukyri* to say anything against Rigvar, and she was a *stodadrakkeyn* woman! We all know that Rigvar has a habit of using his magic to make people like him, to sway crowds to his way of thinking. What do you *think* was going on here?"

The officiator turned to Rigvar. "Speak," he said. "What do you have to say in your defense?"

"I wasn't..." Rigvar said, pale, eyes wide and haunted. "I would never! I know the laws of the moot. I am *Istian*. I would never violate the most sacred of our customs... I certainly wouldn't cause any Istian to lie for any purpose! Brigar, you know me."

"I could feel it," Iskari said. "I could feel your magic trying to work on my mind, but you've never been able to sway me before, and you still haven't succeeded."

"Iskari, honestly!" Rigvar said. He spun suddenly toward me. "I may hate you, Taumir, and wish you as far from Istia as the sea could carry you, but I would never try to *cheat* my way into power!"

"You're saying you had nothing to do with Eyid's murder, then?" I asked, very quietly.

Everyone heard me. There was a general uproar, and Rigvar's face turned, slowly, a death-white shade.

"I didn't..." he said. "I didn't kill your father."

"But you allowed it to happen?"

He stumbled a step back, eyes wide and horrified. "How could you even know something like that?"

"I make it my business to know what people pray I *never* find out about."

"*Veka*," he said.

I said nothing, just watched him expectantly.

"Rigvar, is this true?" Brigar asked. "You were assigned to Godar Eyid's protection. I have always wondered how someone slipped past your watch."

"I didn't know," he whispered, desperate, pleading. "Honestly. I got a message. Anonymous. Someone telling me to leave Eyid's house in the evening, and meet them at the lodging house. I thought it was..." His eyes widened suddenly and he bowed his head, one hand lifted as a sign of honesty. "No. I suspected it came from someone who meant harm to Eyid, and that the invitation was a ruse. I went anyway. When I came back, Eyid was dead. But I don't know who did it. And that is the solemn truth."

All around us, the *sodthari* were shifting their weight, muttering to each other, trying to make sense of what was happening. A little corner of my heart wished I could just let their accusations stand, and take it as a reason to withdraw from the pursuit of the *aydrding*. But I couldn't do that.

I could feel the mood of the crowd shifting around me, like the turning of a tide. It was time to take control. Drawing a thin breath, I slammed a mental hand down over the crowd, over the magic that held them enthralled, and watched as it fractured, and broke, and fell away. All around me *sodthari* stumbled, some of them clutching their heads. Iskari shook his head and stared at Rigvar, who was looking around just as startled as everyone else.

"Taumir," someone cried—the woman who had accused me of making fishnets from guts, I realized. "Forgive me! I...I don't know why I said those things."

Other voices piped up pleas for forgiveness. The officiator flung his hands in the air.

"What is this *skatrdrakkeyn* mess?" he cried.

"Taumir!" someone shouted. "Godar!"

I winced and closed my eyes.

*You've thwarted him,* whispered the voice in the back of my thoughts. *Bested him at his own game.*

The words fell in my mind like a hammer stroke, and I froze, eyes wide, dread coiling through me. It was too easy. That was exactly what Aroden would want me to think. If he wanted the Crown of Cavnal, then he would need me to stay in Istia, and not come back and challenge him for the throne. He would make me feel like I had defeated him, all the while playing directly into his hand.

"No," I said, shaking my head faintly.

The crowd fell silent, uneasy. Even Rigvar, who was crouched on the ground with his head in his arms, looked up at me in puzzlement. I reached out my hand to him and he flinched back, but when I just offered it again, he swallowed and took it. I tempered the static charge so that a bare flutter of a shock passed between us, and helped him to his feet. He looked at our joined hands, then at me.

"How did you—"

"I am the master of my sea," I said, with a grim smile. Then, to the *sodthari* I said, "Rigvar did not wield the magic that twisted your thoughts."

A mutter of surprise chased through the crowd and Iskari looked bewildered, but I turned my attention back to Rigvar.

"You were as much a victim as everyone else, of a magic that this world hasn't seen the likes of in perhaps a hundred years. For my part, I have unfinished business with the mage who wielded it." I bent my head and drew a long breath, then met his gaze again and said, "Will you promise to rule Istia fairly, to honor her treaties so hard-won by my father, and defend her allies in their hour of need? Will you promise to give up this foolish idea that Istia can stand apart from the rest of the world and not suffer for it?"

Rigvar studied me a long moment in silence, looking for a lie, finding none. "I promise it," he said.

"Then I withdraw my claim to the *aydrding*, and salute you as my Godar. And I would humbly ask the *sodthari* here present to do the same."

"Taumir," Iskari hissed.

I ignored him; I clasped Rigvar by the shoulders and said, "Be patient with the Cavnish ambassador, will you? You're apt to scare the wits out of him."

Then I kissed him once on each cheek, and, for the first time in my life, I lowered myself in a bow of obeisance.

# CHAPTER 18 ~ TARIK

WE LEFT RIGVAR WEARING THE *AYDRDING*, LYING PROSTRATE BEFORE THE *Vekahratha* as he begged Wake's blessing on his rule.

The bewildered *sodthari* slowly dissipated, but I was already halfway across the hollow, heading back toward the place where we had left Nika and Agnir. They were both on their feet as I strode up, Iskari close on my heels, and their faces were equal pictures of anticipation.

"Well?" Agnir asked, reaching for my arm. I stalked straight past him, not giving him a chance to grab hold of me. "What happened?"

"He bloody *caved in* to Rigvar," Iskari said, only just softer than a shout. "He had the whole *stodadrakkeyn* moot in the palm of his hand and he bowed out. He gave it all up." When Agnir and Nika just stared at him he flung a hand toward me and said, "They were in the process of hailing him Godar and he *surrendered*."

I spun and grabbed him by the shoulders, giving him a solid shove backwards. "I didn't surrender," I hissed. "You wouldn't understand if I explained it."

"What, that you're a coward and you have a habit of running away from your duties?"

I shoved him again for good measure, and only Nika's hand on my wrist stopped me from following it with a blow to his jaw. "This isn't my fight," I said. "I was sent to lead Istia and this is the best way I know how to do it. But I realized that Aroden *wanted* me to win the *aydrding*, to keep me safely tied up in obligations to another nation while he reaps *chaos* on the rest of the *skatrdrakkeyn* world."

"Aroden!" he echoed.

"Rigvar wasn't manipulating the crowd," I said. "Aroden was. He could have manipulated them to lean toward me from the outset, but he knew that would never have convinced anyone. He was counting on you to recognize the signs of magic, and he was counting on me to play the dutiful mage and free everyone from his control—and letting guilt do the rest. Don't you understand? There is only one person who can stop what Aroden is doing, and that's me. And I can only do it if I am free." I looked from one to the other. "And now I have to get back to Cavnal, to stop that bloody lunatic from sending us all straight to the Seven Circles."

"So you're going to abandon us," Nika said. "Just like that. After all you've been through...after all *we've* been through with you, you're just going to walk away and leave Istia to its fate?"

"What I do, I do for Istia, and Cavnal, and for mages everywhere," I said. I clasped her shoulder. "I know it's hard to understand. I am sorry. I wish I could have done this in a way that didn't...disappoint you. But..."

"Let us come with you," she said suddenly. "So many things, so many *difficult* things have happened in Cavnal for you lately. Take us with you as your allies, to face the unknown with you."

I hesitated, then shook my head faintly. "Cavnal is on the bleeding edge of the war. If it comes, it will hit southern Cavnal before it hits the rest of the world. Don't ask me to bring you into danger."

"If you think Istians shirk from danger, *or* war, you don't know us at all," she said, with a toss of her head.

I looked at Iskari and Agnir, shrugging. "Your choice. I won't try to make it for you."

"I'll stay," Agnir said, "and make sure Rigvar has good advisors, and doesn't renege on any promises he made you."

I nodded my thanks. "Make sure he doesn't back out of supporting Cavnal. For my part, I *will not* allow Cavnal to back out of an alliance with Istia."

I turned to Iskari, who gave me a mad grin and said, "I'll go, of course."

"You two will be useless," I muttered. "You both speak Cavnish as well as a pair of two-year-olds."

"Shut up," Nika said.

Iskari said, "Bastard."

I grinned. "Then are you ready? I don't have time to dawdle, so grab what you need and let's go."

Iskari rifled through his belongings and strapped the sheath of his hunting knife on his thigh. Nika drew a pair of ivory-handled short blades from her bag and slipped them into two sheaths on her back that I had never even noticed.

"That's it?" I asked, skeptical. When they nodded, I shook my head and muttered, "*Ganthiskur* Istians." They just grinned at me like a pair of mad cats. "We're traveling my way, now, so hold on tight and don't let go. Agnir, I hope we see each other again soon."

"When you come back, bring me a damn ship," he said, clasping my forearm, then pulling me into a brief embrace. "Godspeed, Eyidson," he murmured.

I nodded, and wrapped an arm around Iskari and Nika's shoulders, and dragged us out of the world.

TRYING TO MOVE WITH THEM BOTH clinging to me was worlds worse than trying to haul just Mirin, but at least in that strange realm beyond, weight seemed irrelevant, so even Iskari hanging from me like a sack of bricks didn't slow me down. In just ten steps I reached a bright, clear spot in the wall of the world—Borokhev. I studied it a moment, then lifted my hand and gently drew it across the window, shifting its focus to another part of the facility. I wasn't sure yet if I wanted to make a grand entrance or not; I decided the more prudent thing would be to try to discover what was going on before barging in.

"Hold on," I said.

Iskari and Nika both hung on to me like limp dolls, which made me wonder if they could even hear me, if they were even aware of their passage through Wake's realm. I drew my focus in a little closer, until I was on the ground in the building where I had found Hayli. It was a chaos of activity—Krigs, Bridnow's grenadier friend, was leaning over a long table, pressing a headset from a wireless relayer to his ear, jotting down notes on a slim sheaf of paper with the dull stump of a pencil. Bridnow stood on the other side of the table from him, reviewing the papers as Krigs shoved them across to him.

"Meritac is making demands," Bridnow said, to the other people in the room—I saw Anuk and Scorch, Coins and a handful of others.

"They're acknowledging the authority of the new King, but they're asking him to deliver the mage known as the Zealot as a peace gesture in recompense for the King dismissing their ambassadors. If not, they're threatening to get rid of him themselves. We know what that means."

"Do they know he isn't here?" Anuk asked.

At almost the same moment, Coins said, "Would they withdraw if we did?"

My heart stung with a sharp, bitter pang at his words, and Bridnow dropped the paper on the table to glare at him.

"Just asking what the terms are! What they're promising in return, right?"

"In one sense it doesn't really matter, Coins, because Tulay has her fleet toe to toe with our blockade in the Grafton Straits, and we've already had to call about half the ships of the blockade away to meet the Meritian fleet south of Ridgemark. If we give up Shade to Meritac, Tulay *will* attack."

"Damn," Anuk muttered. "This is such a…damn…*mess*."

The door suddenly slammed open, and Jig bolted in, hair wild, eyes terribly wide. "He's here," he said.

Bridnow swore, told Krigs to stay put, and grabbed his coat as the others all piled out of the building. I frowned and flicked my wrist, my fingertips grazing the window in the world, and followed them out into the Borokhev courtyard. There, to my dismay and horror, I saw Hayli, and standing beside her, Aroden. At least he looked like Aroden, and not like me, but the sight of him standing there still curdled my blood. Hayli looked weary, I thought, and worried, but she faced Bridnow with her chin lifted.

*Did Bridnow approve of this scheme of putting Aroden on the throne?* I wondered. *How many people were involved in that?*

"Give me one good reason why I shouldn't put a bullet in your head right now," Bridnow said, striding straight up to Aroden with his revolver raised in his right hand.

*Guess he didn't approve.*

"Bridnow!" Hayli cried. "He's got news."

"Besides the fact that you've effectively undermined any chance we had at peace?"

"Tarik," Aroden said, holding up his hands. "Shade, Taumir, whatever you want to call him. He was dismissed from the *eyltheng* in

Istia. Rigvar Karvarson is the new Godar."

"Dismissed!" Bridnow echoed.

"How could you possibly know that?" Anuk asked, his voice deadly low, but Aroden didn't even glance his way.

I could see the horror in Bridnow's eyes all too plainly. I knew what he was thinking—if he knew anything about Rigvar, he would know that Rigvar meant to sever his nation's old alliances in the name of Istian supremacy. If he was counting on Istia being an ally that could help dissuade Meritac from launching Alokin's doomsday weapon, then Rigvar's accession was a knife through the heart of that hope.

"I know you don't want to hear it," Aroden said, his face a picture of very convincing distress, "but he has gone completely mad. And it's not just a mental issue. He is so deeply in the clutches of the mad god…he *is* his Scion, and he will be making whatever grab for power he can to turn this world to chaos. The Istians recognized that at the last minute, and drove him out of the moot. He will bring us all to ruin."

"Funny," I said, stepping through the veil between the worlds, "that's not at all how I remember it happening. Though your attempt to sway the *sodthari* from a thousand miles away was fairly impressive."

I allowed myself to revel briefly in the utter shock on everyone's faces as they whirled to face me—especially Aroden's, whose face had gone completely white.

"Shade," Hayli whispered, a strange, strangled sound.

I released Iskari and Nika, who took a moment to shake themselves out of their daze. Because I couldn't bear to look at Hayli, I looked at Iskari instead, putting a hand on his shoulder as he prodded his fingertips against his forehead.

"You said it would be quick," he muttered. "That was *drakkeyn* horrific."

"Poor little Istian," I said, patting his shoulder. "I had to do a bit of reconnaissance work first. Standing over there in the rather elegant suit…that's Aroden."

Iskari's hand went instantly to the hilt of his knife, but I shook my head subtly.

"You wouldn't stand a chance," I murmured. "And that's not a criticism of your abilities."

He nodded and let go of the knife, and I turned back to the shocked

and silent faces staring at me.

"You look like you've seen a Ghost," I said, hiding a smile at my own humor.

Bridnow was the first to move. He strode up to me and saluted, and said, very pointedly, "Your Majesty." I nodded—more to acknowledge his loyalty than the claim—and he said, "They told us you weren't coming back."

"Who would make up such a lie?" I asked, scanning the crowd, deliberately not looking at Hayli.

"I told them," Aothir said suddenly, his hand pressed against his head. "That's what Thane told me. And...we heard about the two men and then...Thane..."

"Thane was a traitor," Iskari said, in Istian, to Aothir. "Or at least very easily persuaded. *I* killed him. Taumir had nothing to do with that, since he was, at that particular moment, completely incapable of defending himself."

Aothir's eyes widened in horror, and he turned from Iskari to look at me. "I'm so sorry," he whispered. "I had no idea. I only knew what he showed me."

I lifted a hand dismissively and stepped past Bridnow, coming closer to the rest of the group with Iskari and Nika close on my heels. A crowd of the other Borokhev folks had gathered around, but they stayed well back from the people in the center. I looked at each of them in turn—Coins, Anuk, Jig, Scorch. Derrin. Shiver. Zip with tears in his eyes. Griff, hands in his pockets, head bent to hide his look of guilt. Hayli, staring at me like she could make me disappear by wishing hard enough.

"I leave for a month," I said, "and you lot send the place straight to hell. What am I to make of that?"

"I think it's you who sent the place to hell," Aroden said. "And the question is, what are you going to do about it? You claim that I was the one manipulating the people at the moot, but why don't you tell everyone the truth? *You* were the one who did it. Contrived the whole bloody thing so you could end up looking like the hero who refuses power when it's offered him!"

Iskari frowned; I wondered how much of that he'd understood.

I said, "You know rather a lot about what happened at the *eyltheng*, Aroden. Things you couldn't possibly know unless you were watching what happened there very closely."

"Of course I was watching! It matters very much to me what happens in Istia."

"Did you do it?" Griff asked me suddenly. "Did you use magic to sway the outcome of the moot?"

I stared at him as if he were a stranger. "Farro," I said, "no. Of *course* not. How can you even—"

"Meritac is asking for an answer!" Krigs suddenly shouted from the door behind me. "But the bloody *King* has gone miss—Oh." He edged outside and came closer to the group, staring first at me, then at Aroden. "Oh hell," he said. "Both of you." He reached out and gripped my arm. "Shade, they've armed the device."

"Alokin's weapon?" I asked. "It targets magic."

"That's the theory. Doesn't just destroy magic, though. Destroys every bloody thing in its area of detonation."

I turned and grinned at Aroden. "Well, I guess we know exactly where it will land."

"I told you, he is *mad*," Aroden hissed.

"How can we stop them?" Hayli suddenly asked, shoving her way forward, her attention all on Krigs.

"They're demanding we turn *him* over," Krigs said, jerking his head toward me. "But that'll just bring war on us from the east. Tulay will attack."

"Istia won't," Aroden said, smirking. "Rigvar won't lift a finger in our plight. I doubt Tulay will risk a war on three fronts without Istia's support. I say we give him to Meritac."

I'd told Rigvar not to abandon Cavnal, on the promise that I wouldn't let Cavnal abandon Istia. But if Cavnal turned me over to Meritac, then that is exactly what Cavnal would be doing. But if I didn't let Cavnal turn me over, then the Meritian battleship would fire that twice-cursed weapon, and we would all die anyway.

"I'm sure the mad god is pleased with what you've done here," I said to Aroden.

"Well, you would know, wouldn't you?" At my surprised look he smiled and took a step closer to me, wincing a little as if just the proximity pained him. "We all know how he has you under his thumb."

"The mad god has no claims on me," I growled, "which can't be said for you."

"Lies!" Aroden hissed. "You hear how he lies! The mad god is a master of deceit, and he and his Scion can make people believe whatever they want, even that they are not the enemy! How eloquently he could claim to be Wake's Zealot, even, and how quickly so many would fall to believe him!"

"Because it's true," Nika shouted suddenly. "We know who Scion is, and not Taumir."

"She has a sword for a tongue," Aroden said, smirking. "Is that why you keep her around, *Taumir*, or is it just for her lovely looks?"

From the corner of my eye I saw Hayli's cheeks flush a deep red, and my heart ached with a pang of loss and grief and twisted regret.

*Oh Hayli, how could you doubt me so quickly? You know I can't lose my heart to anyone else, ever, no matter what you do.*

Nika gave Aroden a wide, half-mad grin, then, before he could so much as twitch, she was inches from him with one of her small blades pressed against his throat.

"Neither, *stodadrakkim*."

"You're threatening the King of Cavnal," he hissed.

Her smile grew even colder, and crueler. "No," she said. "I think not. You don't look anything like him."

"I hate to interrupt," Krigs said. He was sweating profusely. "I have a line to Minister Farro. I can relay a message to him...we need to respond now, or Meritac isn't going to wait."

# CHAPTER 19 ~~ HAYLI

I WATCHED, MY MIND AN AGONY OF DOUBT AND FEAR AND CONFUSION, AS SHADE spun suddenly and grabbed Krigs by the arm. He walked with him toward the Rookery, his head bent close to Krigs's ear as he whispered something to him. At the door he stopped, and Krigs glanced up at him with wide eyes, then nodded, clasped his arm, and disappeared inside. Shade swung around and came back to us then, walking with that strange predatory grace I'd almost forgot he could have. The air prickled all around me as he got closer, and I could sense some of the other mages getting a bit fitsy too.

Aroden retreated from the fierce blonde girl, watching her knife hand warily the whole time, until he stood next to me again. "Wake," he whispered suddenly. "Shade's going to try to use that weapon."

He spun to face me, eyes wild with fright. I drew a step away from him before I could stop myself.

"What?" I said. "How can he use it?"

"That weapon *is* power. Look, Shade could stop those Chernayi guns, couldn't he? He could withstand the Hunter, and still keep his magic. You think he is powerful now? You think it's difficult to stand too near him now? Just imagine what would happen if he stole power from that weapon! He would be unstoppable."

My poor brain didn't want to make sense of his words. I frowned at him for a good long tick, trying to sort out what he was suggesting, but nothing made sense.

"Ask him," Aroden urged. "Ask him what he means to do, and

you'll understand."

I swallowed, and shook my hair away from my face, and forced myself to walk toward Shade. He wasn't facing me, but I got the sense he knew I was coming, and was waiting for me. The beautiful girl at his shoulder glared coldly at me the whole time I approached, making me feel about two feet smaller than I was. With the energy in the air around Shade pitching to a chaos, I realized the girl must not be a mage—not if she was comfortable standing that close to him.

I was at once relieved and seized with a horrible, ugly jealousy.

The taller man was watching me too as I got closer. There was a wildness about him that intrigued me, but his stare was just as frigid as the girl's.

"Shade," I whispered.

His jaw tightened, and still he wouldn't face me. Then he said, very softly, "Why would you do this?"

"They said...you weren't coming back."

He glanced at me then, a grief in his eyes that scraped at my heart like bits of broken glass. "You believed them?"

"You told me...you told me the same."

"*Yet*, Hayli. I said I couldn't come back *yet*." He pressed his fingertips against his forehead. "Well, what did your pet King send you over to ask me?"

I winced. Fought the impulse to reach out and take his hand. *Dangerous*, whispered the voice in the back of my mind. *He could make you believe anything.*

"What do you mean to do?" I asked. "What did you tell Krigs?"

His mouth lifted in a feral kind of smile. "I told him to tell Farro that Shade is here with the King, and that he will take care of the weapon."

"What?"

He turned to face me then, coming so close I felt the hairs on my arms stand straight on end. "I will destroy that weapon and stop Meritac's attack," he said, "and if I survive that, I'm going to come back here and clean up this mess, and take back my damn crown."

He jabbed a finger in Aroden's direction as he spoke, and my insides shuddered. Part of me had no doubt at all that he could do it, could do exactly what he said without even blinking.

I just couldn't bear to think what it would mean if he did.

"The mad god's been lying to you," I whispered. "You gotta

see that. It ain't Wake. I know you're confused, but please, you gotta believe me."

"Why?" he asked. He leaned toward me, close enough to kiss me, but instead he said, "Because Aroden said so?"

"I read the book," I said, recoiling, heart hammering. "I know all about the Scion."

"You really don't." His hand went into his coat pocket, then reappeared holding the fat book. His gaze went to someone behind me—I thought it was Aroden, but then I glanced over my shoulder and saw it was Rivano. Shade's smile got even colder, and he held up the book where Rivano, and Aroden, were sure to see it. "I read it too."

And then, before I could do aught to stop him, before anyone could do aught to stop him, the book erupted in flames. Rivano started forward, eyes wide with horror, and Aroden just watched him, aghast, and didn't move. Shade held the burning book up as the flames licked over his hands. Even the two Istians drew back a little from the heat of the burning pages.

"It's just a madman's quest for sanity," Shade said. He looked straight at Rivano, then at Aroden. "But in the wrong hands, a weapon."

"You fool," Aroden hissed.

"Well, it's already done what damage it could do, so, it really has no more value." He walked past me, toward Rivano, still carrying the smoking, burning book. Ashes fluttered in his wake like macabre petals. "I am the one who follows," he said, "and walks through chaos like a reaper through the harvest."

"Hayli!" Aroden cried. "You have to stop him…he's…"

"*You*," Shade said, flinging the book down. It disintegrated as soon as it hit the pavement, curling into a sad heap of smoldering embers. "Don't move."

Aroden, who'd started to move toward him, stopped suddenly, face contorting in surprise. I shied away from Shade, fear hammering through my veins. It was one thing to Push someone, or Pull a gun across the floor—but that wasn't what I saw in Aroden's eyes. Shade had simply…*commanded* him, and Aroden had no choice but obey. What kind of mage had that much power over someone?

What kind of mage would willingly use it?

Shade nodded approvingly at his handiwork, then turned back to the Istians, who, to my surprise, were watching without the least bit of shock. Instead they wore matching grim smiles, as if they were in on some kind of private joke that none of us understood.

He said something to them in Istian that I couldn't understand, and nodded toward Bridnow, then clapped the young man on the shoulder. The girl—I stared, because she suddenly had tears in her eyes, and she was trying to argue with Shade about something. His mouth quirked in a half-smile, but he just clasped her arm briefly and turned away.

And came straight over to me.

I bit my lip hard to stop its quivering, willing myself not to let him see how scared I was, how torn I was, how I wanted to run to him, how I wanted to run as far from him as I could possibly get. Somehow I thought he read all of it in my eyes, because his face grew sad, his storm-grey eyes dark with regret.

"Hayli," he said. "I wish…"

"They just launched the missile!" Krigs bellowed from the Rookery door.

Shade jerked his gaze from mine to look at Krigs, then he nodded once. Smiling sadly, he reached out and touched my cheek, just barely, just the whisper of a touch. I braced myself for a surge of enervating power, but the pulse I felt from his fingertips was gentle, the faintest butterfly-wing flutter of electricity.

He said, "Goodbye."

And then he was gone.

Aroden, still frozen behind me where Shade had left him, screamed, "Hayli, stop him!"

Without thinking I ran and grabbed Derrin's arm. He didn't even need to ask what I wanted. He just wrapped his arms around me and dragged me from the world, Bridnow's warning shout still echoing in my ears.

# CHAPTER 20 ~ TARIK

HALFWAY TO THE SEA, I FROZE IN MY MAD RACE THROUGH WAKE'S REALM AND turned to look behind me. Wake stood there, wild and bright and stern, his hands held out toward me like an invitation.

"The weapon will kill you," he said. "It was made just for you."

"Better me than my people," I said, choking on the words.

"Is that your choice to make, Tarik? Do you really think your death would serve the world half as well as your life?"

"Well, I really don't have any idea about that," I said, "since half the world wants me to believe that you're really the mad god, scheming ruin at my hands."

"You're wiser than that."

I laughed. "Am I?" I shook my head and turned away. "I have to go. That missile is in the air, and…with me trapped here, it will go straight toward Aroden, and everyone I love."

"It doesn't have to hurt you, you know," he said, his voice following me as I moved away. "The Zealot could dispel its power."

I pushed his voice aside and came to the end of my path, where I could see the port of Ridgemark through the clear glass of the tunnel's wall. Without hesitating, I pushed through and stepped out onto the docks, ignoring the startled screams of a handful of civilians hurrying for safety.

The docks were a frenzy of activity, as naval officers and seamen raced for their ships, and warning sirens droned from a nearby tower. I paced along the edge of the water, my mind tearing a million directions at once. I couldn't Ghost to the missile; I'd never seen it before; I didn't know where it was. I certainly didn't have the skill to commandeer a vessel and sail it out toward the Meritian fleet. But if I stood here for long, the weapon would come straight to me, and the city of Ridgemark would be laid waste.

That vision I had seen flashed before my eyes again—a city in ruins, the dead unburied in the streets. A swath of destruction all across my land. I bent my head, fear and dread turning all my bones to jelly.

*Take control of the missile,* Death's voice suddenly purred into my thoughts, *and direct it back toward the Meritian fleet. They sail their vessels close together as a rule. That missile could tear a hole through half its ships. The fleet would be crippled for years to come. Open your hand to my power, and the devastation could embrace the entire fleet. At your command.*

*I thought I told you to leave me.*

*I'm giving you a second chance. Will you do it?*

*I can't,* I said. *It targets magic. It would never work—Meritac has no mages of its own.*

*It's what you told Hayli you would do.*

*Not exactly.*

I shook my head, driving her voice from my thoughts, and strode to the quay wall. My heart ached as I stepped up onto the low stones, and I spread my fingers to catch the breeze. This time I knew that the wind curling around me was my own—my grief, my anger, my fear.

*They say you shouldn't fear death,* I heard Zagger say again. *They were wrong.*

"Oh, God," I whispered.

"Shade!" someone screamed behind me.

I dropped my eyes closed, weariness settling over me, then turned to see Hayli and Derrin standing behind me, the wind whipping Hayli's hair across her face.

"What are you doing here?" I called. "Go back."

"You can't do this," she said. I could see she was weeping, and she pressed the back of her hand against her mouth. "I know what you plan to do. You can't. Don't give up."

"It's the only way."

"Don't we mean anything to you?"

I recoiled, staring at her in puzzlement. "Of course," I said. "That's why I have no choice."

She just stared at me, frozen in grief, and I turned back to the sea. My mind carried me back to the belfry arch, and I spread my arms, my gaze on the churning water below.

*I'm a Blood*, I told myself. *I'm a Blood. That means…*

A smile spread across my face of its own accord, and I glanced one last time over my shoulder. But in that moment I didn't see Hayli and Derrin; I saw Zagger, impossibly young again, in his long black trencher, running to catch me before I fell into the sea. My throat tightened, and I turned away.

I looked at Wake, who stood beside me, and said, "I'll take another step."

Then I threw myself from the wall.

# CHAPTER 21 ～ HAYLI

ONE MINUTE SHADE WAS ON THE QUAY WALL, FACING THE ENDLESS SEA, HIS face turned a little to the side with his mouth tracing a sad smile, the next…he let himself fall, and was gone.

"Shade!" I screamed.

I jerked away from Derrin and ran for the wall, sure I would see his body dashed on the stones below. But I'd barely reached the wall when a flurry of wings erupted in front of me, and I startled back so violently I fell, wrenching my wrist as I landed on the cold stone. I watched, disbelieving, as the most beautiful golden hawk I'd ever seen rose to beat its wings in front of me. Its bright eyes seemed to see straight into my soul for one endless moment, then with a keening cry, it wheeled and climbed higher and higher into the sky.

*Stop him,* I heard Aroden's voice echoing in my thoughts.

*Oh stars, I have to stop him.*

Without thinking, I cast myself into the wind to follow him.

*I FLY HARDER THAN I HAVE ever flown before, but not because of what Hayli fears Shade is planning, but because of what I know he is planning. And they are not at all the same.*

*The hawk has the brightness of Shade's spirit all around it, even in the gleam of his eye as he cants his head back to look at me. But they are still too new—the hawk has never flown before. I beat my wings faster, and come above him, then careen down to snatch at the feathers on his back. He twists in the air, talons outstretched, and his wings sweep toward me like whips, trying to cut me from the air. I plummet, dodging his attack, and he, undeterred, keeps straight on toward the south, toward the fleet, toward the scent of destruction I can already taste on the wind. I wonder if he can sense it too. I wonder if he is as terrified as I am.*

*I streak after him, shouting for him, but he never turns and he never slows. He doesn't understand me, he doesn't understand my despair—we don't even speak the same language now. I dive toward his back once more, this time latching on with my claws and twisting. The effort sends us both into free fall, losing the currents of the air as we hurtle, spinning, a blur of wings and talons, toward the sea. He gives a piercing scream and rights himself, batting at me with his long wings as he takes to the skies again. With stubborn determination I follow once more, but he is climbing straight into the air, higher, higher. I chase him until the air grows thin around me, and the world wobbles in inky streams of violet light far, far below me.*

*I am too high. I know I am not meant to climb this high, but I cannot leave him.*

*I fly on, helpless, trying to keep pace with him from hundreds of feet below him, though I can hardly see him now among the clouds so far above. I can feel him, though, but his presence is slowly fading.*

*And then, as if I'd been hit by a rogue wind, I falter, and my wings falter, and I almost lose my grip on the air, because there, streaking from the horizon like a comet of fire and smoke, is the missile.*

*It is heading straight for Shade's hawk, latched on like a tug rope.*

*I scream and fly as fast as I can. My heart is hammering so hard I fear it will break. I can't reach him.*

*I know I will never reach him in time.*

# CHAPTER 22 ~ TARIK

I CAN SEE THE MISSILE ALREADY, A SLEEK BLACK BULLET TRAILING TEARS OF FLAME *and smoke as it streaks across the sky. Every instinct inside me wants to turn, to flee, but Tarik drives me on with stern determination.*

*I cannot understand his will for his own ruin.*

*I know, as surely he must know, that I have no magic of my own. I cannot do what Death urged him to do—take control of the missile, and send it back to the fleet I can just see in the far distance, like bits of flotsam on the waves. There are only two ways this can end, and both of them fill me with fear.*

*In the back of my mind I can hear the voice of Wake, terrible and brilliant and beautiful. He is speaking to Tarik, but Tarik is stubbornly refusing to listen. I listen instead, though I feel keenly that I am reaching above my nature.*

*"It will not hurt you," he says. "It cannot hurt you, if you would only stop resisting my power. Do you think there is anything in this world that can harm if you if my hand is protecting you? The mark of my sigil will shield you. You will stand, safe, at the eye of the storm when it breaks."*

*"No," Tarik answers finally. "I cannot. I cannot…become everything they fear."*

*I can hear the roar of the missile now. My heart quakes and my wings falter, but Tarik's will is like a goad in my mind, and I fly forward with grim resolve.*

*Of course, it would be that the first time that Tarik recognized my presence would be the last time we would fly together. I have only just tasted freedom, and life, and I see it snatched from my talons in the breadth of a heartbeat.*

*"I cannot become everything they hate," Tarik adds.*

"You will abandon them to the schemes of the mad god's Scion," Wake says. "Do you truly believe Aroden will stop…do you believe this war will stop with you gone?"

Please listen to him, *I whisper.*

*I can feel Tarik jolt, shuddering. Maybe he didn't realize I would have a voice of my own.*

You can't see it, because you're a human, and you've been wounded, but Hayli needs you.

Don't you dare, *he says.* Don't you dare use Hayli to deter me.

You can still stop the weapon, *I say,* and go on to try to quell the war, but just…stop being a damned stubborn fool and do what Wake is asking you!

Don't you see, *he says,* I've lost her either way.

Well then, do me a favor, and don't die, *I say.* I happen to want to taste the thrill of the winds more than once in my life, since you've kept me shackled all these years.

*The missile has almost reached us. I falter, I can't help it. Maybe it's Tarik's will that has faltered.*

Please, *I whisper.*

*I feel the turmoil in his spirit, the agony, desire mixed with an animal fear I understand all too well. The fear of loss. The fear of death. The fear of fear itself.*

*The longing for life.*

*But suddenly I realize what he has already realized—Hayli is too close. If Wake's power protects us…it will utterly destroy her.*

*Then Tarik's will slams down over mine, and his scream and mine are the same.*

# CHAPTER 23 ~ HAYLI

FOR ONE MOMENT, I ALMOST BELIEVE SHADE WILL TRY TO OUTSMART THE MISSILE. Lead it back to the Meritian fleet and use it to destroy their ships. Drag it down to the sea where it could do no harm. But then I realize the horrible truth—the hawk may be faster than me, but there is no way he can outfly the missile.

And just as suddenly as I know the truth, I hear the hawk scream. I watch, paralyzed with fear, as he draws up, beating the air with his wings. And waits.

It's over before I realize what has happened.

There is a brilliant blaze of light, so powerful it bleaches my vision. A terrible wind hits me first, and I lose its currents, blown back in a sickening somersault until I regain my wings. Then a shockwave of energy ruptures the sky with a noise like thunder, coming closer and closer. I can almost feel it unmaking me from the inside as it closes in on me.

Then, abruptly, it stops.

I know it is all over without anyone telling me. There, at the heart of the ring of fire, I don't see the hawk at all. I see Shade's body, his back arced in agony, hanging suspended in the air like he has been pinioned to the sky by a spear of light.

I am flying desperately toward him when the air tears around me again. The fire and the energy and the light are all pulling back, faster and faster, like it is being sucked into a vortex...

Into Shade.

All of the power vanishes within his hanging body, and for one split *second, there is absolutely quiet, absolute calm.*

*Then there is nothing but light.*

*It bursts from Shade's body, from every inch of him, from the tips of his fingers and the bottoms of his feet, from his forehead and his heart and his stomach, from every inch of his arms and legs. Even from his eyes the brightness blazes, like the afterimage of lightning.*

*I can hardly move. I can hardly keep myself in the air.*

*No! Hayli is screaming, over and over again.*

*But I can only watch, helpless, hoping, circling around and around as I try to inch my way closer to him.*

*And then, just when the hope starts to blossom in my heart, the light vanishes, and Shade's body crumples, and falls.*

*I scream and plummet after him, but he is too far away from me. Too far, but too close…I can see every line of agony on his face.*

*I can see the tears on his cheeks.*

*The scorch marks on his hands.*

*The front of his shirt burned away, the bloody ruin of his torso beneath.*

*And he just falls, and falls, straight for the sea below. I am still fifty feet above the water when he hits the surface of the sea with a sickening crack. I tuck my wings and dive, claws outstretched, as if I could do anything at all, but then I reach the water and my claws snatch nothing but the cold and briny sea.*

*I pluck desperately at the waves, my heart fluttering uselessly in my chest. I want to plunge into the depths, but I cannot. I can't see him. I cannot even feel the brilliant pulse of his spirit any more. I feel nothing but a great and hollow emptiness.*

*Deep in my mind, Hayli is silent. I can feel her heart breaking along with mine. It is a grief too great for words.*

THE WAVES DRIFT BY IN ENDLESS *repetition, always the same, always different, flowing ever and always onward. I circle the spot where Shade was lost to the sea, again, and again, as I have now for almost an hour. I am near the end of my strength, and miles from the coast. It may be I have made my last flight, but there is nowhere I would rather make my final roost than the place where I lost Shade.*

*But it isn't fair to Hayli. I resent her with a burning fire, for all the ways she doubted Shade, for her stubborn refusal to listen to me, but she is my Hayli, and I will never see harm come to her by my wings and claws.*

658

*With one last grieving cry, I dip my wings and brush the surface of the waves, and then turn, soul-weary, and make my way slowly, slowly north.*

PIPER WAS ALMOST DEAD WITH EXHAUSTION when we reached the docks of the shore city—I never asked Derrin where we were, but, from all the ships in the harbor, I guessed it was Ridgemark. He was still waiting for me when we got back, and as soon as he saw me Shift he was on his feet, and I threw myself in his arms and sobbed like my heart was breaking all over again.

"Stars, Hayli," he murmured, pressing his cheek against my hair. "What happened? We saw the light, but..."

"I dan' na," I wept. "I dan' na what happened. The missile...and Shade stopped it...but he fell..." I clung to him, burying my face against his chest, shoulders heaving. "He's *gone*, Derrin. He's gone...and he never knew. I div'n want...oh God, I div'n want..."

He just held me tighter, and then, before I knew what he was doing, he had pulled me back into that white nothingness outside the world. I'd barely found the breath to collect myself when the whiteness faded and I found myself back in Borokhev's courtyard, stumbling beside Derrin. Everyone turned to look at us. Aroden. Jig, and Scorch. Anuk. Shiver and Coins and Griff. The Istians. Commandant Bridnow.

Derrin kept his arm around me, holding me up.

"Hayli," Bridnow said, the calmness of his voice cutting through the wild chaos of my grief. "Report."

I tried to stand straight. I looked at him and lifted my chin, and yet all I could see, over and over again, was Shade plummeting to the depths of the sea.

"I tried," I whispered. My breath caught, strangled somewhere far deeper than my throat. "I tried to stop him."

"Where is Shade?" he asked, taking two steps toward me. "Hayli, *where is he?*"

I stared at him, not seeing him. "Gone," I said.

Aroden started forward, disbelief waging a war with relief in his eyes, and the fact that he was moving freely was enough to bring the tears to my eyes again.

"Hayli," he said. "You did it. You stopped him."

"Dan' say that!" I cried. "Dan' you lay this at...at my feet..."

"You, back, now," Bridnow said, whirling on Aroden and driving him back with a pointed finger. "Before I put you in cuffs again myself, *Your Majesty.*"

Then he came closer to me, and I saw tears at the corners of his eyes, and the way he tried so hard to fight them back.

"You're sure he's...gone?"

"I looked for hours," I said, and bit down hard on my knuckles. "He fell into the sea. He never...he never came back up. Commandant, I'm so sorry."

He wrapped his arms around me and held me briefly, but I knew when he released me that he didn't forgive me. Not really. I tore my gaze from his face and looked around at the others—the rest of Tarik's crew, who were all still gathered around, still watching me. Anuk turned away, arms tight across his chest. The Istians looked at me like they were caught in a nightmare they couldn't escape from.

If only I knew how to escape.

"What do we do now?" Coins asked, softly.

No one had an answer. I buried myself in Derrin's arms again, and a few of the people drifted away, irresolute, confused, many of them unabashedly wiping their eyes. Some time later—I wasn't sure how long, Krigs stepped out of the Rookery, looking pale and exhausted.

"Istia," he said, and closed his eyes, bracing one hand on the doorframe. "Godar Rigvar just used one of his Knacks to relay a message to the Istian ambassador at the Palace. Istia stands with Cavnal. So does Tulay. Meritac and Cromis will have no choice but back down, unless they want to see their navy completely decimated."

Aroden's face registered his shock, then he bent his head. Somehow the look of relief on his face didn't quite match the hard light in his eyes.

# CHAPTER 24 — TARIK

"MY ZEALOT, WHAT HAVE YOU DONE?"
Wake's voice humming in the back of my mind was the first thing I became aware of. The second was the press of water all around me, cold, unconquerable. My eyes flew open and I tried to gasp, and choked on the sea instead. I couldn't see anything but darkness above me, a depth of water so great I could feel it crushing my lungs.

With one desperate effort I brought my hands in front of my face and blew a little air from my lungs, slowly. The bubbles brushed past my fingers, traveling toward my feet, so I flipped myself around and kicked out, and pushed toward what I could only hope was the ocean's surface.

It felt like I swam forever. Just when I thought I couldn't hold my breath for another second, when my lungs were seizing and tugging, begging for air, I thrashed free of the waves. The sun was in front of me, tumbling toward the horizon in a red cascade, and around me the waves were gentle, buoying me up. I floated on my back, my gaze on the sky, my mind a terrifying blank.

I couldn't remember what had happened. Vaguely I could recall the thrill of flight...a struggle... Wake's voice, insistent, pleading. I swallowed and closed my eyes. The last thing I could remember was the will to live. The will to win.

"Did you save me?" I asked Wake, saltwater teasing the corners of my lips.

The emptiness inside me lasted far too long, then I heard him say,

"Did you ask me to?"

I pressed my hand over my eyes, fighting tears. "Yes."

"But one moment too late," he said.

At first I didn't know what he meant, then I remembered. He had told me that his sigil was a shield the weapon's energy could never breach, but I hadn't let him protect me. I hadn't dispelled the weapon's power at all.

I'd let it consume me.

"No," Wake said, and I thought he sounded sad. "You, my sea, consumed it."

I let my fingers drift over the shredded fabric of my shirt, the shredded skin of my chest. The salt water burned inside the wounds with a pain so intense I stopped feeling anything at all—not the cold, not the agony, not the grief, not the fear.

"And Hayli?" I whispered, afraid to hear the answer. Afraid to hear that, in spite of everything I'd done, I'd failed to protect her.

"She is alive," Wake said, but the words were etched in sorrow.

I closed my eyes, letting the waves wash over me until I couldn't tell my tears from the sea. I don't know how long I floated adrift, but suddenly I heard the sound of shouting, the creak of planks, the splash of a heavy rope. Then a larger splash followed, and someone's arms were around me, dragging me through the water.

I held perfectly still as I felt myself drifting upwards, then, blessedly, I felt solid wood beneath my cheek, my hands. For too long I didn't even breathe, then I realized I wasn't breathing, and my lungs opened to drag in one broken, gasping, choking breath. Almost as soon as I did, I coughed and spat saltwater, and felt rough hands on my shoulders rolling me onto my side.

I coughed and retched water until both my lungs and my stomach were empty, then I rolled onto my back again.

"Steady on, steady on," said a Cavnish voice above me, with the thick accent of Greydowns. "Take it slow, man. You've got a lungful of the drink in you. Danna y'try too hard to move now. C'mon Tillen, give us a hand."

Other hands reached down to grab me under the arms, but no sooner had they touched me than they tore away again.

"Oh God!" someone wept.

I gasped, feeling a surge of light and strength and power welling up deep inside me, building and building until I thought I would burst with it. My eyes flew open, and latched on the face of a sobbing man clutching his hands to his chest.

"I lost 'em!" he cried, wringing his hands.

"Lost what, Tillen? Stars, man, y'look a ghost!"

"I lost the currents...the currents! I cannee find them!"

Another face appeared above me, then just as quickly jerked back.

"Dear God," he whispered. "Your eyes, my lord...your eyes..."

I struggled to lift a hand to my forehead, passing it over my eyes. My skin felt hot in spite of the coldness of the saltwater I'd been floating in, and I shuddered with the feeling of energy prickling beneath it, through every vein and muscle.

"Your eyes..." the man wept again.

I tried to sit upright, but no one moved to help me.

"My lord, spare us," another man said. He was on his knees, shielding his face. "We dan' want harm to come to you...just dan' hurt us. We only wished to help..."

"Where are we?" I asked, my voice hoarse and raw from the sea.

"Not far sou'west of Ridgemark, my lord. We tried to get clear of the enemy fleet, but our boat dan' sail so fast."

"It's all right," I said. "Your boat is safe now. The fleet won't be coming."

"Oh God," the first man gasped again.

I looked at him, disturbed, and finally bent to lift him to his feet. His forearms were traced with tattoos of swirling water, but when I clasped his arms, I felt nothing at all. I stumbled away from him, dread pooling in the pit of stomach.

"You're a mage?"

At that the man doubled over, clutching his head in his hands. "I lost the currents. What did I do to offend you? What did I ever do to you?"

"I don't know," I said. "I didn't mean... Was it me? Did I do this to you?"

He looked at me then, bitterly. "Aye," he said. "When I touched you, my lord. It just...shattered like glass, and then it was gone. What've you *done* to me? You've broken me..."

I staggered back until I hit the rail of the ship, and bent my gaze to my hands. Beneath the surface of my skin, little traces of light rippled, like sunlight on broken water. I clenched my hands in fists and shoved them under my armpits, as if hiding them could change the truth of it.

"I'm so sorry," I whispered. "I truly am. I never meant to hurt you. I hope you believe that."

But he just stared at me in horror and hatred, and I bent my head and closed my eyes, and pulled myself away from the vessel, away from the world.

In the white in-between, I stood face to face with Wake, my heart crumbling within me.

"Is this what it means," I said, "to be your Zealot?"

"This is the consequence of your choice," he said. "I will help you endure it, but take care that the thirst for power doesn't consume you. If it does, I will withdraw my sigil from you and raise up another Zealot to work your ruin."

"Power," I whispered, and shook my head. "You said all your gifts would be mine if I became your Zealot, but it's all chaos and shadows inside. This is the only gift I could find. What of your promise?"

"You've been torn apart and pieced back together," he said gently. "And you're still suffering from the weapon's effects. If I unlocked my power in your soul now, you would truly drown."

He held his hands up between us, palms up, an invitation.

For one endless moment I held his gaze, a war raging in my soul. Then I swallowed and lifted my hands, and placed them against his. A blazing spike of energy stung my palms, shooting up my arms and burying fast in my broken heart.

I fell to my knees.

Bowing my head, I whispered, "Then I am yours. What would you have your Zealot do?"

"Now," he said, lifting me to my feet, "we will remake the world."

I pushed past him, stumbling, pressing toward the clear light that outlined the prison town of Borokhev.

I knew it was the last place I should go, but I had to.

I had nowhere else to go.

# CHAPTER 25 ~ HAYLI

KRIGS DISAPPEARED BACK INTO THE ROOKERY, LEAVING US STANDING IN uncertain silence. But he was only gone a few moments—no one had made up their mind what to say or do when he walked back out to join us, swiping his hat off and kneading his fingers against his forehead.

"It's over," he said. "Meritac is withdrawing their fleet. Cromis is standing down."

Bridnow let out all his breath in one shattered sigh of relief. Someone started to weep, but I couldn't see who. Aroden measured Krigs a long while in silence, face unreadable. Me, I was too numb to even know what to think. I clung to Derrin, and let my mind drift among the clouds and currents of the wind.

"I should return to the palace," Aroden said at last. "They'll be wondering where I am."

Derrin pushed me gently away, and I swiped the tears from my cheeks. More than aught else I wanted to get away, to hide somewhere alone with my grief and make sense of what had just happened, but I couldn't leave. Not now. Not the way everyone crowded so close around us, desperate for stability, for guidance.

Bridnow met Aroden's leave-taking with his lip lifted in what looked dangerously like a snarl, and even I couldn't stop him from surging toward Aroden with both hands in fists.

"You get back there," he said, "and you make sure that this alliance with Tulay and Istia holds. If it doesn't, if I hear one whisper that you've gone and reneged on it, I will personally hunt you down and kill you."

"Steady," Aroden said, holding up his hands and backing a step away, as if Bridnow were a watchdog he'd got on the wrong side of. "I'll do my duty, never fear. My job will be easier, anyway, now that the mad god's Scion has been dealt with."

"You liar!" the Istian girl shouted. "*You* the Scion, you *vingathur stodadrakkim!*"

I looked at her in surprise, and even Aroden seemed a bit taken aback by the violence of her words. Then his face softened and he took a few steps toward her, which made her retreat a half step toward the dark-haired man.

"Friends," he said, "I know you were lied to as much as anyone by the mage you knew as Taumir. But that is all past. You don't have to be enslaved to his deceptions any more."

She spat at his feet, her hands toying over the hilts of her short knives. "Taumir is Istian," she snapped. "Not a *liar*. Not like *you*."

Aroden lifted his hands. "Well, it hardly matters now, does it? He's dead, and you're stranded, and half these people here believe you walked in with what was very nearly their doom." Her brow wrinkled, probably trying to translate all of what he'd said, and Aroden lifted his hands. "You were friends with Taumir," he said, "who almost got them all killed."

The knife blade was out before anyone could stop her, but she only pointed the tip at him—still, nobody would've made the mistake of thinking she wasn't a hair's breadth from burying the thing in Aroden's chest. I watched, frozen and helpless, from ten feet away.

"Get the foreigners!" someone shouted. "She's threatening our King!"

Griff and Coins moved without a word, circling closer to her, but it was Bridnow who stepped up to her. He didn't try to stop her, though. He held his hands out toward the lads, his face fixed in a look of absolute fury.

"You two, stand down, *now*."

"They are allies of the Scion!" another person cried.

Coins said, rather feebly, "They're enemies."

"Enemies of whom?" Bridnow shouted. Bridnow shouting was enough to make anyone back down. Coins subsided, looking a bit sheepish, and Bridnow slammed one fist into his other palm in warning. "They are not our enemies." He speared a glance at Aroden. "Well, maybe they're *his* enemies, but—"

"And he is our King," someone said.

"False King," the Istian man growled. "A thief and usurper."

He gasped suddenly and staggered back, and though I never saw what hit him, he pulled a hand away from his chest slick with red blood. The girl turned a ghastly shade of pale, and rushed to his side as he dropped to a knee.

"Iskari!" she whispered. "*Veka...Veka...*"

Aroden suddenly gave a cry and spun away, his hands clamped over his ears. A moment later I felt what he must have felt, a dangerous surge of electricity, the heavy press of power like a hand clamping down on my soul. Every mage in the crowd cried out, and I, with my hands over my ears, twisted to look around for the source.

I almost missed the figure in the dark coat standing just inside Borokhev's front gate, his hood drawn up, hands in front of him as if they were poised on a still pool of water. Everything inside me recoiled on instinct, but I couldn't move to get away. I could hear the hum of power in the air all around him, and even from where I stood, I could see the ripples of light under the skin of his hands.

One by one, other gazes followed mine, until we were all staring at the figure who stood staring at us.

"Stars," someone said. "What is that?"

The figure moved suddenly, and everyone inched a little further away, watching in spellbound silence as the light-traced hands reached up and brushed back the deep hood.

A hood, I realized too late, I recognized all too clearly.

My breath escaped in a shattered sob.

That was Tarik, with his white hair and his pale skin, his mouth forever hiding a secret. But his eyes weren't Tarik's dark eyes. They blazed like lightning, like the hottest core of flame. There were tears on his cheeks—in the light from his eyes, they glimmered like streaks of silver.

He didn't try to come near us.

His gaze fixed on me, and in a low, sea-wild voice, he said, "Help me."

# CHAPTER 26 ~ TARIK

THEY WERE ALL STARING AT ME. IN HORROR. IN FEAR. In hatred.

I wanted to go to them, but they cringed away from me like whipped dogs, and it was all I could do not to turn and walk away again. Then, slowly, Bridnow made his way toward me, hands held cautiously at his sides. A sudden fear spiked inside me, and I help up my own hands, desperate to ward him away.

"Bridnow, no," I whispered. "Don't come near me."

But he didn't stop. I could feel the strength of his power as he came closer, and my hands curled reflexively as a hunger stirred somewhere much deeper than the pit of my stomach, snapping at my soul with a longing I'd never felt before. I tore my hands back, clutching them around my head. Bridnow stumbled, and looked at me in confusion.

"Get away," I said. "Please...I can't stop it."

He staggered back a few steps, and I felt the burning draw from his power begin to fade. I let out a shattered breath and looked away, my palm pressed hard against my forehead.

"What happened?" Bridnow asked, hoarse.

I bent my head; again I felt that moment of nothingness, that desperate effort to wall in the destruction...the surge of power and life and ecstatic glory, which I knew had nothing to do with the weapon's energy, and everything to do with the hand of Wake on my soul. And then the darkness. The fall. Fading into the sea. I wished I could have stayed there forever. I wished that was where it had ended.

"I tried to stop it," I said, too numb, too weary to lie. "I tried...to save you."

From somewhere in the depth of the crowd, Aroden cried, "He is *lying*. He has been manipulating this situation from the very beginning. As soon as he heard about Alokin's weapon, he has been working to secure the circumstances that would force Meritac's hand, so he could steal the weapon's power for himself. He's only *ever* wanted to become that weapon himself." He spun toward Hayli. "It is *exactly* what I told you he would do!"

"Aroden..." Hayli said. She looked terrible—eyes red and swollen, framed by dark circles.

*Did you mourn me?* I wondered, bitterly.

"Think about it," Aroden went on. "He could have been elected Godar and prevented this situation from ever arising, but instead he arranged the whole thing to bring us to the very brink of ruin, so then he could absorb the weapon's power and claim that he saved us all *and* stopped the war in the process. How could anyone refuse to give obeisance to such a powerful and compassionate *overlord*?"

"What are you saying?" I asked, baffled. "Look at me! Do you think I wanted this? Do you imagine anyone will believe you?"

"Look around," he said. "Who do you think won't? But I tell you this now, as King of Cavnal—we will *never* bow down to you, Scion."

"I am not the Scion," I said. I hardly had the strength now to protest. I just shook my head, lifting one hand between us. Half the people in the crowd cringed away as I did. "What have I done to you?" I asked them. "What have I done to deserve your hatred? I never wanted this power. I swear to you...I never wanted it."

For a moment there was absolute silence, then one voice said, softly, "Of course you did."

Those words could well have been a bullet to the heart. I turned, slowly, and met Hayli's gaze. "What?"

"Shade, you know you never could stand to be ruled by anyone but yourself. Would you've bowed down to Aroden, as your King?" She pressed her lips together, then she shook her hair back from her face and said, "You know you wouldn't. You never would. So you set yourself above him, just like he said you would."

"Hayli," I said.

I couldn't say anything else.

She held my gaze as I pleaded with her in the silence of my mind, but I never saw the answer in her eyes. Holding my breath to cage in my grief, I turned to look at Iskari and Nika.

"And you? Do you believe her?"

Nika glared at her and stalked over to my side, staring a challenge at the rest of the crowd. Iskari followed more slowly. He had his arms folded tight across his chest, but he couldn't hide the gleam of blood on the front of his shirt. I grabbed his shoulder, catching his eye.

"What happened to you?"

He shook his head, very faintly. "I don't know. One minute I was fine. The next...I just felt this burning, tearing pain, and...*this*."

He moved his arm, revealing the bloodstain.

"The same as what happened to me?" I asked softly, and he nodded. "Are you all right?"

"Just a little light-headed."

"I can't put blood back in your body," I said.

"Not asking you to."

The sight of the blood reminded me of something I'd read in Arnthor's book, but of course, I'd gone and burned the damn thing so I couldn't look it up again.

*"It will be a harvest of blood..."*

I looked at Aroden, eyes narrowed, and he met my gaze with an open challenge in his eyes. For one long moment we stared across the courtyard at each other, and all the world held its breath around us.

Jig suddenly moved from his place along the edge of the crowd, moving toward me first, then shifting abruptly toward Aroden. He had his arms crossed like Iskari, and as he turned, I saw the glint of the little knife he held hidden, pressed against his side. I saw the glint of rage in his eyes.

"Jig!" I shouted, alarm flaring inside me. "Wait. Come here."

I didn't mean to put a Command in the word, but he froze, and then, with one spiteful glance back, he walked straight up to me and looked me in the eye.

"Never believed a word that creepy knave said about you," he said. "I'd've happily gutted him for you, y' know."

"He would have killed you," I said. "He's too strong for you."

"For you?"

I flexed my fingers. "For now." From the corner of my eye I saw

Scorch heading toward me, his amber-gold eyes fixed on me, fever-bright in a way I couldn't quite understand. I held my hand desperately toward him. "No. Stay back. I don't know what's wrong with me, but if you come any closer, I'll…" I bent my head, and finished, "I'll rob your magic if you come too close."

Scorch hesitated, face tight with emotion. His gaze drifted back to the crowd, and I realized a moment too late that he was looking at Luce, who had her hands pressed to her mouth, tears streaking her cheeks. I wanted to tell him to go to her, to leave me while he had the chance, but I couldn't force the voice from my throat. And then he shook his head faintly, and before I could stop him, he strode up to me and clasped my hands in both his own. A blaze of bright fire surged up inside me, endless and ragged as the heart of the sun.

"My power is yours, lord," he said.

I shuddered even while I savored the rush and ecstatic burn of power, and I tried to pull my hands away, but couldn't before he'd pressed his lips to the back of my right hand.

God, I wanted to walk away.

I felt like a spectator trapped in my own nightmare.

My gaze snagged on Anuk and Coins where they stood side by side, watching the scene unfold in front of them with just as much horror as me.

"Coins?" I whispered. "Anuk, please…" I felt sick at heart. All I wanted was to push them away, but instead I heard myself saying, "Don't abandon me, please. Not now. Not when I need you the most."

Anuk took a step forward, but Coins reached out and grabbed his arm. "Anuk, don't. Look at him. Look at what he's become. He'll *destroy* you. Who knows what he'll do…what he'll do to the world next."

I'd never seen Coins so serious. I wanted to shake him. I wanted to beg him for his ridiculous made-up phrases. I wanted to give him a whole handful of half-smoked cigos if only he wouldn't forget who I was. But he just shook his head faintly at Anuk, a desperate plea. With a muttered curse Anuk jerked his arm free and walked slowly across the yard.

Coins turned away, hiding his face behind the hand he scrubbed relentlessly through his hair.

"Damn it, Shade," Anuk said as he joined me. "I've never doubted you yet. Can't say I understand what's happening, but I'll stand with you." He hesitated, then added, "Always."

I nodded, and my gaze, almost against my will, drifted toward Griff. He had moved to stand near Hayli, and his cheeks were streaked with tears.

"Farro," I said. "What are you doing over there? Are you afraid of me? I can't do anything to you."

He shook his head, tongue-tied.

"Brother, please," I said.

Griff made a strangled noise and shook his head again. "Oh stars," he whispered suddenly. "Tarik, I…I can't." He closed his eyes, shoulders heaving, then said, "You have always been my Prince, but I can't follow you down this road."

I closed my eyes. *Wake, how could you do this to me? You've cast me off from everything I love. Why? Didn't I do what you asked?*

But Wake was silent.

Griff turned before he could see my misery and walked away, slowly, toward the long building where Krigs had been posted. Derrin followed him without a last glance in my direction. Then it was just Hayli facing me across the courtyard, wind-tossed and wild, a war raging behind her eyes.

"Stars, girl," I whispered. "Don't you know how much I need you?"

From the corner of my eye I saw Aroden circling toward her, like a bird of prey drawing in on its quarry. He stopped close beside her and she didn't even flinch, didn't even try to draw away. And more than anything I wanted to walk straight up to him and devour every last fragment of his power and leave him a broken, empty shell, but he was too close to Hayli; I couldn't reach him without robbing her of her magic too. I almost imagined that was why he'd gone to stand beside her. Bastard.

"Hayli, don't come near me," I said. "Just please…tell me you're with me. I need your strength."

She hesitated.

"He's lying," Aroden said, loud enough that I could hear. "He will tell you anything to lure you in, to make you believe him. But look at him. Look at his eyes. There's nothing *human* left in him. He doesn't care about you. He doesn't care about anybody. He will only care if you get in his way. Did you see how he welcomed the offer of power from Scorch? That is what he will do to you. That is the only reason he wants you—he wants to rob your power. He will use you up, and he will cast you off when he's done with you."

Hayli stared at me, and I held her gaze, pleading.

Then she took a step back.

"Please," I whispered.

She stepped back again, and shook her head. Just once.

She never said a word.

With the world caving in around me, I wrapped the little band of my followers in a web of magic, and stepped away from the world.

# EPILOGUE — HAYLI

Too long after Shade had vanished, I waited, frozen, staring at the place where he'd stood. My whole body was trembling, but I didn't have any tears left, or any strength to cry them.

A thin sleet began to fall, gathering in the little hollows in the paving stones where the snow had just started to melt, soaking through the wool of my watchcap, but still I didn't move.

We'd gotten a reprieve from the war, and—maybe for just this one day, maybe for just one month—we were at peace. But the cost was breaking my heart.

I couldn't make sense of what had happened to Shade. Nothing about it seemed possible. Aroden's warnings wove endlessly through my mind, but I couldn't forget the look in Shade's eyes when he'd begged me not to abandon him.

I didn't know if Shade was the Zealot, or if he was the Scion, or if he was something entirely new. I didn't know if he was dangerous. I didn't know if he meant to save us all, or cast us all to ruin. All I knew was that I loved him.

I loved him, and I had turned my back on him.

Aroden laid a hand gently on my shoulder. "I know that was a hard decision," he murmured. "I know how devoted you were to Shade. And I know you probably don't want to hear this, but...you did the right thing. Funny how the right thing and the easy thing are so seldom the same."

I startled and looked at him, wondering how he could have known those words—those words that I had once imagined in Zagger's voice to give me strength.

At the thought of Zagger my heart shuddered and I dropped to a crouch, hugging my arms around my knees.

*Oh, Zagger, I'm so sorry. If only you'd been here. You never would've let him fall. But I wasn't enough. I wasn't enough to stop him.*

Aroden crouched beside me and wrapped his arms around me, and I let him hold me as my body shook with broken grief, as the shadows fell, and the sleet fell, and the long empty silence.

As twilight settled over Borokhev, and the lamps in the windows winked out one by one, there was only one truth I saw with any clarity.

*I will save him,* I thought, *or I will destroy him.*

# ACKNOWLEDGEMENTS

Without the support of you, my readers, I could never have gotten through writing this book. You waited patiently while I muddled through nursing school, and kept encouraging me to continue writing even when I couldn't dredge up a single drop of creative juice. I hope that you've found the experience worth the wait, and I promise the next volume of this mad adventure will not take quite so long to write.

Once again, I want to thank my beta readers who have provided me such invaluable feedback and support. I could never do this without you! You are true treasures.

# Did You Enjoy the Book?

Don't forget to leave a review on your favorite site to
let others know what you think!

Reviews are incredibly valuable to all authors…but we also just
love to hear from you!

If you haven't done it yet, be sure to scan here to sign
up for my email newsletter!

Get the latest news and updates, plus sneak peeks at my WIPs,
bonus scenes, deleted scenes, artwork, and much more…
but I promise I'll never spam you!

Just for signing up you get a free copy of my
Writers of the Future semifinalist short story,
*The Silence Between.*

# BOOKS BY J. LEIGH BRALICK

## THE LOST ROAD CHRONICLES

*Down a Lost Road* (Lost Road Chronicles #1)
*Subverter* (Lost Road Chronicles #2)
*Prism* (Lost Road Chronicles #3)
*Down a Lost Road: Special Extended Edition*
*The Lost Road Chronicles: The Complete Series*

## THE MADNESS METHOD

*The Madness Project* (Madness Method #1)
*A Dark So Deep* (Madness Method #2)
*A Sea Like Glass* (Madness Method #3)
*The Hollow King* (Madness Method #4 - coming soon!)
*Untitled* (madness Method #5 - coming later!)

## CHAOS LIES BENEATH THE NIGHT

*Episode 1: Gifts*
*Episode 2: Omens*

## SHORT STORIES

*Of Smoke and Wind*
*The Silence Between*

*Scan here to learn more about my books and where to get them!*